PENGUIN CLASSICS

THE LIFE AND OPINIONS OF
TRISTRAM SHANDY, GENTLEMAN

LAURENCE STERNE was born in 1713 at Clonmel, Ireland, the son of an army ensign. From 1723 until his father's death in 1731 he was sent to school in Halifax, Yorkshire, and in 1733 he entered as a sizar at Jesus College, Cambridge, receiving his BA in 1737. With the help of his uncle Jaques, precentor and canon at York, Sterne procured his livings. He took holy orders and in 1738 obtained the living of Sutton-on-the-Forest, near York, and a prebend in the cathedral. In 1741 he received the neighbouring benefice of Stillington and he was married, although his marriage was generally unhappy. Sterne wrote forty-five sermons, of which four volumes were published during his lifetime and three were published posthumously in 1769. His literary career began late and he wrote his first pamphlet, *A Political Romance*, in 1759, but it was suppressed because of its controversial satirical content. In the same year he began his masterpiece, *The Life and Opinions of Tristram Shandy*. The first two volumes made him a celebrity and he visited London, where he was lavishly fêted. Between 1761 and 1767 he brought out a further seven volumes. Sterne was dogged by ill-health for much of his life and during his later years he alternated bouts of being lionized in London with recuperative continental travels and trips back to York, where he always returned to write his next instalment. *A Sentimental Journey* represents Sterne's observations and experiences of two tours of the continent and is largely based on his time spent in France. The book was published in February 1768, barely three weeks before his death in London on 18 March 1768.

MELVYN NEW is Professor of English at the University of Florida. He has been writing about Laurence Sterne for thirty years and his recent work includes an edition of Sterne's sermons, which comprise volumes four and five of the Florida Edition of *The Works of Laurence Sterne* (1996); *Telling New Lies: Essays in Fiction, Past and Present* (1992), a collection of essays; and *Tristram Shandy: A Book for Free Spirits* (1994). In 1993 he also edited the novels and selected writings of the Anglo-Jewish author Amy Levy (1861–1889).

JOAN NEW, who has taught at the University of Florida, is a poet as well as co-editor of volumes one and two of the Florida Edition of *The Works of Laurence Sterne; Tristram Shandy: The Text* (1978). In addition to numerous appearances in literary magazines, her collection *The River Bend* was published in 1993.

CHRISTOPHER RICKS teaches at Boston University, and is a Fellow of the British Academy and of the American Academy of Arts and Sciences. His recent publications include *Beckett's Dying Words* (1993) and *Essays in Appreciation* (1996), and he is also editor and general editor of numerous Penguin editions.

Laurence Sterne

THE LIFE AND OPINIONS
OF TRISTRAM SHANDY,
GENTLEMAN

Edited by MELVYN NEW *and* JOAN NEW
with an introductory essay by CHRISTOPHER RICKS
and an introduction and notes by MELVYN NEW

PENGUIN BOOKS

PENGUIN BOOKS

Published by the Penguin Group
Penguin Books Ltd, 27 Wrights Lane, London w8 5TZ, England
Penguin Putnam Inc., 375 Hudson Street, New York, New York 10014, USA
Penguin Books Australia Ltd, Ringwood, Victoria, Australia
Penguin Books Canada Ltd, 10 Alcorn Avenue, Toronto, Ontario, Canada M4V 3B2
Penguin Books (NZ) Ltd, Private Bag 102902, NSMC, Auckland, New Zealand

Penguin Books Ltd, Registered Offices: Harmondsworth, Middlesex, England

First published 1759–67
This edition of the text first published in the Florida Edition of
The Works of Laurence Sterne by the University Presses of Florida 1978
Introductory essay by Christopher Ricks first published in the
Penguin English Library edition of *Tristram Shandy* 1967
This edition published in Penguin Classics 1997

5 7 9 10 8 6 4

Set in 9.5/12pt Postscript Monotype Janson
Typeset by Rowland Phototypesetting Ltd, Bury St Edmunds, Suffolk
Printed in England by Clays Ltd, St Ives plc

Contents

Introductory Essay

by CHRISTOPHER RICKS

Tristram Shandy is the greatest shaggy-dog story in the language. Like all
the best shaggy-dog stories, it is somewhat bawdy, preposterously comic,
brazenly exasperating, and very shrewd in its understanding of human
responses. Laurence Sterne himself has a concluding friendly jibe at
his readers by insisting that they have been spending their time on a
cock-and-bull story. Since Sterne's world is one of delightful topsy-
turvydom, it is hardly surprising that a good starting-point should be the
novel's closing words. We have been told how Uncle Toby's amours have
faded into unconsummated nothingness, and now we hear that the parish
bull is not up to its work – you could say that the bull breeds nothing but
disappointment. At which the novel ends, with one of the characters
voicing just that mingled irritation and affection which Sterne has dexterously created in his readers:

> L--d! said my mother, what is all this story about?——
>   A COCK and a BULL, said Yorick——And one of the best of its kind, I ever
> heard.

The shaggy-dog story and the cock-and-bull story are cousins of the
'Irish bull', and Sterne was brought up in Ireland. So it is not surprising
that one of Sterne's earliest commentators, John Ferriar, should have been
put in mind of the 'Irish bull'. Ferriar mentioned the famous opening
paragraph of Swift's first *Drapier's Letter*: 'Read this Paper with the utmost
Attention, or get it read to you by others'; and he went on to speak of 'the
old story in the jest books, where a templar leaves a note in the key-hole,
directing the finder, if he cannot read it, to carry it to the stationer at the
gate, who will read it for him'. That comic illogicality, expanded and
varied in a thousand ways, is – as Ferriar saw – the stuff of *Tristram Shandy.*

From the moment of publication, *Tristram Shandy* had its enemies. Its
fame in the 1760s might sweep England, and make the author famous and
rich, fêted in London and Paris. But there were voices saying that the
book was obscene, or pointless, or deficient in everything that a novel

ought to provide. The fact that pointlessness was one of Sterne's points, that he was out to flout and taunt humdrum expectations – this meant little. By 1776 the greatest critic of the age, Dr Johnson, could asseverate that 'Nothing odd will do long. *Tristram Shandy* did not last.' A Cambridge don in 1765 had been as massively confident about the fate of this nonsensical book:

> Mark my words, and remember what I say to you; however much it may be talked about at present, yet, depend upon it, in the course of twenty years, should any one wish to refer to the book in question, he will be obliged to go to an antiquary to inquire for it.

The don it was that died. *Tristram Shandy* goes marching on – or, in Sterne's mockingly seedy words, it has managed to 'swim down the gutter of Time'.

Sterne inveigles us into a predicament, and so neatly that we cannot help joining in his laughter at us. Just what the predicament is can be seen from a standard work of reference, the *Oxford Companion to English Literature*. It sets out to summarize *Tristram Shandy* for us:

> In spite of the title, the book gives us very little of the life, and nothing of the opinions, of the nominal hero, who gets born only in vol. iv, and breeched in vol. vi, and then disappears from the story. Instead we have a group of humorous figures: Walter Shandy of Shandy Hall, Tristram's father, peevish but frank and generous, full of paradoxical notions, which he defends with great show of learning; 'my uncle Toby', his brother, wounded in the groin at the siege of Namur, whose hobby is the science of attacking fortified towns, which he studies by means of miniature scarps, ravelins, and bastions on his bowling-green, a man 'of unparalleled modesty' and amiability; Corporal Trim, his servant, wounded in the knee at Landen, devoted to his master and sharing his enthusiasm for the military art, voluble but respectful. Behind these three major figures, the minor characters, Yorick the parson, Dr Slop, Mrs Shandy, and the widow Wadman, play a more elusive part. . . .

Sterne would have relished the fact that such a summary, useful though it is, suggests a man throwing up his hands or throwing in the sponge.

That Sterne was a creative genius was not evident till he was in his forty-seventh year. It was then, in 1759, that he published the first two books of *Tristram Shandy*. Till then he had been merely a Yorkshire priest who dabbled in writing. A few sermons; a satirical squib called *A Political*

Romance (later *The History of a Good Warm Watch Coat*), attacking ecclesiastical chicanery in York – these are not evidence of genius, and they had not brought him fame.

He was born on 24 November 1713, in Clonmel in Ireland, the son of an ensign in the army. (His memories of military life may have influenced the characterization of Uncle Toby.) His father died in 1731, and his mother stayed in Ireland. His opportunity to attend Jesus College, Cambridge, was provided by a generous cousin. Sterne did not prove a distinguished student, but he read widely – and he made a lifelong friend, John Hall (later Hall-Stevenson), rich, eccentric, dissolute, and the future patron of a revelling set which Sterne attended, 'the Demoniacs'. Already, while still at the university, Sterne suffered a haemorrhage of the lungs; ill-health was to dog him, and to produce some of the most courageously humorous passages in *Tristram Shandy*. With the help of uncle Jaques, precentor and canon of York, Sterne earned his livings. He took holy orders, became a priest in 1738, and was presented to the vicarage of Sutton-on-the-Forest near York. His experiences during twenty years were to furnish or at least suggest those of Parson Yorick, a veiled self-portrait, mocking but not self-lacerating. He progressed to a prebendal stall at York, and then to a richer one, and in 1741 he married Elizabeth Lumley, whom he had courted for two years. It was not to be the happiest of marriages.

His life was unobtrusive and cultivated. An amateur painter and musician (these other arts are wittily invoked in *Tristram Shandy*), he was also something of a writer. But it was not until 1759 – immediately following the suppression of *The Good Warm Watch Coat*, which had offended local susceptibilities – that he began *The Life and Opinions of Tristram Shandy, Gentleman*. His marriage was crumbling, and his wife was temporarily insane. It was against this grim background that he flung himself into a work of exuberant humour. After six weeks he had reached Chapter 18; after six months, the first two volumes were completed. His offer to the publisher Dodsley was at first rejected. But a small edition was put out, and Sterne found himself famous. Acclaimed by men as different as David Garrick and Bishop Warburton, Sterne had hospitality and flattery lavished on him. He was commissioned to supply fresh volumes. He was invited to Windsor. His portrait was painted by Sir Joshua Reynolds. 'I wrote, not to be *fed* but to be *famous*', he said.

The Sermons of Mr. Yorick were rushed out in 1760, scandalizing many people, not by their substance, but by their title. Yet Sterne delighted in scandalizing people, and scandal is a form of fame. He did not relax; Volumes III and IV of *Tristram Shandy* were finished by the end of 1760, and Volumes V and VI by the end of 1761. The strain can hardly have helped his health, and he was sent to the south of France to recuperate. The recuperation included being idolized by Parisian society. Mrs Sterne and the daughter Lydia were sent for, and Sterne spent more than a year in Toulouse. (His foreign travel was adapted for Volume VII of *Tristram Shandy*.) The family moved about France, and in 1764 Sterne was 'heartily tired' of it. He returned to England, leaving his family at their request. He had been away for more than two and a half years. But *Tristram Shandy* had by no means been neglected in England, though increasingly deplored, vilified, and sniffed at. Volumes VII and VIII were published in 1765. Still in ill-health, Sterne took a trip of seven months in France and Italy, from which he was to create *A Sentimental Journey*, a traveller's tale of great charm, which he planned after the completion of Volume IX of *Tristram Shandy* in 1766.

Visiting London in 1766, he met Mrs Eliza Draper, then in her twenties. With her he engaged in a sentimental and flowery love-affair, broken after a few months by her return to her middle-aged husband in Bombay. (Sterne's mawkish *Journal to Eliza* was not published until 1904.) The homecoming of Mrs Sterne did not improve matters, but she was persuaded to return to France. *A Sentimental Journey* was completed, and published in February 1768. A month later, Sterne was fatally ill; influenza became pleurisy, and he died on 18 March 1768. His brief but hectic writing life was over, and he left debts of £1,100 and assets of £400. Fortunately he had also left a comic masterpiece.

The tradition of 'learned wit' came down to Sterne from Rabelais and from Burton's *Anatomy of Melancholy*. D. W. Jefferson has written excellently on what such a tradition meant to Sterne, with its mockery of mustiness, its half-loving ridicule of learning run mad, its profane zest for theological speculation. Hence Sterne's delighted proffering of documentation: the legal argument about where Tristram's mother would have to lie in; the medical-cum-theological arguments about whether or not a child can be baptized before it is born; the gigantic curse of Bishop Ernulphus. All this, with a battery of learning (real and fake), with translations on facing pages, and with contemptuous gusto.

Another tradition – the book as a physical object, with all the conventions and paraphernalia of printing – has been well commented on by Hugh Kenner. It is Jonathan Swift who stands behind the brilliant versatility and trickery of Sterne's juggling with the book itself. As Kenner has pointed out, you can't *say* a footnote. Sterne exploits just this gulf, so that, although his style is superbly conversational, a reader is continually being teased into realizing that writing is not, after all, the same as conversation. When Dr Slop crosses himself, a cross (✝) suddenly pops up in print – how do you speak that? Or indicate by an inflection of the speaking voice that such-and-such is in square brackets? Sterne took all such jokes and precisions as far as they can go: his black page when Yorick dies; his squiggly graphs to show the narrative line which he had accomplished; the blank page for a chapter torn out, and the blank page (very different) upon which the reader may inscribe his own description of Widow Wadman's beauty; the chapters misplaced but turning up in the end – all this is a serious reminder of the difference between literature and life; but it is first and foremost superbly funny. We are never allowed to forget that a book, among other things, is a solid object:

WE'LL not stop two moments, my dear Sir,—only, as we have got thro' these five volumes, (do, Sir, sit down upon a set——they are better than nothing) . . .

It was Sterne who saw the possibilities of combining 'learned wit' and book-making with the ordinary novelistic pleasures, often thwarted in *Tristram Shandy* but not invariably.

Not that it is easy to define Sterne's originality. Wayne C. Booth, in a very important study, has shown that the novels of the 1750s made many attempts at self-conscious narration, with a comically intrusive writer preoccupied by the problems of writing. Just as Wordsworth's *Lyrical Ballads* were not in fact revolutionary but rather a late indemnifying of some feeble predecessors, so *Tristram Shandy* is the culmination of a decade of such experiment.

Sterne was fascinated by the problems which have come to dominate our recent art, especially the problems about *deception* in a work of art, about what kind of credence we are to place in art itself. He would have been amused at a recent development, the paintings of Jim Dine, who – as John Richardson has said –

is obsessed with problems of art and illusion, shadow and substance, image and reality. In his earlier pictures he contrasted different kinds of reality. He would take an actual shoe and set it off against its painted image and its name – SHOE.... And to give this assemblage an extra degree of reality Dine has embedded a real light-switch in the canvas and plugged a real lamp into it.

For any critic confronted with such heterogeneous material it is natural to murmur 'I don't know where to begin.' But then, that, Sterne insisted, was exactly the problem, whether in writing or in anything else: where do you begin? And at once we come up against the central paradox about his novel: that it hugely widened the potentialities of the novel-form and yet that, unlike most novels, it is concerned explicitly with reminding us that there are things which you cannot expect a novel to do. The greatness of Sterne is that, with humour and sensitivity, he insists all the time that novels cannot save us. In other words he never used his gifts without recalling to our attention the limitations of all such gifts. He has, for example, a wonderful gift for characterization – one thinks of Walter Shandy, with his bizarre theories on names and on noses, or of Uncle Toby, who combines the most gentle of temperaments with an unceasing preoccupation with war. Certainly Sterne is able to let us know a very great deal about these people, but his unusual strength lies in the fact that at the same time he insists – without getting either mystical or servile about it – that in the end everybody is unknowable.

Certainly the rise of the novel was a great achievement, but Sterne seems to have been one of the first to realize that a novelist, just because he was indeed creating, might be tempted to think himself endued with godlike powers of scrutiny. So instead of the omniscient, omnipotent narrator humorously deployed by Fielding, Sterne substitutes the vague half-knowledge and frustrated impotence of Tristram. Of course the result is very funny and not at all despairing; the book has an unquenchable optimism and vitality, despite all the sufferings of Sterne's own life. But all the same the limits of a novelist's (and indeed any man's) knowledge and power are wittily, and resolutely, insisted on. The novelist, like the rest of us, is committed to the idea of getting to know people, but he must not get too confident about his ability to know what makes so-and-so tick. Sterne ('Alas, poor Yorick!') returned again and again to echoes of *Hamlet*; he may have remembered Hamlet's remonstrance when Guildenstern treats him as a simple musical instrument: 'Why looke you now, how unworthy a thing you make of me: you would play upon mee; you would seem to know my stops: you would pluck out the heart of my Mysterie.'

That is any man to any man – and particularly any character to his creator. These days, Sterne is often reproached for immorality, but he seems to me triumphant in this most basic morality of all. He neither despairs nor anatomizes. In *Tristram Shandy* we hear Sterne's voice behind Tristram's in the discussion of '*Momus*'s glass in the human breast', by which we should be able to gaze into people:

> had the said glass been there set up, nothing more would have been wanting, in order to have taken a man's character, but to have taken a chair and gone softly, as you would to a dioptrical bee-hive, and look'd in.

(Notice 'taken a man's character', as casual as 'taken a chair'.) 'But', he adds drily, 'this is an advantage not to be had by the biographer in this planet'. Sterne, whatever his faults of taste, was never guilty of reducing men to bees, of believing that we can pluck the heart out of their mystery, of becoming a private detective spying on his own characters. 'Taking a man's character' is not something that much resembles the Day of Judgement.

Needless to say, Sterne's humorous humility wouldn't be worth much if it weren't combined with its opposite: a determined ability to show us as much about his characters as can truly be shown. Tristram may make, and with truth, a disclaimer:

> As many pictures as have been given of my father, how like him soever in different airs and attitudes,—not one, or all of them, can ever help the reader to any kind of preconception of how my father would think, speak, or act, upon any untried occasion or occurrence of life.

And of course this is a good joke. But it is more than a joke, since it doesn't merely mock a novelist's pretensions. What it does is insist on setting limits to a novelist's optimism. The novel may have been for Sterne and his contemporaries an excitingly new form, but Sterne manages to bring home to the reader what a novel could *not* do as well as what it could. Which is why the best criticism of Sterne's characters is that which brings out, very simply, how real and how incomprehensible they are. Particularly Coleridge's account of Walter Shandy's character,

> the essence of which is a craving for sympathy in exact proportion to the oddity and unsympathizability of what he proposes; – this coupled with an instinctive desire to be at least disputed with, or rather, both in one, to dispute and yet to agree.

Sterne achieves what this kind of novel can achieve, and insists on the limits of such an achievement. And this was noted, in a way, by even as unsympathetic a critic as the Victorian, Walter Bagehot. Bagehot complains of Sterne's characters that they are 'unintelligibilities, foreign to the realm of true art. But' – he goes on, contrasting other characters – 'as soon as they can be explained to us . . .' Yet that is exactly the point of view which Sterne writes against: that the novel can simply 'explain' people to us, that it has no truck with unintelligibilities, that there *is* such a thing as what Bagehot here called 'the *optional* world of literature, which we can make as we please'. Walter Shandy and Uncle Toby, like all people, imaginary or otherwise, are in some ways intelligible (Sterne shows us that), and also ultimately unintelligible (he shows us that too).

There is a similar dilemma in literature itself. From one point of view, to the writer nothing matters more than writing. From another, writing is ultimately as nothing compared to living. Sterne belonged to an age which was increasingly tempted to look upon literature as an ultimate good, and he was writing in a form – the novel – which quite rightly thought that it was fitted to accomplish literary tasks in some ways more profound, more true, and more complete than any literature that had preceded it. But Sterne, with a comedy that is a million miles from preaching or sententiousness, manages to bring out, simultaneously, that we must hold to two opposing points of view.

Yeats said that 'words alone are certain good', and there is a sense in which every writer would have to agree. But Sterne's brilliant tactic was to bring out all the time how severe the limits of words are. The potential arrogance of literature – in its relations to the other arts, to the sciences, to religion, to life – is put wittily before us, and by a man who writes so well that he can hardly be suspected of denigrating a skill which he himself lacks.

It is this which is the serious reason for the wonderfully comic pages that are given to the other intellectual disciplines: the pages about the law, science (particularly medicine), religion, history, psychology, even psychiatry. All of these are presented to us in the book, and in every case we cannot help reflecting that despite their excesses or absurdities they do embody truthful and essential ways of dealing with life that are not the way of literature. Law, history, psychology, science – they are in their turn judged by literature, and *their* limits, the potentialities and even the actuality of *their* arrogance, are all the time insisted on. The juxtaposition of literature with all those other ways of understanding humanity performs the two-fold task: it shows that literature can never be the be-all and end-all of human existence, and it shows that there is no substitute for literature.

And despite the affectionate ridicule of the absurdities of them all, there is no suggestion in *Tristram Shandy* that we can dismiss them as a waste of time. In this Sterne is very different from a writer to whom he owed a great deal: Jonathan Swift. To Swift the scientific experiments of the Royal Society, the cogitations of philosophers and theologians, were more or less a waste of time. To Sterne, they are for one thing more genially comic; for another, they are shown to minister to permanent human needs. There is a magnificent saying of St Augustine, one which a modern writer influenced by Sterne, Samuel Beckett, has quoted with particular relish and sadness: 'Do not despair, one of the thieves was saved; do not presume, one of the thieves was damned.' Admittedly those words speak of a world very different from Sterne's, and if Beckett were not an important heir of Sterne it would be altogether far-fetched to quote them. And yet there is a sense in which Sterne's great comic novel urged his exasperated readers: 'Do not despair, do not presume' – and that at the moment in history when literature, particularly the novel, was becoming much tempted to presume.

Hence Sterne's delighted use of the other arts in his novel. The theatre is present in the repeated stage directions, and in the vocabulary which speaks all the time of the 'stage', of 'lifting the curtain' and so on. Often with invocations to Sterne's friend, the greatest actor of his day, David Garrick. Once again, though, the effect is many-sided. By speaking of the drama, Sterne not only reminds us of the essential limitations of the novelist's method – even one who takes as many liberties as he does. We cannot help being reminded that if the intention really is to set figures unmistakably before us in the flesh, then the novel just cannot do it as well as the drama. Even when Sterne lavishes all his skill on a minute description of Trim's physical posture. On stage, Trim would simply stand there. But conversely, the inherent limitations of the drama are not forgotten in *Tristram Shandy* – as soon as Sterne modestly invokes the dramatist's art, we are reminded of how superbly the novelist, and the novelist alone, can make us aware of the faintly tenuous and hesitating currents of internal thought and emotion.

There is a similar reminder in Sterne's incorporation of the pictorial arts. He himself painted, and it is not surprising that again and again he resorted to the vocabulary of drawing, sketching, and so on. His allusions to Hogarth, to Raphael, to Sir Joshua Reynolds, are all deliciously comic – there is a fetching lunacy about trying to rival the brush with the pen. Sterne played the violin and the cello, and that vocabulary too he employed continuously. Throughout the novel there is a consistent use of musical metaphor and of music, and in particular there is Uncle Toby's habit of whistling *Lillabullero* whenever something particularly tries his temper or understanding. Of course, like the painting analogies, all this has a broadly comic effect – it allows Sterne to show off outrageously, and it makes his novel delightfully encyclopedic. But basically there is the same concern to praise literature for what it alone can do, and to insist at the same time that literature is only one among many arts.

But let me get back to the idea 'I don't know where to begin'. Tristram is setting out to record 'the life and opinions of Tristram Shandy'. But where ought he to start? At birth? No, because much of his life was shaped before then. For one thing, Tristram shares his father's notion (widely held in the seventeenth and eighteenth centuries) that the moment of conception affects the embryo. So we need to know about Mr Shandy and his notions. For another thing, Tristram's whole life has been affected by the fact that his nose was crushed at birth by Dr Slop's forceps. So we need to know how this came about. That is why the famous and unforgettable first chapter of *Tristram Shandy* begins and ends like this:

I WISH either my father or my mother, or indeed both of them, as they were in duty both equally bound to it, had minded what they were about when they begot me; had they duly consider'd how much depended upon what they were then doing; . . .

Pray, my dear, quoth my mother, *have you not forgot to wind up the clock?*——*Good G*——*!* cried my father, making an exclamation, but taking care to moderate his voice at the same time,——*Did ever woman, since the creation of the world, interrupt a man with such a silly question?* Pray, what was your father saying?——Nothing.

And there we are – Mr Shandy's animal spirits dispersed just at the vital moment. Such was the price he paid for his habit of winding the family clock on the first Sunday night of each month, and taking care of 'some other little family concernments' at the same time. Already on the first page, Sterne's themes are fairly before us. Association of ideas as the cause of folly and peril; the comic frustrations caused by time (it *would* be a clock); our unwary habit of thinking that communication means speaking ('Pray, what was your father saying?——Nothing'). That mention of the creation of the world, and the oath ('Good G—'), bring already into focus Sterne's curious interpenetration of the sacred and the profane. But then Mr Shandy, in his way, was creating a world – and later in the novel we hear, again with the same *double entendre*, that the first Sunday of the month was always 'a sacrament day'.

Sterne's first page, in fact, alerts us to almost all his concerns, and it does so with a technical audacity that matches its subject-matter. Plus the fact that it is also, at the same time, about writing a novel (or autobiography). This witty trick has now gone stale on us, simply because it has been so often done. I, for one, groan when I find Alexander Trocchi's novel *Cain's Book* is about a man who is writing a novel called *Cain's Book*, and that Nathalie Sarraute's novel *The Golden Fruits* is about a novel called *The Golden Fruits*. But we cannot blame Sterne, we must not visit on the father the sins of the children. Sterne tells us these anecdotes, and he tells us about telling them, which is why the opening is perfectly apt. The conception of Tristram is the conception of the book, and when Mr Shandy mentions the creation of the world, we are indeed in at the creation of a world: the creation of Tristram leads to the creation by Tristram of the world of *Tristram Shandy*. Indeed, as Sterne brings out at one point by a sly emphasis on a Latin quotation ('*Quod omne animal post coitum est* triste'), Tristram's name is to be connected with the idea that 'After coition every animal is sad'. The joke is that poor Tristram is sad for the rest of his life, not because of his own but because of his parents' coition.

For Tristram (as for us), the concatenation of circumstances, the pressure of a million imponderables, is such that life is a gigantically tangled skein. The problem of where his life and opinions really begin continues to dog him; after about three hundred pages, he decides that it really begins with the death of his brother:

FROM this moment I am to be considered as heir-apparent to the Shandy family—and it is from this point properly, that the story of my LIFE and my OPINIONS sets out; with all my hurry and precipitation I have but been clearing the ground to raise the building—and such a building do I foresee it will turn out, as never was planned, and as never was executed since *Adam*.

And there we are, back at the first page and 'the creation of the world'. It is, after all, a time-honoured analogy that sees God as the great *architect* or the *author* of our being (Tristram himself refers to 'the Supreme Maker and Designer'), and which therefore sees a human creator as sharing in the great act of creation. Sterne thought that authors might get above themselves. Coleridge, in all solemnity, was to speak of the Imagination as 'a repetition in the finite mind of the eternal act of creation in the infinite I AM'.

Sterne was already aware of the novelist's predicament – one which touched all artists but pressed particularly on those who claimed with more emphasis that they showed life in all its circumstantiality. As Henry James said in his preface to *Roderick Hudson*:

Really, universally, relations stop nowhere, and the exquisite problem of the artist is eternally but to draw, by a geometry of his own, the circle within which they shall happily *appear* to do so. He is in the perpetual predicament that the continuity of things is the whole matter, for him, of comedy and tragedy; that this continuity is never, by the space of an instant or an inch, broken, and that, to do anything at all, he has at once intensely to consult and intensely to ignore it.

Tristram Shandy certainly looks delightfully unkempt beside the elegance of James's classic formulation. But Sterne confronts the problem, not – as James recommends – by drawing the circle within which relations 'happily appear' to come to an end; but, on the contrary, by bringing out how indisputably they do no such thing. The innovation and the value of *Tristram Shandy* – and it is a comically artistic value as well as a moral one – are that it reminds us of what novelists may, too singlemindedly, insist that we utterly forget. (If it is the novelist's duty to posit a beginning and an end, it is also his antithetical duty to keep before us some sense of life's multifariousness, life's difference from art.) Sterne reminds us that there is no such thing as a beginning, middle, and end. That, even in a minutely faithful novel, we cannot find out enough about people to be sure how they would behave. That all art is artifice. That a conversational style is not a conversation. And – most important – that words cannot do nearly as much as we should like to think. The influence of Locke was here very strong, though Sterne is a light-hearted plagiarist rather than a disciple. 'What little knowledge is got by mere words,' says Sterne cheerfully – and it is, in a way, an odd thing to say since it is said with words. When Corporal Trim flourishes his stick, we are given not words but a twirling line on the page:

Whilst a man is free—cried the Corporal, giving a flourish with his stick thus——

A thousand of my father's most subtle syllogisms could not have said more for celibacy.

A fine comic stroke, and of course the flourish shows that 'a man is *free*', because to incorporate such a diagram is in itself an act of unexpected freedom by the writer.

Even Sterne's notorious habits of obscenity and sentimentality often have the same foundation in a sense of the limits of language. Most of the time his obscenity seems to me wonderfully comic, and it could be argued that one of his most important innovations was that he made bawdy jokes at home in the novel. But in any case a remark by Mr Shandy makes explicit the connection between the subject of sex and the scepticism about language. More than on any other subject, the vocabulary of sex is impoverished, inadequate, or laughable:

for what reason is it, that all the parts thereof—the congredients—the preparations—the instruments, and whatever serves thereto, are so held as to be conveyed to a cleanly mind by no language, translation, or periphrasis whatever?

Of course Sterne also took pleasure in obscene puns for their own sake. But their sake often coincided with the sake of his novel. And so did his sentimentality, which is perfectly at one with the capacious generosity of his novel's structure:

> Here,——but why here,——rather than in any other part of my story,——I am not able to tell;——but here it is,——my heart stops me to pay to thee, my dear uncle *Toby*, once for all, the tribute I owe thy goodness.

Amusingly handled, but aptly too – because the tribute to Toby's spontaneous and impulsive goodness must itself be spontaneous and impulsive. 'But why here?' – because the heart has its reasons which the reason knows nothing of. 'My heart stops me.' Such a moment is itself an example of what it is writing about, and such a device – wheels within wheels – goes to make up the intricate structure of *Tristram Shandy* and is a major technical innovation in itself.

Take the moment (only a few pages from the end of the book) when Uncle Toby learns a truth about womankind. He has been courting Widow Wadman while Corporal Trim courts Bridget. Bridget never takes the least interest in the terrible wound which Trim had in his knee – whereas Widow Wadman is solicitude itself when it comes to inquiring about the wound which Toby had – in the groin. For Toby, what could be clearer proof of Widow Wadman's loving compassion? 'Was I her brother, Trim, a thousand fold, she could not make more constant or more tender enquiries after my sufferings——though now no more.' But Trim strips him of the illusion:

> The Corporal had advanced too far to retire——in three words he told the rest——
>
> My uncle Toby laid down his pipe as gently upon the fender, as if it had been spun from the unravellings of a spider's web——
>
> ——Let us go to my brother Shandy's, said he.

This is beautifully done, with all Sterne's perceptiveness about the way in which an ordinary gesture (laying down a pipe) can be charged with feeling and with character (and with innuendo). Notice, too, the comic but touching modulation by which we pass from the sexual innocence of

'Was I her brother', to 'Let us go to my brother Shandy's, said he'. Toby does not reel at the shock, he simply becomes even more gently courteous than ever, so that one remembers Hazlitt's praise of Toby's characterization as 'one of the finest compliments ever paid to human nature'. But this mention of the spider's web does even more than that – more than catch delicately a physical gesture, an innuendo, a man's character, and a fine-spun illusion. The unravellings of a spider's web: that applies, too, to the incident itself. Trim has unravelled for Toby the web of female solicitude, and so Toby escapes from Widow Wadman's invitation to come into her parlour. It is not an accident that one of the most famous moments in the book shows us that Toby would not hurt a fly; he lets one out of the window exclaiming 'This world surely is wide enough to hold both thee and me.'

Sterne's greatness is not simply that he wrote a novel about writing a novel; his triumph is due to the fact that (unlike most of his imitators) he gave as much of his genius to his invented world (the characters of Mr Shandy and Toby) as to the theme of inventing it. Wheels within wheels – but each as well-made as the others, and none buckled. So that the final threads of that wonderfully suggestive 'spider's web' touch the writing of the book itself. Trim unravels the web of Toby's amours, and it is this unravelling itself which unravels the whole novel and brings it – a few pages later – to an end. The *dénouement* – that is, literally, the unravelling. To think, or to write, is both to spin and to unravel. As Tristram says of his father's book, the *Tristra-paedia*, 'My father spun his, every thread of it, out of his own brain, – or reeled and cross-twisted what all other spinners and spinsters had spun before him.'

All the implications of Uncle Toby's spider's web, then, are delightfully apt, and handled with a correct self-consciousness that never becomes inhibiting. Sterne's whole attempt was to create a web as beautifully wrought, as strong, and as delicate – one which, in catching the consciousness of the characters, would at the same time express the consciousness of their creator. He is fascinated by the fluctuating and undulating impulses of thought and feeling. In *The Art of Fiction*, Henry James said:

> Experience is never limited, and it is never complete; it is an immense sensibility, a kind of huge spider-web of the finest silken threads suspended in the chamber of consciousness and catching every air-borne particle in its tissue.

Sterne takes all such patterns of wheels-within-wheels as far as they can go. There is his outcry against plagiarism and the making of books:

> Shall we for ever make new books, as apothecaries make new mixtures, by pouring only out of one vessel into another?
> Are we for ever to be twisting, and untwisting the same rope?

But the joke – as John Ferriar pointed out one hundred and fifty years ago – is that Sterne has himself lifted all this from Burton's *Anatomy of Melancholy*. Sterne plagiarizes in order to speak against plagiarism – and in any case Burton himself, it seems, had borrowed most of it. There could hardly be a more witty, or more telling, illustration of the point which Sterne was so concerned to make: that, at every moment, an infinite regression lies in wait for the unwary. Such vertiginous regressions, mirrors reflected in mirrors, are a characteristic anxiety of modern literature. There is William Empson's poem 'Dissatisfaction with Metaphysics':

> Two mirrors with Infinity to dine
> Drink him below the table when they please.

There are the Chinese-boxes of guilt and self-reproach which trap Patrick Standish, the hero of Kingsley Amis's *Take a Girl Like You*:

> But I'm not trying to get credit with you by saying I know I'm a bastard. Nor by saying I'm not trying to get credit. Nor by saying I'm not trying to by saying ... trying ... you know what I mean. Nor by saying that. Nor by saying that.

There is Thom Gunn's poem, 'Carnal Knowledge', with its regressive refrain: 'I know you know I know you know I know'. Sterne seems to have been one of the first to catch this glimpse of a comic situation of which we can also say, that way madness lies. His vitality creates from these wheels-within-wheels a sense of dizzying but comic speed. There are, for instance, all the hitherto unpublished books which Tristram keeps mentioning: his father's life of Socrates, or his system of education for his son Tristram, the *Tristra-paedia* (rivalling Xenophon's *Cyropaedia*, the training of Cyrus the Great). The *Tristra-paedia* is a perfect example of the perils of regression, since Tristram grows faster than the book. Mr Shandy

was three years and something more, indefatigably at work, and at last, had scarce compleated, by his own reckoning, one half of his undertaking: the misfortune was, that I was all that time totally neglected and abandoned to my mother; and what was almost as bad, by the very delay, the first part of the work, upon which my father had spent the most of his pains, was rendered entirely useless,——every day a page or two became of no consequence.——

Farfetched? But it is uncommonly like the parent who is so interested in reading about the duties of parenthood that he never has time actually to speak to his children. In this doomed and heroically absurd battle against time, the *Tristra-paedia* is of course the brother to *Tristram Shandy* itself. Tristram's appalled glee when he realizes the real predicament of an autobiographer anticipates the best of Lewis Carroll's philosophical paradoxes:

I am this month one whole year older than I was this time twelve-month; and having got, as you perceive, almost into the middle of my fourth volume—and no farther than to my first day's life—'tis demonstrative that I have three hundred and sixty-four days more life to write just now, than when I first set out; so that instead of advancing, as a common writer, in my work with what I have been doing at it—on the contrary, I am just thrown so many volumes back—was every day of my life to be as busy a day as this—And why not?—and the transactions and opinions of it to take up as much description—And for what reason should they be cut short? as at this rate I should just live 364 times faster than I should write— It must follow, an' please your worships, that the more I write, the more I shall have to write—and consequently, the more your worships read, the more your worships will have to read.

Will this be good for your worships eyes?

Sterne's courageous humour keeps these wheels as circles of the happy, but it would not take much change of perspective to see them as circles of the damned – as they become in Samuel Beckett. What Beckett calls 'the poisonous ingenuity of Time in the science of affliction' might be viewed by Sterne as the delicious ingenuity of Time in the science of entertainment.

This is why *Tristram Shandy* is full of incidents or images which relate, at one and the same time, to the characters and to the novel itself. When Dr Slop's obstetrical bag has been trussed with a dozen knots so that it won't rattle, and then poor Dr Slop has to wrestle hurriedly with them (the baby is being born), we are aware not only of Dr Slop, but of the fact that Tristram has created – as part of the novel – exactly this 'multiplicity of round-abouts and intricate cross turns, with a hard knot at every intersection or point where the strings met'. The incident *within* the novel (for Dr Slop) acts just as it does *in* the novel (for the reader). The greatness of Sterne is in his doing justice to both, with equal fidelity and awareness. It is not that he pretends to gaze on them both but is really interested only in the knots of his novel-writing; no, his gaze is genuinely bifocal even if that often means a comic squint. When Corporal Trim hands Toby a book, a sermon drops out of it – in exactly the same way as it drops out of the book *Tristram Shandy* itself. (A further spin is given to the wheels by the fact that it was a sermon which Laurence Sterne had already published.) The neatest triumph comes for both Tristram and Sterne when Tristram exclaims, 'For in talking of my digression——I declare before heaven I have made it!' And a similar point is made by the mysterious appearance, from time to time, of an editor of the book, whose footnotes correct Tristram and open up yet another vista of regression.

When we hear how 'the learned Peireskius' walked five hundred miles to see a sailing chariot, the book itself trudges off as valiantly and absurdly as did Peireskius. When we are told that the parson Yorick (i.e. Sterne) once wrote the word 'Bravo' at the foot of one of his sermons, but in a later ink crossed the word out – then we see in a flash that the word 'Bravo!' is in effect being written at the foot of the telling of this anecdote: and then retracted? When Corporal Trim tries, again and again, to tell Toby the story of the King of Bohemia, only to be foiled and finally left to a series of false starts – we think too of *Tristram Shandy* itself, a book which promised us his life and opinions and which finally back-pedals so that it concludes four years before Tristram was born. The frustrating of the story of the King of Bohemia – like that of *Tristram Shandy* – is incomparably comic. But here too it is easy to be reminded of the pain and even madness which Sterne's humour fends off. When Sterne's wife temporarily went out of her mind, she believed that she was the Queen of Bohemia.

Goethe praised Sterne's 'contentedness' – a quality which we are now likely to regard with some suspicion. Surely the writer's business is not to be contented, but to rouse us to discontent? But this is another place where modern literature has tended to throw all its weight on one arm of the paradox about literature, dangerously one-sided. Yes, from one point of view, we do ask that literature will make us more aware, more sensitive about the suffering of the world. But if thoughtlessness, lack of imagination, callousness – if these are an enemy of literature and of life, they are not the only enemy. What about madness? What about being so sensitive to the suffering of the world that you in effect opt out of the world? No, Sterne's 'contentedness' may be attacked as complacency, but it is something very different: a necessary resilience. When Mr Shandy hears of the death of his son Bobby, it is not long before the exhilaration of making a flowing speech on death has allowed him to forget the actual death. Sterne does not snicker at the ability of the human mind to behave in such a way – on the contrary, he finds it something to admire and to be grateful for. And if Sterne's writing seems unthinkably far from the world of madness, we have only to think of how Uncle Toby behaves – and of how Sterne's wife went mad. Dr Johnson thought Sterne a sordid writer, but Sterne's work bears out Johnson's magnificent judgement that 'The only end of writing is to enable the readers better to enjoy life, or better to endure it'. *Tristram Shandy* enables us to do both.

CHRISTOPHER RICKS

Editor's Introduction
by MELVYN NEW

> The reader who demands to know exactly what Sterne really thinks of a thing ...
> must be given up for lost.   Friedrich Nietzsche, *Human, All Too Human*

Thirty years have passed – a generation – since Christopher Ricks wrote his fine introduction to the first Penguin edition of *Tristram Shandy* (1967), and it is a mark of its worthiness that it can be reprinted without apology. As Sterne himself well knew ('of all the cants which are canted in this canting world ... the cant of criticism is the most tormenting' [III.xii]), criticism, whether of literature or painting, music or dramatic performance, can only rarely hope to survive its hour. Thirty years is a lifetime for almost all artistic endeavours, ample time to be born and to die; for critical endeavours, and especially in this present age of frenzied academic commentary, thirty years might well seem an eternity.

The enduring masterpieces of literature, the classics of any tradition, find their power not in some mystical transcendence of the fugacity of critical commentary, but, quite the contrary, in their capacity to relish the rapid succession of ideas about themselves, much as a fire feeds upon – even as it destroys – whatever fuels its existence. The smaller but no less difficult accomplishment of literary criticism is to survive long enough to be a moment – to change my metaphor – in the collective train of witnesses to that endurance, even while succumbing to those changes in times, tastes, and temperaments that announce a commentary's individual demise.

It is no coincidence, then, that in the list of Further Reading following this Introduction only four of thirty titles are dated earlier than 1967. Unlike some who would despair over this evidence of criticism's short life-span, I see in the currency of my list no cause for complaint. Indeed, one might rather suggest a small celebration is in order, for the list assures us that the critical conversation accompanying *Tristram* into the twenty-first century is spirited and plentiful: a 'classic' ought not to hope for a better complement/compliment from its commentary. More than either complaint or celebration, however, this fecundity of commentary calls for our need to acknowledge the unending process of change by which one generation's insights become another generation's blindness.

It will be useful to begin this acknowledgement with two contributions to Sterne scholarship since 1967 that may have somewhat longer 'shelf-lives' than most commentaries. The first is Arthur H. Cash's monumental two-volume biography of Sterne (Methuen, 1975, 1986), replacing the biography by Wilbur Cross, first written in 1909, revised in 1925, and again in 1929. Biography, too, is subject to tastes and times; questions we ask about a writer's life today are different in many respects from those asked by Cross. Still, as one reads Cash's account of Sterne's life, so carefully and minutely chronicled as to event and environment, there develops a strong sense that additional information and new perspectives will not alter greatly the biographical information we have now accumulated about Laurence Sterne. The story will be retold for future generations, but these retellings will, without doubt, rely heavily upon the work of Cash; and while new materials may continue to appear – as, for example, political and other ephemeral writings possibly by Sterne, as suggested by Kenneth Monkman in issues of *The Shandean: An Annual Volume Devoted to Laurence Sterne and his Works* from 1989 to 1992 – they will almost certainly not change in significant ways the broad outlines of Sterne's life story. One simply expects Cash's splendid biography to suffice for much of the next century.

I must be far more careful in my claims concerning the second commentary; as Sterne warns us, quoting Bishop Joseph Hall, 'it is an abominable thing for a man to commend himself'. Let it simply be noted that the text of *Tristram Shandy* in this edition is taken from the Florida Edition of *The Works of Laurence Sterne* (Vols. I and II, 1978), the result of an extensive study of the textual history of the work; this Penguin edition is the first trade edition to make a fully acknowledged use of the information garnered by that study. It is, as well, the first trade edition able to rely on the 500 pages of annotations that comprise the third volume of the Florida *Tristram Shandy* (1984).

Since James A. Work's valuable textbook edition published in 1940, subsequent annotators, prior to the Florida Edition, have in large measure merely duplicated his work (often with inadequate credit), scattering a new finding here and there, but, presumably for reasons of space, skimping elsewhere. Work's annotations, another instance of a more enduring scholarly effort, in themselves or their reappearance in other textbook editions, have served *Tristram* readers for more than half a century; indeed, as the Florida annotators (myself, Richard A. Davies, and W. G. Day) pointed out, few if any eighteenth-century fiction writers have been better served in being made available to a general reading audience than Sterne. Without doubt, Work's influence continues to be felt throughout the Florida *Notes*, and hence again in these new Penguin annotations. Still, Work's primary efforts were historical and pedagogical: he identified historical and contemporary personages mentioned by Sterne, defined 'difficult' and foreign words and phrases, and elucidated allusions that a modern audience could not be expected to grasp. The Florida *Notes* serves several additional purposes.

Most important, perhaps, the Florida *Notes* provides the full text of passages from which Sterne borrowed, so that comparisons can conveniently be made, without recourse to sources available only in the largest libraries. Sterne's manipulation of the borrowed materials that constitute so significant a portion of *Tristram*'s texture is one key to understanding the work. Although it was impossible to proffer all of the Florida materials in this edition, significant and sufficient examples are provided, so that general readers may explore for themselves this important aspect of Sterne's creative process.

The Florida *Notes* also expands the list of Sterne's borrowings, helped immensely by generations of scholars, from the first serious inquirer into Sterne's borrowings, John Ferriar in 1798, to Theodore Baird, who in 1936 uncovered Sterne's source for most of his historical and military details (Nicolas Tindal's translation and continuation of Paul Rapin de Thoyras's *Histoire d'Angleterre*, a source surprisingly ignored by Work, and hence by subsequent editors as well), to the important discovery of Sterne's use of Pierre Charron's *De la Sagesse* (*Of Wisdome*) by Françoise Pellan in 1972. As in the Florida *Notes*, every effort has been made in my notes herein to acknowledge previous scholarship, although limitations of space may perhaps have led to some unfortunate lapses. In that I opened this Introduction with a discussion of criticism's evanescence, let me note here that one may also argue that nothing written about a classic work ever completely disappears. Certainly from the annotator's viewpoint, an awareness that one is building on the work of others, named or unnamed, is paramount. All annotated editions, in this regard, are variorums, celebrating the enterprise of commentary almost as much as the work on which they comment; every annotator, in brief, is a 'dwarf', standing on the shoulders of the 'giant' of accumulated commentary.

The Florida *Notes* also offers many 'parallel' passages from sources contemporary to Sterne, where no single source could be identified, but where it was felt to be unwise to label an image, topic, method, or discussion as 'uniquely' Shandean. Here annotation serves not so much to elucidate a text as to put in question readings that claim a work is *sui generis*, a label that bespeaks a reader's lack of knowledge more frequently than it records the true status of the work. Readers for whom any critical restraint is an unfair imposition on the career of their hobby-horses will find all annotation irksome, and these 'parallels' particularly so; on the other hand, the old-fashioned study of 'analogues' can often forestall inept commentary, particularly of the sort that insists an author's sole significance comes from being uniquely out of joint with his or her own time or place, and hence, uniquely, one of 'us' and not one of 'them'.

Two illustrations will suffice. In Volume IV, chapter xvii, Sterne writes: 'But mark, madam, we live amongst riddles and mysteries—the most obvious things, which come in our way, have dark sides, which the quickest sight cannot penetrate into; and even the clearest and most exalted understandings amongst us find ourselves puzzled and at a loss in almost every cranny of nature's works ...' Perhaps no other passage in *Tristram Shandy* has been more often invoked by critics over the past twenty-five years, as they have applied various postmodern theories of indeterminacy to Sterne's eighteenth-century novel. The typical argument moves in this direction: Fielding and Richardson lived in an essentialist world of certainty, dominated by Christian absolutes; Sterne, on the other hand, lived in the modern solipsistic world where there are no absolutes, where all value is created by the human being. His world is, in short, a confusion of 'riddles and mysteries', akin to our own indeterminate and undecidable universe. What then, the annotator may ask, are we to make of the fact that the 'riddles and mysteries' passage very closely echoes two of Sterne's sermons, in both of which the context clearly suggests Sterne is restating a commonplace Christian belief in the limitations of the postlapsarian human mind? One year after the Florida *Notes* appeared, it was pointed out that a passage in Locke's *Essay Concerning Human Understanding* (IV.3.22) underlies all three passages; and more recently, while annotating the sermons, I located Sterne's actual verbatim source in the theologian John Norris of Bemerton, a passage in his *Practical Discourses upon Several Divine Subjects, Volume Two* (1691). In each instance, from Locke to Norris to Sterne, the context of the passage is not postmodern angst, but 1 Corinthians 13:12:

'For now we see through a glass, darkly: but then face to face: now I know in part; but then shall I know even as also I am known.' Perhaps there has never been a period in history in which the human mind has not confronted the limitations of knowledge; perhaps – as twentieth-century intellectuals – we are unique only in believing we are unique.

A second illustration comes from the final chapter of *Tristram Shandy*, Walter's lament over human sexuality. In annotating the passage, I have quoted Sterne's source, Pierre Charron's *Of Wisdome*, at length, because both the passage *and* its source seem of great importance for our understanding of Sterne. Professor Ricks also singles out Walter's lament, as have numerous modern commentators, most of whom – even after 1972 and Pellan's recovery of the debt to Charron – still do not account for the fact that the words are not Sterne's but Charron's, who was, in turn, rephrasing Montaigne, his mentor. Professor Ricks's intuitive linking of the passage with 'scepticism' takes on important new life when the source is known. That one can comment on the passage brilliantly without knowing of Charron's influence is not to be gainsaid (though 'brilliant' commentary is, indeed, a very rare occurrence). However, since we now know of Charron's influence on the passage, a reading without acknowledging his presence is equivalent to reading an 'abridged' version; good readers, I believe, always prefer the 'complete' text – with the understanding, of course, that 'completion' is always a grace beyond the reach of criticism.

Finally, the present notes follow the Florida *Notes* in providing illustrative passages from Sterne's other writings, *A Sentimental Journey*, the forty-five sermons, the correspondence, and the minor works, when they seem to contribute usefully to our understanding of *Tristram Shandy*. Here, too, one is deeply indebted to previous scholarly work, especially Gardner D. Stout's 1967 edition of the *Journey* (California), and Lewis Perry Curtis's 1935 edition of the *Letters* (Oxford). The sermons are also now available in a scholarly edition (the Florida Edition, Vols. IV and V [1996]) that was not available to the Florida *Tristram Shandy* editors. Some materials from its 400 pages of annotations have contributed to the present annotations, but the sermons remain a relatively untapped source of insight into Sterne's fiction. Indeed, one hope in annotating the sermons so extensively – a hidden agenda, except that the purpose is self-evident – was to raise Sterne's clerical career in the consciousness of literary commentators who have heretofore largely ignored this aspect of his life; the outcome of this endeavour awaits the passage of time.

If the Florida *Sermons* has a not-so-hidden agenda, the annotations to *Tristram Shandy* should also come under suspicion, for few if any 'novels' in the short history of the novel (a genre that emerged in western literature only in Sterne's day and may already be in rapid retreat) require this kind of extensive annotation. When fictional emphasis is on the understanding of character and relationships through the orderly (sequential) enactment of narrated events, when these events establish their own internal context for comprehension, indeed, when authors are guided, consciously or unconsciously, by the drive for the '*novelty*' buried in their genre's name, and therefore separate their work from, rather than connect it to, sources of meaning outside its self-creating 'real' world, annotation takes on a sparse form. As in modern scholarly editions of Fielding or Smollett, novels require that historical figures be identified and that commonplaces unfamiliar to our age, but not to the author's, be explained; good narratives eschew additional annotation, and in the best narratives one would actually resent being driven away from the story to a footnote for an explanation. The annotations to the Wesleyan edition of *Tom Jones* provide a good example, especially because of the disproportionate number of notes required for Fielding's famous introductory chapters – which have a certain kinship with the self-conscious narration of *Tristram Shandy* – while the narrative itself is by and large self-explanatory. Maugham's infamous abridgement of *Tom Jones*, where he cut the introductory chapters in order to highlight the narrative, comes to mind.

Sterne's writing, like Fielding's introductory chapters, demands a different mode of annotation, one arising from its embeddedness (often masked) in a literary past, the literary existence of its narrator (Tristram's primary occupation as an adult is to write his book), and its digressive texture, so often consisting of borrowed documents and pseudo-documents, counter-narratives and parodies. Professor Ricks points to the ways in which this structure might serve as a riposte to the developing history of the novel and that is certainly the way many (if not most) readers encounter *Tristram Shandy* today, that is, as students in a course in the eighteenth-century *novel*, in which Sterne comes after Defoe, Richardson, and Fielding, and before Smollett, sharing with them a chronological time-line and the length of their books – and little else, except by way of contrast.

Interestingly, Sterne never mentions Defoe, Richardson, or Fielding anywhere in his canon, and mentions Smollett only as a miserable tourist, the Smelfungus of *A Sentimental Journey.* The authors he does frequently cite as his forebears come from another tradition, and Sterne invokes that tradition often enough to put the notion that he was writing a *novel* or even writing 'against' the *novel* into some question – assuming that we mean something more than 'a long work in prose' when we use the generic term. Sterne's major sources, Rabelais, Montaigne, Burton, Cervantes, and Swift, when taken together, reflect a tradition of prose writing I prefer to label *satire*, especially in so far as these immensely variegated sources indicate that *satire* is not a mode of writing practised only by cynics and misanthropes. Satire and comedy often march hand in hand, as in the Restoration comedies of Wycherley and Congreve, for example, and in *Don Quixote*; and satire has also shared a comfortable bed with gentle, though telling, wit and urbanity, as in Horace and Montaigne.

Sterne consistently singles out Swift among his English-writing predecessors; and when he decided to include a sermon in Volume II, it is important to recognize that he chose one in which significant portions are borrowed from a very similar sermon on the subject of conscience by Swift. Critics intent on separating Sterne from Swift in order to pursue a reading of *Tristram Shandy* within the novel tradition (or as part of the emerging secularism that the novel heralds) have found it necessary to paint Swift very darkly; his satire – and the author – are painted as the psychological aberrations of a black misanthrope. I find this portrait absurd, if only because Swift – like Sterne – so often makes me laugh at human absurdity (rather, say, than gnash my teeth). More to the point, however one reads *A Tale of a Tub*, it seems to me a work absolutely central, as both literary *and* religious satire, to any meaningful reading of *Tristram Shandy*. As is the case with *Tristram Shandy* and Charron, I would similarly argue that reading *Tristram* without Swift's *Tale* in mind is equivalent to reading an abridged version. Whatever shape the tree finally took over the nine years of its growth, it is necessary to recognize, I believe, that the seed of *Tristram Shandy* was embedded in the Augustan satirists of the age preceding Sterne's own, and not in the mid-century novelists with whom he is too often thoughtlessly contextualized.

Even before questions of literary influence can be raised, however, a good reader of *Tristram Shandy* must confront Sterne's twenty-two-year career as a village vicar. His primary writing during this period, and perhaps his primary reading as well, was of sermons, the predominant reading of much of the mid-century population. In his forty-five sermons which have survived, Sterne demonstrates a commitment to Christian belief as defined by the centrist Anglicanism of his age and taught in the Cambridge of the 1730s, when he was in residence. His sermons are typically balanced appeals to reason and emotion, the head and the heart, and to religion (the institution) and revelation (Scripture). He is rarely if ever innovative, certainly not about doctrine or truth, nor would he have wanted to stray from established positions. He attacks Roman Catholics and enthusiasts (Methodists) with some meanness, but little fire; he celebrates the congregation's virtues when he seeks charitable contributions, and highlights their vices when he prepares them for Communion. Above all, he denies the possibility of happiness or morality without religion, and asserts again and again the Providential design of the world (and the special Providence accorded England), from the first Adam's fall to the second Adam's (Christ's) redemptive sacrifice. That this preaching follows the lead of the great Restoration preachers, most particularly John Tillotson, in its embrace of plainness, simplicity, practical moral teaching, and a quiet yet sincere emotionalism, has deceived some readers of Sterne (and of Tillotson for that matter) into equating this mode of Anglicanism with socinianism, deism, even secularism, but nothing could be further from its own sense of itself as the continuation of Christ's original church, now flourishing under His guidance and after a century of bloody Christian warfare, in the growing prosperity and religious peace of eighteenth-century England.

Had Sterne died in 1758, his forty-fifth year, he would have done so unnoticed by the world then – and certainly unrecognized by it today. But when a silly dispute over church prerogatives broke out in the York establishment at the end of that year, Sterne was inspired to join the quarrel with a little pamphlet he entitled *A Political Romance*. It is a reductive satire and echoes two other writers, Rabelais and Swift, who satirized the Church not to bring it down but to reform it. The guiding spirit, however, was a third satirist, Horace, who is given pride of place on the title-page: '*Ridiculum acri / Fortius et melius magnas plerumque secat Res*' (Ridicule often cuts hard knots more forcefully and effectively than gravity). A link is thus forged between Sterne's long clerical career and the onset of his nine-year career as a writer.

The same link is evident in his next creative attempt, his 'Fragment in the Manner of Rabelais', two chapters of an aborted parodic work on how to write sermons, modelled, it seems clear, on Pope's manual of instruction in bad writing, *Peri Bathous; or, The Art of Sinking in Poetry*. Again, the recourse to Pope seems no stray gesture, but an indication that Sterne's literary interests were rooted in the same age from which he took his theological direction – and, perhaps, for many of the same reasons. To my mind, these reasons, enormously complex by any measure, may be reduced (and I emphasize that this is a 'reduction') to one particular observation about reading *Tristram Shandy*. The real community of the Shandy world is not, as is so often maintained by the 'novelistic' school of criticism, the Shandy brothers or the Shandy household; rather, community in *Tristram Shandy* is represented by all the authors and books summoned by Sterne, all the documents and cultures and artifacts from which he erects his edifice, in short, all that illustrates to us what it means to live in a world written by God, and hence always approximated – but never finalized – by the same human endeavour. At times the documents are necessarily ludicrous, as is so much human effort in the face of the infinite, but at other times they are useful and perhaps even profound, as human effort can also be. Sterne keeps us aware of both possibilities, and aware above all that while every attempt to create a world of certainty and truth will fail, the attempt is what ties us to the community of humanity, what offers us the equivalent of communion with our legacy. This legacy produces neither God's world (the theocracies of the seventeenth century) nor a world in which we are God (the novels of the nineteenth century); rather, in its mass of fragments, we confront the world of human endeavours towards truth and certainty (God), we weigh them, and we find them always wanting, at times comically wanting, at times tragically. In thus measuring our legacy (as good a definition of satire as any other), we are inextricably linked to the past, but we are also taught much about the limitations of our future. Birth and death are indeed important subjects in *Tristram Shandy*, but as markers of the human condition, rather than frames of narration.

Reading and writing seem to have been activities Sterne delighted in, not as epistemological experiences, but ontological ones. He was not, that is to say, as concerned as we are today with knowledge and ignorance, certainty and indeterminacy, because truth (the Truth, the Word, the Logos) was already known (revealed). The human problem he confronted was that our path to this Truth is littered with fictions and follies, and that, far from allowing these scatterings to discourage us, we must accept that they are the sole contents of truth's discourse in the human condition – beginning with the scattering of 'animal spirits' that announces Tristram's begetting. The point of validation by which this babel of competing visions and visionary constructs is to be evaluated is found within Sterne's Christian faith, which explained for him the origins of human folly and failure, the fragmentary and unfulfilled nature of all human endeavour; and which offered, by the sacrifices of redeeming charity and love, a plan of human reconciliation with the divine, but never *here* and never *now*: 'Hope springs eternal in the human breast / Man never Is, but always To be blest.'

Tristram Shandy is neither parable nor allegory, but it shares with these older (and enduring) modes of fiction a belief that fictions can ultimately represent elements of Truth, and not merely other fictions. As a satire, however, another older (and equally enduring) mode of narrative, *Tristram* rides athwart this belief, much as Don Quixote tilts at windmills, and Pantagruelians set forth for the oracle of the bottle: reality – precious and beautiful precisely because it is not autonomous, not indeterminate, not existential – is found in the impossible journey of postlapsarian humanity towards truth.

The questions we ask about a text are rarely if ever generated solely by the text itself; indeed, before we read the first page, we are enmeshed in a web of preconceptions and preconditions from which our questions emerge. The length of the work, the appearance of the printed page, the date, the author's name and the information we associate with it, the publisher, the prefatory materials such as Professor Ricks and I are supplying all play a part in weaving that web, as do the conditions under which we read, the book(s) we read just prior to this one, and, of course, such personal factors as age, education, disposition, experience. Finally, and overarching all these considerations, is the era in which we live. One hundred years ago, for example, questions about the indecency of Sterne's fiction were uppermost in readers' minds; today, we actually *compel* students – for educational purposes – to read *Tristram Shandy*.

Prefacers can hope to influence the construction of this web, but they weave only one strand of many. Surely, however, the important point is for readers to learn to recognize the *pretextual* nature of their questions; and, equally important, to reject the most fundamental *pretext* of literary commentary, that a text generates its own valid questioning. Good reading, it might be suggested, is as much an examination of origins as of conclusions; in this light, the origins of an author, of a work of art, and of a critic's questions are intricately intertwined, and asking ourselves about the origins of an author's preconceptions leads us to the origins of our own. Hence, when we contemplate the possibility of *Tristram Shandy*'s origins in Sterne's clerical career and his invocations of Horace and Rabelais, Swift and Pope, we may find ourselves in a better position than heretofore to investigate our own origins as readers. As twentieth-century readers, for example, it is difficult to escape the fact that many of our critical questions originate in our secular outlook, which, in academic circles at least, often takes a strong anti-clerical hue, an implicit belief that intelligent people cannot sincerely hold to an organized religious faith. Or, from a different tack, we might come to recognize what Northrop Frye has labelled our mistaken novel-centred view of the fictional universe, that we tend to define our expectations for any long prose work by its relationship to Dickens, Flaubert, Henry James. In both instances, we can immediately note in our 'origins' the makings of some significant conflicts with Sterne's.

The most interesting readings of Sterne in the past quarter-century, to my mind, are readings against the grain of these two dominant precon-ceptions of many twentieth-century readers. In recent years, the approaches of criticism, whether new historicist or feminist, Marxist or postmodernist, have all encouraged reading against the formerly prevailing tendencies, 'suspicious' or 'anti-*author*itarian' or 'revolutionary' readings that tend to discover a complicity in repression among all previous writers and critics alike. The readings produced by this viewpoint are in many ways numb-ingly similar: works of art are all culpably less 'radical' than the commen-tator, with radicalism (anti-establishmentarianism, not quite to revive an old shibboleth) taken as the *sine qua non* of achievement. But precisely because Sterne in earlier criticism was the 'radical' – the disrupter of the 'novel form', the lewd cleric, the promoter of theories of life, language, and narrative that connected him to the most avant-garde thought and practice of western culture – to read Sterne *against the grain* at the end of this century means to read him in alternative contexts, and the best criticism in recent years has done just that. Put another way, the universal scepticism undergirding criticism in the past quarter-century has every-where challenged 'received wisdom', and since the received wisdom about *Tristram Shandy* had to do with its radicalness, the 'new' wisdom argues the traditional nature of Sterne's enterprise, his embeddedness in his own time and place. It is a paradox he might have enjoyed.

None of this is to deny, of course, that among eighteenth-century English fiction writers, Sterne is perhaps the most important figure in terms of influence on modern writers. When James Joyce wanted to explain

Finnegans Wake, his most experimental fiction, he invoked Sterne: 'Time and the river and the mountain are the real heroes of my book. Yet the elements are exactly what every novelist might use: man and woman, birth, childhood, night, sleep, marriage, prayer, death. There is nothing paradoxical about this. Only I am trying to build as many planes of narrative with a single esthetic purpose. Did you ever read Laurence Sterne?' And when Thomas Mann tried to explain the achievement of his great *Joseph* saga, he also invoked Sterne: 'There is a symptom for the innate character of a work, for the category toward which it strives . . . : that is the reading matter which the author prefers and which he considers helpful while working on it. . . . Well then, such strengthening reading during the last Joseph years was provided by two books: Laurence Sterne's "Tristram Shandy" and Goethe's "Faust" . . . and in this connection it was a pleasure for me to know that Goethe had held Sterne in very high esteem.' More recently, Salman Rushdie in *Midnight's Children*, Juan Goytisolo in *Juan the Landless*, and Carlos Fuentes in *Christopher Unborn* have all written major fictions of national identity, the roots of which are buried in *Tristram Shandy*. No other eighteenth-century fiction can claim so specific, so glorious, a progeny. But even when one can agree that these authors were all influenced by Sterne, one can also dispute, as I have been doing, the notion that Sterne's achievement was to herald our secular, existential, autonomous world, or to 'create' a new shape to the 'novel'. What, alternatively, might be Sterne's purchase on modernity?

I would begin a brief answer with the notion that Sterne reinforces a great Renaissance tradition of 'unknowingness' (with roots deep enough to touch Solomon and Aristophanes), a tradition under dire challenge in his century, and in ours until quite recently – the challenge of rationalism. For the rationalist, the possibility that one can encounter a problem or contradiction and fail to resolve it is most unsettling; reason, logic, human progress, and mental wellbeing all suggest the need to resolve contradictions, make determinations, reconcile all conflicts as part of some larger and better design. This faith in the systematic resolution of problematic conflicts (the practice of science) became the dominant mode of thinking in Europe during the eighteenth century and continued to dominate western civilization until, perhaps, the devastations to notions of human progress made evident by twentieth-century totalitarianism. Sterne's importance, I suspect, is that he offers a lively, witty, joyous opposition to this new drummer, a stubborn way of looking at contradictions within a context of human limitations and worldly complexities that modern authors, in full retreat from nineteenth-century notions of secular progress, find both instructive and appealing. It is the same world-view (sceptical and Christian, as each seeks reinforcement from the other) that emerges in Rabelais and Montaigne, in Erasmus, Robert Burton, and Cervantes, and in the Augustan satirists, particularly Pope and Swift, for whom Cervantic 'gravity' was a fundamental mask. Resolution and positiveness are the tempting and inevitable vices of this shared world-view; suspension and doubt, its difficult, if not impossible, virtues.

And it is not merely contradictions and puzzlements in character or subject-matter that *Tristram Shandy* illustrates; indeed, far more important is the contradiction of Sterne's artistry, the carefully crafted impression of carelessness and abandon. Sterne is the eminently 'sane' writer pretending to be 'mad' (a formal lesson he learned from Cervantes and Swift, and helped pass on to Joyce and Mann, Rushdie and Fuentes), one of the primary aesthetic defences of modern art and artists against an insane world insisting on its own 'rationalities'. In a world gone mad with the infinite hypocrisies of 'problem-solving' (which Sterne characterizes as *gravity*, Swift as *hypocrisy*, but totalitarians as *final solutions*), the artist must insist, in John Keats's famous formulation, on the vast energies and joys to be found in the infinite contradictions of 'negative capability': 'At once it struck me, what quality went to form a Man of Achievement especially in Literature & which Shakespeare possessed so enormously – I mean *Negative Capability*, that is when man is capable of being in uncertainties, Mysteries, doubts, without any irritable reaching after fact & reason.' Because every fibre of our being cries out to resolve the painful and threatening mysteries surrounding us, the artist whose work embodies a countervailing tendency has much to teach us. Sterne's ever-increasing reputation strongly suggests that modern readers and writers alike feel an urgent need to understand and cultivate Sterne's antirationalism as this most rational – and murderous – century draws to a close.

To remain undecisive in our interpretations is the most difficult goal we can set for ourselves, one we violate with almost every word we speak, just as Christians directed by Jesus's revision of the Ten Commandments may be found to violate their moral goals with almost every thought they have (the lesson, as Sterne the preacher might have pointed out, of Matthew 5:21–48). Virtue and undecisiveness are defined by the human inadequacy in achieving either, and to elide that difficulty in the latter instance by suggesting an idealistic embrace of scholarly impartiality or universal tolerance of all ideas is simply the opening gambit of an often successful (but always deceptive) rhetorical strategy in defence of one's own convictions and interpretations. Friedrich Nietzsche, who called Sterne 'the most liberated spirit of all time, in comparison with whom all others seem stiff, square, intolerant and boorishly direct', comments in the same work, *Human, All Too Human*, that 'It is not conflict of opinions that has made history so violent but conflict of belief in opinions, that is to say conflict of convictions.' Readers of *Tristram Shandy* will immediately recognize the sentiment as an offspring of Sterne's motto, via Epictetus, to Volumes I and II of *Tristram Shandy*: 'We are tormented with the opinions we have of things, and not by things themselves.' Donald Greene, observing the play in the original Greek between *pragmata* and *dogmata*, has suggested a more telling translation: 'Human beings are not troubled by practicalities, but by their dogmas concerning them.' The temptation is, of course, to draw a straight line between Sterne and Nietzsche, between Sterne and the father of modern scepticism; surely, we would argue to ourselves, this neat concurrence of views, along with Nietzsche's great enthusiasm for Sterne, suggests the 'way' to read *Tristram Shandy*, indeed, quite the way I have all along been suggesting is the way I read the work.

But the straight line of conviction, as Sterne illustrates at the conclusion of Volume VI, is always the danger we must most fear, even when – especially when – we are on the verge of embracing, wholeheartedly, the notion that, again quoting Nietzsche, convictions 'are more dangerous enemies of truth than lies'. It is far better, but also far more difficult, not to be convinced by that argument either. One would like, in brief, to write a commentary (by way of introduction, afterword, or exegesis) that would leave the reader, as Toby leaves the Widow Wadman, completely unsatisfied. Toby's motives for doing so, however, are as suspicious as are the Widow's for wanting to charge, helter-skelter, pell-mell, into the very '*curtin* of the *place*' (IX.xxxi), to attack the unknown and render it her own. We are too much like the Widow, each and every reader; every text is, for us, a fortress to be penetrated, a mystery revealed, a riddle solved. Then again, Toby's 'virginity' may people heaven, but it leaves the world unpopulated and Mrs Wadman very unhappy. Another modern enthusiast of Sterne, Milan Kundera, in *Testaments Betrayed* (1995), points towards one way to balance Toby's accounts with all others (though he is writing here not about *Tristram Shandy* but about Stravinsky's so-called 'poverty of heart'): 'Are not vile acts committed as often with the heart's help as without it? ... Will we ever be done with this imbecile sentimental Inquisition, the heart's Reign of Terror?' Only another Nietzschean aphorism, from the voice of Zarathustra, can rescue us and *Tristram Shandy* at this critical juncture, when even dear uncle Toby comes under question: 'That I have to be struggle and becoming and goal and conflict of goals; ah, he who divines my will surely divines, too, along what *crooked* paths it has to go!'

MELVYN NEW

Further Reading

Entries marked with an asterisk are collected in *Tristram Shandy: Contemporary Critical Essays*, ed. Melvyn New (Macmillan, 1992).

*Booth, Wayne C., 'The Self-Conscious Narrator in Comic Fiction before *Tristram Shandy*', *PMLA* 67 (1952), 163–85.

*Brady, Frank, '*Tristram Shandy*: Sexuality, Morality, and Sensibility', *Eighteenth-Century Studies* 4 (1970), 41–56.

*Burckhardt, Sigurd, '*Tristram Shandy*'s Law of Gravity', *ELH* 28 (1961), 70–88.

Cash, Arthur H., 'The Birth of Tristram Shandy: Sterne and Dr. Burton', in *Studies in the Eighteenth Century*, ed. R. F. Brissenden (Australian National University Press, 1968), 133–54.

——, *Laurence Sterne: The Early and Middle Years* (Methuen, 1975).

——, *Laurence Sterne: The Later Years* (Methuen, 1986).

Ehlers, Leigh A., 'Mrs. Shandy's "Lint and Basilicon": The Importance of Women in *Tristram Shandy*', *South Atlantic Review* 46 (1981), 61–75.

*Harries, Elizabeth W., 'Sterne's Novels: Gathering Up the Fragments', *ELH* 49 (1982), 35–49.

*Jefferson, D. W., '*Tristram Shandy* and the Tradition of Learned Wit', *Essays in Criticism* 1 (1951), 225–48.

Lamb, Jonathan, 'Sterne's Use of Montaigne', *Comparative Literature* 32 (1980), 1–41.

——, 'Sterne's System of Imitation', *Modern Language Review* 76 (1981), 794–810.

——, *Sterne's Fiction and the Double Principle* (Cambridge University Press, 1989).

Loscocco, Paula, 'Can't Live Without 'em: Walter Shandy and the Woman Within', *Eighteenth Century: Theory and Interpretation* 32 (1991), 166–79.

McMaster, Juliet, 'Walter Shandy, Sterne, and Gender: A Feminist Foray', *English Studies in Canada* 15 (1989), 441–58.

Mullan, John, 'Laurence Sterne and the "Sociality" of the Novel', in

Sentiment and Sociability: The Language of Feeling in the Eighteenth Century (Clarendon Press, 1988).

New, Melvyn, *Laurence Sterne as Satirist: A Reading of 'Tristram Shandy'* (University of Florida Press, 1969).

——, 'Sterne, Warburton, and the Burden of Exuberant Wit', *Eighteenth-Century Studies* 15 (1982), 245–74.

——, 'Sterne and the Narrative of Determinateness', *Eighteenth-Century Fiction* 4 (1992), 315–29.

——, 'Swift and Sterne: Two Tales, Several Sermons, and a Relationship Revisited', in *Critical Essays on Jonathan Swift*, ed. Frank Palmeri (G. K. Hall, 1993), 164–86.

——, *'Tristram Shandy': A Book for Free Spirits* (Twayne/Macmillan, 1994).

*Ostovich, Helen, 'Reader as Hobby-Horse in *Tristram Shandy*', *Philological Quarterly* 68 (1989), 325–42.

Parnell, J. T., 'Swift, Sterne, and the Skeptical Tradition', *Studies in Eighteenth-Century Culture* 23 (1994), 221–42.

Rosenblum, Michael, 'Why What Happens in Shandy Hall Is Not "A Matter for the Police"', *Eighteenth-Century Fiction* 7 (1995), 147–64.

Schulze, Fritz W., 'In the Margin of the Florida Edition of Sterne', in *Wege Amerikanischer Kultur*, ed. Renate von Bardeleben (Peter Lang, 1989), 47–68.

Smyth, John Vignaux, 'Sterne', in *A Question of Eros: Irony in Sterne, Kierkegaard, and Barthes* (University of Florida Press, 1986).

Soud, Stephen, ' "Weavers, gardeners, and gladiators": Labyrinths in *Tristram Shandy*', *Eighteenth-Century Studies* 28 (1995), 397–411.

Thomas, Calvin, *'Tristram Shandy*'s Consent to Incompleteness: Discourse, Disavowal, Disruption', *Literature & Psychology* 36 (1990), 44–62.

Traugott, John, *Tristram Shandy's World: Sterne's Philosophical Rhetoric* (University of California Press, 1954).

*Wehrs, Donald R., 'Sterne, Cervantes, Montaigne: Fideistic Skepticism and the Rhetoric of Desire', *Comparative Literature Studies* 25 (1988), 127–51.

*Zimmerman, Everett, *'Tristram Shandy* and Narrative Representation', *Eighteenth Century: Theory and Interpretation* 28 (1987), 127–47.

A Note on the Text

The text herein is based on the Florida Edition of *The Works of Laurence Sterne: Tristram Shandy: The Text*, ed. Melvyn New and Joan New, 2 vols. (University Press of Florida, 1978).

Tristram Shandy was first published serially between 1759 and 1767 as follows:

December 1759 Vols. I and II – in York by Ann Ward
January 1761 Vols. III and IV – in London by Dodsley
December 1761 Vols. V and VI – in London by Becket and DeHondt
January 1765 Vols. VII and VIII – in London by Becket and DeHondt
January 1767 Vol. IX – in London by Becket and DeHondt

After the first instalment took London by storm, Dodsley published a second edition in April 1760; before Sterne's death in March 1768, four additional editions were required. Volumes III–VIII also had a second edition during Sterne's lifetime. For the Florida *Text*, multiple copies of these lifetime editions were carefully collated and the results recorded in two appendices, a 'List of Emendations' and an 'Historical Collation'. Sterne had a slight hand in the second editions of Volumes I, II, and III; and he seems to have added two sentences to the second edition of Volume V (see n. 11 to V.xlii); in no other editions is his hand evident. Because of this minimal activity, and the absence of manuscripts, it was clear that the first edition of all nine volumes was the best choice for the copy-text for the Florida Edition.

The Florida *Text* is not a facsimile edition, but it does demonstrate considerable editorial reserve in emending the copy-text. After studying the surviving manuscripts of *A Sentimental Journey* and *A Journal to Eliza*, the editors decided that normalizing Sterne's erratic spellings, grammar, and punctuation would, in too many instances, possibly confuse his intentions. Did he, for example, alter 'Rugians' (the name of a Germanic tribe correctly spelled in his source) to 'Bugians' to create a bawdy play (see n. 1 to VI.xvii), or did the compositor, unfamiliar with 'Rugians', make a simple error? Is Sterne showing his poor command of French when he writes '*a le pere*', as many correcting editors seem to believe; or is he making a deliberate error, designed to echo '*à la mere*' (see nn. 4 and 5 to I.xx)? Conjectures multiply around many such puzzlements in *Tristram Shandy*, and an editor's choice among them will rarely satisfy all readers. Still, almost twenty years after publishing the Florida *Text*, I found only two changes I definitely wanted to make for the Penguin text: 'Lacerna' emends Florida's 'Lacema' (see n. 4 to VI.xix), because it now seems to me that I preserved a likely compositorial error for a Latin word probably familiar to Sterne, since it was taught to schoolboys; and 'wistfully' emends 'wishfully' (p. 353) on the basis of a recovered portion of manuscript, as explained below.

In most instances, substantive emendations to the copy-text have been made only in self-evident instances, the correction of obvious inadvertencies in the printed text. Some few emendations, however, do require explanation (as do some failures to emend), and I have explained these decisions in the notes. Conjectural alternative readings are indicated in the notes by an italic question mark.

During the preparation of the Florida *Text* no manuscript of *Tristram* could be found. In 1990, however, the lost fair copy of the Le Fever episode that Sterne gave to his patron, Lady Spencer, resurfaced in the British Library (see my essay in *Scriblerian* 23 (1991)). A collation of that manuscript with the printed version showed many differences in the accidentals, and several substantive differences as well, one of which, 'wistfully' for 'wishfully', has been accepted into this edition (see p. 353). Reading the manuscript proved a humbling experience; as I wrote in 1990, 'the difficulty of establishing a "true" text may be beautifully brought home by observing the slight difference between "wishfully" and "wistfully" ... and then acknowledging that extrapolation would argue over one hundred such buried and irrecoverable "misreadings" in the printed text – one every seven or eight pages of the Florida edition. The Le Fever manuscript might well bring a tear to the eye.'

To be sure, one takes some consolation in remembering, as Professor Ricks notes in his introduction, that Sterne had a highly developed sense of the 'bookishness' of his enterprise, the fact that a work 'in print' develops a character of its own. It is one's offspring, to use a favourite Shandean metaphor, and even when we can place ourselves at the precise scene of conception, delivery is turned over to a plethora of competing egos and instruments. It is – Dr Slop might opine – a wonder that any book gets born; and yet – Toby might reply – what prodigious libraries we have!

In the Florida *Text*, Greek words were photographically reproduced from the first edition in order to emphasize that for Sterne the *appearance* of Greek in the middle of his text (or in a footnote) had a visual significance that ought not to be ignored; the same practice is used for this edition. Sterne's often incorrect accenting has been preserved; such details can help mark the extent of his command of Greek and, as well, help identify his sources. Sterne's other foreign language borrowings are discussed at length in Appendices 6 and 8 of the Florida *Text*. Generally speaking, where it was felt (for example, in the Sorbonne Memoire) that Sterne would have used a photocopy had the technology been available, the copy-text was emended to conform to his source; otherwise, his errors, particularly in accenting, have usually been allowed to stand.

Sterne's varied dash-lengths have been preserved, including the use of two to five hyphens rather than the usual em and two-em dashes, a usage particularly evident in the York-printed volumes, when Sterne may have overseen the printing with some care. Other vagaries of punctuation have also been preserved. Silent changes to the copy-text include (1) consistently setting in italics the opening and closing parentheses around an italic word, as well as colons, question marks, and exclamation points after italic words; (2) consistently setting in roman the possessive 's' after an italicized name (these changes follow the usual practice of the copy-text); (3) modernizing the long 's' of the copy-text; (4) silently omitting running quotation marks in the left margin.

Beginning in Volume VII, Sterne's compositors abandoned the uniform italicizing of proper names, and I have followed suit; while it may take readers a few pages to adjust to the difference, the pause serves to remind us that Sterne published *Tristram* with three different houses over an eight-year period.

Finally, it should be noted that *Tristram Shandy* in any one-volume edition is not the work Sterne's contemporaries knew. They received it in small octavo volumes, measuring perhaps 3.5 by 7 inches, usually fewer than 200 pages, each page containing some 200 words. It was, in short, a pleasant little book well suited to the large pockets of eighteenth-century dress, and to a rapid and joyful reading, perhaps with one's elbow propped on the mantelpiece, and a year's wait (at least) for the sequel. We read *Tristram Shandy* in a much different format today, but one must not blame Sterne for that.

T H E

L I F E

A N D

O P I N I O N S

O F

TRISTRAM SHANDY,
GENTLEMAN.

Ταρασσει τὲς Ἀνθρώπες ἐ τὰ Πράγμαϊα,
αλλα τὰ περι τῶν Πραγμάϊων, Δογμαϊα.

VOL. I.

1760.

(Height of original type-page 123 mm.)

To the Right Honourable
Mr. PITT.[1]

SIR,

NEVER poor Wight of a Dedicator had less hopes from his Dedication, than I have from this of mine; for it is written in a bye corner[2] of the kingdom, and in a retired thatch'd house, where I live in a constant endeavour to fence against the infirmities of ill health,[3] and other evils of life, by mirth; being firmly persuaded that every time a man smiles,—but much more so, when he laughs, that it adds something to this Fragment of Life.

I humbly beg, Sir, that you will honour this book by taking it——(not under your Protection,——it must protect itself, but)—into the country with you; where, if I am ever told, it has made you smile, or can conceive it has beguiled you of one moment's pain——I shall think myself as happy as a minister of state;——perhaps much happier than any one (one only excepted) that I have ever read or heard of.

I am, great Sir,
(and what is more to your Honour,)
I am, good Sir,
Your Well-wisher,
and most humble Fellow-Subject,

THE AUTHOR.

THE

LIFE and OPINIONS

OF

TRISTRAM SHANDY, Gent.

CHAP. I.

I Wish either my father or my mother, or indeed both of them, as
they were in duty both equally bound to it, had minded what they were
about when they begot me;[1] had they duly consider'd how much depended upon what they were then doing;——that not only the production
of a rational Being was concern'd in it, but that possibly the happy formation and temperature[2] of his body, perhaps his genius and the very cast of
his mind;——and, for aught they knew to the contrary, even the fortunes
of his whole house might take their turn from the humours[3] and dispositions which were then uppermost:——Had they duly weighed
and considered all this, and proceeded accordingly,——I am verily persuaded I should have made a quite different figure in the world, from
that, in which the reader is likely to see me.——Believe me, good folks,
this is not so inconsiderable a thing as many of you may think it;——you
have all, I dare say, heard of the animal spirits,[4] as how they are trans-
fused from father to son, &c. &c.——and a great deal to that purpose:——
Well, you may take my word, that nine parts in ten of a man's sense or
his nonsense, his successes and miscarriages in this world depend upon
their motions and activity, and the different tracks and trains you put them
into; so that when they are once set a-going, whether right or wrong, 'tis
not a halfpenny matter,--away they go cluttering like hey-go-mad; and
by treading the same steps over and over again, they presently make a
road of it, as plain and as smooth as a garden-walk, which, when they are

once used to, the Devil himself sometimes shall not be able to drive them off it.

Pray, my dear, quoth my mother, *have you not forgot to wind up the clock?*——*Good G——!* cried my father, making an exclamation, but taking care to moderate his voice at the same time,——*Did ever woman, since the creation of the world, interrupt a man with such a silly question?* Pray, what was your father saying?——Nothing.

CHAP. II.

——Then, positively, there is nothing in the question, that I can see, either good or bad.——Then let me tell you, Sir, it was a very unseasonable question at least,—because it scattered and dispersed the animal spirits, whose business it was to have escorted and gone hand-in-hand with the *HOMUNCULUS*, and conducted him safe to the place destined for his reception.[1]

The HOMUNCULUS, Sir, in how-ever low and ludicrous a light he may appear, in this age of levity, to the eye of folly or prejudice;—to the eye of reason in scientifick research, he stands confess'd—a BEING guarded and circumscribed with rights:——The minutest philosophers,[2] who, by the bye, have the most enlarged understandings, (their souls being inversely as their enquiries) shew us incontestably, That the HOMUNCULUS is created by the same hand,—engender'd in the same course of nature,—endowed with the same loco-motive powers and faculties with us:——That he consists, as we do, of skin, hair, fat, flesh, veins, arteries, ligaments, nerves, cartileges, bones, marrow, brains, glands, genitals, humours, and articulations;[3]——is a Being of as much activity,——and, in all senses of the word, as much and as truly our fellow-creature as my Lord Chancellor[4] of England.—He may be benefited, he may be injured,—he may obtain redress;—in a word, he has all the claims and rights of humanity, which *Tully, Puffendorff,*[5] or the best ethick writers allow to arise out of that state and relation.

Now, dear Sir, what if any accident had befallen him in his way alone?——or that, thro' terror of it, natural to so young a traveller, my little gentleman had got to his journey's end miserably spent;——his muscular strength and virility worn down to a thread;—his own animal spirits ruffled beyond description,—and that in this sad disorder'd state of nerves, he had laid down a prey to sudden starts, or a series of melancholy dreams and fancies for nine long, long months together.——I tremble to think what a foundation had been laid for a thousand weaknesses both of body and mind, which no skill of the physician or the philosopher could ever afterwards have set thoroughly to rights.

CHAP. III.

TO my uncle Mr. *Toby Shandy* do I stand indebted for the preceding anecdote, to whom my father, who was an excellent natural philosopher, and much given to close reasoning upon the smallest matters, had oft, and heavily, complain'd of the injury; but once more particularly, as my uncle *Toby* well remember'd, upon his observing a most unaccountable obliquity, (as he call'd it) in my manner of setting up my top, and justifying the principles upon which I had done it,—the old gentleman shook his head, and in a tone more expressive by half of sorrow than reproach,—he said his heart all along foreboded, and he saw it verified in this, and from a thousand other observations he had made upon me, That I should neither think nor act like any other man's child:——*But alas!* continued he, shaking his head a second time, and wiping away a tear which was trickling down his cheeks, *My Tristram's misfortunes began nine months before ever he came into the world.*

——My mother, who was sitting by, look'd up,—but she knew no more than her backside what my father meant,--but my uncle, Mr. *Toby Shandy*, who had been often informed of the affair,—understood him very well.

CHAP. IV.

I Know there are <u>readers</u> in the world, as well as many other good people in it, who are <u>no readers</u> at all,—who find themselves <u>ill at ease</u>, unless they are let into the whole secret from first to last, of every thing which concerns you.

It is in <u>pure compliance</u> with this humour of theirs, and <u>from a backward-ness</u> in my nature to disappoint any one soul living, that I have been so very <u>particular</u> already. As my <u>life and opinions</u> are likely to make some noise in the world, and, if I conjecture right, will take in all ranks, professions, and denominations of men whatever,—be no less read than the *Pilgrim's Progress*[1] itself---and, in the end, prove the very thing which *Montaigne*[2] dreaded his essays should turn out, that is, a book for a parlour-window;—I find it <u>necessary to consult</u> every one a little in his turn; and therefore <u>must beg pardon for going on a little further</u> in the same way: For which cause, right glad I am, that I have begun the history of myself in the way I have done; and that <u>I am able to go on tracing every thing in it</u>, as *Horace* says, *ab Ovo*.[3]

Horace, I know, does not recommend this fashion altogether: But that gentleman is speaking <u>only of an epic poem</u> or a tragedy;—(I forget which)—besides, if it was not so, I should beg Mr. *Horace*'s pardon;—for in writing what I have set about, I shall confine myself neither to his rules, <u>nor to any man's rules that ever lived</u>.

To such, however, as do <u>not choose to go so far back into these things</u>, I can give no better advice, than that they <u>skip</u> over the remaining part of this Chapter; for I declare before hand, 'tis <u>wrote only for the curious and inquisitive</u>.

──────────────── Shut the door. ────────────────

<u>I was begot in the night</u>, betwixt the first *Sunday* and the first *Monday* in the month of *March*, in the year of our Lord one thousand seven hundred and eighteen. <u>I am positive I was</u>.—But how I came to be so very <u>particular</u> in my account of a thing which happened before I was born, is owing to <u>another small</u> anecdote known only in our own family, but now made public[4] for the better clearing up this point.

My father, you must know, who was originally a *Turky* <u>merchant</u>,[5] but had left off business for some years, in order to retire to, and die upon, his paternal estate in the county of————, was, I believe, one of the most regular men in every thing he did, whether 'twas matter of business, or matter of amusement, that ever lived. As a small specimen of this extreme exactness of his, to which he was in truth a slave,—he had made it a rule for many years of his life,—on the first *Sunday night* of every month throughout the whole year,—as certain as ever the *Sunday night* came, ————to wind up a large house-clock which we had standing upon the back-stairs head, with his own hands:——And being somewhere between fifty and sixty years of age, at the time I have been speaking of,—he had likewise gradually brought some other little family concernments to the same period, in order, as he would often say to my uncle *Toby*, to get them all out of the way at one time, and be no more plagued and pester'd with them the rest of the month.

It was attended but with one misfortune, which, in a great measure, fell upon myself, and the effects of which I fear I shall carry with me to my grave; namely, that, from an unhappy association of ideas which have no connection in nature, it so fell out at length, that my poor mother could never hear the said clock wound up,—but the thoughts of some other things unavoidably popp'd into her head,—*& vice versâ:*—which strange combination of ideas, the sagacious *Locke*,[6] who certainly understood the nature of these things better than most men, affirms to have produced more wry actions than all other sources of prejudice whatsoever.

But this by the bye.

Now it appears, by a memorandum in my father's pocket-book, which now lies upon the table, "That on *Lady-Day*,[7] which was on the 25th of the same month in which I date my geniture,—my father set out upon his journey to *London* with my eldest brother *Bobby*, to fix him at *Westminster* school;"[8] and, as it appears from the same authority, "That he did not get down to his wife and family till the *second week* in *May* following,"—it brings the thing almost to a certainty. However, what follows in the beginning of the next chapter puts it beyond all possibility of doubt.

————But pray, Sir, What was your father doing all *December*,— *January*, and *February?*——Why, Madam,—he was all that time afflicted with a Sciatica.[9]

CHAP. V.

O N the fifth day of *November*, 1718, which to the æra fixed on, was as near nine kalendar months as any husband could in reason have expected,[1]—was I *Tristram Shandy*, Gentleman, brought forth into this scurvy and disasterous[2] world of ours.—I wish I had been born in the Moon, or in any of the planets, (except *Jupiter* or *Saturn*, because I never could bear cold weather) for it could not well have fared worse with me in any of them (tho' I will not answer for *Venus*) than it has in this vile, dirty planet of ours,—which o' my conscience, with reverence be it spoken, I take to be made up of the shreds and clippings of the rest;——not but the planet is well enough, provided a man could be born in it to a great title or to a great estate; or could any how contrive to be called up to publick charges, and employments of dignity or power;—but that is not my case;----and therefore every man will speak of the fair as his own market has gone in it;—for which cause I affirm it over again to be one of the vilest worlds that ever was made;---for I can truly say, that from the first hour I drew my breath in it, to this, that I can now scarce draw it at all, for an asthma I got in scating against the wind in *Flanders*;--I have been the continual sport of what the world calls Fortune; and though I will not wrong her by saying, She has ever made me feel the weight of any great or signal evil;---yet with all the good temper in the world, I affirm it of her, That in every stage of my life, and at every turn and corner where she could get fairly at me, the ungracious Duchess has pelted me with a set of as pitiful misadventures and cross accidents[3] as ever small HERO sustained.

CHAP. VI.

IN the beginning of the last chapter, I inform'd you exactly *when* I was born;—but I did not inform you, *how. No*; that particular was reserved entirely for a chapter by itself;—besides, Sir, as you and I are in a manner perfect strangers to each other, it would not have been proper to have let you into too many circumstances relating to myself all at once.—You must have a little patience. I have undertaken, you see, to write not only my life, but my opinions also; hoping and expecting that your knowledge of my character, and of what kind of a mortal I am, by the one, would give you a better relish for the other: As you proceed further with me, the slight acquaintance which is now beginning betwixt us, will grow into familiarity; and that, unless one of us is in fault, will terminate in friendship. —— *O diem præclarum!*[1] —— then nothing which has touched me will be thought trifling in its nature, or tedious in its telling. Therefore, my dear friend and companion, if you should think me somewhat sparing of my narrative on my first setting out,—bear with me,—and let me go on, and tell my story my own way:—— or if I should seem now and then to trifle upon the road,—— or should sometimes put on a fool's cap with a bell to it, for a moment or two as we pass along,--don't fly off,—but rather courteously give me credit for a little more wisdom than appears upon my outside;—and as we jogg on, either laugh with me, or at me, or in short, do any thing,—— only keep your temper.

CHAP. VII.

IN the same village where my father and my mother dwelt, dwelt also a thin, upright, motherly, notable, good old body of a midwife,[1] who, with the help of a little plain good sense, and some years full employment in her business, in which she had all along trusted little to her own efforts, and a great deal to those of dame nature,—had acquired, in her way, no small degree of reputation in the world;—by which word *world*, need I in this place inform your worship, that I would be understood to mean no more of it, than a small circle described upon the circle of the great world, of four *English* miles diameter, or thereabouts, of which the cottage where the good old woman lived, is supposed to be the centre.——She had been left, it seems, a widow in great distress, with three or four small children, in her forty-seventh year; and as she was at that time a person of decent carriage,—grave deportment,——a woman moreover of few words, and withall an object of compassion, whose distress and silence under it call'd out the louder for a friendly lift: the wife of the parson of the parish was touch'd with pity; and having often lamented an inconvenience, to which her husband's flock had for many years been exposed, inasmuch, as there was no such thing as a midwife, of any kind or degree to be got at, let the case have been never so urgent, within less than six or seven long miles riding; which said seven long miles in dark nights and dismal roads, the country thereabouts being nothing but a deep clay, was almost equal to fourteen; and that in effect was sometimes next to having no midwife at all; it came into her head, that it would be doing as seasonable a kindness to the whole parish, as to the poor creature herself, to get her a little instructed in some of the plain principles of the business, in order to set her up in it. As no woman thereabouts was better qualified to execute the plan she had formed than herself, the Gentlewoman very charitably undertook it; and having great influence over the female part of the parish, she found no difficulty in effecting it to the utmost of her wishes. In truth, the parson join'd his interest with his wife's in the whole affair; and in order to do things as they should be, and give the poor soul as good a title by law to practise, as his wife had given by institution,——he chearfully paid the fees for the ordinaries licence himself, amounting, in the whole, to the sum of eighteen shillings and fourpence; so that, betwixt them both, the good woman was fully invested in the real and corporal possession of her office, together with all its *rights, members, and appurtenances whatsoever.*[2]

These last words, you must know, were not according to the old form in which such licences, faculties, and powers usually ran, which in like cases had heretofore been granted to the sisterhood. But it was according to a neat *Formula* of *Didius*[3] his own devising, who having a particular turn for taking to pieces, and new framing over again, all kind of instruments in that way, not only hit upon this dainty amendment, but coax'd many of the old licensed matrons in the neighbourhood, to open their faculties afresh, in order to have this whim-wham[4] of his inserted.

I own I never could envy *Didius* in these kinds of fancies of his:—But every man to his own taste.—Did not Dr. *Kunastrokius*,[5] that great man, at his leisure hours, take the greatest delight imaginable in combing of asses tails, and plucking the dead hairs out with his teeth, though he had tweezers always in his pocket? Nay, if you come to that, Sir, have not the wisest of men in all ages, not excepting *Solomon* himself,—have they not had their HOBBY-HORSES;[6]—their running horses,[7]—their coins and their cockle-shells, their drums and their trumpets, their fiddles, their pallets,[8]——their maggots[9] and their butterflies?—and so long as a man rides his HOBBY-HORSE peaceably and quietly along the King's high-way, and neither compels you or me to get up behind him,——pray, Sir, what have either you or I to do with it?

CHAP. VIII.

—*De gustibus non est disputandum*;[1]—that is, there is no disputing against HOBBY-HORSES; and, for my part, I seldom do; nor could I with any sort of grace, had I been an enemy to them at the bottom; for happening, at certain intervals and changes of the Moon, to be both fiddler and painter,[2] according as the fly stings:---Be it known to you, that I keep a couple of pads[3] myself, upon which, in their turns, (nor do I care who knows it) I frequently ride out and take the air;—tho' sometimes, to my shame be it spoken, I take somewhat longer journies than what a wise man would think altogether right.----But the truth is,---I am not a wise man;—— and besides am a mortal of so little consequence in the world, it is not much matter what I do; so I seldom fret or fume at all about it: Nor does it much disturb my rest when I see such great Lords and tall Personages as hereafter follow;---such, for instance, as my Lord A, B, C, D, E, F, G, H, I, K, L, M, N, O, P, Q, and so on, all of a row, mounted upon their several horses;--some with large stirrups, getting on in a more grave and sober pace;----others on the contrary, tuck'd up to their very chins, with whips across their mouths, scouring and scampering it away like so many little party-colour'd devils astride a mortgage,——and as if some of them were resolved to break their necks.—So much the better—say I to myself;—for in case the worst should happen, the world will make a shift to do excellently well without them;—and for the rest,----why,----God speed them,----e'en let them ride on without any opposition from me; for were their lordships unhorsed this very night,——'tis ten to one but that many of them would be worse mounted by one half before to-morrow morning.

Not one of these instances therefore can be said to break in upon my rest.—But there is an instance, which I own puts me off my guard, and that is, when I see one born for great actions, and, what is still more for his honour, whose nature ever inclines him to good ones;----when I behold such a one, my Lord, like yourself, whose principles and conduct are as generous and noble as his blood, and whom, for that reason, a corrupt world cannot spare one moment;—when I see such a one, my Lord, mounted, though it is but for a minute beyond the time which my love to my country has prescribed to him, and my zeal for his glory wishes,— then, my Lord, I cease to be a philosopher, and in the first transport of an honest impatience, I wish the HOBBY-HORSE, with all his fraternity, at the Devil.

My Lord,

66 I Maintain this to be a dedication, notwithstanding its singularity in the three great essentials of matter, form, and place: I beg, therefore, you will accept it as such, and that you will permit me to lay it, with the most respectful humility, at your Lordship's feet,--when you are upon them,--which you can be when you please;----and that is, my Lord, when ever there is occasion for it, and I will add, to the best purposes too. I have the honour to be,

My Lord,

Your Lordship's most obedient,

and most devoted,

and most humble servant,

TRISTRAM SHANDY."

CHAP. IX.

I Solemnly declare to all mankind, that the above dedication was made for no one Prince, Prelate, Pope, or Potentate,—Duke, Marquis, Earl, Viscount, or Baron of this, or any other Realm in Christendom;-----nor has it yet been hawk'd about, or offered publickly or privately, directly or indirectly, to any one person or personage, great or small; but is honestly a true Virgin-Dedication untried on, upon any soul living.

I labour this point so particularly, merely to remove any offence or objection which might arise against it, from the manner in which I propose to make the most of it;---which is the putting it up fairly to publick sale; which I now do.

——Every author has a way of his own, in bringing his points to bear;--for my own part, as I hate chaffering and higgling for a few guineas in a dark entry;---I resolved within myself, from the very beginning, to deal squarely and openly with your Great Folks in this affair, and try whether I should not come off the better by it.

If therefore there is any one Duke, Marquis, Earl, Viscount, or Baron, in these his Majesty's dominions, who stands in need of a tight, genteel dedication, and whom the above will suit, (for by the bye, unless it suits in some degree, I will not part with it)——it is much at his service for fifty guineas;——which I am positive is twenty guineas less than it ought to be afforded for, by any man of genius.

My Lord, if you examine it over again, it is far from being a gross piece of daubing,[1] as some dedications are. The design, your Lordship sees, is good, the colouring transparent,—the drawing not amiss;—or to speak more like a man of science,—and measure my piece in the painter's scale,[2] divided into 20,—I believe, my Lord, the out-lines will turn out as 12,—the composition as 9,—the colouring as 6,—the expression 13 and a half,—and the design,—if I may be allowed, my Lord, to understand my own *design*, and supposing absolute perfection in designing, to be as 20,—I think it cannot well fall short of 19. Besides all this,—there is keeping in it, and the dark strokes in the HOBBY-HORSE, (which is a secondary figure, and a kind of back-ground to the whole) give great force to the principal lights in your own figure, and make it come off wonderfully;——and besides, there is an air of originality in the *tout ensemble*.[3]

Be pleased, my good Lord, to order the sum to be paid into the hands of Mr. *Dodsley*,[4] for the benefit of the author; and in the next edition care shall be taken that this chapter be expunged, and your Lordship's titles, distinctions, arms and good actions, be placed at the front of the preceding chapter: All which, from the words, *De gustibus non est disputandum*, and whatever else in this book relates to HOBBY-HORSES, but no more, shall stand dedicated to your Lordship.---The rest I dedicate to the MOON, who, by the bye, of all the PATRONS or MATRONS I can think of, has most power to set my book a-going, and make the world run mad after it.

Bright Goddess,

If thou art not too busy with CANDID and Miss CUNEGUND's affairs,[5]--take *Tristram Shandy*'s under thy protection also.

CHAP. X.

WHatever degree of small merit, the act of benignity in favour of the midwife, might justly claim, or in whom that claim truly rested,——at first sight seems not very material to this history;——certain however it was, that the gentlewoman, the parson's wife, did run away at that time with the whole of it: And yet, for my life, I cannot help thinking but that the parson himself, tho' he had not the good fortune to hit upon the design first,——yet, as he heartily concurred in it the moment it was laid before him, and as heartily parted with his money to carry it into execution, had a claim to some share of it,——if not to a full half of whatever honour was due to it.

The world at that time was pleased to determine the matter otherwise.

Lay down the book, and I will allow you half a day to give a probable guess at the grounds of this procedure.

Be it known then, that, for about five years before the date of the midwife's licence, of which you have had so circumstantial an account,——the parson we have to do with, had made himself a country-talk by a breach of all decorum, which he had committed against himself, his station, and his office;——and that was, in never appearing better, or otherwise mounted, than upon a lean, sorry, jack-ass of a horse, value about one pound fifteen shillings; who, to shorten all description of him, was full brother to *Rosinante*,[1] as far as similitude congenial could make him; for he answered his description to a hair-breadth in every thing,——except that I do not remember 'tis any where said, that *Rosinante* was broken winded; and that, moreover, *Rosinante*, as is the happiness of most *Spanish* horses, fat or lean,——was undoubtedly a horse at all points.

I know very well that the HERO's horse was a horse of chaste deportment,[2] which may have given grounds for a contrary opinion: But it is as certain at the same time, that *Rosinante*'s continency (as may be demonstrated from the adventure of the *Yanguesian* carriers) proceeded from no bodily defect or cause whatsoever, but from the temperance and orderly current of his blood.——And let me tell you, Madam, there is a great deal of very good chastity in the world, in behalf of which you could not say more for your life.

Let that be as it may, as my purpose is to do exact justice to every creature brought upon the stage of this dramatic work,——I could not stifle this distinction in favour of Don *Quixote*'s horse;——in all other points the parson's horse, I say, was just such another,——for he was as lean, and as lank, and as sorry a jade, as HUMILITY herself could have bestrided.

In the estimation of here and there a man of weak judgment, it was greatly in the parson's power to have helped the figure of this horse of his,——for he was master of a very handsome demi-peak'd[3] saddle, quilted on the seat with green plush, garnished with a double row of silver-headed studs, and a noble pair of shining brass stirrups, with a housing altogether suitable, of grey superfine cloth, with an edging of black lace, terminating in a deep, black, silk fringe, *poudrè d'or*,[4]——all which he had purchased in the pride and prime of his life, together with a grand embossed bridle, ornamented at all points as it should be.——But not caring to banter his beast, he had hung all these up behind his study door;——and, in lieu of them, had seriously befitted him with just such a bridle and such a saddle, as the figure and value of such a steed might well and truly deserve.

In the several sallies about his parish, and in the neighbouring visits to the gentry who lived around him,——you will easily comprehend, that the parson, so appointed, would both hear and see enough to keep his philosophy from rusting. To speak the truth, he never could enter a village, but he caught the attention of both old and young.----Labour stood still as he pass'd,---the bucket hung suspended in the middle of the well, ——the spinning-wheel forgot its round,———even chuck-farthing and shuffle-cap[5] themselves stood gaping till he had got out of sight; and as his movement was not of the quickest, he had generally time enough upon his hands to make his observations,--to hear the groans of the serious, ——and the laughter of the light-hearted;—all which he bore with excellent tranquility.—His character was,——he loved a jest in his heart—and as he saw himself in the true point of ridicule,[6] he would say, he could not be angry with others for seeing him in a light, in which he so strongly saw himself: So that to his friends, who knew his foible was not the love of money, and who therefore made the less scruple in bantering the extravagance of his humour,—instead of giving the true cause,—— he chose rather to join in the laugh against himself; and as he never carried one single ounce of flesh upon his own bones, being altogether as spare a figure as his beast,—he would sometimes insist upon it, that the horse was as good as the rider deserved;—that they were, centaur-like,---both of a piece. At other times, and in other moods, when his spirits were above the temptation of false wit,—he would say, he found himself going off fast in a consumption; and, with great gravity, would pretend, he could not bear the sight of a fat horse without a dejection of heart, and a sensible alteration in his pulse; and that he had made choice of the lean one he rode upon, not only to keep himself in countenance, but in spirits.

At different times he would give fifty humourous and opposite reasons for riding a meek-spirited jade of a broken-winded horse, preferably to one of mettle;—for on such a one he could sit mechanically, and meditate as delightfully *de vanitate mundi et fugâ sæculi*,[7] as with the advantage of a death's head[8] before him;—that, in all other exercitations, he could spend his time, as he rode slowly along,——to as much account as in his study;— that he could draw up an argument in his sermon,—or a hole in his breeches, as steadily on the one as in the other;—that brisk trotting and slow argumentation, like wit and judgment,[9] were two incompatible movements.--But that, upon his steed—he could unite and reconcile every thing,—he could compose his sermon,—he could compose his cough,[10]——and, in case nature gave a call that way, he could likewise compose himself to sleep.—In short, the parson upon such encounters would assign any cause, but the true cause,—and he with-held the true one, only out of a nicety of temper, because he thought it did honour to him.

But the truth of the story was as follows: In the first years of this gentleman's life, and about the time when the superb saddle and bridle were purchased by him, it had been his manner, or vanity, or call it what you will,——to run into the opposite extream.——In the language of the county where he dwelt, he was said to have loved a good horse, and generally had one of the best in the whole parish standing in his stable always ready for saddling; and as the nearest midwife, as I told you, did not live nearer to the village than seven miles, and in a vile country,—— it so fell out that the poor gentleman was scarce a whole week together without some piteous application for his beast; and as he was not an unkind-hearted man, and every case was more pressing and more distressful than the last,—as much as he loved his beast, he had never a heart to refuse him; the upshot of which was generally this, that his horse was either clapp'd, or spavin'd, or greaz'd;—or he was twitter-bon'd, or broken-winded,[11] or something, in short, or other had befallen him which would let him carry no flesh;—so that he had every nine or ten months a bad horse to get rid of,—and a good horse to purchase in his stead.

What the loss in such a balance might amount to, *communibus annis*,[12] I would leave to a special jury of sufferers in the same traffic, to determine;— but let it be what it would, the honest gentleman bore it for many years without a murmur, till at length, by repeated ill accidents of the kind, he found it necessary to take the thing under consideration; and upon weighing the whole, and summing it up in his mind, he found it not only dispro- portion'd to his other expences, but withall so heavy an article in itself, as to disable him from any other act of generosity in his parish: Besides this he considered, that, with half the sum thus galloped away, he could do ten times as much good;——and what still weighed more with him than all other considerations put together, was this, that it confined all his charity into one particular channel, and where, as he fancied, it was the least wanted, namely, to the child-bearing and child-getting part of his parish; reserving nothing for the impotent,---nothing for the aged,--- nothing for the many comfortless scenes he was hourly called forth to visit, where poverty, and sickness, and affliction dwelt together.

For these reasons he resolved to discontinue the expence; and there appeared but two possible ways to extricate him clearly out of it;—and these were, either to make it an irrevocable law never more to lend his steed upon any application whatever,—or else be content to ride the last poor devil, such as they had made him, with all his aches and infirmities, to the very end of the chapter.

As he dreaded his own constancy in the first,——he very chearfully betook himself to the second; and tho' he could very well have explain'd it, as I said, to his honour,—yet, for that very reason, he had a spirit above it; choosing rather to bear the contempt of his enemies, and the laughter of his friends, than undergo the pain of telling a story, which might seem a panygeric upon himself.

I have the highest idea of the spiritual and refined sentiments of this reverend gentleman, from this single stroke in his character, which I think comes up to any of the honest refinements of the peerless knight of *La Mancha*,[13] whom, by the bye, with all his follies, I love more, and would actually have gone further to have paid a visit to, than the greatest hero of antiquity.

But this is not the moral of my story: The thing I had in view was to shew the temper of the world in the whole of this affair.—For you must know, that so long as this explanation would have done the parson credit,— the devil a soul could find it out,—I suppose his enemies would not, and that his friends could not.——But no sooner did he bestir himself in behalf of the midwife, and pay the expences of the ordinary's licence to set her up,—but the whole secret came out; every horse he had lost, and two horses more than ever he had lost, with all the circumstances of their destruction, were known and distinctly remembered.—The story ran like wild-fire.—"The parson had a returning fit of pride which had just seized him; and he was going to be well mounted once again in his life; and if it was so, 'twas plain as the sun at noon-day, he would pocket the expence of the licence, ten times told the very first year:——so that every body was left to judge what were his views in this act of charity."

What were his views in this, and in every other action of his life,—or rather what were the opinions which floated in the brains of other people concerning it, was a thought which too much floated in his own, and too often broke in upon his rest, when he should have been sound asleep.

About ten years ago this gentleman had the good fortune to be made entirely easy upon that score,——it being just so long since he left his parish,——and the whole world at the same time behind him,--and stands accountable to a judge of whom he will have no cause to complain.

But there is a fatality attends the actions of some men:[14] Order them as they will, they pass thro' a certain medium which so twists and refracts them from their true directions————that, with all the titles to praise which a rectitude of heart can give, the doers of them are nevertheless forced to live and die without it.

Of the truth of which this gentleman was a painful example.——But to know by what means this came to pass,----and to make that knowledge of use to you, I insist upon it that you read the two following chapters, which contain such a sketch of his life and conversation, as will carry its moral along with it.--When this is done, if nothing stops us in our way, we will go on with the midwife.

CHAP. XI.

YORICK[1] was this parson's name, and, what is very remarkable in it, (as appears from a most antient account of the family, wrote upon strong vellum, and now in perfect preservation) it had been exactly so spelt for near,——I was within an ace of saying nine hundred years;—— but I would not shake my credit in telling an improbable truth, however indisputable in itself;——and therefore I shall content myself with only saying,---It had been exactly so spelt, without the least variation or transposition of a single letter, for I do not know how long; which is more than I would venture to say of one half of the best surnames in the kingdom; which, in a course of years, have generally undergone as many chops and changes as their owners.——Has this been owing to the pride, or to the shame of the respective proprietors?——In honest truth, I think, sometimes to the one, and sometimes to the other, just as the temptation has wrought. But a villainous affair it is, and will one day so blend and confound us all together, that no one shall be able to stand up and swear, "That his own great grand father was the man who did either this or that."

This evil had been sufficiently fenced against by the prudent care of the *Yorick*'s family, and their religious preservation of these records I quote, which do further inform us, That the family was originally of *Danish* extraction, and had been transplanted into *England* as early as in the reign of *Horwendillus*,[2] king of *Denmark*, in whose court it seems, an ancestor of this Mr. *Yorick*'s, and from whom he was lineally descended, held a considerable post to the day of his death. Of what nature this considerable post was, this record saith not;—it only adds, That, for near two centuries, it had been totally abolished as altogether unnecessary, not only in that court, but in every other court of the Christian world.

It has often come into my head, that this post could be no other than that of the king's chief Jester;---and that *Hamlet*'s *Yorick*, in our *Shakespear*, many of whose plays, you know, are founded upon authenticated facts,--was certainly the very man.

I have not the time to look into *Saxo-Grammaticus*'s *Danish* history, to know the certainty of this;—but if you have leisure, and can easily get at the book, you may do it full as well yourself.

I had just time, in my travels through *Denmark* with Mr. *Noddy*'s[3] eldest son, whom, in the year 1741, I accompanied as governor, riding along with him at a prodigious rate thro' most parts of *Europe*, and of which original journey perform'd by us two, a most delectable narrative[4] will be given in the progress of this work. I had just time, I say, and that was all, to prove the truth of an observation made by a long sojourner in that country;----namely, "That nature was neither very lavish, nor was she very stingy in her gifts of genius and capacity to its inhabitants;--but, like a discreet parent, was moderately kind to them all; observing such an equal tenor in the distribution of her favours, as to bring them, in those points, pretty near to a level with each other; so that you will meet with few instances in that kingdom of refin'd parts; but a great deal of good plain houshold understanding amongst all ranks of people, of which every body has a share;" which is, I think, very right.

With us, you see, the case is quite different;—we are all ups and downs in this matter;—you are a great genius;--or 'tis fifty to one, Sir, you are a great dunce and a blockhead;---not that there is a total want of intermediate steps,—no,—we are not so irregular as that comes to;—but the two extremes are more common, and in a greater degree in this unsettled island, where nature, in her gifts and dispositions of this kind, is most whimsical and capricious; fortune herself not being more so in the bequest of her goods and chattels[5] than she.

This is all that ever stagger'd my faith in regard to *Yorick*'s extraction, who, by what I can remember of him, and by all the accounts I could ever get of him, seem'd not to have had one single drop of *Danish* blood in his whole crasis;[6] in nine hundred years, it might possibly have all run out:----I will not philosophize one moment with you about it; for happen how it would, the fact was this:—That instead of that cold phlegm and exact regularity of sense and humours, you would have look'd for, in one so extracted;---he was, on the contrary, as mercurial and sublimated a composition,----as heteroclite a creature in all his declensions;[7]-----with as much life and whim, and *gaité de cœur*[8] about him, as the kindliest climate could have engendered and put together. With all this sail, poor *Yorick* carried not one ounce of ballast; he was utterly unpractised in the world; and, at the age of twenty-six, knew just about as well how to steer his course in it, as a romping, unsuspicious girl of thirteen: So that upon his first setting out, the brisk gale of his spirits, as you will imagine, ran him foul ten times in a day of some body's tackling; and as the grave and more slow-paced were oftenest in his way,-----you may likewise imagine, 'twas with such he had generally the ill luck to get the most entangled. For aught I know there might be some mixture of unlucky wit at the bottom of such *Fracas:*---For, to speak the truth, *Yorick* had an invincible dislike and opposition in his nature to gravity;----not to gravity as such;---- for where gravity was wanted, he would be the most grave or serious of mortal men for days and weeks together;---but he was an enemy to the affectation of it, and declared open war against it, only as it appeared a cloak for ignorance, or for folly; and then, whenever it fell in his way, however sheltered and protected, he seldom gave it much quarter.

Sometimes, in his wild way of talking, he would say, That gravity was an errant scoundrel; and he would add,—of the most dangerous kind too,----because a sly one; and that, he verily believed, more honest, well-meaning people were bubbled[9] out of their goods and money by it in one twelve-month, than by pocket-picking and shop-lifting in seven. In the naked temper which a merry heart discovered, he would say, There was no danger,--but to itself:—whereas the very essence of gravity was design, and consequently deceit;---'twas a taught trick to gain credit of the world for more sense and knowledge than a man was worth; and that, with all its pretensions,---it was no better, but often worse, than what a *French* wit[10] had long ago defined it,---*viz. A mysterious carriage of the body to cover the defects of the mind*;—which definition of gravity, *Yorick*, with great imprudence, would say, deserved to be wrote in letters of gold.

But, in plain truth,[11] he was a man unhackneyed[12] and unpractised in the world, and was altogether as indiscreet and foolish on every other subject of discourse where policy is wont to impress restraint. *Yorick* had no impression but one, and that was what arose from the nature of the deed spoken of; which impression he would usually translate into plain *English* without any periphrasis,——and too oft without much distinction of either personage, time, or place;---so that when mention was made of a pitiful or an ungenerous proceeding,---he never gave himself a moment's time to reflect who was the Hero of the piece,----what his station,----or how far he had power to hurt him hereafter;---but if it was a dirty action,-----without more ado,-----The man was a dirty fellow,---and so on:---And as his comments had usually the ill fate to be terminated either in a *bon mot*,[13] or to be enliven'd throughout with some drollery or humour of expression, it gave wings to *Yorick*'s indiscretion. In a word, tho' he never sought, yet, at the same time, as he seldom shun'd occasions of saying what came uppermost, and without much ceremony;----he had but too many temptations in life, of scattering his wit and his humour,— his gibes and his jests[14] about him.----They were not lost for want of gathering.

What were the consequences, and what was *Yorick*'s catastrophe there-upon, you will read in the next chapter.

CHAP. XII.

T HE *Mortgager* and *Mortgageé* differ the one from the other, not more in length of purse, than the *Jester* and *Jesteé* do, in that of memory. But in this the comparison between them runs, as the scholiasts call it, upon all-four;[1] which, by the bye, is upon one or two legs more, than some of the best of *Homer*'s can pretend to;—namely, That the one raises a sum and the other a laugh at your expence, and think no more about it. Interest, however, still runs on in both cases;----the periodical or accidental payments of it, just serving to keep the memory of the affair alive; till, at length, in some evil hour,----pop comes the creditor upon each, and by demanding principal upon the spot, together with full interest to the very day, makes them both feel the full extent of their obligations.

As the reader (for I hate your *ifs*) has a thorough knowledge of human nature, I need not say more to satisfy him, that my Hero could not go on at this rate without some slight experience of these incidental mementos. To speak the truth, he had wantonly involved himself in a multitude of small book-debts[2] of this stamp, which, notwithstanding *Eugenius*'s[3] frequent advice, he too much disregarded; thinking, that as not one of them was contracted thro' any malignancy;---but, on the contrary, from an honesty of mind, and a mere jocundity of humour, they would all of them be cross'd out in course.

Eugenius would never admit this; and would often tell him, that one day or other he would certainly be reckoned with; and he would often add, in an accent of sorrowful apprehension,---to the uttermost mite. To which *Yorick*, with his usual carelesness of heart, would as often answer with a pshaw!---and if the subject was started in the fields,---with a hop, skip, and a jump, at the end of it; but if close pent up in the social chimney corner, where the culprit was barricado'd in, with a table and a couple of arm chairs, and could not so readily fly off in a tangent,----*Eugenius* would then go on with his lecture upon discretion, in words to this purpose, though somewhat better put together.

Trust me, dear *Yorick*, this unwary pleasantry of thine will sooner or later bring thee into scrapes and difficulties, which no after-wit can extricate thee out of.——In these sallies, too oft, I see, it happens, that a person laugh'd at, considers himself in the light of a person injured, with all the rights of such a situation belonging to him; and when thou viewest him in that light too, and reckons up his friends, his family, his kindred, and allies,----and musters up with them the many recruits which will list under him from a sense of common danger;---'tis no extravagant arithmetic to say, that for every ten jokes,---thou hast got a hundred enemies; and till thou hast gone on, and raised a swarm of wasps about thy ears, and art half stung to death by them, thou will never be convinced it is so.

I cannot suspect it in the man whom I esteem, that there is the least spur from spleen or malevolence of intent in these sallies.——I believe and know them to be truly honest and sportive:---But consider, my dear lad, that fools cannot distinguish this,--and that knaves will not; and thou knowest not what it is, either to provoke the one, or to make merry with the other,--whenever they associate for mutual defence, depend upon it, they will carry on the war in such a manner against thee, my dear friend, as to make thee heartily sick of it, and of thy life too.

REVENGE from some baneful corner shall level a tale of dishonour at thee, which no innocence of heart or integrity of conduct shall set right.

——The fortunes of thy house shall totter,---thy character, which led the way to them, shall bleed on every side of it,--thy faith questioned,--thy works belied,--thy wit forgotten,--thy learning trampled on. To wind up the last scene of thy tragedy, CRUELTY and COWARDICE, twin ruffians, hired and set on by MALICE in the dark, shall strike together at all thy infirmities and mistakes:---the best of us, my dear lad, lye open there,---and trust me,----trust me, *Yorick, When to gratify a private appetite, it is once resolved upon, that an innocent and an helpless creature shall be sacrificed, 'tis an easy matter to pick up sticks enew from any thicket where it has strayed, to make a fire to offer it up with.*[4]

Yorick scarce ever heard this sad vaticination of his destiny read over to him, but with a tear stealing from his eye, and a promissory look attending it, that he was resolved, for the time to come, to ride his tit[5] with more sobriety.——But, alas, too late!---a grand confederacy, with ***** and ***** at the head of it, was form'd before the first prediction of it.----The whole plan of the attack, just as *Eugenius* had foreboded, was put in execution all at once,-----with so little mercy on the side of the allies,---and so little suspicion in *Yorick*, of what was carrying on against him,---that when he thought, good easy man! full surely preferment was o'ripening,--they had smote his root, and then he fell, as many a worthy man had fallen before him.[6]

Yorick, however, fought it out with all imaginable gallantry for some time; till, over-power'd by numbers, and worn out at length by the calamities of the war,----but more so, by the ungenerous manner in which it was carried on,---he threw down the sword; and though he kept up his spirits in appearance to the last,----he died, nevertheless, as was generally thought, quite broken hearted.

What inclined *Eugenius* to the same opinion, was as follows:

A few hours before *Yorick* breath'd his last, *Eugenius* stept in with an intent to take his last sight and last farewell of him: Upon his drawing *Yorick*'s curtain, and asking how he felt himself, *Yorick*, looking up in his face, took hold of his hand,----and, after thanking him for the many tokens of his friendship to him, for which, he said, if it was their fate to meet hereafter,---he would thank him again and again.——He told him, he was within a few hours of giving his enemies the slip for ever.-----I hope not, answered *Eugenius*, with tears trickling down his cheeks, and with the tenderest tone that ever man spoke,---I hope not, *Yorick*, said he.--*Yorick* replied, with a look up, and a gentle squeeze of *Eugenius*'s hand, and that was all,--but it cut *Eugenius* to his heart.--Come,--come, *Yorick*, quoth *Eugenius*, wiping his eyes, and summoning up the man within him,-----my dear lad, be comforted,---let not all thy spirits and fortitude forsake thee at this crisis when thou most wants them;——who knows what resourses are in store, and what the power of God may yet do for thee?—— *Yorick* laid his hand upon his heart, and gently shook his head;---for my part, continued *Eugenius*, crying bitterly as he uttered the words,—I declare I know not, *Yorick*, how to part with thee,——and would gladly flatter my hopes, added *Eugenius*, chearing up his voice, that there is still enough left of thee to make a bishop,---and that I may live to see it.——I beseech thee, *Eugenius*, quoth *Yorick*, taking off his night-cap as well as he could with his left hand,——his right being still grasped close in that of *Eugenius*, ——I beseech thee to take a view of my head.----I see nothing that ails it, replied *Eugenius*. Then, alas! my friend, said *Yorick*, let me tell you, that 'tis so bruised and misshapen'd with the blows which ***** and *****, and some others have so unhandsomely given me in the dark, that I might say with *Sancho Pança*,[7] that should I recover, and "Mitres thereupon be suffer'd to rain down from heaven as thick as hail, not one of 'em would fit it." ———— *Yorick*'s last breath was hanging upon his trembling lips ready to depart as he uttered this;---yet still it was utter'd with something of a *cervantick* tone;[8]--and as he spoke it, *Eugenius* could perceive a stream of lambent fire lighted up for a moment in his eyes;----faint picture of those flashes of his spirit, which (as *Shakespear* said of his ancestor) were wont to set the table in a roar![9]

Eugenius was convinced from this, that the heart of his friend was broke; he squeez'd his hand,——and then walk'd softly out of the room, weeping as he walk'd. *Yorick* followed *Eugenius* with his eyes to the door,----he then closed them,—and never opened them more.

He lies buried in a corner of his church-yard, in the parish of———, under a plain marble slabb, which his friend *Eugenius*, by leave of his executors, laid upon his grave, with no more than these three words of inscription serving both for his epitaph and elegy.

Alas, poor Y O R I C K![10]

Ten times in a day has *Yorick*'s ghost the consolation to hear his monumental inscription read over with such a variety of plaintive tones, as denote a general pity and esteem for him;——a foot-way crossing the church-yard close by the side of his grave,—not a passenger goes by without stopping to cast a look upon it,——and sighing as he walks on,

Alas, poor Y O R I C K !

CHAPTER XIII

CHAP. XIII.

IT is so long since the reader of this rhapsodical work[1] has been parted from the midwife, that it is high time to mention her again to him, merely to put him in mind that there is such a body still in the world, and whom, upon the best judgment I can form upon my own plan at present,---I am going to introduce to him for good and all: But as fresh matter may be started, and much unexpected business fall out betwixt the reader and myself, which may require immediate dispatch;-----'twas right to take care that the poor woman should not be lost in the mean time;---because when she is wanted we can no way do without her.

I think I told you that this good woman was a person of no small note and consequence throughout our whole village and township;---that her fame had spread itself to the very out-edge[2] and circumference of that circle of importance, of which kind every soul living, whether he has a shirt to his back or no,----has one surrounding him;--which said circle, by the way, whenever 'tis said that such a one is of great weight and importance in the *world*,——I desire may be enlarged or contracted in your worship's fancy, in a compound-ratio[3] of the station, profession, knowledge, abilities, height and depth (measuring both ways) of the personage brought before you.

In the present case, if I remember, I fixed it at about four or five miles, which not only comprehended the whole parish, but extended itself to two or three of the adjacent hamlets in the skirts of the next parish; which made a considerable thing of it. I must add, That she was, moreover, very well looked on at one large grange-house and some other odd houses and farms within two or three miles, as I said, from the smoke of her own chimney:----But I must here, once for all, inform you, that all this will be more exactly delineated and explain'd in a map, now in the hands of the engraver, which, with many other pieces and developments to this work, will be added to the end of the twentieth volume,---not to swell the work,——I detest the thought of such a thing;——but by way of comment-ary,[4] scholium, illustration, and key to such passages, incidents, or inuendos as shall be thought to be either of private interpretation, or of dark or doubtful meaning after my life and my opinions shall have been read over, (now don't forget the meaning of the word) by all the *world*;--which, betwixt you and me, and in spight of all the gentlemen reviewers in *Great-Britain*, and of all that their worships shall undertake to write or say to the contrary,----I am determined shall be the case.——I need not tell your worship, that all this is spoke in confidence.

CHAP. XIV.

U PON looking into my mother's marriage settlement, in order to satisfy myself and reader in a point necessary to be clear'd up, before we could proceed any further in this history;---I had the good fortune to pop upon the very thing I wanted before I had read a day and a half straight forwards,--it might have taken me up a month;--which shews plainly, that when a man sits down to write a history,---tho' it be but the history of *Jack Hickathrift* or *Tom Thumb*,[1] he knows no more than his heels what lets and confounded hinderances he is to meet with in his way,---or what a dance he may be led, by one excursion or another, before all is over. Could a historiographer drive on his history, as a muleteer drives on his mule,—straight forward;----for instance, from *Rome* all the way to *Loretto*,[2] without ever once turning his head aside either to the right hand or to the left,—he might venture to foretell you to an hour when he should get to his journey's end;[3]-----but the thing is, morally speaking, impossible: For, if he is a man of the least spirit, he will have fifty deviations from a straight line to make with this or that party as he goes along, which he can no ways avoid. He will have views and prospects[4] to himself perpetually solliciting his eye, which he can no more help standing still to look at than he can fly; he will moreover have various

Accounts to reconcile:
Anecdotes to pick up:
Inscriptions to make out:
Stories to weave in:
Traditions to sift:
Personages to call upon:
Panygericks to paste up at this door:

Pasquinades at that:——All which both the man and his mule are quite exempt from. To sum up all; there are archives at every stage to be look'd into, and rolls, records, documents, and endless genealogies, which justice ever and anon calls him back to stay the reading of:----In short, there is no end of it;-----for my own part, I declare I have been at it these six weeks, making all the speed I possibly could,—and am not yet born:--I have just been able, and that's all, to tell you *when* it happen'd, but not *how*;---so that you see the thing is yet far from being accomplished.

These unforeseen stoppages, which I own I had no conception of when I first set out;---but which, I am convinced now, will rather increase than diminish as I advance,---have struck out a hint which I am resolved to follow;---and that is,---not to be in a hurry;---but to go on leisurely, writing and publishing two volumes of my life every year;----which, if I am suffered to go on quietly, and can make a tolerable bargain with my bookseller, I shall continue to do as long as I live.

CHAP. XV.

THE article in my mother's marriage settlement, which I told the reader I was at the pains to search for, and which, now that I have found it, I think proper to lay before him,—is so much more fully express'd in the deed itself, than ever I can pretend to do it, that it would be barbarity to take it out of the lawyer's hand:—It is as follows.

"**And this Indenture further witnesseth,** That the said *Walter Shandy*, merchant, in consideration of the said intended marriage to be had, and, by God's blessing, to be well and truly solemnized and consummated between the said *Walter Shandy* and *Elizabeth Mollineux* aforesaid, and divers other good and valuable causes and considerations him thereunto specially moving,—doth grant, covenant, condescend, consent, conclude, bargain, and fully agree to and with *John Dixon* and *James Turner*, Esqrs. the above-named trustees, *&c. &c.*—**to wit,**—That in case it should hereafter so fall out, chance, happen, or otherwise come to pass,—That the said *Walter Shandy*, merchant, shall have left off business before the time or times, that the said *Elizabeth Mollineux* shall, according to the course of nature, or otherwise, have left off bearing and bringing forth children;—and that, in consequence of the said *Walter Shandy* having so left off business, shall, in despight, and against the free will, consent, and good-liking of the said *Elizabeth Mollineux*,—make a departure from the city of *London*, in order to retire to, and dwell upon, his estate at *Shandy-Hall*, in the county of ——, or at any other country seat, castle, hall, mansion-house, messuage, or grainge-house, now purchased, or hereafter to be purchased, or upon any part or parcel thereof:—That then, and as often as the said *Elizabeth Mollineux* shall happen to be enceint with child or children severally and lawfully begot, or to be begotten, upon the body of the said *Elizabeth Mollineux* during her said coverture,——he the said *Walter Shandy* shall, at his own proper cost and charges, and out of his own proper monies, upon good and reasonable notice, which is hereby agreed to be within six weeks of her the said *Elizabeth Mollineux*'s full reckoning, or time of supposed and computed delivery,—pay, or cause to be paid, the sum of one hundred and twenty pounds of good and lawful money, to *John Dixon* and *James Turner*, Esqrs. or assigns,—upon TRUST and confidence, and for and unto the use and uses, intent, end, and purpose following:—**That is to say,**—That the said sum of one hundred and twenty pounds shall be paid into the hands of the said *Elizabeth Mollineux*, or to be otherwise applied by them the said trustees, for the well and truly hiring of one coach, with able and sufficient horses, to carry and convey the body of the said *Elizabeth Mollineux* and the child or children which she shall be then and there enceint and pregnant with,—unto the city of *London*; and for the further paying and defraying of all other incidental costs, charges, and expences whatsoever,—in and about, and for, and relating to her said intended delivery and lying-in, in the said city or suburbs thereof. And that the said *Elizabeth Mollineux* shall and may, from time to time, and at all such time and times as are here covenanted and agreed upon,—peaceably and quietly hire the said coach and horses, and have free ingress, egress, and regress[1] throughout her journey, in and from the said coach, according to the tenor, true intent, and meaning of these presents, without any let, suit, trouble, disturbance, molestation, discharge, hinderance, forfeiture, eviction, vexation, interruption, or incumberance whatsoever.—And that it shall moreover be lawful to and for the said *Elizabeth Mollineux*, from time to time, and as oft or often as she shall well and truly be advanced in her said pregnancy, to the time heretofore stipulated and agreed upon,—to live and reside in such place or places, and in such family or families, and with such relations, friends, and other persons within the said city of *London*, as she, at her own will and pleasure, notwithstanding her present coverture, and as if she was a *femme sole*[2] and unmarried,—shall think fit.—𝕬𝖓𝖉 𝖙𝖍𝖎𝖘 𝕴𝖓𝖉𝖊𝖓𝖙𝖚𝖗𝖊 𝖋𝖚𝖗𝖙𝖍𝖊𝖗 𝖜𝖎𝖙𝖓𝖊𝖘𝖘𝖊𝖙𝖍, That for the more effectually carrying of the said covenant into execution, the said *Walter Shandy*, merchant, doth hereby grant, bargain, sell, release, and confirm unto the said *John Dixon* and *James Turner*, Esqrs. their heirs, executors, and assigns, in their actual possession now being, by virtue of an indenture of bargain and sale for a year to them the said *John Dixon* and *James Turner*, Esqrs. by him the said *Walter Shandy*, merchant, thereof made; which said bargain and sale for a year, bears date the day next before the date of these presents, and by force and virtue of the statute for transferring of uses into possession,———𝕬𝖑𝖑 that the manor and lordship of *Shandy* in the county of ———, with all the rights, members, and appurtenances thereof; and all and every the messuages, houses, buildings, barns, stables, orchards, gardens, backsides, tofts, crofts, garths, cottages, lands, meadows, feedings, pastures, marshes, commons, woods, underwoods, drains, fisheries, waters, and water-courses;—together with all rents, reversions, services, annuities, fee-farms, knights fees, views of frank-pledge, escheats, reliefs, mines, quarries, goods and chattels of felons and fugitives, felons of themselves, and put in exigent, deodands, free warrens, and all other royalties and seignories, rights and jurisdictions, privileges and hereditaments whatsoever.———𝕬𝖓𝖉 𝖆𝖑𝖘𝖔 the advowson, donation, presentation and free disposition of the rectory or parsonage of *Shandy* aforesaid, and all and every the tenths, tythes, glebe-lands" ——In three words,——"My mother was to lay in, (if she chose it) in *London*."

But in order to put a stop to the practice of any unfair play on the part of my mother, which a marriage article of this nature too manifestly opened a door to, and which indeed had never been thought of at all, but for my uncle *Toby Shandy*;--a clause was added in security of my father, which was this:—"That in case my mother hereafter should, at any time, put my father to the trouble and expence of a *London* journey upon false cries and tokens;——that for every such instance she should forfeit all the right and title which the covenant gave her to the next turn;——but to no more,--and so on, *toties quoties*,[3] in as effectual a manner, as if such a covenant betwixt them had not been made."—This, by the way, was no more than what was reasonable;—and yet, as reasonable as it was, I have ever thought it hard that the whole weight of the article should have fallen entirely, as it did, upon myself.

But I was begot and born to misfortunes;—for my poor mother, whether it was wind or water,—or a compound of both,—or neither;----or whether it was simply the mere swell of imagination[4] and fancy in her;—or how far a strong wish and desire to have it so, might mislead her judgment;—in short, whether she was deceived or deceiving in this matter, it no way becomes me to decide. The fact was this, That, in the latter end of *September*, 1717, which was the year before I was born, my mother having carried my father up to town much against the grain,—he peremptorily insisted upon the clause;----so that I was doom'd, by marriage articles, to have my nose squeez'd as flat to my face, as if the destinies had actually spun me without one.

How this event came about,---and what a train of vexatious disappointments, in one stage or other of my life, have pursued me from the mere loss, or rather compression, of this one single member,---shall be laid before the reader all in due time.

CHAP. XVI.

M Y father, as any body may naturally imagine, came down with my mother into the country, in but a pettish kind of a humour. The first twenty or five-and-twenty miles he did nothing in the world but fret and teaze himself, and indeed my mother too, about the cursed expence, which he said might every shilling of it have been saved;—then what vexed him more than every thing else was the provoking time of the year, ——which, as I told you, was towards the end of *September*, when his wall-fruit,[1] and green gages especially, in which he was very curious, were just ready for pulling:——"Had he been whistled up to *London*, upon a *Tom Fool*'s errand in any other month of the whole year, he should not have said three words about it."

For the next two whole stages, no subject would go down, but the heavy blow he had sustain'd from the loss of a son, whom it seems he had fully reckon'd upon in his mind, and register'd down in his pocket-book, as a second staff for his old age, in case *Bobby* should fail him. "The disappoint-ment of this, he said, "was ten times more to a wise man than all the money which the journey, *&c.* had cost him, put together,---rot the hundred and twenty pounds,——he did not mind it a rush."

From *Stilton*, all the way to *Grantham*,[2] nothing in the whole affair provoked him so much as the condolences of his friends, and the foolish figure they should both make at church the first *Sunday*;——of which, in the satirical vehemence of his wit, now sharpen'd a little by vexation, he would give so many humorous and provoking descriptions,---and place his rib and self in so many tormenting lights and attitudes in the face of the whole congregation;---that my mother declared, these two stages were so truly tragicomical, that she did nothing but laugh and cry in a breath, from one end to the other of them all the way.

From *Grantham*, till they had cross'd the *Trent*, my father was out of all kind of patience at the vile trick and imposition which he fancied my mother had put upon him in this affair.---"Certainly, he would say to himself, over and over again, "the woman could not be deceived herself;——if she could,———what weakness!"——tormenting word! which led his imagination a thorny dance, and, before all was over, play'd the duce and all with him;——for sure as ever the word *weakness* was uttered, and struck full upon his brain,—so sure it set him upon running divisions[3] upon how many kinds of weaknesses there were;——that there was such a thing as weakness of the body,——as well as weakness of the mind,----and then he would do nothing but syllogize within himself for a stage[4] or two together, How far the cause of all these vexations might, or might not, have arisen out of himself.

In short, he had so many little subjects of disquietude springing out of this one affair, all fretting successively in his mind as they rose up in it, that my mother, whatever was her journey up, had but an uneasy journey of it down.——In a word, as she complained to my uncle *Toby*, he would have tired out the patience of any flesh alive.

CHAP. XVII.

THough my father travelled homewards, as I told you, in none of the best of moods,---pshaw-ing and pish-ing all the way down,----yet he had the complaisance to keep the worst part of the story still to himself;—which was the resolution he had taken of doing himself the justice, which my uncle *Toby*'s clause in the marriage settlement empowered him; nor was it till the very night in which I was begot, which was thirteen months after,[1] that she had the least intimation of his design;---when my father, happening, as you remember, to be a little chagrin'd and out of temper,——took occasion as they lay chatting gravely in bed afterwards, talking over what was to come,——to let her know that she must accommodate herself as well as she could to the bargain made between them in their marriage deeds; which was to lye-in of her next child in the country to balance the last year's journey.

My father was a gentleman of many virtues,—but he had a strong spice of that in his temper which might, or might not, add to the number.----'Tis known by the name of perseverance in a good cause,—and of obstinacy in a bad one:[2] Of this my mother had so much knowledge, that she knew 'twas to no purpose to make any remonstrance,—so she e'en resolved to sit down quietly, and make the most of it.

CHAP. XVIII.

AS the point was that night agreed, or rather determin'd, that my mother should lye-in of me in the country, she took her measures accordingly; for which purpose, when she was three days, or thereabouts, gone with child, she began to cast her eyes upon the midwife, whom you have so often heard me mention; and before the week was well got round, as the famous Dr. *Maningham*[1] was not to be had, she had come to a final determination in her mind,——notwithstanding there was a scientifick operator[2] within so near a call as eight miles of us, and who, moreover, had expressly wrote a five shillings book upon the subject of midwifery, in which he had exposed, not only the blunders of the sisterhood itself, ——but had likewise superadded many curious improvements for the quicker extraction of the fœtus in cross births, and some other cases of danger which belay us in getting into the world; notwithstanding all this, my mother, I say, was absolutely determined to trust her life and mine with it, into no soul's hand but this old woman's only.—Now this I like;— when we cannot get at the very thing we wish,-----never to take up with the next best in degree to it;---no; that's pitiful beyond description;—it is no more than a week from this very day, in which I am now writing this book for the edification of the world,---which is *March* 9, 1759,[3]—— that my dear, dear *Jenny*[4] observing I look'd a little grave, as she stood cheapening a silk of five-and-twenty shillings a yard,—told the mercer, she was sorry she had given him so much trouble;—and immediately went and bought herself a yard-wide stuff of ten-pence a yard.—'Tis the duplication of one and the same greatness of soul; only what lessen'd the honour of it somewhat, in my mother's case, was, that she could not heroine it[5] into so violent and hazardous an extream, as one in her situation might have wish'd, because the old midwife had really some little claim to be depended upon,—as much, at least, as success could give her; having, in the course of her practice of near twenty years in the parish, brought every mother's son of them into the world without any one slip or accident which could fairly be laid to her account.

These facts, tho' they had their weight, yet did not altogether satisfy some few scruples and uneasinesses which hung upon my father's spirits in relation to this choice.—To say nothing of the natural workings of humanity and justice,—or of the yearnings of parental and connubial love, all which prompted him to leave as little to hazard as possible in a case of this kind;——he felt himself concern'd in a particular manner, that all should go right in the present case;—from the accumulated sorrow he lay open to, should any evil betide his wife and child in lying-in at *Shandy-Hall.* ——He knew the world judged by events, and would add to his afflictions in such a misfortune, by loading him with the whole blame of it.—— "Alas o'day!—had Mrs. *Shandy*, poor gentlewoman! had but her wish in going up to town just to lye-in and come down again;---which, they say, she begg'd and pray'd for upon her bare knees,——and which, in my opinion, considering the fortune which Mr. *Shandy* got with her,—was no such mighty matter to have complied with, the lady and her babe might both of 'em have been alive at this hour."

This exclamation, my father knew was unanswerable;----and yet, it was not merely to shelter himself,—nor was it altogether for the care of his offspring and wife that he seem'd so extremely anxious about this point;—my father had extensive views of things,——and stood, moreover, as he thought, deeply concern'd in it for the publick good, from the dread he entertained of the bad uses an ill-fated instance might be put to.

He was very sensible that all political writers upon the subject had unanimously agreed and lamented, from the beginning of Queen *Elizabeth*'s reign down to his own time, that the current of men and money towards the metropolis, upon one frivolous errand or another,—set in so strong,— as to become dangerous to our civil rights;—tho', by the bye,——a *current* was not the image he took most delight in,--a *distemper* was here his favourite metaphor, and he would run it down into a perfect allegory, by maintaining it was identically the same in the body national as in the body natural, where blood and spirits were driven up into the head faster than they could find their ways down;——a stoppage of circulation must ensue, which was death in both cases.[6]

There was little danger, he would say, of losing our liberties by *French* politicks or *French* invasions;——nor was he so much in pain of a consumption from the mass of corrupted matter and ulcerated humours in our constitution,—which he hoped was not so bad as it was imagined;—but he verily feared, that in some violent push, we should go off, all at once, in a state-apoplexy;—and then he would say, *The Lord have mercy upon us all*.

My father was never able to give the history of this distemper,---without the remedy along with it.

"Was I an absolute prince, he would say, pulling up his breeches with both his hands, as he rose from his arm-chair, "I would appoint able judges, at every avenue of my metropolis, who should take cognizance of every fool's business who came there;---and if, upon a fair and candid hearing, it appeared not of weight sufficient to leave his own home, and come up, bag and baggage, with his wife and children, farmers sons, *&c. &c.* at his backside, they should be all sent back, from constable to constable, like vagrants as they were, to the place of their legal settlements. By this means, I shall take care, that my metropolis totter'd not thro' its own weight;— that the head be no longer too big for the body;---that the extreams, now wasted and pin'd in, be restored to their due share of nourishment, and regain, with it, their natural strength and beauty:--I would effectually provide, That the meadows and corn-fields, of my dominions, should laugh and sing;—that good chear and hospitality flourish once more;—and that such weight and influence be put thereby into the hands of the Squirality[7] of my kingdom, as should counterpoise what I perceive my Nobility are now taking from them.

"Why are there so few palaces and gentlemen's seats, he would ask, with some emotion, as he walked a-cross the room, "throughout so many delicious provinces in *France?* Whence is it that the few remaining *Chateaus* amongst them are so dismantled,—so unfurnished, and in so ruinous and desolate a condition?—Because, Sir, (he would say) "in that kingdom no man has any country-interest[8] to support;---the little interest of any kind, which any man has any where in it, is concentrated in the court, and the looks of the Grand Monarch;[9] by the sun-shine of whose countenance, or the clouds which pass a-cross it, every *French* man lives or dies."

Another political reason which prompted my father so strongly to guard against the least evil accident in my mother's lying-in in the country,—— was, That any such instance would infallibly throw a balance of power, too great already, into the weaker vessels[10] of the gentry, in his own, or higher stations;----which, with the many other usurped rights which that part of the constitution was hourly establishing,—would, in the end, prove fatal to the monarchical system of domestick government established in the first creation of things by God.

In this point he was entirely of Sir *Robert Filmer*'s opinion,[11] That the plans and institutions of the greatest monarchies in the eastern parts of the world, were, originally, all stolen from that admirable pattern and prototype of this houshold and paternal power;---which, for a century, he said, and more, had gradually been degenerating away into a mix'd government;——the form of which, however desirable in great combinations of the species,——was very troublesome in small ones,—and seldom produced any thing, that he saw, but sorrow and confusion.

For all these reasons, private and publick, put together,—my father was for having the man-midwife by all means,---my mother by no means. My father begg'd and intreated, she would for once recede from her prerogative in this matter, and suffer him to choose for her;—my mother, on the contrary, insisted upon her privilege in this matter, to choose for herself,—and have no mortal's help but the old woman's.—What could my father do? He was almost at his wit's end;——talked it over with her in all moods;—placed his arguments in all lights;—argued the matter with her like a christian,—like a heathen,—like a husband,—like a father,—like a patriot,—like a man:—My mother answered every thing only like a woman; which was a little hard upon her;—for as she could not assume and fight it out behind such a variety of characters,—'twas no fair match;—'twas seven to one.—What could my mother do?——She had the advantage (otherwise she had been certainly overpowered) of a small reinforcement of chagrin personal at the bottom which bore her up, and enabled her to dispute the affair with my father with so equal an advantage,——that both sides sung *Te Deum*.[12] In a word, my mother was to have the old woman,—and the operator was to have licence to drink a bottle of wine with my father and my uncle *Toby Shandy* in the back parlour,—for which he was to be paid five guineas.

I must beg leave, before I finish this chapter, to enter a caveat in the breast of my fair reader;—and it is this:——Not to take it absolutely for granted from an unguarded word or two which I have dropp'd in it,—— "That I am a married man."---I own the tender appellation of my dear, dear *Jenny*,----with some other strokes of conjugal knowledge, interspersed here and there, might, naturally enough, have misled the most candid judge in the world into such a determination against me.---All I plead for, in this case, Madam, is strict justice, and that you do so much of it, to me as well as to yourself,—as not to prejudge or receive such an impression of me, till you have better evidence, than I am positive, at present, can be produced against me:---Not that I can be so vain or unreasonable, Madam, as to desire you should therefore think, that my dear, dear *Jenny* is my kept mistress;—no,—that would be flattering my character in the other extream, and giving it an air of freedom, which, perhaps, it has no kind of right to. All I contend for, is the utter impossibility for some volumes, that you, or the most penetrating spirit upon earth, should know how this matter really stands.----It is not impossible, but that my dear, dear *Jenny!* tender as the appellation is, may be my child.——Consider,—I was born in the year eighteen.—Nor is there any thing unnatural or extravagant in the supposition, that my dear *Jenny* may be my friend.——Friend!— My friend.—Surely, Madam, a friendship between the two sexes may subsist, and be supported without——Fy! Mr. *Shandy:*—Without any thing, Madam, but that tender and delicious sentiment, which ever mixes in friendship, where there is a difference of sex.[13] Let me intreat you to

study the pure and sentimental[14] parts of the best *French* Romances;——
it will really, Madam, astonish you to see with what a variety of chaste
expression this delicious sentiment, which I have the honour to speak of,
is dress'd out.

CHAP. XIX.

I Would sooner undertake to explain the hardest problem in Geometry,
than pretend to account for it, that a gentleman of my father's great
good sense,——knowing, as the reader must have observed him, and
curious too, in philosophy,--wise also in political reasoning,—and in
polemical (as he will find) no way ignorant,---could be capable of entertaining a notion in his head, so out of the common track,---that I fear the
reader, when I come to mention it to him, if he is the least of a cholerick
temper, will immediately throw the book by; if mercurial, he will laugh
most heartily at it;—and if he is of a grave and saturnine cast, he will, at
first sight, absolutely condemn as fanciful and extravagant; and that was
in respect to the choice and imposition of Christian names,[1] on which he
thought a great deal more depended than what superficial minds were
capable of conceiving.

His opinion, in this matter, was, That there was a strange kind of magick
bias, which good or bad names, as he called them, irresistibly impress'd
upon our characters and conduct.

The Hero of *Cervantes* argued not the point with more seriousness,----
nor had he more faith,----or more to say on the powers of Necromancy
in dishonouring his deeds,—or on DULCINEA's[2] name, in shedding lustre
upon them, than my father had on those of TRISMEGISTUS[3] or ARCHI-
MEDES,[4] on the one hand,—or of NYKY and SIMKIN[5] on the other. How
many CÆSARS and POMPEYS, he would say, by mere inspiration of the
names, have been render'd worthy of them? And how many, he would
add, are there who might have done exceeding well in the world, had not
their characters and spirits been totally depress'd and NICODEMUS'D[6] into
nothing.

I see plainly, Sir, by your looks, (or as the case happen'd) my father would say,—that you do not heartily subscribe to this opinion of mine,— which, to those, he would add, who have not carefully sifted it to the bottom,—I own has an air more of fancy than of solid reasoning in it;----and yet, my dear Sir, if I may presume to know your character, I am morally assured, I should hazard little in stating a case to you,---not as a party in the dispute,—but as a judge, and trusting my appeal upon it to your own good sense and candid disquisition in this matter;——you are a person free from as many narrow prejudices of education[7] as most men;—and, if I may presume to penetrate further into you,—of a liberality of genius above bearing down an opinion, merely because it wants friends. Your son!---your dear son,---from whose sweet and open temper you have so much to expect.—Your BILLY, Sir!—would you, for the world, have called him JUDAS?—Would you, my dear Sir, he would say, laying his hand upon your breast, with the genteelest address,---and in that soft and irresistible *piano*[8] of voice, which the nature of the *argumentum ad hominem*[9] absolutely requires,—Would you, Sir, if a *Jew* of a godfather had proposed the name for your child, and offered you his purse along with it, would you have consented to such a desecration of him?——O my God! he would say, looking up, if I know your temper right, Sir,--- you are incapable of it;——you would have trampled upon the offer; ---you would have thrown the temptation at the tempter's head with abhorrence.

Your greatness of mind in this action, which I admire, with that generous contempt of money which you shew me in the whole transaction, is really noble;---and what renders it more so, is the principle of it;---the workings of a parent's love upon the truth and conviction of this very hypothesis, namely, That was your son called JUDAS,---the sordid and treacherous idea, so inseparable from the name, would have accompanied him thro' life like his shadow, and, in the end, made a miser and a rascal of him, in spight, Sir, of your example.

I never knew a man able to answer this argument.——But, indeed, to speak of my father as he was;—he was certainly irresistible, both in his orations and disputations;—he was born an orator;—Θεοδιδακ]Θ.[10]— Persuasion hung upon his lips, and the elements of Logick and Rhetorick were so blended up in him,—and, withall, he had so shrewd guess at the weaknesses and passions of his respondent,——that NATURE might have stood up and said,—"This man is eloquent."[11] In short, whether he was on the weak or the strong side of the question, 'twas hazardous in either case to attack him:—And yet, 'tis strange, he had never read *Cicero* nor *Quintilian de Oratore*, nor *Isocrates*, nor *Aristotle*, nor *Longinus* amongst the antients;——nor *Vossius*, nor *Skioppius*, nor *Ramus*, nor *Farnaby* amongst the moderns;—and what is more astonishing, he had never in his whole life the least light or spark of subtilty struck into his mind, by one single lecture upon *Crackenthorp* or *Burgersdicius*, or any *Dutch* logician or commentator;[12]—he knew not so much as in what the difference of an argument *ad ignorantiam*,[13] and an argument *ad hominem* consisted; so that I well remember, when he went up along with me to enter my name at *Jesus College*[14] in * * * *,—it was a matter of just wonder with my worthy tutor, and two or three fellows of that learned society,---that a man who knew not so much as the names of his tools, should be able to work after that fashion with 'em.

To work with them in the best manner he could, was what my father was, however, perpetually forced upon;——for he had a thousand little sceptical notions of the comick kind to defend,——most of which notions, I verily believe, at first enter'd upon the footing of mere whims, and of a *vive la Bagatelle*;[15] and as such he would make merry with them for half an hour or so, and having sharpen'd his wit upon 'em, dismiss them till another day.

I mention this, not only as matter of hypothesis or conjecture upon the progress and establishment of my father's many odd opinions,--but as a warning to the learned reader against the indiscreet reception of such guests, who, after a free and undisturbed enterance, for some years, into our brains,—at length claim a kind of settlement there,——working sometimes like yeast;—but more generally after the manner of the gentle passion, beginning in jest,—but ending in downright earnest.

Whether this was the case of the singularity of my father's notions,—or that his judgment, at length, became the dupe of his wit;—or how far, in many of his notions, he might, tho' odd, be absolutely right;——the reader, as he comes at them, shall decide. All that I maintain here, is, that in this one, of the influence of Christian names, however it gain'd footing, he was serious;—he was all uniformity;—he was systematical, and, like all systematick reasoners, he would move both heaven and earth, and twist and torture every thing in nature to support his hypothesis. In a word, I repeat it over again;—he was serious;—and, in consequence of it, he would lose all kind of patience whenever he saw people, especially of condition, who should have known better,——as careless and as indifferent about the name they imposed upon their child,—or more so, than in the choice of *Ponto* or *Cupid* for their puppy dog.

This, he would say, look'd ill;—and had, moreover, this particular aggravation in it, *viz*. That when once a vile name was wrongfully or injudiciously given, 'twas not like the case of a man's character, which, when wrong'd, might hereafter be clear'd;——and, possibly, sometime or other, if not in the man's life, at least after his death,—be, somehow or other, set to rights with the world: But the injury of this, he would say, could never be undone;---nay, he doubted even whether an act of parliament could reach it:——He knew as well as you, that the legislature assum'd a power over surnames;—but for very strong reasons, which he could give, it had never yet adventured, he would say, to go a step further.

It was observable, that tho' my father, in consequence of this opinion, had, as I have told you, the strongest likings and dislikings towards certain names;—that there were still numbers of names which hung so equally in the balance before him, that they were absolutely indifferent to him. *Jack*, *Dick*, and *Tom* were of this class: These my father call'd neutral names;—affirming of them, without a satyr, That there had been as many knaves and fools, at least, as wise and good men, since the world began, who had indifferently borne them;---so that, like equal forces acting against each other in contrary directions, he thought they mutually destroyed each others effects; for which reason, he would often declare, He would not give a cherry-stone to choose amongst them. *Bob*, which was my brother's name, was another of these neutral kinds of Christian names, which operated very little either way; and as my father happen'd to be at *Epsom*,[16] when it was given him,—he would oft times thank heaven it was no worse. *Andrew* was something like a negative quantity in Algebra with him;---'twas worse, he said, than nothing.---*William* stood pretty high:-----*Numps* again was low with him;--and *Nick*,[17] he said, was the Devil.

But, of all the names in the universe, he had the most unconquerable aversion for Tristram;---he had the lowest and most contemptible opinion of it of any thing in the world,---thinking it could possibly produce nothing in *rerum naturâ*,[18] but what was extreamly mean and pitiful: So that in the midst of a dispute on the subject, in which, by the bye, he was frequently involved,-----he would sometimes break off in a sudden and spirited Epiphonema, or rather Erotesis,[19] raised a third, and sometimes a full fifth, above the key of the discourse,——and demand it categorically of his antagonist, Whether he would take upon him to say, he had ever remember'd,-----whether he had ever read,---or even whether he had ever heard tell of a man, call'd *Tristram*, performing any thing great or worth recording?—No---, he would say,---TRISTRAM!---The thing is impossible.

What could be wanting in my father but to have wrote a book to publish this notion of his to the world? Little boots it to the subtle speculatist to stand single in his opinions,----unless he gives them proper vent:---It was the identical thing which my father did;—for in the year sixteen, which was two years before I was born, he was at the pains of writing an express DISSERTATION simply upon the word *Tristram*,—shewing the world, with great candour and modesty, the grounds of his great abhorrence to the name.

When this story is compared with the title-page,---Will not the gentle reader pity my father from his soul?----to see an orderly and well-disposed gentleman, who tho' singular,—yet inoffensive in his notions,—so played upon in them by cross purposes;——to look down upon the stage, and see him baffled and overthrown in all his little systems and wishes; to behold a train of events perpetually falling out against him, and in so critical and cruel a way, as if they had purposedly been plann'd and pointed against him, merely to insult his speculations.——In a word, to behold such a one, in his old age, ill-fitted for troubles, ten times in a day suffering sorrow;—ten times in a day calling the child of his prayers TRISTRAM! ——Melancholy dissyllable of sound! which, to his ears, was unison to *Nicompoop*, and every name vituperative under heaven.——By his ashes! I swear it,—if ever malignant spirit took pleasure, or busied itself in traversing the purposes of mortal man,---it must have been here;---and if it was not necessary I should be born before I was christened, I would this moment give the reader an account of it.

CHAP. XX.

————How could you, Madam, be so inattentive in reading the last chapter? I told you in it, *That my mother was not a papist.*——Papist! You told me no such thing, Sir. Madam, I beg leave to repeat it over again, That I told you as plain, at least, as words, by direct inference, could tell you such a thing.——Then, Sir, I must have miss'd a page.--No, Madam,——you have not miss'd a word.——Then I was asleep, Sir.——My pride, Madam, cannot allow you that refuge.——Then, I declare, I know nothing at all about the matter.——That, Madam, is the very fault I lay to your charge; and as a punishment for it, I do insist upon it, that you immediately turn back, that is, as soon as you get to the next full stop, and read the whole chapter over again.

I have imposed this penance upon the lady, neither out of wantonness or cruelty, but from the best of motives; and therefore shall make her no apology for it when she returns back:——'Tis to rebuke a vicious taste which has crept into thousands besides herself,——of reading straight forwards, more in quest of the adventures, than of the deep erudition and knowledge which a book of this cast, if read over as it should be, would infallibly impart with them.——The mind should be accustomed to make wise reflections, and draw curious conclusions as it goes along; the habitude of which made *Pliny*[1] the younger affirm, "That he never read a book so bad, but he drew some profit from it." The stories of *Greece* and *Rome*, run over without this turn and application,——do less service, I affirm it, than the history of *Parismus* and *Parismenus*,[2] or of the Seven Champions of *England*,[3] read with it.

————But here comes my fair Lady. Have you read over again the chapter, Madam, as I desired you?——You have: And did you not observe the passage, upon the second reading, which admits the inference?——Not a word like it! Then, Madam, be pleased to ponder well the last line but one of the chapter, where I take upon me to say, "It was *necessary* I should be born before I was christen'd." Had my mother, Madam, been a Papist, that consequence did not follow.*

---

*The *Romish* Rituals[4] direct the baptizing of the child, in cases of danger, *before* it is born;—but upon this proviso, That some part or other of the child's body be seen by the baptizer:

It is a terrible misfortune for this same book of mine, but more so to the Republick of Letters;—so that my own is quite swallowed up in the consideration of it,--that this self-same vile pruriency for fresh adventures in all things, has got so strongly into our habit and humours,—and so wholly intent are we upon satisfying the impatience of our concupiscence that way,—that nothing but the gross and more carnal parts of a composition will go down:—The subtle hints and sly communications of science fly off, like spirits, upwards;——the heavy moral escapes downwards; and both the one and the other are as much lost to the world, as if they were still left in the bottom of the ink-horn.

I wish the male-reader has not pass'd by many a one, as quaint and curious as this one, in which the female-reader has been detected. I wish it may have its effects;—and that all good people, both male and female, from her example, may be taught to think as well as read.

Memoire presenté a Messieurs les Docteurs de Sorbonne[*].

U N Chirurgien Accoucheur, represente à Messieurs les Docteurs de Sorbonne, qu'il y a des cas, quoique très-rares, où une mere ne sçauroit accoucher, & même où l'enfant est tellement renfermé dans le sein de sa mere, qu'il ne fait paroître aucune partie de son corps, ce qui seroit un cas, suivant les rituels, de lui conferer, du moins sous condition, le baptême. Le chirurgien, qui consulte, prétend, par le moyen d'une petite canulle, de pouvoir baptiser immediatement l'enfant, sans faire aucun tort à la mere.——Il demande si ce moyen, qu'il vient de proposer, est permis & legitime, & s'il peut s'en servir dans le cas qu'il vient d'exposer.

[*] Vide Deventer. Paris Edit. 4to. 1734, p. 366.

———But the Doctors of the *Sorbonne*, by a deliberation held amongst them, *April* 10, 1733,—have enlarged the powers of the midwives, by determining, That tho' no part of the child's body should appear,——that baptism shall, nevertheless, be administered to it by injection,—*par le moyen d'une petite Canulle.*—Anglicé, *a squirt.*——'Tis very strange that St. *Thomas Aquinas*, who had so good a mechanical head, both for tying and untying the knots of school-divinity,—should, after so much pains bestowed upon this,—give up the point at last, as a second *La chose impossible*;—"Infantes in maternis uteris existentes (quoth St. *Thomas*) baptizari possunt *nullo modo.*"—O *Thomas! Thomas!*

If the reader has the curiosity to see the question upon baptism, *by injection*, as presented to the Doctors of the *Sorbonne*,—with their consultation thereupon, it is as follows.

RÉPONSE.

*L*E *conseil estime, que la question proposée souffre de grandes difficultés. Les theologiens posent d'un côté pour principe, que le baptême, qui est une naissance spirituelle, suppose une premiere naissance; il faut être né dans le monde, pour renaître en* Jesus Christ, *comme ils l'enseignent.* S. Thomas, 3ᵃ. part. quæst. 68. artic. II. *suit cette doctrine comme une verité constante; l'on ne peut, dit ce* S. *docteur, baptiser les enfans qui sont renfermés dans le sein de leurs meres, et* S. Thomas *est fondé sur ce, que les enfans ne sont point nés, & ne peuvent être comptés parmi les autres hommes; d'où il conclud, qu'ils ne peuvent être l'objet d'une action exterieure, pour recevoir par leur ministere les sacremens nécessaires au salut:* pueri in maternis uteris existentes nondum prodierunt in lucem ut cum aliis hominibus vitam ducant; unde non possunt subjici actioni humanæ, ut per eorum ministerium sacramenta recipiant ad salutem. *Les rituels ordonnent dans la pratique ce que les theologiens ont établi sur les mêmes matieres, & ils deffendent tous d'une maniere uniforme de baptiser les enfans qui sont renfermés dans le sein de leurs meres, s'ils ne font paroître quelque partie de leurs corps. Le concours des theologiens, & des rituels, qui sont les regles des dioceses, paroît former une autorité qui termine la question presente; cependant le conseil de conscience considerant d'un côté, que le raisonnement des theologiens est uniquement fondé sur une raison de convenance, & que la deffense des rituels, suppose que l'on ne peut baptiser immediatement les enfans ainsi renfermés dans le sein de leurs meres, ce qui est contre la supposition presente; & d'un autre côté, considerant que les mêmes theologiens enseignent, que l'on peut risquer les sacremens qu'* Jesus Christ *a établis comme des moyens faciles, mais nécessaires pour sanctifier les hommes; & d'ailleurs estimant, que les enfans renfermés dans le sein de leurs meres, pourroient être capables de salut, parce qu'ils sont capables de damnation;—pour ces considerations, & eu égard à l'exposé, suivant lequel on assure avoir trouvé un moyen certain de baptiser ces enfans ainsi renfermés, sans faire aucun tort à la mere, le conseil estime que l'on pourroit se servir du moyen proposé, dans la confiance qu'il a, que Dieu n'a point laissé ces sortes d'enfans sans aucuns secours, & supposant, comme il est exposé, que le moyen dont il s'agit est propre à leur procurer le baptême; cependant comme il s'agiroit, en autorisant la pratique proposée, de changer une regle universellement établie, le conseil croit que celui qui consulte doit s'adresser à son evêque, à qui il appartient de juger de l'utilité, & du danger du moyen proposé, & comme, sous le bon plaisir de l'evêque, le conseil estime qu'il faudroit recourir au Pape, qui a le droit d'expliquer les regles de l'eglise, & d'y déroger dans les cas, où la loi ne sçauroit obliger, quelque* *sage & quelque utile que paroisse la maniere de baptiser dont il s'agit, le conseil ne pourroit l'approuver sans le concours de ces deux autorités. On conseille au moins à celui qui consulte, de s'adresser à son evêque, & de lui faire part de la presente décision, afin que, si le prélat entre dans les raisons sur lesquelles les docteurs soussignés s'appuyent, il puisse être autorisé dans le cas de nécessité, ou il risqueroit trop d'attendre que la permission fût demandée & accordée d'employer le moyen qu'il propose si avantageux au salut de l'enfant. Au reste le conseil, en estimant que l'on pourroit s'en servir, croit cependant que, si les enfans dont il s'agit venoient au monde, contre l'esperance de ceux qui se seroient servis du même moyen, il seroit nécessaire de les baptiser* sous condition, *& en cela, le conseil se conforme à tous les rituels, qui, en autorisant le baptême d'un enfant qui fait paroître quelque partie de son corps, enjoignent neanmoins, & ordonnent de le baptiser* sous condition, *s'il vient heureusement au monde.*

Déliberé en *Sorbonne*, le 10 *Avril*, 1733.

A. Le Moyne,
L. De Romigny,
De Marcilly.

Mr. *Tristram Shandy*'s compliments to Messrs. *Le Moyne*, *De Romigny*, and *De Marcilly*, hopes they all rested well the night after so tiresome a consultation.—He begs to know, whether, after the ceremony of marriage, and before that of consummation, the baptizing all the Homunculi at once, slap-dash, by *injection*, would not be a shorter and safer cut still; on condition, as above, That if the Homunculi do well and come safe into the world after this, That each and every of them shall be baptized again *(sous condition.)*——And provided, in the second place, That the thing can be done, which Mr. *Shandy* apprehends it may, *par le moyen d'une* petite canulle, and, *sans faire aucun tort a le pere.*[5]

CHAP. XXI.

———I wonder what's all that noise, and running backwards and forwards for, above stairs, quoth my father, addressing himself, after an hour and a half's silence, to my uncle *Toby*,——who you must know, was sitting on the opposite side of the fire, smoking his social pipe all the time, in mute contemplation of a new pair of black-plush-breeches which he had got on;—What can they be doing brother? quoth my father,—we can scarce hear ourselves talk.

I think, replied my uncle *Toby*, taking his pipe from his mouth, and striking the head of it two or three times upon the nail of his left thumb, as he began his sentence,[1]——I think, says he:——But to enter rightly into my uncle *Toby*'s sentiments upon this matter, you must be made to enter first a little into his character, the out-lines of which I shall just give you, and then the dialogue between him and my father will go on as well again.

——Pray what was that man's name,---for I write in such a hurry, I have no time to recollect or look for it,——who first made the observation, "That there was great inconstancy in our air and climate?" Whoever he was, 'twas a just and good observation in him.----But the corollary drawn from it, namely, "That it is this which has furnished us with such a variety of odd and whimsical characters;"—that was not his;----it was found out by another man, at least a century and a half after him:—Then again,—that this copious store-house of original materials, is the true and natural cause that our Comedies are so much better than those of *France*, or any others that either have, or can be wrote upon the Continent;——that discovery was not fully made till about the middle of king *William*'s reign,---when the great *Dryden*,[2] in writing one of his long prefaces, (if I mistake not) most fortunately hit upon it. Indeed towards the latter end of queen *Anne*, the great *Addison*[3] began to patronize the notion, and more fully explained it to the world in one or two of his Spectators;—but the discovery was not his.—Then, fourthly and lastly, that this strange irregularity in our climate, producing so strange an irregularity in our characters,——doth thereby, in some sort, make us amends, by giving us somewhat to make us merry with when the weather will not suffer us to go out of doors,--that observation is my own;--and was struck out by me this very rainy day, *March* 26, 1759, and betwixt the hours of nine and ten in the morning.

Thus,---thus my fellow labourers and associates in this great harvest of our learning, now ripening before our eyes; thus it is, by slow steps of casual increase, that our knowledge physical, metaphysical, physiological, polemical, nautical, mathematical, ænigmatical, technical, biographical, romantical, chemical, and obstetrical, with fifty other branches of it, (most of 'em ending, as these do, in *ical*) have, for these two last centuries and more, gradually been creeping upwards towards that Aκμή [4] of their perfections, from which, if we may form a conjecture from the advances of these last seven years, we cannot possibly be far off.

When that happens, it is to be hoped, it will put an end to all kind of writings whatsoever;—the want of all kind of writing will put an end to all kind of reading;---and that in time, *As war begets poverty, poverty peace,*[5] ——must, in course, put an end to all kind of knowledge,---and then ——we shall have all to begin over again; or, in other words, be exactly where we started.

————Happy! thrice happy Times! I only wish that the æra of my begetting, as well as the mode and manner of it, had been a little alter'd,--or that it could have been put off with any convenience to my father or mother, for some twenty or five-and-twenty years longer, when a man in the literary world might have stood some chance.————

But I forget my uncle *Toby*, whom all this while we have left knocking the ashes out of his tobacco pipe.

His humour was of that particular species, which does honour to our atmosphere; and I should have made no scruple of ranking him amongst one of the first-rate productions of it, had not there appear'd too many strong lines in it of a family-likeness, which shewed that he derived the singularity of his temper more from blood, than either wind or water, or any modifications or combinations of them whatever: And I have, therefore, oft times wondered, that my father, tho' I believe he had his reasons for it, upon his observing some tokens of excentricity in my course when I was a boy,—should never once endeavour to account for them in this way; for all the SHANDY FAMILY were of an original character throughout; ——I mean the males,—the females had no character at all,[6]—except, indeed, my great aunt DINAH,[7] who, about sixty years ago, was married and got with child by the coachman, for which my father, according to his hypothesis of Christian names, would often say, She might thank her godfathers and godmothers.

It will seem very strange,——and I would as soon think of dropping a riddle in the reader's way, which is not my interest to do, as set him upon guessing how it could come to pass, that an event of this kind, so many years after it had happened, should be reserved for the interruption of the peace and unity, which otherwise so cordially subsisted, between my father and my uncle *Toby*. One would have thought, that the whole force of the misfortune should have spent and wasted itself in the family at first,—as is generally the case:—But nothing ever wrought with our family after the ordinary way. Possibly at the very time this happened, it might have something else to afflict it; and as afflictions are sent down for our good, and that as this had never done the SHANDY FAMILY any good at all, it might lye waiting till apt times and circumstances should give it an opportunity to discharge its office.———Observe, I determine nothing upon this.———My way is ever to point out to the curious, different tracts of investigation, to come at the first springs of the events I tell;— not with a pedantic *Fescue*,[8]—or in the decisive Manner of *Tacitus*,[9] who outwits himself and his reader;—but with the officious humility of a heart devoted to the assistance merely of the inquisitive;--to them I write,—— and by them I shall be read,——if any such reading as this could be supposed to hold out so long, to the very end of the world.

Why this cause of sorrow, therefore, was thus reserved for my father and uncle, is undetermined by me. But how and in what direction it exerted itself, so as to become the cause of dissatisfaction between them, after it began to operate, is what I am able to explain with great exactness, and is as follows:

My uncle TOBY SHANDY, Madam, was a gentleman, who, with the virtues which usually constitute the character of a man of honour and rectitude,—possessed one in a very eminent degree, which is seldom or never put into the catalogue; and that was a most extream and unparallel'd modesty of nature;[10]——tho' I correct the word nature, for this reason, that I may not prejudge a point which must shortly come to a hearing; and that is, Whether this modesty of his was natural or acquir'd.——— Which ever way my uncle *Toby* came by it, 'twas nevertheless modesty in the truest sense of it; and that is, Madam, not in regard to words, for he was so unhappy as to have very little choice in them,—but to things; ——and this kind of modesty so possess'd him, and it arose to such a height in him, as almost to equal, if such a thing could be, even the modesty of a woman: That female nicety, Madam, and inward cleanliness of mind and fancy, in your sex, which makes you so much the awe of ours.

You will imagine, Madam, that my uncle *Toby* had contracted all this from this very source;----that he had spent a great part of his time in converse with your sex; and that, from a thorough knowledge of you, and the force of imitation which such fair examples render irresistable,---he had acquired this amiable turn of mind.

I wish I could say so,----for unless it was with his sister-in-law, my father's wife and my mother,——my uncle *Toby* scarce exchanged three words with the sex in as many years;——no, he got it, Madam, by a blow. ——A blow!---Yes, Madam, it was owing to a blow from a stone, broke off by a ball from the parapet of a horn-work at the siege of *Namur*,[11] which struck full upon my uncle *Toby*'s groin.---Which way could that effect it? The story of that, Madam, is long and interesting;----but it would be running my history all upon heaps to give it you here.——'Tis for an episode hereafter; and every circumstance relating to it in its proper place, shall be faithfully laid before you:----'Till then, it is not in my power to give further light into this matter, or say more than what I have said already,-----That my uncle *Toby* was a gentleman of unparallel'd modesty, which happening to be somewhat subtilized and rarified by the constant heat of a little family-pride,-----they both so wrought together within him, that he could never bear to hear the affair of my aunt DINAH touch'd upon, but with the greatest emotion.——The least hint of it was enough to make the blood fly into his face;---but when my father enlarged upon the story in mixed companies, which the illustration of his hypothesis frequently obliged him to do,----the unfortunate blight of one of the fairest branches of the family, would set my uncle *Toby*'s honour and modesty o'bleeding; and he would often take my father aside, in the greatest concern imaginable, to expostulate and tell him, he would give him any thing in the world, only to let the story rest.

My father, I believe, had the truest love and tenderness for my uncle *Toby*, that ever one brother bore towards another, and would have done any thing in nature, which one brother in reason could have desir'd of another, to have made my uncle *Toby*'s heart easy in this, or any other point. But this lay out of his power.

——My father, as I told you, was a philosopher in grain,—specula-tive,—systematical;—and my aunt *Dinah*'s affair was a matter of as much

consequence to him, as the retrogradation of the planets[12] to *Copernicus:*—
The backslidings of *Venus* in her orbit fortified the *Copernican* system, call'd
so after his name; and the backslidings of my aunt *Dinah* in her orbit, did
the same service in establishing my father's system, which, I trust, will for
ever hereafter be call'd the *Shandean System*, after his.

In any other family dishonour, my father, I believe, had as nice a sense
of shame as any man whatever;——and neither he, nor, I dare say,
Copernicus, would have divulged the affair in either case, or have taken the
least notice of it to the world, but for the obligations they owed, as they
thought, to truth.—*Amicus Plato*, my father would say, construing the
words to my uncle *Toby*, as he went along, *Amicus Plato*; that is, DINAH
was my aunt;—*sed magis amica veritas*——but TRUTH is my sister.[13]

This contrariety of humours betwixt my father and my uncle, was the
source of many a fraternal squabble. The one could not bear to hear the
tale of family disgrace recorded,——and the other would scarce ever
let a day pass to an end without some hint at it.

For God's sake, my uncle *Toby* would cry,——and for my sake, and
for all our sakes, my dear brother *Shandy*,—do let this story of our aunt's
and her ashes sleep in peace;——how can you,——how can you have
so little feeling and compassion for the character of our family:——What
is the character of a family to an hypothesis? my father would reply.——
Nay, if you come to that—what is the life of a family:——The life of
a family!—my uncle *Toby* would say, throwing himself back in his arm-
chair, and lifting up his hands, his eyes, and one leg.——Yes the life,
——my father would say, maintaining his point. How many thousands of
'em are there every year that comes cast away, (in all civilized countries
at least)——and consider'd as nothing but common air, in competition
of an hypothesis. In my plain sense of things, my uncle *Toby*, would answer,
——every such instance is downright MURDER, let who will commit it.
——There lies your mistake, my father would reply;——for, in *Foro
Scientiæ*[14] there is no such thing as MURDER,——'tis only DEATH,[15]
brother.

My uncle *Toby* would never offer to answer this by any other kind of
argument, than that of whistling half a dozen bars of *Lillabullero*.[16]——
You must know it was the usual channel thro' which his passions got vent,
when any thing shocked or surprised him;——but especially when any
thing, which he deem'd very absurd, was offer'd.

As not one of our logical writers, nor any of the commentators upon them, that I remember, have thought proper to give a name to this particular species of argument,—I here take the liberty to do it myself, for two reasons. First, That, in order to prevent all confusion in disputes, it may stand as much distinguished for ever, from every other species of argument,———as the *Argumentum ad Verecundiam*,[17] *ex Absurdo*,[18] *ex Fortiori*,[19] or any other argument whatsoever:———And, secondly, That it may be said by my children's children, when my head is laid to rest,----that their learned grand-father's head had been busied to as much purpose once, as other people's:—That he had invented a name,---and generously thrown it into the TREASURY of the *Ars Logica*,[20] for one of the most unanswerable arguments in the whole science. And if the end of disputation[21] is more to silence than convince,--they may add, if they please, to one of the best arguments too.

I do therefore, by these presents, strictly order and command, That it be known and distinguished by the name and title of the *Argumentum Fistulatorium*,[22] and no other;---and that it rank hereafter with the *Argumentum Baculinum*,[23] and the *Argumentum ad Crumenam*,[24] and for ever hereafter be treated of in the same chapter.

As for the *Argumentum Tripodium*,[25] which is never used but by the woman against the man;---and the *Argumentum ad Rem*, which, contrarywise, is made use of by the man only against the woman:—As these two are enough in conscience for one lecture;———and, moreover, as the one is the best answer to the other,---let them likewise be kept apart, and be treated of in a place by themselves.

CHAP. XXII.

THE learned Bishop *Hall*,[1] I mean the famous Dr. *Joseph Hall*, who was Bishop of *Exeter* in King *James* the first's reign, tells us in one of his *Decads*, at the end of his divine art of meditation, imprinted at *London*, in the year 1610, by *John Beal*, dwelling in *Aldersgate-street*, "That it is an abominable thing for a man to commend himself;"---and I really think it is so.

And yet, on the other hand, when a thing is executed in a masterly kind of a fashion, which thing is not likely to be found out;---I think it is full as abominable, that a man should lose the honour of it, and go out of the world with the conceit of it rotting in his head.

This is precisely my situation.

For in this long digression which I was accidentally led into, as in all my digressions (one only excepted) there is a master-stroke of digressive skill,[2] the merit of which has all along, I fear, been overlooked by my reader,--not for want of penetration in him,—but because 'tis an excellence seldom looked for, or expected indeed, in a digression;---and it is this: That tho' my digressions are all fair, as you observe,—and that I fly off from what I am about, as far and as often too as any writer in *Great-Britain*; yet I constantly take care to order affairs so, that my main business does not stand still in my absence.

I was just going, for example, to have given you the great out-lines of my uncle *Toby*'s most whimsical character;—when my aunt *Dinah* and the coachman came a-cross us, and led us a vagary some millions of miles into the very heart of the planetary system: Notwithstanding all this, you perceive that the drawing of my uncle *Toby*'s character went on gently all the time;---not the great contours of it,—that was impossible,---but some familiar strokes and faint designations of it, were here and there touch'd in, as we went along, so that you are much better acquainted with my uncle *Toby* now than you was before.

By this contrivance the machinery of my work is of a species by itself; two contrary motions are introduced into it, and reconciled, which were thought to be at variance with each other. In a word, my work is digressive, and it is progressive too,—and at the same time.

This, Sir, is a very different story from that of the earth's moving round her axis, in her diurnal rotation, with her progress in her elliptick orbit which brings about the year, and constitutes that variety and vicissitude of seasons we enjoy;---though I own it suggested the thought,—as I believe the greatest of our boasted improvements and discoveries have come from some such trifling hints.

Digressions, incontestably, are the sun-shine;——they are the life, the soul of reading;---take them out of this book for instance,--you might as well take the book along with them;—one cold eternal winter would reign in every page of it; restore them to the writer;-----he steps forth like a bridegroom,[3]—bids All hail; brings in variety, and forbids the appetite to fail.[4]

All the dexterity is in the good cookery and management of them, so as to be not only for the advantage of the reader, but also of the author, whose distress, in this matter, is truely pitiable: For, if he begins a digression,---from that moment, I observe, his whole work stands stock-still;—and if he goes on with his main work,----then there is an end of his digression.

—— This is vile work.—For which reason, from the beginning of this, you see, I have constructed the main work and the adventitious parts of it with such intersections, and have so complicated and involved the digressive and progressive movements, one wheel within another, that the whole machine, in general, has been kept a-going;---and, what's more, it shall be kept a-going these forty years, if it pleases the fountain of health to bless me so long with life and good spirits.

CHAP. XXIII.

I Have a strong propensity in me to begin this chapter very nonsensically, and I will not balk my fancy.—Accordingly I set off thus.

If the fixure of *Momus*'s glass,[1] in the human breast, according to the proposed emendation of that arch-critick, had taken place,——first, This foolish consequence would certainly have followed,--That the very wisest and the very gravest of us all, in one coin or other, must have paid window-money[2] every day of our lives.

And, secondly, That had the said glass been there set up, nothing more would have been wanting, in order to have taken a man's character, but to have taken a chair and gone softly, as you would to a dioptrical[3] bee-hive, and look'd in,--view'd the soul stark naked;---observ'd all her motions,—her machinations;—traced all her maggots from their first engendering to their crawling forth;---watched her loose in her frisks, her gambols, her capricios; and after some notice of her more solemn deportment, consequent upon such frisks, *&c.*——then taken your pen and ink and set down nothing but what you had seen, and could have sworn to:---But this is an advantage not to be had by the biographer in this planet,—in the planet *Mercury*[4] (belike) it may be so, if not better still for him;----for there the intense heat of the country, which is proved by computators, from its vicinity to the sun, to be more than equal to that of red hot iron,— must, I think, long ago have vitrified the bodies of the inhabitants, (as the efficient cause) to suit them for the climate (which is the final cause);[5] so that, betwixt them both, all the tenements of their souls, from top to bottom, may be nothing else, for aught the soundest philosophy can shew to the contrary, but one fine transparent body of clear glass (bating the umbilical knot);---so, that till the inhabitants grow old and tolerably wrinkled, whereby the rays of light, in passing through them, become so monstrously refracted,-----or return reflected from their surfaces in such transverse lines to the eye, that a man cannot be seen thro';---his soul might as well, unless, for more[6] ceremony,---or the trifling advantage which the umbilical point gave her,----might, upon all other accounts, I say, as well play the fool out o'doors as in her own house.[7]

But this, as I said above, is not the case of the inhabitants of this earth;— our minds shine not through the body, but are wrapt up here in a dark covering of uncrystalized flesh and blood; so that if we would come to the specifick characters of them, we must go some other way to work.

Many, in good truth, are the ways which human wit has been forced to take to do this thing with exactness.

Some, for instance, draw all their characters with wind instruments.— *Virgil* takes notice of that way in the affair of *Dido* and *Æneas*;[8]—but it is as fallacious as the breath of fame;—and, moreover, bespeaks a narrow genius. I am not ignorant that the *Italians*[9] pretend to a mathematical exactness in their designations of one particular sort of character among them, from the *forte* or *piano*[10] of a certain wind instrument they use,— which they say is infallible.—I dare not mention the name of the instrument in this place;--'tis sufficient we have it amongst us,—but never think of making a drawing by it;---this is ænigmatical, and intended to be so, at least, *ad populum*:[11]---And therefore I beg, Madam, when you come here, that you read on as fast as you can, and never stop to make any inquiry about it.

There are others again, who will draw a man's character from no other helps in the world, but merely from his evacuations;—but this often gives a very incorrect out-line,---unless, indeed, you take a sketch of his repletions too; and by correcting one drawing from the other, compound one good figure out of them both.

I should have no objection to this method, but that I think it must smell too strong of the lamp,—and be render'd still more operose, by forcing you to have an eye to the rest of his *Non-Naturals*.[12]——Why the most natural actions of a man's life should be call'd his Non-Naturals,---is another question.

There are others, fourthly, who disdain every one of these expedients;—not from any fertility of their own, but from the various ways of doing it, which they have borrowed from the honourable devices which the Pentagraphic[13] Brethren* of the brush have shewn in taking copies.—These, you must know, are your great historians.

One of these you will see drawing a full-length character *against the light*;—that's illiberal,----dishonest,----and hard upon the character of the man who sits.

Others, to mend the matter, will make a drawing of you in the *Camera*;[14] ---that is most unfair of all,---because, *there* you are sure to be represented in some of your most ridiculous attitudes.

To avoid all and every one of these errors, in giving you my uncle *Toby*'s character, I am determin'd to draw it by no mechanical help whatever;——nor shall my pencil[15] be guided by any one wind instrument which ever was blown upon, either on this, or on the other side of the *Alps*;—nor will I consider either his repletions or his discharges,—or touch upon his Non-Naturals;---but, in a word, I will draw my uncle *Toby*'s character from his HOBBY-HORSE.[16]

CHAP. XXIV.

IF I was not morally sure that the reader must be out of all patience for my uncle *Toby*'s character,——I would here previously have convinced him, that there is no instrument so fit to draw such a thing with, as that which I have pitch'd upon.

A man and his HOBBY-HORSE, tho' I cannot say that they act and re-act exactly after the same manner in which the soul and body do upon each other: Yet doubtless there is a communication between them of some kind,

---

*Pentagraph, an instrument to copy prints and pictures mechanically, and in any proportion.

and my opinion rather is, that there is something in it more of the manner of electrified bodies,--and that by means of the heated parts of the rider, which come immediately into contact with the back of the HOBBY-HORSE.—By long journies and much friction, it so happens that the body of the rider is at length fill'd as full of HOBBY-HORSICAL matter as it can hold;----so that if you are able to give but a clear description of the nature of the one, you may form a pretty exact notion of the genius and character of the other.

Now the HOBBY-HORSE which my uncle *Toby* always rode upon, was, in my opinion, an HOBBY-HORSE well worth giving a description of, if it was only upon the score of his great singularity; for you might have travelled from *York* to *Dover*,——from *Dover* to *Penzance* in *Cornwall*, and from *Penzance* to *York* back again, and not have seen such another upon the road; or if you had seen such a one, whatever haste you had been in, you must infallibly have stopp'd to have taken a view of him. Indeed, the gait and figure of him was so strange, and so utterly unlike was he, from his head to his tail, to any one of the whole species, that it was now and then made a matter of dispute,—— whether he was really a HOBBY-HORSE or no: But as the Philosopher would use no other argument to the sceptic, who disputed with him against the reality of motion,[1] save that of rising up upon his legs, and walking a-cross the room;—so would my uncle *Toby* use no other argument to prove his HOBBY-HORSE was a HOBBY-HORSE indeed, but by getting upon his back and riding him about;—leaving the world after that to determine the point as it thought fit.

In good truth, my uncle *Toby* mounted him with so much pleasure, and he carried my uncle *Toby* so well,——that he troubled his head very little with what the world either said or thought about it.

It is now high time, however, that I give you a description of him:— But to go on regularly, I only beg you will give me leave to acquaint you first, how my uncle *Toby* came by him.

CHAP. XXV.

THE wound in my uncle *Toby*'s groin, which he received at the siege of *Namur*, rendering him unfit for the service, it was thought expedient he should return to *England*, in order, if possible, to be set to rights.

He was four years totally confined,—part of it to his bed, and all of it to his room; and in the course of his cure, which was all that time in hand, suffer'd unspeakable miseries,—owing to a succession of exfoliations from the *oss pubis*, and the outward edge of that part of the *coxendix* called the *oss illeum*,¹——both which bones were dismally crush'd, as much by the irregularity of the stone, which I told you was broke off the parapet,—as by its size,—(though it was pretty large) which inclined the surgeon all along to think, that the great injury which it had done my uncle *Toby*'s groin, was more owing to the gravity of the stone itself, than to the projectile force of it,—which he would often tell him was a great happiness.

My father at that time was just beginning business in *London*, and had taken a house;—and as the truest friendship and cordiality subsisted between the two brothers,—and that my father thought my uncle *Toby* could no where be so well nursed and taken care of as in his own house, ——he assign'd him the very best apartment in it.—And what was a much more sincere mark of his affection still, he would never suffer a friend or an acquaintance to step into the house on any occasion, but he would take him by the hand, and lead him up stairs to see his brother *Toby*, and chat an hour by his bed side.

The history of a soldier's wound² beguiles the pain of it;—my uncle's visiters at least thought so, and in their daily calls upon him, from the courtesy arising out of that belief, they would frequently turn the discourse to that subject,—and from that subject the discourse would generally roll on to the siege itself.

These conversations were infinitely kind; and my uncle *Toby* received great relief from them, and would have received much more, but that they brought him into some unforeseen perplexities, which, for three months together, retarded his cure greatly; and if he had not hit upon an expedient to extricate himself out of them, I verily believe they would have laid him in his grave.

What these perplexities of my uncle *Toby* were,——'tis impossible for you to guess;—if you could,—I should blush; not as a relation,—not as a man,—nor even as a woman,—but I should blush as an author; inasmuch as I set no small store by myself upon this very account, that my reader has never yet been able to guess at any thing. And in this, Sir, I am of so nice and singular a humour, that if I thought you was able to form the least judgment or probable conjecture to yourself, of what was to come in the next page,—I would tear it out of my book.

END of the First Volume.

THE

LIFE

AND

OPINIONS

OF

TRISTRAM SHANDY,
GENTLEMAN.

Ταρασσει τὲς Ἀνθρώπες ἐ τὰ Πράγμαῖα,
αλλα τὰ περι των Πραγμαῖων, Δογμαῖα·

VOL. II.

1760.

(Height of original type-page 123 mm.)

THE

LIFE and OPINIONS

OF

TRISTRAM SHANDY, Gent.

CHAP. I.

I Have begun a new book, on purpose that I might have room enough to explain the nature of the perplexities in which my uncle *Toby* was involved, from the many discourses and interrogations about the siege of *Namur*,[1] where he received his wound.

I must remind the reader, in case he has read the history of King *William*'s wars,—but if he has not,--I then inform him, that one of the most memorable attacks in that siege, was that which was made by the *English* and *Dutch* upon the point of the advanced counterscarp, before the gate of *St. Nicolas*, which inclosed the great sluice or water-stop, where the *English* were terribly exposed to the shot of the counter-guard and demi-bastion of *St. Roch:* The issue of which hot dispute, in three words, was this; That the *Dutch* lodged themselves upon the counter-guard,---and that the *English* made themselves masters of the covered way before *St. Nicolas*'s gate, notwithstanding the gallantry of the *French* officers, who exposed themselves upon the glacis sword in hand.

As this was the principal attack of which my uncle *Toby* was an eye-witness at *Namur*,——the army of the besiegers being cut off, by the confluence of the *Maes* and *Sambre*, from seeing much of each other's operations,—my uncle *Toby* was generally more eloquent and particular in his account of it; and the many perplexities he was in, arose out of the almost insurmountable difficulties he found in telling his story intelligibly, and giving such clear ideas of the differences and distinctions between the scarp and counterscarp,——the glacis and covered way,——the half-moon and ravelin,——as to make his company fully comprehend where and what he was about.

Writers themselves are too apt to confound these terms;——so that you will the less wonder, if in his endeavours to explain them, and in opposition to many misconceptions, that my uncle *Toby* did oft times puzzle his visiters; and sometimes himself too.

To speak the truth, unless the company my father led up stairs were tolerably clear-headed, or my uncle *Toby* was in one of his best explanatory moods, 'twas a difficult thing, do what he could, to keep the discourse free from obscurity.

What rendered the account of this affair the more intricate to my uncle *Toby*, was this,——that in the attack of the counterscarp before the gate of *St. Nicolas*, extending itself from the bank of the *Maes*, quite up to the great water-stop;——the ground was cut and cross-cut with such a multitude of dykes, drains, rivulets, and sluices, on all sides,——and he would get so sadly bewilder'd and set fast amongst them, that frequently he could neither get backwards or forwards to save his life; and was oft times obliged to give up the attack upon that very account only.

These perplexing rebuffs gave my uncle *Toby Shandy* more perturbations than you would imagine; and as my father's kindness to him was continually dragging up fresh friends and fresh inquirers,——he had but a very uneasy task of it.

No doubt my uncle *Toby* had great command of himself,——and could guard appearances, I believe, as well as most men;——yet any one may imagine, that when he could not retreat out of the ravelin without getting into the half-moon, or get out of the covered way without falling down the counterscarp, nor cross the dyke without danger of slipping into the ditch, but that he must have fretted and fumed inwardly:——He did so;—— and these little and hourly vexations, which may seem trifling and of no account to the man who has not read *Hippocrates*,[2] yet, whoever has read *Hippocrates*, or Dr. *James Mackenzie*,[3] and has considered well the effects which the passions and affections of the mind have upon the digestion,[4]—— (Why not of a wound as well as of a dinner?)——may easily conceive what sharp paroxisms and exacerbations of his wound my uncle *Toby* must have undergone upon that score only.

——My uncle *Toby* could not philosophize upon it;——'twas enough he felt it was so,——and having sustained the pain and sorrows of it for three months together, he was resolved some way or other to extricate himself.

He was one morning lying upon his back in his bed, the anguish and nature of the wound upon his groin suffering him to lye in no other position, when a thought came into his head, that if he could purchase such a thing, and have it pasted down upon a board, as a large map of the fortifications of the town and citadel of *Namur*, with its environs, it might be a means of giving him ease.—I take notice of his desire to have the environs along with the town and citadel, for this reason,—because my uncle *Toby*'s wound was got in one of the traverses, about thirty toises from the returning angle of the trench, opposite to the salient angle of the demi-bastion of *St. Roch*;——so that he was pretty confident he could stick a pin upon the identical spot of ground where he was standing in when the stone struck him.

All this succeeded to his wishes, and not only freed him from a world of sad explanations, but, in the end, it prov'd the happy means, as you will read, of procuring my uncle *Toby* his HOBBY-HORSE.

CHAP. II.

THERE is nothing so foolish, when you are at the expence of making an entertainment of this kind, as to order things so badly, as to let your criticks and gentry of refined taste run it down: Nor is there any thing so likely to make them do it, as that of leaving them out of the party, or, what is full as offensive, of bestowing your attention upon the rest of your guests in so particular a way, as if there was no such thing as a critick (by occupation) at table.

———I guard against both; for, in the first place, I have left half a dozen places purposely open for them;—and, in the next place, I pay them all court,—Gentlemen, I kiss your hands,—I protest no company could give me half the pleasure,—by my soul I am glad to see you,——I beg only you will make no strangers of yourselves, but sit down without any ceremony, and fall on heartily.

I said I had left six places, and I was upon the point of carrying my complaisance so far, as to have left a seventh open for them,—and in this very spot I stand on;—but being told by a critick, (tho' not by occupation,---but by nature) that I had acquitted myself well enough, I shall fill it up directly, hoping, in the mean time, that I shall be able to make a great deal of more room next year.

————How, in the name of wonder! could your uncle *Toby*, who, it seems, was a military man, and whom you have represented as no fool, ----be at the same time such a confused, pudding-headed, muddle-headed fellow, as---Go look.

So, Sir Critick, I could have replied; but I scorn it.————'Tis language unurbane,----and only befitting the man who cannot give clear and satisfactory accounts of things, or dive deep enough into the first causes of human ignorance and confusion. It is moreover the reply valiant,----and therefore I reject it; for tho' it might have suited my uncle *Toby*'s character as a soldier excellently well,---and had he not accustomed himself, in such attacks, to whistle the *Lillabullero*,----as he wanted no courage, 'tis the very answer he would have given; yet it would by no means have done for me. You see as plain as can be, that I write as a man of erudition;---that even my similies, my allusions, my illustrations, my metaphors, are erudite,----and that I must sustain my character properly, and contrast it properly too,---else what would become of me? Why, Sir, I should be undone;----at this very moment that I am going here to fill up one place against a critick,-----I should have made an opening for a couple.

————Therefore I answer thus:

Pray, Sir, in all the reading which you have ever read, did you ever read such a book as *Locke*'s Essay upon the Human Understanding?[1]———— Don't answer me rashly,--because many, I know, quote the book, who have not read it,---and many have read it who understand it not:---If either of these is your case, as I write to instruct, I will tell you in three words what the book is.——It is a history.——A history! of who? what? where? when? Don't hurry yourself.————It is a history-book, Sir, (which may possibly recommend it to the world) of what passes in a man's own mind; and if you will say so much of the book, and no more, believe me, you will cut no contemptible figure in a metaphysic circle.

But this by the way.

Now if you will venture to go along with me, and look down into the bottom of this matter, it will be found that the cause of obscurity and confusion, in the mind of man, is threefold.

Dull organs, dear Sir, in the first place. Secondly, slight and transient impressions made by objects when the said organs are not dull. And, thirdly, a memory like unto a sieve, not able to retain what it has received. ----Call down *Dolly* your chamber-maid, and I will give you my cap and bell along with it, if I make not this matter so plain that *Dolly* herself shall understand it as well as *Malbranch*.[2] —— When *Dolly* has indited her epistle to *Robin*, and has thrust her arm into the bottom of her pocket hanging by her right side;—take that opportunity to recollect that the organs and faculties of perception, can, by nothing in this world, be so aptly typified and explained as by that one thing which *Dolly*'s hand is in search of.— Your organs are not so dull that I should inform you---'tis an inch, Sir, of red seal-wax.

When this is melted and dropp'd upon the letter,—if *Dolly* fumbles too long for her thimble, till the wax is over harden'd, it will not receive the mark of her thimble from the usual impulse which was wont to imprint it. Very well: If *Dolly*'s wax, for want of better, is bees-wax, or of a temper too soft,—tho' it may receive,---it will not hold the impression, how hard soever *Dolly* thrusts against it; and last of all, supposing the wax good, and eke the thimble, but applied thereto in careless haste, as her Mistress rings the bell;——in any one of these three cases, the print, left by the thimble, will be as unlike the prototype as a brass-jack.[3]

Now you must understand that not one of these was the true cause of the confusion in my uncle *Toby*'s discourse; and it is for that very reason I enlarge upon them so long, after the manner of great physiologists,—to shew the world what it did *not* arise from.

What it did arise from, I have hinted above, and a fertile source of obscurity it is,---and ever will be,---and that is the unsteady uses of words which have perplexed the clearest and most exalted understandings.

It is ten to one, (at *Arthur*'s)[4] whether you have ever read the literary histories of past ages;—if you have,—what terrible battles, 'yclept[5] logo-machies, have they occasioned and perpetuated with so much gall and ink-shed,---that a good natured man cannot read the accounts of them without tears in his eyes.

Gentle critick! when thou hast weigh'd all this, and consider'd within thyself how much of thy own knowledge, discourse, and conversation has been pestered and disordered, at one time or other, by this, and this only: —— What a pudder and racket in COUNCILS about ἐσία and ὑπόςασις; and in the SCHOOLS of the learned about power and about spirit;—about essences, and about quintessences;—— about substances, and about space.[6]

71

——What confusion in greater THEATRES from words of little meaning, and as indeterminate a sense;---when thou considers this, thou wilt not wonder at my uncle *Toby*'s perplexities,—thou wilt drop a tear of pity upon his scarp and his counterscarp;—his glacis and his covered-way;—his ravelin and his half-moon: 'Twas not by ideas,——by heaven! his life was put in jeopardy by words.

CHAP. III.

WHEN my uncle *Toby* got his map of *Namur* to his mind, he began immediately to apply himself, and with the utmost diligence, to the study of it; for nothing being of more importance to him than his recovery, and his recovery depending, as you have read, upon the passions and affections of his mind, it behoved him to take the nicest care to make himself so far master of his subject, as to be able to talk upon it without emotion.

In a fortnight's close and painful application, which, by the bye, did my uncle *Toby*'s wound, upon his groin, no good,—he was enabled, by the help of some marginal documents at the feet of the elephant,[1] together with *Gobesius*'s[2] military architecture and pyroballogy, translated from the *Flemish*, to form his discourse with passable perspicuity; and, before he was two full months gone,—he was right eloquent upon it, and could make not only the attack of the advanced counterscarp with great order;——but having, by that time, gone much deeper into the art, than what his first motive made necessary,—my uncle *Toby* was able to cross the *Maes* and *Sambre*; make diversions as far as *Vauban*'s line, the abbey of *Salsines*,[3] &c. and give his visiters as distinct a history of each of their attacks, as of that of the gate of *St. Nicolas*, where he had the honour to receive his wound.

But the desire of knowledge, like the thirst of riches, increases ever with the acquisition of it. The more my uncle *Toby* pored over his map, the more he took a liking to it;—by the same process and electrical assimilation,[4] as I told you, thro' which I ween the souls of connoisseurs themselves, by long friction and incumbition,[5] have the happiness, at length, to get all be-virtu'd,—be-pictur'd,—be-butterflied, and be-fiddled.

The more my uncle *Toby* drank of this sweet fountain of science, the greater was the heat and impatience of his thirst, so that, before the first year of his confinement had well gone round, there was scarce a fortified town in *Italy* or *Flanders*, of which, by one means or other, he had not procured a plan, reading over as he got them, and carefully collating therewith the histories of their sieges, their demolitions, their improvements and new works, all which he would read with that intense application and delight, that he would forget himself, his wound, his confinement, his dinner.

In the second year my uncle *Toby* purchased *Ramelli* and *Cataneo*, translated from the *Italian*;——likewise *Stevinus*, *Marolis*, the Chevalier *de Ville*, *Lorini*, *Coehorn*, *Sheeter*, the Count de *Pagan*, the Marshal *Vauban*, Mons. *Blondel*,[6] with almost as many more books of military architecture, as Don *Quixote* was found to have of chivalry, when the curate and barber invaded his library.[7]

Towards the beginning of the third year,[8] which was in *August*, ninety-nine, my uncle *Toby* found it necessary to understand a little of projectiles:—And having judged it best to draw his knowledge from the fountain-head, he began with *N. Tartaglia*,[9] who it seems was the first man who detected the imposition of a cannon-ball's doing all that mischief under the notion of a right line.—This *N. Tartaglia* proved to my uncle *Toby* to be an impossible thing.

————Endless is the Search of Truth!

No sooner was my uncle *Toby* satisfied which road the cannon-ball did not go, but he was insensibly led on, and resolved in his mind to enquire and find out which road the ball did go: For which purpose he was obliged to set off afresh with old *Maltus*, and studied him devoutly.—He proceeded next to *Gallileo* and *Torricellius*, wherein, by certain geometrical rules, infallibly laid down, he found the precise path to be a PARABOLA,—or else an HYPERBOLA,—and that the parameter, or *latus rectum*,[10] of the conic section of the said path, was to the quantity and amplitude in a direct *ratio*, as the whole line to the sine of double the angle of incidence, form'd by the breech upon an horizontal plane;—and that the semi-parameter,————stop! my dear uncle *Toby*,—stop!—go not one foot further into this thorny and bewilder'd track,—intricate are the steps! intricate are the mases[11] of this labyrinth! intricate are the troubles which the pursuit of this bewitching phantom, KNOWLEDGE, will bring upon thee.—O my uncle! fly--fly--fly from it as from a serpent.[12]—Is it fit, good-natur'd man! thou should'st sit up, with the wound upon thy groin, whole nights baking thy blood with hectic watchings?—Alas! 'twill exasperate thy symptoms,—check thy perspirations,—evaporate thy spirits, —waste thy animal strength,—dry up thy radical moisture,—bring thee into a costive habit of body, impair thy health,—and hasten all the infirmities of thy old age.[13]—O my uncle! my uncle *Toby*.

CHAP. IV.

I Would not give a groat[1] for that man's knowledge in pen-craft, who does not understand this,——That the best plain narrative in the world, tack'd very close to the last spirited apostrophe to my uncle *Toby*,—would have felt both cold and vapid upon the reader's palate;—therefore I forthwith put an end to the chapter,—though I was in the middle of my story.

——Writers of my stamp have one principle in common with painters.—Where an exact copying makes our pictures less striking, we choose the less evil; deeming it even more pardonable to trespass against truth, than beauty.—This is to be understood *cum grano salis*;[2] but be it as it will,——as the parallel is made more for the sake of letting the apostrophe cool, than any thing else,—'tis not very material whether upon any other score the reader approves of it or not.

In the latter end of the third year, my uncle *Toby* perceiving that the parameter and semi-parameter of the conic section, angered his wound, he left off the study of projectiles in a kind of a huff, and betook himself to the practical part of fortification only; the pleasure of which, like a spring held back, returned upon him with redoubled force.

It was in this year that my uncle began to break in upon the daily regularity of a clean shirt,[3]——to dismiss his barber unshaven,——and to allow his surgeon scarce time sufficient to dress his wound, concerning himself so little about it, as not to ask him once in seven times dressing how it went on: When, lo!—all of a sudden, for the change was as quick as lightening, he began to sigh heavily for his recovery,—complain'd to my father, grew impatient with the surgeon;—and one morning as he heard his foot coming up stairs, he shut up his books, and thrust aside his instruments, in order to expostulate with him upon the protraction of his cure, which, he told him, might surely have been accomplished at least by that time:—He dwelt long upon the miseries he had undergone, and the sorrows of his four years melancholy imprisonment;—adding, that had it not been for the kind looks, and fraternal chearings of the best of brothers,—he had long since sunk under his misfortunes.—My father was by: My uncle *Toby*'s eloquence brought tears into his eyes;—'twas unexpected.—My uncle *Toby*, by nature, was not eloquent;——it had the greater effect.—The Surgeon was confounded;—not that there wanted grounds for such, or greater, marks of impatience,—but 'twas unexpected too; in the four years he had attended him, he had never seen any thing like it in my uncle *Toby*'s carriage;—he had never once dropp'd one fretful or discontented word;—he had been all patience,—all submission.

—We lose the right of complaining sometimes by forbearing it;—— but we oftener treble the force:—The Surgeon was astonished;—but much more so, when he heard my uncle *Toby* go on, and peremptorily insist upon his healing up the wound directly,——or sending for Monsieur *Ronjat*,[4] the King's Serjeant-Surgeon, to do it for him.

The desire of life and health is implanted in man's nature;—the love of liberty and enlargement is a sister passion to it: These my uncle *Toby* had in common with his species;——and either of them had been sufficient to account for his earnest desire to get well and out of doors;—but I have told you before that nothing wrought with our family after the common way;—and from the time and manner in which this eager desire shew'd itself in the present case, the penetrating reader will suspect there was some other cause or crotchet for it in my uncle *Toby*'s head:—There was so, and 'tis the subject of the next chapter to set forth what that cause and crotchet was. I own, when that's done, 'twill be time to return back to the parlour fire-side, where we left my uncle *Toby* in the middle of his sentence.

CHAP. V.

WHEN a man gives himself up to the government of a ruling passion,——or, in other words, when his HOBBY-HORSE grows head-strong,——farewell cool reason and fair discretion![1]

My uncle *Toby*'s wound was near well, and as soon as the surgeon recovered his surprize, and could get leave to say as much—he told him, 'twas just beginning to incarnate;[2] and that if no fresh exfoliation happen'd, which there was no signs of,—it would be dried up in five or six weeks. The sound of as many olympiads twelve hours before, would have convey'd an idea of shorter duration to my uncle *Toby*'s mind.[3]—The succession of his ideas was now rapid,—he broil'd with impatience to put his design in execution;—and so, without consulting further with any soul living, ——which, by the bye, I think is right, when you are predetermined to take no one soul's advice,—he privately ordered *Trim*, his man, to pack up a bundle of lint and dressings, and hire a chariot and four to be at the door exactly by twelve o'clock that day, when he knew my father would be upon 'Change.[4]——So leaving a bank-note upon the table for the surgeon's care of him, and a letter of tender thanks for his brother's,—— he pack'd up his maps, his books of fortification, his instruments, *&c.*— and, by the help of a crutch on one side, and *Trim* on the other,——my uncle *Toby* embark'd for *Shandy-Hall*.

The reason, or rather the rise, of this sudden demigration,[5] was as follows:

The table in my uncle *Toby*'s room, and at which, the night before this change happened, he was sitting with his maps, *&c.* about him,—being somewhat of the smallest, for that infinity of great and small instruments of knowledge which usually lay crouded upon it;—he had the accident, in reaching over for his tobacco-box, to throw down his compasses, and in stooping to take the compasses up, with his sleeve he threw down his case of instruments and snuffers;—and as the dice took a run against him, in his endeavouring to catch the snuffers in falling,—he thrust Monsieur *Blondel* off the table and Count de *Pagan* o'top of him.

'Twas to no purpose for a man, lame as my uncle *Toby* was, to think of redressing all these evils by himself,—he rung his bell for his man *Trim*;—

Trim! quoth my uncle *Toby*, pri'thee see what confusion I have here been making.——I must have some better contrivance, *Trim*.——Can'st not thou take my rule and measure the length and breadth of this table, and then go and bespeak me one as big again?——Yes, an' please your Honour, replied *Trim*, making a bow;——but I hope your Honour will be soon well enough to get down to your country seat, where,——as your Honour takes so much pleasure in fortification, we could manage this matter to a T.

I must here inform you, that this servant of my uncle *Toby*'s, who went by the name of *Trim*, had been a Corporal in my uncle's own company, ——his real name was *James Butler*,[6]——but having got the nick-name of *Trim* in the regiment, my uncle *Toby*, unless when he happened to be very angry with him, would never call him by any other name.

The poor fellow had been disabled for the service, by a wound on his left knee by a musket-bullet, at the battle of *Landen*, which was two years before the affair of *Namur*;——and as the fellow was well beloved in the regiment, and a handy fellow into the bargain, my uncle *Toby* took him for his servant, and of excellent use was he, attending my uncle *Toby* in the camp and in his quarters as valet, groom, barber, cook, sempster, and nurse; and indeed, from first to last, waited upon him and served him with great fidelity and affection.

My uncle *Toby* loved the man in return, and what attached him more to him still, was the similitude of their knowledge:——For Corporal *Trim*, (for so, for the future, I shall call him) by four years occasional attention to his Master's discourse upon fortified towns, and the advantage of prying and peeping continually into his Master's plans, *&c.* exclusive and besides what he gained HOBBY-HORSICALLY, as a body-servant, *Non Hobby-Horsical per se*;——had become no mean proficient in the science; and was thought, by the cook and chamber-maid, to know as much of the nature of strong-holds as my uncle *Toby* himself.

I have but one more stroke to give to finish Corporal *Trim*'s character,--and it is the only dark line in it.——The fellow lov'd to advise,—— or rather to hear himself talk; his carriage, however, was so perfectly respectful, 'twas easy to keep him silent when you had him so; but set his tongue a-going,——you had no hold of him;——he was voluble;--the eternal interlardings of *your Honour*, with the respectfulness of Corporal *Trim*'s manner, interceeding so strong in behalf of his elocution,——that tho' you might have been incommoded,——you could not well be angry. My uncle

Toby was seldom either the one or the other with him,—or, at least, this fault, in *Trim*, broke no squares[7] with 'em. My uncle *Toby*, as I said, loved the man;—and besides, as he ever looked upon a faithful servant,——but as a humble friend,—he could not bear to stop his mouth.——Such was Corporal *Trim*.

If I durst presume, continued *Trim*, to give your Honour my advice, and speak my opinion in this matter.—Thou art welcome, *Trim*, quoth my uncle *Toby*,—speak,—speak what thou thinkest upon the subject, man, without fear. Why then, replied *Trim*, (not hanging his ears and scratching his head like a country lout, but) stroking his hair back from his forehead, and standing erect as before his division.——I think, quoth *Trim*, advancing his left, which was his lame leg, a little forwards,—and pointing with his right hand open towards a map of *Dunkirk*, which was pinn'd against the hangings,—I think, quoth Corporal *Trim*, with humble submission to your Honour's better judgment,—that these ravelins, bastions, curtins, and horn-works make but a poor, contemptible, fiddle faddle piece of work of it here upon paper, compared to what your Honour and I could make of it, were we in the country by ourselves, and had but a rood, or a rood and a half of ground to do what we pleased with: As summer is coming on, continued *Trim*, your Honour might sit out of doors, and give me the nography——(call it ichnography,[8] quoth my uncle)—of the town or citadel, your Honour was pleased to sit down before,[9]—and I will be shot by your Honour upon the glacis of it, if I did not fortify it to your Honour's mind.—I dare say thou would'st *Trim*, quoth my uncle.—For if your Honour, continued the Corporal, could but mark me the polygon,[10] with its exact lines and angles,——that I could do very well, quoth my uncle.—I would begin with the fossé, and if your Honour could tell me the proper depth and breadth,—I can to a hair's breadth, *Trim*, replied my uncle,—I would throw out the earth upon this hand towards the town for the scarp,—and on that hand towards the campaign[11] for the counterscarp,—very right, *Trim*, quoth my uncle *Toby*,—and when I had sloped them to your mind,—an' please your Honour, I would face the glacis, as the finest fortifications are done in *Flanders*, with sods,—and as your Honour knows they should be,——and I would make the walls and parapets with sods too;—the best engineers call them gazons, *Trim*, said my uncle *Toby*;—whether they are gazons or sods, is not much matter, replied *Trim*, your Honour knows they are ten times beyond a facing either of brick or stone;——I know they are, *Trim*, in some respects,—

quoth my uncle *Toby*, nodding his head;—for a cannon-ball enters into the gazon right onwards, without bringing any rubbish down with it, which might fill the fossé, (as was the case at *St. Nicolas's Gate*) and facilitate the passage over it.

Your Honour understands these matters, replied Corporal *Trim*, better than any officer in his Majesty's service;——but would your Honour please to let the bespeaking of the table alone, and let us but go into the country, I would work under your Honour's directions like a horse, and make fortifications for you something like a tansy,[12] with all their batteries, saps, ditches, and pallisadoes, that it should be worth all the world's riding twenty miles to go and see it.

My uncle *Toby* blushed as red as scarlet[13] as *Trim* went on;—but it was not a blush of guilt,—of modesty,—or of anger;—it was a blush of joy;—he was fired with Corporal *Trim's* project and description.—*Trim!* said my uncle *Toby*, thou hast said enough.—We might begin the campaign, continued *Trim*, on the very day that his Majesty and the Allies take the field, and demolish 'em town by town as fast as——*Trim*, quoth my uncle *Toby*, say no more.—Your Honour, continued *Trim*, might sit in your arm-chair, (pointing to it) this fine weather, giving me your orders, and I would——Say no more, *Trim*, quoth my uncle *Toby*.——Besides, your Honour would get not only pleasure and good pastime,—but good air, and good exercise, and good health,—and your Honour's wound would be well in a month. Thou hast said enough, *Trim*,—quoth my uncle *Toby*, (putting his hand into his breeches-pocket)—I like thy project mightily;—and if your Honour pleases, I'll, this moment, go and buy a pioneer's spade to take down with us, and I'll bespeak a shovel and a pick-ax, and a couple of——Say no more, *Trim*, quoth my uncle *Toby*, leaping up upon one leg, quite overcome with rapture,——and thrusting a guinea into *Trim's* hand.——*Trim*, said my uncle *Toby*, say no more;--but go down, *Trim*, this moment, my lad, and bring up my supper this instant.

Trim ran down and brought up his Master's supper,—to no purpose:——*Trim's* plan of operation ran so in my uncle *Toby's* head, he could not taste it.—*Trim*, quoth my uncle *Toby*, get me to bed;—'twas all one.—Corporal *Trim's* description had fired his imagination,—my uncle *Toby* could not shut his eyes.--The more he consider'd it, the more bewitching the scene appeared to him;—so that, two full hours before day-light, he had come to a final determination, and had concerted the whole plan of his and Corporal *Trim's* decampment.

My uncle *Toby* had a little neat country-house of his own, in the village where my father's estate lay at *Shandy*, which had been left him by an old uncle, with a small estate of about one hundred pounds a-year. Behind this house, and contiguous to it, was a kitchen-garden of about half an acre;—and at the bottom of the garden, and cut off from it by a tall yew hedge, was a bowling-green,[14] containing just about as much ground as Corporal *Trim* wished for;—so that as *Trim* uttered the words, "A rood and a half of ground to do what they would with:"——This identical bowling-green instantly presented itself, and became curiously painted, all at once, upon the retina[15] of my uncle *Toby*'s fancy;——which was the physical cause of making him change colour, or at least, of heightening his blush to that immoderate degree I spoke of.

Never did lover post down to a belov'd mistress with more heat and expectation, than my uncle *Toby* did, to enjoy this self-same thing in private;—I say in private;—for it was sheltered from the house, as I told you, by a tall yew hedge, and was covered on the other three sides, from mortal sight, by rough holly and thickset flowering shrubs;—so that the idea of not being seen, did not a little contribute to the idea of pleasure preconceived in my uncle *Toby*'s mind.—Vain thought! however thick it was planted about,——or private soever it might seem,—to think, dear uncle *Toby*, of enjoying a thing which took up a whole rood and a half of ground,—and not have it known!

How my uncle *Toby* and Corporal *Trim* managed this matter,—with the history of their campaigns, which were no way barren of events,—may make no uninteresting under-plot in the epitasis[16] and working up of this drama.—At present the scene must drop,—and change for the parlour fire-side.

CHAP. VI.

——What can they be doing, brother? said my father.—I think, replied my uncle *Toby*,—taking, as I told you, his pipe from his mouth, and striking the ashes out of it as he began his sentence;----I think, replied he,—it would not be amiss, brother, if we rung the bell.

Pray, what's all that racket over our heads, *Obadiah?*—quoth my father;—my brother and I can scarce hear ourselves speak.

Sir, answer'd *Obadiah*, making a bow towards his left shoulder,—my Mistress is taken very badly;—and where's *Susannah* running down the garden there, as if they were going to ravish her.[1]——Sir, she is running the shortest cut into the town, replied *Obadiah*, to fetch the old midwife. ——Then saddle a horse, quoth my father, and do you go directly for Dr. *Slop*, the man-midwife, with all our services,—and let him know your Mistress is fallen into labour,—and that I desire he will return with you with all speed.

It is very strange, says my father, addressing himself to my uncle *Toby*, as *Obadiah* shut the door,—as there is so expert an operator as Dr. *Slop* so near---that my wife should persist to the very last in this obstinate humour of hers, in trusting the life of my child, who has had one misfortune already, to the ignorance of an old woman;——and not only the life of my child, brother,—but her own life, and with it the lives of all the children I might, peradventure, have begot out of her hereafter.

Mayhap, brother, replied my uncle *Toby*, my sister does it to save the expence:—A pudding's end,[2]—replied my father,—the Doctor must be paid the same for inaction as action,—if not better,—to keep him in temper.

—Then it can be out of nothing in the whole world, quoth my uncle *Toby*, in the simplicity of his heart,—but MODESTY:—My sister, I dare say, added he, does not care to let a man come so near her****.[3] I will not say whether my uncle *Toby* had compleated the sentence or not;—'tis for his advantage to suppose he had,—as, I think, he could have added no ONE WORD which would have improved it.

If, on the contrary, my uncle *Toby* had not fully arrived at his period's end,—then the world stands indebted to the sudden snapping of my father's tobacco-pipe, for one of the neatest examples of that ornamental figure in oratory, which Rhetoricians stile the *Aposiopesis*.[4]—Just heaven! how does the *Poco piu* and the *Poco meno*[5] of the *Italian* artists;—the insensible MORE or LESS, determine the precise line of beauty in the sentence, as well as in the statue! How do the slight touches of the chisel, the pencil, the pen, the fiddle-stick, *et cætera*,[6]—give the true swell, which gives the true pleasure!—O my countrymen!—be nice;—be cautious of your language;——and never, O! never let it be forgotten upon what small particles your eloquence and your fame depend.

——"My sister, mayhap, quoth my uncle *Toby*, does not choose to let

a man come so near her****" Make this dash,——'tis an Aposiopesis.—
Take the dash away, and write Backside,—'tis Bawdy.—Scratch Backside
out, and put *Cover'd-way* in,—'tis a Metaphor;—and, I dare say, as fortification ran so much in my uncle *Toby*'s head, that if he had been left to have
added one word to the sentence,—that word was it.

But whether that was the case or not the case;—or whether the snapping
of my father's tobacco-pipe so critically, happened thro' accident or
anger,—will be seen in due time.

CHAP. VII.

THO' my father was a good natural philosopher,[1]——yet he was
something of a moral philosopher too; for which reason, when his
tobacco-pipe snapp'd short in the middle,——he had nothing to do,—
as such,—but to have taken hold of the two pieces, and thrown them
gently upon the back of the fire.—He did no such thing;—he threw them
with all the violence in the world;—and, to give the action still more
emphasis,--he started up upon both his legs to do it.

This look'd something like heat;—and the manner of his reply to what
my uncle *Toby* was saying prov'd it was so.

—"Not choose, quoth my father, (repeating my uncle *Toby*'s words)
to let a man come so near her——" By heaven, brother *Toby!* you would
try the patience of a *Job*;—and I think I have the plagues of one already, without it.——Why?——Where?——Wherein?——Where-
fore?—Upon what account, replied my uncle *Toby*, in the utmost astonish-
ment.——To think, said my father, of a man living to your age, brother,
and knowing so little about women!—I know nothing at all about them,—
replied my uncle *Toby*; and I think, continued he, that the shock I received
the year after the demolition of *Dunkirk*,[2] in my affair with widow *Wadman*;—which shock you know I should not have received, but from my
total ignorance of the sex,---has given me just cause to say, That I neither
know, nor do pretend to know, any thing about 'em, or their concerns
either.——Methinks, brother, replied my father, you might, at least, know
so much as the right end of a woman from the wrong.

It is said in *Aristotle's Master-Piece*,[3] "That when a man doth think of any thing which is past,---he looketh down upon the ground;---but that when he thinketh of something which is to come, he looketh up towards the heavens."

My uncle *Toby*, I suppose, thought of neither,---for he look'd horizont-ally.----Right end,---quoth my uncle *Toby*, muttering the two words low to himself, and fixing his two eyes insensibly as he muttered them, upon a small crevice, form'd by a bad joint in the chimney-piece.—Right end of a woman!——I declare, quoth my uncle, I know no more which it is, than the man in the moon;--and if I was to think, continued my uncle *Toby*, (keeping his eye still fix'd upon the bad joint) this month together, I am sure I should not be able to find it out.

Then brother *Toby*, replied my father, I will tell you.

Every thing in this world, continued my father, (filling a fresh pipe)----every thing in this earthly world, my dear brother *Toby*, has two handles;--not always, quoth my uncle *Toby*;---at least, replied my father, every one has two hands,----which comes to the same thing.----Now, if a man was to sit down coolly, and consider within himself the make, the shape, the construction, com-at-ability, and convenience of all the parts which constitute the whole of that animal, call'd Woman, and compare them analogically—I never understood rightly the meaning of that word,---quoth my uncle *Toby*.——ANALOGY,[4] replied my father, is the certain relation and agreement, which different—Here a Devil of a rap at the door snapp'd my father's definition (like his tobacco-pipe) in two,---and, at the same time, crushed the head of as notable and curious a dissertation as ever was engendered in the womb of speculation;—it was some months before my father could get an opportunity to be safely deliver'd of it:—And, at this hour, it is a thing full as problematical as the subject of the dissertation itself,--(considering the confusion and distresses of our domestick misadventures, which are now coming thick one upon the back of another) whether I shall be able to find a place for it in the third volume or not.

CHAP. VIII.

IT is about an hour and a half's tolerable good reading since my uncle
Toby rung the bell,[1] when *Obadiah* was order'd to saddle a horse, and
go for Dr. *Slop*, the man-midwife;---so that no one can say, with reason,
that I have not allowed *Obadiah* time enough, poetically speaking, and
considering the emergency too, both to go and come;----tho', morally
and truly speaking, the man, perhaps, has scarce had time to get on his
boots.

If the hypercritick will go upon this; and is resolved after all to take a
pendulum, and measure the true distance betwixt the ringing of the bell
and the rap at the door;—and, after finding it to be no more than two
minutes, thirteen seconds, and three fifths,----should take upon him to
insult over me for such a breach in the unity, or rather probability, of
time;[2]—I would remind him, that the idea of duration and of its simple
modes, is got merely from the train and succession of our ideas,[3]---and is
the true scholastick pendulum,----and by which, as a scholar, I will be
tried in this matter,----abjuring and detesting the jurisdiction of all other
pendulums whatever.

I would, therefore, desire him to consider that it is but poor eight miles
from *Shandy-Hall* to Dr. *Slop*, the man-midwife's house;—and that whilst
Obadiah has been going those said miles and back, I have brought my uncle
Toby from *Namur*, quite across all *Flanders*, into *England:*---That I have
had him ill upon my hands near four years;---and have since travelled
him and Corporal *Trim*, in a chariot and four, a journey of near two
hundred miles down into *Yorkshire*;—all which put together, must have
prepared the reader's imagination for the enterance of Dr. *Slop* upon the
stage,——as much, at least, (I hope) as a dance, a song, or a concerto
between the acts.[4]

If my hypercritick is intractable,—alledging, that two minutes and
thirteen seconds are no more than two minutes and thirteen seconds,---
when I have said all I can about them;——and that this plea, tho' it might
save me dramatically, will damn me biographically, rendering my book,
from this very moment, a profess'd ROMANCE, which, before, was a book
apocryphal:——If I am thus pressed—I then put an end to the whole

objection and controversy about it all at once,---by acquainting him, that *Obadiah* had not got above threescore yards from the stable-yard before he met with Dr. *Slop*;—and indeed he gave a dirty proof that he had met with him,-----and was within an ace of giving a tragical one too.

Imagine to yourself;——but this had better begin a new chapter.

CHAP. IX.

IMagine to yourself a little, squat, uncourtly figure of a Doctor *Slop*, of about four feet and a half perpendicular height,[1] with a breadth of back, and a sesquipedality[2] of belly, which might have done honour to a Serjeant in the Horse-Guards.

Such were the out-lines of Dr. *Slop*'s figure, which,—if you have read *Hogarth*'s analysis of beauty, and if you have not, I wish you would;—you must know, may as certainly be caracatur'd, and convey'd to the mind by three strokes[3] as three hundred.

Imagine such a one,—for such, I say, were the out-lines of Dr. *Slop*'s figure, coming slowly along, foot by foot, waddling thro' the dirt upon the vertebræ of a little diminutive pony,—of a pretty colour;---but of strength,---alack!——scarce able to have made an amble of it, under such a fardel,[4] had the roads been in an ambling condition.----They were not. ——Imagine to yourself, *Obadiah* mounted upon a strong monster of a coach-horse, prick'd into a full gallop, and making all practicable speed the adverse way.

Pray, Sir, let me interest you a moment in this description.[5]

Had Dr. *Slop* beheld *Obadiah* a mile off, posting in a narrow lane directly towards him, at that monstrous rate,—splashing and plunging like a devil thro' thick and thin, as he approach'd, would not such a phænomenon, with such a vortex of mud and water moving along with it, round its axis,—have been a subject of juster apprehension to Dr. *Slop* in his situation, than the *worst* of *Whiston*'s comets?[6]—To say nothing of the NUCLEUS; that is, of *Obadiah* and the coach-horse.—In my idea, the vortex alone of 'em was enough to have involved and carried, if not the Doctor, at least the Doctor's pony quite away with it. What then do you think must the terror and hydrophobia[7] of Dr. *Slop* have been, when you read, (which you are just going to do) that he was advancing thus warily along towards *Shandy-Hall*, and had approach'd to within sixty yards of it, and within five yards of a sudden turn, made by an acute angle of the garden wall,—and in the dirtiest part of a dirty lane,—when *Obadiah* and his coach-horse turn'd the corner, rapid, furious,---pop,---full upon him!-----Nothing, I think, in nature, can be supposed more terrible, than such a Rencounter,--so imprompt![8] so ill prepared to stand the shock of it as Dr. *Slop* was!

What could Dr. *Slop* do?---He cross'd himself ✝——Pugh!----but the Doctor, Sir, was a Papist.——No matter; he had better have kept hold of the pummel.—He had so;—nay, as it happen'd, he had better have done nothing at all;---for in crossing himself he let go his whip,——and in attempting to save his whip betwixt his knee and his saddle's skirt, as it slipp'd, he lost his stirrup,—in losing which, he lost his seat;——and in the multitude of all these losses, (which, by the bye, shews what little advantage there is in crossing) the unfortunate Doctor lost his presence of mind. So that, without waiting for *Obadiah*'s onset, he left his pony to its destiny, tumbling off it diagonally, something in the stile and manner of a pack of wool, and without any other consequence from the fall, save that of being left, (as it would have been) with the broadest part of him sunk about twelve inches deep in the mire.

Obadiah pull'd off his cap twice to Dr. *Slop*;——once as he was falling, ----and then again when he saw him seated.---Ill timed complaisance!——had not the fellow better have stopp'd his horse, and got off and help'd him?——Sir, he did all that his situation would allow;---but the MOMENTUM of the coach-horse was so great, that *Obadiah* could not do it all at once;——he rode in a circle three times round Dr. *Slop*, before he could fully accomplish it any how;---and at the last, when he did stop his beast, 'twas done with such an explosion of mud, that *Obadiah* had better have been a league off. In short, never was a Dr. *Slop* so beluted,[9] and so transubstantiated, since that affair came into fashion.

CHAP. X.

WHEN Dr. *Slop* entered the back parlour, where my father and my uncle *Toby* were discoursing upon the nature of women,——it was hard to determine whether Dr. *Slop*'s figure, or Dr. *Slop*'s presence, occasioned more surprize to them; for as the accident happened so near the house, as not to make it worth while for *Obadiah* to remount him,----*Obadiah* had led him in as he was, *unwiped, unappointed, unanealed*, with all his stains and blotches on him.[1]——He stood like *Hamlet*'s ghost, motionless and speechless, for a full minute and a half, at the parlour door, *(Obadiah* still holding his hand) with all the majesty of mud.[2] His hinder parts, upon which he had received his fall, totally besmear'd,----and in every other part of him, blotched over in such a manner with *Obadiah*'s explosion, that you would have sworn, (without mental reservation)[3] that every grain of it had taken effect.

Here was a fair opportunity for my uncle *Toby* to have triumph'd over my father in his turn;---for no mortal, who had beheld Dr. *Slop* in that pickle, could have dissented from so much, at least, of my uncle *Toby*'s opinion, "That mayhap his sister might not care to let such a Dr. *Slop* come so near her****" But it was the *Argumentum ad hominem*;[4] and if my uncle *Toby* was not very expert at it, you may think, he might not care to use it.——No; the reason was,——'twas not his nature to insult.

Dr. *Slop*'s presence, at that time, was no less problematical than the mode of it; tho', it is certain, one moment's reflection in my father might have solved it; for he had apprized Dr. *Slop* but the week before, that my mother was at her full reckoning; and as the Doctor had heard nothing since, 'twas natural and very political too in him, to have taken a ride to *Shandy-Hall*, as he did, merely to see how matters went on.

But my father's mind took unfortunately a wrong turn in the investigation; running, like the hypercritick's, altogether upon the ringing of the bell and the rap upon the door,--measuring their distance,——and keeping his mind so intent upon the operation, as to have power to think of nothing else,---common-place infirmity of the greatest mathematicians! working with might and main at the demonstration, and so wasting all their strength upon it, that they have none left in them to draw the corollary, to do good with.

The ringing of the bell and the rap upon the door, struck likewise strong upon the sensorium[5] of my uncle *Toby*,—but it excited a very different train of thoughts;—the two irreconcileable pulsations instantly brought *Stevinus*,[6] the great engineer, along with them, into my uncle *Toby*'s mind:
——What business *Stevinus* had in this affair,—is the greatest problem of all;—it shall be solved,—but not in the next chapter.

CHAP. XI.

W Riting, when properly managed, (as you may be sure I think mine is) is but a different name for conversation: As no one, who knows what he is about in good company, would venture to talk all;—so no author, who understands the just boundaries of decorum and good breeding, would presume to think all: The truest respect which you can pay to the reader's understanding, is to halve this matter amicably, and leave him something to imagine, in his turn, as well as yourself.

For my own part, I am eternally paying him compliments of this kind, and do all that lies in my power to keep his imagination as busy as my own.

'Tis his turn now;—I have given an ample description of Dr. *Slop*'s sad overthrow, and of his sad appearance in the back parlour;—his imagination must now go on with it for a while.

Let the reader imagine then, that Dr. *Slop* has told his tale;——and in what words, and with what aggravations his fancy chooses:——Let him suppose that *Obadiah* has told his tale also, and with such rueful looks of affected concern, as he thinks will best contrast the two figures as they stand by each other: Let him imagine that my father has stepp'd up stairs to see my mother:—And, to conclude this work of imagination,—let him imagine the Doctor wash'd,——rubb'd down,—condoled with,—felicitated,—got into a pair of *Obadiah*'s pumps,[1] stepping forwards towards the door, upon the very point of entering upon action.

Truce!—truce, good Dr. *Slop!*—stay thy obstetrick hand;[2]—return it safe into thy bosom to keep it warm;—little do'st thou know what obstacles;—little do'st thou think what hidden causes retard its operation!—Hast thou, Dr. *Slop,*—hast thou been intrusted with the secret articles of this solemn treaty which has brought thee into this place?—Art thou aware that, at this instant, a daughter of *Lucina*[3] is put obstetrically over thy head? Alas! 'tis too true.—Besides, great son of *Pilumnus!*[4] what can'st thou do?—Thou has come forth unarm'd;—thou hast left thy *tire-tête,*—thy new-invented *forceps,*—thy *crotchet,*—thy *squirt,* and all thy instruments of salvation and deliverance behind thee.[5]——By heaven! at this moment they are hanging up in a green bays[6] bag, betwixt thy two pistols, at thy bed's head!—Ring;—call;—send *Obadiah* back upon the coach-horse to bring them with all speed.

—Make great haste, *Obadiah,* quoth my father, and I'll give thee a crown;—and, quoth my uncle *Toby,* I'll give him another.

CHAP. XII.

YOUR sudden and unexpected arrival, quoth my uncle *Toby,* addressing himself to Dr. *Slop,* (all three of them sitting down to the fire together, as my uncle *Toby* began to speak)----instantly brought the great *Stevinus* into my head, who, you must know, is a favourite author with me.——Then, added my father, making use of the argument *Ad Crumenam,*[1]---I will lay twenty guineas to a single crown piece, (which will serve to give away to *Obadiah* when he gets back) that this same *Stevinus* was some engineer or other,----or has wrote something or other, either directly or indirectly, upon the science of fortification.

He has so,—replied my uncle *Toby.*—I knew it, said my father;—tho', for the soul of me, I cannot see what kind of connection there can be betwixt Dr. *Slop*'s sudden coming, and a discourse upon fortification;—yet I fear'd it.—Talk of what we will, brother,—or let the occasion be never so foreign or unfit for the subject,---you are sure to bring it in: I would not, brother *Toby,* continued my father,---I declare I would not have my head so full of curtins and horn-works.—That, I dare say, you would not, quoth Dr. *Slop*, interrupting him, and laughing most immoderately at his pun.

Dennis[2] the critick could not detest and abhor a pun, or the insinuation of a pun, more cordially than my father;——he would grow testy upon it at any time;--but to be broke in upon by one, in a serious discourse, was as bad, he would say, as a fillip upon the nose;—he saw no difference.

Sir, quoth my uncle *Toby*, addressing himself to Dr. *Slop*,——the curtins[3] my brother *Shandy* mentions here, have nothing to do with bed-steads;— tho', I know, *Du Cange* says, "That bed-curtains, in all probability, have taken their name from them;"---nor have the horn-works, he speaks of, any thing in the world to do with the horn-works of cuckoldom:—But the *curtin*, Sir, is the word we use in fortification, for that part of the wall or rampart which lies between the two bastions and joins them.----Besiegers seldom offer to carry on their attacks directly against the curtin, for this reason, because they are so well *flanked*; ('tis the case of other curtins, quoth Dr. *Slop*, laughing) however, continued my uncle *Toby*, to make them sure, we generally choose to place ravelins before them, taking care only to extend them beyond the fossé or ditch:—The common men, who know very little of fortification, confound the ravelin and the half-moon together,---tho' they are very different things;---not in their figure or construction, for we make them exactly alike in all points;---for they always consist of two faces, making a salient angle, with the gorges, not straight, but in form of a crescent.—Where then lies the difference? (quoth my father, a little testily)--In their situations, answered my uncle *Toby*:--For when a ravelin, brother, stands before the curtin, it is a ravelin; and when a ravelin stands before a bastion, then the ravelin is not a ravelin;--it is a half-moon;—a half-moon likewise is a half-moon, and no more, so long as it stands before its bastion;—but was it to change place, and get before the curtin,—'twould be no longer a half-moon; a half-moon, in that case, is not a half-moon;—'tis no more than a ravelin.—I think, quoth my father, that the noble science of defence has its weak sides,----as well as others.

—As for the horn-works (high! ho! sigh'd my father) which, continued my uncle *Toby*, my brother was speaking of, they are a very considerable part of an outwork;---they are called by the *French* engineers, *Ouvrage á corne*, and we generally make them to cover such places as we suspect to be weaker than the rest;--'tis form'd by two epaulments or demi-bastions,—they are very pretty, and if you will take a walk, I'll engage to shew you one well worth your trouble.——I own, continued my uncle *Toby*, when we crown them,—they are much stronger, but then they are very expensive, and take up a great deal of ground; so that, in my opinion, they are most of use to cover or defend the head of a camp; otherwise the double tenaille————By the mother who bore us!——brother *Toby*, quoth my father, not able to hold out any longer,—you would provoke a saint;—here have you got us, I know not how, not only souse into the middle of the old subject again:—But so full is your head of these confounded works, that tho' my wife is this moment in the pains of labour,—and you hear her cry out,—yet nothing will serve you but to carry off the man-midwife.——*Accoucheur*,[4]—if you please, quoth Dr. *Slop*.---With all my heart, replied my father, I don't care what they call you,——but I wish the whole science of fortification, with all its inventors, at the Devil;—it has been the death of thousands,——and it will be mine, in the end.--I would not, I would not, brother *Toby*, have my brains so full of saps, mines, blinds, gabions, palisadoes, ravelins, half-moons, and such trumpery, to be proprietor of *Namur*, and of all the towns in *Flanders* with it.

My uncle *Toby* was a man patient of injuries;—not from want of courage,—I have told you in the fifth chapter[5] of this second book, "That he was a man of courage:"——And will add here, that where just occasions presented, or called it forth,---I know no man under whose arm I would sooner have taken shelter; nor did this arise from any insensibility or obtuseness of his intellectual parts;--for he felt this insult of my father's as feelingly as a man could do;----but he was of a peaceful, placid nature,—no jarring element in it,—all was mix'd up so kindly within him; my uncle *Toby* had scarce a heart to retalliate upon a fly.

—Go,---says he, one day at dinner, to an over-grown one which had buzz'd about his nose, and tormented him cruelly all dinner-time,—and which, after infinite attempts, he had caught at last, as it flew by him;---I'll not hurt thee, says my uncle *Toby*, rising from his chair, and going a-cross the room, with the fly in his hand,---I'll not hurt a hair of thy head:---Go, says he, lifting up the sash, and opening his hand as he spoke, to let it escape;—go poor Devil, get thee gone, why should I hurt thee?----This world surely is wide enough to hold both thee and me.

I was but ten years old when this happened;—but whether it was, that the action itself was more in unison to my nerves at that age of pity, which instantly set my whole frame into one vibration of most pleasurable sensation;—or how far the manner and expression of it might go towards it;—or in what degree, or by what secret magick,—a tone of voice and harmony of movement, attuned by mercy, might find a passage to my heart, I know not;—this I know, that the lesson of universal good-will then taught and imprinted by my uncle *Toby*, has never since been worn out of my mind: And tho' I would not depreciate what the study of the *Literæ humaniores*,[6] at the university, have done for me in that respect, or discredit the other helps of an expensive education bestowed upon me, both at home and abroad since;—yet I often think that I owe one half of my philanthropy[7] to that one accidental impression.

☞ This is to serve for parents and governors instead of a whole volume upon the subject.

I could not give the reader this stroke in my uncle *Toby*'s picture, by the instrument with which I drew the other parts of it,—that taking in no more than the mere HOBBY-HORSICAL likeness;—this is a part of his moral character. My father, in this patient endurance of wrongs, which I mention, was very different, as the reader must long ago have noted; he had a much more acute and quick sensibility of nature, attended with a little soreness of temper; tho' this never transported him to any thing which looked like malignancy;—yet, in the little rubs and vexations of life, 'twas apt to shew itself in a drollish and witty kind of peevishness:— He was, however, frank and generous in his nature,——at all times open to conviction; and in the little ebullitions of this subacid humour towards others, but particularly towards my uncle *Toby*, whom he truly loved;— he would feel more pain, ten times told, (except in the affair of my aunt *Dinah*, or where an hypothesis was concerned) than what he ever gave.

The characters of the two brothers, in this view of them, reflected light upon each other, and appear'd with great advantage in this affair which arose about *Stevinus*.

I need not tell the reader, if he keeps a HOBBY-HORSE,--that a man's HOBBY-HORSE is as tender a part as he has about him; and that these unprovoked strokes, at my uncle *Toby*'s could not be unfelt by him.— No;—as I said above, my uncle *Toby* did feel them, and very sensibly too.

Pray, Sir, what said he?—How did he behave?—Oh, Sir!—it was great: For as soon as my father had done insulting his HOBBY-HORSE,—he turned his head, without the least emotion, from Dr. *Slop*, to whom he was addressing his discourse, and look'd up into my father's face, with a countenance spread over with so much good nature;—so placid;—so fraternal;—so inexpressibly tender towards him;—it penetrated my father to his heart: He rose up hastily from his chair, and seizing hold of both my uncle *Toby*'s hands as he spoke:—Brother *Toby*, said he,—I beg thy pardon;—forgive, I pray thee, this rash humour which my mother gave me.[8]—My dear, dear brother, answer'd my uncle *Toby*, rising up by my father's help, say no more about it;—you are heartily welcome, had it been ten times as much, brother. But 'tis ungenerous, replied my father, to hurt any man;—a brother worse;—but to hurt a brother of such gentle manners,—so unprovoking,—and so unresenting;—'tis base:— By heaven, 'tis cowardly.——You are heartily welcome, brother, quoth my uncle *Toby*,—had it been fifty times as much.——Besides, what have I to do, my dear *Toby*, cried my father, either with your amusements or your pleasures, unless it was in my power (which it is not) to increase their measure?

—Brother *Shandy*, answer'd my uncle *Toby*, looking wistfully in his face,—you are much mistaken in this point;—for you do increase my pleasure very much, in begetting children for the *Shandy* Family at your time of life.——But, by that, Sir, quoth Dr. *Slop*, Mr. *Shandy* increases his own.———Not a jot, quoth my father.

CHAP. XIII.

MY brother does it, quoth my uncle *Toby*, out of *principle*.—In a family-way,[1] I suppose, quoth Dr. *Slop*.—Pshaw!—said my father,—'tis not worth talking of.

CHAP. XIV.

AT the end of the last chapter, my father and my uncle *Toby* were left both standing, like *Brutus* and *Cassius* at the close of the scene making up their accounts.

As my father spoke the three last words,—he sat down;—my uncle *Toby* exactly followed his example, only, that before he took his chair, he rung the bell, to order Corporal *Trim*, who was in waiting, to step home for *Stevinus*;---my uncle *Toby* 's house being no further off than the opposite side of the way.

Some men would have dropp'd the subject of *Stevinus*;—but my uncle *Toby* had no resentment in his heart, and he went on with the subject, to shew my father that he had none.

Your sudden appearance, Dr. *Slop*, quoth my uncle, resuming the discourse, instantly brought *Stevinus* into my head. (My father, you may be sure, did not offer to lay any more wagers upon *Stevinus* 's head)——Because, continued my uncle *Toby*, the celebrated sailing chariot,[1] which belonged to Prince *Maurice*, and was of such wonderful contrivance and velocity, as to carry half a dozen people thirty *German* miles, in I don't know how few minutes,—was invented by *Stevinus*, that great mathematician and engineer.

You might have spared your servant the trouble, quoth Dr. *Slop*, (as the fellow is lame) of going for *Stevinus* 's account of it, because, in my return from *Leyden* thro' the *Hague*, I walked as far as *Schevling*, which is two long miles, on purpose to take a view of it.

—That's nothing, replied my uncle *Toby*, to what the learned *Peireskius* did, who walked a matter of five hundred miles, reckoning from *Paris* to *Schevling*, and from *Schevling* to *Paris* back again, in order to see it,—and nothing else.

Some men cannot bear to be out-gone.

The more fool *Peireskius*, replied Dr. *Slop*. But mark,--'twas out of no contempt of *Peireskius* at all;—but that *Peireskius* 's indefatigable labour in trudging so far on foot out of love for the sciences, reduced the exploit of Dr. *Slop*, in that affair, to nothing;—the more fool *Peireskius*, said he again:—Why so?—replied my father, taking his brother's part, not only to make reparation as fast as he could for the insult he had given him, which sat still upon my father's mind;—but partly, that my father began really to interest himself in the discourse;——Why so?—said he. Why is *Peireskius*, or any man else, to be abused for an appetite for that, or any other morsel of sound knowledge? For, notwithstanding I know nothing of the chariot in question, continued he, the inventor of it must have had a very mechanical head; and tho' I cannot guess upon what principles of philosophy he has atchiev'd it;—yet certainly his machine has been constructed upon solid ones, be they what they will, or it could not have answer'd at the rate my brother mentions.

It answered, replied my uncle *Toby*, as well, if not better; for, as *Peireskius* elegantly expresses it, speaking of the velocity of its motion, *Tam citus erat, quam erat ventus*; which, unless I have forgot my Latin, is, that it was as swift as the wind itself.

But pray, Dr. *Slop*, quoth my father, interrupting my uncle, (tho' not without begging pardon for it, at the same time) upon what principles was this self-same chariot set a-going?----Upon very pretty principles to be sure, replied Dr. *Slop*;—and I have often wondered, continued he, evading the question, why none of our Gentry, who live upon large plains like this of ours,---(especially they whose wives are not past child-bearing) attempt nothing of this kind; for it would not only be infinitely expeditious upon sudden calls, to which the sex is subject,—if the wind only served,—but would be excellent good husbandry to make use of the winds, which cost nothing, and which eat nothing, rather than horses, which (the Devil take 'em) both cost and eat a great deal.

For that very reason, replied my father, "Because they cost nothing, and because they eat nothing,"—the scheme is bad;—it is the consumption of our products, as well as the manufactures of them, which gives bread to the hungry, circulates trade,—brings in money, and supports the value of our lands;—and tho', I own, if I was a Prince, I would generously recompence the scientifick head which brought forth such contrivances;—yet I would as peremptorily suppress the use of them.

My father here had got into his element,—and was going on as prosperously with his dissertation upon trade, as my uncle *Toby* had before, upon his of fortification;—but, to the loss of much sound knowledge, the destinies in the morning had decreed that no dissertation of any kind should be spun by my father that day;——for as he opened his mouth to begin the next sentence,

CHAP. XV.

IN popp'd Corporal *Trim* with *Stevinus:*—But 'twas too late,—all the discourse had been exhausted without him, and was running into a new channel.

—You may take the book home again, *Trim*, said my uncle *Toby*, nodding to him.

But pri'thee, Corporal, quoth my father, drolling,—look first into it, and see if thou can'st spy aught of a sailing chariot in it.

Corporal *Trim*, by being in the service, had learned to obey,—and not to remonstrate;——so taking the book to a side-table, and running over the leaves; an' please your Honour, said *Trim*, I can see no such thing;—however, continued the Corporal, drolling a little in his turn, I'll make sure work of it, an' please your Honour;—so taking hold of the two covers of the book, one in each hand, and letting the leaves fall down, as he bent the covers back, he gave the book a good sound shake.

There is something fallen out, however, said *Trim*, an' please your Honour; but it is not a chariot, or any thing like one:—Pri'thee Corporal, said my father, smiling, what is it then?—I think, answered *Trim*, stooping to take it up,—'tis more like a sermon,—for it begins, with a text of scripture, and the chapter and verse;—and then goes on, not as a chariot,—but like a sermon directly.

The company smiled.

I cannot conceive how it is possible, quoth my uncle *Toby*, for such a thing as a sermon to have got into my *Stevinus*.

I think 'tis a sermon, replied *Trim*;—but if it please your Honours, as it is a fair hand, I will read you a page;—for *Trim*, you must know, loved to hear himself read almost as well as talk.

I have ever a strong propensity, said my father, to look into things which cross my way, by such strange fatalities as these;—and as we have nothing better to do, at least till *Obadiah* gets back, I should be obliged to you, brother, if Dr. *Slop* has no objection to it, to order the Corporal to give us a page or two of it,—if he is as able to do it, as he seems willing. An' please your Honour, quoth *Trim*, I officiated two whole campaigns in *Flanders*, as Clerk to the Chaplain of the Regiment.—He can read it, quoth my uncle *Toby*, as well as I can.— *Trim*, I assure you, was the best scholar in my company, and should have had the next Halberd,[1] but for the poor fellow's misfortune. Corporal *Trim* laid his hand upon his heart, and made a humble bow to his Master;--then laying down his hat upon the floor, and taking up the sermon in his left hand, in order to have his right at liberty,—he advanced, nothing doubting, into the middle of the room, where he could best see, and be best seen by, his audience.

CHAP. XVI.

——If you have any objection,—said my father, addressing himself to Dr. *Slop:* Not in the least, replied Dr. *Slop*;—for it does not appear on which side of the question it is wrote;——it may be a composition of a divine of our church, as well as yours,—so that we run equal risks.—— 'Tis wrote upon neither side, quoth *Trim*, for 'tis only upon *Conscience*, an' please your Honours.

Trim's reason put his audience into good humour,—all but Dr. *Slop*, who, turning his head about towards *Trim*, look'd a little angry.

Begin, *Trim*,——and read distinctly, quoth my father;—I will, an' please your Honour, replied the Corporal, making a bow, and bespeaking attention with a slight movement of his right hand.

CHAP. XVII.

——But before the Corporal begins, I must first give you a description of his attitude;[1]——otherwise he will naturally stand represented, by your imagination, in an uneasy posture,—stiff,—perpendicular,—dividing the weight of his body equally upon both legs;—his eye fix'd, as if on duty;— his look determined,—clinching the sermon in his left hand, like his firelock:—In a word, you would be apt to paint *Trim*, as if he was standing in his platoon ready for action:——His attitude was as unlike all this as you can conceive.

He stood before them with his body swayed, and bent forwards just so far, as to make an angle of 85 degrees and a half upon the plain of the horizon;——which sound orators, to whom I address this, know very well, to be the true persuasive angle of incidence;—in any other angle you may talk and preach;—'tis certain,—and it is done every day;—but with what effect,—I leave the world to judge!

The necessity of this precise angle of 85 degrees and a half to a mathematical exactness,—does it not shew us, by the way,—how the arts and sciences mutually befriend each other?

How the duce Corporal *Trim*, who knew not so much as an acute angle from an obtuse one, came to hit it so exactly;—or whether it was chance or nature, or good sense or imitation, *&c.* shall be commented upon in that part of this cyclopædia of arts and sciences,[2] where the instrumental parts of the eloquence of the senate, the pulpit, the bar, the coffee-house, the bed-chamber, and fire-side, fall under consideration.

He stood,—for I repeat it, to take the picture of him in at one view, with his body sway'd, and somewhat bent forwards,—his right leg firm under him, sustaining seven-eighths of his whole weight,—the foot of his left leg, the defect of which was no disadvantage to his attitude, advanced a little,—not laterally, nor forwards, but in a line betwixt them;—his knee bent, but that not violently,—but so as to fall within the limits of the line of beauty;[3]—and I add, of the line of science too;—for consider, it had one eighth part of his body to bear up;—so that in this case the position of the leg is determined,—because the foot could be no further advanced, or the knee more bent, than what would allow him, mechanically, to receive an eighth part of his whole weight under it,—and to carry it too.

☞ This I recommend to painters;—need I add,—to orators?—I think not; for, unless they practise it,—they must fall upon their noses.

So much for Corporal *Trim*'s body and legs.—He held the sermon loosely,—not carelessly, in his left hand, raised something above his stomach, and detach'd a little from his breast;—his right arm falling negligently by his side, as nature and the laws of gravity order'd it,—but with the palm of it open and turned towards his audience, ready to aid the sentiment, in case it stood in need.

Corporal *Trim*'s eyes and the muscles of his face were in full harmony with the other parts of him;—he look'd frank,—unconstrained,—something assured,—but not bordering upon assurance.

Let not the critick ask how Corporal *Trim* could come by all this; I've told him it shall be explained;—but so he stood before my father, my uncle *Toby*, and Dr. *Slop*,—so swayed his body, so contrasted his limbs, and with such an oratorical sweep throughout the whole figure,—a statuary might have modell'd from it;——nay, I doubt whether the oldest Fellow of a College,—or the *Hebrew* Professor himself, could have much mended it.

Trim made a bow, and read as follows:

The SERMON.[4]

HEBREWS xiii. 18.

——— *For we* trust *we have a good Conscience.*———

"T Rust!—Trust we have a good conscience!"

[Certainly, *Trim*, quoth my father, interrupting him, you give that sentence a very improper accent; for you curl up your nose, man, and read it with such a sneering tone, as if the Parson was going to abuse the Apostle.

He is, an' please your Honour, replied *Trim*. Pugh! said my father, smiling.

Sir, quoth Dr. *Slop*, *Trim* is certainly in the right; for the writer, (who I perceive is a Protestant) by the snappish manner in which he takes up the Apostle, is certainly going to abuse him,—if this treatment of him has not done it already. But from whence, replied my father, have you concluded so soon Dr. *Slop*, that the writer is of our Church?—for aught I can see yet,—he may be of any Church:—Because, answered Dr. *Slop*, if he was of ours,—he durst no more take such a licence,—than a bear by his beard:
——If, in our communion, Sir, a man was to insult an Apostle,——a saint,—or even the paring of a saint's nail,—he would have his eyes scratched out.——What, by the saint? quoth my uncle *Toby*. No; replied Dr. *Slop*,—he would have an old house over his head.[5] Pray is the Inquisition an antient building, answered my uncle *Toby*, or is it a modern one?—I know nothing of architecture[6] replied Dr. *Slop*.——An' please your Honours, quoth *Trim*, the Inquisition is the vilest——Pri'thee spare thy description, *Trim*, I hate the very name of it, said my father.—No matter

for that, answered Dr. *Slop*,—it has its uses; for tho' I'm no great advocate for it, yet in such a case as this, he would soon be taught better manners; and I can tell him, if he went on at that rate, would be flung into the Inquisition for his pains. God help him then, quoth my uncle *Toby*. Amen, added *Trim*; for, heaven above knows, I have a poor brother who has been fourteen years a captive in it.--I never heard one word of it before,[7] said my uncle *Toby*, hastily:—How came he there, *Trim*?——O, Sir! the story will make your heart bleed,—as it has made mine a thousand times;—but it is too long to be told now;—your Honour shall hear it from first to last some day when I am working besides you in our fortifications;——but the short of the story is this:——That my brother *Tom* went over a servant to *Lisbon*,—and then married a *Jew*'s widow, who kept a small shop, and sold sausages, which, some how or other, was the cause of his being taken in the middle of the night out of his bed, where he was lying with his wife and two small children, and carried directly to the Inquisition, where, God help him, continued *Trim*, fetching a sigh from the bottom of his heart,—the poor honest lad lies confined at this hour;—he was as honest a soul, added *Trim*, (pulling out his handkerchief) as ever blood warm'd.——

——The tears trickled down *Trim*'s cheeks faster than he could well wipe them away:—A dead silence in the room ensued for some minutes.——Certain proof of pity!

Come, *Trim*, quoth my father, after he saw the poor fellow's grief had got a little vent,—read on,—and put this melancholy story out of thy head:—I grieve that I interrupted thee;—but pri'thee begin the sermon again;—for if the first sentence in it is matter of abuse, as thou sayest, I have a great desire to know what kind of provocation the Apostle has given.

Corporal *Trim* wiped his face, and returning his handkerchief into his pocket, and, making a bow as he did it,—he began again.]

The SERMON.

HEBREWS xiii. 18.

——*For we* trust *we have a good Conscience.*——

"TRust! trust we have a good conscience! Surely if there is any thing in this life which a man may depend upon, and to the knowledge of which he is capable of arriving upon the most indisputable evidence, it must be this very thing,—whether he has a good conscience or no."

[I am positive I am right quoth Dr. *Slop*.]

"If a man thinks at all, he cannot well be a stranger to the true state of this account;—he must be privy to his own thoughts and desires;—he must remember his past pursuits, and know certainly the true springs and motives which, in general, have governed the actions of his life."

[I defy him, without an assistant, quoth Dr. *Slop*.]

"In other matters we may be deceived by false appearances; and, as the Wise Man complains, *hardly do we guess aright at the things that are upon the earth, and with labour do we find the things that are before us.*[8] But here the mind has all the evidence and facts within herself;--is conscious of the web she has wove;—knows its texture and fineness, and the exact share which every passion has had in working upon the several designs which virtue or vice has plann'd[9] before her."

[The language is good, and I declare *Trim* reads very well, quoth my father.]

"Now,—as conscience is nothing else but the knowledge which the mind has within herself of this; and the judgment, either of approbation or censure, which it unavoidably makes upon the successive actions of our lives; 'tis plain you will say, from the very terms of the proposition,—whenever this inward testimony goes against a man, and he stands self-accused,—that he must necessarily be a guilty man.—And, on the contrary, when the report is favourable on his side, and his heart condemns him not;—that it is not a matter of *trust*, as the Apostle intimates,—but a matter of *certainty* and fact, that the conscience is good, and that the man must be good also."[10]

[Then the Apostle is altogether in the wrong, I suppose, quoth Dr. *Slop*, and the Protestant divine is in the right. Sir, have patience, replied my father, for I think it will presently appear that St. *Paul* and the Protestant divine are both of an opinion.—As nearly so, quoth Dr. *Slop*, as East is to West;—but this, continued he, lifting both hands, comes from the liberty of the press.

It is no more, at the worst, replied my uncle *Toby*, than the liberty of the pulpit; for it does not appear that the sermon is printed, or ever likely to be.

Go on, *Trim*, quoth my father.]

"At first sight this may seem to be a true state of the case; and I make no doubt but the knowledge of right and wrong is so truly impressed upon the mind of man,—that did no such thing ever happen, as that the conscience of a man, by long habits of sin, might (as the scripture assures it may)[11] insensibly become hard;—and, like some tender parts of his body, by much stress and continual hard usage, lose, by degrees, that nice sense and perception with which God and nature endow'd it:——Did this never happen;—or was it certain that self-love could never hang the least bias upon the judgment;—or that the little interests below, could rise up and perplex the faculties of our upper regions, and encompass them about with clouds and thick darkness:[12]—Could no such thing as favour and affection enter this sacred COURT:—Did WIT disdain to take a bribe in it;—or was asham'd to shew its face as an advocate for an unwarrantable enjoyment:——Or, lastly, were we assured, that INTEREST stood always unconcern'd whilst the cause was hearing,—and that PASSION never got into the judgment-seat, and pronounc'd sentence in the stead of reason, which is supposed always to preside and determine upon the case:—Was this truly so, as the objection must suppose;—no doubt then, the religious and moral state of a man would be exactly what he himself esteem'd it;—and the guilt or innocence of every man's life could be known, in general, by no better measure, than the degrees of his own approbation and censure.

"I own, in one case, whenever a man's conscience does accuse him, (as it seldom errs on that side) that he is guilty; and, unless in melancholy and hypochondriack cases, we may safely pronounce upon it, that there is always sufficient grounds for the accusation.

"But the converse of the proposition will not hold true;——namely, that whenever there is guilt the conscience must accuse; and if it does not, that a man is therefore innocent.—This is not fact:—So that the common consolation which some good christian or other, is hourly administering to himself,—that he thanks God his mind does not misgive him; and that, consequently, he has a good conscience, because he has a quiet one,—is fallacious;—and as current as the inference is, and as infallible as the rule appears at first sight, yet, when you look nearer to it, and try the truth of this rule upon plain facts,—you see it liable to so much error from a false application;——the principle upon which it goes so often perverted;—the whole force of it lost, and sometimes so vilely cast away, that it is painful to produce the common examples from human life which confirm the account.

"A man shall be vicious and utterly debauched in his principles;—exceptionable in his conduct to the world; shall live shameless, in the open commission of a sin which no reason or pretence can justify;—a sin, by which, contrary to all the workings of humanity, he shall ruin for ever the deluded partner of his guilt;—rob her of her best dowry; and not only cover her own head with dishonour,—but involve a whole virtuous family in shame and sorrow for her sake.—Surely, you will think conscience must lead such a man a troublesome life;—he can have no rest night or day from its reproaches.

"Alas! CONSCIENCE had something else to do, all this time, than break in upon him; as *Elijah* reproached the God *Baal*,—this domestick God *was either talking, or pursuing, or was in a journey, or peradventure he slept and could not be awoke.*[13]

"Perhaps HE was gone out in company with HONOUR to fight a duel;—to pay off some debt at play;——or dirty annuity, the bargain of his lust: Perhaps CONSCIENCE all this time was engaged at home, talking loud against petty larceny, and executing vengeance upon some such puny crimes as his fortune and rank in life secured him against all temptation of committing; so that he lives as merrily, [if he was of our church tho', quoth Dr. *Slop*, he could not]—"sleeps as soundly in his bed;—and at last meets death as unconcernedly;—perhaps much more so than a much better man."

[All this is impossible with us, quoth Dr. *Slop*, turning to my father,—the case could not happen in our Church.——It happens in ours, however, replied my father, but too often.—I own, quoth Dr. *Slop*, (struck a little with my father's frank acknowledgment)—that a man in the *Romish* Church may live as badly;—but then he cannot easily die so.—'Tis little matter, replied my father, with an air of indifference,—how a rascal dies.—I mean, answer'd Dr. *Slop*, he would be denied the benefits of the last sacraments.---Pray how many have you in all, said my uncle *Toby*,—for I always forget?——Seven,[14] answered Dr. *Slop*.—Humph!—said my uncle *Toby*;--tho' not accented as a note of acquiescence,—but as an interjection of that particular species of surprize, when a man, in looking into a drawer, finds more of a thing than he expected.--Humph! replied my uncle *Toby*. Dr. *Slop*, who had an ear, understood my uncle *Toby* as well as if he had wrote a whole volume against the seven sacraments.——Humph! replied Dr. *Slop*, (stating my uncle *Toby*'s argument over again to him)—Why, Sir, are there not seven cardinal virtues?—Seven mortal sins?—Seven golden candle-sticks?—Seven heavens?—'Tis more than I know, replied my uncle *Toby*.—Are there not seven wonders of the world?——Seven days of the creation?—Seven planets?[15]—Seven plagues?—That there are, quoth my father, with a most affected gravity. But pri'thee, continued he, go on with the rest of thy characters, *Trim*.]

"Another is sordid, unmerciful, (here *Trim* waved his right hand) a strait-hearted, selfish wretch, incapable either of private friendship or publick spirit. Take notice how he passes by the widow and orphan in their distress, and sees all the miseries incident to human life without a sigh or a prayer." [And please your Honours, cried *Trim*, I think this is a viler man than the other.]

"Shall not conscience rise up and sting him on such occasions?——No; thank God there is no occasion; *I pay every man his own;—I have no fornication to answer to my conscience;—no faithless vows or promises to make up;—I have debauched no man's wife or child; thank God, I am not as other men, adulterers, unjust, or even as this libertine, who stands before me.*[16]

"A third is crafty and designing in his nature. View his whole life; ——'tis nothing but a cunning contexture of dark arts and unequitable subterfuges, basely to defeat the true intent of all laws,—plain dealing and the safe enjoyment of our several properties.——You will see such a one working out a frame of little designs upon the ignorance and perplexities of the poor and needy man;—shall raise a fortune upon the inexperience of a youth, or the unsuspecting temper of his friend who would have trusted him with his life.

"When old age comes on, and repentance calls him to look back upon this black account, and state it over again with his conscience,——CONSCIENCE looks into the STATUTES at LARGE;—finds no express law broken by what he has done;—perceives no penalty or forfeiture of goods and chattels incurred;--sees no scourge waving over his head, or prison opening his gates upon him:—What is there to affright his conscience?—Conscience has got safely entrenched behind the Letter of the Law;[17] sits there invulnerable, fortified with **Cafes** and **Reports** so strongly on all sides,—that it is not preaching can dispossess it of its hold."

[Here Corporal *Trim* and my uncle *Toby* exchanged looks with each other.--Aye,—aye, *Trim!* quoth my uncle *Toby*, shaking his head,—these are but sorry fortifications, *Trim*.——O! very poor work, answered *Trim*, to what your Honour and I make of it.——The character of this last man, said Dr. *Slop*, interrupting *Trim*, is more detestable than all the rest;—and

seems to have been taken from some pettifogging Lawyer amongst you:—
Amongst us a man's conscience could not possibly continue so long
blinded;—three times in a year, at least, he must go to confession. Will
that restore it to sight, quoth my uncle *Toby?*—Go on, *Trim*, quoth my
father, or *Obadiah* will have got back before thou hast got to the end of
thy sermon;—'tis a very short one, replied *Trim*.—I wish it was longer,
quoth my uncle *Toby*, for I like it hugely.— *Trim* went on.]

"A fourth man shall want even this refuge;—shall break through all
this ceremony of slow chicane;——scorns the doubtful workings of secret
plots and cautious trains to bring about his purpose:—See the bare-faced
villain, how he cheats, lies, perjures, robs, murders.——Horrid!——But
indeed much better was not to be expected, in the present case,—the
poor man was in the dark!—his priest had got the keeping of his conscience;—and all he would let him know of it, was, That he must believe
in the Pope;—go to Mass;—cross himself;—tell his beads;—be a good
Catholick, and that this, in all conscience, was enough to carry him to
heaven. What;—if he perjures!—Why;—he had a mental reservation[18]
in it.—But if he is so wicked and abandoned a wretch as you represent
him;—if he robs,—if he stabs,——will not conscience, on every such
act, receive a wound itself? Aye,—but the man has carried it to confession;—the wound digests there,[19] and will do well enough, and in a
short time be quite healed up by absolution. O Popery! what hast thou to
answer for?—when, not content with the too many natural and fatal ways,
thro' which the heart of man is every day thus treacherous to itself above
all things;[20]—thou hast wilfully set open this wide gate of deceit before
the face of this unwary traveller, too apt, God knows, to go astray of
himself; and confidently speak peace to himself, when there is no peace.[21]

"Of this the common instances which I have drawn out of life, are too
notorious to require much evidence. If any man doubts the reality of them,
or thinks it impossible for a man to be such a bubble to himself,—I must
refer him a moment to his own reflections, and will then venture to trust
my appeal with his own heart.

"Let him consider in how different a degree of detestation, numbers of
wicked actions stand *there*, tho' equally bad and vicious in their own
natures;—he will soon find that such of them, as strong inclination and
custom have prompted him to commit, are generally dress'd out and
painted with all the false beauties, which a soft and a flattering hand can
give them;—and that the others, to which he feels no propensity, appear,

at once, naked and deformed, surrounded with all the true circumstances of folly and dishonour.[22]

"When *David* surprized *Saul* sleeping in the cave, and cut off the skirt of his robe,—we read his heart smote him for what he had done:—But in the matter of *Uriah*, where a faithful and gallant servant, whom he ought to have loved and honoured, fell to make way for his lust,—where conscience had so much greater reason to take the alarm, his heart smote him not. A whole year had almost passed from the first commission of that crime, to the time *Nathan* was sent to reprove him; and we read not once of the least sorrow or compunction of heart which he testified, during all that time, for what he had done.[23]

"Thus conscience, this once able monitor,—placed on high as a judge within us, and intended by our maker as a just and equitable one too,—by an unhappy train of causes and impediments, takes often such imperfect cognizance of what passes,—does its office so negligently,—sometimes so corruptly,—that it is not to be trusted alone; and therefore we find there is a necessity, an absolute necessity of joining another principle with it to aid, if not govern, its determinations.

"So that if you would form a just judgment of what is of infinite importance to you not to be misled in,——namely, in what degree of real merit you stand either as an honest man, an useful citizen, a faithful subject to your King, or a good servant to your God,--call in religion and morality.—Look,--What is written in the law of God?—How readest thou?——Consult calm reason and the unchangeable obligations of justice and truth;—what say they?[24]

"Let CONSCIENCE determine the matter upon these reports;—and then if thy heart condemns thee not, which is the case the Apostle supposes,—the rule will be infallible, (here Dr. *Slop* fell asleep) *thou wilt have confidence towards God*;[25]—that is, have just grounds to believe the judgment thou hast past upon thyself, is the judgment of God; and nothing else but an anticipation of that righteous sentence which will be pronounced upon thee hereafter by that Being, to whom thou art finally to give an account of thy actions.

"*Blessed is the man*, indeed then, as the author of the book of *Ecclesiasticus* expresses it, *who is not prick'd with the multitude of his sins: Blessed is the man whose heart hath not condemn'd him; whether he be rich, or whether he be poor, if he have a good heart,* (a heart thus guided and informed) *he shall at all times rejoice in a chearful countenance; his mind shall tell him more than seven watch-men*

that sit above upon a tower on high.[26]———[A tower has no strength, quoth my uncle *Toby*, unless 'tis flank'd.] In the darkest doubts it shall conduct him safer than a thousand casuists, and give the state he lives in a better security for his behaviour than all the clauses and restrictions put together, which law-makers are forced to multiply:—*Forced*, I say, as things stand; human laws not being a matter of original choice, but of pure necessity, brought in to fence against the mischievous effects of those consciences which are no law unto themselves; well intending, by the many provisions made,—that in all such corrupt and misguided cases, where principles and the checks of conscience will not make us upright,—to supply their force, and, by the terrors of gaols and halters, oblige us to it."

[I see plainly, said my father, that this sermon has been composed to be preach'd at the Temple,[27]—or at some Assize.—I like the reasoning,—and am sorry that Dr. *Slop* has fallen asleep before the time of his conviction;—for it is now clear, that the Parson, as I thought at first, never insulted St. *Paul* in the least;—nor has there been, brother, the least difference between them.—A great matter, if they had differed, replied my uncle *Toby*,—the best friends in the world may differ sometimes.—True,—brother *Toby*, quoth my father, shaking hands with him,—we'll fill our pipes, brother, and then *Trim* shall go on.

Well,—what do'st thou think of it? said my father, speaking to Corporal *Trim*, as he reach'd his tobacco-box.

I think, answered the Corporal, that the seven watch-men upon the tower, who, I suppose, are all centinels there,—are more, an' please your Honour, than were necessary;—and, to go on at that rate, would harrass a regiment all to pieces, which a commanding officer, who loves his men, will never do, if he can help it; because two centinels, added the Corporal, are as good as twenty.—I have been a commanding officer myself in the *Corps de Garde*[28] a hundred times, continued *Trim*, rising an inch higher in his figure, as he spoke,———and all the time I had the honour to serve his Majesty King *William*, in relieving the most considerable posts, I never left more than two in my life.———Very right, *Trim*, quoth my uncle *Toby*;—but you do not consider *Trim*, that the towers, in *Solomon*'s days, were not such things as our bastions, flank'd and defended by other works;—this, *Trim*, was an invention since *Solomon*'s death; nor had they horn-works, or ravelins before the curtin, in his time;—or such a fossé as we make with a cuvette in the middle of it, and with cover'd-ways and counterscarps pallisadoed along it, to guard against a *Coup de main:*[29]—So that the seven men upon the tower were a party, I dare say, from the *Corps de Garde*, set there, not only to look out, but to defend it.—They could be no more, an' please your Honour, than a Corporal's Guard.—My father smiled inwardly,—but not outwardly;—the subject between my uncle *Toby* and Corporal *Trim* being rather too serious, considering what had happened, to make a jest of:—So, putting his pipe into his mouth, which he had just lighted,—he contented himself with ordering *Trim* to read on. He read on as follows:]

"To have the fear of God before our eyes, and, in our mutual dealings with each other, to govern our actions by the eternal measures of right and wrong:—The first of these will comprehend the duties of religion;——the second, those of morality, which are so inseparably connected together, that you cannot divide these two *tables*,[30] even in imagination, (tho' the attempt is often made in practice) without breaking and mutually destroying them both.

"I said the attempt is often made, and so it is;—there being nothing more common than to see a man who has no sense at all of religion,—— and indeed has so much honesty as to pretend to none, who would take it as the bitterest affront, should you but hint at a suspicion of his moral character,--or imagine he was not conscientiously just and scrupulous to the uttermost mite.

"When there is some appearance that it is so,—tho' one is unwilling even to suspect the appearance of so amiable a virtue as moral honesty, yet were we to look into the grounds of it, in the present case, I am persuaded we should find little reason to envy such a one the honour of his motive.

"Let him declaim as pompously as he chooses upon the subject, it will be found to rest upon no better foundation than either his interest, his pride, his ease, or some such little and changeable passion as will give us but small dependence upon his actions in matters of great stress.

"I will illustrate this by an example.

"I know the banker I deal with, or the physician I usually call in [there is no need, cried Dr. *Slop*, (waking) to call in any physician in this case] to be neither of them men of much religion: I hear them make a jest of it every day, and treat all its sanctions with so much scorn, as to put the matter past doubt. Well;—notwithstanding this, I put my fortune into the hands of the one;—and, what is dearer still to me, I trust my life to the honest skill of the other.

"Now, let me examine what is my reason for this great confidence.——— Why, in the first place, I believe there is no probability that either of them will employ the power I put into their hands to my disadvantage;—I consider that honesty serves the purposes of this life:—I know their success in the world depends upon the fairness of their characters.—In a word,— I'm persuaded that they cannot hurt me, without hurting themselves more.

"But put it otherwise, namely, that interest lay, for once, on the other side; that a case should happen, wherein the one, without stain to his reputation, could secrete my fortune, and leave me naked in the world;— or that the other could send me out of it, and enjoy an estate by my death, without dishonour to himself or his art:—In this case, what hold have I of either of them?—Religion, the strongest of all motives, is out of the question:—Interest, the next most powerful motive in the world, is strongly against me:—What have I left to cast into the opposite scale to balance this temptation?--Alas! I have nothing,—nothing but what is lighter than a bubble.—I must lay at the mercy of HONOUR, or some such capricious principle.——— Strait security for two of my most valuable blessings!— my property and my life.[31]

"As, therefore, we can have no dependence upon morality without religion;—so, on the other hand, there is nothing better to be expected from religion without morality;—nevertheless, 'tis no prodigy to see a man whose real moral character stands very low, who yet entertains the highest notion of himself, in the light of a religious man.

"He shall not only be covetous, revengeful, implacable,——but even wanting in points of common honesty; yet, inasmuch as he talks aloud against the infidelity of the age,—is zealous for some points of religion, ——goes twice a day to church,—attends the sacraments,—and amuses himself with a few instrumental parts of religion,[32]—shall cheat his conscience into a judgment that, for this, he is a religious man, and has discharged truly his duty to God: And you will find that such a man, thro' force of this delusion, generally looks down with spiritual pride upon every other man who has less affectation of piety,--tho', perhaps, ten times more moral honesty than himself.

"*This likewise is a sore evil under the sun*;[33] and I believe there is no one mistaken principle which, for its time, has wrought more serious mischiefs.—For a general proof of this,—examine the history of the *Romish* Church;[34]—[Well, what can you make of that, cried Dr. *Slop?*]— see what scenes of cruelty, murders, rapines, blood-shed, [They may thank their own obstinacy, cried Dr. *Slop*] have all been sanctified by a religion not strictly governed by morality.

"In how many kingdoms of the world, [Here *Trim* kept waving his right hand from the sermon to the extent of his arm, returning it backwards and forwards to the conclusion of the paragraph.]

"In how many kingdoms of the world has the crusading sword of this misguided saint-errant[35] spared neither age, or merit, or sex, or condition?—and, as he fought under the banners of a religion which set him loose from justice and humanity, he shew'd none; mercilessly trampled upon both,——heard neither the cries of the unfortunate, nor pitied their distresses."

[I have been in many a battle, an' please your Honour, quoth *Trim*, sighing, but never in so melancholy a one as this.—I would not have drawn a tricker[36] in it, against these poor souls,——to have been made a general officer.—Why, what do you understand of the affair? said Doctor *Slop*, looking towards *Trim* with something more contempt[37] than the Corporal's honest heart deserved.—What do you know, friend, about this battle you talk of?——I know, replied *Trim*, that I never refused quarter in my life to any man who cried out for it;—but to a woman or a child, continued *Trim*, before I would level my musket at them, I would lose my life a thousand times.—Here's a crown for thee, *Trim*, to drink with *Obadiah* to-night, quoth my uncle *Toby*, and I'll give *Obadiah* another too.--God bless your Honour, replied *Trim*,—I had rather these poor women and children had it.—Thou art an honest fellow, quoth my uncle *Toby*.----My father nodded his head,—as much as to say,—and so he is.——

But pri'thee, *Trim*, said my father, make an end,—for I see thou hast but a leaf or two left.]

Corporal Trim read on.

"If the testimony of past centuries in this matter is not sufficient,—— consider, at this instant, how the votaries of that religion are every day thinking to do service and honour to God, by actions which are a dishonour and scandal to themselves.

"To be convinced of this, go with me for a moment into the prisons of the inquisition. [God help my poor brother *Tom*.]——Behold *Religion*, with *Mercy* and *Justice* chained down under her feet,——there sitting ghastly upon a black tribunal, propp'd up with racks and instruments of torment. Hark!—hark! what a piteous groan! [Here *Trim*'s face turned as pale as ashes.] See the melancholy wretch who utter'd it—[Here the tears began to trickle down] just brought forth to undergo the anguish of a mock trial, and endure the utmost pains that a studied system of cruelty has been able to invent.—[D—n them all, quoth *Trim*, his colour returning into his face as red as blood.]—Behold this helpless victim delivered up to his tormentors,——his body so wasted with sorrow and confinement— [Oh! 'tis my brother, cried poor *Trim* in a most passionate exclamation, dropping the sermon upon the ground, and clapping his hands together ——I fear 'tis poor *Tom*. My father's and my uncle *Toby*'s hearts yearn'd with sympathy for the poor fellow's distress,——even *Slop* himself acknowledged pity for him.—Why, *Trim*, said my father, this is not a history,—'tis a sermon thou art reading;—pri'thee begin the sentence again.]—Behold this helpless victim deliver'd up to his tormentors,—his body so wasted with sorrow and confinement, you will see every nerve and muscle as it suffers.

"Observe the last movement of that horrid engine! [I would rather face a cannon, quoth *Trim*, stamping.]——See what convulsions it has thrown him into!——Consider the nature of the posture in which he now lies stretched,—what exquisite tortures he endures by it!——[I hope 'tis not in *Portugal*.]³⁸—'Tis all nature can bear! Good God! see how it keeps his weary soul hanging upon his trembling lips! [I would not read another line of it, quoth *Trim*, for all this world;—I fear, an' please your Honours, all this is in *Portugal*, where my poor brother *Tom* is. I tell thee, *Trim*, again, quoth my father, 'tis not an historical account,—'tis a description. —'Tis only a description, honest man, quoth *Slop*, there's not a word of truth in it.—That's another story, replied my father.—However, as *Trim* reads it with so much concern,—'tis cruelty to force him to go on with it.--Give me hold of the sermon, *Trim*,--I'll finish it for thee, and thou may'st go. I must stay and hear it too, replied *Trim*, if your Honour will allow me;—tho' I would not read it myself for a Colonel's pay.——Poor *Trim!* quoth my uncle *Toby*. My father went on.]

—"Consider the nature of the posture in which he now lies stretch'd,— what exquisite torture he endures by it!—'Tis all nature can bear!—Good God! See how it keeps his weary soul hanging upon his trembling lips,— willing to take its leave,——but not suffered to depart!——Behold the unhappy wretch led back to his cell! [Then, thank God, however, quoth *Trim*, they have not killed him]—See him dragg'd out of it again to meet the flames, and the insults in his last agonies, which this principle,—this principle, that there can be religion without mercy, has prepared for him. [Then, thank God,—he is dead, quoth *Trim*,—he is out of his pain,—and they have done their worst at him.—O Sirs!—Hold your peace, *Trim*, said my father, going on with the sermon, lest *Trim* should incense Dr. *Slop*,—we shall never have done at this rate.]

"The surest way to try the merit of any disputed notion is, to trace down the consequences such a notion has produced, and compare them with the spirit of Christianity;—'tis the short and decisive rule which our Saviour hath left us, for these and such-like cases, and it is worth a thousand arguments,—— *By their fruits ye shall know them*.[39]

"I will add no further to the length of this sermon, than, by two or three short and independent rules deducible from it.

"*First*, Whenever a man talks loudly against religion,—always suspect that it is not his reason, but his passions which have got the better of his CREED. A bad life and a good belief are disagreeable and troublesome neighbours, and where they separate, depend upon it, 'tis for no other cause but quietness sake.

"*Secondly*, When a man, thus represented, tells you in any particular instance,—— That such a thing goes *against* his conscience,—always believe he means exactly the same thing, as when he tells you such a thing goes *against* his stomach;—a present want of appetite being generally the true cause of both.

"In a word,—trust that man in nothing, who has not a CONSCIENCE in every thing.

"And, in your own case, remember this plain distinction, a mistake in which has ruined thousands,—that your conscience is not a law:--No, God and reason made the law, and have placed conscience within you to determine;—not like an *Asiatick* Cadi,[40] according to the ebbs and flows of his own passions,—but like a *British* judge in this land of liberty and good sense, who makes no new law, but faithfully declares that law which he knows already written."

FINIS.

Thou hast read the sermon extremely well, *Trim*, quoth my father.— If he had spared his comments, replied Dr. *Slop*, he would have read it much better. I should have read it ten times better, Sir, answered *Trim*, but that my heart was so full.—That was the very reason, *Trim*, replied my father, which has made thee read the sermon as well as thou hast done; and if the clergy of our church, continued my father, addressing himself to Dr. *Slop*, would take part in what they deliver, as deeply as this poor fellow has done,—as their compositions are fine, (I deny it, quoth Dr. *Slop*) I maintain it, that the eloquence of our pulpits,[41] with such subjects to inflame it,—would be a model for the whole world:—But, alas! continued my father, and I own it, Sir, with sorrow, that, like *French* politicians in this respect, what they gain in the cabinet they lose in the field.——— 'Twere a pity, quoth my uncle, that this should be lost. I like the sermon well, replied my father,—'tis dramatic,——and there is something in that way of writing, when skilfully managed, which catches the attention. ———We preach much in that way with us, said Dr. *Slop*.—I know that very well, said my father,—but in a tone and manner which disgusted Dr. *Slop*, full as much as his assent, simply, could have pleased him.-----But in this, added Dr. *Slop*, a little piqued,——our sermons have greatly the advantage, that we never introduce any character into them below a patriarch or a patriarch's wife, or a martyr or a saint.—There are some very bad characters in this, however, said my father, and I do not think the sermon a jot the worse for 'em.———But pray, quoth my uncle *Toby*, ——who's can this be?—How could it get into my *Stevinus?* A man must be as great a conjurer as *Stevinus*, said my father, to resolve the second question:—The first, I think, is not so difficult;—for unless my judgment greatly deceives me,——I know the author, for 'tis wrote, certainly, by the parson of the parish.

The similitude of the stile and manner of it, with those my father constantly had heard preach'd in his parish-church, was the ground of his conjecture,—proving it as strongly, as an argument *a priori*,[42] could prove such a thing to a philosophic mind, That it was *Yorick* 's and no one's else: ——It was proved to be so *a posteriori*, the day after, when *Yorick* sent a servant to my uncle *Toby* 's house to enquire after it.

It seems that *Yorick*, who was inquisitive after all kinds of knowledge, had borrowed *Stevinus* of my uncle *Toby*, and had carelesly popp'd his sermon, as soon as he had made it, into the middle of *Stevinus*; and, by an act of forgetfulness, to which he was ever subject, he had sent *Stevinus* home, and his sermon to keep him company.

Ill-fated sermon! Thou wast lost, after this recovery of thee, a second time, dropp'd thro' an unsuspected fissure in thy master's pocket, down into a treacherous and a tatter'd lining,—trod deep into the dirt by the left hind foot of his Rosinante, inhumanly stepping upon thee as thou falledst;—buried ten days in the mire,—raised up out of it by a beggar, sold for a halfpenny to a parish-clerk,—transferred to his parson,—lost for ever to thy own, the remainder of his days,—nor restored to his restless MANES till this very moment, that I tell the world the story.[43]

Can the reader believe, that this sermon of *Yorick*'s was preach'd at an assize, in the cathedral of *York*, before a thousand witnesses, ready to give oath of it, by a certain prebendary of that church, and actually printed by him when he had done,——and within so short a space as two years and three months after *Yorick*'s death.— *Yorick*, indeed, was never better served in his life!——but it was a little hard to male-treat him before, and plunder him after he was laid in his grave.

However, as the gentleman who did it, was in perfect charity with *Yorick*,—and, in conscious justice, printed but a few copies to give away;—and that, I am told, he could moreover have made as good a one himself, had he thought fit,—I declare I would not have published this anecdote to the world;—nor do I publish it with an intent to hurt his character and advancement in the church;——I leave that to others;——but I find myself impell'd by two reasons, which I cannot withstand.

The first is, That, in doing justice, I may give rest to *Yorick*'s ghost;— which, as the country people,—and some others, believe,—— *still walks.*[44]

The second reason is, That, by laying open this story to the world, I gain an opportunity of informing it,——That in case the character of parson *Yorick*, and this sample of his sermons[45] is liked,—that there are now in the possession of the *Shandy* Family, as many as will make a handsome volume, at the world's service,—and much good may they do it.

CHAP. XVIII.

OBADIAH gain'd the two crowns without dispute; for he came in jingling, with all the instruments in the green bays bag we spoke of, slung across his body, just as Corporal *Trim* went out of the room.

It is now proper, I think, quoth Dr. *Slop*, (clearing up his looks) as we are in a condition to be of some service to Mrs. *Shandy*, to send up stairs to know how she goes on.

I have ordered, answered my father, the old midwife to come down to us upon the least difficulty;——for you must know, Dr. *Slop*, continued my father, with a perplexed kind of a smile upon his countenance, that by express treaty, solemnly ratified between me and my wife, you are no more than an auxiliary in this affair,——and not so much as that,——unless the lean old mother of a midwife above stairs cannot do without you.—— Women have their particular fancies, and in points of this nature, continued my father, where they bear the whole burden, and suffer so much acute pain for the advantage of our families, and the good of the species,——they claim a right of deciding, *en Soveraines*,[1] in whose hands, and in what fashion, they chuse to undergo it.

They are in the right of it,——quoth my uncle *Toby*. But, Sir, replied Dr. *Slop*, not taking notice of my uncle *Toby*'s opinion, but turning to my father,——they had better govern in other points;——and a father of a family, who wished its perpetuity, in my opinion, had better exchange this prerogative with them, and give up some other rights in lieu of it.——I know not, quoth my father, answering a little too testily, to be quite dispassionate in what he said,——I know not, quoth he, what we have left to give up, in lieu of who shall bring our children into the world,—— unless that,——of who shall beget them.——One would almost give up any thing, replied Dr. *Slop*.——I beg your pardon,——answered my uncle *Toby*.——Sir, replied Dr. *Slop*, it would astonish you to know what Improvements we have made of late years in all branches of obstetrical knowledge, but particularly in that one single point of the safe and expeditious extraction of the *fœtus*,——which has received such lights, that, for my part, (holding up his hands) I declare I wonder how the world has——I wish, quoth my uncle *Toby*, you had seen what prodigious armies we had in *Flanders*.

CHAP. XIX.

I Have dropp'd the curtain over this scene for a minute,—to remind you of one thing,—and to inform you of another.

What I have to inform you, comes, I own, a little out of its due course;— for it should have been told a hundred and fifty pages ago, but that I foresaw then 'twould come in pat hereafter, and be of more advantage here than elsewhere.[1]----Writers had need look before them to keep up the spirit and connection of what they have in hand.

When these two things are done,—the curtain shall be drawn up again, and my uncle *Toby*, my father, and Dr. *Slop* shall go on with their discourse, without any more interruption.

First, then, the matter which I have to remind you of, is this;—that from the specimens of singularity in my father's notions in the point of Christian-names, and that other point previous thereto,—you was led, I think, into an opinion, (and I am sure I said as much) that my father was a gentleman altogether as odd and whimsical in fifty other opinions. In truth, there was not a stage in the life of man, from the very first act of his begetting,—down to the lean and slipper'd pantaloon in his second childishness,[2] but he had some favourite notion to himself, springing out of it, as sceptical, and as far out of the high-way of thinking, as these two which have been explained.

——Mr. *Shandy*, my father, Sir, would see nothing in the light in which others placed it;—he placed things in his own light;—he would weigh nothing in common scales;—no,—he was too refined a researcher to lay open to so gross an imposition.——To come at the exact weight of things in the scientific steel-yard,[3] the fulcrum, he would say, should be almost invisible, to avoid all friction from popular tenets;—without this the minutiæ of philosophy, which should always turn the balance, will have no weight at all.——Knowledge, like matter, he would affirm, was divisible *in infinitum*;[4]—that the grains and scruples were as much a part of it, as the gravitation of the whole world.——In a word, he would say, error was error,—no matter where it fell,—whether in a fraction,—or a pound,— 'twas alike fatal to truth, and she was kept down at the bottom of her well[5] as inevitably by a mistake in the dust of a butterfly's wing,—as in the disk of the sun, the moon, and all the stars of heaven put together.

He would often lament that it was for want of considering this properly, and of applying it skilfully to civil matters, as well as to speculative truths, that so many things in this world were out of joint;[6]—that the political arch was giving way;—and that the very foundations of our excellent constitution in church and state, were so sapp'd as estimators had reported.

You cry out, he would say, we are a ruined, undone people.——Why?—he would ask, making use of the sorites[7] or syllogism of *Zeno* and *Chrysippus*, without knowing it belonged to them.—Why? why are we a ruined people?—Because we are corrupted.[8]——Whence is it, dear Sir, that we are corrupted?—Because we are needy;—our poverty, and not our wills, consent.[9]——And wherefore, he would add,—are we needy?——From the neglect, he would answer, of our pence and our halfpence:——Our bank-notes, Sir, our guineas,--nay our shillings, take care of themselves.

'Tis the same, he would say, throughout the whole circle of the sciences;—the great, the established points of them, are not to be broke in upon.—The laws of nature will defend themselves;—but error—(he would add, looking earnestly at my mother)—error, Sir, creeps in thro' the minute-holes, and small crevices, which human nature leaves unguarded.

This turn of thinking in my father, is what I had to remind you of:——The point you are to be informed of, and which I have reserved for this place, is as follows:

Amongst the many and excellent reasons, with which my father had urged my mother to accept of Dr. *Slop*'s assistance preferably to that of the old woman,—there was one of a very singular nature; which, when he had done arguing the matter with her as a Christian, and came to argue it over again with her as a philosopher,—he had put his whole strength to, depending indeed upon it as his sheet anchor.——It failed him; tho' from no defect in the argument itself; but that, do what he could, he was not able for his soul to make her comprehend the drift of it.——Cursed luck!—said he to himself, one afternoon, as he walk'd out of the room, after he had been stating it for an hour and a half to her, to no manner of purpose;—cursed luck! said he, biting his lip as he shut the door,—for a man to be master of one of the finest chains of reasoning in nature,—and have a wife at the same time with such a head-piece, that she cannot hang up a single inference within side of it, to save his soul from destruction.

This argument, though it was intirely lost upon my mother,—had more weight with him, than all his other arguments joined together:——I will therefore endeavour to do it justice,—and set it forth with all the perspicuity I am master of.

My father set out upon the strength of these two following axioms:

First, That an ounce of a man's own wit, was worth a tun of other people's;[10] and,

Secondly, (Which, by the bye, was the ground-work of the first axiom,—tho' it comes last)—That every man's wit must come from every man's own soul,—and no other body's.

Now, as it was plain to my father, that all souls were by nature equal,—and that the great difference between the most acute and the most obtuse understanding,—was from no original sharpness or bluntness of one thinking substance above or below another,——but arose merely from the lucky or unlucky organization of the body, in that part where the soul principally took up her residence,—he had made it the subject of his enquiry to find out the identical place.

Now, from the best accounts he had been able to get of this matter, he was satisfied it could not be where *Des Cartes* had fixed it, upon the top of the *pineal* gland of the brain; which, as he philosophised, form'd a cushion for her about the size of a marrow pea;—tho', to speak the truth, as so many nerves did terminate all in that one place,[11]—'twas no bad conjecture;—and my father had certainly fallen with that great philosopher plumb into the center of the mistake, had it not been for my uncle *Toby*, who rescued him out of it, by a story he told him of a *Walloon* Officer at the battle of *Landen*,[12] who had one part of his brain shot away by a musket-ball,—and another part of it taken out after by a *French* Surgeon; and, after all, recovered, and did his duty very well without it.

If death, said my father, reasoning with himself, is nothing but the separation of the soul from the body;—and if it is true that people can walk about and do their business without brains,—then certes the soul does not inhabit there. Q. E. D.[13]

As for that certain very thin, subtle, and very fragrant juice which *Coglionissimo Borri*, the great *Milaneze* physician, affirms, in a letter to *Bartholine*,[14] to have discovered in the cellulæ of the occipital parts of the cerebellum, and which he likewise affirms to be the principal seat of the reasonable soul (for, you must know, in these latter and more enlightened ages, there are two souls in every man living,—the one according to the great *Metheglingius*,[15] being called the *Animus*, the other the *Anima*);[16]—as for this opinion, I say, of *Borri*,——my father could never subscribe to it by any means; the very idea of so noble, so refined, so immaterial, and so exalted a being as the *Anima*, or even the *Animus*, taking up her residence, and sitting dabbling, like a tad-pole, all day long, both summer and winter, in a puddle,—or in a liquid of any kind, how thick or thin soever, he would say, shock'd his imagination; he would scarce give the doctrine a hearing.

What, therefore, seem'd the least liable to objections of any, was, that the chief sensorium, or head-quarters of the soul, and to which place all intelligences were referred, and from whence all her mandates were issued,—was in, or near, the cerebellum,--or rather some-where about the *medulla oblongata*, wherein it was generally agreed by *Dutch* anatomists,[17] that all the minute nerves from all the organs of the seven senses[18] concentered, like streets and winding alleys, into a square.

So far there was nothing singular in my father's opinion,—he had the best of philosophers, of all ages and climates, to go along with him.—— But here he took a road of his own, setting up another *Shandean* hypothesis upon these corner-stones they had laid for him;—and which said hypothesis equally stood its ground; whether the subtilty and fineness of the soul depended upon the temperature and clearness of the said liquor, or of the finer net-work and texture in the cerebellum itself; which opinion he favoured.

He maintained, that next to the due care to be taken in the act of propagation of each individual, which required all the thought in the world, as it laid the foundation of this incomprehensible contexture in which wit, memory, fancy, eloquence, and what is usually meant by the name of good natural parts, do consist;—that next to this and his Christian-name, which were the two original and most efficacious causes of all;—that the third cause, or rather what logicians call the *Causa sine quâ non*,[19] and without which all that was done was of no manner of significance,--was the preservation of this delicate and fine-spun web, from the havock which was generally made in it by the violent compression and crush which the head was made to undergo, by the nonsensical method of bringing us into the world by that part foremost.

——This requires explanation.

My father, who dipp'd into all kinds of books, upon looking into

Lithopædus Senonesis de Partu difficili*,[20] published by *Adrianus Smelvogt*, had found out, That the lax and pliable state of a child's head in parturition, the bones of the cranium having no sutures at that time, was such,—that by force of the woman's efforts, which, in strong labour-pains, was equal, upon an average, to a weight of 470 pounds[21] averdupoise acting perpendicularly upon it;—it so happened that, in 49 instances out of 50, the said head was compressed and moulded into the shape of an oblong conical piece of dough,[22] such as a pastry-cook generally rolls up in order to make a pye of.——Good God! cried my father, what havock and destruction must this make in the infinitely fine and tender texture of the cerebellum!—Or if there is such a juice as *Borri* pretends,—is it not enough to make the clearest liquor in the world both feculent and mothery?[23]

But how great was his apprehension, when he further understood, that this force, acting upon the very vertex of the head, not only injured the brain itself or cerebrum,——but that it necessarily squeez'd and propell'd the cerebrum towards the cerebellum, which was the immediate seat of the understanding.—Angels and Ministers of grace defend us![24] cried my father,—can any soul withstand this shock?—No wonder the intellectual web is so rent and tatter'd as we see it; and that so many of our best heads are no better than a puzzled skein of silk,---all perplexity,—all confusion within side.

But when my father read on, and was let into the secret, that when a child was turn'd topsy-turvy, which was easy for an operator to do, and was extracted by the feet;[25]—that instead of the cerebrum being propell'd towards the cerebellum, the cerebellum, on the contrary, was propell'd simply towards the cerebrum where it could do no manner of hurt:—By heavens! cried he, the world is in a conspiracy to drive out what little wit God has given us,—and the professors of the obstetrick art are listed into the same conspiracy.—What is it to me which end of my son comes foremost into the world, provided all goes right after, and his cerebellum escapes uncrushed?

It is the nature of an hypothesis, when once a man has conceived it,

---

*The author is here twice mistaken;—for *Lithopædus* should be wrote thus, *Lithopædii Senonensis Icon.* The second mistake is, that this *Lithopædus* is not an author, but a drawing of a petrified child. The account of this, published by *Albosius*, 1580, may be seen at the end of *Cordæus*'s works in *Spachius*. Mr. *Tristram Shandy* has been led into this error, either from seeing *Lithopædus*'s name of late in a catalogue of learned writers in Dr. ——, or by mistaking *Lithopædus* for *Trinecavellius*,—from the too great similitude of the names.

that it assimulates every thing to itself as proper nourishment; and, from the first moment of your begetting it, it generally grows the stronger by every thing you see, hear, read, or understand. This is of great use.

When my father was gone with this about a month, there was scarce a phænomenon of stupidity or of genius, which he could not readily solve by it;—it accounted for the eldest son being the greatest blockhead in the family.--Poor Devil, he would say,--he made way for the capacity of his younger brothers.--It unriddled the observation of drivellers and monstrous heads,—shewing, *a priori*, it could not be otherwise,—unless **** I don't know what. It wonderfully explain'd and accounted for the acumen of the *Asiatick* genius, and that sprightlier turn, and a more penetrating intuition of minds, in warmer climates; not from the loose and common-place solution of a clearer sky, and a more perpetual sun-shine, *&c.*—which, for aught he knew, might as well rarify and dilute the faculties of the soul into nothing, by one extreme,—as they are condensed in colder climates by the other;—but he traced the affair up to its spring-head;—shew'd that, in warmer climates, nature had laid a lighter tax upon the fairest parts of the creation;---their pleasures more;—the necessity of their pains less, insomuch that the pressure and resistance upon the vertex was so slight, that the whole organization of the cerebellum was preserved;—nay, he did not believe, in natural births, that so much as a single thread of the net-work was broke or displaced,—so that the soul might just act as she liked.

When my father had got so far,—what a blaze of light did the accounts of the *Cæsarian* section,[26] and of the towering geniuses who had come safe into the world by it, cast upon this hypothesis? Here you see, he would say, there was no injury done to the sensorium;—no pressure of the head against the pelvis;—no propulsion of the cerebrum towards the cerebellum, either by the *oss pubis* on this side, or the *oss coxcygis*[27] on that;—and, pray, what were the happy consequences? Why, Sir, your *Julius Cæsar*, who gave the operation a name;—and your *Hermes Trismegistus*, who was born so before ever the operation had a name;—your *Scipio Africanus*; your *Manlius Torquatus*; our *Edward* the sixth,——who, had he lived, would have done the same honour to the hypothesis:——These, and many more, who figur'd high in the annals of fame,—all came *side-way*, Sir, into the world.

This incision of the *abdomen* and *uterus*, ran for six weeks together in my father's head;—he had read, and was satisfied, that wounds in the *epigastrium*, and those in the *matrix*, were not mortal;—so that the belly of the mother might be opened extremely well to give a passage to the child.—He mentioned the thing one afternoon to my mother,—merely as a matter of fact;—but seeing her turn as pale as ashes at the very mention of it, as much as the operation flattered his hopes,—he thought it as well to say no more of it,—contenting himself with admiring—what he thought was to no purpose to propose.

This was my father Mr. *Shandy*'s hypothesis; concerning which I have only to add, that my brother *Bobby* did as great honour to it (whatever he did to the family) as any one of the great heroes we spoke of:—For happening not only to be christen'd, as I told you, but to be born too, when my father was at *Epsom*,--being moreover my mother's *first* child,--coming into the world with his head *foremost*,—and turning out afterwards a lad of wonderful slow parts,—my father spelt all these together into his opinion; and as he had failed at one end,—he was determined to try the other.

This was not to be expected from one of the sisterhood, who are not easily to be put out of their way,—and was therefore one of my father's great reasons in favour of a man of science, whom he could better deal with.

Of all men in the world, Dr. *Slop* was the fittest for my father's purpose;—for tho' his new-invented forceps was the armour he had proved, and what he maintained, to be the safest instrument of deliverance,—yet, it seems, he had scattered a word or two in his book, in favour of the very thing which ran in my father's fancy;—tho' not with a view to the soul's good in extracting by the feet, as was my father's system,—but for reasons merely obstetrical.

This will account for the coallition betwixt my father and Dr. *Slop*, in the ensuing discourse, which went a little hard against my uncle *Toby*.——In what manner a plain man, with nothing but common sense, could bear up against two such allies in science,—is hard to conceive.——You may conjecture upon it, if you please,—and whilst your imagination is in motion, you may encourage it to go on, and discover by what causes and effects in nature it could come to pass, that my uncle *Toby* got his modesty by the wound he received upon his groin.—You may raise a system to account for the loss of my nose by marriage articles,——and shew the world how it could happen, that I should have the misfortune to be called TRISTRAM, in opposition to my father's hypothesis, and the wish of the whole family, God-fathers and God-mothers not excepted.—These, with fifty other points left yet unravelled, you may endeavour to solve if you have time;—but I tell you before-hand it will be in vain,—for not the sage *Alquife*, the magician in Don *Belianis* of *Greece*, nor the no less famous *Urganda*, the sorceress his wife, (were they alive) could pretend to come within a league of the truth.[28]

The reader will be content to wait for a full explanation of these matters till the next year,—when a series of things will be laid open which he little expects.

END of the SECOND VOLUME.

W. Hogarth inv.   *F. Ravenet sculp.*

THE
LIFE
AND
OPINIONS
OF
TRISTRAM SHANDY,
GENTLEMAN.

Multitudinis imperitæ non formido judicia; meis
tamen, rogo, parcant opusculis —— in quibus
fuit propofiti femper, a jocis ad feria, a feriis
viciffim ad jocos tranfire.

JOAN. SARESBERIENSIS,
Epifcopus Lugdun.

VOL. III.

LONDON:

Printed for R. and J. DODSLEY in *Pall-Mall.*
M.DCC.LXI.

(Height of original type-page 119 mm.)

CHAP. I.

"*I* Wish, Dr. *Slop*," quoth my uncle *Toby* (repeating his wish for Dr. *Slop* a second time, and with a degree of more zeal and earnestness in his manner of wishing, than he had wished it at first*)——— "*I wish, Dr. Slop*," quoth my uncle *Toby*, "*you had seen what prodigious armies we had in Flanders.*"

My uncle *Toby*'s wish did Dr. *Slop* a disservice which his heart never intended any man,——Sir, it confounded him—and thereby putting his ideas first into confusion, and then to flight, he could not rally them again for the soul of him.

In all disputes,——male or female,——whether for honour, for profit or for love,——it makes no difference in the case;—nothing is more dangerous, madam, than a wish coming sideways in this unexpected manner upon a man: the safest way in general to take off the force of the wish, is, for the party wished at, instantly to get up upon his legs—and wish the *wisher* something in return, of pretty near the same value,——so balancing the account upon the spot, you stand as you were—nay sometimes gain the advantage of the attack by it.

This will be fully illustrated to the world in my chapter of wishes.[1]———

Dr. *Slop* did not understand the nature of this defence;——he was

---

*Vid. Vol. II. p. 159. (Page 116 in present volume.)

puzzled with it, and it put an entire stop to the dispute for four minutes and a half;——five had been fatal to it:——my father saw the danger—— the dispute was one of the most interesting disputes in the world, "Whether the child of his prayers and endeavours should be born without a head or with one:"——he waited to the last moment to allow Dr. *Slop*, in whose behalf the wish was made, his right of returning it; but perceiving, I say, that he was confounded, and continued looking with that perplexed vacuity of eye which puzzled souls generally stare with,——first in my uncle *Toby*'s face——then in his——then up——then down——then east ——east and by east, and so on,——coasting it along by the plinth of the wainscot till he had got to the opposite point of the compass,——and that he had actually begun to count the brass nails upon the arm of his chair——my father thought there was no time to be lost with my uncle *Toby*, so took up the discourse as follows.

CHAP. II.

"——WHAT prodigious armies you had in *Flanders!*"—— Brother *Toby*, replied my father, taking his wig from off his head with his right hand, and with his *left* pulling out a striped *India* handkerchief[1] from his right coat pocket, in order to rub his head, as he argued the point with my uncle *Toby*.——

——Now, in this I think my father was much to blame; and I will give you my reasons for it.

Matters of no more seeming consequence in themselves than, "*Whether my father should have taken off his wig with his right hand or with his left,*"—— have divided the greatest kingdoms, and made the crowns of the mon-archs who governed them, to totter upon their heads.——But need I tell you, Sir, that the circumstances with which every thing in this world is begirt, give every thing in this world its size and shape;——and by tightening it, or relaxing it, this way or that, make the thing to be, what it is—great—little—good—bad—indifferent or not indifferent, just as the case happens.

As my father's *India* handkerchief was in his right coat pocket, he should by no means have suffered his right hand to have got engaged: on the contrary, instead of taking off his wig with it, as he did, he ought to have committed that entirely to the left; and then, when the natural exigency my father was under of rubbing his head, call'd out for his handkerchief, he would have had nothing in the world to have done, but to have put his right hand into his right coat pocket and taken it out;—which he might have done without any violence, or the least ungraceful twist in any one tendon or muscle of his whole body.

In this case, (unless indeed, my father had been resolved to make a fool of himself by holding the wig stiff in his left hand—or by making some nonsensical angle or other at his elbow joint, or arm-pit)—his whole attitude had been easy—natural—unforced: *Reynolds*[2] himself, as great and gracefully as he paints, might have painted him as he sat.

Now, as my father managed this matter,——consider what a devil of a figure my father made of himself.

—In the latter end of Queen *Anne*'s reign, and in the beginning of the reign of King *George* the first—"*Coat pockets were cut very low down in the skirt.*"——I need say no more——the father of mischief, had he been hammering at it a month, could not have contrived a worse fashion for one in my father's situation.

CHAP. III.

IT was not an easy matter in any king's reign, (unless you were as lean a subject as myself) to have forced your hand diagonally, quite across your whole body, so as to gain the bottom of your opposite coat-pocket.— In the year, one thousand seven hundred and eighteen, when this happened, it was extremely difficult; so that when my uncle *Toby* discovered the transverse zig-zaggery[1] of my father's approaches towards it, it instantly brought into his mind those he had done duty in, before the gate of St. *Nicholas*;——the idea of which drew off his attention so entirely from the subject in debate, that he had got his right hand to the bell to ring up *Trim*, to go and fetch his map of *Namur*, and his compasses and sector along with it, to measure the returning angles of the traverses of that attack,—but particularly of that one, where he received his wound upon his groin.

My father knit his brows, and as he knit them, all the blood in his body seemed to rush up into his face——my uncle *Toby* dismounted immediately.

—I did not apprehend your uncle *Toby* was o'horseback.——

CHAP. IV.

A Man's body and his mind, with the utmost reverence to both I speak it, are exactly like a jerkin, and a jerkin's lining;—rumple the one— you rumple the other. There is one certain exception however in this case, and that is, when you are so fortunate a fellow, as to have had your jerkin made of a gum-taffeta,[1] and the body-lining to it, of a sarcenet or thin persian.

Zeno, Cleanthes, Diogenes Babylonius, Dyonisius Heracleotes, Antipater, Panætius and *Possidonius* amongst the *Greeks*;— *Cato* and *Varro* and *Seneca* amongst the *Romans*;— *Pantenus* and *Clemens Alexandrinus* and *Montaigne*[2] amongst the Christians; and a score and a half of good honest, unthinking, *Shandean* people as ever lived, whose names I can't recollect,—all pretended that their jerkins were made after this fashion,——you might have rumpled and crumpled, and doubled and creased, and fretted and fridged the outsides of them all to pieces;—in short, you might have played the very devil with them, and at the same time, not one of the insides of 'em would have been one button the worse, for all you had done to them.

I believe in my conscience that mine is made up somewhat after this sort:—for never poor jerkin has been tickled off, at such a rate as it has been these last nine months together,[3]——and yet I declare the lining to it,——as far as I am a judge of the matter, it is not a three-penny piece the worse;—pell mell, helter skelter, ding dong, cut and thrust, back stroke and fore stroke, side way and long way, have they been trimming it for me:—had there been the least gumminess in my lining,——by heaven! it had all of it long ago been fray'd and fretted to a thread.

—You Messrs. the monthly Reviewers![4]——how could you cut and slash my jerkin as you did?——how did you know, but you would cut my lining too?

Heartily and from my soul, to the protection of that Being who will injure none of us, do I recommend you and your affairs,——so God bless you;——only next month, if any one of you should gnash his teeth, and storm and rage at me, as some of you did last MAY, (in which I remember the weather was very hot)——don't be exasperated, if I pass it by again with good temper,——being determined as long as I live or write (which in my case means the same thing) never to give the honest gentleman a worse word or a worse wish, than my uncle *Toby* gave the fly which buzz'd about his nose all *dinner time*,——"Go,——go poor devil," quoth he, "——get thee gone,——why should I hurt thee? This world is surely wide enough to hold both thee and me."

CHAP. V.

ANY man, madam, reasoning upwards, and observing the prodigious suffusion of blood in my father's countenance,——by means of which, (as all the blood in his body seemed to rush up into his face, as I told you) he must have redden'd, pictorically and scientintically speaking, six whole tints and a half, if not a full octave above his natural colour:[1]——any man, madam, but my uncle *Toby*, who had observed this, together with the violent knitting of my father's brows, and the extravagant contortion of his body during the whole affair,——would have concluded my father in a rage; and taking that for granted,——had he been a lover of such kind of concord as arises from two such instruments being put into exact tune,—— he would instantly have skrew'd up his, to the same pitch;——and then the devil and all had broke loose——the whole piece, madam, must have been played off like the sixth of Avison's Scarlatti[2]——*con furia*,——like mad. ——Grant me patience!——What has *con furia*,——*con strepito*,——or any other hurlyburly word whatever to do with harmony?

Any man, I say, madam, but my uncle *Toby*, the benignity of whose heart interpreted every motion of the body in the kindest sense the motion would admit of, would have concluded my father angry and blamed him too. My uncle *Toby* blamed nothing but the taylor who cut the pocket-hole;——so sitting still, till my father had got his handkerchief out of it, and looking all the time up in his face with inexpressible good will——my father at length went on as follows.

CHAP. VI.

——"WHAT prodigious armies you had in *Flanders!*"——Brother *Toby*, quoth my father, I do believe thee to be as honest a man, and with as good and as upright a heart as ever God created;——nor is it thy fault, if all the children which have been, may, can, shall, will or ought to be begotten, come with their heads foremost into the world:——but believe me, dear *Toby*, the accidents which unavoidably way-lay them, not only in the article of our begetting 'em,——though these in my opinion, are well worth considering,——but the dangers and difficulties our children are beset with, after they are got forth into the world, are enow,——little need is there to expose them to unnecessary ones in their passage to it.——Are these dangers, quoth my uncle *Toby*, laying his hand upon my father's knee, and looking up seriously in his face for an answer,——are these dangers greater now o'days, brother, than in times past? Brother *Toby*, answered my father, if a child was but fairly begot, and born alive, and healthy, and the mother did well after it,——our forefathers never looked further.——My uncle *Toby* instantly withdrew his hand from off my father's knee, reclined his body gently back in his chair, raised his head till he could just see the cornish[1] of the room, and then directing the buccinatory[2] muscles along his cheeks, and the orbicular muscles around his lips to do their duty——he whistled *Lillabullero*.

CHAP. VII.

WHILST my uncle *Toby* was whistling Lillabullero to my father,—— Dr. *Slop* was stamping, and cursing and damning at *Obadiah* at a most dreadful rate;——it would have done your heart good, and cured you, Sir, for ever, of the vile sin of swearing to have heard him.——I am determined therefore to relate the whole affair to you.

When Dr. *Slop*'s maid delivered the green bays bag, with her master's instruments in it, to *Obadiah*, she very sensibly exhorted him to put his head and one arm through the strings, and ride with it slung across his body: so undoing the bow-knot, to lengthen the strings for him, without any more ado, she helped him on with it. However, as this, in some measure, unguarded the mouth of the bag, lest any thing should bolt out in galloping back at the speed *Obadiah* threatened, they consulted to take it off again; and in the great care and caution of their hearts, they had taken the two strings and tied them close (pursing up the mouth of the bag first) with half a dozen hard knots, each of which, *Obadiah*, to make all safe, had twitched and drawn together with all the strength of his body.

This answered all that *Obadiah* and the maid intended; but was no remedy against some evils which neither he or she foresaw. The instruments, it seems, as tight as the bag was tied above, had so much room to play in it, towards the bottom, (the shape of the bag being conical) that *Obadiah* could not make a trot of it, but with such a terrible jingle, what with the *tire-tête*, *forceps* and *squirt*, as would have been enough, had *Hymen*[1] been taking a jaunt that way, to have frightened him out of the country; but when *Obadiah* accelerated this motion, and from a plain trot assayed to prick his coach-horse into a full gallop—by heaven! Sir,—the jingle was incredible.

As *Obadiah* had a wife and three children—the turpitude of fornication, and the many other political ill consequences of this jingling, never once entered his brain,——he had however his objection, which came home to himself, and weighed with him, as it has oft-times done with the greatest patriots.[2]——"*The poor fellow, Sir, was not able to hear himself whistle.*"

CHAP. VIII.

AS *Obadiah* loved wind musick preferably to all the instrumental musick he carried with him,—he very considerately set his imagination to work, to contrive and to invent by what means he should put himself in a condition of enjoying it.

In all distresses (except musical) where small cords are wanted,——nothing is so apt to enter a man's head, as his hat-band:——the philosophy of this is so near the surface—I scorn to enter into it.

As *Obadiah*'s was a mix'd case,——mark, Sirs,—I say, a mix'd case; for it was obstretical,[1]—*scrip*-tical,—squirtical, papistical,—and as far as the coach-horse was concerned in it,—caball-istical[2]—and only partly musical;—*Obadiah* made no scruple of availing himself of the first expedient which offered;—so taking hold of the bag and instruments, and gripeing them hard together with one hand, and with the finger and thumb of the other, putting the end of the hat-band betwixt his teeth, and then slipping his hand down to the middle of it,—he tied and cross-tied them all fast together from one end to the other (as you would cord a trunk) with such a multiplicity of round-abouts and intricate cross turns, with a hard knot at every intersection or point where the strings met,—that Dr. *Slop* must have had three fifths of *Job*'s patience at least to have unloosed them.— I think in my conscience, that had NATURE been in one of her nimble moods, and in humour for such a contest——and she and Dr. *Slop* both fairly started together—there is no man living who had seen the bag with all that *Obadiah* had done to it,—and known likewise, the great speed the goddess can make when she thinks proper, who would have had the least doubt remaining in his mind——which of the two would have carried off the prize. My mother, madam, had been delivered sooner than the green bag infallibly—at least by twenty *knots*.——Sport of small accidents, *Tristram Shandy!* that thou art, and ever will be! had that trial been made for thee, and it was fifty to one but it had,——thy affairs had not been so depress'd—(at least by the depression of thy nose) as they have been; nor had the fortunes of thy house and the occasions of making them, which have so often presented themselves in the course of thy life, to thee, been so often, so vexatiously, so tamely, so irrecoverably abandoned—as thou hast been forced to leave them!—but 'tis over,—all but the account of 'em, which cannot be given to the curious till I am got out into the world.

CHAP. IX.

GREAT wits jump:[1] for the moment Dr. *Slop* cast his eyes upon his bag (which he had not done till the dispute with my uncle *Toby* about midwifery put him in mind of it)—the very same thought occurred. ——'Tis God's mercy, quoth he, (to himself) that Mrs. *Shandy* has had so bad a time of it,—else she might have been brought to bed seven times told, before one half of these knots could have got untied.——But here, you must distinguish——the thought floated only in Dr. *Slop*'s mind, without sail or ballast to it, as a simple proposition; millions of which, as your worship knows, are every day swiming quietly in the middle of the thin juice of a man's understanding, without being carried backwards or forwards, till some little gusts of passion or interest drive them to one side.[2]

A sudden trampling in the room above, near my mother's bed, did the proposition the very service I am speaking of. By all that's unfortunate, quoth Dr. *Slop*, unless I make haste, the thing will actually befall me as it is.

CHAP. X.

IN the case of *knots*,——by which, in the first place, I would not be understood to mean slip-knots,——because in the course of my life and opinions,——my opinions concerning them will come in more properly when I mention the catastrophe of my great uncle Mr. *Hammond Shandy*,[1]——a little man,——but of high fancy:——he rushed into the duke of *Monmouth*'s affair:[2]——nor, secondly, in this place, do I mean that particular species of knots, called bow-knots;——there is so little address, or skill, or patience, required in the unloosing them, that they are below my giving any opinion at all about them.——But by the knots I am speaking of, may it please your reverences to believe, that I mean good, honest, devilish tight, hard knots, made *bona fide*, as *Obadiah* made his;—in which there is no quibbling provision made by the duplication and return of the two ends of the strings through the annulus or noose made by the second *implication*[3] of them—to get them slipp'd and undone by———I hope you apprehend me.

In the case of these *knots*[4] then, and of the several obstructions, which, may it please your reverences, such knots cast in our way in getting through life——every hasty man can whip out his penknife and cut through them.——'Tis wrong. Believe me, Sirs, the most virtuous way, and which both reason and conscience dictate—is to take our teeth or our fingers to them.——Dr. *Slop* had lost his teeth—his favourite instrument, by extracting in a wrong direction, or by some misapplication of it, unfortunately slipping, he had formerly in a hard labour, knock'd out three of the best of them, with the handle of it:—he tried his fingers— alas! the nails of his fingers and thumbs were cut close.[5]—The deuce take it! I can make nothing of it either way, cried Dr. *Slop*.——The trampling over head near my mother's bed side increased.—Pox take the fellow! I shall never get the knots untied as long as I live.—My mother gave a groan—Lend me your penknife—I must e'en cut the knots at last----- pugh!---psha!---Lord! I have cut my thumb[6] quite across to the very bone ——curse the fellow——if there was not another man midwife within fifty miles—I am undone for this bout——I wish the scoundrel hang'd ——I wish he was shot——I wish all the devils in hell had him for a blockhead——

My father had a great respect for *Obadiah*, and could not bear to hear him disposed of in such a manner——he had moreover some little respect for himself——and could as ill bear with the indignity offer'd to himself in it.

Had Dr. *Slop* cut any part about him, but his thumb——my father had pass'd it by——his prudence had triumphed: as it was, he was determined to have his revenge.

Small curses, Dr. *Slop*, upon great occasions, quoth my father, (condoling with him first upon the accident) are but so much waste of our strength and soul's health to no manner of purpose.—I own it, replied Dr. *Slop*.

——They are like sparrow shot, quoth my uncle *Toby*, (suspending his whistling) fired against a bastion.——They serve, continued my father, to stir the humours—but carry off none of their acrimony:—for my own part, I seldom swear or curse at all——I hold it bad—but if I fall into it, by surprize, I generally retain so much presence of mind (right, quoth my uncle *Toby*) as to make it answer my purpose—that is, I swear on, till I find myself easy. A wise and a just man however would always endeavour to proportion the vent given to these humours, not only to the degree of them stirring within himself—but to the size and ill intent of the offence upon which they are to fall.——"*Injuries come only from the heart*,"[7]—— quoth my uncle *Toby*. For this reason, continued my father, with the most *Cervantick* gravity,[8] I have the greatest veneration in the world for that gentleman, who, in distrust of his own discretion in this point, sat down and composed (that is at his leisure) fit forms of swearing suitable to all cases, from the lowest to the highest provocations which could possibly happen to him,—which forms being well consider'd by him, and such moreover as he could stand to, he kept them ever by him on the chimney piece, within his reach, ready for use.——I never apprehended, replied Dr. *Slop*, that such a thing was ever thought of,——much less executed. I beg your pardon—answered my father; I was reading, though not using, one of them to my brother *Toby* this morning, whilst he pour'd out the tea—'tis here upon the shelf over my head;——but if I remember right, 'tis too violent for a cut of the thumb.——Not at all, quoth Dr. *Slop*— the devil take the fellow.—Then answered my father, 'Tis much at your service, Dr. *Slop*——on condition you will read it aloud;——so rising up and reaching down a form of excommunication[9] of the church of *Rome*, a copy of which, my father (who was curious in his collections) had procured out of the leger-book of the church of *Rochester*, writ by ERNULPHUS the bishop—with a most affected seriousness of look and voice, which might have cajoled ERNULPHUS himself,—he put it into Dr. *Slop*'s hands.—Dr. *Slop* wrapt his thumb up in the corner of his handkerchief, and with a wry face, though without any suspicion, read aloud, as follows,—my uncle *Toby* whistling *Lillabullero*, as loud as he could, all the time.

Textus de Ecclesiâ Roffensi, per Ernulfum Episcopum.

CAP. XXXV.
EXCOMMUNICATIO.

E X auctoritate Dei omnipotentis, Patris, et Filij, et Spiritus Sancti, et sanctorum canonum, sanctæque et intemeratæ Virginis Dei genetricis Mariæ,

————Atque omnium cœlestium virtutum, angelorum, archangelorum, thronorum, dominationum, potestatuum, cherubin ac seraphin, & sanctorum patriarcharum, prophetarum, & omnium apostolorum et evangelistarum, & sanctorum innocentum, qui in conspectu Agni soli digni inventi sunt canticum cantare novum, et sanctorum martyrum, et sanctorum confessorum, et sanctarum virginum, atque omnium simul sanctorum et electorum Dei,—Excommunicamus, et anathematizamus

---

As the genuineness of the consultation of the *Sorbonne* upon the question of baptism, was doubted by some, and denied by others,———'twas thought proper to print the original of this excommunication; for the copy of which Mr. *Shandy* returns thanks to the chapter clerk of the dean and chapter of *Rochester*.

CHAP. XI.

"BY the authority of God Almighty, the Father, Son, and Holy Ghost, and of the holy canons, and of the undefiled Virgin *Mary*, mother and patroness of our Saviour." I think there is no necessity, quoth Dr. *Slop*, dropping the paper down to his knee, and addressing himself to my father, ——as you have read it over, Sir, so lately, to read it aloud;—and as Captain *Shandy* seems to have no great inclination to hear it,——I may as well read it to myself. That's contrary to treaty, replied my father,—besides, there is something so whimsical, especially in the latter part of it, I should grieve to lose the pleasure of a second reading. Dr. *Slop* did not altogether like it,— but my uncle *Toby* offering at that instant to give over whistling, and read it himself to them;——Dr. *Slop* thought he might as well read it under the cover of my uncle *Toby*'s whistling,—as suffer my uncle *Toby* to read it alone;—so raising up the paper to his face, and holding it quite parallel to it, in order to hide his chagrin,—he read it aloud as follows,——my uncle *Toby* whistling Lillabullero, though not quite so loud as before.

"By the authority of God Almighty, the Father, Son, and Holy Ghost, and of the undefiled Virgin *Mary*, mother and patroness of our Saviour, and of all the celestial virtues, angels, archangels, thrones, dominions, powers, cherubins and seraphins, and of all the holy patriarchs, prophets, and of all the apostles and evangelists, and of the holy innocents, who in the sight of the holy Lamb, are found worthy to sing the new song, of the holy martyrs and holy confessors, and of the holy virgins, and of all the saints together, with the holy and elect of God.——May he," *(Obadiah)* "be damn'd," (for tying these knots.)—— "We excommunicate, and anathematise him, and from the thresholds of the holy church of God Almighty *vel* os[1]   s   *vel* os   s

hunc furem, vel hunc malefactorem, N.N. et a liminibus sanctæ Dei
                                                    vel i   n
ecclesiæ sequestramus ut æternis suppliciis excruciandus, mancipetur, cum
Dathan et Abiram, et cum his qui dixerunt Domino Deo, Recede à nobis,
scientiam viarum tuarum nolumus: et sicut aquâ ignis extinguitur, sic
          vel eorum
extinguatur lucerna ejus in secula seculorum nisi resipuerit, et ad satisfac-
            n
tionem venerit. Amen.

                    os   os
Maledicat illum Deus Pater qui hominem creavit. Maledicat illum Dei
                                        os
Filius qui pro homine passus est. Maledicat illum Spiritus Sanctus qui in
                                        os
baptismo effusus est. Maledicat illum sancta crux, quam Christus pro nostrâ
salute hostem triumphans, ascendit.

                    os
Maledicat illum sancta Dei genetrix et perpetua Virgo Maria. Maledicat
os   os
illum sanctus Michael, animarum susceptor sacrarum. Maledicant illum
omnes angeli et archangeli, principatus et potestates, omnisque militia
cœlestis.

                    os
Maledicat illum patriarcharum et prophetarum laudabilis numerus.
                os
Maledicat illum sanctus Johannes præcursor et Baptista Christi, et sanctus
Petrus, et sanctus Paulus, atque sanctus Andreas, omnesque Christi apostoli,
simul et cæteri discipuli, quatuor quoque evangelistæ, qui sua prædicatione
                                                    os
mundum universum converterunt. Maledicat illum cuneus martyrum et
confessorum mirificus, qui Deo bonis operibus placitus inventus est.

                    os
Maledicant illum sacrarum virginum chori, quæ mùndi vana causa
                                                    os
honoris Christi respuenda contempserunt. Maledicant illum omnes sancti
qui ab initio mundi usque in finem seculi Deo dilecti inveniuntur.

                os
Maledicant illum cœli et terra, et omnia sancta in eis manentia.

we sequester him, that he may be tormented, disposed and delivered over with *Dathan* and *Abiram*,[2] and with those who say unto the Lord God, Depart from us, we desire none of thy ways. And as fire is quenched with water, so let the light of him be put out for evermore, unless it shall repent him" (Obadiah, of the knots which he has tied) "and make satisfaction" (for them.) Amen.

"May the Father who created man, curse him.— May the Son who suffered for us, curse him.— May the Holy Ghost who was given to us in baptism, curse him (Obadiah.)— May the holy cross which Christ for our salvation triumphing over his enemies, ascended,— curse him.

"May the holy and eternal *Virgin Mary*, mother of God, curse him.— May St. *Michael* the advocate of holy souls, curse him.— May all the angels and archangels, principalities and powers, and all the heavenly armies,[3] curse him." [Our armies swore terribly in *Flanders*, cried my uncle *Toby*,— but nothing to this.— For my own part, I could not have a heart to curse my dog so.]

"May St. John the præ-cursor, and St. John the Baptist,[4] and St. Peter and St. Paul, and St. Andrew, and all other Christ's apostles, together curse him. And may the rest of his disciples and four evangelists, who by their preaching converted the universal world,— and may the holy and wonderful company of martyrs and confessors, who by their holy works are found pleasing to God Almighty, curse him (Obadiah.)

"May the holy choir of the holy virgins, who for the honour of Christ have despised the things of the world, damn him.— May all the saints who from the beginning of the world to everlasting ages are found to be beloved of God, damn him.— May the heavens and earth, and all the holy things remaining therein, damn him," (Obadiah) "or her," (or whoever else had a hand in tying these knots.)

n n
Maledictus sit ubicunque fuerit, sive in domo, sive in agro, sive in viâ, sive in semitâ, sive in silvâ, sive in aquâ, sive in ecclesiâ.

Maledictus sit vivendo, moriendo, —————————————————————————— manducando, bibendo, esuriendo, sitiendo, jejunando, dormitando, dormiendo, vigilando, ambulando, stando, sedendo, jacendo, operando, quiescendo, mingendo, cacando, flebotomando.

i n
Maledictus sit in totis viribus corporis.

Maledictus sit intus et exterius.

Maledictus sit in capillis; maledictus sit in cerebro. Maledictus sit in vertice, in temporibus, in fronte, in auriculis, in superciliis, in oculis, in genis, in maxillis, in naribus, in dentibus, mordacibus sive molaribus, in labiis, in gutture, in humeris, in harmis, in brachiis, in manibus, in digitis, in pectore, in corde, et in omnibus interioribus stomacho tenus, in renibus, in inguinibus, in femore, in genitalibus, in coxis, in genubus, in cruribus, in pedibus, et in unguibus.

Maledictus sit in totis compagibus membrorum, a vertice capitis, usque ad plantam pedis——non sit in eo sanitas.

Maledicat illum Christus Filius Dei vivi toto suæ majestatis imperio

"May he (Obadiah) be damn'd where-ever he be,—whether in the house or the stables, the garden or the field, or the highway, or in the path, or in the wood, or in the water, or in the church.—May he be cursed in living, in dying." [Here my uncle *Toby* taking the advantage of a *minim*⁵ in the second barr of his tune, kept whistling one continual note to the end of the sentence——Dr. *Slop* with his division of curses moving under him, like a running bass all the way.] "May he be cursed in eating and drinking, in being hungry, in being thirsty, in fasting, in sleeping, in slumbering, in walking, in standing, in sitting, in lying, in working, in resting, in pissing, in shitting, and in blood-letting."

"May he *(Obadiah)* be cursed in all the faculties of his body.

"May he be cursed inwardly and outwardly.—May he be cursed in the hair of his head.—May he be cursed in his brains, and in his vertex," (that is a sad curse, quoth my father) "in his temples, in his forehead, in his ears, in his eye-brows, in his cheeks, in his jaw-bones, in his nostrils, in his foreteeth and grinders, in his lips, in his throat, in his shoulders, in his wrists, in his arms, in his hands, in his fingers.

"May he be damn'd in his mouth, in his breast, in his heart and purtenance, down to the very stomach.

"May he be cursed in his reins, and in his groin," (God in heaven forbid, quoth my uncle *Toby*)—"in his thighs, in his genitals," (my father shook his head) "and in his hips, and in his knees, his legs, and feet, and toe-nails.

"May he be cursed in all the joints and articulations of his members, from the top of his head to the soal of his foot, may there be no soundness in him.

"May the Son of the living God, with all the glory of his Majesty"—— [Here my uncle *Toby* throwing back his head, gave a monstrous, long, loud Whew—w—w——something betwixt the interjectional whistle of *Hey day!* and the word itself.——

——et insurgat adversus illum cœlum cum omnibus virtutibus quæ in eo moventur ad *damnandum* eum, nisi penituerit et ad satisfactionem venerit. Amen. Fiat, fiat. Amen.

——By the golden beard of *Jupiter*—and of *Juno*, (if her majesty wore one), and by the beards of the rest of your heathen worships, which by the bye was no small number, since what with the beards of your celestial gods, and gods aerial and aquatick,—to say nothing of the beards of town-gods and country-gods, or of the celestial goddesses your wives, or of the infernal goddesses your whores and concubines, (that is in case they wore 'em)——all which beards, as *Varro* tells me, upon his word and honour, when mustered up together, made no less than thirty thousand effective beards upon the pagan establishment;[6]——every beard of which claimed the rights and privileges of being stroked and sworn by,—by all these beards together then,——I vow and protest, that of the two bad cassocks I am worth in the world, I would have given the better of them, as freely as ever *Cid Hamet*[7] offered his,——only to have stood by, and heard my uncle *Toby*'s accompanyment.]

——"Curse him,"——continued Dr. *Slop*,——"and may heaven with all the powers which move therein, rise up against him, curse and damn him (Obadiah) unless he repent and make satisfaction. Amen. So be it,— so be it. Amen."

I declare, quoth my uncle *Toby*, my heart would not let me curse the devil himself with so much bitterness.——He is the father of curses, replied Dr. *Slop*.——So am not I, replied my uncle.——But he is cursed, and damn'd already, to all eternity,[8]——replied Dr. *Slop*.

I am sorry for it, quoth my uncle *Toby*.

Dr. *Slop* drew up his mouth, and was just beginning to return my uncle *Toby* the compliment of his Whu—u—u——or interjectional whistle, ——when the door hastily opening in the next chapter but one——put an end to the affair.

CHAP. XII.

NOW don't let us give ourselves a parcel of airs, and pretend that the oaths we make free with in this land of liberty of ours are our own; and because we have the spirit to swear them,——imagine that we have had the wit to invent them too.

I'll undertake this moment to prove it to any man in the world, except to a connoisseur;——though I declare I object only to a connoisseur in swearing,——as I would do to a connoisseur in painting, &c. &c. the whole set of 'em are so hung round and *befetish'd*[1] with the bobs and trinkets of criticism,——or to drop my metaphor, which by the bye is a pity,—— for I have fetch'd it as far as from the coast of *Guinea*;——their heads, Sir, are stuck so full of rules and compasses, and have that eternal propensity to apply them upon all occasions, that a work of genius had better go to the devil at once, than stand to be prick'd and tortured to death by 'em.

——And how did *Garrick*[2] speak the soliloquy last night?——Oh, against all rule, my Lord,——most ungrammatically! betwixt the substantive and the adjective, which should agree together in *number, case* and *gender*, he made a breach thus,——stopping, as if the point wanted settling;——and betwixt the nominative case, which your lordship knows should govern the verb, he suspended his voice in the epilogue a dozen times, three seconds and three fifths by a stop-watch, my Lord, each time.—— Admirable grammarian!——But in suspending his voice——was the sense suspended likewise? Did no expression of attitude or countenance fill up the chasm?—Was the eye silent? Did you narrowly look?—I look'd only at the stop-watch, my Lord.——Excellent observer!

And what of this new book[3] the whole world makes such a rout about?— Oh! 'tis out of all plumb, my Lord,——quite an irregular thing!—not one of the angles at the four corners was a right angle.——I had my rule and compasses, &c. my Lord, in my pocket.——Excellent critic!

—And for the epick poem, your lordship bid me look at;—upon taking the length, breadth, height, and depth of it, and trying them at home upon an exact scale of *Bossu* 's,[4]—'tis out, my Lord, in every one of its dimensions. ——Admirable connoisseur!

—And did you step in, to take a look at the grand picture, in your way back?——'Tis a melancholy daub!⁵ my Lord; not one principle of the *pyramid* in any one group!⁶——and what a price!——for there is nothing of the colouring of *Titian*,——the expression of *Rubens*,—the grace of *Raphael*,——the purity of *Dominichino*,—the *corregiescity* of *Corregio*,—the learning of *Poussin*,—the airs of *Guido*,—the taste of the *Carrachi*'s,—or the grand contour of *Angelo*.⁷———Grant me patience, just heaven!—— Of all the cants which are canted in this canting world,——though the cant of hypocrites may be the worst,—the cant of criticism is the most tormenting!

I would go fifty miles on foot, for I have not a horse worth riding on, to kiss the hand of that man whose generous heart will give up the reins of his imagination into his author's hands,——be pleased he knows not why, and cares not wherefore.⁸

Great *Apollo!*⁹ if thou art in a giving humour,——give me,——I ask no more, but one stroke of native humour, with a single spark of thy own fire along with it,——and send *Mercury*, with the *rules and compasses*, if he can be spared, with my compliments to——no matter.

Now to any one else, I will undertake to prove, that all the oaths and imprecations, which we have been puffing off upon the world for these two hundred and fifty years last past, as originals,——except St. *Paul*'s *thumb*,——*God*'s *flesh and God*'s *fish*,¹⁰ which were oaths monarchical, and, considering who made them, not much amiss; and as kings oaths, 'tis not much matter whether they were fish or flesh;——else, I say, there is not an oath, or at least a curse amongst them, which has not been copied over and over again out of *Ernulphus*, a thousand times: but, like all other copies, how infinitely short of the force and spirit of the original!——It is thought to be no bad oath,——and by itself passes very well——"*G---d damn you.*"——Set it beside *Ernulphus*'s——"God Almighty the Father damn you,—God the Son damn you,—God the Holy Ghost damn you,"——you see 'tis nothing.——There is an orientality¹¹ in his, we cannot rise up to: besides, he is more copious in his invention,——possess'd more of the excellencies of a swearer,——had such a thorough knowledge of the human frame, its membranes, nerves, ligaments, knittings of the joints, and articulations,—that when *Ernulphus* cursed,—no part escaped him.—'Tis true, there is something of a *hardness* in his manner,—and, as in *Michael Angelo*, a want of *grace*,——but then there is such a greatness of *gusto!*—

My father, who generally look'd upon every thing in a light very different from all mankind,——would, after all, never allow this to be an original.

——He consider'd rather *Ernulphus*'s anathema, as an institute of swearing, in which, as he suspected, upon the decline of *swearing* in some milder pontificate, *Ernulphus*, by order of the succeeding pope, had with great learning and diligence collected together all the laws of it;——for the same reason that *Justinian*, in the decline of the empire, had ordered his chancellor *Tribonian* to collect the *Roman* or civil laws all together into one code or digest,[12]——lest through the rust of time,——and the fatality of all things committed to oral tradition, they should be lost to the world for ever.

For this reason my father would oft-times affirm, there was not an oath, from the great and tremendous oath of *William* the Conqueror, *(By the splendour of God)*[13] down to the lowest oath of a scavenger, *(Damn your eyes)* which was not to be found in *Ernulphus*.——In short, he would add,——I defy a man to swear *out* of it.

The hypothesis is, like most of my father's, singular and ingenious too;——nor have I any objection to it, but that it overturns my own.

CHAP. XIII.

—B LESS my soul!——my poor mistress is ready to faint,——and her pains are gone,——and the drops are done,——and the bottle of julap[1] is broke,——and the nurse has cut her arm,——(and I, my thumb, cried Dr. *Slop*) and the child is where it was, continued *Susannah*, ——and the midwife has fallen backwards upon the edge of the fender, and bruised her hip as black as your hat.——I'll look at it, quoth Dr. *Slop*. ——There is no need of that, replied *Susannah*,——you had better look at my mistress,——but the midwife would gladly first give you an account how things are, so desires you would go up stairs and speak to her this moment.

Human nature is the same in all professions.

The midwife had just before been put over Dr. *Slop* 's head.—He had not digested it.—No, replied Dr. *Slop*, 'twould be full as proper, if the midwife came down to me.—I like subordination, quoth my uncle *Toby*,—and but for it, after the reduction of *Lisle*, I know not what might have become of the garrison of *Ghent*, in the mutiny for bread, in the year Ten.[2]

————Nor, replied Dr. *Slop*, (parodying my uncle *Toby*'s hobby-horsical reflection, though full as hobby-horsically himself)——do I know, Captain *Shandy*, what might have become of the garrison above stairs, in the mutiny and confusion I find all things are in at present, but for the subordination of fingers and thumbs to ******——the application of which, Sir, under this accident of mine, comes in so *a propos*, that without it, the cut upon my thumb might have been felt by the *Shandy* family, as long as the *Shandy* family had a name.

CHAP. XIV.

LET us go back to the ******——in the last chapter.

It is a singular stroke of eloquence (at least it was so, when eloquence flourished at *Athens* and *Rome*, and would be so now, did orators wear mantles) not to mention the name of a thing, when you had the thing about you, *in petto*,[1] ready to produce, pop, in the place you want it. A scar, an axe, a sword, a pink'd-doublet, a rusty helmet, a pound and a half of pot-ashes in an urn, or a three-halfpenny pickle pot,——but above all, a tender infant royally accoutred.——Tho' if it was too young, and the oration as long as *Tully*'s second *Philippick*,[2]——it must certainly have beshit the orator's mantle.——And then again, if too old,——it must have been unwieldy and incommodious to his action,——so as to make him lose by his child almost as much as he could gain by it.——Otherwise, when a state orator has hit the precise age to a minute,——hid his BAMBINO in his mantle so cunningly that no mortal could smell it,——and produced it so critically, that no soul could say, it came in by head and shoulders,[3] ——Oh, Sirs! it has done wonders.——It has open'd the sluices, and turn'd the brains, and shook the principles, and unhinged the politicks of half a nation.

These feats however are not to be done, except in those states and times, I say, where orators wore mantles,——and pretty large ones too, my brethren, with some twenty or five and twenty yards of good purple, superfine, marketable cloth in them,——with large flowing folds and doubles, and in a great stile of design.————All which plainly shews, may it please your worships, that the decay of eloquence, and the little good service it does at present, both within, and without doors, is owing to nothing else in the world, but short coats, and the disuse of *trunk-hose*.[4] ————We can conceal nothing under ours, Madam, worth shewing.

CHAP. XV.

D R. *Slop* was within an ace of being an exception to all this argumentation: for happening to have his green bays bag upon his knees, when he began to parody my uncle *Toby*,————'twas as good as the best mantle in the world to him: for which purpose, when he foresaw the sentence would end in his new invented *forceps*, he thrust his hand into the bag in order to have them ready to clap in, where your reverences took so much notice of the * * * * * *, which had he managed,——my uncle *Toby* had certainly been overthrown: the sentence and the argument in that case jumping closely in one point, so like the two lines which form the salient angle of a raveline,——Dr. *Slop* would never have given them up;——and my uncle *Toby* would as soon thought of flying, as taking them by force: but Dr. *Slop* fumbled so vilely in pulling them out, it took off the whole effect, and what was a ten times worse evil (for they seldom come alone in this life) in pulling out his *forceps*, his *forceps* unfortunately drew out the *squirt* along with it.

When a proposition can be taken in two senses,——'tis a law in disputation That the respondent may reply to which of the two he pleases, or finds most convenient for him.——This threw the advantage of the argument quite on my uncle *Toby*'s side.——"Good God!" cried my uncle *Toby*, "*are children brought into the world with a squirt?*"

CHAP. XVI.

—UPON my honour, Sir, you have tore every bit of the skin quite off the back of both my hands with your forceps, cried my uncle *Toby*,—and you have crush'd all my knuckles into the bargain with them, to a jelly. 'Tis your own fault, said Dr. *Slop*,——you should have clinch'd your two fists together into the form of a child's head, as I told you, and sat firm.——I did so, answered my uncle *Toby*.——Then the points of my forceps have not been sufficiently arm'd, or the rivet wants closing— or else the cut on my thumb has made me a little aukward,——or possibly ——'Tis well, quoth my father, interrupting the detail of possibilities,—— that the experiment was not first made upon my child's head piece.—— It would not have been a cherry stone the worse, answered Dr. *Slop*. I maintain it, said my uncle *Toby*, it would have broke the cerebellum, (unless indeed the skull had been as hard as a granado) and turned it all into a perfect posset. Pshaw! replied Dr. *Slop*, a child's head is naturally as soft as the pap of an apple;——the sutures give way,——and besides, I could have extracted by the feet after.——Not you, said she.—I rather wish you would begin that way, quoth my father.

Pray do, added my uncle *Toby*.

CHAP. XVII.

—AND pray, good woman, after all, will you take upon you to say, it may not be the child's hip, as well as the child's head?—— 'Tis most certainly the head, replied the midwife. Because, continued Dr. *Slop*, (turning to my father) as positive as these old ladies generally are,——'tis a point very difficult to know,[1]—and yet of the greatest consequence to be known;——because, Sir, if the hip is mistaken for the head,—there is a possibility (if it is a boy) that the forceps *.

—— What the possibility was, Dr. *Slop* whispered very low to my father, and then to my uncle *Toby*.—— There is no such danger, continued he, with the head.—No, in truth, quoth my father,—but when your possibility has taken place at the hip,——you may as well take off the head too.

—— It is morally impossible the reader should understand this,——'tis enough Dr. *Slop* understood it;——so taking the green bays bag in his hand, with the help of *Obadiah*'s pumps, he tripp'd pretty nimbly, for a man of his size, across the room to the door,——and from the door was shewn the way, by the good old midwife, to my mother's apartment.

CHAP. XVIII.

IT is two hours, and ten minutes,—and no more,——cried my father, looking at his watch, since Dr. *Slop* and *Obadiah* arrived,——and I know not how it happens, brother *Toby*,——but to my imagination it seems almost an age.

—— Here——pray, Sir, take hold of my cap,—nay, take the bell along with it, and my pantoufles[1] too.——

Now, Sir, they are all at your service; and I freely make you a present of 'em, on condition, you give me all your attention to this chapter.

Though my father said, "*he knew not how it happen'd*," ——yet he knew very well, how it happen'd;——and at the instant he spoke it, was pre-determined in his mind, to give my uncle *Toby* a clear account of the matter by a metaphysical dissertation upon the subject of *duration and its simple modes*,[2] in order to shew my uncle *Toby*, by what mechanism and mensurations in the brain it came to pass, that the rapid succession[3] of their ideas, and the eternal scampering of the discourse from one thing to another, since Dr. *Slop* had come into the room, had lengthened out so short a period, to so inconceivable an extent.——"I know not how it happens,——cried my father,——"but it seems an age."

—'Tis owing, entirely, quoth my uncle *Toby*, to the succession of our ideas.

My father, who had an itch in common with all philosophers, of reasoning upon every thing which happened, and accounting for it too,——proposed infinite pleasure to himself in this, of the succession of ideas, and had not the least apprehension of having it snatch'd out of his hands by my uncle *Toby*, who (honest man!) generally took every thing as it happened;—— and who, of all things in the world, troubled his brain the least with abstruse thinking;—the ideas of time and space,——or how we came by those ideas,——or of what stuff they were made,—or whether they were born with us,[4]——or we pick'd them up afterwards as we went along,—or whether we did it in frocks,—or not till we had got into breeches,—with a thousand other inquiries and disputes about INFINITY, PRESCIENCE, LIBERTY, NECESSITY,[5] and so forth, upon whose desperate and unconquerable theories, so many fine heads have been turned and crack'd,—never did my uncle *Toby*'s the least injury at all; my father knew it,——and was no less surprised, than he was disappointed with my uncle's fortuitous solution.

Do you understand the theory of that affair? replied my father.

Not I, quoth my uncle.

——But you have some ideas, said my father, of what you talk about.——

No more than my horse, replied my uncle *Toby*.

Gracious heaven! cried my father, looking upwards, and clasping his two hands together,——there is a worth in thy honest ignorance, brother *Toby*,—'twere almost a pity to exchange it for a knowledge.———But I'll tell thee.——

To understand what *time* is aright, without which we never can comprehend *infinity*, insomuch as one is a portion of the other,——we ought seriously to sit down and consider what idea it is, we have of *duration*, so as to give a satisfactory account, how we came by it.——What is that to any body? quoth my uncle *Toby*. **For if you will turn your eyes inwards upon your mind*, continued my father, *and observe attentively, you will perceive, brother, that whilst you and I are talking together, and thinking and smoaking our pipes: or whilst we receive successively ideas in our minds, we know that we do exist, and so we estimate the existence, or the continuation of the existence of ourselves, or any thing else commensurate to the succession of any ideas in our minds, the duration of ourselves, or any such other thing co existing with our thinking,——and so*

---

*Vid. Locke.

according to that preconceived [6]——You puzzle me to death, cried my uncle *Toby*.——

——'Tis owing to this, replied my father, that in our computations of *time*, we are so used to minutes, hours, weeks, and months,——and of clocks (I wish there was not a clock in the kingdom) to measure out their several portions to us, and to those who belong to us,——that 'twill be well, if in time to come, the *succession of our ideas* be of any use or service to us at all.[7]

Now, whether we observe it or no, continued my father, in every sound man's head, there is a regular succession of ideas of one sort or other, which follow each other in train just like——A train of artillery? said my uncle *Toby*.——A train of a fiddle stick!—quoth my father,—which follow and succeed one another in our minds at certain distances, just like the images in the inside of a lanthorn turned round by the heat of a candle.[8]—— I declare, quoth my uncle *Toby*, mine are more like a smoak-jack.[9]—— Then, brother *Toby*, I have nothing more to say to you upon the subject, said my father.

CHAP. XIX.

—— WHAT a conjuncture was here lost!——My father in one of his best explanatory moods,—in eager pursuit of a metaphysic point into the very regions where clouds and thick darkness would soon have encompassed it about;——my uncle *Toby* in one of the finest dispositions for it in the world;—his head like a smoak-jack;——the funnel unswept, and the ideas whirling round and round about in it, all obfuscated and darkened over with fuliginous matter!——By the tomb stone of *Lucian*——if it is in being,——if not, why then, by his ashes! by the ashes of my dear *Rabelais*, and dearer *Cervantes*,[1]——my father and my uncle *Toby*'s discourse upon TIME and ETERNITY,—was a discourse devoutly to be wished for![2] and the petulancy of my father's humour in putting a stop to it, as he did, was a robbery of the *Ontologic*[3] *treasury*, of such a jewel, as no coalition of great occasions and great men, are ever likely to restore to it again.

CHAP. XX.

THO' my father persisted in not going on with the discourse,—yet he could not get my uncle *Toby*'s smoak-jack out of his head,— piqued as he was at first with it;——there was something in the comparison at the bottom, which hit his fancy; for which purpose resting his elbow upon the table, and reclining the right side of his head upon the palm of his hand,——but looking first stedfastly in the fire,——he began to commune with himself and philosophize about it: but his spirits being wore out with the fatigues of investigating new tracts, and the constant exertion of his faculties upon that variety of subjects which had taken their turn in the discourse,——the idea of the smoak-jack soon turned all his ideas upside down,——so that he fell asleep almost before he knew what he was about.

As for my uncle *Toby*, his smoak-jack had not made a dozen revolutions, before he fell asleep also.——Peace be with them both.——Dr. *Slop* is engaged with the midwife, and my mother above stairs.— *Trim* is busy in turning an old pair of jack-boots into a couple of mortars to be employed in the siege of *Messina*[1] next summer,——and is this instant boring the touch holes with the point of a hot poker.——All my heroes are off my hands;——'tis the first time I have had a moment to spare,—and I'll make use of it, and write my preface.

THE
Author's PREFACE.

NO, I'll not say a word about it,—here it is;——in publishing it, ——I have appealed to the world,——and to the world I leave it; ——it must speak for itself.

All I know of the matter is,——when I sat down, my intent was to write a good book; and as far as the tenuity of my understanding would hold out,——a wise, aye, and a discreet,——taking care only, as I went along, to put into it all the wit and the judgment (be it more or less) which the great author and bestower of them had thought fit originally to give me,——so that, as your worships see,—'tis just as God pleases.

Now, *Agelastes*[2] (speaking dispraisingly) sayeth, That there may be some wit in it, for aught he knows,——but no judgment at all. And *Triptolemus*[3] and *Phutatorius*[4] agreeing thereto, ask, How is it possible there should? for that wit and judgment[5] in this world never go together; inasmuch as they are two operations differing from each other as wide as east is from west.—So, says *Locke*,—so are farting and hickuping, say I. But in answer to this, *Didius* the great church lawyer, in his code *de fartandi et illustrandi fallaciis*,[6] doth maintain and make fully appear, That an illustration is no argument,—nor do I maintain the wiping of a looking-glass clean, to be a syllogism;——but you all, may it please your worships, see the better for it,——so that the main good these things do, is only to clarify the understanding, previous to the application of the argument itself, in order to free it from any little motes, or specks of opacular[7] matter, which if left swiming therein, might hinder a conception and spoil all.

Now, my dear Anti-Shandeans, and thrice able critics,[8] and fellow-labourers, (for to you I write this Preface)——and to you, most subtle statesmen and discreet doctors (do—pull off your beards) renowned for gravity and wisdom;—*Monopolos*, my politician,—*Didius*, my counsel; *Kysarcius*, my friend;—*Phutatorius*, my guide;—*Gastripheres*, the preserver of my life; *Somnolentius*,[9] the balm and repose of it,—not forgetting all others as well sleeping as waking,—ecclesiastical as civil, whom for brevity, but out of no resentment to you, I lump all together.——Believe me, right worthy,

My most zealous wish and fervent prayer in your behalf, and in my own too, in case the thing is not done already for us,——is, that the great gifts and endowments both of wit and judgment, with every thing which usually goes along with them,——such as memory, fancy, genius, eloquence, quick parts, and what not, may this precious moment without stint or measure, let or hinderance, be poured down warm as each of us could bear it,—scum and sediment an' all; (for I would not have a drop lost) into the several receptacles, cells, cellules, domiciles, dormitories, refectories, and spare places of our brains,—in such sort, that they might continue to be injected and tunn'd into, according to the true intent and meaning of my wish, until every vessel of them, both great and small, be so replenished, saturated and fill'd up therewith, that no more, would it save a man's life, could possibly be got either in or out.[10]

Bless us!—what noble work we should make!——how should I tickle it off!——and what spirits should I find myself in, to be writing away for such readers!—and you,—just heaven!——with what raptures would you sit and read,——but oh!——'tis too much,——I am sick,——I faint away deliciously at the thoughts of it!——'tis more than nature can bear!—— lay hold of me,—I am giddy,—I am stone blind,——I'm dying,——I am gone.——Help! Help! Help!——But hold,—I grow something better again, for I am beginning to foresee, when this is over, that as we shall all of us continue to be great wits,—we should never agree amongst ourselves, one day to an end:——there would be so much satire and sarcasm,[11]—— scoffing and flouting, with raillying and reparteeing of it,——thrusting and parrying in one corner or another,——there would be nothing but mischief amongst us.—Chaste stars! what biting and scratching, and what a racket and a clatter we should make, what with breaking of heads, and rapping of knuckles, and hitting of sore places,——there would be no such thing as living for us.

But then again, as we should all of us be men of great judgment, we should make up matters as fast as ever they went wrong; and though we should abominate each other, ten times worse than so many devils or devilesses, we should nevertheless, my dear creatures, be all courtesy and kindness,——milk and honey,[12]——'twould be a second land of promise, ——a paradise upon earth, if there was such a thing to be had,—so that upon the whole we should have done well enough.

All I fret and fume at, and what most distresses my invention at present, is how to bring the point itself to bear; for as your worships well know, that of these heavenly emanations of *wit* and *judgment*, which I have so bountifully wished both for your worships and myself,—there is but a certain *quantum* stored up for us all, for the use and behoof of the whole race of mankind; and such small *modicums* of 'em are only sent forth into this wide world, circulating here and there in one by corner or another,— and in such narrow streams, and at such prodigious intervals from each other, that one would wonder how it holds out, or could be sufficient for the wants and emergencies of so many great states, and populous empires.

Indeed there is one thing to be considered, that in *Nova Zembla, North Lapland*, and in all those cold and dreary tracts of the globe, which lie more directly under the artick and antartick circles,——where the whole province of a man's concernments lies for near nine months together, within the narrow compass of his cave,[13]——where the spirits are compressed almost to nothing,——and where the passions of a man, with every thing which belongs to them, are as frigid as the zone itself;[14]—there the least quantity of *judgment* imaginable does the business,—and of *wit*,—there is a total and an absolute saving,—for as not one spark is wanted,——so not one spark is given. Angels and ministers of grace defend us![15] What a dismal thing would it have been to have governed a kingdom, to have fought a battle, or made a treaty, or run a match,[16] or wrote a book, or got a child, or held a provincial chapter there, with so *plentiful a lack* of wit and judgment about us! for mercy's sake! let us think no more about it, but travel on as fast as we can southwards into *Norway*,——crossing over *Swedeland*, if you please, through the small triangular province of *Angermania* to the lake of *Bothnia*; coasting along it through east and west *Bothnia*, down to *Carelia*, and so on, through all those states and provinces which border upon the far side of the *Gulf* of *Finland*, and the north east of the *Baltick*, up to *Petersbourg*, and just stepping into *Ingria*;——then stretching over directly from thence through the north parts of the *Russian* empire—leaving *Siberia* a little upon the left hand till we get into the very heart of *Russian* and *Asiatick Tartary*.[17]

Now throughout this long tour which I have led you, you observe the good people are better off by far, than in the polar countries which we have just left:—for if you hold your hand over your eyes, and look very attentively, you may perceive some small glimmerings (as it were) of wit, with a comfortable provision of good plain *houshold* judgment, which taking the quality and quantity of it together, they make a very good shift with,—and had they more of either the one or the other, it would destroy the proper ballance betwixt them, and I am satisfied moreover they would want occasions to put them to use.

Now, Sir, if I conduct you home again into this warmer and more luxuriant island,[18] where you perceive the spring tide of our blood and humours runs high,—where we have more ambition, and pride, and envy, and lechery, and other whoreson passions upon our hands to govern and subject to reason,—the *height* of our wit and the *depth* of our judgment, you see, are exactly proportioned to the *length* and *breadth* of our necessities,[19]—and accordingly, we have them sent down amongst us in such a flowing kind of decent and creditable plenty, that no one thinks he has any cause to complain.

It must however be confessed on this head, that, as our air blows hot and cold,——wet and dry, ten times in a day, we have them in no regular and settled way;——so that sometimes for near half a century together, there shall be very little wit or judgment, either to be seen or heard of amongst us:——the small channels of them shall seem quite dried up,—then all of a sudden the sluices shall break out, and take a fit of running again like fury,——you would think they would never stop:——and then it is, that in writing and fighting, and twenty other gallant things, we drive all the world before us.

It is by these observations, and a wary reasoning by analogy in that kind of argumentative process, which *Suidas* calls *dialectick induction*,[20]——that I draw and set up this position as most true and veritable:

That of these two luminaries, so much of their irradiations are suffered from time to time to shine down upon us; as he, whose infinite wisdom which dispenses every thing in exact weight and measure, knows will just serve to light us on our way in this night of our obscurity; so that your reverences and worships[21] now find out, nor is it a moment longer in my power to conceal it from you, That the fervent wish in your behalf with which I set out, was no more than the first insinuating *How d'ye*[22] of a caressing prefacer stifling his reader, as a lover sometimes does a coy mistress into silence. For alas! could this effusion of light have been as easily procured, as the exordium wished it—I tremble to think how many thousands for it, of benighted travellers (in the learned sciences at least) must have groped and blundered on in the dark, all the nights of their lives,—running their heads against posts, and knocking out their brains without ever getting to their journies end;——some falling with their noses perpendicularly into stinks,—others horizontally with their tails into kennels.[23] Here one half of a learned profession tilting full butt[24] against the other half of it, and then tumbling and rolling one over the other in the dirt like hogs.[25]——Here the brethren, of another profession, who should have run in opposition to each other, flying on the contrary like a flock of wild geese, all in a row the same way.—What confusion!—what mistakes!—fiddlers and painters judging by their eyes and ears,—admirable!—trusting to the passions excited in an air sung, or a story painted to the heart,——instead of measuring them by a quadrant.

In the foreground of this picture, a *statesman* turning the political wheel, like a brute, the wrong way round—*against* the stream of corruption,—by heaven!—instead of *with* it.

In this corner, a son of the divine *Esculapius*, writing a book against predestination; perhaps worse,—feeling his patient's pulse, instead of his apothecary's—a brother of the faculty in the back ground upon his knees in tears,—drawing the curtains of a mangled victim to beg his forgiveness;—offering a fee,—instead of taking one.[26]

In that spacious HALL, a coalition of the gown,[27] from all the barrs of it, driving a damn'd, dirty, vexatious cause before them, with all their might and main, the wrong way;——kicking it *out* of the great doors, instead of, *in*,——and with such fury in their looks, and such a degree of inveteracy in their manner of kicking it, as if the laws had been originally made for the peace and preservation of mankind:—perhaps a more enormous mistake committed by them still,—a litigated point fairly hung up;—— for instance, Whether *John o'Nokes* his nose, could stand in *Tom o'Stiles*[28] his face, without a trespass, or not,—rashly determined by them in five and twenty minutes, which, with the cautious pro's and con's required in so intricate a proceeding, might have taken up as many months,—and if carried on upon a military plan, as your honours know, an ACTION should be, with all the stratagems practicable therein,—such as feints,—forced marches,—surprizes,—ambuscades,—mask-batteries, and a thousand other strokes of generalship which consist in catching at all advantages on both sides,——might reasonably have lasted them as many years, finding food and raiment all that term for a centumvirate[29] of the profession.

As for the clergy———No——If I say a word against them, I'll be shot.—I have no desire,—and besides, if I had,——I durst not for my soul touch upon the subject,——with such weak nerves and spirits, and in the condition I am in at present, 'twould be as much as my life was worth, to deject and contrist[30] myself with so bad and melancholy an account,——and therefore, 'tis safer to draw a curtain across, and hasten from it, as fast as I can, to the main and principal point I have undertaken to clear up,——and that is, How it comes to pass, that your men of least *wit* are reported to be men of most *judgment.*——But mark,—I say, *reported to be,*——for it is no more, my dear Sirs, than a report, and which like twenty others taken up every day upon trust, I maintain to be a vile and a malicious report into the bargain.

This by the help of the observations already premised, and I hope already weighed and perpended by your reverences and worships, I shall forthwith make appear.

I hate set dissertations,——and above all things in the world, 'tis one of the silliest things in one of them, to darken your hypothesis by placing a number of tall, opake words, one before another, in a right line, betwixt your own and your readers conception,——when in all likelihood, if you had looked about, you might have seen something standing, or hanging up, which would have cleared the point at once,——"for what hinderance, hurt or harm, doth the laudable desire of knowledge bring to any man, if even from a sot, a pot, a fool, a stool, a winter-mittain, a truckle for a pully, the lid of a goldsmith's crucible, an oyl bottle, an old slipper, or a cane chair,"[31]——I am this moment sitting upon one. Will you give me leave to illustrate this affair of wit and judgment, by the two knobs on the top of the back of it,——they are fasten'd on, you see, with two pegs stuck slightly into two gimlet-holes, and will place what I have to say in so clear a light, as to let you see through the drift and meaning of my whole preface, as plainly as if every point and particle of it was made up of sun beams.

I enter now directly upon the point.

——Here stands *wit*,——and there stands *judgment*, close beside it, just like the two knobbs I'm speaking of, upon the back of this self same chair on which I am sitting.

——You see, they are the highest and most ornamental parts of its *frame*,——as wit and judgment are of *ours*,——and like them too, indubitably both made and fitted to go together, in order as we say in all such cases of duplicated embellishments,—— *to answer one another.*[32]

Now for the sake of an experiment, and for the clearer illustrating this matter,—let us for a moment, take off one of these two curious ornaments (I care not which) from the point or pinacle of the chair it now stands on; ——nay, don't laugh at it.——But did you ever see in the whole course of your lives such a ridiculous business as this has made of it?——Why, 'tis as miserable a sight as a sow with one ear;[33] and there is just as much sense and symmetry in the one, as in the other:—do,—pray, get off your seats, only to take a view of it.——Now would any man who valued his character a straw, have turned a piece of work out of his hand in such a condition?——nay, lay your hands upon your hearts, and answer this plain question, Whether this one single knobb which now stands here like a blockhead by itself, can serve any purpose upon earth, but to put one in mind of the want of the other;——and let me further ask, in case the chair was your own, if you would not in your consciences think, rather than be as it is, that it would be ten times better without any knobb at all.

Now these two knobs——or top ornaments of the mind of man, which crown the whole entablature,—being, as I said, wit and judgment, which of all others, as I have proved it, are the most needful,—the most priz'd, ——the most calamitous to be without, and consequently the hardest to come at,——for all these reasons put together, there is not a mortal amongst us, so destitute of a love of good fame or feeding,[34]——or so ignorant of what will do him good therein,—who does not wish and stedfastly resolve in his own mind, to be, or to be thought at least master of the one or the other, and indeed of both of them, if the thing seems any way feasible, or likely to be brought to pass.

Now your graver gentry having little or no kind of chance in aiming at the one,—unless they laid hold of the other,——pray what do you think would become of them?—Why, Sirs, in spight of all their *gravities*, they must e'en have been contented to have gone with their insides naked:— this was not to be borne, but by an effort of philosophy not to be supposed in the case we are upon,——so that no one could well have been angry with them, had they been satisfied with what little they could have snatched up and secreted under their cloaks and great perrywigs, had they not raised a *hue* and *cry* at the same time against the lawful owners.

I need not tell your worships, that this was done with so much cunning and artifice,—that the great *Locke*, who was seldom outwitted by false sounds,——was nevertheless bubbled here. The cry, it seems, was so deep and solemn a one, and what with the help of great wigs, grave faces, and other implements of deceit, was rendered so general a one against the *poor wits* in this matter, that the philosopher himself was deceived by it,—it was his glory to free the world from the lumber of a thousand vulgar errors;[35]——but this was not of the number; so that instead of sitting down cooly, as such a philosopher should have done, to have examined the matter of fact before he philosophised upon it;——on the contrary, he took the fact for granted, and so joined in with the cry, and halloo'd it as boisterously as the rest.

This has been made the *Magna Charta* of stupidity ever since,—but your reverences plainly see, it has been obtained in such a manner, that the title to it is not worth a groat;——which by the bye is one of the many and vile impositions which gravity and grave folks have to answer for hereafter.

As for great wigs, upon which I may be thought to have spoken my mind too freely,——I beg leave to qualify whatever has been unguardedly said to their dispraise or prejudice, by one general declaration——That I have no abhorrence whatever, nor do I detest and abjure either great wigs or long beards,——any further than when I see they are bespoke and let grow on purpose to carry on this self-same imposture——for any purpose,—peace be with them;—☞ mark only,—I write not for them.

CHAP. XXI.

EVERY day for at least ten years together did my father resolve to have it mended,——'tis not mended yet;——no family but ours would have borne with it an hour,—and what is most astonishing, there was not a subject in the world upon which my father was so eloquent, as upon that of door-hinges.——And yet at the same time, he was certainly one of the greatest bubbles to them, I think, that history can produce: his rhetoric and conduct were at perpetual handy-cuffs.[1]——Never did the parlour-door open—but his philosophy or his principles fell a victim to it;——three drops of oyl with a feather, and a smart stroke of a hammer, had saved his honour for ever.

——Inconsistent soul that man is![2]—languishing under wounds, which he has the power to heal!—his whole life a contradiction to his know-ledge!—his reason, that precious gift of God to him—(instead of pouring in oyl)[3] serving but to sharpen his sensibilities,——to multiply his pains and render him more melancholy and uneasy under them!—poor unhappy creature, that he should do so!——are not the necessary causes of misery in this life enow, but he must add voluntary ones to his stock of sorrow;——struggle against evils which cannot be avoided, and submit to others, which a tenth part of the trouble they create him, would remove from his heart for ever?

By all that is good and virtuous! if there are three drops of oyl to be got, and a hammer to be found within ten miles of *Shandy-Hall*,—the parlour-door hinge shall be mended this reign.

CHAP. XXII.

WHEN corporal *Trim* had brought his two mortars to bear, he was delighted with his handy-work above measure; and knowing what a pleasure it would be to his master to see them, he was not able to resist the desire he had of carrying them directly into the parlour.

Now next to the moral lesson I had in view in mentioning the affair of *hinges*, I had a speculative consideration arising out of it, and it is this.

Had the parlour-door open'd and turn'd upon its hinges, as a door should do———

—Or for example, as cleverly as our government has been turning upon its hinges,[1]———(that is, in case things have all along gone well with your worship,—otherwise I give up my simile)—in this case, I say, there had been no danger either to master or man, in corporal *Trim*'s peeping in: the moment, he had beheld my father and my uncle *Toby* fast asleep, ———the respectfulness of his carriage was such, he would have retired as silent as death, and left them both in their arm-chairs, dreaming as happy as he had found them: but the thing was morally speaking so very impracticable, that for the many years in which this hinge was suffered to be out of order, and amongst the hourly grievances my father submitted to upon its account,—this was one; that he never folded his arms to take his nap after dinner, but the thoughts of being unavoidably awakened by the first person who should open the door, was always uppermost in his imagination, and so incessantly step'd in betwixt him and the first balmy presage of his repose, as to rob him, as he often declared, of the whole sweets of it.

"*When things move upon bad hinges*, an' please your lordships, *how can it be otherwise?*"

Pray what's the matter? Who is there? cried my father, waking, the moment the door began to creak.———I wish the smith would give a peep at that confounded hinge.———'Tis nothing, an' please your honour, said *Trim*, but two mortars I am bringing in.———They shan't make a clatter with them here, cried my father hastily.———If Dr. *Slop* has any drugs to pound, let him do it in the kitchen.———May it please your honour, cried *Trim*,—they are two mortar-pieces for a siege next summer, which I have been making out of a pair of jack-boots,[2] which *Obadiah* told me your honour had left off wearing.——By heaven! cried my father, springing out of his chair, as he swore,—I have not one appointment belonging to me, which I set so much store by, as I do by these jack-boots,——they were our great-grandfather's, brother *Toby*,——they were *hereditary*. Then I fear, quoth my uncle *Toby*, *Trim* has cut off the entail.[3]——I have only cut off the tops, an' please your honour, cried *Trim*.——I hate *perpetuities* as much as any man alive, cried my father,——but these jack-boots, continued he, (smiling, though very angry at the same time) have been in the family, brother, ever since the civil wars;——Sir *Roger Shandy* wore them at the battle of *Marston-Moor*.[4]—I declare I would not have taken ten pounds for them.——I'll pay you the money, brother *Shandy*, quoth my uncle *Toby*, looking at the two mortars with infinite pleasure, and putting his hand into his breeches-pocket, as he viewed them.——I'll pay you the ten pounds this moment with all my heart and soul.——

Brother *Toby*, replied my father, altering his tone, you care not what money you dissipate and throw away, provided, continued he, 'tis but upon a SIEGE.—Have I not a hundred and twenty pounds a year, besides my half-pay? cried my uncle *Toby*.——What is that, replied my father, hastily,—to ten pounds for a pair of jack-boots?——twelve guineas for your *pontoons*;——half as much for your *Dutch*-draw-bridge;—to say nothing of the train of little brass-artillery you bespoke last week, with twenty other preparations for the siege of *Messina*; believe me, dear brother *Toby*, continued my father, taking him kindly by the hand,—these military operations of yours are above your strength;—you mean well, brother,—but they carry you into greater expences than you were first aware of,—and take my word,——dear *Toby*, they will in the end quite ruin your fortune, and make a beggar of you.——What signifies it if they do, brother, replied my uncle *Toby*, so long as we know 'tis for the good of the nation.—

My father could not help smiling for his soul;—his anger at the worst was never more than a spark,—and the zeal and simplicity of *Trim*,——and the generous (tho' hobby-horsical) gallantry of my uncle *Toby*, brought him into perfect good humour with them in an instant.

Generous souls!—God prosper you both, and your mortar-pieces too, quoth my father to himself.

CHAP. XXIII.

ALL is quiet and hush, cried my father, at least above stairs,—I hear not one foot stirring.——Prithee, *Trim*, who is in the kitchen? There is no one soul in the kitchen, answered *Trim*, making a low bow as he spoke, except Dr. *Slop*.——Confusion! cried my father, (getting up upon his legs a second time)——not one single thing has gone right this day! had I faith in astrology, brother, (which by the bye, my father had) I would have sworn some retrograde planet[1] was hanging over this unfortunate house of mine, and turning every individual thing in it out of its place. ——Why, I thought Dr. *Slop* had been above stairs with my wife, and so said you.—What can the fellow be puzzling about in the kitchen?—— He is busy, an' please your honour, replied *Trim*, in making a bridge.—— 'Tis very obliging in him, quoth my uncle *Toby*;——pray give my humble service to Dr. *Slop*, *Trim*, and tell him I thank him heartily.

You must know, my uncle *Toby* mistook the bridge as widely as my father mistook the mortars;——but to understand how my uncle *Toby* could mistake the bridge,—I fear I must give you an exact account of the road which led to it;——or to drop my metaphor, (for there is nothing more dishonest in an historian, than the use of one,)——in order to conceive the probability of this error in my uncle *Toby* aright, I must give you some account of an adventure of *Trim*'s, though much against my will. I say much against my will, only because the story, in one sense, is certainly out of its place here; for by right it should come in, either amongst the anecdotes of my uncle *Toby*'s amours with widow *Wadman*, in which corporal *Trim* was no mean actor,—or else in the middle of his and my uncle *Toby*'s campaigns on the bowling green,——for it will do very well in either place;——but then if I reserve it for either of those parts of my story,—I ruin the story I'm upon,—and if I tell it here—I anticipate matters, and ruin it there.

—What would your worships have me to do in this case?

—Tell it, Mr. *Shandy*, by all means.——You are a fool, *Tristram*, if you do.

O ye Powers! (for powers ye are, and great ones too)—which enable mortal man to tell a story worth the hearing,—that kindly shew him, where he is to begin it,—and where he is to end it,—what he is to put into it,—and what he is to leave out,—how much of it he is to cast into shade,—and whereabouts he is to throw his light!——Ye, who preside over this vast empire of biographical freebooters, and see how many scrapes and plunges your subjects hourly fall into;—will you do one thing?

I beg and beseech you, (in case you will do nothing better for us) that where-ever, in any part of your dominions it so falls out, that three several roads meet in one point, as they have done just here,—that at least you set up a guide-post, in the center of them, in mere charity to direct an uncertain devil, which of the three he is to take.

CHAP. XXIV.

THO' the shock my uncle *Toby* received the year after the demolition of *Dunkirk*, in his affair with widow *Wadman*, had fixed him in a resolution, never more to think of the sex,——or of aught which belonged to it;—yet corporal *Trim* had made no such bargain with himself. Indeed in my uncle *Toby*'s case there was a strange and unaccountable concurrence of circumstances which insensibly drew him in, to lay siege to that fair and strong citadel.——In *Trim*'s case there was a concurrence of nothing in the world, but of him and *Bridget*[1] in the kitchen;——though in truth, the love and veneration he bore his master was such, and so fond was he of imitating him in all he did, that had my uncle *Toby* employed his time and genius in tagging of points,[2]——I am persuaded the honest corporal would have laid down his arms, and followed his example with pleasure. When therefore my uncle *Toby* sat down before the mistress,—corporal *Trim* incontinently took ground before the maid.

Now, my dear friend *Garrick*, whom I have so much cause to esteem and honour,—(why, or wherefore, 'tis no matter)—can it escape your penetration,—I defy it,—that so many play-wrights, and opificers[3] of chit chat have ever since been working upon *Trim*'s and my uncle *Toby*'s pattern.—I care not what *Aristotle*, or *Pacuvius*, or *Bossu*, or *Ricaboni*[4] say,—(though I never read one of them)——there is not a greater difference between a single-horse chair and madam *Pompadour*'s *vis a vis*,[5] than betwixt a single amour, and an amour thus nobly doubled, and going upon all four, prancing throughout a grand drama.——Sir, a simple, single, silly affair of that kind,——is quite lost in five acts,——but that is neither here or there.

After a series of attacks and repulses in a course of nine months on my uncle *Toby*'s quarter, a most minute account of every particular of which shall be given in its proper place, my uncle *Toby*, honest man! found it necessary to draw off his forces, and raise the siege somewhat indignantly.

Corporal *Trim*, as I said, had made no such bargain either with himself ——or with any one else,——the fidelity however of his heart not suffering him to go into a house which his master had forsaken with disgust,—— he contented himself with turning his part of the siege into a blockade; ——that is, he kept others off,—for though he never after went to the house, yet he never met *Bridget* in the village, but he would either nod or wink, or smile, or look kindly at her,—or (as circumstances directed), he would shake her by the hand,——or ask her lovingly how she did,—— or would give her a ribban,——and now and then, though never but when it could be done with decorum, would give *Bridget* a ———

Precisely in this situation, did these things stand for five years; that is, from the demolition of *Dunkirk* in the year 13, to the latter end of my uncle *Toby*'s campaign in the year 18, which was about six or seven weeks before the time I'm speaking of.—When *Trim*, as his custom was, after he had put my uncle *Toby* to bed, going down one moon-shiny night to see that every thing was right at his fortifications,——in the lane separated from the bowling-green with flowering shrubs and holly,—he espied his *Bridget*.

As the corporal thought there was nothing in the world so well worth shewing as the glorious works which he and my uncle *Toby* had made, *Trim* courteously and gallantly took her by the hand, and led her in: this was not done so privately, but that the foul-mouth'd trumpet of Fame[6] carried it from ear to ear, till at length it reached my father's, with this untoward circumstance along with it, that my uncle *Toby*'s curious draw-bridge, constructed and painted after the *Dutch* fashion, and which went quite across the ditch,—was broke down, and some how or other crush'd all to pieces that very night.

My father, as you have observed, had no great esteem for my uncle *Toby*'s hobby-horse,—he thought it the most ridiculous horse that ever gentleman mounted, and indeed unless my uncle *Toby* vexed him about it, could never think of it once, without smiling at it,——so that it never could get lame or happen any mischance, but it tickled my father's imagination beyond measure; but this being an accident much more to his humour than any one which had yet befall'n it, it proved an inexhaustible fund of entertainment to him.——Well,——but dear *Toby!* my father would say, do tell me seriously how this affair of the bridge happened. ——How can you teaze me so much about it? my uncle *Toby* would reply,—I have told it you twenty times, word for word as *Trim* told it me.—Prithee, how was it then, corporal? my father would cry, turning to *Trim.*—It was a mere misfortune, an' please your honour,——I was shewing Mrs. *Bridget* our fortifications, and in going too near the edge of the fossè, I unfortunately slip'd in.——Very well *Trim!* my father would cry,—(smiling mysteriously, and giving a nod,——but without interrupting him)———and being link'd fast, an' please your honour, arm in arm with Mrs. *Bridget*, I dragg'd her after me, by means of which she fell backwards soss[7] against the bridge,——and *Trim*'s foot, (my uncle *Toby* would cry, taking the story out of his mouth) getting into the cuvette, he tumbled full against the bridge too.—It was a thousand to one, my uncle *Toby* would add, that the poor fellow did not break his leg.[8]—Ay truly! my father would say,——a limb is soon broke, brother *Toby*, in such encounters.——And so, an' please your honour, the bridge, which your honour knows was a very slight one, was broke down betwixt us, and splintered all to pieces.

At other times, but especially when my uncle *Toby* was so unfortunate as to say a syllable about cannons, bombs or petards,——my father would exhaust all the stores of his eloquence (which indeed were very great) in a panegyric upon the BATTERING-RAMS[9] of the ancients,—the VINEA which *Alexander* made use of at the siege of *Tyre.*——He would tell my uncle *Toby* of the CATAPULTÆ of the *Syrians* which threw such monstrous stones so many hundred feet, and shook the strongest bulwarks from their very foundation;—he would go on and describe the wonderful mechanism of the BALLISTA, which *Marcellinus* makes so much rout about,—the terrible effects of the PYRABOLI,—which cast fire,——the danger of the TEREBRA and SCORPIO, which cast javelins.—But what are these, he would say, to the destructive machinery of corporal *Trim?*—Believe me, brother *Toby*, no bridge, or bastion, or sally port[10] that ever was constructed in this world, can hold out against such artillery.

My uncle *Toby* would never attempt any defence against the force of this ridicule, but that of redoubling the vehemence of smoking his pipe;

in doing which, he raised so dense a vapour one night after supper, that it set my father, who was a little phthisical, into a suffocating fit of violent coughing: my uncle *Toby* leap'd up without feeling the pain upon his groin,——and, with infinite pity, stood beside his brother's chair, tapping his back with one hand, and holding his head with the other, and from time to time, wiping his eyes with a clean cambrick handkerchief, which he pull'd out of his pocket.——The affectionate and endearing manner in which my uncle *Toby* did these little offices,——cut my father thro' his reins, for the pain he had just been giving him.——May my brains be knock'd out with a battering ram or a catapulta, I care not which, quoth my father to himself,——if ever I insult this worthy soul more.

CHAP. XXV.

THE draw-bridge being held irreparable, *Trim* was ordered directly to set about another,——but not upon the same model; for cardinal *Alberoni*'s intrigues[1] at that time being discovered, and my uncle *Toby* rightly foreseeing that a flame would inevitably break out betwixt *Spain* and the Empire, and that the operations of the ensuing campaign must in all likelihood be either in *Naples* or *Scicily*,——he determined upon an *Italian* bridge,—(my uncle *Toby*, by the bye, was not far out in his conjectures)——but my father, who was infinitely the better politician, and took the lead as far of my uncle *Toby* in the cabinet, as my uncle *Toby* took it of him in the field,—convinced him, that if the King of *Spain* and the Emperor went together by the ears, that *England* and *France* and *Holland* must, by force of their pre-engagements, all enter the lists too;——and if so, he would say, the combatants, brother *Toby*, as sure as we are alive, will fall to it again, pell-mell, upon the old prize-fighting stage of *Flanders*; ——then what will you do with your *Italian* bridge?

——We will go on with it then, upon the old model, cried my uncle *Toby*.

When corporal *Trim* had about half finished it in that stile,——my uncle *Toby* found out a capital defect in it, which he had never thoroughly considered before. It turned, it seems, upon hinges at both ends of it, opening in the middle, one half of which turning to one side of the fossè, and the other, to the other; the advantage of which was this, that by dividing the weight of the bridge into two equal portions, it impowered my uncle *Toby* to raise it up or let it down with the end of his crutch, and with one hand, which, as his garrison was weak, was as much as he could well spare,——but the disadvantages of such a construction were insurmountable,——for by this means, he would say, I leave one half of my bridge in my enemy's possession,——and pray of what use is the other?

The natural remedy for this, was no doubt to have his bridge fast only at one end with hinges, so that the whole might be lifted up together, and stand bolt upright,——but that was rejected for the reason given above.

For a whole week after he was determined in his mind to have one of that particular construction which is made to draw back horizontally, to hinder a passage; and to thrust forwards again to gain a passage,——of which sorts your worships might have seen three famous ones at *Spires* before its destruction,——and one now at *Brisac*, if I mistake not;——but my father advising my uncle *Toby*, with great earnestness, to have nothing more to do with thrusting bridges,——and my uncle foreseeing moreover that it would but perpetuate the memory of the corporal's misfortune,—— he changed his mind, for that of the marquis *d'Hôpital* 's invention, which the younger *Bernouilli* has so well and learnedly described, as your worships may see,——*Act. Erud. Lips.* an. 1695,——to these a lead weight is an eternal ballance, and keeps watch as well as a couple of centinels, inasmuch as the construction of them was a curve-line approximating to a cycloid, ——if not a cycloid itself.[2]

My uncle *Toby* understood the nature of a parabola as well as any man in *England*,——but was not quite such a master of the cycloid;——he talked however about it every day;——the bridge went not forwards.——We'll ask somebody about it, cried my uncle *Toby* to *Trim*.

CHAP. XXVI.

WHEN *Trim* came in and told my father, that Dr. *Slop* was in the kitchen, and busy in making a bridge,——my uncle *Toby*,——the affair of the jack-boots having just then raised a train of military ideas in his brain,——took it instantly for granted that Dr. *Slop* was making a model of the marquis *d'Hôpital*'s bridge.——'Tis very obliging in him, quoth my uncle *Toby*;——pray give my humble service to Dr. *Slop*, *Trim*, and tell him I thank him heartily.

Had my uncle *Toby*'s head been a *Savoyard*'s box,[1] and my father peeping in all the time at one end of it,——it could not have given him a more distinct conception of the operations in my uncle *Toby*'s imagination, than what he had; so notwithstanding the catapulta and battering-ram, and his bitter imprecation about them, he was just beginning to triumph———

When *Trim*'s answer, in an instant, tore the laurel from his brows, and twisted it to pieces.

CHAP. XXVII.

——THIS unfortunate draw-bridge of yours, quoth my father— God bless your honour, cried *Trim*, 'tis a bridge for master's nose.——In bringing him into the world with his vile instruments, he has crush'd his nose, *Susannah* says, as flat as a pancake to his face, and he is making a false bridge with a piece of cotton and a thin piece of whalebone out of *Susannah*'s stays, to raise it up.

———Lead me, brother *Toby*, cried my father, to my room this instant.

CHAP. XXVIII.

FROM the first moment I sat down to write my life for the amusement of the world, and my opinions for its instruction, has a cloud insensibly been gathering over my father.——A tide of little evils and distresses has been setting in against him.——Not one thing, as he observed himself, has gone right: and now is the storm thicken'd, and going to break, and pour down full upon his head.

I enter upon this part of my story in the most pensive and melancholy frame of mind, that ever sympathetic breast was touched with.———My nerves relax as I tell it.———Every line I write, I feel an abatement of the quickness of my pulse, and of that careless alacrity with it, which every day of my life prompts me to say and write a thousand things I should not.——And this moment that I last dipp'd my pen into my ink, I could not help taking notice what a cautious air of sad composure and solemnity there appear'd in my manner of doing it.——Lord! how different from the rash jerks, and hare-brain'd squirts thou art wont, *Tristram!* to transact it with in other humours,——dropping thy pen,—spurting thy ink about thy table and thy books,——as if thy pen and thy ink, thy books and thy furniture cost thee nothing.

CHAP. XXIX.

——I WON'T go about to argue the point with you,—'tis so,—and I am persuaded of it, madam, as much as can be, "That both man and woman bear pain or sorrow, (and, for aught I know, pleasure too) best in a horizontal position."

The moment my father got up into his chamber, he threw himself prostrate across his bed in the wildest disorder imaginable, but at the same time, in the most lamentable attitude of a man borne down with sorrows, that ever the eye of pity dropp'd a tear for.——The palm of his right hand, as he fell upon the bed, receiving his forehead, and covering the greatest part of both his eyes, gently sunk down with his head (his elbow giving way backwards) till his nose touch'd the quilt;——his left arm hung insensible over the side of the bed, his knuckles reclining upon the handle of the chamber pot, which peep'd out beyond the valance,——his right leg (his left being drawn up towards his body) hung half over the side of the bed, the edge of it pressing upon his shin-bone.——He felt it not. A fix'd, inflexible sorrow took possession of every line of his face.—He sigh'd once,——heaved his breast often,—but utter'd not a word.

An old set-stitch'd chair, valanced and fringed around with party-colour'd worsted bobs, stood at the bed's head, opposite to the side where my father's head reclined.——My uncle *Toby* sat him down in it.

Before an affliction is digested,——consolation ever comes too soon;——and after it is digested,——it comes too late: so that you see, madam, there is but a mark between these two, as fine almost as a hair, for a comforter to take aim at: my uncle *Toby* was always either on this side, or on that of it, and would often say, He believed in his heart, he could as soon hit the longitude;[1] for this reason, when he sat down in the chair, he drew the curtain a little forwards, and having a tear at every one's service,—he pull'd out a cambrick handkerchief,——gave a low sigh,——but held his peace.

CHAP. XXX.

——"*ALL is not gain that is got into the purse.*"——So that notwithstanding my father had the happiness of reading the oddest books in the universe, and had moreover, in himself, the oddest way of thinking, that ever man in it was bless'd with, yet it had this drawback upon him after all,——that it laid him open to some of the oddest and most whimsical distresses; of which this particular one which he sunk under at present is as strong an example as can be given.

No doubt, the breaking down of the bridge of a child's nose, by the edge of a pair of forceps,——however scientifically applied,——would vex any man in the world, who was at so much pains in begetting a child, as my father was,——yet it will not account for the extravagance of his affliction, or will it justify the unchristian manner he abandoned and surrender'd himself up to it.

To explain this, I must leave him upon the bed for half an hour,—— and my good uncle *Toby* in his old fringed chair sitting beside him.

CHAP. XXXI.

——I THINK it a very unreasonable demand,——cried my great grandfather, twisting up the paper, and throwing it upon the table. ——By this account, madam, you have but two thousand pounds fortune, and not a shilling more,——and you insist upon having three hundred pounds a year jointure for it.——

——"Because," replied my great grandmother, "you have little or no nose, Sir."———

Now, before I venture to make use of the word *Nose*[1] a second time, ——to avoid all confusion in what will be said upon it, in this interesting part of my story, it may not be amiss to explain my own meaning, and define, with all possible exactness and precision, what I would willingly be understood to mean by the term: being of opinion, that 'tis owing to the negligence and perverseness of writers, in despising this precaution, and to nothing else,——That all the polemical writings in divinity, are not as clear and demonstrative as those upon *a Will o' the Wisp*, or any other sound part of philosophy, and natural pursuit; in order to which, what have you to do, before you set out, unless you intend to go puzzling on to the day of judgment,———but to give the world a good definition, and stand to it, of the main word you have most occasion for,—changing it, Sir, as you would a guinea, into small coin?—which done,—let the father of confusion puzzle you, if he can; or put a different idea either into your head, or your reader's head, if he knows how.

In books of strict morality and close reasoning, such as this I am engaged in,—the neglect is inexcusable; and heaven is witness, how the world has revenged itself upon me for leaving so many openings to equivocal strictures,——and for depending so much as I have done, all along, upon the cleanliness of my reader's imaginations.

——————Here are two senses, cried *Eugenius*, as we walk'd along, pointing with the fore finger of his right hand to the word *Crevice*, in the fifty-second page of the second volume* of this book of books,——here are two senses, ——quoth he.——And here are two roads, replied I, turning short upon him,——a dirty and a clean one,——which shall we take?——The clean,—by all means, replied *Eugenius*. *Eugenius*, said I, stepping before him, and laying my hand upon his breast,——to define——is to distrust. ——Thus I triumph'd over *Eugenius*; but I triumph'd over him as I always do, like a fool.——'Tis my comfort however, I am not an obstinate one; therefore

I define a nose, as follows,——intreating only beforehand, and beseeching my readers, both male and female, of what age, complexion, and condition soever, for the love of God and their own souls, to guard against the temptations and suggestions of the devil, and suffer him by no art or wile to put any other ideas into their minds, than what I put into my definition.——For by the word *Nose*, throughout all this long chapter of noses, and in every other part of my work, where the word *Nose* occurs,—— I declare, by that word I mean a Nose, and nothing more, or less.

CHAP. XXXII.

——"BECAUSE," quoth my great grandmother, repeating the words again,——"you have little or no nose, Sir"——

S'death! cried my great grandfather, clapping his hand upon his nose,—'tis not so small as that comes to;—'tis a full inch longer than my father's.——Now, my great grandfather's nose was for all the world like unto the noses of all the men, women, and children, whom *Pantagruel* found dwelling upon the island of ENNASIN.[1]——By the way, if you would know the strange way of getting a-kin amongst so flat-nosed a

---

*Page 83 in the present edition.

people,——you must read the book;—find it out yourself, you never can.——

——'Twas shaped, Sir, like an ace of clubs.

——'Tis a full inch, continued my great grandfather, pressing up the ridge of his nose with his finger and thumb; and repeating his assertion, ——'tis a full inch longer, madam, than my father's—. You must mean your uncle's, replied my great grandmother.

——My great grandfather was convinced.—He untwisted the paper, and signed the article.

CHAP. XXXIII.

WHAT an unconscionable jointure, my dear, do we pay out of this small estate of ours, quoth my grandmother to my grandfather.

My father, replied my grandfather, had no more nose, my dear, saving the mark,[1] than there is upon the back of my hand.——

——Now, you must know, that my great grandmother outlived my grandfather twelve years; so that my father had the jointure to pay, a hundred and fifty pounds half yearly——(on *Michaelmas* and *Lady day*)[2]— during all that time.

No man discharged pecuniary obligations with a better grace than my father.———And as far as the hundred pounds went, he would fling it upon the table, guinea by guinea, with that spirited jerk of an honest welcome, which generous souls, and generous souls only, are able to fling down money: but as soon as ever he enter'd upon the odd fifty,—he generally gave a loud *Hem!*—rubb'd the side of his nose leisurely with the flat part of his fore finger,——inserted his hand cautiously betwixt his head and the cawl[3] of his wig,—look'd at both sides of every guinea, as he parted with it,—and seldom could get to the end of the fifty pounds, without pulling out his handkerchief, and wiping his temples.

Defend me, gracious heaven! from those persecuting spirits who make no allowances for these workings within us.—Never,—O never may I lay down in their tents,[4] who cannot relax the engine, and feel pity for the force of education, and the prevalence of opinions long derived from ancestors!

For three generations at least, this *tenet* in favour of long noses had gradually been taking root in our family.——TRADITION was all along on its side, and INTEREST was every half year stepping in to strengthen it; so that the whimsicality of my father's brain was far from having the whole honour of this, as it had of almost all his other strange notions.—— For in a great measure he might be said to have suck'd this in, with his mother's milk.[5] He did his part however.——If education planted the mistake, (in case it was one) my father watered it, and ripened it to perfection.

He would often declare, in speaking his thoughts upon the subject, that he did not conceive how the greatest family in *England* could stand it out against an uninterrupted succession of six or seven short noses.—And for the contrary reason, he would generally add, That it must be one of the greatest problems in civil life, where the same number of long and jolly noses following one another in a direct line, did not raise and hoist it up into the best vacancies in the kingdom.——He would often boast that the *Shandy* family rank'd very high in king *Harry* the VIIIth's time, but owed its rise to no state engine,—he would say,—but to that only;—— but that, like other families, he would add,—it had felt the turn of the wheel, and had never recovered the blow of my great grandfather's nose. ——It was an ace of clubs indeed, he would cry, shaking his head,—— and as vile a one for an unfortunate family, as ever turn'd up trumps.[6]

——Fair and softly, gentle reader!——where is thy fancy carrying thee?——If there is truth in man, by my great grandfather's nose, I mean the external organ of smelling, or that part of man which stands prominent in his face,—and which painters say, in good jolly noses and well-proportioned faces, should comprehend a full third,—that is, measuring downwards from the setting on of the hair.——

——What a life of it has an author, at this pass!

CHAP. XXXIV.

IT is a singular blessing, that nature has form'd the mind of man with the same happy backwardness and renitency against conviction, which is observed in old dogs,——"of not learning new tricks."

What a shuttlecock of a fellow would the greatest philosopher that ever existed, be whisk'd into at once, did he read such books, and observe such facts, and think such thoughts, as would eternally be making him change sides!

Now, my father, as I told you last year, detested all this.——He pick'd up an opinion, Sir, as a man in a state of nature picks up an apple.——It becomes his own,——and if he is a man of spirit, he would lose his life rather than give it up.——

I am aware, that *Didius* the great civilian, will contest this point; and cry out against me, Whence comes this man's right to this apple? *ex confesso,*[1] he will say,——things were in a state of nature.——The apple, as much *Frank*'s apple, as *John*'s. Pray, Mr. *Shandy*, what patent has he to shew for it? and how did it begin to be his? was it, when he set his heart upon it? or when he gather'd it? or when he chew'd it? or when he roasted it? or when he peel'd? or when he brought it home? or when he digested?—— or when he——?——. For 'tis plain, Sir, if the first picking up of the apple, made it not his,——that no subsequent act could.[2]

Brother *Didius, Tribonius*[3] will answer,——(now *Tribonius* the civilian and church lawyer's beard being three inches and a half and three eighths longer than *Didius* his beard,——I'm glad he takes up the cudgels for me, so I give myself no further trouble about the answer.)——Brother *Didius, Tribonius* will say, it is a decreed case, as you may find it in the fragments of *Gregorius* and *Hermogenes*'s codes, and in all the codes from *Justinian*'s down to the codes of *Louis* and *Des Eaux*,[4]——That the sweat of a man's brows, and the exsudations[5] of a man's brains, are as much a man's own property, as the breeches upon his backside;——which said exsudations, *&c.* being dropp'd upon the said apple by the labour of finding it, and picking it up; and being moreover indissolubly wafted,[6] and as indissolubly annex'd by the picker up, to the thing pick'd up, carried home, roasted, peel'd, eaten, digested, and so on;——'tis evident that the gatherer of the apple, in so doing, has mix'd up something which was his own, with the apple which was not his own, by which means he has acquired a property;—or, in other words, the apple is *John*'s apple.

By the same learned chain of reasoning my father stood up for all his opinions: he had spared no pains in picking them up, and the more they lay out of the common way, the better still was his title.——No mortal claim'd them: they had cost him moreover as much labour in cooking and digesting as in the case above, so that they might well and truely be said to be his own goods and chattles.——Accordingly he held fast by 'em, both by teeth and claws,——would fly to whatever he could lay his hands on,——and in a word, would intrench and fortify them round with as many circumvallations and breast-works, as my uncle *Toby* would a citadel.

There was one plaguy rub in the way of this,——the scarcity of materials to make any thing of a defence with, in case of a smart attack; inasmuch as few men of great genius had exercised their parts in writing books upon the subject of great noses: by the trotting of my lean horse, the thing is incredible! and I am quite lost in my understanding when I am considering what a treasure of precious time and talents together has been wasted upon worse subjects,——and how many millions of books in all languages, and in all possible types and bindings, have been fabricated upon points not half so much tending to the unity and peace-making of the world. What was to be had, however, he set the greater store by; and though my father would oft-times sport with my uncle *Toby*'s library, ——which, by the bye, was ridiculous enough,—yet at the very same time he did it, he collected every book and treatise which had been systematically wrote upon noses, with as much care as my honest uncle *Toby* had done those upon military architecture.——'Tis true, a much less table would have held them,—but that was not thy transgression, my dear uncle.——

Here,——but why here,——rather than in any other part of my story, ——I am not able to tell;——but here it is,——my heart stops me to pay to thee, my dear uncle *Toby*, once for all, the tribute I owe thy goodness. ——Here let me thrust my chair aside, and kneel down upon the ground, whilst I am pouring forth the warmest sentiments of love for thee, and veneration for the excellency of thy character, that ever virtue and nature kindled in a nephew's bosom.——Peace and comfort rest for evermore upon thy head!—Thou envied'st no man's comforts,——insulted'st no man's opinions.——Thou blackened'st no man's character,——devoured'st no man's bread: gently with faithful *Trim* behind thee, didst thou amble round the little circle of thy pleasures, jostling no creature in thy way;——for each one's service,[7] thou hadst a tear,——for each man's need, thou hadst a shilling.

Whilst I am worth one, to pay a weeder,——thy path from thy door to thy bowling green shall never be grown up.——Whilst there is a rood and a half of land in the *Shandy* family, thy fortifications, my dear uncle *Toby*, shall never be demolish'd.

CHAP. XXXV.

MY father's collection was not great, but to make amends, it was curious; and consequently, he was some time in making it; he had the great good fortune however to set off well, in getting *Bruscambille*'s prologue[1] upon long noses, almost for nothing,—for he gave no more for *Bruscambille* than three half crowns; owing indeed to the strong fancy which the stall-man saw my father had for the book the moment he laid his hands upon it.——There are not three *Bruscambilles* in *Christendom*,——said the stall-man, except what are chain'd up in the libraries of the curious. My father flung down the money as quick as lightening,—took *Bruscambille* into his bosom,——hyed home from *Piccadilly* to *Coleman*-street[2] with it, as he would have hyed home with a treasure, without taking his hand once off from *Bruscambille* all the way.

To those who do not yet know of which gender *Bruscambille* is,—— inasmuch as a prologue upon long noses might easily be done by either, ——'twill be no objection against the simile,—to say, That when my father got home, he solaced himself with *Bruscambille* after the manner, in which, 'tis ten to one, your worship solaced yourself with your first mistress,[3]——that is, from morning even unto night: which by the bye, how delightful soever it may prove to the inamorato,—is of little, or no entertainment at all, to by-standers,—Take notice, I go no farther with the simile,—my father's eye was greater than his appetite,—his zeal greater than his knowledge,——he cool'd——his affections became divided,——he got hold of *Prignitz*,—purchased *Scroderus*, *Andrea Paræus*,

Bouchet's Evening Conferences, and above all, the great and learned *Hafen Slawkenbergius*; of which, as I shall have much to say by and bye,——I will say nothing now.

CHAP. XXXVI.

O F all the tracts my father was at the pains to procure and study in support of his hypothesis, there was not any one wherein he felt a more cruel disappointment at first, than in the celebrated dialogue[1] between *Pamphagus* and *Cocles*, written by the chaste pen of the great and venerable *Erasmus*, upon the various uses and seasonable applications of long noses.
——Now don't let Satan, my dear girl, in this chapter, take advantage of any one spot of rising-ground to get astride of your imagination, if you can any ways help it; or if he is so nimble as to slip on,——let me beg of you, like an unback'd filly, *to frisk it, to squirt it, to jump it, to rear it, to bound it,—and to kick it, with long kicks and short kicks*, till like *Tickletoby*'s mare,[2] you break a strap or a crupper, and throw his worship into the dirt.————
You need not kill him.——

——And pray who was *Tickletoby*'s mare?—'tis just as discreditable and unscholar-like a question, Sir, as to have asked what year *(ab. urb. con.)*[3] the second Punic war broke out.—Who was *Tickletoby*'s mare!—Read, read, read, read, my unlearned reader! read,[4]—or by the knowledge of the great saint *Paraleipomenon*[5]—I tell you before-hand, you had better throw down the book at once; for without *much reading*, by which your reverence knows, I mean *much knowledge*, you will no more be able to penetrate the moral[6] of the next marbled page (motly[7] emblem of my work!) than the world with all its sagacity has been able to unraval the many opinions, transactions and truths which still lie mystically hid under the dark veil of the black one.

CHAPTER XXXVII

CHAP. XXXVII.

" *NIHIL me pœnitet hujus nasi*," quoth *Pamphagus*;—that is,——"My nose has been the making of me."——"*Nec est cur pœniteat*," replies *Cocles*; that is, "How the duce should such a nose fail?"[1]

The doctrine, you see, was laid down by *Erasmus*, as my father wished it, with the utmost plainness; but my father's disappointment was, in finding nothing more from so able a pen, but the bare fact itself; without any of that speculative subtilty or ambidexterity[2] of argumentation upon it, which heaven had bestow'd upon man on purpose to investigate truth and fight for her on all sides.——My father pish'd and pugh'd at first most terribly,—'tis worth something to have a good name. As the dialogue was of *Erasmus*, my father soon came to himself, and read it over and over again with great application, studying every word and every syllable of it thro' and thro' in its most strict and literal interpretation,—he could still make nothing of it, that way. Mayhaps there is more meant, than is said in it, quoth my father.—Learned men, brother *Toby*, don't write dialogues upon long noses for nothing.——I'll study the mystic and the allegoric sense,——here is some room to turn a man's self in, brother.

My father read on.——

Now, I find it needful to inform your reverences and worships, that besides the many nautical uses[3] of long noses enumerated by *Erasmus*, the dialogist affirmeth that a long nose is not without its domestic conveniences also, for that in a case of distress,—and for want of a pair of bellows, it will do excellently well, *ad excitandum focum*, (to stir up the fire.)

Nature had been prodigal in her gifts to my father beyond measure, and had sown the seeds of verbal criticism as deep within him, as she had done the seeds of all other knowledge,—so that he had got out his penknife, and was trying experiments upon the sentence, to see if he could not scratch some better sense into it.—I've got within a single letter, brother *Toby*, cried my father, of *Erasmus* his mystic meaning.—You are near enough, brother, replied my uncle, in all conscience.——Pshaw! cried my father, scratching on,—I might as well be seven miles off.—I've done it,——said my father, snapping his fingers.—See, my dear brother *Toby*, how I have mended the sense.—But you have marr'd a word, replied my uncle *Toby.*—My father put on his spectacles,—bit his lip,—and tore out the leaf in a passion.

CHAP. XXXVIII.

O *Slawkenbergius!* thou faithful analyzer of my *Disgrázias,*[1]——thou sad foreteller of so many of the whips and short turns, which in one stage or other of my life have come slap upon me from the shortness of my nose, and no other cause, that I am conscious of.——Tell me, *Slawkenbergius!* what secret impulse was it? what intonation of voice? whence came it? how did it sound in thy ears?—art thou sure thou heard'st it?—which first cried out to thee,—go,—go, *Slawkenbergius!* dedicate the labours of thy life,——neglect thy pastimes,—call forth all the powers and faculties of thy nature,——macerate thyself in the service of mankind, and write a grand FOLIO for them, upon the subject of their noses.

How the communication was conveyed into *Slawkenbergius*'s sensorium, ——so that *Slawkenbergius* should know whose finger touch'd the key, ——and whose hand it was that blew the bellows,——as *Hafen Slawkenbergius* has been dead and laid in his grave above fourscore and ten years, ——we can only raise conjectures.

Slawkenbergius was play'd upon, for aught I know, like one of *Whitfield*'s disciples,[2]——that is, with such a distinct intelligence, Sir, of which of the two *masters* it was, that had been practising upon his *instrument,*—— as to make all reasoning upon it needless.

——For in the account which *Hafen Slawkenbergius* gives the world of his motives and occasions for writing, and spending so many years of his life upon this one work—towards the end of his prologomena, which by the bye should have come first,——but the bookbinder has most injudiciously placed it betwixt the analitical contents of the book, and the book itself,——he informs his reader, that ever since he had arrived at the age of discernment, and was able to sit down coolly, and consider within himself the true state and condition of man, and distinguish the main end and design of his being;——or,——to shorten my translation, for *Slawkenbergius*'s book is in *Latin,* and not a little prolix in this passage,

—— ever since I understood, quoth *Slawkenbergius*, any thing,—— or rather *what was what*,—— and could perceive that the point of long noses had been too loosely handled by all who had gone before;—— have I, *Slawkenbergius*, felt a strong impulse, with a mighty and an unresistible call within me, to gird up myself[3] to this undertaking.

And to do justice to *Slawkenbergius*, he has entered the list with a stronger lance, and taken a much larger career in it, than any one man who had ever entered it before him,—— and indeed, in many respects, deserves to be *en-nich'd* as a prototype for all writers, of voluminous works at least, to model their books by,—— for he has taken in, Sir, the whole subject,— examined every part of it, *dialectically*,— then brought it into full day; dilucidating[4] it with all the light which either the collision of his own natural parts could strike,—— or the profoundest knowledge of the sciences had impowered him to cast upon it,—— collating, collecting and compiling,— begging, borrowing, and stealing, as he went along, all that had been wrote or wrangled thereupon in the schools and porticos of the learned: so that *Slawkenbergius* his book may properly be considered, not only as a model,— but as a thorough-stitch'd DIGEST and regular institute of *noses*; comprehending in it, all that is, or can be needful to be known about them.

For this cause it is, that I forbear to speak of so many (otherwise) valuable books and treatises of my father's collecting, wrote either, plump upon noses,— or collaterally touching them;—— such for instance as *Prignitz*, now lying upon the table before me, who with infinite learning, and from the most candid and scholar-like examination of above four thousand different skulls, in upwards of twenty charnel houses in *Silesia*,[5] which he had rummaged,— has informed us, that the mensuration and configuration of the osseous or boney parts of human noses, in any *given* tract of country, except *Crim Tartary*,[6] where they are all crush'd down by the thumb, so that no judgment can be formed upon them,—— are much nearer alike, than the world imagines;—— the difference amongst them, being, he says, a mere trifle, not worth taking notice of,—— but that the size and jollity of every individual nose, and by which one nose ranks above another, and bears a higher price, is owing to the cartilagenous and muscular parts of it, into whose ducts and sinuses the blood and animal spirits being impell'd, and driven by the warmth and force of the imagination, which is but a step from it, (bating the case of ideots, whom *Prignitz*, who had lived many years in *Turky*, supposes under the more immediate tutelage of heaven)[7]—— it so happens, and ever must, says *Prignitz*, that the excellency of the nose is in a direct arithmetical proportion to the excellency of the wearer's fancy.

It is for the same reason, that is, because 'tis all comprehended in *Slawkenbergius*, that I say nothing likewise of *Scroderus (Andrea)* who all the world knows, set himself to oppugn *Prignitz* with great violence,—— proving it in his own way, first *logically*, and then by a series of stubborn facts, "That so far was *Prignitz* from the truth, in affirming that the fancy begat the nose, that on the contrary,—the nose begat the fancy."

——The learned suspected *Scroderus*, of an indecent sophism in this,—— and *Prignitz* cried out aloud in the dispute, that *Scroderus* had shifted the idea upon him,—but *Scroderus* went on, maintaining his thesis.——

My father was just balancing within himself, which of the two sides he should take in this affair; when *Ambrose Paræus*[8] decided it in a moment, and by overthrowing the systems, both of *Prignitz* and *Scroderus*, drove my father out of both sides of the controversy at once.

Be witness——

I don't acquaint the learned reader,—in saying it, I mention it only to shew the learned, I know the fact myself.——

That this *Ambrose Paræus* was chief surgeon and nose-mender to *Francis* the ninth of *France*, and in high credit with him and the two preceding, or succeeding kings (I know not which)—and that except in the slip he made in his story of *Taliacotius*'s noses, and his manner of setting them on,—— was esteemed by the whole college of physicians at that time, as more knowing in matters of noses, than any one who had ever taken them in hand.

Now *Ambrose Paræus* convinced my father, that the true and efficient cause[9] of what had engaged so much the attention of the world, and upon which *Prignitz* and *Scroderus* had wasted so much learning and fine parts,—— was neither this nor that,——but that the length and goodness of the nose was owing simply to the softness and flaccidity in the nurse's breast,—— as the flatness and shortness of *puisne*[10] noses was, to the firmness and elastic repulsion of the same organ of nutrition in the hale and lively,— which, tho' happy for the woman, was the undoing of the child, inasmuch as his nose was so snubb'd, so rebuff'd, so rebated, and so refrigerated thereby, as never to arrive *ad mensuram suam legitimam*;[11]——but that in case of the flaccidity and softness of the nurse or mother's breast,—by sinking into it, quoth *Paræus*, as into so much butter, the nose was comforted, nourish'd, plump'd up, refresh'd, refocillated,[12] and set a growing for ever.

I have but two things to observe of *Paræus*; first, that he proves and explains all this with the utmost chastity and decorum of expression:— for which may his soul for ever rest in peace!

And, secondly, that besides the systems of *Prignitz* and *Scroderus*, which *Ambrose Paræus* his hypothesis effectually overthrew,——it overthrew at the same time the system of peace and harmony of our family; and for three days together, not only embroiled matters between my father and my mother, but turn'd likewise the whole house and every thing in it, except my uncle *Toby*, quite upside down.

Such a ridiculous tale of a dispute between a man and his wife, never surely in any age or country got vent through the key-hole of a street-door.

My mother, you must know,——but I have fifty things more necessary to let you know first,——I have a hundred difficulties which I have promised to clear up, and a thousand distresses and domestic misadventures crouding in upon me thick and three-fold, one upon the neck of another,——a cow broke in (to-morrow morning) to my uncle *Toby*'s fortifications, and eat up two ratios[13] and half of dried grass, tearing up the sods with it, which faced his horn-work and covered way.— *Trim* insists upon being tried by a court-martial,—the cow to be shot,— *Slop* to be *crucifix'd*,[14]— myself to be *tristram'd*, and at my very baptism made a martyr of;—— poor unhappy devils that we all are!—I want swaddling,——but there is no time to be lost in exclamations.——I have left my father lying across his bed, and my uncle *Toby* in his old fringed chair, sitting beside him, and promised I would go back to them in half an hour, and five and thirty minutes are laps'd already.——Of all the perplexities a mortal author was ever seen in,——this certainly is the greatest, for I have *Hafen Slawkenberg-ius*'s folio, Sir, to finish——a dialogue between my father and my uncle *Toby*, upon the solution of *Prignitz, Scroderus, Ambrose Paræus, Ponocrates* and *Grangousier*[15] to relate,—a tale out of *Slawkenbergius* to translate, and all this in five minutes less, than no time at all;—such a head!—would to heaven! my enemies only saw the inside of it.

CHAP. XXXIX.

THERE was not any one scene more entertaining in our family,——and to do it justice in this point;——and I here put off my cap and lay it upon the table close beside my ink-horn, on purpose to make my declaration to the world concerning this one article, the more solemn,——that I believe in my soul, (unless my love and partiality to my understanding blinds me) the hand of the supreme Maker and first Designer of all things, never made or put a family together, (in that period at least of it, which I have sat down to write the story of)——where the characters of it were cast or contrasted with so dramatic a felicity as ours was, for this end; or in which the capacities of affording such exquisite scenes, and the powers of shifting them perpetually from morning to night, were lodged and intrusted with so unlimited a confidence, as in the SHANDY-FAMILY.

Not any one of these was more diverting, I say, in this whimsical theatre of ours,——than what frequently arose out of this self-same chapter of long noses,——especially when my father's imagination was heated with the enquiry, and nothing would serve him but to heat my uncle *Toby*'s too.

My uncle *Toby* would give my father all possible fair play in this attempt; and with infinite patience would sit smoking his pipe for whole hours together, whilst my father was practising upon his head, and trying every accessible avenue to drive *Prignitz* and *Scroderus*'s solutions into it.

Whether they were above my uncle *Toby*'s reason,——or contrary to it,——or that his brain was like *damp* tinder, and no spark could possibly take hold,——or that it was so full of saps, mines, blinds, curtins, and such military disqualifications to his seeing clearly into *Prignitz* and *Scroderus*'s doctrines,——I say not,——let school-men—scullions, anatomists, and engineers, fight for it amongst themselves.——

'Twas some misfortune, I make no doubt, in this affair, that my father had every word of it to translate for the benefit of my uncle *Toby*, and render out of *Slawkenbergius*'s *Latin*, of which, as he was no great master, his translation was not always of the purest,——and generally least so where 'twas most wanted,——this naturally open'd a door to a second misfortune;——that in the warmer paroxisms of his zeal to open my uncle *Toby*'s eyes——my father's ideas run on, as much faster than the translation, as the translation outmoved my uncle *Toby*'s;——neither the one or the other added much to the perspicuity of my father's lecture.

CHAP. XL.

THE gift of ratiocination and making syllogisms,—I mean in man,—for in superior classes of beings, such as angels and spirits,—'tis all done, may it please your worships, as they tell me, by INTUITION;—and beings inferior, as your worships all know,——syllogize by their noses:[1] though there is an island swiming in the sea, though not altogether at its ease, whose inhabitants, if my intelligence deceives me not, are so wonderfully gifted, as to syllogize after the same fashion, and oft-times to make very well out too:——but that's neither here nor there——

The gift of doing it as it should be, amongst us,—or the great and principal act of ratiocination in man, as logicians tell us, is the finding out the agreement or disagreement of two ideas one with another, by the intervention of a third; (called the *medius terminus)* just as a man, as *Locke* well observes, by a yard, finds two mens nine-pin-alleys to be of the same length, which could not be brought together, to measure their equality, by *juxta-position*.[2]

Had the same great reasoner looked on, as my father illustrated his systems of noses, and observed my uncle *Toby*'s deportment,—what great attention he gave to every word,—and as oft as he took his pipe from his mouth, with what wonderful seriousness he contemplated the length of it,—surveying it transversely as he held it betwixt his finger and his thumb,—then foreright,—then this way, and then that, in all its possible directions and foreshortenings,——he would have concluded my uncle *Toby* had got hold of the *medius terminus*; and was syllogizing and measuring with it the truth of each hypothesis of long noses, in order as my father laid them before him. This by the bye, was more than my father wanted,—his aim in all the pains he was at in these philosophic lectures,—was to enable my uncle *Toby* not to *discuss*,——but *comprehend*——to *hold* the grains and scruples of learning,—not to *weigh* them.—My uncle *Toby*, as you will read in the next chapter, did neither the one or the other.

CHAP. XLI.

'TIS a pity, cried my father one winter's night, after a three hours painful translation of *Slawkenbergius*,—'tis a pity, cried my father, putting my mother's thread-paper into the book for a mark, as he spoke ——that truth, brother *Toby*, should shut herself up in such impregnable fastnesses, and be so obstinate as not to surrender herself sometimes up upon the closest siege.——

Now it happened then, as indeed it had often done before, that my uncle *Toby*'s fancy, during the time of my father's explanation of *Prignitz* to him,——having nothing to stay it there, had taken a short flight to the bowling-green;——his body might as well have taken a turn there too, ——so that with all the semblance of a deep school-man intent upon the *medius terminus*,——my uncle *Toby* was in fact as ignorant of the whole lecture, and all its pro's and con's, as if my father had been translating *Hafen Slawkenbergius* from the *Latin* tongue into the *Cherokeè*. But the word *siege*, like a talismanic power, in my father's metaphor, wafting back my uncle *Toby*'s fancy, quick as a note could follow the touch,——he open'd his ears,—and my father observing that he took his pipe out of his mouth, and shuffled his chair nearer the table, as with a desire to profit,—my father with great pleasure began his sentence again,——changing only the plan, and dropping the metaphor of the siege of it, to keep clear of some dangers my father apprehended from it.

'Tis a pity, said my father, that truth can only be on one side, brother *Toby*,—considering what ingenuity these learned men have all shewn in their solutions of noses.——Can noses be dissolved? replied my uncle *Toby*.

——My father thrust back his chair,——rose up,——put on his hat, ——took four long strides to the door,—jerked it open,—thrust his head half way out,—shut the door again,—took no notice of the bad hinge,— returned to the table,—pluck'd my mother's thread-paper out of *Slawkenbergius*'s book,—went hastily to his bureau,—walk'd slowly back, twisting my mother's thread-paper about his thumb,—unbutton'd his waistcoat, ——threw my mother's thread-paper into the fire,—bit her sattin pin-cushion in two, fill'd his mouth with bran,—confounded it;—but mark!—

the oath of confusion was levell'd at my uncle *Toby*'s brain,——which was e'en confused enough already,——the curse came charged only with the bran,—the bran, may it please your honours,—was no more than powder to the ball.

'Twas well my father's passions lasted not long; for so long as they did last, they led him a busy life on't, and it is one of the most unaccountable problems that ever I met with in my observations of human nature, that nothing should prove my father's mettle so much, or make his passions go off so like gun-powder, as the unexpected strokes his science met with from the quaint simplicity of my uncle *Toby*'s questions.——Had ten dozen of hornets stung him behind in so many different places all at one time,—he could not have exerted more mechanical functions in fewer seconds,—or started half so much, as with one single *quære*[1] of three words unseasonably popping in full upon him in his hobbyhorsical career.

'Twas all one to my uncle *Toby*,—he smoaked his pipe on, with unvaried composure,—his heart never intended offence to his brother,—and as his head could seldom find out where the sting of it lay,——he always gave my father the credit of cooling by himself.——He was five minutes and thirty-five seconds about it in the present case.

By all that's good! said my father, swearing, as he came to himself, and taking the oath out of *Ernulphus*'s digest of curses,—(though to do my father justice it was a fault (as he told Dr. *Slop* in the affair of *Ernulphus)* which he as seldom committed as any man upon earth.)——By all that's good and great! brother *Toby*, said my father, if it was not for the aids of philosophy, which befriend one so much as they do,—you would put a man beside all temper.—Why, by the *solutions* of noses, of which I was telling you, I meant as you might have known, had you favoured me with one grain of attention, the various accounts which learned men of different kinds of knowledge have given the world, of the causes of short and long noses.—There is no cause but one, replied my uncle *Toby*,—why one man's nose is longer than another's, but because that God pleases to have it so.—That is *Grangousier*'s solution,[2] said my father.—'Tis he, continued my uncle *Toby*, looking up, and not regarding my father's interruption, who makes us all, and frames and puts us together in such forms and proportions, and for such ends, as is agreeable to his infinite wisdom.—— 'Tis a pious account, cried my father, but not philosophical,—there is more religion in it than sound science. 'Twas no inconsistent part of my uncle *Toby*'s character,——that he feared God, and reverenced religion.

——So the moment my father finished his remark,——my uncle *Toby* fell a whistling *Lillabullero*, with more zeal (though more out of tune) than usual.——

What is become of my wife's thread-paper?

CHAP. XLII.

NO matter,——as an appendage to seamstressy, the thread-paper might be of some consequence to my mother,——of none to my father, as a mark in *Slawkenbergius*. *Slawkenbergius* in every page of him was a rich treasury of inexhaustible knowledge to my father,——he could not open him amiss; and he would often say in closing the book, that if all the arts and sciences in the world, with the books which treated of them, were lost,——should the wisdom and policies of governments, he would say, through disuse, ever happen to be forgot, and all that statesmen had wrote, or caused to be written, upon the strong or the weak sides of courts and kingdoms, should they be forgot also,——and *Slawkenbergius* only left,—— there would be enough in him in all conscience, he would say, to set the world a-going again. A treasure therefore was he indeed! an institute of all that was necessary to be known of noses, and every thing else,——at *matin*, noon, and vespers was *Hafen Slawkenbergius* his recreation and delight: 'twas for ever in his hands,——you would have sworn, Sir, it had been a canon's prayer-book,——so worn, so glazed, so contrited and attrited[1] was it with fingers and with thumbs in all its parts, from one end even unto the other.

I am not such a bigot to *Slawkenbergius*, as my father;——there is a fund in him, no doubt; but in my opinion, the best, I don't say the most profitable, but the most amusing part of *Hafen Slawkenbergius*, is his tales,——and, considering he was a *German*, many of them told not without fancy:—— these take up his second book, containing nearly one half of his folio, and are comprehended in ten decads, each decad containing ten tales.—— Philosophy is not built upon tales; and therefore 'twas certainly wrong in *Slawkenbergius* to send them into the world by that name;——there are a few of them in his eighth, ninth, and tenth decads, which I own seem rather playful and sportive, than speculative,—but in general they are to be looked upon by the learned as a detail of so many independent facts, all of them turning round somehow or other upon the main hinges of his subject, and collected by him with great fidelity, and added to his work as so many illustrations upon the doctrines of noses.

As we have leisure enough upon our hands,—if you give me leave, madam, I'll tell you the ninth tale of his tenth decad.

THE END OF THE THIRD VOLUME.

THE

L I F E

A N D

O P I N I O N S

O F

TRISTRAM SHANDY,

G E N T L E M A N.

Multitudinis imperitæ non formido judicia; meis
tamen, rogo, parcant opufculis —— in quibus
fuit propofiti femper, a jocis ad feria, a feriis
·viciffim ad jocos tranfire.

JOAN. SARESBERIENSIS,
Epifcopus Lugdun.

V O L. IV.

L O N D O N:
Printed for R. and J. DODSLEY in *Pall-Mall.*
M. DCC. LXI.

(Height of original type-page 121 mm.)

SLAWKENBERGII
Fabella.*[1]

VESPERA quâdam frigidulâ, posteriori in parte mensis Augusti, *peregrinus, mulo fusco colore insidens, manticâ a tergo, paucis indusijs, binis calceis, braccisque sericis coccinejs repletâ* Argentoratum *ingressus est.*

Militi eum percontanti, quum portus intraret, dixit, se apud Nasorum promontorium fuisse, Francofurtum proficisci, et Argentoratum, transitu ad fines Sarmatiæ mensis intervallo, reversurum.

Miles peregrini in faciem suspexit—Di boni, nova forma nasi!

At multum mihi profuit, inquit peregrinus, carpum amento extrahens, e quo pependit acinaces: Loculo manum inseruit; & magnâ cum urbanitate, pilei parte anteriore tactâ manu sinistrâ, ut extendit dextram, militi florinum dedit et processit.

Dolet mihi, ait miles, tympanistam nanum et valgum alloquens, virum adeo urbanum vaginam perdidisse; itinerari haud poterit nudâ acinaci, neque vaginam toto Argentorato, *habilem inveniet.—Nullam unquam habui, respondit peregrinus respiciens,—seque comiter inclinans—hoc more gesto, nudam acinacem elevans, mulo lentò progrediente, ut nasum tueri possim.*

Non immerito, benigne peregrine, respondit miles.
Nihili æstimo, ait ille tympanista, e pergamenâ factitius est.

---

* As *Hafen Slawkenbergius de Nasis* is extremely scarce, it may not be unacceptable to the learned reader to see the specimen of a few pages of his original; I will make no reflection upon it, but that his story-telling Latin is much more concise than his philosophic—and, I think, has more of Latinity in it.

SLAWKENBERGIUS'S
TALE.

IT was one cool refreshing evening, at the close of a very sultry day, in the latter end of the month of *August*, when a stranger, mounted upon a dark mule, with a small cloak-bag behind him, containing a few shirts, a pair of shoes, and a crimson-sattin pair of breeches, entered the town of *Strasburg.*[2]

He told the centinel, who questioned him as he entered the gates, that he had been at the promontory of Noses—was going on to *Frankfort*—and should be back again at *Strasburg* that day month, in his way to the borders of *Crim-Tartary.*

The centinel looked up into the stranger's face—never saw such a nose in his life!

—I have made a very good venture of it, quoth the stranger—so slipping his wrist out of the loop of a black ribban, to which a short scymetar was hung: He put his hand into his pocket, and with great courtesy touching the forepart of his cap with his left-hand, as he extended his right—he put a florin into the centinel's hand, and passed on.

It grieves me, said the centinel, speaking to a little dwarfish bandy-leg'd drummer, that so courteous a soul should have lost his scabbard[3]—he cannot travel without one to his scymetar, and will not be able to get a scabbard to fit it in all *Strasburg.*——I never had one, replied the stranger, looking back to the centinel, and putting his hand up to his cap as he spoke——I carry it, continued he, thus—holding up his naked scymetar, his mule moving on slowly all the time, on purpose to defend my nose.

It is well worth it, gentle stranger, replied the centinel.

—'Tis not worth a single stiver, said the bandy-leg'd drummer—'tis a nose of parchment.

Prout christianus sum, inquit miles, nasus ille, ni sexties major sit, meo esset conformis.

Crepitare[4] audivi ait tympanista.

Mehercule! sanguinem emisit, respondit miles.

Miseret me, inquit tympanista, qui non ambo tetigimus!

Eodem temporis puncto, quo hæc res argumentata fuit inter militem et tympanistam, disceptabatur ibidem tubicine & uxore suâ, qui tunc accesserunt, et peregrino prætereunte, restiterunt.

Quantus nasus! æque longus est, ait tubicina, ac tuba.

Et ex eodem metallo, ait tubicen, velut sternutamento audias.

Tantum abest, respondit illa, quod fistulam dulcedine vincit.

Æneus est, ait tubicen.

Nequaquam, respondit uxor.

Rursum affirmo, ait tubicen, quod æneus est.

Rem penitus explorabo;[5] prius, enim digito tangam, ait uxor, quam dormivero.

Mulus peregrini, gradu lento progressus est, ut unumquodque verbum controversiæ, non tantum inter militem et tympanistam, verum etiam inter tubicinem et uxorem ejus, audiret.

Nequaquam, ait ille, in muli collum fræna demittens, & manibus ambabus in pectus positis, (mulo lentè progrediente) nequaquam ait ille, respiciens, non necesse est ut res isthæc dilucidata foret. Minime gentium! meus nasus nunquam tangetur, dum spiritus hos reget artus—ad quid agendum? ait uxor burgomagistri.

Peregrinus illi non respondit. Votum faciebat tunc temporis sancto Nicolao, quo facto, sinum dextram inserens, e quâ negligenter pependit acinaces, lento gradu processit per plateam Argentorati latam quæ ad diversorium templo ex adversum ducit.

Peregrinus mulo descendens stabulo includi, & manticam inferri jussit:

As I am a true catholic—except that it is six times as big—'tis a nose, said the centinel, like my own.

—I heard it crackle, said the drummer.

By dunder, said the centinel, I saw it bleed.

What a pity, cried the bandy-legg'd drummer, we did not both touch it!

At the very time that this dispute was maintaining by the centinel and the drummer—was the same point debating betwixt a trumpeter and a trumpeter's wife, who were just then coming up, and had stopped to see the stranger pass by.

Benedicity![6]——What a nose! 'tis as long, said the trumpeter's wife, as a trumpet.

And of the same mettle, said the trumpeter, as you hear by its sneezing.

—'Tis as soft as a flute, said she.

—'Tis brass, said the trumpeter.

—'Tis a pudding's end—said his wife.

I tell thee again, said the trumpeter, 'tis a brazen nose.

I'll know the bottom of it, said the trumpeter's wife, for I will touch it with my finger before I sleep.

The stranger's mule moved on at so slow a rate, that he heard every word of the dispute, not only betwixt the centinel and the drummer; but betwixt the trumpeter and the trumpeter's wife.

No! said he, dropping his reins upon his mule's neck, and laying both his hands upon his breast, the one over the other in a saint-like position (his mule going on easily all the time) No! said he, looking up,—I am not such a debtor to the world—slandered and disappointed as I have been——as to give it that conviction—no! said he, my nose shall never be touched whilst heaven gives me strength—To do what? said a burgo-master's wife.

The stranger took no notice of the burgomaster's wife—he was making a vow to saint *Nicolas*;[7] which done, having uncrossed his arms with the same solemnity with which he crossed them, he took up the reins of his bridle with his left-hand, and putting his right-hand into his bosom, with his scymetar hanging loosely to the wrist of it, he rode on as slowly as one foot of the mule could follow another thro' the principal streets of *Strasburg*, till chance brought him to the great inn in the market-place over-against the church.

The moment the stranger alighted, he ordered his mule to be led into *quâ apertâ et coccineis sericis femoralibus extractis cum argenteo laciniato* Περιζομαῖε,[8] *his sese induit, statimque, acinaci in manu, ad forum deambulavit.*

Quod ubi peregrinus esset ingressus, uxorem tubicinis obviam euntem aspicit; illico cursum flectit, metuens ne nasus suus exploraretur, atque ad diversorium regressus est—exuit se vestibus; braccas coccineas sericas manticæ imposuit mulumque educi jussit.

Francofurtum proficiscor, ait ille, et Argentoratum quatuor abhinc hebdomadis revertar.
Bene curasti hoc jumentum (ait) muli faciem manu demulcens——me, manticamque meam, plus sexcentis mille passibus portavit.

Longa via est! respondit hospes, nisi plurimum esset negoti.——Enimvero ait peregrinus a nasorum promontorio redij, et nasum speciosissimum, egregiosissimumque quem unquam quisquam sortitus est, acquisivi!

Dum peregrinus hanc miram rationem, de seipso reddit, hospes et uxor ejus, oculis intentis, peregrini nasum contemplantur—Per sanctos, sanctasque omnes, ait hospitis uxor, nasis duodecim maximis, in toto Argentorato major est!—estne ait illa mariti in aurem insusurrans, nonne est nasus prægrandis?

Dolus inest, anime mi, ait hospes—nasus est falsus.—

Verus est, respondit uxor.—
Ex abiete factus est, ait ille, terebinthinum olet——
Carbunculus inest, ait uxor.
Mortuus est nasus, respondit hospes.
Vivus est, ait illa,—— & si ipsa vivam tangam.

Votum feci sancto Nicolao, ait peregrinus, nasum meum intactum fore usque ad—Quodnam tempus? illico respondit illa.

Minime tangetur,[9] inquit ille (manibus in pectus compositis) usque ad illam the stable, and his cloak-bag to be brought in; then opening, and taking out of it, his crimson-sattin breeches, with a silver-fringed——(appendage to them, which I dare not translate)——he put his breeches, with his fringed cod-piece on, and forthwith with his short scymetar in his hand, walked out to the grand parade.

The stranger had just taken three turns upon the parade, when he perceived the trumpeter's wife at the opposite side of it—so turning short, in pain lest his nose should be attempted, he instantly went back to his inn——undressed himself, packed up his crimson-sattin breeches, &c. in his cloak-bag, and called for his mule.

I am going forwards, said the stranger, for *Frankfort*——and shall be back at *Strasburg* this day month.

I hope, continued the stranger, stroking down the face of his mule with his left-hand as he was going to mount it, that you have been kind to this faithful slave of mine——it has carried me and my cloak-bag, continued he, tapping the mule's back, above six hundred leagues.

—'Tis a long journey, Sir, replied the master of the inn——unless a man has great business.—Tut! tut! said the stranger, I have been at the promontory of Noses; and have got me one of the goodliest and jolliest, thank heaven, that ever fell to a single man's lot.

Whilst the stranger was giving this odd account of himself, the master of the inn and his wife kept both their eyes fixed full upon the stranger's nose—By saint *Radagunda*,[10] said the inn-keeper's wife to herself, there is more of it than in any dozen of the largest noses put together in all *Strasburg!* is it not, said she, whispering her husband in his ear, is it not a noble nose?

'Tis an imposture, my dear, said the master of the inn—'tis a false nose.—

'Tis a true nose, said his wife.—

'Tis made of fir-tree, said he,—I smell the turpentine.[11]—

There's a pimple on it, said she.

'Tis a dead nose, replied the inn-keeper.

'Tis a live nose, and if I am alive myself, said the inn-keeper's wife, I will touch it.

I have made a vow to saint *Nicolas* this day, said the stranger, that my nose shall not be touched till——Here the stranger, suspending his voice, looked up—Till when? said she hastily.

It never shall be touched, said he, clasping his hands and bringing

horam—Quam horam? ait illa.—Nullam, respondit peregrinus, donec pervenio,
ad—Quem locum,—obsecro? ait illa—Peregrinus nil respondens mulo consenso
discessit.

them close to his breast, till that hour——What hour? cried the inn-keeper's wife.——Never!—never! said the stranger, never till I am got—For heaven sake into what place? said she.—The stranger rode away without saying a word.

The stranger had not got half a league on his way towards *Frankfort*, before all the city of *Strasburg* was in an uproar about his nose. The *Compline*-bells were just ringing to call the *Strasburgers* to their devotions, and shut up the duties of the day in prayer:——no soul in all *Strasburg* heard 'em—the city was like a swarm of bees——men, women, and children (the *Compline*-bells tinkling all the time) flying here and there—in at one door, out at another—this way and that way—long ways and cross ways—up one street, down another street—in at this ally, out at that——did you see it? did you see it? did you see it? O! did you see it?—who saw it? who did see it? for mercy's sake, who saw it?

Alack o'day! I was at vespers!——I was washing, I was starching, I was scouring, I was quilting—GOD help me! I never saw it—I never touch'd it!——would I had been a centinel, a bandy-leg'd drummer, a trumpeter, a trumpeter's wife, was the general cry and lamentation in every street and corner of *Strasburg*.

Whilst all this confusion and disorder triumphed throughout the great city of *Strasburg*, was the courteous stranger going on as gently upon his mule in his way to *Frankfort*, as if he had had no concern at all in the affair—talking all the way he rode in broken sentences, sometimes to his mule—sometimes to himself——sometimes to his Julia.

O Julia, my lovely Julia!—nay I cannot stop to let thee bite that thistle—that ever the suspected tongue of a rival should have robbed me of enjoyment when I was upon the point of tasting it.—

—Pugh!—'tis nothing but a thistle—never mind it—thou shalt have a better supper at night.—

——Banish'd from my country—my friends—from thee.—

Poor devil, thou'rt sadly tired with thy journey!—come—get on a little faster—there's nothing in my cloak-bag but two shirts—a crimson-sattin pair of breeches, and a fringed—Dear Julia!

—But why to *Frankfort*?—is it that there is a hand unfelt, which secretly is conducting me through these meanders and unsuspected tracts?—

—Stumbling! by saint *Nicolas!* every step——why at this rate we shall be all night in getting in——

—To happiness—or am I to be the sport of fortune and slander—

destined to be driven forth unconvicted—unheard—untouched——if so, why did I not stay at *Strasburg*, where justice——but I had sworn!—Come, thou shalt drink—to *St. Nicolas*—O Julia!——What dost thou prick up thy ears at?—'tis nothing but a man, *&c.*——

The stranger rode on communing in this manner with his mule and Julia—till he arrived at his inn, where, as soon as he arrived, he alighted—saw his mule, as he had promised it, taken good care of——took off his cloak-bag, with his crimson-sattin breeches, *&c.* in it——called for an omelet to his supper, went to his bed about twelve o'clock, and in five minutes fell fast asleep.

It was about the same hour when the tumult in *Strasburg* being abated for that night,——the *Strasburgers* had all got quietly into their beds—but not like the stranger, for the rest either of their minds or bodies; queen *Mab*,[12] like an elf as she was, had taken the stranger's nose, and without reduction of its bulk, had that night been at the pains of slitting and dividing it into as many noses of different cuts and fashions, as there were heads in *Strasburg* to hold them. The abbess of *Quedlingberg*,[13] who, with the four great dignitaries of her chapter, the prioress, the deaness, the sub-chantress, and senior canoness, had that week come to *Strasburg* to consult the university upon a case of conscience relating to their placket holes[14]—was ill all the night.

The courteous stranger's nose had got perched upon the top of the pineal gland of her brain, and made such rousing work in the fancies of the four great dignitaries of her chapter, they could not get a wink of sleep the whole night thro' for it——there was no keeping a limb still amongst them—in short, they got up like so many ghosts.

The penitentiaries of the third order of saint *Francis*[15]——the nuns of mount *Calvary*[16]—the *Præmonstratenses*[17]——the *Clunienses**[18]—the *Carthusians*,[19] and all the severer orders of nuns who lay that night in blankets or hair-cloth, were still in a worse condition than the abbess of *Quedlingberg*—by tumbling and tossing, and tossing and tumbling from one side of their beds to the other the whole night long—the several sisterhoods had scratch'd and mawl'd themselves all to death—they got out of their beds almost flead[20] alive—every body thought saint *Antony* had visited them for probation with his fire[21]——they had never

---

* *Hafen Slawkenbergius* means the Benedictine nuns of *Cluny*, founded in the year 940, by *Odo*, abbé de *Cluny*.

once, in short, shut their eyes the whole night long from vespers to matins.

The nuns of saint *Ursula*[22] acted the wisest—they never attempted to go to bed at all.

The dean of *Strasburg*, the prebendaries, the capitulars[23] and domiciliars[24] (capitularly assembled in the morning to consider the case of butter'd buns)[25] all wished they had followed the nuns of saint *Ursula*'s example.

——In the hurry and confusion every thing had been in the night before, the bakers had all forgot to lay their leaven—there were no butter'd buns to be had for breakfast in all *Strasburg*—the whole close of the cathedral was in one eternal commotion—such a cause of restlessness and disquietude, and such a zealous inquiry into the cause of that restlessness, had never happened in *Strasburg*, since *Martin Luther*, with his doctrines, had turned the city up-side down.

If the stranger's nose took this liberty of thrusting itself thus into the dishes* of religious orders, *&c*. what a carnival did his nose make of it, in those of the laity!—'tis more than my pen, worn to the stump as it is, has power to describe; tho' I acknowledge, *(cries* Slawkenbergius, *with more gaiety of thought than I could have expected from him)* that there is many a good simile now subsisting in the world which might give my countrymen some idea of it; but at the close of such a folio as this, wrote for their sakes, and in which I have spent the greatest part of my life—tho' I own to them the simile is in being, yet would it not be unreasonable in them to expect I should have either time or inclination to search for it? Let it suffice to say, that the riot and disorder it occasioned in the *Strasburgers* fantacies was so general—such an overpowering mastership had it got of all the faculties of the *Strasburgers* minds—so many strange things, with equal confidence on all sides, and with equal eloquence in all places, were spoken and sworn to concerning it, that turned the whole stream of all discourse and wonder towards it—every soul, good and bad—rich and poor—learned and unlearned—doctor and student—mistress and maid—gentle and simple—nun's flesh and woman's flesh in *Strasburg* spent their time in hearing tidings about it—every eye in *Strasburg* languished to see it——every finger—every thumb in *Strasburg* burned to touch it.

---

*Mr. *Shandy*'s compliments to orators—is very sensible that *Slawkenbergius* has here changed his metaphor—which he is very guilty of;—that as a translator, Mr. *Shandy* has all along done what he could to make him stick to it—but that here 'twas impossible.

Now what might add, if any thing may be thought necessary to add to so vehement a desire—was this, that the centinel, the bandy-legg'd drummer, the trumpeter, the trumpeter's wife, the burgo-master's widow, the master of the inn, and the master of the inn's wife, how widely soever they all differed every one from another in their testimonies and descriptions of the stranger's nose—they all agreed together in two points—namely, that he was gone to *Frankfort*, and would not return to *Strasburg* till that day month; and secondly, whether his nose was true or false, that the stranger himself was one of the most perfect paragons of beauty—the finest made man!—the most genteel!—the most generous of his purse—the most courteous in his carriage that had ever entered the gates of *Strasburg*—that as he rode, with his scymetar slung loosely to his wrist, thro' the streets—and walked with his crimson-sattin breeches across the parade—'twas with so sweet an air of careless modesty, and so manly withal—as would have put the heart in jeopardy (had his nose not stood in his way) of every virgin who had cast her eyes upon him.

I call not upon that heart which is a stranger to the throbs and yearnings of curiosity, so excited, to justify the abbess of *Quedlingberg*, the prioress, the deaness and subchantress for sending at noon-day for the trumpeter's wife: she went through the streets of *Strasburg* with her husband's trumpet in her hand;—the best apparatus the straitness of the time would allow her, for the illustration of her theory—she staid no longer than three days.

The centinel and the bandy-legg'd drummer!—nothing on this side of old *Athens* could equal them! they read their lectures under the city gates to comers and goers, with all the pomp of a *Chrysippus* and a *Crantor* [26] in their porticos.

The master of the inn, with his ostler on his left-hand, read his also in the same stile,—under the portico or gateway of his stable-yard—his wife, hers more privately in a back room: all flocked to their lectures; not promiscuously—but to this or that, as is ever the way, as faith and credulity marshal'd them—in a word, each *Strasburger* came crouding for intelligence—and every *Strasburger* had the intelligence he wanted.

'Tis worth remarking, for the benefit of all demonstrators in natural philosophy, *&c.* that as soon as the trumpeter's wife had finished the abbess of *Quedlinberg*'s private lecture, and had begun to read in public, which she did upon a stool in the middle of the great parade—she incommoded the other demonstrators mainly, by gaining incontinently the most fashionable part of the city of *Strasburg* for her auditory—But when a demonstrator in philosophy (cries *Slawkenbergius)* has a *trumpet* for an apparatus, pray what rival in science can pretend to be heard besides him?

Whilst the unlearned, thro' these conduits of intelligence, were all busied in getting down to the bottom of the well,[27] where TRUTH keeps her little court—were the learned in their way as busy in pumping her up thro' the conduits of dialect induction—they concerned themselves not with facts—they reasoned—

Not one profession had thrown more light upon this subject than the faculty[28]—had not all their disputes about it run into the affair of *Wens* and œdematous swellings, they could not keep clear of them for their bloods and souls—the stranger's nose had nothing to do either with wens or œdematous swellings.

It was demonstrated however very satisfactorily, that such a ponderous mass of heterogenious matter could not be congested and conglomerated to the nose, whilst the infant was *in Utero*, without destroying the statical balance of the fœtus, and throwing it plump upon its head nine months before the time.[29]——

—The opponents granted the theory—they denied the consequences.

And if a suitable provision of veins, arteries, *&c.* said they, was not laid in, for the due nourishment of such a nose, in the very first stamina[30] and rudiments of its formation before it came into the world (bating the case of Wens) it could not regularly grow and be sustained afterwards.

This was all answered by a dissertation upon nutriment, and the effect which nutriment had in extending the vessels, and in the increase and prolongation of the muscular parts to the greatest growth and expansion imaginable—In the triumph of which theory, they went so far as to affirm, that there was no cause in nature, why a nose might not grow to the size of the man himself.

The respondents satisfied the world this event could never happen to them so long as a man had but one stomach and one pair of lungs—For the stomach, said they, being the only organ destined for the reception of food, and turning it into chyle,—and the lungs the only engine of sanguification—it could possibly work off no more, than what the appetite brought it: or admitting the possibility of a man's overloading his stomach, nature had set bounds however to his lungs—the engine was of a determined size and strength, and could elaborate but a certain quantity in a given time—that is, it could produce just as much blood as was sufficient for one single man, and no more; so that, if there was as much nose as man—they proved a mortification must necessarily ensue; and forasmuch as there could not be a support for both, that the nose must either fall off from the man, or the man inevitably fall off from his nose.

Nature accommodates herself to these emergencies, cried the opponents—else what do you say to the case of a whole stomach—a whole pair of lungs, and but *half* a man, when both his legs have been unfortunately shot off?—

He dies of a plethora, said they—or must spit blood, and in a fortnight or three weeks go off in a consumption—

—It happens otherways—replied the opponents.——

It ought not, said they.

The more curious and intimate inquirers after nature and her doings, though they went hand in hand a good way together, yet they all divided about the nose at last, almost as much as the faculty itself.

They amicably laid it down, that there was a just and geometrical arrangement and proportion of the several parts of the human frame to its several destinations, offices, and functions, which could not be transgressed but within certain limits—that nature, though she sported— she sported within a certain circle;—and they could not agree about the diameter of it.

The logicians stuck much closer to the point before them than any of the classes of the literati;—they began and ended with the word nose; and had it not been for a *petitio principii*,[31] which one of the ablest of them ran his head against in the beginning of the combat, the whole controversy had been settled at once.

A nose, argued the logician, cannot bleed without blood—and not only blood—but blood circulating in it to supply the phænomenon with a succession of drops—(a stream being but a quicker succession of drops, that is included, said he)—Now death, continued the logician, being nothing but the stagnation of the blood[32]—

I deny the definition—Death is the separation of the soul from the body, said his antagonist—Then we don't agree about our weapon, said the logician—Then there is an end of the dispute, replied the antagonist.

The civilians[33] were still more concise; what they offered being more in the nature of a decree—than a dispute.

—Such a monstrous nose, said they, had it been a true nose, could not possibly have been suffered in civil society—and if false—to impose upon society with such false signs and tokens, was a still greater violation of its rights, and must have had still less mercy shewn it.

The only objection to this was, that if it proved any thing, it proved the stranger's nose was neither true nor false.

This left room for the controversy to go on. It was maintained by the advocates of the ecclesiastic court, that there was nothing to inhibit a decree, since the stranger *ex mero motu*[34] had confessed he had been at the Promontory of Noses, and had got one of the goodliest, *&c. &c.*—To this it was answered, it was impossible there should be such a place as the Promontory of Noses, and the learned be ignorant where it lay. The commissary of the bishop of *Strasburg* undertook the advocates, explained this matter in a treatise upon proverbial phrases, shewing them, that the Promontory of Noses was a mere allegoric expression, importing no more than that nature had given him a long nose: in proof of which, with great learning, he cited the underwritten authorities*, which had decided the point incontestably, had it not appeared that a dispute about some franchises of dean and chapter-lands had been determined by it nineteen years before.

It happened—I must not say unluckily for Truth, because they were giving her a lift another way in so doing; that the two universities[35] of *Strasburg*—the *Lutheran*, founded in the year 1538 by *Jacobus Sturmius*, counsellor of the senate,—and the *Popish*, founded by *Leopold*, arch-duke of *Austria*, were, during all this time, employing the whole depth of their knowledge (except just what the affair of the abbess of *Quedlinburg*'s placket-holes required)—in determining the point of *Martin Luther*'s damnation.[36]

The *Popish* doctors had undertaken to demonstrate *a priori*; that from the necessary influence of the planets on the twenty-second day of *October* 1483——when the moon was in the twelfth house—*Jupiter, Mars*, and *Venus* in the third, the *Sun, Saturn*, and *Mercury* all got together in the

---

*Nonnulli ex nostratibus eadem loquendi formulâ utun. Quinimo et Legistæ & Canonistæ—Vid. Parce Bar & Jas in d. L. Provincial. Constitut. de conjec. vid. Vol. Lib. 4. Titul. 1. N. 7. quà etiam in re conspir. Om. de Promontorio Nas. Tichmak. ff. d. tit. 3. fol. 189. passim. Vid. Glos. de contrahend. empt. *&c.* nec non J. Scrudr. in cap. §. refut. ff. per totum. cum his cons. Rever. J. Tubal, Sentent. & Prov. cap. 9. ff. 11, 12. obiter. V. et Librum, cui Tit. de Terris & Phras. Belg. ad finem, cum Comment. N. Bardy Belg. Vid. Scrip. Argentoratens. de Antiq. Ecc. in Episc. Archiv. fid. coll. per Von Jacobum Koinshoven Folio Argent. 1583, præcip. ad finem. Quibus add. Rebuff in L. obvenire de Signif. Nom. ff. fol. & de Jure, Gent. & Civil. de prohib. aliena feud. per federa, test. Joha. Luxius in prolegom. quem velim videas, de Analy. Cap. 1, 2, 3. Vid. Idea.[37]

fourth—that he must in course, and unavoidably be a damn'd man—and that his doctrines, by a direct corollary, must be damn'd doctrines too.

By inspection into his horoscope, where five planets were in coition all at once with scorpio* (in reading this my father would always shake his head) in the ninth house which the *Arabians* allotted to religion—it appeared that *Martin Luther* did not care one stiver about the matter—and that from the horoscope directed to the conjunction of *Mars*—they made it plain likewise he must die cursing and blaspheming—with the blast of which his soul (being steep'd in guilt) sailed before the wind, into the lake of hell fire.

The little objection of the *Lutheran* doctors to this, was, that it must certainly be the soul of another man, born *Oct.* 22, 1483, which was forced to sail down before the wind in that manner—inasmuch as it appeared from the register of *Islaben* in the county of *Mansfelt*, that *Luther* was not born in the year 1483, but in 84; and not on the 22d day of *October*, but on the 10th of *November*, the eve of *Martinmas*-day, from whence he had the name of *Martin*.

[—I must break off my translation for a moment; for if I did not, I know I should no more be able to shut my eyes in bed, than the abbess of *Quedlinburg*—It is to tell the reader, that my father never read this passage of *Slawkenbergius* to my uncle *Toby* but with triumph—not over my uncle *Toby*, for he never opposed him in it—but over the whole world.

—Now you see, brother *Toby*, he would say, looking up, "that christian names are not such indifferent things;"—had *Luther* here been called by any other name but *Martin*, he would have been damned to all eternity—Not that I look upon *Martin*, he would add, as a good name—far from it—'tis something better than a neutral, and but a little—yet little as it is, you see it was of some service to him.

My father knew the weakness of this prop to his hypothesis, as well as the best logician could shew him—yet so strange is the weakness of man

---

*Hæc mira, satisque horrenda. 5 Planetarum coitio sub Scorpio Asterismo in nonâ cœli statione, quam Arabes religioni deputabant effecit *Martinum Lutherum* sacrilegum hereticum, christianæ religiosinis hostem acerrimum atque prophanum, ex horoscopi directione ad Martis coitum, religiosissimus obiit, ejus Anima scelestissima ad infernos navigavit—ab Alecto, Tisiphone et Megera flagellis igneis cruciata perenniter.

—Lucas Gauricus in Tractatu astrologico de præteritis multorum hominum accidentibus per genituras examinatis.

at the same time, as it fell in his way, he could not for his life but make use of it; and it was certainly for this reason, that though there are many stories in *Hafen Slawkenbergius*'s Decads full as entertaining as this I am translating, yet there is not one amongst them which my father read over with half the delight—it flattered two of his strangest hypotheses together—his NAMES and his NOSES—I will be bold to say, he might have read all the books in the *Alexandrian* library,[38] had not fate taken other care of them, and not have met with a book or a passage in one, which hit two such nails as these upon the head at one stroke.]

The two universities of *Strasburg* were hard tugging at this affair of *Luther*'s navigation. The Protestant doctors had demonstrated, that he had not sailed right before the wind, as the Popish doctors had pretended; and as every one knew there was no sailing full in the teeth of it,—they were going to settle, in case he had sailed, how many points he was off; whether *Martin* had doubled the cape,[39] or had fallen upon a lee-shore; and no doubt, as it was an enquiry of much edification, at least to those who understood this sort of NAVIGATION, they had gone on with it in spite of the size of the stranger's nose, had not the size of the stranger's nose drawn off the attention of the world from what they were about—it was their business to follow.——

The abbess of *Quedlinburg* and her four dignitaries was no stop; for the enormity of the stranger's nose running full as much in their fancies as their case of conscience—The affair of their placket-holes kept cold— In a word, the printers were ordered to distribute their types[40]—all controversies dropp'd.

'Twas a square cap[41] with a silk tassel upon the crown of it—to a nut shell—to have guessed on which side of the nose the two universities would split.

'Tis above reason, cried the doctors on one side.

'Tis below reason, cried the others.

'Tis faith, cried the one.

'Tis a fiddle-stick, said the other.

'Tis possible, cried the one.

'Tis impossible, said the other.

God's power is infinite, cried the Nosarians, he can do any thing.

He can do nothing, replied the Antinosarians, which implies contradictions.[42]

He can make matter think, said the Nosarians.

As certainly as you can make a velvet cap out of a sow's ear, replied the Antinosarians.

He can make two and two five,[43] replied the Popish doctors.—'Tis false, said their opponents.—

Infinite power is infinite power, said the doctors who maintained the *reality* of the nose.——It extends only to all possible things, replied the *Lutherans*.

By God in heaven, cried the Popish doctors, he can make a nose, if he thinks fit, as big as the steeple of *Strasburg*.[44]

Now the steeple of *Strasburg* being the biggest and the tallest church-steeple to be seen in the whole world, the Antinosarians denied that a nose of 575 geometrical feet in length could be worn, at least by a middle-siz'd man—The Popish doctors swore it could—The *Lutheran* doctors said No;—it could not.

This at once started a new dispute, which they pursued a great way upon the extent and limitation of the moral and natural attributes of God—That controversy led them naturally into *Thomas Aquinas*, and *Thomas Aquinas* to the devil.

The stranger's nose was no more heard of in the dispute—it just served as a frigate to launch them into the gulph of school-divinity,—and then they all sailed before the wind.

Heat is in proportion to the want of true knowledge.

The controversy about the attributes, *&c.* instead of cooling, on the contrary had inflamed the *Strasburgers* imaginations to a most inordinate degree—The less they understood of the matter, the greater was their wonder about it—they were left in all the distresses of desire unsatisfied—saw their doctors, the *Parchmentarians*,[45] the *Brassarians*, the *Turpentarians*, on one side—the Popish doctors on the other, like *Pantagruel* and his companions in quest of the oracle of the bottle, all embarked and out of sight.[46]

——The poor *Strasburgers* left upon the beach!

—What was to be done?—No delay—the uproar increased—every one in disorder—the city gates set open.—

Unfortunate *Strasburgers!* was there in the store-house of nature—was there in the lumber-rooms of learning—was there in the great arsenal of chance, one single engine left undrawn forth to torture your curiosities, and stretch your desires, which was not pointed by the hand of fate to play upon your hearts?—I dip not my pen into my ink to excuse the surrender of yourselves—'tis to write your panegyrick. Shew me a city so macerated with expectation—who neither eat, or drank, or slept, or prayed, or hearkened to the calls either of religion or nature for seven and twenty days together, who could have held out one day longer.

On the twenty-eighth the courteous stranger had promised to return to *Strasburg*.

Seven thousand coaches *(Slawkenbergius* must certainly have made some mistake in his numerical characters) 7000 coaches—15000 single horse chairs——20000 waggons, crouded as full as they could all hold with senators, counsellors, syndicks—beguines,[47] widows, wives, virgins, canons, concubines, all in their coaches—The abbess of *Quedlinburg*, with the prioress, the deaness and sub-chantress leading the procession in one coach, and the dean of *Strasburg*, with the four great dignitaries of his chapter on her left-hand—the rest following higglety-pigglety as they could; some on horseback——some on foot—some led—some driven—some down the *Rhine*—some this way—some that—all set out at sun-rise to meet the courteous stranger on the road.

Haste we now towards the catastrophe of my tale—I say *Catastrophe* (cries *Slawkenbergius)* inasmuch as a tale, with parts rightly disposed, not only rejoiceth *(gaudet)* in the *Catastrophe* and *Peripeitia* of a DRAMA, but rejoiceth moreover in all the essential and integrant parts of it—it has its *Protasis, Epitasis, Catastasis*, its *Catastrophe* or *Peripeitia* growing one out of the other in it, in the order *Aristotle* first planted them[48]—without which a tale had better never be told at all, says *Slawkenbergius*, but be kept to a man's self.

In all my ten tales, in all my ten decads, have I, *Slawkenbergius*, tied down every tale of them as tightly to this rule, as I have done this of the stranger and his nose.

—From his first parley with the centinel, to his leaving the city of *Strasburg*, after pulling off his crimson-sattin pair of breeches, is the *Protasis* or first entrance——where the characters of the *Personæ Dramatis* are just touched in, and the subject slightly begun.

The *Epitasis*, wherein the action is more fully entered upon and heightened, till it arrives at its state or height called the *Catastasis*, and which usually takes up the 2d and 3d act, is included within that busy period of my tale, betwixt the first night's uproar about the nose, to the conclusion of the trumpeter's wife's lectures upon it in the middle of the grand parade; and from the first embarking of the learned in the dispute—to the doctors finally sailing away, and leaving the *Strasburgers* upon the beach in distress, is the *Catastasis* or the ripening of the incidents and passions for their bursting forth in the fifth act.

This commences with the setting out of the *Strasburgers* in the *Frankfort* road, and terminates in unwinding the labyrinth and bringing the hero out of a state of agitation (as *Aristotle* calls it) to a state of rest and quietness.[49]

This, says *Hafen Slawkenbergius*, constitutes the catastrophe or peripeitia of my tale—and that is the part of it I am going to relate.

We left the stranger behind the curtain asleep—he enters now upon the stage.

—What dost thou prick up thy ears at?—'tis nothing but a man upon a horse—was the last word the stranger uttered to his mule. It was not proper then to tell the reader, that the mule took his master's word for it; and without any more *ifs* or *ands*, let the traveller and his horse pass by.

The traveller was hastening with all diligence to get to *Strasburg* that night——What a fool am I, said the traveller to himself, when he had rode about a league farther, to think of getting into *Strasburg* this night— *Strasburg!*—the great *Strasburg!*—*Strasburg*, the capital of all *Alsatia! Strasburg*, an imperial city! *Strasburg*, a sovereign state! *Strasburg*, garrisoned with five thousand of the best troops in all the world!—Alas! if I was at the gates of *Strasburg* this moment, I could not gain admittance into it for a ducat,—nay a ducat and half—'tis too much—better go back to the last inn I have passed—than lie I know not where—or give I know not what. The traveller, as he made these reflections in his mind, turned his horse's head about, and three minutes after the stranger had been conducted into his chamber, he arrived at the same inn.

—We have bacon in the house, said the host, and bread——and till eleven o'clock this night had three eggs in it—but a stranger, who arrived an hour ago, has had them dressed into an omlet, and we have nothing.———

—Alas! said the traveller, harrassed as I am, I want nothing but a bed— I have one as soft as is in *Alsatia*, said the host.

—The stranger, continued he, should have slept in it, for 'tis my best bed, but upon the score of his nose—He has got a defluxion, said the traveller—Not that I know, cried the host—But 'tis a camp-bed, and *Jacinta*, said he, looking towards the maid, imagined there was not room in it to turn his nose in—Why so? cried the traveller starting back—It is so long a nose, replied the host—The traveller fixed his eyes upon *Jacinta*, then upon the ground—kneeled upon his right knee—had just got his hand laid upon his breast—Trifle not with my anxiety, said he, rising up again—'Tis no trifle, said *Jacinta*, 'tis the most glorious nose!—The traveller fell upon his knee again—laid his hand upon his breast—then said he, looking up to heaven! thou hast conducted me to the end of my pilgrimage——'Tis *Diego!*

The traveller was the brother of the Julia, so often invoked that night by the stranger as he rode from *Strasburg* upon his mule; and was come, on her part, in quest of him. He had accompanied his sister from *Valadolid*[50] across the *Pyrenean* mountains thro' *France*, and had many an entangled skein to wind off in pursuit of him thro' the many meanders and abrupt turnings of a lover's thorny tracks.

—Julia had sunk under it—and had not been able to go a step farther than to *Lyons*, where, with the many disquietudes of a tender heart, which all talk of—but few feel—she sicken'd, but had just strength to write a letter to *Diego*; and having conjured her brother never to see her face till he had found him out, and put the letter into his hands, Julia took to her bed.

Fernandez (for that was her brother's name)—tho' the camp-bed was as soft as any one in *Alsace*, yet he could not shut his eyes in it.—As soon as it was day he rose, and hearing *Diego* was risen too, he enter'd his chamber, and discharged his sister's commission.

The letter was as follows:

Seig. DIEGO.

"Whether my suspicions of your nose were justly excited or not—'tis not now to inquire—it is enough I have not had firmness to put them to farther tryal.

"How could I know so little of myself, when I sent my *Duena* to forbid your coming more under my lattice? or how could I know so little of you, *Diego*, as to imagine you would not have staid one day in *Valadolid* to have given ease to my doubts?—Was I to be abandoned, *Diego*, because I was deceived? or was it kind to take me at my word, whether my suspicions were just or no, and leave me, as you did, a prey to much uncertainty and sorrow.

"In what manner Julia has resented this—my brother, when he puts this letter into your hands, will tell you: He will tell you in how few moments she repented of the rash message she had sent you—in what frantic haste she flew to her lattice, and how many days and nights together she leaned immoveably upon her elbow, looking thro' it towards the way which *Diego* was wont to come.

"He will tell you, when she heard of your departure—how her spirits deserted her—how her heart sicken'd—how piteously she mourn'd—how low she hung her head. O *Diego!* how many weary steps has my brother's pity led me by the hand languishing to trace out yours! how far has desire carried me beyond strength—and how oft have I fainted by the way, and sunk into his arms, with only power to cry out—O my *Diego!*

"If the gentleness of your carriage has not belied your heart, you will fly to me, almost as fast as you fled from me—haste as you will, you will arrive but to see me expire.—'Tis a bitter draught, *Diego*, but oh! 'tis embitter'd still more by dying un——."[51]

She could proceed no farther.

Slawkenbergius supposes the word intended was *unconvinced*, but her strength would not enable her to finish her letter.

The heart of the courteous *Diego* overflowed as he read the letter—he ordered his mule forthwith and *Fernandez* 's horse to be saddled; and as no vent in prose is equal to that of poetry in such conflicts—chance, which as often directs us to remedies as to *diseases*, having thrown a piece of charcoal into the window—*Diego* availed himself of it, and whilst the ostler was getting ready his mule, he eased his mind[52] against the wall as follows.

ODE.

> *Harsh and untuneful are the notes of love,*
> > *Unless my Julia strikes the key,*
> *Her hand alone can touch the part,*
> > *Whose dulcet move-*
> *ment charms the heart,*
> > *And governs all the man with sympathetic sway.*

2d.

O Julia!

The lines were very natural—for they were nothing at all to the purpose, says *Slawkenbergius*, and 'tis a pity there were no more of them;

but whether it was that Seig. *Diego* was slow in composing verses—or the ostler quick in saddling mules—is not averred; certain it was, that *Diego*'s mule and *Fernandez*'s horse were ready at the door of the inn, before *Diego* was ready for his second stanza; so without staying to finish his ode, they both mounted, sallied forth, passed the *Rhine*, traversed *Alsace*, shaped their course towards *Lyons*, and before the *Strasburgers* and the abbess of *Quedlinberg* had set out on their cavalcade, had *Fernandez*, *Diego*, and his *Julia*, crossed the *Pyrenean* mountains, and got safe to *Valadolid*.

'Tis needless to inform the geographical reader, that when *Diego* was in *Spain*, it was not possible to meet the courteous stranger in the *Frankfort* road; it is enough to say, that of all restless desires, curiosity being the strongest—the *Strasburgers* felt the full force of it; and that for three days and nights they were tossed to and fro in the *Frankfort* road, with the tempestuous fury of this passion, before they could submit to return home—When alas! an event was prepared for them, of all others the most grievous that could befal a free people.

As this revolution of the *Strasburgers* affairs is often spoken of, and little understood, I will, in ten words, says *Slawkenbergius*, give the world an explanation of it, and with it put an end to my tale.[53]

Every body knows of the grand system of Universal Monarchy,[54] wrote by order of Mons. *Colbert*, and put in manuscript into the hands of *Lewis* the fourteenth, in the year 1664.

'Tis as well known, that one branch out of many of that system, was the getting possession of *Strasburg*, to favour an entrance at all times into *Suabia*, in order to disturb the quiet of *Germany*—and that in consequence of this plan, *Strasburg* unhappily fell at length into their hands.

It is the lot of few to trace out the true springs of this and such like revolutions—The vulgar look too high for them—Statesmen look too low—Truth (for once) lies in the middle.

What a fatal thing is the popular pride of a free city! cries one historian—The *Strasburgers* deemed it a diminution of their freedom to receive an imperial garrison—and so fell a prey to a *French* one.

The fate, says another, of the *Strasburgers*, may be a warning to all free people to save their money—They anticipated their revenues—brought themselves under taxes, exhausted their strength, and in the end became so weak a people, they had not strength to keep their gates shut, and so the *French* pushed them open.

Alas! alas! cries *Slawkenbergius*, 'twas not the *French*—'twas CURIOSITY pushed them open—The *French* indeed, who are ever upon the catch, when they saw the *Strasburgers*, men, women, and children, all marched out to follow the stranger's nose—each man followed his own, and marched in.

Trade and manufactures have decayed and gradually grown down ever since—but not from any cause which commercial heads have assigned; for it is owing to this only, that Noses have ever so run in their heads, that the *Strasburgers* could not follow their business.

Alas! alas! cries *Slawkenbergius*, making an exclamation—it is not the first—and I fear will not be the last fortress that has been either won——or lost by Noses.

The END of
Slawkenbergius's Tale.

CHAPTER I

CHAP. I.

WITH all this learning upon Noses running perpetually in my father's fancy—with so many family prejudices—and ten decads of such tales running on for ever along with them—how was it possible with such exquisite—was it a true nose?—That a man with such exquisite feelings as my father had, could bear the shock at all below stairs—or indeed above stairs, in any other posture, but the very posture I have described.

—Throw yourself down upon the bed, a dozen times—taking care only to place a looking-glass first in a chair on one side of it, before you do it——But was the stranger's nose a true nose—or was it a false one?

To tell that before-hand, madam, would be to do injury to one of the best tales in the christian world; and that is the tenth of the tenth decad which immediately follows this.

This tale, crieth *Slawkenbergius* somewhat exultingly, has been reserved by me for the concluding tale of my whole work; knowing right well, that when I shall have told it, and my reader shall have read it thro'—'twould be even high time for both of us to shut up the book; inasmuch, continues *Slawkenbergius*, as I know of no tale which could possibly ever go down after it.

—'Tis a tale indeed!

This sets out with the first interview in the inn at *Lyons*, when *Fernandez* left the courteous stranger and his sister *Julia* alone in her chamber, and is overwritten,

The INTRICACIES
of
Diego and *Julia*.

Heavens! thou art a strange creature *Slawkenbergius!* what a whimsical view of the involutions of the heart of woman hast thou opened! how this can ever be translated, and yet if this specimen of *Slawkenbergius*'s tales, and the exquisiteness of his moral should please the world—translated shall a couple of volumes be.—Else, how this can ever be translated into good *English*, I have no sort of conception.——There seems in some passages to want a sixth sense to do it rightly.——What can he mean by the lambent pupilability[1] of slow, low, dry chat, five notes below the natural tone,—which you know, madam, is little more than a whisper? The moment I pronounced the words, I could perceive an attempt towards a vibration in the strings, about the region of the heart.—The brain made no acknowledgment.—There's often no good understanding betwixt 'em.—I felt as if I understood it.——I had no ideas.—The movement could not be without cause.—I'm lost. I can make nothing of it,—unless, may it please your worships, the voice, in that case being little more than a whisper, unavoidably forces the eyes to approach not only within six inches of each other—but to look into the pupils—is not that dangerous?—But it can't be avoided—for to look up to the cieling, in that case the two chins unavoidably meet—and to look down into each others laps, the foreheads come into immediate contact, which at once puts an end to the conference—I mean to the sentimental part of it.——What is left, madam, is not worth stooping for.[2]

CHAP. II.

M Y father lay stretched across the bed as still as if the hand of death had pushed him down, for a full hour and a half, before he began to play upon the floor with the toe of that foot which hung over the bed-side; my uncle *Toby*'s heart was a pound lighter for it.—In a few moments, his left-hand, the knuckles of which had all the time reclined upon the handle of the chamber-pot, came to its feeling—he thrust it a little more within the valance—drew up his hand, when he had done, into his bosom—gave a hem!—My good uncle *Toby*, with infinite pleasure, answered it; and full gladly would have ingrafted a sentence of consolation upon the opening it afforded; but having no talents, as I said, that way, and fearing moreover that he might set out with something which might make a bad matter worse, he contented himself with resting his chin placidly upon the cross of his crutch.

Now whether the compression shortened my uncle *Toby*'s face into a more pleasureable oval,—or that the philanthropy of his heart, in seeing his brother beginning to emerge out of the sea of his afflictions, had braced up his muscles,—so that the compression upon his chin only doubled the benignity which was there before, is not hard to decide.—My father, in turning his eyes, was struck with such a gleam of sun-shine in his face, as melted down the sullenness of his grief in a moment.

He broke silence as follows.

CHAP. III.

DID ever man, brother *Toby*, cried my father, raising himself up upon his elbow, and turning himself round to the opposite side of the bed where my uncle *Toby* was sitting in his old fringed chair, with his chin resting upon his crutch—did ever a poor unfortunate man, brother *Toby*, cried my father, receive so many lashes?——The most I ever saw given, quoth my uncle *Toby*, (ringing the bell at the bed's head for *Trim)* was to a grenadier, I think in *Makay*'s regiment.[1]

—Had my uncle *Toby* shot a bullet thro' my father's heart, he could not have fallen down with his nose upon the quilt more suddenly.

Bless me! said my uncle *Toby*.

CHAP. IV.

WAS it *Makay*'s regiment, quoth my uncle *Toby*, where the poor grenadier was so unmercifully whipp'd at *Bruges* about the ducats.—— O Christ! he was innocent! cried *Trim* with a deep sigh.——And he was whipp'd, may it please your honour, almost to death's door.—They had better have shot him outright as he begg'd, and he had gone directly to heaven, for he was as innocent as your honour.——I thank thee, *Trim*, quoth my uncle *Toby*. I never think of his, continued *Trim*, and my poor brother *Tom*'s misfortunes, for we were all three school-fellows, but I cry like a coward.—Tears are no proof of cowardice, *Trim.*—I drop them oft-times myself, cried my uncle *Toby.*—I know your honour does, replied *Trim*, and so am not ashamed of it myself.—But to think, may it please your honour, continued *Trim*, a tear stealing into the corner of his eye as he spoke—to think of two virtuous lads with hearts as warm in their bodies, and as honest as God could make them—the children of honest people, going forth with gallant spirits to seek their fortunes in the world—and fall into such evils!—poor *Tom!* to be tortured upon a rack for nothing—but marrying a *Jew*'s widow who sold sausages—honest *Dick Johnson*'s soul to be scourged out of his body, for the ducats another man put into his knapsack!—O!—these are misfortunes, cried *Trim*, pulling out his handkerchief—these are misfortunes, may it please your honour, worth lying down and crying over.

—My father could not help blushing.

—'Twould be a pity, *Trim*, quoth my uncle *Toby*, thou shouldst ever feel sorrow of thy own—thou feelest it so tenderly for others.—Alack-o-day, replied the corporal, brightening up his face—your honour knows I have neither wife or child——I can have no sorrows in this world.[1]—My father could not help smiling.—As few as any man, *Trim*, replied my uncle *Toby*; nor can I see how a fellow of thy light heart can suffer, but from the distress of poverty in thy old age—when thou art passed all services, *Trim*,—and hast out-lived thy friends—An' please your honour, never fear, replied *Trim* chearily—But I would have thee never fear, *Trim*, replied my uncle; and therefore, continued my uncle *Toby*, throwing down his crutch, and getting up upon his legs as he uttered the word *therefore*—in recompence, *Trim*, of thy long fidelity to me, and that goodness of thy heart I have had such proofs of—whilst thy master is worth a shilling—thou shalt never ask elsewhere, *Trim*, for a penny. *Trim* attempted to thank my uncle *Toby*,—but had not power—tears trickled down his cheeks faster than he could wipe them off—He laid his hands upon his breast—made a bow to the ground, and shut the door.

—I have left *Trim* my bowling-green, cried my uncle *Toby*—My father smiled—I have left him moreover a pension, continued my uncle *Toby*—My father looked grave.

CHAP. V.

IS this a fit time, said my father to himself, to talk of PENSIONS and GRENADIERS?

CHAP. VI.

WHEN my uncle *Toby* first mentioned the grenadier, my father, I said, fell down with his nose flat to the quilt, and as suddenly as if my uncle *Toby* had shot him; but it was not added, that every other limb and member of my father instantly relapsed with his nose into the same precise attitude in which he lay first described; so that when corporal *Trim* left the room, and my father found himself disposed to rise off the bed,— he had all the little preparatory movements to run over again, before he could do it.—Attitudes are nothing, madam,—'tis the transition from one attitude to another—like the preparation and resolution of the discord into harmony, which is all in all.[1]

For which reason my father played the same jig over again with his toe upon the floor—pushed the chamber-pot still a little farther within the valance—gave a hem—raised himself up upon his elbow—and was just beginning to address himself to my uncle *Toby*—when recollecting the unsuccessfulness of his first effort in that attitude,—he got upon his legs, and in making the third turn across the room, he stopped short before my uncle *Toby*; and laying the three first fingers of his right-hand in the palm of his left, and stooping a little, he addressed himself to my uncle *Toby* as follows.

CHAP. VII.

WHEN I reflect, brother *Toby*, upon MAN; and take a view of that dark side of him which represents his life as open to so many causes of trouble—when I consider, brother *Toby*, how oft we eat the bread of affliction, and that we are born to it, as to the portion of our inheritance[1]—I was born to nothing, quoth my uncle *Toby*, interrupting my father—but my commission. Zooks![2] said my father, did not my uncle leave you a hundred and twenty pounds a year?—What could I have done without it? replied my uncle *Toby*.—That's another concern, said my father testily—But I say, *Toby*, when one runs over the catalogue of all the cross reckonings and sorrowful *items* with which the heart of man is overcharged, 'tis wonderful by what hidden resources the mind is enabled to stand it out, and bear itself up, as it does against the impositions laid upon our nature.——'Tis by the assistance of Almighty God,[3] cried my uncle *Toby*, looking up, and pressing the palms of his hands close together—'tis not from our own strength, brother *Shandy*—a sentinel in a wooden centry-box, might as well pretend to stand it out against a detachment of fifty men,—we are upheld by the grace and the assistance of the best of Beings.

—That is cutting the knot,[4] said my father, instead of untying it.—But give me leave to lead you, brother *Toby*, a little deeper into this mystery.

With all my heart, replied my uncle *Toby*.

My father instantly exchanged the attitude he was in, for that in which *Socrates* is so finely painted by *Raffael* in his school of *Athens*;[5] which your connoisseurship knows is so exquisitely imagined, that even the particular manner of the reasoning of *Socrates* is expressed by it—for he holds the fore-finger of his left-hand between the fore-finger and the thumb of his right, and seems as if he was saying to the libertine he is reclaiming—"*You grant me* this—and this: and this, and this, I don't ask of you—they follow of themselves in course."

So stood my father, holding fast his fore-finger betwixt his finger and his thumb, and reasoning with my uncle *Toby* as he sat in his old fringed chair, valanced around with party-coloured worsted bobs—O *Garrick!*[6]

what a rich scene of this would thy exquisite powers make! and how gladly would I write such another to avail myself of thy immortality, and secure my own behind it.

CHAP. VIII.

THOUGH man is of all others the most curious vehicle, said my father, yet at the same time 'tis of so slight a frame and so totteringly put together, that the sudden jerks and hard jostlings it unavoidably meets with in this rugged journey, would overset and tear it to pieces a dozen times a day—was it not, brother *Toby*, that there is a secret spring within us[1]—Which spring, said my uncle *Toby*, I take to be Religion.—Will that set my child's nose on? cried my father, letting go his finger, and striking one hand against the other—It makes every thing straight for us, answered my uncle *Toby*—Figuratively speaking, dear *Toby*, it may, for aught I know, said my father; but the spring I am speaking of, is that great and elastic power within us of counterbalancing evil, which like a secret spring in a well-ordered machine, though it can't prevent the shock—at least it imposes upon our sense of it.

Now, my dear brother, said my father, replacing his fore-finger, as he was coming closer to the point,—had my child arrived safe into the world, unmartyr'd in that precious part of him—fanciful and extravagant as I may appear to the world in my opinion of christian names, and of that magic bias which good or bad names irresistably impress upon our characters and conducts—heaven is witness! that in the warmest transports of my wishes for the prosperity of my child, I never once wished to crown his head with more glory and honour, than what GEORGE or EDWARD[2] would have spread around it.

But alas! continued my father, as the greatest evil has befallen him—I must counteract and undo it with the greatest good.

He shall be christened *Trismegistus*,[3] brother.

I wish it may answer—replied my uncle *Toby*, rising up.

CHAP. IX.

WHAT a chapter of chances, said my father, turning himself about upon the first landing, as he and my uncle *Toby* were going down stairs——what a long chapter of chances do the events of this world lay open to us! Take pen and ink in hand, brother *Toby*, and calculate it fairly—I know no more of calculations than this balluster, said my uncle *Toby*, (striking short of it with his crutch, and hitting my father a desperate blow souse upon his shin-bone)—'Twas a hundred to one—cried my uncle *Toby*.——I thought, quoth my father, (rubbing his shin) you had known nothing of calculations, brother *Toby*.—'Twas a meer chance, said my uncle *Toby*—Then it adds one to the chapter—replied my father.

The double success of my father's repartees tickled off the pain of his shin at once—it was well it so fell out—(chance! again)—or the world to this day had never known the subject of my father's calculation—to guess it—there was no chance—What a lucky chapter of chances has this turned out! for it has saved me the trouble of writing one express, and in truth I have anew already upon my hands without it——Have not I promised the world a chapter of knots? two chapters upon the right and the wrong end of a woman? a chapter upon whiskers? a chapter upon wishes?—a chapter of noses?—No, I have done that—a chapter upon my uncle *Toby*'s modesty? to say nothing of a chapter upon chapters, which I will finish before I sleep—by my great grandfather's whiskers, I shall never get half of 'em through this year.

Take pen and ink in hand, and calculate it fairly, brother *Toby*, said my father, and it will turn out a million to one, that of all the parts of the body, the edge of the forceps should have the ill luck just to fall upon and break down that one part, which should break down the fortunes of our house with it.

It might have been worse, replied my uncle *Toby*—I don't comprehend, said my father—Suppose the hip had presented, replied my uncle *Toby*, as Dr. *Slop* foreboded.

My father reflected half a minute—looked down—touched the middle of his forehead slightly with his finger—

—True, said he.

CHAP. X.

IS it not a shame to make two chapters of what passed in going down one pair of stairs? for we are got no farther yet than to the first landing, and there are fifteen more steps down to the bottom; and for aught I know, as my father and my uncle *Toby* are in a talking humour, there may be as many chapters as steps;—let that be as it will, Sir, I can no more help it than my destiny:—A sudden impulse comes across me——drop the curtain, *Shandy*—I drop it——Strike a line here across the paper, *Tristram*—I strike it—and hey for a new chapter!

The duce of any other rule have I to govern myself by in this affair—and if I had one—as I do all things out of all rule—I would twist it and tear it to pieces, and throw it into the fire when I had done—Am I warm? I am, and the cause demands it—a pretty story! is a man to follow rules—or rules to follow him?

Now this, you must know, being my chapter upon chapters, which I promised to write before I went to sleep, I thought it meet to ease my conscience entirely before I lay'd down, by telling the world all I knew about the matter at once: Is not this ten times better than to set out dogmatically with a sententious parade of wisdom, and telling the world a story of a roasted horse[1]—that chapters relieve the mind—that they assist—or impose upon the imagination—and that in a work of this dramatic cast they are as necessary as the shifting of scenes—with fifty other cold conceits,[2] enough to extinguish the fire which roasted him.—O! but to understand this, which is a puff at the fire of *Diana*'s temple—you must read *Longinus*[3]—read away—if you are not a jot the wiser by reading him the first time over—never fear—read him again—*Avicenna* and *Licetus*,[4] read *Aristotle*'s metaphysicks forty times through a piece, and never understood a single word.—But mark the consequence—*Avicenna* turned out a desperate writer at all kinds of writing—for he wrote books *de omni scribili*;[5] and for *Licetus (Fortunio)* though all the world knows he was born a fœtus*, of no more than five inches and a half in length, yet

---

* *Ce Fœtus* n'etoit pas plus grand que la paúme de la main; mais son pere l'ayant éxaminè en qualitè de Médecin, & ayant trouvé que c'etoit quelque chose de plus qu'un Embryon, le fit

he grew to that astonishing height in literature, as to write a book with a title as long as himself——the learned know I mean his *Gonopsychanthropologia*, upon the origin of the human soul.

So much for my chapter upon chapters, which I hold to be the best chapter in my whole work; and take my word, whoever reads it, is full as well employed, as in picking straws.[6]

CHAP. XI.

WE shall bring all things to rights, said my father, setting his foot upon the first step from the landing——This *Trismegistus*, continued my father, drawing his leg back, and turning to my uncle *Toby*—was the greatest *(Toby)* of all earthly beings—he was the greatest king—the greatest lawgiver—the greatest philosopher—and the greatest priest——and engineer—said my uncle *Toby*.—

——In course, said my father.

---

transporter tout vivant à Rapallo, ou il le fit voir à Jerôme Bardi & à d'autres Medecins du lieu. On trouva qu'il ne lui manquoit rien d'essentiel a la vie; & son pere pour faire voir un essai de son expérience, entreprit d'achever l'ouvrage de la Nature, & de travailler a la formation de l'Enfant avec le même artifice que celui dont on se sert pour faire éclorre les Poulets en Egypte. Il instruisit une Nourrisse de tout ce qu'elle avoit à faire, & ayant fait mettre son fils dans un four proprement accommodè, il reussit à l'élever et a lui faire prendre ses accroissemens necessaires, par l'uniformité d'une chaleur étrangére mesurée éxactement sur les dégrés d'un Thermométre, ou d'un autre instrument équivalent. (Vide Mich. Giustinian, ne gli Scritt. Liguri á Cart. 223. 488.)

On auroit toujours été très-satisfait de l'industrie d'un Pere si experimenté dans l'Art de la Generation, quand il n'auroit pû prolonger la vie a son fils que pour quelques mois, ou pour peu d'années.

Mais quand on se represente que l'Enfant a vecu pres de quatre-vingts ans, & que il a composé quatre-vingts Ouvrages differents tous fruits d'une longue lecture,—il faut convenir que tout ce qui est incroyable n'est pas toujours faux, & que la *Vraisemblance n'est pas toujours du coté de la Veritè.*

Il n'avoit que dix-neuf ans lors qu'il composa Gonopsychanthropologia de Origine Animæ humanæ.

(Les Enfans celebres, revûs & corriges par M. De la Monnoye de l'Academie Françoise.)

CHAP. XII.

—AND how does your mistress? cried my father, taking the same step over again from the landing, and calling to *Susannah*, whom he saw passing by the foot of the stairs with a huge pin-cushion in her hand—how does your mistress? As well, said *Susannah*, tripping by, but without looking up, as can be expected—What a fool am I, said my father! drawing his leg back again—let things be as they will, brother *Toby*, 'tis ever the precise answer—And how is the child, pray?—No answer. And where is doctor *Slop?* added my father, raising his voice aloud, and looking over the ballusters—*Susannah* was out of hearing.

Of all the riddles of a married life, said my father, crossing the landing, in order to set his back against the wall, whilst he propounded it to my uncle *Toby*—of all the puzzling riddles, said he, in a marriage state,—of which you may trust me, brother *Toby*, there are more asses loads than all *Job*'s stock of asses[1] could have carried—there is not one that has more intricacies in it than this—that from the very moment the mistress of the house is brought to bed, every female in it, from my lady's gentlewoman down to the cinder-wench, becomes an inch taller for it; and give themselves more airs upon that single inch, than all their other inches put together.

I think rather, replied my uncle *Toby*, that 'tis we who sink an inch lower.——If I meet but a woman with child—I do it—'Tis a heavy tax upon that half of our fellow-creatures, brother *Shandy*, said my uncle *Toby*—'Tis a piteous burden upon 'em, continued he, shaking his head.—Yes, yes, 'tis a painful thing—said my father, shaking his head too—but certainly since shaking of heads came into fashion, never did two heads shake together, in concert, from two such different springs.

God bless } 'em all—said my uncle *Toby* and my father, each to
Duce take } himself.

CHAP. XIII.

HOLLA!—you chairman![1]—here's sixpence—do step into that bookseller's shop, and call me a *day-tall*[2] critick. I am very willing to give any one of 'em a crown to help me with his tackling, to get my father and my uncle *Toby* off the stairs, and to put them to bed.—

—'Tis even high time; for except a short nap, which they both got whilst *Trim* was boring the jack-boots—and which, by the bye, did my father no sort of good upon the score of the bad hinge—they have not else shut their eyes, since nine hours before the time that doctor *Slop* was led into the back parlour in that dirty pickle by *Obadiah*.

Was every day of my life to be as busy a day as this,—and to take up,—truce—

I will not finish that sentence till I have made an observation upon the strange state of affairs between the reader and myself, just as things stand at present—an observation never applicable before to any one biographical writer[3] since the creation of the world, but to myself—and I believe will never hold good to any other, until its final destruction——and therefore, for the very novelty of it alone, it must be worth your worships attending to.

I am this month one whole year older than I was this time twelve-month; and having got, as you perceive, almost into the middle of my fourth volume—and no farther than to my first day's life—'tis demonstrative that I have three hundred and sixty-four days more life to write just now, than when I first set out; so that instead of advancing, as a common writer, in my work with what I have been doing at it—on the contrary, I am just thrown so many volumes back—was every day of my life to be as busy a day as this—And why not?—and the transactions and opinions of it to take up as much description—And for what reason should they be cut short? as at this rate I should just live 364 times faster than I should write—It must follow, an' please your worships, that the more I write, the more I shall have to write—and consequently, the more your worships read, the more your worships will have to read.

Will this be good for your worships eyes?

It will do well for mine; and, was it not that my OPINIONS will be the death of me, I perceive I shall lead a fine life of it out of this self-same life of mine; or, in other words, shall lead a couple of fine lives together.

As for the proposal of twelve volumes a year, or a volume a month, it no way alters my prospect—write as I will, and rush as I may into the middle of things, as *Horace* advises,[4]—I shall never overtake myself—whipp'd and driven to the last pinch, at the worst I shall have one day the start of my pen—and one day is enough for two volumes—and two volumes will be enough for one year.—

Heaven prosper the manufactures of paper under this propitious reign,[5] which is now open'd to us,—as I trust its providence will prosper every thing else in it that is taken in hand.—

As for the propagation of Geese—I give myself no concern—Nature is all bountiful—I shall never want tools to work with.

—So then, friend! you have got my father and my uncle *Toby* off the stairs, and seen them to bed?—And how did you manage it?—You dropp'd a curtain at the stairs foot—I thought you had no other way for it—Here's a crown for your trouble.

CHAP. XIV.

—THEN reach me my breeches off the chair, said my father to *Susannah*—There is not a moment's time to dress you, Sir, cried *Susannah*—the child is as black in the face as my—As your, what? said my father, for like all orators, he was a dear searcher into comparisons—Bless me, Sir, said *Susannah*, the child's in a fit—And where's Mr. *Yorick*—Never where he should be, said *Susannah*, but his curate's in the dressing-room, with the child upon his arm, waiting for the name——and my mistress bid me run as fast as I could to know, as captain *Shandy* is the godfather, whether it should not be called after him.

Were one sure, said my father to himself, scratching his eye-brow, that the child was expiring, one might as well compliment my brother *Toby* as not—and 'twould be a pity, in such a case, to throw away so great a name as *Trismegistus* upon him—But he may recover.

No, no,—said my father to *Susannah*, I'll get up——There is no time, cried *Susannah*, the child's as black as my shoe. *Trismegistus*, said my father—But stay—thou art a leaky vessel, *Susannah*, added my father; canst thou carry *Trismegistus* in thy head, the length of the gallery without scattering—Can I? cried *Susannah*, shutting the door in a huff—If she can, I'll be shot, said my father, bouncing out of bed in the dark, and groping for his breeches.

Susannah ran with all speed along the gallery.

My father made all possible speed to find his breeches.

Susannah got the start, and kept it—'Tis *Tris*—something, cried *Susannah*—There is no christian name in the world, said the curate, beginning with *Tris*—but *Tristram*. Then 'tis *Tristram-gistus*, quoth *Susannah*.

—There is no *gistus* to it, noodle!—'tis my own name, replied the curate, dipping his hand as he spoke into the bason—*Tristram!* said he, &c. &c. &c. &c. so *Tristram* was I called, and *Tristram* shall I be to the day of my death.

My father followed *Susannah* with his night-gown across his arm, with nothing more than his breeches on, fastened through haste with but a single button, and that button through haste thrust only half into the button-hole.

—She has not forgot the name, cried my father, half opening the door— No, no, said the curate, with a tone of intelligence—And the child is better, cried *Susannah*—And how does your mistress? As well, said *Susannah*, as can be expected—Pish! said my father, the button of his breeches slipping out of the button-hole—So that whether the interjection was levelled at *Susannah*, or the button-hole,—whether pish was an interjection of contempt or an interjection of modesty, is a doubt, and must be a doubt till I shall have time to write the three following favorite chapters, that is, my chapter of *chamber-maids*—my chapter of *pishes*, and my chapter of *button-holes*.

All the light I am able to give the reader at present is this, that the moment my father cried Pish! he whisk'd himself about—and with his breeches held up by one hand, and his night-gown thrown across the arm of the other, he returned along the gallery to bed, something slower than he came.

W.Hogarth inv.ᵗ del.   J.Ryland sculp

CHAP. XV.

I Wish I could write a chapter upon sleep.

A fitter occasion could never have presented itself, than what this moment offers, when all the curtains of the family are drawn—the candles put out—and no creature's eyes are open but a single one, for the other has been shut these twenty years, of my mother's nurse.

It is a fine subject!

And yet, as fine as it is, I would undertake to write a dozen chapters upon button-holes, both quicker and with more fame than a single chapter upon this.

Button-holes!——there is something lively in the very idea of 'em— and trust me, when I get amongst 'em—You gentry with great beards— look as grave as you will—I'll make merry work with my button- holes—I shall have 'em all to myself—'tis a maiden subject—I shall run foul of no man's wisdom or fine sayings in it.

But for sleep[1]—I know I shall make nothing of it before I begin—I am no dab at your fine sayings in the first place—and in the next, I cannot for my soul set a grave face upon a bad matter,[2] and tell the world—'tis the refuge of the unfortunate—the enfranchisement of the prisoner—the downy lap of the hopeless, the weary and the broken-hearted; nor could I set out with a lye in my mouth, by affirming, that of all the soft and delicious functions of our nature, by which the great Author of it, in his bounty, has been pleased to recompence the sufferings wherewith his justice and his good pleasure has wearied us,—that this is the chiefest (I know pleasures worth ten of it) or what a happiness it is to man, when the anxieties and passions of the day are over, and he lays down upon his back, that his soul shall be so seated within him, that which ever way she turns her eyes, the heavens shall look calm and sweet above her—no desire—or fear—or doubt that troubles the air, nor any difficulty pass'd, present, or to come, that the imagination may not pass over without offence, in that sweet secession.

—"God's blessing, said *Sancho Panca*, "be upon the man who first invented this self-same thing called sleep——it covers a man all over like a cloak."[3] Now there is more to me in this, and it speaks warmer to my heart and affections, than all the dissertations squeez'd out of the heads of the learned together upon the subject.

——Not that I altogether disapprove of what *Montaigne* advances[4] upon it——'tis admirable in its way.——(I quote by memory.)

The world enjoys other pleasures, says he, as they do that of sleep, without tasting or feeling it as it slips and passes by——We should study and ruminate upon it, in order to render proper thanks to him who grants it to us——for this end I cause myself to be disturbed in my sleep, that I may the better and more sensibly relish it——And yet I see few, says he again, who live with less sleep when need requires; my body is capable of a firm, but not of a violent and sudden agitation——I evade of late all violent exercises——I am never weary with walking——but from my youth, I never liked to ride upon pavements. I love to lie hard and alone, and even without my wife——This last word may stagger the faith of the world——but remember, "La Vraisemblance (as *Baylet* says in the affair of *Liceti*) n'est pas toujours du Cotè de la Verité." And so much for sleep.

CHAP. XVI.

IF my wife will but venture him——brother *Toby*, *Trismegistus* shall be dress'd and brought down to us, whilst you and I are getting our breakfasts together.——

——Go, tell *Susannah*, *Obadiah*, to step here.

She is run up stairs, answered *Obadiah*, this very instant, sobbing and crying, and wringing her hands as if her heart would break.——

We shall have a rare month of it, said my father, turning his head from *Obadiah*, and looking wistfully in my uncle *Toby*'s face for some time—— we shall have a devilish month of it, brother *Toby*, said my father, setting his arms a-kimbo, and shaking his head; fire, water, women, wind——brother *Toby!*——'Tis some misfortune, quoth my uncle *Toby*——That it is, cried my father,——to have so many jarring elements breaking loose, and riding triumph in every corner of a gentleman's house——Little boots it to the peace of a family, brother *Toby*, that you and I possess ourselves, and sit here silent and unmoved,—whilst such a storm is whistling over our heads.——

——And what's the matter, *Susannah?* They have called the child *Tristram*——and my mistress is just got out of an hysterick fit about it——No!—'tis not my fault, said *Susannah*—I told him it was *Tristram-gistus*.

——Make tea for yourself, brother *Toby*, said my father, taking down his hat—but how different from the sallies and agitations of voice and members which a common reader would imagine!

——For he spake in the sweetest modulation—and took down his hat with the gentlest movement of limbs, that ever affliction harmonized and attuned together.

——Go to the bowling-green for corporal *Trim*, said my uncle *Toby*, speaking to *Obadiah*, as soon as my father left the room.

CHAP. XVII.

WHEN the misfortune of my NOSE fell so heavily upon my father's head,—the reader remembers that he walked instantly up stairs, and cast himself down upon his bed; and from hence, unless he has a great insight into human nature, he will be apt to expect a rotation of the same ascending and descending movements from him, upon this misfortune of my NAME;——no.

The different weight, dear Sir,—nay even the different package of two vexations of the same weight,—makes a very wide difference in our manners of bearing and getting through with them.——It is not half an hour ago, when (in the great hurry and precipitation of a poor devil's writing for daily bread) I threw a fair sheet, which I had just finished, and carefully wrote out, slap into the fire, instead of the foul one.

Instantly I snatch'd off my wig, and threw it perpendicularly, with all imaginable violence, up to the top of the room—indeed I caught it as it fell—but there was an end of the matter; nor do I think any thing else in *Nature*, would have given such immediate ease: She, dear Goddess, by an instantaneous impulse, in all *provoking cases*, determines us to a sally of this or that member—or else she thrusts us into this or that place, or posture of body, we know not why—But mark, madam, we live amongst riddles and mysteries[1]—the most obvious things, which come in our way, have dark sides, which the quickest sight cannot penetrate into; and even the clearest and most exalted understandings amongst us find ourselves puzzled and at a loss in almost every cranny of nature's works; so that this, like a thousand other things, falls out for us in a way, which tho' we cannot reason upon it,—yet we find the good of it, may it please your reverences and your worships—and that's enough for us.

Now, my father could not lie down with this affliction for his life—nor could he carry it up stairs like the other—He walked composedly out with it to the fish-pond.

Had my father leaned his head upon his hand, and reasoned an hour which way to have gone—reason, with all her force, could not have directed him to any thing like it: there is something, Sir, in fish-ponds—but what it is, I leave to system builders and fish pond diggers betwixt 'em to find out—but there is something, under the first disorderly transport of the humours, so unaccountably becalming in an orderly and a sober walk towards one of them, that I have often wondered that neither *Pythagoras*, nor *Plato*, nor *Solon*, nor *Licurgus*, nor *Mahomet*,[2] nor any of your noted lawgivers, ever gave order about them.

CHAP. XVIII.

YOUR honour, said *Trim*, shutting the parlour door before he began to speak, has heard, I imagine, of this unlucky accident——O yes, *Trim!* said my uncle *Toby*, and it gives me great concern—I am heartily concerned too, but I hope your honour, replied *Trim*, will do me the justice to believe, that it was not in the least owing to me—To thee—*Trim!*—cried my uncle *Toby*, looking kindly in his face—'twas *Susannah*'s and the curate's folly betwixt them—What business could they have together, an' please your honour, in the garden?—In the gallery, thou meanest, replied my uncle *Toby*.

Trim found he was upon a wrong scent, and stopped short with a low bow—Two misfortunes, quoth the corporal to himself, are twice as many at least as are needful to be talked over at one time,—the mischief the cow has done in breaking into the fortifications, may be told his honour hereafter—*Trim*'s casuistry and address, under the cover of his low bow, prevented all suspicion in my uncle *Toby*, so he went on with what he had to say to *Trim* as follows.

—For my own part, *Trim*, though I can see little or no difference betwixt my nephew's being called *Tristram* or *Trismegistus*—yet as the thing sits so near my brother's heart, *Trim*,—I would freely have given a hundred pounds rather than it should have happened—A hundred pounds, an' please your honour, replied *Trim*,—I would not give a cherry-stone to boot—Nor would I, *Trim*, upon my own account, quoth my uncle *Toby*—but my brother, whom there is no arguing with in this case— maintains that a great deal more depends, *Trim*, upon christian names, than what ignorant people imagine;——for he says there never was a great or heroic action performed since the world began by one called *Tristram*—nay he will have it, *Trim*, that a man can neither be learned, or wise, or brave—'Tis all a fancy, an' please your honour—I fought just as well, replied the corporal, when the regiment called me *Trim*, as when they called me *James Butler* [1]—And for my own part, said my uncle *Toby*, though I should blush to boast of myself, *Trim*,—yet had my name been *Alexander*, I could have done no more at *Namur* than my duty—Bless your honour! cried *Trim*, advancing three steps as he spoke, does a man think of his christian name when he goes upon the attack?—Or when he stands in the trench, *Trim*? cried my uncle *Toby*, looking firm—Or when he enters a breach? said *Trim*, pushing in between two chairs—Or forces the lines? cried my uncle, rising up, and pushing his crutch like a pike—Or facing a platoon, cried *Trim*, presenting his stick like a firelock—Or when he marches up the glacis, cried my uncle *Toby*, looking warm and setting his foot upon his stool.——

CHAP. XIX.

M Y father was returned from his walk to the fish-pond—and opened the parlour-door in the very height of the attack, just as my uncle *Toby* was marching up the glacis—*Trim* recovered his arms—never was my uncle *Toby* caught riding at such a desperate rate in his life! Alas! my uncle *Toby!* had not a weightier matter called forth all the ready eloquence of my father—how hadst thou then and thy poor HOBBY-HORSE too have been insulted!

My father hung up his hat with the same air he took it down; and after giving a slight look at the disorder of the room, he took hold of one of the chairs which had formed the corporal's breach, and placing it over-against my uncle *Toby*, he sat down in it, and as soon as the tea-things were taken away and the door shut, he broke out in a lamentation as follows.

MY FATHER'S LAMENTATION.

I T is in vain longer, said my father, addressing himself as much to *Ernulphus*'s curse, which was laid upon the corner of the chimney-piece,—as to my uncle *Toby* who sat under it—it is in vain longer, said my father, in the most querulous monotone imaginable, to struggle as I have done against this most uncomfortable of human persuasions—I see it plainly, that either for my own sins, brother *Toby*, or the sins and follies of the *Shandy*-family,[1] heaven has thought fit to draw forth the heaviest of its artillery against me; and that the prosperity of my child is the point upon which the whole force of it is directed to play——Such a thing would batter the whole universe about our ears, brother *Shandy*, said my uncle *Toby*,—if it was so—Unhappy *Tristram!* child of wrath![2] child of decrepitude! interruption! mistake! and discontent! What one misfortune or disaster in the book of embryotic evils,[3] that could unmechanize thy frame, or entangle thy filaments! which has not fallen upon thy head, or ever thou camest into the world—what evils in thy passage into it!— What evils since!—produced into being, in the decline of thy father's days—when the powers of his imagination and of his body were waxing feeble——when radical heat[4] and radical moisture, the elements which should have temper'd thine, were drying up; and nothing left to found thy stamina[5] in, but negations——'tis pitiful——brother *Toby*, at the best, and called out for all the little helps that care and attention on both sides could give it. But how were we defeated! You know the event, brother *Toby*,——'tis too melancholy a one to be repeated now,——when the few animal spirits I was worth in the world, and with which memory, fancy, and quick parts should have been convey'd,——were all dispersed, confused, confounded, scattered, and sent to the devil.——

Here then was the time to have put a stop to this persecution against him;——and tried an experiment at least——whether calmness and serenity of mind in your sister, with a due attention, brother *Toby*, to her evacuations and repletions——and the rest of her non-naturals,[6] might not, in a course of nine months gestation, have set all things to rights.——My child was bereft of these!——What a teazing life did she lead herself, and consequently her fœtus too, with that nonsensical anxiety of hers about lying in in town? I thought my sister submitted with the greatest patience, replied my uncle *Toby*——I never heard her utter one fretful word about it——She fumed inwardly, cried my father; and that, let me tell you, brother, was ten times worse for the child——and then! what battles did she fight with me, and what perpetual storms about the midwife——There she gave vent,[7] said my uncle *Toby*——Vent! cried my father, looking up——

But what was all this, my dear *Toby*, to the injuries done us by my child's coming head foremost into the world, when all I wished in this general wreck of his frame, was to have saved this little casket unbroke, unrifled——

With all my precautions, how was my system turned topside turvy in the womb with my child! his head exposed to the hand of violence, and a pressure of 470 pounds averdupois weight acting so perpendicularly upon its apex——that at this hour 'tis ninety *per Cent.* insurance, that the fine network of the intellectual web be not rent and torn to a thousand tatters.

——Still we could have done.——Fool, coxcomb, puppy——give him but a NOSE——Cripple, Dwarf, Driviller, Goosecap——(shape him as you will) the door of Fortune stands open——O *Licetus! Licetus!* had I been blest with a fœtus five inches long and a half, like thee——fate might have done her worst.

Still, brother *Toby*, there was one cast of the dye left for our child after all——O *Tristram! Tristram! Tristram!*

We will send for Mr. *Yorick*, said my uncle *Toby*.

——You may send for whom you will, replied my father.

CHAP. XX.

WHAT a rate have I gone on at, curvetting and frisking it away, two up and two down for four volumes together, without looking once behind, or even on one side of me, to see whom I trod upon!—I'll tread upon no one,—quoth I to myself when I mounted—I'll take a good rattling gallop; but I'll not hurt the poorest jack-ass upon the road—So off I set—up one lane—down another, through this turn-pike—over that, as if the arch-jockey of jockeys had got behind me.

Now ride at this rate with what good intention and resolution you may,—'tis a million to one you'll do some one a mischief, if not yourself—He's flung—he's off—he's lost his seat—he's down—he'll break his neck—see!—if he has not galloped full amongst the scaffolding of the undertaking criticks![1]—he'll knock his brains out against some of their posts—he's bounced out!—look—he's now riding like a madcap full tilt through a whole crowd of painters, fiddlers, poets, biographers, physicians, lawyers, logicians, players, schoolmen, churchmen, statesmen, soldiers, casuists, connoisseurs, prelates, popes, and engineers—Don't fear, said I—I'll not hurt the poorest jack-ass upon the king's high-way—But your horse throws dirt; see you've splash'd a bishop[2]—I hope in God, 'twas only *Ernulphus*, said I—But you have squirted full in the faces of Mess. *Le Moyne, De Romigny,* and *De Marcilly,* doctors of the Sorbonne[3]—That was last year, replied I—But you have trod this moment upon a king.——Kings have bad times on't, said I, to be trod upon by such people as me.

—You have done it, replied my accuser.

I deny it, quoth I, and so have got off, and here am I standing with my bridle in one hand, and with my cap in the other, to tell my story—And what is it? You shall hear in the next chapter.

CHAP. XXI.

AS *Francis* the first of *France* was one winterly night warming himself over the embers of a wood fire, and talking with his first minister of sundry things for the good of the state*[1]—it would not be amiss, said the king, stirring up the embers with his cane, if this good understanding betwixt ourselves and *Switzerland* was a little strengthened—There is no end, Sire, replied the minister, in giving money to these people—they would swallow up the treasury of *France*—Poo! poo! answered the king——there are more ways, Mons. *le Premier*, of bribing states, besides that of giving money——I'll pay *Switzerland* the honour of standing godfather for my next child—Your majesty, said the minister, in so doing, would have all the grammarians in *Europe* upon your back;—*Switzerland*, as a republick, being a female, can in no construction be godfather—She may be godmother, replied *Francis*, hastily—so announce my intentions by a courier to morrow morning.

I am astonished, said *Francis* the First, (that day fortnight) speaking to his minister as he entered the closet, that we have had no answer from *Switzerland*—Sire, I wait upon you this moment, said Mons. *le Premier*, to lay before you my dispatches upon that business.—They take it kindly? said the king—They do, Sire, replied the minister, and have the highest sense of the honour your majesty has done them—but the republick, as godmother, claims her right in this case, of naming the child.

In all reason, quoth the king—she will christen him *Francis*, or *Henry*, or *Lewis*, or some name that she knows will be agreeable to us. Your majesty is deceived, replied the minister—I have this hour received a dispatch from our resident, with the determination of the republick on that point also—And what name has the republick fixed upon for the Dauphin?—*Shadrach*, *Mesech*, and *Abed-nego*,[2] replied the minister—By saint *Peter*'s girdle,[3] I will have nothing to do with the *Swiss*, cried *Francis* the First, pulling up his breeches[4] and walking hastily across the floor.

Your majesty, replied the minister calmly, cannot bring yourself off.

We'll pay them in money—said the king.

*Vide Menagiana, vol. I.

Sire, there are not sixty thousand crowns in the treasury, answered the minister——I'll pawn the best jewel in my crown, quoth *Francis* the First.

Your honour stands pawn'd already in this matter, answered Monsieur *le Premier*.

Then, Mons. *le Premier*, said the king, by ——— we'll go to war with 'em.

CHAP. XXII.

ALBEIT, gentle reader, I have lusted earnestly, and endeavoured carefully (according to the measure of such slender skill as God has vouchsafed me, and as convenient leisure from other occasions of needful profit and healthful pastime have permitted) that these little books, which I here put into thy hands, might stand instead of many bigger books— yet have I carried myself towards thee in such fanciful guise of careless disport,[1] that right sore am I ashamed now to entreat thy lenity seriously— in beseeching thee to believe it of me, that in the story of my father and his christen-names,—I had no thoughts of treading upon *Francis* the First—nor in the affair of the nose—upon *Francis* the Ninth[2]—nor in the character of my uncle *Toby*—of characterizing the militiating spirits of my country—the wound upon his groin, is a wound to every comparison of that kind,—nor by *Trim*,—that I meant the duke of *Ormond*[3]—or that my book is wrote against predestination, or free will, or taxes—If 'tis wrote against any thing,——'tis wrote, an' please your worships, against the spleen; in order, by a more frequent and a more convulsive elevation and depression of the diaphragm, and the succussations of the intercostal and abdominal muscles in laughter, to drive the *gall* and other *bitter juices* from the gall bladder, liver and sweet-bread of his majesty's subjects, with all the inimicitious passions which belong to them, down into their duodenums.[4]

CHAP. XXIII.

—BUT can the thing be undone, *Yorick?* said my father—for in my opinion, continued he, it cannot. I am a vile canonist, replied *Yorick*—but of all evils, holding suspense to be the most tormenting, we shall at least know the worst of this matter. I hate these great dinners[1] — said my father—The size of the dinner is not the point, answered *Yorick*— we want, Mr. *Shandy*, to dive into the bottom of this doubt, whether the name can be changed or not—and as the beards of so many commissaries, officials, advocates, proctors, registers, and of the most able of our school-divines, and others, are all to meet in the middle of one table, and *Didius* has so pressingly invited you,——who in your distress would miss such an occasion? All that is requisite, continued *Yorick*, is to apprize *Didius*, and let him manage a conversation after dinner so as to introduce the subject—Then my brother *Toby*, cried my father, clapping his two hands together, shall go with us.

—Let my old tye wig, quoth my uncle *Toby*, and my laced regimentals, be hung to the fire all night, *Trim.*

CHAP. XXV.

—NO doubt, Sir—there is a whole chapter wanting here—and a chasm of ten pages[1] made in the book by it—but the book-binder is neither a fool, or a knave, or a puppy—nor is the book a jot more imperfect, (at least upon that score)—but, on the contrary, the book is more perfect and complete by wanting the chapter, than having it, as I shall demonstrate to your reverences in this manner—I question first by the bye, whether the same experiment might not be made as successfully upon sundry other chapters——but there is no end, an' please your reverences, in trying experiments upon chapters—we have had enough of it—So there's an end of that matter.

But before I begin my demonstration, let me only tell you, that the chapter which I have torn out, and which otherwise you would all have been reading just now, instead of this,—was the description of my father's, my uncle *Toby*'s, *Trim*'s, and *Obadiah*'s setting out and journeying to the visitations at ****.

We'll go in the coach, said my father—Prithee, have the arms been altered, *Obadiah?*—It would have made my story much better, to have begun with telling you, that at the time my mother's arms were added to the *Shandy*'s, when the coach was repainted upon my father's marriage, it had so fallen out, that the coach-painter, whether by performing all his works with the left-hand, like *Turpilius* the *Roman*, or *Hans Holbein* of *Basil*[2]—or whether 'twas more from the blunder of his head than hand—or whether, lastly, it was from the sinister turn, which every thing relating to our family was apt to take—It so fell out, however, to our reproach, that instead of the *bend dexter*,[3] which since *Harry* the Eighth's reign was honestly our due——a *bend sinister*, by some of these fatalities, had been drawn quite across the field of the *Shandy*-arms. 'Tis scarce credible that the mind of so wise a man as my father was, could be so much incommoded with so small a matter. The word coach—let it be whose it would—or coach-man, or coach-horse, or coach-hire, could never be named in the family, but he constantly complained of carrying this vile mark of Illegitimacy upon the door of his own; he never once was able to step into the coach, or out of it, without turning round to take a view of the arms, and making a vow at the same time, that it was the last time he would ever set his foot in it again, till the *bend-sinister* was taken out—but like the affair of the hinge, it was one of the many things which the *Destinies* had set down in their books—ever to be grumbled at (and in wiser families than ours)—but never to be mended.

—Has the *bend-sinister* been brush'd out, I say? said my father—There has been nothing brush'd out, Sir, answered *Obadiah*, but the lining. We'll go o'horse-back, said my father, turning to *Yorick*—Of all things in the world, except politicks, the clergy know the least of heraldry, said *Yorick* —No matter for that, cried my father—I should be sorry to appear with a blot in my escutcheon⁴ before them——Never mind the *bend-sinister*, said my uncle *Toby*, putting on his tye-wig—No, indeed, said my father,—you may go with my aunt *Dinah* to a visitation with a *bend-sinister*, if you think fit—My poor uncle *Toby* blush'd. My father was vexed at himself—No—my dear brother *Toby*, said my father, changing his tone—but the damp of the coach-lining about my loins, may give me the Sciatica again, as it did *December*, *January*, and *February* last winter—so if you please you shall ride my wife's pad—and as you are to preach, *Yorick*, you had better make the best of your way before,— and leave me to take care of my brother *Toby*, and to follow at our own rates.

Now the chapter I was obliged to tear out, was the description of this cavalcade, in which corporal *Trim* and *Obadiah*, upon two coach-horses a-breast, led the way as slow as a patrole—whilst my uncle *Toby*, in his laced regimentals and tye-wig, kept his rank with my father, in deep roads and dissertations alternately upon the advantage of learning and arms, as each could get the start.

—But the painting of this journey, upon reviewing it, appears to be so much above the stile and manner of any thing else I have been able to paint in this book, that it could not have remained in it, without depreciating every other scene; and destroying at the same time that necessary equipoise and balance, (whether of good or bad) betwixt chapter and chapter, from whence the just proportions and harmony of the whole work results. For my own part, I am but just set up in the business, so know little about it—but, in my opinion, to write a book is for all the world like humming a song—be but in tune with yourself, madam, 'tis no matter how high or how low you take it.—

—This is the reason, may it please your reverences, that some of the lowest and flattest compositions pass off very well—(as *Yorick* told my uncle *Toby* one night) by siege[5]—My uncle *Toby* looked brisk at the sound of the word *siege,* but could make neither head or tail of it.

I'm to preach at court next Sunday, said *Homenas*[6]—run over my notes—so I humm'd over doctor *Homenas*'s notes—the modulation's very well—'twill do, *Homenas,* if it holds on at this rate—so on I humm'd—and a tolerable tune I thought it was; and to this hour, may it please your reverences, had never found out how low, how flat, how spiritless and jejune it was, but that all of a sudden, up started an air in the middle of it, so fine, so rich, so heavenly—it carried my soul up with it into the other world; now had I, (as *Montaigne* complained[7] in a parallel accident)—had I found the declivity easy, or the ascent accessible—certes I had been outwitted—Your notes, *Homenas,* I should have said, are good notes,— but it was so perpendicular a precipice—so wholly cut off from the rest of the work, that by the first note I humm'd, I found myself flying into the other world, and from thence discovered the vale from whence I came, so deep, so low, and dismal, that I shall never have the heart to descend into it again.

☞ A dwarf who brings a standard along with him to measure his own size—take my word, is a dwarf in more articles than one—And so much for tearing out of chapters.

CHAP. XXVI.

SEE if he is not cutting it all into slips, and giving them about him to light their pipes![1]—'Tis abominable, answered *Didius*; it should not go unnoticed, said doctor *Kysarcius*[2]—☞ he was of the *Kysarcij* of the low countries.

Methinks, said *Didius,* half rising from his chair, in order to remove a bottle and a tall decanter, which stood in a direct line betwixt him and *Yorick*—you might have spared this sarcastick stroke, and have hit upon a more proper place, Mr. *Yorick*—or at least upon a more proper occasion to have shewn your contempt of what we have been about: If the Sermon is of no better worth than to light pipes with—'twas certainly, Sir, not good enough to be preached before so learned a body; and if 'twas good enough to be preached before so learned a body—'twas certainly, Sir, too good to light their pipes with afterwards.

—I have got him fast hung up, quoth *Didius* to himself, upon one of the two horns of my dilemma—let him get off as he can.

I have undergone such unspeakable torments, in bringing forth this sermon, quoth *Yorick*, upon this occasion,—that I declare, *Didius*, I would suffer martyrdom—and if it was possible my horse with me, a thousand times over, before I would sit down and make such another: I was delivered of it at the wrong end of me—it came from my head instead of my heart[3]—and it is for the pain it gave me, both in the writing and preaching of it, that I revenge myself of it, in this manner.—To preach, to shew the extent of our reading, or the subtleties of our wit—to parade it in the eyes of the vulgar with the beggarly accounts of a little learning, tinseled over with a few words which glitter, but convey little light and less warmth—is a dishonest use of the poor single half hour in a week which is put into our hands—'Tis not preaching the gospel—but ourselves— For my own part, continued *Yorick*, I had rather direct five words point blank to the heart[4]—

As *Yorick* pronounced the word *point blank*, my uncle *Toby* rose up to say something upon projectiles——when a single word, and no more, uttered from the opposite side of the table, drew every one's ears towards it—a word of all others in the dictionary the last in that place to be expected—a word I am ashamed to write—yet must be written—must be read;—illegal—uncanonical—guess ten thousand guesses, multiplied into themselves—rack—torture your invention for ever, you're where you was—In short, I'll tell it in the next chapter.

CHAP. XXVII.

Z OUNDS![1] ————————————————————

————————————————————————————

————————————————————— Z——ds! cried *Phutatorius*,[2] partly to himself—and yet high enough to be heard—and what seemed odd, 'twas uttered in a construction of look, and in a tone of voice, somewhat between that of a man in amazement, and of one in bodily pain.

One or two who had very nice ears, and could distinguish the expression and mixture of the two tones as plainly as a *third* or a *fifth*, or any other chord in musick—were the most puzzled and perplexed with it—the *concord* was good in itself—but then 'twas quite out of the key, and no way applicable to the subject started;—so that with all their knowledge, they could not tell what in the world to make of it.

Others who knew nothing of musical expression, and merely lent their ears to the plain import of the *word*, imagined that *Phutatorius*, who was somewhat of a cholerick spirit, was just going to snatch the cudgels out of *Didius*'s hands, in order to bemawl *Yorick* to some purpose—and that the desperate monosyllable Z——ds was the exordium to an oration, which, as they judged from the sample, presaged but a rough kind of handling of him; so that my uncle *Toby*'s good nature felt a pang for what *Yorick* was about to undergo. But seeing *Phutatorius* stop short, without any attempt or desire to go on—a third party began to suppose, that it was no more than an involuntary respiration, casually forming itself into the shape of a twelve-penny oath[3]—without the sin or substance of one.

Others, and especially one or two who sat next him, looked upon it on the contrary, as a real and substantial oath propensly formed against *Yorick*, to whom he was known to bear no good liking—which said oath, as my father philosophized upon it, actually lay fretting and fuming at that very time in the upper regions of *Phutatorius*'s purtenance; and so was naturally, and according to the due course of things, first squeezed out by the sudden influx of blood, which was driven into the right ventricle of *Phutatorius*'s heart, by the stroke of surprize which so strange a theory of preaching had excited.

How finely we argue upon mistaken facts!

There was not a soul busied in all these various reasonings upon the monosyllable which *Phutatorius* uttered,—who did not take this for granted, proceeding upon it as from an axiom, namely, that *Phutatorius*'s mind was intent upon the subject of debate which was arising between *Didius* and *Yorick*; and indeed as he looked first towards the one, and then towards the other, with the air of a man listening to what was going forwards,—who would not have thought the same? But the truth was, that *Phutatorius* knew not one word or one syllable of what was passing—but his whole thoughts and attention were taken up with a transaction which was going forwards at that very instant within the precincts of his own *Galligaskins*, and in a part of them, where of all others he stood most interested to watch accidents: So that notwithstanding he looked with all the attention in the world, and had gradually skrewed up every nerve and muscle in his face, to the utmost pitch the instrument would bear, in order, as it was thought, to give a sharp reply to *Yorick*, who sat over-against him—Yet I say, was *Yorick* never once in any one domicile of *Phutatorius*'s brain—but the true cause of his exclamation lay at least a yard below.[4]

This I will endeavour to explain to you with all imaginable decency.

You must be informed then, that *Gastripheres*,[5] who had taken a turn into the kitchen a little before dinner, to see how things went on—observing a wicker-basket of fine chesnuts standing upon the dresser, had ordered that a hundred or two of them might be roasted and sent in, as soon as dinner was over—*Gastripheres* inforcing his orders about them, that *Didius*, but *Phutatorius* especially, were particularly fond of 'em.

About two minutes before the time that my uncle *Toby* interrupted *Yorick*'s harangue—*Gastripheres*'s chesnuts were brought in—and as *Phutatorius*'s fondness for 'em, was uppermost in the waiter's head, he laid them directly before *Phutatorius*, wrapt up hot in a clean damask napkin.

Now whether it was physically impossible, with half a dozen hands all thrust into the napkin at a time—but that some one chesnut, of more life and rotundity than the rest, must be put in motion—it so fell out, however, that one was actually sent rolling off the table; and as *Phutatorius* sat straddling under—it fell perpendicularly into that particular aperture of *Phutatorius*'s breeches, for which, to the shame and indelicacy of our language be it spoke, there is no chaste word throughout all *Johnson*'s dictionary[6]—let it suffice to say—it was that particular aperture, which in all good societies, the laws of decorum do strictly require, like the temple of *Janus*[7] (in peace at least) to be universally shut up.

The neglect of this punctilio in *Phutatorius* (which by the bye should be a warning to all mankind) had opened a door to this accident.—

—Accident, I call it, in compliance to a received mode of speaking,—but in no opposition to the opinion either of *Acrites* or *Mythogeras*[8] in this matter; I know they were both prepossessed and fully persuaded of it—and are so to this hour, That there was nothing of accident in the whole event—but that the chesnut's taking that particular course, and in a manner of its own accord—and then falling with all its heat directly into that one particular place, and no other——was a real judgment upon

Phutatorius, for that filthy and obscene treatise *de Concubinis retinendis*,[9] which *Phutatorius* had published about twenty years ago—and was that identical week going to give the world a second edition of.

It is not my business to dip my pen in this controversy——much undoubtedly may be wrote on both sides of the question—all that concerns me as an historian, is to represent the matter of fact, and render it credible to the reader, that the hiatus in *Phutatorius*'s breeches was sufficiently wide to receive the chesnut;—and that the chesnut, some how or other, did fall perpendicularly and piping hot into it, without *Phutatorius*'s perceiving it, or any one else at that time.

The genial warmth which the chesnut imparted, was not undelectable for the first twenty or five and twenty seconds,—and did no more than gently solicit *Phutatorius*'s attention towards the part:—But the heat gradually increasing, and in a few seconds more getting beyond the point of all sober pleasure, and then advancing with all speed into the regions of pain,—the soul of *Phutatorius*, together with all his ideas, his thoughts, his attention, his imagination, judgment, resolution, deliberation, ratiocination, memory, fancy, with ten batallions of animal spirits, all tumultuously crouded down, through different defiles and circuits, to the place in danger, leaving all his upper regions, as you may imagine, as empty as my purse.

With the best intelligence which all these messengers could bring him back, *Phutatorius* was not able to dive into the secret of what was going forwards below, nor could he make any kind of conjecture, what the devil was the matter with it: However, as he knew not what the true cause might turn out, he deemed it most prudent, in the situation he was in at present, to bear it, if possible, like a stoick; which, with the help of some wry faces and compursions[10] of the mouth, he had certainly accomplished, had his imagination continued neuter—but the sallies of the imagination are ungovernable in things of this kind—a thought instantly darted into his mind, that tho' the anguish had the sensation of glowing heat—it might, notwithstanding that, be a bite as well as a burn; and if so, that possibly a *Newt* or an *Asker*,[11] or some such detested reptile, had crept up, and was fastening his teeth—the horrid idea of which, with a fresh glow of pain arising that instant from the chesnut, seized *Phutatorius* with a sudden panick, and in the first terrifying disorder of the passion it threw him, as it has done the best generals upon earth, quite off his guard;—the effect of which was this, that he leapt incontinently up, uttering as he rose that interjection of surprise so much discanted upon, with the aposiopestick-

break[12] after it, marked thus, Z——ds—which, though not strictly canonical, was still as little as any man could have said upon the occasion;——
and which, by the bye, whether canonical or not, *Phutatorius* could no
more help than he could the cause of it.

Though this has taken up some time in the narrative, it took up little
more time in the transaction, than just to allow time for *Phutatorius* to draw
forth the chesnut, and throw it down with violence upon the floor—and
for *Yorick*, to rise from his chair, and pick the chesnut up.

It is curious to observe the triumph of slight incidents over the mind:—
What incredible weight they have in forming and governing our opinions,
both of men and things,—that trifles light as air,[13] shall waft a belief into the
soul, and plant it so immoveably within it,—that *Euclid*'s demonstrations,[14]
could they be brought to batter it in breach, should not all have power to
overthrow it.

Yorick, I said, picked up the chesnut which *Phutatorius*'s wrath had flung
down—the action was trifling—I am ashamed to account for it—he did
it, for no reason, but that he thought the chesnut not a jot worse for the
adventure—and that he held a good chesnut worth stooping for.[15]—But
this incident, trifling as it was, wrought differently in *Phutatorius*'s head:
He considered this act of *Yorick*'s, in getting off his chair, and picking up
the chesnut, as a plain acknowledgment in him, that the chesnut was
originally his,—and in course, that it must have been the owner of the
chesnut, and no one else, who could have plaid him such a prank with it:
What greatly confirmed him in this opinion, was this, that the table being
parallelogramical and very narrow, it afforded a fair opportunity for *Yorick*,
who sat directly over-against *Phutatorius*, of slipping the chesnut in—and
consequently that he did it. The look of something more than suspicion,
which *Phutatorius* cast full upon *Yorick* as these thoughts arose, too evidently
spoke his opinion—and as *Phutatorius* was naturally supposed to know
more of the matter than any person besides, his opinion at once became
the general one;—and for a reason very different from any which have
been yet given—in a little time it was put out of all manner of dispute.

When great or unexpected events fall out upon the stage of this sub-
lunary world—the mind of man, which is an inquisitive kind of a
substance, naturally takes a flight, behind the scenes, to see what is the
cause and first spring of them—The search was not long in this instance.

It was well known that *Yorick* had never a good opinion of the treatise
which *Phutatorius* had wrote *de Concubinis retinendis*, as a thing which he

feared had done hurt in the world—and 'twas easily found out, that there was a mystical meaning in *Yorick*'s prank—and that his chucking the chesnut hot into *Phutatorius*'s ***—*****, was a sarcastical fling at his book—the doctrines of which, they said, had inflamed many an honest man in the same place.

This conceit awaken'd *Somnolentus*—made *Agelastes* smile—and if you can recollect the precise look and air of a man's face intent in finding out a riddle—it threw *Gastripheres*'s into that form—and in short was thought by many to be a master-stroke of arch-wit.

This, as the reader has seen from one end to the other, was as groundless as the dreams of philosophy: *Yorick*, no doubt, as *Shakespear* said of his ancestor—*"was a man of jest,"*[16] but it was temper'd with something which withheld him from that, and many other ungracious pranks, of which he as undeservedly bore the blame;—but it was his misfortune all his life long to bear the imputation of saying and doing a thousand things of which (unless my esteem blinds me) his nature was incapable. All I blame him for—or rather, all I blame and alternately like him for, was that singularity of his temper, which would never suffer him to take pains to set a story right with the world, however in his power. In every ill usage of that sort, he acted precisely as in the affair of his lean horse—he could have explained it to his honour, but his spirit was above it; and besides he ever looked upon the inventor, the propagator and believer of an illiberal report alike so injurious to him,—he could not stoop to tell his story to them— and so trusted to time and truth to do it for him.

This heroic cast produced him inconveniences in many respects—in the present, it was followed by the fixed resentment of *Phutatorius*, who, as *Yorick* had just made an end of his chesnut, rose up from his chair a second time, to let him know it—which indeed he did with a smile; saying only—that he would endeavour not to forget the obligation.

But you must mark and carefully separate and distinguish these two things in your mind.

—The smile was for the company.

—The threat was for *Yorick*.

CHAP. XXVIII.

—CAN you tell me, quoth *Phutatorius*, speaking to *Gastripheres* who sat next to him,—for one would not apply to a surgeon in so foolish an affair,—can you tell me, *Gastripheres*, what is best to take out the fire?[1]—Ask *Eugenius*, said *Gastripheres*—That greatly depends, said *Eugenius*, pretending ignorance of the adventure, upon the nature of the part—If it is a tender part, and a part which can conveniently be wrapt up—It is both the one and the other, replied *Phutatorius*, laying his hand as he spoke, with an emphatical nod of his head upon the part in question, and lifting up his right leg at the same time to ease and ventilate it—If that is the case, said *Eugenius*, I would advise you, *Phutatorius*, not to tamper with it by any means; but if you will send to the next printer, and trust your cure to such a simple thing as a soft sheet of paper just come off the press—you need do nothing more than twist it round—The damp paper, quoth *Yorick* (who sat next to his friend *Eugenius)* though I know it has a refreshing coolness in it—yet I presume is no more than the vehicle—and that the oil and lamp-black with which the paper is so strongly impregnated, does the business—Right, said *Eugenius*, and is of any outward application I would venture to recommend the most anodyne and safe.

Was it my case, said *Gastripheres*, as the main thing is the oil and lamp-black, I should spread them thick upon a rag, and clap it on directly. That would make a very devil[2] of it, replied *Yorick*—And besides, added *Eugenius*, it would not answer the intention, which is the extreame neatness and elegance of the prescription, which the faculty hold to be half in half—for consider, if the type is a very small one, (which it should be) the sanative particles, which come into contact in this form, have the advantage of being spread so infinitely thin and with such a mathematical equality (fresh paragraphs and large capitals excepted) as no art or manage-ment of the spatula can come up to. It falls out very luckily, replied *Phutatorius*, that the second edition of my treatise *de Concubinis retinendis*, is at this instant in the press—You may take any leaf of it, said *Eugenius*—No matter which—provided, quoth *Yorick*, there is no bawdry in it—

They are just now, replied *Phutatorius*, printing off the ninth chapter—which is the last chapter but one in the book—Pray what is the title to that chapter, said *Yorick*, making a respectful bow to *Phutatorius* as he spoke—I think, answered *Phutatorius*, 'tis that, *de re concubinariâ*.[3]

For heaven's sake keep out of that chapter, quoth *Yorick*.

—By all means—added *Eugenius*.

CHAP. XXIX.

—NOW, quoth *Didius*, rising up, and laying his right-hand with his fingers spread upon his breast—had such a blunder about a christian-name happened before the reformation—(It happened the day before yesterday, quoth my uncle *Toby* to himself) and when baptism was administer'd in *Latin*——('Twas all in *English*, said my uncle)—Many things might have coincided with it, and upon the authority of sundry decreed cases, to have pronounced the baptism null, with a power of giving the child a new name—Had a priest, for instance, which was no uncommon thing, through ignorance of the *Latin* tongue, baptized a child of Tom-o'Stiles, *in nomino patriæ & filia & spiritum sanctos*,—the baptism was held null—I beg your pardon, replied *Kysarcius*,—in that case, as the mistake was only in the *terminations*, the baptism was valid—and to have rendered it null, the blunder of the priest should have fallen upon the first syllable of each noun—and not, as in your case, upon the last.[1]—

My father delighted in subtleties of this kind, and listen'd with infinite attention.

Gastripheres, for example, continued *Kysarcius*, baptizes a child of *John Stradling*'s,[2] *in Gomine gatris*, *&c. &c.* instead of *in Nomine patris*, *&c.*—Is this a baptism? No,—say the ablest canonists; inasmuch as the radix of each word is hereby torn up, and the sense and meaning of them removed and changed quite to another object; for *Gomine* does not signify a name, nor *gatris* a father—What do they signify? said my uncle *Toby*—Nothing at all—quoth *Yorick*—Ergo, such a baptism is null, said *Kysarcius*—In course, answered *Yorick*, in a tone two parts jest and one part earnest—

But in the case cited, continued *Kysarcius*, where *patrim* is put for *patris*, *filia* for *filij*, and so on—as it is a fault only in the declension, and the roots of the words continue untouch'd, the inflexions of their branches, either this way or that, does not in any sort hinder the baptism, inasmuch as the same sense continues in the words as before—But then, said *Didius*, the intention of the priest's pronouncing them grammatically, must have been proved to have gone along with it—Right, answered *Kysarcius*; and of this, brother *Didius*, we have an instance in a decree of the decretals of Pope *Leo* the IIId.—But my brother's child, cried my uncle *Toby*, has nothing to do with the Pope—'tis the plain child of a Protestant gentleman, christen'd *Tristram* against the wills and wishes both of its father and mother, and all who are a-kin to it—

If the wills and wishes, said *Kysarcius*, interrupting my uncle *Toby*, of those only who stand related to Mr. *Shandy*'s child, were to have weight in this matter, Mrs. *Shandy*, of all people, has the least to do in it—My uncle *Toby* lay'd down his pipe, and my father drew his chair still closer to the table to hear the conclusion of so strange an introduction.

It has not only been a question, captain *Shandy*, amongst the* best lawyers[3] and civilians[4] in this land, continued *Kysarcius*, "*Whether the mother be of kin to her child,*"—but after much dispassionate enquiry and jactitation[5] of the arguments on all sides,—it has been adjudged for the negative,—namely, "*That the mother is not of kin to her child*†." My father instantly clapp'd his hand upon my uncle *Toby*'s mouth, under colour of whispering in his ear—the truth was, he was alarmed for *Lillabullero*—and having a great desire to hear more of so curious an argument—he begg'd my uncle *Toby*, for heaven's sake, not to disappoint him in it—My uncle *Toby* gave a nod—resumed his pipe, and contenting himself with whistling *Lillabullero* inwardly—*Kysarcius*, *Didius*, and *Triptolemus*[6] went on with the discourse as follows.

This determination, continued *Kysarcius*, how contrary soever it may seem to run to the stream of vulgar ideas, yet had reason strongly on its side; and has been put out of all manner of dispute from the famous case, known commonly by the name of the Duke of *Suffolk*'s case:—It is cited in *Brook*, said *Triptolemus*—And taken notice of by Lord *Coke*,[7] added *Didius*—And you may find it in *Swinburn* on Testaments, said *Kysarcius*.

The case, Mr. *Shandy*, was this.

In the reign of *Edward* the Sixth, *Charles* Duke of *Suffolk* having issue a son by one venter, and a daughter by another venter, made his last will,

---

* Vid. Swinburn on Testaments, Part 7. § 8.

† Vid. Brook Abridg. Tit. Administr. N. 47.

wherein he devised goods to his son, and died; after whose death the son died also—but without will, without wife, and without child—his mother and his sister by the father's side (for she was born of the former venter) then living. The mother took the administration of her son's goods, according to the statute of the 21st of *Harry* the Eighth, whereby it is enacted, That in case any person die intestate, the administration of his goods shall be committed to the next of kin.

The administration being thus (surreptitiously) granted to the mother, the sister by the father's side commenced a suit before the Ecclesiastical Judge, alledging, 1st, That she herself was next of kin; and 2dly, That the mother was not of kin at all to the party deceased; and therefore pray'd the court, that the administration granted to the mother might be revoked, and be committed unto her, as next of kin to the deceased, by force of the said statute.

Hereupon, as it was a great cause, and much depending upon its issue—and many causes of great property likely to be decided in times to come, by the precedent to be then made—the most learned, as well in the laws of this realm, as in the civil law, were consulted together, whether the mother was of kin to her son, or no.—Whereunto not only the temporal lawyers—but the church-lawyers—the juris-consulti[8]—the juris-prudentes[9]—the civilians—the advocates—the commissaries—the judges of the consistory and prerogative courts[10] of *Canterbury* and *York*, with the master of the faculties, were all unanimously of opinion, That the mother was not of * kin to her child—

And what said the Duchess of *Suffolk* to it? said my uncle *Toby*.

The unexpectedness of my uncle *Toby*'s question, confounded *Kysarcius* more than the ablest advocate——He stopp'd a full minute, looking in my uncle *Toby*'s face without replying——and in that single minute *Triptolemus* put by him, and took the lead as follows.

'Tis a ground and principle in the law, said *Triptolemus*, that things do not ascend, but descend in it; and I make no doubt 'tis for this cause, that however true it is, that the child may be of the blood or seed of its parents—that the parents, nevertheless, are not of the blood and seed of it; inasmuch as the parents are not begot by the child, but the child by the parents—For so they write, *Liberi sunt de sanguine patris & matris, sed pater et mater non sunt de sanguine liberorum.*[11]

---

* Mater non numeratur inter consaguineos. Bald. in ult. C. de Verb. signific.[12]

—But this, *Triptolemus*, cried *Didius*, proves too much—for from this authority cited it would follow, not only what indeed is granted on all sides, that the mother is not of kin to her child—but the father likewise ——It is held, said *Triptolemus*, the better opinion; because the father, the mother, and the child, though they be three persons, yet are they but *(una caro*)* one flesh; and consequently no degree of kindred—or any method of acquiring one *in nature*—There you push the argument again too far, cried *Didius*—for there is no prohibition *in nature*, though there is in the levitical law,[13]—but that a man may beget a child upon his grandmother—in which case, supposing the issue a daughter, she would stand in relation both of——But who ever thought, cried *Kysarcius*, of laying with his grandmother?——The young gentleman, replied *Yorick*, whom *Selden*[14] speaks of—who not only thought of it, but justified his intention to his father by the argument drawn from the law of retaliation——"You lay'd, Sir, with my mother, said the lad—why may not I lay with yours?" ——'Tis the *Argumentum commune*,[15] added *Yorick*.—'Tis as good, replied *Eugenius*, taking down his hat, as they deserve.

The company broke up——

CHAP. XXX.

—AND pray, said my uncle *Toby*, leaning upon *Yorick*, as he and my father were helping him leisurely down the stairs—don't be terrified, madam, this stair-case conversation is not so long as the last— And pray, *Yorick*, said my uncle *Toby*, which way is this said[1] affair of *Tristram* at length settled by these learned men? Very satisfactorily, replied *Yorick*; no mortal, Sir, has any concern with it—for Mrs. *Shandy* the mother is nothing at all akin to him—and as the mother's is the surest side—Mr. *Shandy*, in course, is still less than nothing—In short, he is not as much akin to him, Sir, as I am—

—That may well be, said my father, shaking his head.

—Let the learned say what they will, there must certainly, quoth my

---

*Vide Brook Abridg. tit. Administr. N. 47.

uncle *Toby*, have been some sort of consanguinity betwixt the duchess of *Suffolk* and her son—

The vulgar are of the same opinion, quoth *Yorick*, to this hour.

CHAP. XXXI.

THOUGH my father was hugely tickled with the subtleties of these learned discourses—'twas still but like the anointing of a broken bone—The moment he got home, the weight of his afflictions returned upon him but so much the heavier, as is ever the case when the staff we lean on slips from under us—He became pensive—walked frequently forth to the fish-pond—let down one loop of his hat[1]—sigh'd often— forbore to snap—and, as the hasty sparks of temper, which occasion snapping, so much assist perspiration and digestion, as *Hippocrates*[2] tells us—he had certainly fallen ill with the extinction of them, had not his thoughts been critically drawn off, and his health rescued by a fresh train of disquietudes left him, with a legacy of a thousand pounds by my aunt *Dinah*—

My father had scarce read the letter, when taking the thing by the right end, he instantly begun to plague and puzzle his head how to lay it out mostly to the honour of his family—A hundred and fifty odd projects took possession of his brains by turns—he would do this, and that, and t'other—He would go to *Rome*—he would go to law—he would buy stock—he would buy *John Hobson*'s farm—he would new fore-front his house, and add a new wing to make it even—There was a fine water-mill on this side, and he would build a wind-mill[3] on the other side of the river in full view to answer it—But above all things in the world, he would inclose the great *Ox-moor*, and send out my brother *Bobby* immediately upon his travels.

But as the sum was *finite*, and consequently could not do every thing— and in truth very few of these to any purpose,—of all the projects which offered themselves upon this occasion, the two last seemed to make the deepest impression; and he would infallibly have determined upon both at once, but for the small inconvenience hinted at above, which absolutely put him under a necessity of deciding in favour either of the one or the other.

This was not altogether so easy to be done; for though 'tis certain my father had long before set his heart upon this necessary part of my brother's education, and like a prudent man had actually determined to carry it into execution, with the first money that returned from the second creation of actions in the *Missisippi*-scheme,[4] in which he was an adventurer—yet the *Ox-moor*, which was a fine, large, whinny,[5] undrained, unimproved common, belonging to the *Shandy*-estate, had almost as old a claim upon him: He had long and affectionately set his heart upon turning it likewise to some account.

But having never hitherto been pressed with such a conjuncture of things, as made it necessary to settle either the priority or justice of their claims,—like a wise man he had refrained entering into any nice or critical examination about them: So that upon the dismission of every other project at this crisis,——the two old projects, the Ox-moor and my brother, divided him again; and so equal a match were they for each other, as to become the occasion of no small contest in the old gentleman's mind,—which of the two should be set o'going first.

—People may laugh as they will——but the case was this.

It had ever been the custom of the family, and by length of time was almost become a matter of common right, that the eldest son of it should have free ingress, egress, and regress[6] into foreign parts before marriage,—not only for the sake of bettering his own private parts, by the benefit of exercise and change of so much air—but simply for the mere delectation of his fancy, by the feather put into his cap,[7] of having been abroad—*tantum valet*, my father would say, *quantum sonat*.[8]

Now as this was a reasonable, and in course a most christian indulgence—to deprive him of it, without why or wherefore,—and thereby make an example of him, as the first *Shandy* unwhirl'd about *Europe* in a post-chaise, and only because he was a heavy lad—would be using him ten times worse than a *Turk*.

On the other hand, the case of the *Ox-moor* was full as hard.

Exclusive of the original purchase-money, which was eight hundred pounds—it had cost the family eight hundred pounds more in a law-suit about fifteen years before—besides the Lord knows what trouble and vexation.

It had been moreover in possession of the *Shandy*-family ever since the middle of the last century; and though it lay full in view before the house, bounded on one extremity by the water-mill, and on the other by the projected wind-mill spoken of above,—and for all these reasons seemed to have the fairest title of any part of the estate to the care and protection of the family—yet by an unaccountable fatality, common to men, as well as the ground they tread on,—it had all along most shamefully been overlook'd; and to speak the truth of it, had suffered so much by it, that it would have made any man's heart have bled *(Obadiah* said) who understood the value of land, to have rode over it, and only seen the condition it was in.

However, as neither the purchasing this tract of ground—nor indeed the placing of it where it lay, were either of them, properly speaking, of my father's doing—he had never thought himself any way concerned in the affair—till the fifteen years before, when the breaking out of that cursed law-suit mentioned above (and which had arose about its boundaries)—which being altogether my father's own act and deed, it naturally awakened every other argument in its favour; and upon summing them all up together, he saw, not merely in interest, but in honour, he was bound to do something for it—and that now or never was the time.

I think there must certainly have been a mixture of ill-luck in it, that the reasons on both sides should happen to be so equally balanced by each other; for though my father weigh'd them in all humours and conditions— spent many an anxious hour in the most profound and abstracted meditation upon what was best to be done——reading books of farming one day— books of travels another—laying aside all passion whatever—viewing the arguments on both sides in all their lights and circumstances—— communing every day with my uncle *Toby*—arguing with *Yorick*, and talking over the whole affair of the *Ox-moor* with *Obadiah*—yet nothing in all that time appeared so strongly in behalf of the one, which was not either strictly applicable to the other, or at least so far counterbalanced by some consideration of equal weight, as to keep the scales even.

For to be sure, with proper helps, and in the hands of some people, tho' the *Ox-moor* would undoubtedly have made a different appearance in the world from what it did, or ever would do in the condition it lay—yet every tittle of this was true, with regard to my brother *Bobby*—let *Obadiah* say what he would.——

In point of interest—the contest, I own, at first sight, did not appear so undecisive betwixt them; for whenever my father took pen and ink in hand, and set about calculating the simple expence of paring and burning, and fenceing in the *Ox-moor*, &c. &c.—with the certain profit it would bring him in return—the latter turned out so prodigiously in his way of working the account, that you would have sworn the *Ox-moor* would have carried all before it. For it was plain he should reap a hundred lasts of rape, at twenty pounds a last, the very first year—besides an excellent crop of wheat the year following—and the year after that, to speak within bounds, a hundred——but, in all likelihood, a hundred and fifty—if not two hundred quarters of pease and beans—besides potatoes without end— But then, to think he was all this while breeding up my brother like a hog to eat them—knocked all on the head again, and generally left the old gentleman in such a state of suspence—that, as he often declared to my uncle *Toby*—he knew no more than his heels what to do.

No body, but he who has felt it, can conceive what a plaguing thing it is to have a man's mind torn asunder by two projects of equal strength, both obstinately pulling in a contrary direction at the same time: For to say nothing of the havock, which by a certain consequence is unavoidably made by it all over the finer system of the nerves, which you know convey the animal spirits and more subtle juices from the heart to the head, and so on——It is not to be told in what a degree such a wayward kind of friction works upon the more gross and solid parts, wasting the fat and impairing the strength of a man every time as it goes backwards and forwards.

My father had certainly sunk under this evil, as certainly as he had done under that of my CHRISTIAN NAME—had he not been rescued out of it as he was out of that, by a fresh evil—the misfortune of my brother *Bobby*'s death.

What is the life of man! Is it not to shift from side to side?—from sorrow to sorrow?——to button up one cause of vexation!—and unbutton another!

CHAP. XXXII.

FROM this moment I am to be considered as heir-apparent to the *Shandy* family—and it is from this point properly, that the story of my LIFE and my OPINIONS sets out; with all my hurry and precipitation I have but been clearing the ground to raise the building——and such a building do I foresee it will turn out, as never was planned, and as never was executed since *Adam.* In less than five minutes I shall have thrown my pen into the fire, and the little drop of thick ink which is left remaining at the bottom of my ink-horn, after it—I have but half a score things to do in the time——I have a thing to name—a thing to lament—a thing to hope—a thing to promise, and a thing to threaten—I have a thing to suppose—a thing to declare—a thing to conceal—a thing to chuse, and a thing to pray for.—This chapter, therefore, I *name* the chapter of THINGS—and my next chapter to it, that is, the first chapter of my next volume, if I live, shall be my chapter upon WHISKERS, in order to keep up some sort of connection in my works.

The thing I lament is, that things have crowded in so thick upon me, that I have not been able to get into that part of my work, towards which, I have all the way, looked forwards, with so much earnest desire; and that is the campaigns, but especially the amours of my uncle *Toby,* the events of which are of so singular a nature, and so Cervantick a cast, that if I can so manage it, as to convey but the same impressions to every other brain, which the occurrences themselves excite in my own——I will answer for it the book shall make its way in the world, much better than its master has done before it——Oh *Tristram! Tristram!* can this but be once brought about——the credit, which will attend thee as an author, shall counter-balance the many evils which have befallen thee as a man—thou wilt feast upon the one—when thou hast lost all sense and remembrance of the other!——

No wonder I itch so much as I do, to get at these amours—They are the choicest morsel[1] of my whole story! and when I do get at 'em—assure yourselves, good folks,—(nor do I value whose squeamish stomach takes offence at it) I shall not be at all nice in the choice of my words;——and that's the thing I have to *declare.*—I shall never get all through in five minutes, that I fear—and the thing I *hope* is, that your worships and reverences are not offended—if you are, depend upon't I'll give you something, my good gentry, next year, to be offended at——that's my dear *Jenny*'s way—but who my *Jenny* is—and which is the right and which the wrong end of a woman, is the thing to be *concealed*—it shall be told you the next chapter but one, to my chapter of button-holes,—and not one chapter before.

And now that you have just got to the end of these four volumes—— the thing I have to *ask* is, how you feel your heads? my own akes dismally[2]— as for your healths, I know, they are much better——True *Shandeism*,[3] think what you will against it, opens the heart and lungs, and like all those affections which partake of its nature, it forces the blood and other vital fluids of the body to run freely thro' its channels, and makes the wheel of life run long and chearfully round.

Was I left like *Sancho Pança*,[4] to chuse my kingdom, it should not be maritime—or a kingdom of blacks to make a penny of——no, it should be a kingdom of hearty laughing subjects: And as the bilious and more saturnine passions, by creating disorders in the blood and humours, have as bad an influence, I see, upon the body politick as body natural—and as nothing but a habit of virtue can fully govern those passions, and subject them to reason—I should add to my prayer—that God would give my subjects grace to be as WISE as they were MERRY; and then should I be the happiest monarch, and they the happiest people under heaven—

And so, with this moral for the present, may it please your worships and your reverences, I take my leave of you till this time twelve-month, when (unless this vile cough[5] kills me in the mean time) I'll have another pluck at your beards,[6] and lay open a story to the world you little dream of.

FINIS.

THE
LIFE
AND
OPINIONS
OF
TRISTRAM SHANDY,
GENTLEMAN.

Dixero fi quid fortè jocofius, hoc mihi juris
Cum venia dabis.——   HOR.

—Si quis calumnietur levius effe quam decet theo-
logum, aut mordacius quam deceat Chriftia-
num—non Ego, fed Democritus dixit.—
                      ERASMUS.

VOL. V.

LONDON:
Printed for T. BECKET and P. A. DEHONDT,
in the Strand.   M DCC LXII.

(Height of original type-page 121 mm.)

THE
LIFE
AND
OPINIONS
OF
TRISTRAM SHANDY,
GENTLEMAN.

Dixero si quid forte jocosius, hoc mihi juris
Cum venia dabis.——— HOR.

——*Si quis calumnietur levius esse quam decet theologum,*
aut mordacius quam deceat Christianum——non
Ego, sed Democritus dixit——— ERASMUS.

Si quis Clericus, aut Monachus, verba joculatoria,
visum moventia sciebat anathema esto.
Second Council of CARTHAGE.

The SECOND EDITION.

VOL. V.

LONDON.
Printed for T. BECKET and P. A. DEHONDT,
in the Strand. M DCC LXVII.

(Height of original type-page 123 mm.)

To the Right Honourable

JOHN,

Lord Viscount SPENCER.

MY LORD,

I Humbly beg leave to offer you these two Volumes; they are the best my talents, with such bad health as I have, could produce:——had providence granted me a larger stock of either, they had been a much more proper present to your Lordship.

I beg your Lordship will forgive me, if, at the same time I dedicate this work to you, I join Lady SPENCER, in the liberty I take of inscribing the story of *Le Fever* in the sixth volume to her name; for which I have no other motive, which my heart has informed me of, but that the story is a humane one.

> *I am,*
> *My Lord,*
> *Your Lordship's*
> *Most devoted,*
> *And most humble Servant,*
>
> LAUR. STERNE.

CHAP. I.

IF it had not been for those two mettlesome tits, and that madcap of a postilion, who drove them from Stilton to Stamford,[1] the thought had never entered my head. He flew like lightning——there was a slope of three miles and a half——we scarce touched the ground——the motion was most rapid—most impetuous—'twas communicated to my brain— my heart partook of it——By the great God of day, said I, looking towards the sun, and thrusting my arm out of the fore-window of the chaise, as I made my vow, "I will lock up my study door the moment I get home, and throw the key of it ninety feet below the surface of the earth, into the draw-well at the back of my house."

The London waggon confirmed me in my resolution: it hung tottering upon the hill, scarce progressive, drag'd—drag'd up by eight *heavy beasts* ——"by main strength!—quoth I, nodding—but your betters draw the same way—and something of every bodies!——O rare!"

Tell me, ye learned, shall we for ever be adding so much to the *bulk*— so little to the *stock?*

Shall we for ever make new books, as apothecaries make new mixtures, by pouring only out of one vessel into another?

Are we for ever to be twisting, and untwisting the same rope? for ever in the same track—for ever at the same pace?[2]

Shall we be destined to the days of eternity, on holy-days, as well as working-days, to be shewing the *relicks of learning*, as monks do the relicks of their saints—without working one—one single miracle with them?

Who made MAN, with powers which dart him from earth to heaven in a moment—that great, that most excellent, and most noble creature of the world—the *miracle* of nature, as Zoroaster in his book περὶ φύσεως called him—the SHEKINAH of the divine presence, as Chrysostom—the *image* of God, as Moses—the *ray* of divinity, as Plato—the *marvel* of *marvels*, as Aristotle[3]——to go sneaking on at this pitiful—pimping— pettifogging rate?

I scorn to be as abusive as Horace upon the occasion[4]——but if there is no catachresis in the wish, and no sin in it, I wish from my soul, that every imitator in *Great Britain*, *France*, and *Ireland*, had the farcy[5] for his pains; and that there was a good farcical house, large enough to hold— aye—and sublimate them, *shag-rag and bob-tail*,[6] male and female, all together: and this leads me to the affair of *Whiskers*——but, by what chain of ideas—I leave as a legacy in *mort main*[7] to Prudes and Tartufs,[8] to enjoy and make the most of.

Upon Whiskers.

I'm sorry I made it——'twas as inconsiderate a promise as ever entered a man's head——A chapter upon whiskers! alas! the world will not bear it——'tis a delicate world—but I knew not of what mettle it was made— nor had I ever seen the underwritten fragment; otherwise, as surely as noses are noses, and whiskers are whiskers still; (let the world say what it will to the contrary) so surely would I have steered clear of this dangerous chapter.

The Fragment.

* * * * * * * * * * * * *

* * * * * * * * * * *

* * *——You are half asleep, my good lady, said the old gentleman, taking hold of the old lady's hand and giving it a gentle squeeze, as he pronounced the word *Whiskers*——shall we change the subject? By no means, replied the old lady—I like your account of these matters: so throwing a thin gauze handkerchief over her head, and leaning it back upon the chair with her face turned towards him, and advancing her two feet as she reclined herself—I desire, continued she, you will go on.

The old gentleman went on as follows.———Whiskers! cried the queen of *Navarre*,[9] dropping her knotting-ball, as *La Fosseuse* uttered the word——Whiskers; madam, said *La Fosseuse*, pinning the ball to the queen's apron, and making a courtesy as she repeated it.

La Fosseuse's voice was naturally soft and low, yet 'twas an articulate voice: and every letter of the word *whiskers* fell distinctly upon the queen of *Navarre*'s ear—Whiskers! cried the queen, laying a greater stress upon the word, and as if she had still distrusted her ears—Whiskers; replied *La Fosseuse*, repeating the word a third time—There is not a cavalier, madam, of his age in *Navarre*, continued the maid of honour, pressing the page's interest upon the queen, that has so gallant a pair—Of what? cried *Margaret*, smiling——Of whiskers, said *La Fosseuse*, with infinite modesty.

The word whiskers still stood its ground, and continued to be made use of in most of the best companies throughout the little kingdom of *Navarre*, notwithstanding the indiscreet use which *La Fosseuse* had made of it: the truth was, *La Fosseuse* had pronounced the word, not only before the queen, but upon sundry other occasions at court, with an accent which always implied something of a mystery——And as the court of *Margaret*, as all the world knows, was at that time a mixture of gallantry and devotion——and whiskers being as applicable to the one, as the other, the word naturally stood its ground—it gain'd full as much as it lost; that is, the clergy were for it—the laity were against it—and for the women,—— *they* were divided.——

The excellency of the figure and mien of the young Sieur *de Croix*, was at that time beginning to draw the attention of the maids of honour towards the terras before the palace gate, where the guard was mounted. The Lady *de Baussiere* fell deeply in love with him,—*La Battarelle* did the same—it was the finest weather for it, that ever was remembered in *Navarre*—*La Guyol*, *La Maronette*, *La Sabatiere*, fell in love with the Sieur *de Croix* also—*La Rebours* and *La Fosseuse* knew better—*De Croix* had failed in an attempt to recommend himself to *La Rebours*; and *La Rebours* and *La Fosseuse* were inseparable.

The queen of *Navarre* was sitting with her ladies in the painted bow-window, facing the gate of the second court, as *De Croix* passed through it—He is handsome, said the Lady *Baussiere*.—He has a good mien, said *La Battarelle*.—He is finely shaped, said *La Guyol*.—I never saw an officer of the horse-guards in my life, said *La Maronette*, with two such legs—Or who stood so well upon them, said *La Sabatiere*——But he has no whiskers, cried *La Fosseuse*—Not a pile, said *La Rebours*.

The queen went directly to her oratory, musing all the way, as she walked through the gallery, upon the subject; turning it this way and that way in her fancy——*Ave Maria* †—what can *La Fosseuse* mean? said she, kneeling down upon the cushion.

La Guyol, La Battarelle, La Maronette, La Sabatiere, retired instantly to their chambers—Whiskers! said all four of them to themselves, as they bolted their doors on the inside.

The Lady *Carnavallette* was counting her beads with both hands, unsuspected under her farthingal—from St. *Antony* down to St. *Ursula* inclusive, not a saint passed through her fingers without whiskers; St. *Francis*, St. *Dominick*, St. *Bennet*, St. *Basil*, St. *Bridget*,[10] had all whiskers.

The Lady *Baussiere* had got into a wilderness of conceits, with moralizing too intricately upon *La Fosseuse*'s text—She mounted her palfry, her page followed her—the host passed by—the lady *Baussiere* rode on.[11]

One denier, cried the order of mercy[12]—one single denier, in behalf of a thousand patient captives, whose eyes look towards heaven and you for their redemption.

—The Lady *Baussiere* rode on.

Pity the unhappy, said a devout, venerable, hoary-headed man, meekly holding up a box, begirt with iron, in his withered hands——I beg for the unfortunate—good, my lady, 'tis for a prison—for an hospital—'tis for an old man—a poor man undone by shipwreck, by suretyship, by fire ——I call God and all his angels to witness—'tis to cloath the naked— to feed the hungry—'tis to comfort the sick and the broken hearted.

—The Lady *Baussiere* rode on.

A decayed kinsman bowed himself to the ground.

—The Lady *Baussiere* rode on.

He ran begging bare-headed on one side of her palfry, conjuring her by the former bonds of friendship, alliance, consanguinity, *&c.*—Cousin, aunt, sister, mother—for virtue's sake, for your own, for mine, for Christ's sake remember me—pity me.

—The Lady *Baussiere* rode on.

Take hold of my whiskers, said the Lady *Baussiere*——The page took hold of her palfry. She dismounted at the end of the terrace.

There are some trains of certain ideas which leave prints of themselves about our eyes and eye-brows; and there is a consciousness of it, somewhere

about the heart, which serves but to make these etchings the stronger—
we see, spell, and put them together without a dictionary.

Ha, ha! hee, hee! cried *La Guyol* and *La Sabatiere*, looking close at each
others prints——Ho, ho! cried *La Battarelle* and *Maronette*, doing the same:
—Whist! cried one—st, st,—said a second,—hush, quoth a third——
poo, poo, replied a fourth—gramercy! cried the Lady *Carnavallette*;—
'twas she who bewhisker'd St. *Bridget*.

La Fosseuse drew her bodkin from the knot of her hair, and having traced
the outline of a small whisker, with the blunt end of it, upon one side of
her upper lip, put it into *La Rebours*'s hand—*La Rebours* shook her head.

The Lady *Baussiere* cough'd thrice into the inside of her muff—*La Guyol*
smiled—Fy, said the Lady *Baussiere*. The queen of *Navarre* touched her
eye with the tip of her fore finger—as much as to say, I understand you
all.

'Twas plain to the whole court the word was ruined: *La Fosseuse* had
given it a wound, and it was not the better for passing through all these
defiles——It made a faint stand, however, for a few months; by the
expiration of which, the Sieur *de Croix*, finding it high time to leave *Navarre*
for want of whiskers—the word in course became indecent, and (after a
few efforts) absolutely unfit for use.

The best word, in the best language of the best world, must have suffered
under such combinations.[13]—The curate of *d'Estella*[14] wrote a book against
them, setting forth the dangers of accessory ideas, and warning the *Navarois*
against them.

Does not all the world know, said the curate *d'Estella* at the conclusion
of his work, that Noses ran the same fate some centuries ago in most parts
of *Europe*, which Whiskers have now done in the kingdom of *Navarre*—
The evil indeed spread no further then—, but have not beds and bolsters,
and night-caps and chamber-pots stood upon the brink of destruction ever
since? Are not trouse,[15] and placket-holes, and pump-handles—and spigots
and faucets, in danger still, from the same association?—Chastity, by
nature the gentlest of all affections—give it but its head—'tis like a
ramping and a roaring lion.

The drift of the curate *d'Estella*'s argument was not understood.—They
ran the scent the wrong way.—The world bridled his ass at the tail.—
And when the *extreams* of DELICACY, and the *beginnings* of CONCUPISCENCE,
hold their next provincial chapter together, they may decree that bawdy
also.

CHAP. II.

WHEN my father received the letter which brought him the melancholy account of my brother *Bobby*'s death, he was busy calculating the expence of his riding post from *Calais* to *Paris*, and so on to *Lyons*.

'Twas a most inauspicious journey; my father having had every foot of it to travel over again, and his calculation to begin afresh, when he had almost got to the end of it, by *Obadiah*'s opening the door to acquaint him the family was out of yeast—and to ask whether he might not take the great coach-horse early in the morning, and ride in search of some.— With all my heart, *Obadiah*, said my father, (pursuing his journey)—take the coach-horse, and welcome.—But he wants a shoe, poor creature! said *Obadiah*.—Poor creature! said my uncle *Toby*, vibrating the note back again, like a string in unison. Then ride the *Scotch* horse, quoth my father hastily.—He cannot bear a saddle upon his back, quoth *Obadiah*, for the whole world.——The devil's in that horse; then take PATRIOT,[1] cried my father, and shut the door.——PATRIOT is sold, said *Obadiah*.—Here's for you! cried my father, making a pause, and looking in my uncle *Toby*'s face, as if the thing had not been a matter of fact.—Your worship ordered me to sell him last *April*, said *Obadiah*.—Then go on foot for your pains, cried my father.—I had much rather walk than ride, said *Obadiah*, shutting the door.

What plagues! cried my father, going on with his calculation.—But the waters are out, said *Obadiah*,—opening the door again.

Till that moment, my father, who had a map of *Sanson*'s,[2] and a book of the post roads before him, had kept his hand upon the head of his compasses, with one foot of them fixed upon *Nevers*,[3] the last stage he had paid for—purposing to go on from that point with his journey and calculation, as soon as *Obadiah* quitted the room; but this second attack of *Obadiah*'s, in opening the door and laying the whole country under water, was too much.—He let go his compasses—or rather with a mixed motion betwixt accident and anger, he threw them upon the table; and then there was nothing for him to do, but to return back to *Calais* (like many others) as wise as he had set out.

When the letter was brought into the parlour, which contained the news of my brother's death, my father had got forwards again upon his journey to within a stride of the compasses of the very same stage of *Nevers*.—By your leave, Mons. *Sanson*, cried my father, striking the point of his compasses through *Nevers* into the table,—and nodding to my uncle *Toby*, to see what was in the letter,—twice of one night is too much for an *English* gentleman and his son, Mons. *Sanson*, to be turned back from so lousy a town as *Nevers*,—what think'st thou, *Toby*, added my father in a sprightly tone.—Unless it be a garrison town, said my uncle *Toby*,—for then—I shall be a fool, said my father, smiling to himself, as long as I live.—So giving a second nod—and keeping his compasses still upon *Nevers* with one hand, and holding his book of the post-roads in the other—half calculating and half listening, he leaned forwards upon the table with both elbows, as my uncle *Toby* hummed over the letter.

—   —   —   —   —   —

—   —   —   —   —   —

—   —   —   —   —   —

—   —   —   —   —   —   he's gone!
said my uncle *Toby*.—Where—Who? cried my father.—My nephew, said my uncle *Toby*.——What—without leave—without money—— without governor? cried my father in amazement. No:—he is dead, my dear brother, quoth my uncle *Toby*.—Without being ill? cried my father again.—I dare say not, said my uncle *Toby*, in a low voice, and fetching a deep sigh from the bottom of his heart, he has been ill enough, poor lad! I'll answer for him—for he is dead.

When *Agrippina* was told of her son's death, *Tacitus* informs us, that not being able to moderate the violence of her passions, she abruptly broke off her work[4]—My father stuck his compasses into *Nevers*, but so much the faster.—What contrarieties! his, indeed, was matter of calculation— *Agrippina*'s must have been quite a different affair; who else could pretend to reason from history?

How my father went on, in my opinion, deserves a chapter to itself.—

CHAP. III.

———————— ——————— And a chapter it shall have, and a devil of a one too—so look to yourselves.

'Tis either *Plato*, or *Plutarch*, or *Seneca*, or *Xenophon*, or *Epictetus*, or *Theophrastus*, or *Lucian*—or some one perhaps of later date—either *Cardan*, or *Budæus*, or *Petrarch*, or *Stella*—or possibly it may be some divine or father of the church, St. *Austin*, or St. *Cyprian*, or *Barnard*,[1] who affirms that it is an irresistable and natural passion to weep for the loss of our friends or children[2]—and *Seneca* (I'm positive) tells us somewhere, that such griefs evacuate themselves best by that particular channel.[3]—And accordingly we find, that *David* wept for his son *Absolom*—*Adrian* for his *Antinous*—*Niobe* for her children, and that *Apollodorus* and *Crito* both shed tears for *Socrates* before his death.[4]

My father managed his affliction otherwise; and indeed differently from most men either ancient or modern; for he neither wept it away, as the *Hebrews* and the *Romans*—or slept it off, as the *Laplanders*—or hang'd it, as the *English*, or drowned it, as the *Germans*[5]—nor did he curse it, or damn it, or excommunicate it, or rhyme it, or lillabullero it.——

——He got rid of it, however.

Will your worships give me leave to squeeze in a story between these two pages?

When *Tully* was bereft of his dear daughter *Tullia*, at first he laid it to his heart,—he listened to the voice of nature, and modulated his own unto it.—O my *Tullia*! my daughter! my child!—still, still, still,—'twas O my *Tullia*!——my *Tullia*! Methinks I see my *Tullia*, I hear my *Tullia*, I talk with my *Tullia*.—But as soon as he began to look into the stores of philosophy, and consider how many excellent things might be said upon the occasion—no body upon earth can conceive, says the great orator, how happy, how joyful it made me.[6]

My father was as proud of his eloquence as MARCUS TULLIUS CICERO could be for his life, and for aught I am convinced of to the contrary at present, with as much reason: it was indeed his strength—and his weakness too.——His strength—for he was by nature eloquent,—and his weakness—for he was hourly a dupe to it; and provided an occasion in life would but permit him to shew his talents, or say either a wise thing, a witty, or a shrewd one—(bating the case of a systematick misfortune)—he had all he wanted.—A blessing which tied up my father's tongue, and a misfortune which set it loose with a good grace, were pretty equal: sometimes, indeed, the misfortune was the better of the two; for instance, where the pleasure of the harangue was as *ten*, and the pain of the misfortune but as *five*—my father gained half in half, and consequently was as well again off, as it never had befallen him.[7]

This clue will unravel, what otherwise would seem very inconsistent in my father's domestick character; and it is this, that in the provocations arising from the neglects and blunders of servants, or other mishaps unavoidable in a family, his anger, or rather the duration of it, eternally ran counter to all conjecture.

My father had a favourite little mare, which he had consigned over to a most beautiful Arabian horse, in order to have a pad out of her for his own riding: he was sanguine in all his projects; so talked about his pad every day with as absolute a security, as if it had been reared, broke,—and bridled and saddled at his door ready for mounting. By some neglect or other in *Obadiah*, it so fell out, that my father's expectations were answered with nothing better than a mule, and as ugly a beast of the kind as ever was produced.

My mother and my uncle *Toby* expected my father would be the death of *Obadiah*—and that there never would be an end of the disaster.——See here! you rascal, cried my father, pointing to the mule, what you have done!—It was not me, said *Obadiah*.—How do I know that? replied my father.

Triumph swam in my father's eyes, at the repartee—the *Attic* salt [8] brought water into them—and so *Obadiah* heard no more about it.

Now let us go back to my brother's death.

Philosophy has a fine saying for every thing.—For *Death* it has an entire set; the misery was, they all at once rushed into my father's head, that 'twas difficult to string them together, so as to make any thing of a consistent show out of them.—He took them as they came.

" 'Tis an inevitable chance—the first statute in *Magnâ Chartâ*—it is an everlasting act of parliament, my dear brother,—*All must die*.[9]

"If my son could not have died, it had been matter of wonder,—not that he is dead."

"Monarchs and princes dance in the same ring with us."[10]

"——*To die*, is the great debt and tribute due unto nature: tombs and monuments, which should perpetuate our memories, pay it themselves; and the proudest pyramid of them all, which wealth and science have erected, has lost its apex, and stands obtruncated in the traveller's horizon."[11] (My father found he got great ease, and went on)—"Kingdoms and provinces, and towns and cities, have they not their periods? and when those principles and powers, which at first cemented and put them together, have performed their several evolutions, they fall back."—Brother *Shandy*, said my uncle *Toby*, laying down his pipe at the word *evolutions*[12]—Revolutions, I meant, quoth my father,—by heaven! I meant revolutions, brother *Toby*—evolutions is nonsense.—'Tis not nonsense—said my uncle *Toby*.——But is it not nonsense to break the thread of such a discourse, upon such an occasion? cried my father—do not—dear *Toby*, continued he, taking him by the hand, do not—do not, I beseech thee, interrupt me at this crisis.—My uncle *Toby* put his pipe into his mouth.

"Where is *Troy* and *Mycenæ*, and *Thebes* and *Delos*, and *Persepolis*, and *Agrigentum*"—continued my father, taking up his book of post-roads, which he had laid down.—"What is become, brother *Toby*, of *Nineveh* and *Babylon*, of *Cizicum* and *Mitylene?*[13] The fairest towns that ever the sun rose upon, are now no more: the names only are left, and those (for many of them are wrong spelt) are falling themselves by piecemeals to decay, and in length of time will be forgotten, and involved with every thing in a perpetual night: the world itself, brother *Toby*, must—must come to an end.

"Returning out of *Asia*, when I sailed from *Ægina* towards *Megara*," *(when can this have been? thought my uncle Toby)* "I began to view the country round about. *Ægina* was behind me, *Megara* was before, *Pyræus* on the right hand, *Corinth* on the left.—What flourishing towns now prostrate upon the earth! Alas! alas! said I to myself, that man should disturb his soul for the loss of a child, when so much as this lies awfully buried in his presence ——Remember, said I to myself again—remember thou art a man."—

Now my uncle *Toby* knew not that this last paragraph was an extract of *Servius Sulpicius*'s consolatory letter to *Tully*.—He had as little skill, honest man, in the fragments, as he had in the whole pieces of antiquity.—And as my father, whilst he was concerned in the *Turky* trade, had been three or four different times in the *Levant*, in one of which he had staid a whole year and a half at *Zant*,[14] my uncle *Toby* naturally concluded, that in some one of these periods he had taken a trip across the *Archipelago* into *Asia*;

and that all this sailing affair with *Ægina* behind, and *Megara* before, and *Pyræus* on the right hand, *&c. &c.* was nothing more than the true course of my father's voyage and reflections.—'Twas certainly in his *manner*, and many an undertaking critick would have built two stories higher upon worse foundations.—And pray, brother, quoth my uncle *Toby*, laying the end of his pipe upon my father's hand in a kindly way of interruption—but waiting till he finished the account—what year of our Lord was this?—'Twas no year of our Lord, replied my father.—That's impossible, cried my uncle *Toby*.—Simpleton! said my father,—'twas forty years before Christ was born.

My uncle *Toby* had but two things for it; either to suppose his brother to be the wandering *Jew*,[15] or that his misfortunes had disordered his brain.—"May the Lord God of heaven and earth protect him and restore him," said my uncle *Toby*, praying silently for my father, and with tears in his eyes.

—My father placed the tears to a proper account, and went on with his harangue with great spirit.

"There is not such great odds, brother *Toby*, betwixt good and evil, as the world imagines"——(this way of setting off, by the bye, was not likely to cure my uncle *Toby*'s suspicions).—"Labour, sorrow, grief, sickness, want, and woe, are the sauces of life."[16]—Much good may it do them—said my uncle *Toby* to himself.——

"My son is dead![17]—so much the better;—'tis a shame in such a tempest to have but one anchor."[18]

"But he is gone for ever from us!—be it so. He is got from under the hands of his barber before he was bald—he is but risen from a feast before he was surfeited—from a banquet before he had got drunken."

"The *Thracians* wept when a child was born"—(and we were very near it, quoth my uncle *Toby*)—"and feasted and made merry when a man went out of the world;[19] and with reason.—Death opens the gate of fame, and shuts the gate of envy after it,[20]—it unlooses the chain of the captive, and puts the bondsman's task into another man's hands."

"Shew me the man, who knows what life is, who dreads it, and I'll shew thee a prisoner who dreads his liberty."[21]

Is it not better, my dear brother *Toby*, (for mark—our appetites are but diseases)—is it not better not to hunger at all, than to eat?—not to thirst, than to take physick to cure it?

Is it not better to be freed from cares and agues, from love and melancholy, and the other hot and cold fits of life,[22] than like a galled traveller, who comes weary to his inn, to be bound to begin his journey afresh?[23]

There is no terror, brother *Toby*, in its looks, but what it borrows from groans and convulsions—and the blowing of noses, and the wiping away of tears with the bottoms of curtains in a dying man's room.—Strip it of these, what is it—'Tis better in battle than in bed,[24] said my uncle *Toby*.—Take away its herses, its mutes,[25] and its mourning,—its plumes, scutcheons, and other mechanic aids—What is it?—*Better in battle!* continued my father, smiling, for he had absolutely forgot my brother *Bobby*—'tis terrible no way—for consider, brother *Toby*,—when we *are*—death is *not*;—and when death *is*—we are *not*.[26] My uncle *Toby* laid down his pipe to consider the proposition; my father's eloquence was too rapid to stay for any man—away it went,—and hurried my uncle *Toby*'s ideas along with it.——

For this reason, continued my father, 'tis worthy to recollect, how little alteration in great men, the approaches of death have made.—*Vespasian* died in a jest upon his close stool—*Galba* with a sentence—*Septimius Severus* in a dispatch—*Tiberius* in dissimulation, and *Cæsar Augustus* in a compliment.—I hope, 'twas a sincere one—quoth my uncle *Toby*.

—'Twas to his wife,[27]—said my father.

CHAP. IV.

——And lastly—for of all the choice anecdotes which history can produce of this matter, continued my father,—this, like the gilded dome which covers in the fabrick—crowns all.—

'Tis of *Cornelius Gallus*,[1] the prætor—which I dare say, brother *Toby*, you have read.—I dare say I have not, replied my uncle.—He died, said my father, as * * * * * * * * * * * * * —And if it was with his wife, said my uncle *Toby*—there could be no hurt in it.—That's more than I know—replied my father.

CHAP. V.

M Y mother was going very gingerly in the dark along the passage which led to the parlour, as my uncle *Toby* pronounced the word *wife*.—'Tis a shrill, penetrating sound of itself, and *Obadiah* had helped it by leaving the door a little a-jar, so that my mother heard enough of it, to imagine herself the subject of the conversation: so laying the edge of her finger across her two lips—holding in her breath, and bending her head a little downwards, with a twist of her neck—(not towards the door, but from it, by which means her ear was brought to the chink)—she listened with all her powers:——the listening slave,[1] with the Goddess of Silence at his back, could not have given a finer thought for an intaglio.

In this attitude I am determined to let her stand for five minutes: till I bring up the affairs of the kitchen (as *Rapin* does those of the church)[2] to the same period.

CHAP. VI.

T HOUGH in one sense, our family was certainly a simple machine, as it consisted of a few wheels; yet there was thus much to be said for it, that these wheels were set in motion by so many different springs, and acted one upon the other from such a variety of strange principles and impulses,——that though it was a simple machine, it had all the honour and advantages of a complex one,——and a number of as odd movements within it, as ever were beheld in the inside of a *Dutch* silk-mill.

Amongst these there was one, I am going to speak of, in which, perhaps, it was not altogether so singular, as in many others; and it was this, that whatever motion, debate, harangue, dialogue, project, or dissertation, was going forwards in the parlour, there was generally another at the same time, and upon the same subject, running parallel along with it in the kitchen.

Now to bring this about, whenever an extraordinary message, or letter, was delivered in the parlour,—or a discourse suspended till a servant went out—or the lines of discontent were observed to hang upon the brows of my father or mother—or, in short, when any thing was supposed to be upon the tapis[1] worth knowing or listening to, 'twas the rule to leave the door, not absolutely shut, but somewhat a-jar—as it stands just now,—which, under covert of the bad hinge, (and that possibly might be one of the many reasons why it was never mended) it was not difficult to manage; by which means, in all these cases, a passage was generally left, not indeed as wide as the *Dardanells*, but wide enough, for all that, to carry on as much of this windward trade, as was sufficient to save my father the trouble of governing his house;—my mother at this moment stands profiting by it.— *Obadiah* did the same thing, as soon as he had left the letter upon the table which brought the news of my brother's death; so that before my father had well got over his surprize, and entered upon his harangue,—had *Trim* got upon his legs, to speak his sentiments upon the subject.

A curious observer of nature, had he been worth the inventory of all *Job*'s stock—though, by the bye, *your curious observers are seldom worth a groat*—would have given the half of it, to have heard Corporal *Trim* and my father, two orators so contrasted by nature and education, haranguing over the same bier.

My father a man of deep reading—prompt memory—with *Cato*, and *Seneca*, and *Epictetus*, at his fingers ends.—

The corporal—with nothing—to remember—of no deeper reading than his muster-roll—or greater names at his finger's end, than the contents of it.

The one proceeding from period to period, by metaphor and allusion, and striking the fancy as he went along, (as men of wit and fancy do) with the entertainment and pleasantry of his pictures and images.

The other, without wit or antithesis, or point, or turn, this way or that; but leaving the images on one side, and the pictures on the other, going strait forwards as nature could lead him, to the heart. O *Trim!* would to heaven thou had'st a better historian!—would!—thy historian had a better pair of breeches!——O ye criticks! will nothing melt you?

CHAP. VII.

————My young master in *London* is dead! said *Obadiah*.——

——A green sattin night-gown of my mother's, which had been twice scoured, was the first idea which *Obadiah*'s exclamation brought into *Susannah*'s head.——Well might *Locke* write a chapter upon the imperfections of words.[1]——Then, quoth *Susannah*, we must all go into mourning.—— But note a second time: the word *mourning*, notwithstanding *Susannah* made use of it herself—failed also of doing its office; it excited not one single idea, tinged either with grey or black,—all was green.——The green sattin night-gown hung there still.

—O! 'twill be the death of my poor mistress, cried *Susannah*.—My mother's whole wardrobe followed.—What a procession! her red damask,—her orange-tawny,—her white and yellow lutestrings,—her brown taffata,—her bone-laced caps, her bed-gowns, and comfortable under-petticoats.—Not a rag was left behind.—"*No,—she will never look up again*," said *Susannah*.

We had a fat foolish scullion—my father, I think, kept her for her simplicity;—she had been all autumn struggling with a dropsy.—He is dead! said *Obadiah*,—he is certainly dead!—So am not I, said the foolish scullion.

————Here is sad news, *Trim!* cried *Susannah*, wiping her eyes as *Trim* step'd into the kitchen,—master *Bobby* is dead and *buried*,—the funeral was an interpolation of *Susannah*'s,—we shall have all to go into mourning, said *Susannah*.

I hope not, said *Trim*.—You hope not! cried *Susannah* earnestly.—The mourning ran not in *Trim*'s head, whatever it did in *Susannah*'s.—I hope—said *Trim*, explaining himself, I hope in God the news is not true. I heard the letter read with my own ears, answered *Obadiah*; and we shall have a terrible piece of work of it in stubbing the ox-moor.—Oh! he's dead, said *Susannah*.—As sure, said the scullion, as I am alive.

I lament for him from my heart and my soul, said *Trim*, fetching a sigh.—Poor creature!—poor boy! poor gentleman!

—He was alive last *Whitsontide*, said the coachman.—*Whitsontide!* alas! cried *Trim*, extending his right arm, and falling instantly into the same attitude in which he read the sermon,—what is *Whitsontide, Jonathan*, (for that was the coachman's name) or *Shrovetide*, or any tide or time past, to this? Are we not here now, continued the corporal, (striking the end of his stick perpendicularly upon the floor, so as to give an idea of health and stability)—and are we not—(dropping his hat upon the ground) gone! in a moment!—'Twas infinitely striking! *Susannah* burst into a flood of tears. —We are not stocks and stones.—*Jonathan, Obadiah*, the cook-maid, all melted.—The foolish fat scullion herself, who was scouring a fish-kettle upon her knees, was rous'd with it.—The whole kitchen crouded about the corporal.

Now as I perceive plainly, that the preservation of our constitution in church and state,—and possibly the preservation of the whole world— or what is the same thing, the distribution and balance of its property and power, may in time to come depend greatly upon the right understanding of this stroke of the corporal's eloquence[2]—I do demand your attention,— your worships and reverences, for any ten pages together, take them where you will in any other part of the work, shall sleep for it at your ease.

I said, "we were not stocks and stones"—'tis very well. I should have added, nor are we angels, I wish we were,—but men cloathed with bodies, and governed by our imaginations;—and what a junketting piece of work of it there is, betwixt these and our seven senses, especially some of them, for my own part, I own it, I am ashamed to confess.[3] Let it suffice to affirm, that of all the senses, the eye,[4] (for I absolutely deny the touch, though most of your *Barbati*, I know, are for it) has the quickest commerce with the soul,—gives a smarter stroke, and leaves something more inexpressible upon the fancy, than words can either convey—or sometimes get rid of.

—I've gone a little about—no matter, 'tis for health—let us only carry it back in our mind to the mortality of *Trim*'s hat.—"Are we not here now,—and gone in a moment?"—There was nothing in the sentence—'twas one of your self-evident truths we have the advantage of hearing every day; and if *Trim* had not trusted more to his hat than his head—he had made nothing at all of it.

———— "Are we not here now;"—continued the corporal, "and are we not"—(dropping his hat plumb upon the ground—and pausing, before he pronounced the word)——"gone! in a moment?" The descent of the hat was as if a heavy lump of clay had been kneaded into the crown of it. —— Nothing could have expressed the sentiment of mortality, of which it was the type and fore-runner, like it,—his hand seemed to vanish from under it,—it fell dead,—the corporal's eye fix'd upon it, as upon a corps,—and *Susannah* burst into a flood of tears.

Now—Ten thousand, and ten thousand times ten thousand (for matter and motion are infinite) are the ways by which a hat may be dropped upon the ground, without any effect.——Had he flung it, or thrown it, or cast it, or skimmed it, or squirted, or let it slip or fall in any possible direction under heaven,—or in the best direction that could be given to it,—had he dropped it like a goose—like a puppy—like an ass—or in doing it, or even after he had done, had he looked like a fool,—like a ninny—like a nicompoop—it had fail'd, and the effect upon the heart had been lost.

Ye who govern this mighty world and its mighty concerns with the *engines* of eloquence,—who heat it, and cool it, and melt it, and mollify it,——and then harden it again to *your purpose*——

Ye who wind and turn the passions with this great windlass,—and, having done it, lead the owners of them, whither ye think meet—

Ye, lastly, who drive——and why not, Ye also who are driven, like turkeys to market, with a stick and a red clout—meditate—meditate, I beseech you, upon *Trim*'s hat.

CHAP. VIII.

STAY——I have a small account to settle with the reader, before *Trim* can go on with his harangue.—It shall be done in two minutes.

Amongst many other book-debts, all of which I shall discharge in due time,—I own myself a debtor to the world for two items,—a chapter upon *chamber-maids and button-holes*, which, in the former part of my work, I promised and fully intended to pay off this year: but some of your worships and reverences telling me, that the two subjects, especially so connected together, might endanger the morals of the world,—I pray the chapter upon chamber-maids and button-holes may be forgiven me,—and that they will accept of the last chapter in lieu of it; which is nothing, an't please your reverences, but a chapter of *chamber-maids, green-gowns, and old hats.*[1]

Trim took his off the ground,—put it upon his head,—and then went on with his oration upon death, in manner and form following.

CHAP. IX.

——To us, *Jonathan*, who know not what want or care is—who live here in the service of two of the best of masters—(bating in my own case his majesty King *William* the Third, whom I had the honour to serve both in *Ireland* and *Flanders*)—I own it, that from *Whitsontide* to within three weeks of *Christmas*,—'tis not long—'tis like nothing;—but to those, *Jonathan*, who know what death is, and what havock and destruction he can make, before a man can well wheel about—'tis like a whole age.—O *Jonathan!* 'twould make a good-natured man's heart bleed, to consider, continued the corporal, (standing perpendicularly) how low many a brave and upright fellow has been laid since that time!—And trust me, *Susy*, added the corporal, turning to *Susannah*, whose eyes were swiming in water,—before that time comes round again,—many a bright eye will be dim.— *Susannah* placed it to the right side of the page—she wept— but she court'sied too.—Are we not, continued *Trim*, looking still at *Susannah*—are we not like a flower of the field—a tear of pride stole in betwixt every two tears of humiliation—else no tongue could have described *Susannah*'s affliction—is not all flesh grass?—'Tis clay,—'tis dirt.—They all looked directly at the scullion,—the scullion had just been scouring a fish-kettle.—It was not fair.——

—What is the finest face that ever man looked at!—I could hear *Trim* talk so for ever, cried *Susannah*,—what is it! *(Susannah* laid her hand upon *Trim*'s shoulder)—but corruption?[1]—— *Susannah* took it off.

—Now I love you for this—and 'tis this delicious mixture within you which makes you dear creatures what you are—and he who hates you for it———all I can say of the matter, is—That he has either a pumkin for his head[2]—or a pippin for his heart,—and whenever he is dissected 'twill be found so.

CHAP. X.

WHETHER *Susannah*, by taking her hand too suddenly from off the corporal's shoulder, (by the whisking about of her passions) ——broke a little the chain of his reflections——

Or whether the corporal began to be suspicious, he had got into the doctor's quarters, and was talking more like the chaplain than himself——

Or whether – – – – – – – – – – – – – – –

Or whether——for in all such cases a man of invention and parts may with pleasure fill a couple of pages with suppositions——which of all these was the cause, let the curious physiologist, or the curious any body determine——'tis certain, at least, the corporal went on thus with his harangue.

For my own part, I declare it, that out of doors, I value not death at all:—not this .. added the corporal, snapping his fingers,—but with an air which no one but the corporal could have given to the sentiment.— In battle, I value death not this[1] ... and let him not take me cowardly, like poor *Joe Gibbins*, in scouring his gun.—What is he? A pull of a trigger— a push of a bayonet an inch this way or that—makes the difference.— Look along the line—to the right—see! *Jack*'s down! well,—'tis worth a regiment of horse to him.—No—'tis *Dick*. Then *Jack*'s no worse.— Never mind which,—we pass on,—in hot pursuit the wound itself which brings him is not felt,[2]—the best way is to stand up to him,—the man who flies, is in ten times more danger than the man who marches up into his jaws.—I've look'd him, added the corporal, an hundred times in the face,—and know what he is.—He's nothing, *Obadiah*, at all in the field.— But he's very frightful in a house, quoth *Obadiah*.——I never mind it myself, said *Jonathan*, upon a coach-box.—It must, in my opinion, be most natural in bed, replied *Susannah*.—And could I escape him by creeping into the worst calf's skin that ever was made into a knapsack, I would do it there—said *Trim*—but that is nature.[3]

——Nature is nature, said *Jonathan*.—And that is the reason, cried *Susannah*, I so much pity my mistress.—She will never get the better of it.—Now I pity the captain the most of any one in the family, answered

Trim.——Madam will get ease of heart in weeping,—and the Squire in talking about it,—but my poor master will keep it all in silence to himself.—I shall hear him sigh in his bed for a whole month together, as he did for lieutenant *Le Fever.* An' please your honour, do not sigh so piteously, I would say to him as I laid besides him. I cannot help it, *Trim,* my master would say,——'tis so melancholy an accident—I cannot get it off my heart.—Your honour fears not death yourself.—I hope, *Trim,* I fear nothing, he would say, but the doing a wrong thing.——Well, he would add, whatever betides, I will take care of *Le Fever*'s boy.—And with that, like a quieting draught, his honour would fall asleep.

I like to hear *Trim*'s stories about the captain, said *Susannah.*—He is a kindly-hearted gentleman, said *Obadiah,* as ever lived.—Aye,—and as brave a one too, said the corporal, as ever stept before a platoon.—There never was a better officer in the king's army,—or a better man in God's world; for he would march up to the mouth of a cannon, though he saw the lighted match at the very touch-hole,—and yet, for all that, he has a heart as soft as a child for other people.——He would not hurt a chicken.

——I would sooner, quoth *Jonathan,* drive such a gentleman for seven pounds a year—than some for eight.—Thank thee, *Jonathan!* for thy twenty shillings,—as much, *Jonathan,* said the corporal, shaking him by the hand, as if thou hadst put the money into my own pocket.——I would serve him to the day of my death out of love. He is a friend and a brother to me,—and could I be sure my poor brother *Tom* was dead,—continued the corporal, taking out his handkerchief,—was I worth ten thousand pounds, I would leave every shilling of it to the captain.——*Trim* could not refrain from tears at this testamentary proof he gave of his affection to his master.——The whole kitchen was affected.——Do tell us this story of the poor lieutenant, said *Susannah.*——With all my heart, answered the corporal.

Susannah, the cook, *Jonathan, Obadiah,* and corporal *Trim,* formed a circle about the fire; and as soon as the scullion had shut the kitchen door,— the corporal begun.

CHAP. XI.

I Am a *Turk* if I had not as much forgot my mother, as if Nature had plaistered me up, and set me down naked upon the banks of the river *Nile*,[1] without one.——Your most obedient servant, Madam—I've cost you a great deal of trouble,—I wish it may answer;—but you have left a crack in my back,—and here's a great piece fallen off here before,—and what must I do with this foot?——I shall never reach *England* with it.

For my own part I never wonder at any thing;—and so often has my judgment deceived me in my life, that I always suspect it, right or wrong,—at least I am seldom hot upon cold subjects. For all this, I reverence truth as much as any body; and when it has slipped us, if a man will but take me by the hand, and go quietly and search for it, as for a thing we have both lost, and can neither of us do well without,—I'll go to the world's end with him:——But I hate disputes,—and therefore (bating religious points, or such as touch society) I would almost subscribe to any thing which does not choak me in the first passage, rather than be drawn into one——But I cannot bear suffocation,——and bad smells worst of all.——For which reasons, I resolved from the beginning, That if ever the army of martyrs was to be augmented,—or a new one raised,—I would have no hand in it, one way or t'other.

CHAP. XII.

——BUT to return to my mother.

My uncle *Toby*'s opinion, Madam, "that there could be no harm in *Cornelius Gallus*, the *Roman* prætor's lying with his wife;"——or rather the last word of that opinion,—(for it was all my mother heard of it) caught hold of her by the weak part of the whole sex:——You shall not mistake me,—I mean her curiosity,[1]—she instantly concluded herself the subject of the conversation, and with that prepossession upon her fancy, you will readily conceive every word my father said, was accommodated either to herself, or her family concerns.

——Pray, Madam, in what street does the lady live, who would not have done the same?

From the strange mode of *Cornelius*'s death, my father had made a transition to that of *Socrates*, and was giving my uncle *Toby* an abstract of his pleading before his judges;——'twas irresistable:——not the oration of *Socrates*,[2]—but my father's temptation to it.——He had wrote the *Life of *Socrates* [3] himself the year before he left off trade, which, I fear, was the means of hastening him out of it;——so that no one was able to set out with so full a sail, and in so swelling a tide of heroic loftiness upon the occasion, as my father was. Not a period in *Socrates*'s oration, which closed with a shorter word than *transmigration*, or *annihilation*,—or a worse thought in the middle of it than *to be—or not to be*,—the entering upon a new and untried state of things,—or, upon a long, a profound and peaceful sleep, without dreams, without disturbance;—— *That we and our children were born to die, —but neither of us born to be slaves.*——No—there I mistake; that was part of *Eleazer*'s oration, as recorded by *Josephus (de Bell. Judaic.)*—— *Eleazer* owns he had it from the philosophers of *India*;[4] in all likelihood *Alexander* the Great, in his irruption into *India*, after he had over-run *Persia*, amongst the many things he stole,—stole that sentiment also; by which means it was carried, if not all the way by himself, (for we all know he died at *Babylon*)[5] at least by some of his maroders, into *Greece*,—from *Greece* it got to *Rome*,—from *Rome* to *France*,—and from *France* to *England:*——So things come round.[6]——

By land carriage I can conceive no other way.——

By water the sentiment might easily have come down the *Ganges* into the *Sinus Gangeticus*, or *Bay of Bengal*, and so into the *Indian Sea*; and following the course of trade, (the way from *India* by the *Cape of Good Hope* being then unknown) might be carried with other drugs and spices up the *Red Sea* to *Joddah*, the port of *Mekka*, or else to *Tor* or *Sues*, towns at the bottom of the gulf; and from thence by karrawans to *Coptos*,[7] but three days journey distant, so down the *Nile* directly to *Alexandria*, where the SENTIMENT would be landed at the very foot of the great stair-case of the *Alexandrian* library,——and from that store-house it would be fetched. ————Bless me! what a trade was driven by the learned in those days!

* This book my father would never consent to publish; 'tis in manuscript, with some other tracts of his, in the family, all, or most of which will be printed in due time.

CHAP. XIII.

——N OW my father had a way, a little like that of *Job*'s (in case there ever was such a man[1]——if not, there's an end of the matter.——

Though, by the bye, because your learned men find some difficulty in fixing the precise æra in which so great a man lived;—whether, for instance, before or after the patriarchs, &c.——to vote, therefore, that he never lived *at all*, is a little cruel,—'tis not doing as they would be done by— happen that as it may)——My father, I say, had a way, when things went extremely wrong with him, especially upon the first sally of his impatience,—of wondering why he was begot,—wishing himself dead;— sometimes worse:——And when the provocation ran high, and grief touched his lips with more than ordinary powers,—Sir, you scarce could have distinguished him from *Socrates* himself.——Every word would breathe the sentiments of a soul disdaining life, and careless about all its issues; for which reason, though my mother was a woman of no deep reading, yet the abstract of *Socrates*'s oration, which my father was giving my uncle *Toby*, was not altogether new to her.—She listened to it with composed intelligence, and would have done so to the end of the chapter, had not my father plunged (which he had no occasion to have done) into that part of the pleading where the great philosopher reckons up his connections, his alliances, and children; but renounces a security to be so won by working upon the passions of his judges.—"I have friends—I have relations,—I have three desolate children,"—says *Socrates*.—

——Then, cried my mother, opening the door,——you have one more, Mr. *Shandy*, than I know of.

By heaven! I have one less,—said my father, getting up and walking out of the room.

CHAP. XIV.

——They are *Socrates*'s children, said my uncle *Toby*. He has been dead a hundred years ago, replied my mother.

My uncle *Toby* was no chronologer—so not caring to advance a step but upon safe ground, he laid down his pipe deliberately upon the table, and rising up, and taking my mother most kindly by the hand, without saying another word, either good or bad, to her, he led her out after my father, that he might finish the ecclaircissment himself.

CHAP. XV.

HAD this volume been a farce,[1] which, unless every one's life and opinions are to be looked upon as a farce as well as mine, I see no reason to suppose—the last chapter, Sir, had finished the first act of it, and then this chapter must have set off thus.

Ptr . . r . . r . . ing—twing—twang—prut—trut——'tis a cursed bad fiddle.—Do you know whether my fiddle's in tune or no?—trut . . prut . . —They should be *fifths*.——'Tis wickedly strung—tr . . . a.e.i.o.u.–twang.—The bridge is a mile too high, and the sound-post absolutely down,—else—trut . . prut—hark! 'tis not so bad a tone.—Diddle diddle, diddle diddle, diddle diddle, dum. There is nothing in playing before good judges,—but there's a man there—no—not him with the bundle under his arm—the grave man in black.—S'death! not the gentleman with the sword on.—Sir, I had rather play a *Caprichio* to *Calliope*[2] herself, than draw my bow across my fiddle before that very man; and yet, I'll stake my *Cremona* to a *Jew*'s trump, which is the greatest musical odds that ever were laid, that I will this moment stop three hundred and fifty leagues out of tune upon my fiddle, without punishing one single nerve that belongs to him.—Twaddle diddle, tweddle diddle,—twiddle diddle,——twoddle diddle,—twuddle diddle,——prut-trut—krish—

krash—krush.—I've undone you, Sir,—but you see he is no worse,—
and was *Apollo* to take his fiddle after me, he can make him no better.

Diddle diddle, diddle diddle, diddle diddle—hum—dum—drum.

—Your worships and your reverences love musick—and God has
made you all with good ears—and some of you play delightfully yourselves
——trut-prut,—prut-trut.

O! there is—whom I could sit and hear whole days,—whose talents
lie in making what he fiddles to be felt,—who inspires me with his joys
and hopes, and puts the most hidden springs of my heart into motion.
——If you would borrow five guineas of me, Sir,—which is generally
ten guineas more than I have to spare—or you, Messrs. Apothecary and
Taylor, want your bills paying,—that's your time.

CHAP. XVI.

THE first thing which entered my father's head, after affairs were a
little settled in the family, and *Susannah* had got possession of my
mother's green sattin night-gown,—was to sit down cooly, after the
example of *Xenophon*,[1] and write a TRISTRA-*pædia*, or system of education
for me; collecting first for that purpose his own scattered thoughts, counsels,
and notions; and binding them together, so as to form an INSTITUTE for
the government of my childhood and adolescence.[2] I was my father's last
stake—he had lost my brother *Bobby* entirely,—he had lost, by his own
computation, full three fourths of me—that is, he had been unfortunate
in his three first great casts for me—my geniture, nose, and name,—there
was but this one left; and accordingly my father gave himself up to it with
as much devotion as ever my uncle *Toby* had done to his doctrine of
projectils.—The difference between them was, that my uncle *Toby* drew
his whole knowledge of projectils from *Nicholas Tartaglia*[3]—My father
spun his, every thread of it, out of his own brain,—or reeled and cross-
twisted what all other spinners and spinsters had spun before him, that
'twas pretty near the same torture to him.

In about three years, or something more, my father had got advanced
almost into the middle of his work.—Like all other writers, he met with

disappointments.—He imagined he should be able to bring whatever he had to say, into so small a compass, that when it was finished and bound, it might be rolled up in my mother's hussive.[4]—Matter grows under our hands.—Let no man say,—"Come—I'll write a *duodecimo*."

My father gave himself up to it, however, with the most painful diligence, proceeding step by step in every line, with the same kind of caution and circumspection (though I cannot say upon quite so religious a principle) as was used by *John de la Casse*,[5] the lord archbishop of *Benevento*, in compassing his *Galatea*; in which his Grace of *Benevento* spent near forty years of his life; and when the thing came out, it was not of above half the size or the thickness of a *Rider*'s Almanack.[6]—How the holy man managed the affair, unless he spent the greatest part of his time in combing his whiskers, or playing at *primero* with his chaplain,—would pose any mortal not let into the true secret;—and therefore 'tis worth explaining to the world, was it only for the encouragement of those few in it, who write not so much to be fed—as to be famous.[7]

I own had *John de la Casse*, the archbishop of *Benevento*, for whose memory (notwithstanding his *Galatea*) I retain the highest veneration,—had he been, Sir, a slender clerk—of dull wit—slow parts—costive head, and so forth,—he and his *Galatea* might have jogged on together to the age of *Methusalah* for me,—the phænomenon had not been worth a parenthesis.—

But the reverse of this was the truth: *John de la Casse* was a genius of fine parts and fertile fancy; and yet with all these great advantages of nature, which should have pricked him forwards with his *Galatea*, he lay under an impuissance at the same time of advancing above a line and an half in the compass of a whole summer's day: this disability in his Grace arose from an opinion he was afflicted with,—which opinion was this,—*viz.* that whenever a Christian was writing a book (not for his private amusement, but) where his intent and purpose was *bonâ fide*, to print and publish it to the world, his first thoughts were always the temptations of the evil one.—This was the state of ordinary writers: but when a personage of venerable character and high station, either in church or state, once turned author,—he maintained, that from the very moment he took pen in hand—all the devils in hell broke out of their holes to cajole him.—'Twas Term-time[8] with them,—every thought, first and last, was captious;—how specious and good soever,—'twas all one;—in whatever form or colour it presented itself to the imagination,—'twas still a stroke of one or other of 'em levelled at him, and was to be fenced off.—So that the life of a writer,[9] whatever he might fancy to the contrary, was not so much a state of *composition*, as a state of *warfare*; and his probation in it, precisely that of any other man militant upon earth,—both depending alike, not half so much upon the degrees of his WIT—as his RESISTANCE.

My father was hugely pleased with this theory of *John de la Casse*, archbishop of *Benevento*; and (had it not cramped him a little in his creed) I believe would have given ten of the best acres in the *Shandy* estate, to have been the broacher of it.—How far my father actually believed in the devil, will be seen, when I come to speak of my father's religious notions, in the progress of this work: 'tis enough to say here, as he could not have the honour of it, in the literal sense of the doctrine—he took up with the allegory of it;—and would often say, especially when his pen was a little retrograde,[10] there was as much good meaning, truth, and knowledge, couched under the veil of *John de la Casse*'s parabolical representation,—as was to be found in any one poetic fiction, or mystick record of antiquity.—Prejudice of education, he would say, *is the devil,*— and the multitudes of them which we suck in with our mother's milk[11]— *are the devil and all.*——We are haunted with them, brother *Toby*, in all our lucubrations and researches; and was a man fool enough to submit tamely to what they obtruded upon him,—what would his book be? Nothing,—he would add, throwing his pen away with a vengeance,— nothing but a farrago of the clack of nurses, and of the nonsense of the old women (of both sexes) throughout the kingdom.

This is the best account I am determined to give of the slow progress my father made in his *Tristra-pædia*; at which (as I said) he was three years and something more, indefatigably at work, and at last, had scarce compleated, by his own reckoning, one half of his undertaking: the misfortune was, that I was all that time totally neglected and abandoned to my mother; and what was almost as bad, by the very delay, the first part of the work, upon which my father had spent the most of his pains, was rendered entirely useless,——every day a page or two became of no consequence.——

——Certainly it was ordained as a scourge upon the pride of human wisdom, That the wisest of us all, should thus outwit ourselves, and eternally forego our purposes in the intemperate act of pursuing them.

In short, my father was so long in all his acts of resistance,—or in other words,—he advanced so very slow with his work, and I began to live and get forwards at such a rate, that if an event had not happened,——which, when we get to it, if it can be told with decency, shall not be concealed a moment from the reader——I verily believe, I had put by my father, and left him drawing a sun-dial,[12] for no better purpose than to be buried under ground.

CHAP. XVII.

'TWAS nothing,—I did not lose two drops of blood by it—— 'twas not worth calling in a surgeon, had he lived next door to us——thousands suffer by choice, what I did by accident.——Doctor *Slop* made ten times more of it, than there was occasion:——some men rise, by the art of hanging great weights upon small wires,[1]—and I am this day (*August* the 10th, 1761)[2] paying part of the price of this man's reputation.——O 'twould provoke a stone, to see how things are carried on in this world!——The chamber-maid had left no ******* *** under the bed:——Cannot you contrive, master, quoth *Susannah*, lifting up the sash with one hand, as she spoke, and helping me up into the window seat with the other,—cannot you manage, my dear, for a single time to **** *** ** *** ******?

I was five years old.——*Susannah* did not consider that nothing was well hung in our family,——so slap came the sash down like lightening upon us;—Nothing is left,—cried *Susannah*,—nothing is left—for me, but to run my country.——

My uncle *Toby*'s house was a much kinder sanctuary; and so *Susannah* fled to it.

CHAP. XVIII.

WHEN *Susannah* told the corporal the misadventure of the sash, with all the circumstances which attended the *murder* of me,—(as she called it)—the blood forsook his cheeks;—all accessaries in murder, being principals,[1]— *Trim*'s conscience told him he was as much to blame as *Susannah*,—and if the doctrine had been true, my uncle *Toby* had as much of the blood-shed to answer for to heaven, as either of 'em;—so that neither reason or instinct, separate or together, could possibly have guided *Susannah*'s steps to so proper an asylum. It is in vain to leave this to the Reader's imagination:——to form any kind of hypothesis that will render these propositions feasible, he must cudgel his brains sore,—and to do it without,—he must have such brains as no reader ever had before him.——Why should I put them either to tryal or to torture? 'Tis my own affair: I'll explain it myself.

CHAP. XIX.

'TIS a pity, *Trim*, said my uncle *Toby*, resting with his hand upon the corporal's shoulder, as they both stood surveying their works,— that we have not a couple of field pieces to mount in the gorge of that new redoubt;——'twould secure the lines all along there, and make the attack on that side quite complete:——get me a couple cast, *Trim*.

Your honour shall have them, replied *Trim*, before to-morrow morning.

It was the joy of *Trim*'s heart,—nor was his fertile head ever at a loss for expedients in doing it, to supply my uncle *Toby* in his campaigns, with whatever his fancy called for; had it been his last crown, he would have sate down and hammered it into a paderero to have prevented[1] a single wish in his Master. The corporal had already,—what with cutting off the ends of my uncle *Toby*'s spouts—hacking and chiseling up the sides of his leaden gutters,—melting down his pewter shaving bason,—and going at last, like *Lewis* the fourteenth, on to the top of the church, for spare ends, &c.[2]——he had that very campaign brought no less than eight new battering cannons, besides three demi-culverins into the field; my uncle *Toby*'s demand for two more pieces for the redoubt, had set the corporal at work again; and no better resource offering, he had taken the two leaden weights from the nursery window: and as the sash pullies, when the lead was gone, were of no kind of use, he had taken them away also, to make a couple of wheels for one of their carriages.

He had dismantled every sash window in my uncle *Toby*'s house long before, in the very same way,——though not always in the same order; for sometimes the pullies had been wanted, and not the lead,——so then he began with the pullies,——and the pullies being picked out, then the lead became useless,——and so the lead went to pot too.[3]

——A great MORAL might be picked handsomly out of this, but I have not time——'tis enough to say, wherever the demolition began, 'twas equally fatal to the sash window.

CHAP. XX.

THE corporal had not taken his measures so badly in this stroke of artilleryship, but that he might have kept the matter entirely to himself, and left *Susannah* to have sustained the whole weight of the attack, as she could;——true courage is not content with coming off so.——The corporal, whether as general or comptroller of the train,——'twas no matter, ——had done that, without which, as he imagined, the misfortune could never have happened,——*at least in* Susannah's *hands*;——How would your honours have behaved?——He determined at once, not to take shelter behind *Susannah*,——but to give it; and with this resolution upon his mind, he marched upright into the parlour, to lay the whole *manœuvre* before my uncle *Toby*.

My uncle *Toby* had just then been giving *Yorick* an account of the Battle of *Steenkirk*,[1] and of the strange conduct of count *Solmes*[2] in ordering the foot to halt, and the horse to march where it could not act; which was directly contrary to the king's commands, and proved the loss of the day.

There are incidents in some families so pat to the purpose of what is going to follow,—they are scarce exceeded by the invention of a dramatic writer;—I mean of ancient days.————

Trim, by the help of his forefinger, laid flat upon the table, and the edge of his hand striking a-cross it at right angles, made a shift to tell his story so, that priests and virgins might have listened to it;[3]—and the story being told,—the dialogue went on as follows.

CHAP. XXI.

————I would be picquetted[1] to death, cried the corporal, as he concluded *Susannah*'s story, before I would suffer the woman to come to any harm,—'twas my fault, an' please your honour,—not hers.

Corporal *Trim*, replied my uncle *Toby*, putting on his hat which lay upon the table,——if any thing can be said to be a fault, when the service absolutely requires it should be done,—'tis I certainly who deserve the blame,——you obeyed your orders.

Had count *Solmes*, *Trim*, done the same at the battle of *Steenkirk*, said *Yorick*, drolling a little upon the corporal, who had been run over by a dragoon in the retreat,——he had saved thee;——Saved! cried *Trim*, interrupting *Yorick*, and finishing the sentence for him after his own fashion, ——he had saved five battalions, an' please your reverence, every soul of them:——there was *Cutts*'s—continued the corporal, clapping the forefinger of his right hand upon the thumb of his left, and counting round his hand,——there was *Cutts*'s,——*Mackay*'s,——*Angus*'s,—— *Graham*'s——and *Leven*'s,[2] all cut to pieces;——and so had the *English* life-guards too, had it not been for some regiments upon the right, who marched up boldly to their relief, and received the enemy's fire in their faces, before any one of their own platoons discharged a musket,—— they'll go to heaven for it,—added *Trim*.—*Trim* is right, said my uncle *Toby*, nodding to *Yorick*,——he's perfectly right. What signified his marching the horse, continued the corporal, where the ground was so strait, and the *French* had such a nation of hedges, and copses, and ditches, and fell'd trees laid this way and that to cover them; (as they always have.)——

Count *Solmes* should have sent us,——we would have fired muzzle to muzzle with them for their lives.——There was nothing to be done for the horse:——he had his foot shot off however for his pains, continued the corporal, the very next campaign at *Landen*.[3]——Poor *Trim* got his wound there, quoth my uncle *Toby*.——'Twas owing, an' please your honour, entirely to count *Solmes*,——had we drub'd them soundly at *Steenkirk*, they would not have fought us at *Landen*.——Possibly not,—— *Trim*, said my uncle *Toby*;——though if they have the advantage of a wood, or you give them a moment's time to intrench themselves, they are a nation which will pop and pop for ever at you.——There is no way but to march cooly up to them,——receive their fire, and fall in upon them, pell-mell——Ding dong, added *Trim*.——Horse and foot, said my uncle *Toby*.——Helter skelter, said *Trim*.——Right and left, cried my uncle *Toby*.——Blood an' ounds, shouted the corporal;——the battle raged,—— *Yorick* drew his chair a little to one side for safety, and after a moment's pause, my uncle *Toby* sinking his voice a note,—resumed the discourse as follows.

CHAP. XXII.

KING *William*, said my uncle *Toby*, addressing himself to *Yorick*, was so terribly provoked at count *Solmes* for disobeying his orders, that he would not suffer him to come into his presence for many months after. ——I fear, answered *Yorick*, the squire will be as much provoked at the corporal, as the King at the count.——But 'twould be singularly hard in this case, continued he, if corporal *Trim*, who has behaved so diametrically opposite to count *Solmes*, should have the fate to be rewarded with the same disgrace;——too oft in this world, do things take that train.——I would spring a mine, cried my uncle *Toby*, rising up,——and blow up my fortifications, and my house with them, and we would perish under their ruins, ere I would stand by and see it.—— *Trim* directed a slight, ——but a grateful bow towards his master,——and so the chapter ends.

CHAP. XXIII.

——Then, *Yorick*, replied my uncle *Toby*, you and I will lead the way abreast,——and do you, corporal, follow a few paces behind us.——And *Susannah*, an' please your honour, said *Trim*, shall be put in the rear.——'Twas an excellent disposition,——and in this order, without either drums beating, or colours flying, they marched slowly from my uncle *Toby*'s house to *Shandy-hall*.

——I wish, said *Trim*, as they entered the door,——instead of the sash-weights, I had cut off the church-spout, as I once thought to have done.——You have cut off spouts enow, replied *Yorick*.——

CHAP. XXIV.

AS many pictures as have been given of my father, how like him soever in different airs and attitudes,——not one, or all of them, can ever help the reader to any kind of preconception of how my father would think, speak, or act, upon any untried occasion or occurrence of life.——There was that infinitude of oddities in him, and of chances along with it, by which handle he would take a thing,——it baffled, Sir, all calculations.——The truth was, his road lay so very far on one side, from that wherein most men travelled,——that every object before him presented a face and section of itself to his eye, altogether different from the plan and elevation of it seen by the rest of mankind.——In other words, 'twas a different object,——and in course was differently considered:

This is the true reason, that my dear *Jenny* and I, as well as all the world besides us, have such eternal squabbles about nothing.——She looks at her outside,——I, at her in—. How is it possible we should agree about her value?

CHAP. XXV.

'TIS a point settled,—and I mention it for the comfort of *Confucius*,[1] who is apt to get entangled in telling a plain story—that provided he keeps along the line of his story,—he may go backwards and forwards as he will,—'tis still held to be no digression.

This being premised, I take the benefit of the *act of going backwards* myself.

CHAP. XXVI.

FIFTY thousand pannier loads of devils[1]—(not of the Archbishop of *Benevento*'s,—I mean of *Rabelais*'s devils) with their tails chopped off by their rumps, could not have made so diabolical a scream of it, as I did—when the accident befell me: it summoned up my mother instantly into the nursery,—so that *Susannah* had but just time to make her escape down the back stairs, as my mother came up the fore.

Now, though I was old enough to have told the story myself,—and young enough, I hope, to have done it without malignity; yet *Susannah*, in passing by the kitchen, for fear of accidents, had left it in short-hand with the cook—the cook had told it with a commentary to *Jonathan*, and *Jonathan* to *Obadiah*; so that by the time my father had rung the bell half a dozen times, to know what was the matter above,—was *Obadiah* enabled to give him a particular account of it, just as it had happened.—I thought as much, said my father, tucking up his night-gown;—and so walked up stairs.

One would imagine from this——(though for my own part I somewhat question it)—that my father before that time, had actually wrote

---

* Mr. *Shandy* is supposed to mean ***** *** ***, Esq; member for ******,———and not the *Chinese* Legislator.

that remarkable chapter in the *Tristrapædia*, which to me is the most original and entertaining one in the whole book;—and that is the *chapter upon sash-windows*, with a bitter *Philippick*[2] at the end of it, upon the forgetfulness of chamber-maids.—I have but two reasons for thinking otherwise.

First, Had the matter been taken into consideration, before the event happened, my father certainly would have nailed up the sash-window for good an' all;—which, considering with what difficulty he composed books,—he might have done with ten times less trouble, than he could have wrote the chapter: this argument I foresee holds good against his writing the chapter, even after the event; but 'tis obviated under the second reason, which I have the honour to offer to the world in support of my opinion, that my father did not write the chapter upon sash-windows and chamber-pots, at the time supposed,—and it is this.

——That, in order to render the *Tristrapædia* complete,—I wrote the chapter myself.

CHAP. XXVII.

M Y father put on his spectacles—looked,—took them off,—put them into the case—all in less than a statutable minute; and without opening his lips, turned about, and walked precipitately down stairs: my mother imagined he had stepped down for lint and basilicon;[1] but seeing him return with a couple of folios under his arm, and *Obadiah* following him with a large reading desk, she took it for granted 'twas an herbal, and so drew him a chair to the bed side, that he might consult upon the case at his ease.

——If it be but right done,—said my father, turning to the *Section——de sede vel subjecto circumcisionis*,——for he had brought up *Spencer*[2] *de Legibus Hebræorum Ritualibus*—and *Maimonides*,[3] in order to confront and examine us altogether.—

——If it be but right done, quoth he:—Only tell us, cried my mother, interrupting him, what herbs.——For that, replied my father, you must send for Dr. *Slop*.

My mother went down, and my father went on, reading the section as follows.[4]

* * * * * * * * * * * * * * * *

* * * * * * * * * * * * * * * *

* * * * * * *——Very well,—said my father,

* * * * * * * * * * * * * * *

* * * * * * * * * * * * * * *

* * * * * * *——nay, if it has that convenience ——and so without stopping a moment to settle it first in his mind, whether the *Jews* had it from the *Egyptians*, or the *Egyptians* from the *Jews*,—he rose up, and rubbing his forehead two or three times across with the palm of his hand, in the manner we rub out the footsteps of care, when evil has trod lighter upon us than we foreboded,—he shut the book, and walked down stairs.—Nay, said he, mentioning the name of a different great nation upon every step as he set his foot upon it—if the EGYPTIANS,—the SYRIANS,—the PHOENICIANS,—the ARABIANS,—the CAPADOCIANS,[5]——if the COLCHI, and TROGLODYTES did it——if SOLON and PYTHAGORAS[6] submitted,—what is TRISTRAM? ——Who am I, that I should fret or fume one moment about the matter?

CHAP. XXVIII.

DEAR *Yorick*, said my father smiling, (for *Yorick* had broke his rank with my uncle *Toby* in coming through the narrow entry, and so had stept first into the parlour)—this *Tristram* of ours, I find, comes very hardly by all his religious rites.—Never was the son of *Jew*, *Christian*, *Turk*, or *Infidel* initiated into them in so oblique and slovenly a manner.— But he is no worse, I trust, said *Yorick*.—There has been certainly, continued my father, the duce and all to do in some part or other of the ecliptic, when this offspring of mine was formed.—That, you are a better judge of than I, replied *Yorick*.—Astrologers, quoth my father, know better than us both:—the trine and sextil aspects have jumped awry,—or the opposite of their ascendents have not hit it, as they should,—or the lords of the genitures[1] (as they call them) have been at *bo-peep*,—or something has been wrong above, or below with us.

'Tis possible, answered *Yorick*.—But is the child, cried my uncle *Toby*, the worse?—The *Troglodytes* say not, replied my father.—And your theologists, *Yorick*, tell us—Theologically? said *Yorick*,—or speaking after the manner of *apothecaries?—†statesmen?—or ‡washer-women?[2]

——I'm not sure, replied my father,—but they tell us, brother *Toby*, he's the better for it.——Provided, said *Yorick*, you travel him into *Egypt*.

——Of that, answered my father, he will have the advantage, when he sees the *Pyramids*.——

Now every word of this, quoth my uncle *Toby*, is *Arabick* to me.——I wish, said *Yorick*, 'twas so, to half the world.

—¶ILUS,[3] continued my father, circumcised his whole army one morning.—Not without a court martial? cried my uncle *Toby*.——Though the learned, continued he, taking no notice of my uncle *Toby*'s remark, but turning to *Yorick*,—are greatly divided still who *Ilus* was;—some say *Saturn*;—some the supream Being;—others, no more than a brigadier general under *Pharoah-neco*.——Let him be who he will, said my uncle *Toby*, I know not by what article of war he could justify it.

The controvertists, answered my father, assign two and twenty different reasons for it:—others indeed, who have drawn their pens on the opposite side of the question, have shewn the world the futility of the greatest part of them.—But then again, our best polemic divines[4]—I wish there was not a polemic divine, said *Yorick*, in the kingdom;—one ounce of practical divinity[5]—is worth a painted ship load of all their reverences have imported these fifty years.—Pray, Mr. *Yorick*, quoth my uncle *Toby*,—do tell me what a polemic divine is.——The best description, captain *Shandy*, I have ever read, is of a couple of 'em, replied *Yorick*, in the account of the battle fought single hands betwixt *Gymnast* and captain *Tripet*;[6] which I have in my pocket.——I beg I may hear it, quoth my uncle *Toby* earnestly.—You shall, said *Yorick*.—And as the corporal is waiting for me at the door,—and I know the description of a battle, will do the poor fellow more good than his supper,—I beg, brother, you'll give him leave

---

*Χαλιπῆς νόσυ, καὶ δυσιάτυ ἀπαλλαγὴ, ἣν ἄνθραχα καλοῦσιν. PHILO.

†Τὰ τεμνόμενα τῶν ἰθνῶν πολυγονώτατα, καὶ πολυανθρωπότατα εἶναι.

‡Καθαριότητος εἵνεκεν. BOCHART.

¶Ὁ Ιλος, τὰ αἰδοῖα περιτέμνεται. ταυτὸ ποιῆσαι καὶ τὺς ἅμ᾿ αυτῷ συμμάχυς κατανα[σ]κάσας. SANCHUNIATHO.

to come in.—With all my soul, said my father.——*Trim* came in, erect
and happy as an emperour; and having shut the door, *Yorick* took a book
from his right-hand coat pocket, and read, or pretended to read, as follows.

CHAP. XXIX.

——"which words being heard by all the soldiers which were there,
divers of them being inwardly terrified, did shrink back and make room
for the assailant: all this did *Gymnast* very well remark and consider; and
therefore, making as if he would have alighted from off his horse, as he
was poising himself on the mounting side, he most nimbly (with his short
sword by his thigh) shifting his feet in the stirrup and performing the
stirrup-leather feat, whereby, after the inclining of his body downwards,
he forthwith launched himself aloft into the air, and placed both his feet
together upon the saddle, standing upright, with his back turned towards
his horse's head,—Now (said he) my case goes forward. Then suddenly
in the same posture wherein he was, he fetched a gambol upon one foot,
and turning to the left-hand, failed not to carry his body perfectly round,
just into his former position, without missing one jot.——Ha! said *Tripet*,
I will not do that at this time,—and not without cause. Well, said *Gymnast*,
I have failed,—I will undo this leap; then with a marvellous strength and
agility, turning towards the right-hand, he fetched another frisking gambol
as before; which done, he set his right-hand thumb upon the bow of the
saddle, raised himself up, and sprung into the air, poising and upholding
his whole weight upon the muscle and nerve of the said thumb, and so
turned and whirled himself about three times: at the fourth, reversing his
body and overturning it upside-down, and foreside back, without *touching
any thing*, he brought himself betwixt the horse's two ears, and then giving
himself a jerking swing, he seated himself upon the crupper——"

(This can't be fighting, said my uncle *Toby.*——The corporal shook
his head at it.——Have patience, said *Yorick*.)

"Then *(Tripet)* pass'd his right leg over his saddle, and placed himself
en croup.[1]—But, said he, 'twere better for me to get into the saddle; then
putting the thumbs of both hands upon the crupper before him, and

thereupon leaning himself, as upon the only supporters of his body, he incontinently turned heels over head in the air, and straight found himself betwixt the bow of the saddle in a tolerable seat; then springing into the air with a summerset, he turned him about like a wind-mill, and made above a hundred frisks, turns and demi-pommadas."[2]——Good God! cried *Trim*, losing all patience,——one home thrust of a bayonet is worth it all. ——I think so too, replied *Yorick*.——

—I am of a contrary opinion, quoth my father.

CHAP. XXX.

——No,—I think I have advanced nothing, replied my father, making answer to a question which *Yorick* had taken the liberty to put to him,— I have advanced nothing in the *Tristrapædia*, but what is as clear as any one proposition in *Euclid*.[1]—Reach me, *Trim*, that book from off the scrutoir:[2]——it has oft times been in my mind, continued my father, to have read it over both to you, *Yorick*, and to my brother *Toby*, and I think it a little unfriendly in myself, in not having done it long ago:——shall we have a short chapter or two now,—and a chapter or two hereafter, as occasions serve; and so on, till we get through the whole? My uncle *Toby* and *Yorick* made the obeisance which was proper; and the corporal, though he was not included in the compliment, laid his hand upon his breast, and made his bow at the same time.——The company smiled. *Trim*, quoth my father, has paid the full price for staying out the *entertainment*.——He did not seem to relish the play, replied *Yorick*.——'Twas a Tom-fool-battle, an' please your reverence, of captain *Tripet*'s and that other officer, making so many summersets, as they advanced;——the *French* come on capering now and then in that way,—but not quite so much.

My uncle *Toby* never felt the consciousness of his existence with more complacency than what the corporal's, and his own reflections, made him do at that moment;——he lighted his pipe,——*Yorick* drew his chair closer to the table,—*Trim* snuff'd the candle,[3]—my father stir'd up the fire,—took up the book,—cough'd twice, and begun.

CHAP. XXXI.[1]

THE first thirty pages, said my father, turning over the leaves,—are a little dry; and as they are not closely connected with the subject,——for the present we'll pass them by: 'tis a prefatory introduction, continued my father, or an introductory preface (for I am not determined which name to give it) upon political or civil government; the foundation of which being laid in the first conjunction betwixt male and female, for procreation of the species——I was insensibly led into it.——'Twas natural, said *Yorick*.

The original of society, continued my father, I'm satisfied is, what *Politian*[2] tells us, *i.e.* merely conjugal; and nothing more than the getting together of one man and one woman;—to which, (according to *Hesiod*) the philosopher adds a servant:——but supposing in the first beginning there were no men servants born——he lays the foundation of it, in a man,—a woman—and a bull.——I believe 'tis an ox, quoth *Yorick*, quoting the passage (οἶκον μὲν πρῶτιϛα, γυναῖκα τε, βῦν τ᾽ ἀροτῆρα.)—— A bull must have given more trouble than his head was worth.——But there is a better reason still, said my father, (dipping his pen into his ink) for, the ox being the most patient of animals, and the most useful withal in tilling the ground for their nourishment,—was the properest instrument, and emblem too, for the new joined couple, that the creation could have associated with them.—And there is a stronger reason, added my uncle *Toby*, than them all for the ox.—My father had not power to take his pen out of his ink-horn, till he had heard my uncle *Toby*'s reason.—For when the ground was tilled, said my uncle *Toby*, and made worth inclosing, then they began to secure it by walls and ditches, which was the origin of fortification.[3]——True, true; dear *Toby*, cried my father, striking out the bull, and putting the ox in his place.

My father gave *Trim* a nod, to snuff the candle, and resumed his discourse.

——I enter upon this speculation, said my father carelessly, and half shutting the book, as he went on,—merely to shew the foundation of the natural relation between a father and his child; the right and jurisdiction over whom he acquires these several ways—

1st, by marriage.

2d, by adoption.

3d, by legitimation.

And 4th, by procreation; all which I consider in their order.

I lay a slight stress upon one of them; replied *Yorick*——the act, especially where it ends there, in my opinion lays as little obligation upon the child, as it conveys power to the father.—You are wrong,—said my father argutely,[4] and for this plain reason * * * * * * *
* * * * * * * * * * * * * * * *
* * * * * * * * * * * * * *.—I own, added my father, that the offspring, upon this account, is not so under the power and jurisdiction of the *mother.*—But the reason, replied *Yorick*, equally holds good for her.——She is under authority herself, said my father:—and besides, continued my father, nodding his head and laying his finger upon the side of his nose, as he assigned his reason,—*she is not the principal agent,*[5] *Yorick.*—In what? quoth my uncle *Toby*, stopping his pipe.—Though by all means, added my father (not attending to my uncle *Toby*) "*The son ought to pay her respect,*" as you may read, *Yorick*, at large in the first book of the Institutes of *Justinian*,[6] at the eleventh title and the tenth section.—I can read it as well, replied *Yorick*, in the Catechism.

CHAP. XXXII.

*T*RIM can repeat every word of it by heart, quoth my uncle *Toby*.—— Pugh! said my father, not caring to be interrupted with *Trim*'s saying his Catechism. He can upon my honour, replied my uncle *Toby*.—Ask him, Mr. *Yorick*, any question you please.——

——The fifth Commandment, *Trim*—said *Yorick*, speaking mildly, and with a gentle nod, as to a modest Catechumen. The corporal stood silent.— You don't ask him right, said my uncle *Toby*, raising his voice, and giving it rapidly like the word of command;——The fifth——cried my uncle *Toby*.—I must begin with the first, an' please your honour, said the corporal.——

—— *Yorick* could not forbear smiling.—Your reverence does not consider, said the corporal, shouldering his stick like a musket, and marching into the middle of the room, to illustrate his position,—that 'tis exactly the same thing, as doing one's exercise in the field.—

"*Join your right hand to your firelock,*" cried the corporal, giving the word of command, and performing the motion.—

"*Poise your firelock,*" cried the corporal, doing the duty still of both adjutant and private man.—

"*Rest your firelock;*"—one motion, an' please your reverence, you see leads into another.—If his honour will begin but with the *first*—

THE FIRST—cried my uncle *Toby*, setting his hand upon his side—* *.

THE SECOND—cried my uncle *Toby*, waving his tobacco-pipe, as he would have done his sword at the head of a regiment.—The corporal went through his *manual* with exactness; and having *honoured his father and mother*, made a low bow, and fell back to the side of the room.

Every thing in this world, said my father, is big with jest,—and has wit in it, and instruction too,—if we can but find it out.[1]

—Here is the *scaffold work* of INSTRUCTION, its true point of folly, without the BUILDING behind it.—

—Here is the glass for pedagogues, preceptors, tutors, governors, gerund-grinders and bear-leaders[2] to view themselves in, in their true dimensions.—

Oh! there is a husk and shell, *Yorick*, which grows up with learning, which their unskilfulness knows not how to fling away!

—SCIENCES MAY BE LEARNED BY ROTE, BUT WISDOM NOT.[3]

Yorick thought my father inspired.—I will enter into obligations this moment, said my father, to lay out all my aunt *Dinah's* legacy, in charitable uses (of which, by the bye, my father had no high opinion) if the corporal has any one determinate idea annexed[4] to any one word he has repeated.— Prythee, *Trim*, quoth my father, turning round to him,—What do'st thou mean, by "*honouring thy father and mother?*"

Allowing them, an' please your honour, three halfpence a day out of my pay, when they grew old.—And didst thou do that, *Trim?* said *Yorick.*— He did indeed, replied my uncle *Toby.*—Then, *Trim*, said *Yorick*, springing out of his chair, and taking the corporal by the hand, thou art the best commentator upon that part of the *Decalogue*; and I honour thee more for it, corporal *Trim*, than if thou hadst had a hand in the *Talmud*[5] itself.

CHAP. XXXIII.

O Blessed health! cried my father, making an exclamation, as he turned over the leaves to the next chapter,—thou art above all gold and treasure;[1] 'tis thou who enlargest the soul,—and openest all it's powers to receive instruction and to relish virtue.—He that has thee, has little more to wish for;—and he that is so wretched as to want thee,—wants every thing with thee.

I have concentrated all that can be said upon this important head, said my father, into a very little room, therefore we'll read the chapter quite thro'.

My father read as follows.

"The whole secret of health depending upon the due contention for mastery betwixt the radical heat and the radical moisture"[2]—You have proved that matter of fact, I suppose, above, said *Yorick.* Sufficiently, replied my father.

In saying this, my father shut the book,—not as if he resolved to read no more of it, for he kept his forefinger in the chapter:——nor pettishly,—for he shut the book slowly; his thumb resting, when he had done it, upon the upper-side of the cover, as his three fingers supported the lower-side of it, without the least compressive violence.——

I have demonstrated the truth of that point, quoth my father, nodding to *Yorick,* most sufficiently in the preceding chapter.

Now could the man in the moon be told, that a man in the earth had wrote a chapter, sufficiently demonstrating, That the secret of all health depended upon the due contention for mastery betwixt the *radical heat* and the *radical moisture,*—and that he had managed the point so well, that there was not one single word wet or dry upon radical heat or radical moisture, throughout the whole chapter,—or a single syllable in it, *pro* or *con,* directly or indirectly, upon the contention betwixt these two powers in any part of the animal œconomy——

"O thou eternal maker of all beings!"—he would cry, striking his breast with his right hand, (in case he had one)—"Thou whose power and goodness can enlarge the faculties of thy creatures to this infinite degree of excellence and perfection,—What have we Moonites done?"

CHAP. XXXIV.[1]

WITH two strokes, the one at *Hippocrates*, the other at Lord *Verulam*, did my father atchieve it.

The stroke at the prince of physicians, with which he began, was no more than a short insult upon his sorrowful complaint of the *Ars longa,*— and *Vita brevis.*——Life short, cried my father,—and the art of healing tedious! And who are we to thank for both, the one and the other, but the ignorance of quacks themselves,—and the stage-loads[2] of chymical nostrums, and peripatetic lumber, with which in all ages, they have first flatter'd the world, and at last deceived it.

——O my lord *Verulam!* cried my father, turning from *Hippocrates,* and making his second stroke at him, as the principal of nostrum-mongers, and the fittest to be made an example of to the rest,——What shall I say to thee, my great lord *Verulam?* What shall I say to thy internal spirit,— thy opium,—thy salt-petre,——thy greasy unctions, —thy daily purges, —thy nightly glisters,[3] and succedaneums?

——My father was never at a loss what to say to any man, upon any subject; and had the least occasion for the exordium of any man breathing: how he dealt with his lordship's opinion,——you shall see;——but when—I know not:——we must first see what his lordship's opinion was.

CHAP. XXXV.

"THE two great causes, which conspire with each other to shorten life, says lord *Verulam,* are first——

"The internal spirit, which like a gentle flame, wastes the body down to death:—And secondly, the external air, that parches the body up to ashes:—which two enemies attacking us on both sides of our bodies together, at length destroy our organs, and render them unfit to carry on the functions of life."

This being the state of the case; the road to Longevity was plain; nothing more being required, says his lordship, but to repair the waste committed by the internal spirit, by making the substance of it more thick and dense, by a regular course of opiates on one side, and by refrigerating the heat of it on the other, by three grains and a half of salt-petre every morning before you got up.——

Still this frame of ours was left exposed to the inimical assaults of the air without;—but this was fenced off again by a course of greasy unctions, which so fully saturated the pores of the skin, that no spicula[1] could enter;——nor could any one get out.——This put a stop to all perspiration, sensible and insensible, which being the cause of so many scurvy distempers—a course of glisters was requisite to carry off redundant humours,—and render the system compleat.

What my father had to say to my lord of *Verulam*'s opiates, his salt-petre, and greasy unctions and glisters, you shall read,—but not to day—or to morrow: time presses upon me,—my reader is impatient—I must get forwards.——You shall read the chapter at your leisure, (if you chuse it) as soon as ever the *Tristrapædia* is published.——

Sufficeth it at present, to say, my father levelled the hypothesis with the ground, and in doing that, the learned know, he built up and established his own.——

CHAP. XXXVI.

THE whole secret of health, said my father, beginning the sentence again, depending evidently upon the due contention betwixt the radical heat and radical moisture within us;—the least imaginable skill had been sufficient to have maintained it, had not the school-men confounded the task, merely (as *Van Helmont*,[1] the famous chymist, has proved) by all along mistaking the radical moisture for the tallow and fat of animal bodies.

Now the radical moisture is not the tallow or fat of animals, but an oily and balsamous substance; for the fat and tallow, as also the phlegm or watery parts are cold; whereas the oily and balsamous parts are of a lively heat and spirit, which accounts for the observation of *Aristotle*, "*Quod omne animal post coitum est* triste."[2]

Now it is certain, that the radical heat lives in the radical moisture, but whether *vice versâ*, is a doubt: however, when the one decays, the other decays also; and then is produced, either an unnatural heat, which causes an unnatural dryness——or an unnatural moisture, which causes dropsies.

——So that if a child, as he grows up, can but be taught to avoid running into fire or water, as either of 'em threaten his destruction,——'twill be all that is needful to be done upon that head.——

CHAP. XXXVII.

THE description of the siege of *Jerico* itself, could not have engaged the attention of my uncle *Toby* more powerfully than the last chapter;—his eyes were fixed upon my father, throughout it;—he never mentioned radical heat and radical moisture, but my uncle *Toby* took his pipe out of his mouth, and shook his head; and as soon as the chapter was finished, he beckoned to the corporal to come close to his chair, to ask him the following question,—*aside.*——*   *   *
*   *   *   *   *   *   *   *   *. It was at the siege of *Limerick*,[1] an' please your honour, replied the corporal, making a bow.

The poor fellow and I, quoth my uncle *Toby*, addressing himself to my father, were scarce able to crawl out of our tents, at the time the siege of *Limerick* was raised, upon the very account you mention.——Now what can have got into that precious noddle of thine, my dear brother *Toby?* cried my father, mentally.——By Heaven! continued he, communing still with himself, it would puzzle an *Œdipus* to bring it in point.——

I believe, an' please your honour, quoth the corporal, that if it had not been for the quantity of brandy we set fire to every night, and the claret and cinnamon with which I plyed your honour off;—And the geneva, *Trim*, added my uncle *Toby*, which did us more good than all——I verily believe, continued the corporal, we had both, an' please your honour, left our lives in the trenches, and been buried in them too.——The noblest grave, corporal! cried my uncle *Toby*, his eyes sparkling as he spoke, that a soldier could wish to lie down in.——But a pitiful death for him! an' please your honour, replied the corporal.

All this was as much *Arabick* to my father, as the rites of the *Colchi* and *Troglodites* had been before to my uncle *Toby*; my father could not determine whether he was to frown or smile.——

My uncle *Toby*, turning to *Yorick*, resumed the case at *Limerick*, more intelligibly than he had begun it,—and so settled the point for my father at once.

CHAP. XXXVIII.

IT was undoubtedly, said my uncle *Toby*, a great happiness for myself and the corporal, that we had all along a burning fever, attended with a most raging thirst, during the whole five and twenty days the flux was upon us in the camp; otherwise what my brother calls the radical moisture, must, as I conceive it, inevitably have got the better.——My father drew in his lungs top-full of air, and looking up, blew it forth again, as slowly as he possibly could.——

——It was heaven's mercy to us, continued my uncle *Toby*, which put it into the corporal's head to maintain that due contention betwixt the radical heat and the radical moisture, by reinforceing the fever, as he did all along, with hot wine and spices; whereby the corporal kept up (as it were) a continual firing, so that the radical heat stood its ground from the beginning to the end, and was a fair match for the moisture, terrible as it was.——Upon my honour, added my uncle *Toby*, you might have heard the contention within our bodies, brother *Shandy*, twenty toises.—If there was no firing, said *Yorick*.

Well—said my father, with a full aspiration, and pausing a while after the word——Was I a judge, and the laws of the country which made me one permitted it, I would condemn some of the worst malefactors, provided they had had their clergy —————————————————————

—— *Yorick* foreseeing the sentence was likely to end with no sort of mercy, laid his hand upon my father's breast, and begged he would respite it for a few minutes, till he asked the corporal a question.——Prithee, *Trim*, said *Yorick*, without staying for my father's leave,——tell us honestly—what is thy opinion concerning this self-same radical heat and radical moisture?

With humble submission to his honour's better judgment, quoth the corporal, making a bow to my uncle *Toby*—Speak thy opinion freely, corporal, said my uncle *Toby*.——The poor fellow is my servant,—not my slave,—added my uncle *Toby*, turning to my father.——

The corporal put his hat under his left arm, and with his stick hanging upon the wrist of it, by a black thong split into a tassel about the knot, he marched up to the ground where he had performed his catechism; then touching his under jaw with the thumb and fingers of his right hand before he opened his mouth,——he delivered his notion thus.

CHAP. XXXIX.

JUST as the corporal was humming, to begin—in waddled Dr. *Slop*.——'Tis not two-pence matter—the corporal shall go on in the next chapter, let who will come in.——

Well, my good doctor, cried my father sportively, for the transitions of his passions were unaccountably sudden,—and what has this whelp of mine to say to the matter?——

Had my father been asking after the amputation of the tail of a puppy-dog—he could not have done it in a more careless air: the system which Dr. *Slop* had laid down, to treat the accident by, no way allowed of such a mode of enquiry.—He sat down.

Pray, Sir, quoth my uncle *Toby*, in a manner which could not go unanswered,—in what condition is the boy?—'Twill end in a *phimosis*,[1] replied Dr. *Slop*.

I am no wiser than I was, quoth my uncle *Toby*,—returning his pipe into his mouth.——Then let the corporal go on, said my father, with his medical lecture.——The corporal made a bow to his old friend, Dr. *Slop*, and then delivered his opinion concerning radical heat and radical moisture, in the following words.

CHAP. XL.

THE city of *Limerick*, the siege of which was begun under his majesty king *William* himself, the year after I went into the army—lies, an' please your honours, in the middle of a devilish wet, swampy country.—'Tis quite surrounded, said my uncle *Toby*, with the *Shannon*, and is, by its situation, one of the strongest fortified places in *Ireland*.——

I think this is a new fashion, quoth Dr. *Slop*, of beginning a medical lecture.—'Tis all true, answered *Trim*.—Then I wish the faculty would follow the cut of it, said *Yorick*.—'Tis all cut through, an' please your reverence, said the corporal, with drains and bogs; and besides, there was such a quantity of rain fell during the siege, the whole country was like a puddle,—'twas that, and nothing else, which brought on the flux, and which had like to have killed both his honour and myself; now there was no such thing, after the first ten days, continued the corporal, for a soldier to lie dry in his tent, without cutting a ditch round it, to draw off the water;—nor was that enough, for those who could afford it, as his honour could, without setting fire every night to a pewter dish full of brandy, which took off the damp of the air, and made the inside of the tent as warm as a stove.——

And what conclusion dost thou draw, Corporal *Trim*, cried my father, from all these premises?

I infer, an' please your worship, replied *Trim*, that the radical moisture is nothing in the world but ditch-water—and that the radical heat, of those who can go to the expence of it, is burnt brandy—the radical heat and moisture of a private man, an' please your honours, is nothing but ditch-water—and a dram of geneva——and give us but enough of it, with a pipe of tobacco, to give us spirits, and drive away the vapours— we know not what it is to fear death.[1]

I am at a loss, Captain *Shandy*, quoth Doctor *Slop*, to determine in which branch of learning your servant shines most, whether in physiology, or divinity.— *Slop* had not forgot[2] *Trim*'s comment upon the sermon.—

It is but an hour ago, replied *Yorick*, since the corporal was examined in the latter, and pass'd muster with great honour.——

The radical heat and moisture, quoth Doctor *Slop*, turning to my father, you must know, is the basis and foundation of our being,—as the root of a tree is the source and principle of its vegetation.—It is inherent in the seeds of all animals, and may be preserved sundry ways, but principally in my opinion by *consubstantials*, *impriments*, and *occludents*.[3]——Now this poor fellow, continued Dr. *Slop*, pointing to the corporal, has had the misfortune to have heard some superficial emperic discourse [4] upon this nice point.——That he has,—said my father.——Very likely, said my uncle.—I'm sure of it—quoth *Yorick*.——

CHAP. XLI.

D OCTOR *Slop* being called out to look at a cataplasm he had ordered, it gave my father an opportunity of going on with another chapter in the *Tristra-pædia*.——Come! chear up, my lads; I'll shew you land[1] ——for when we have tugged through that chapter, the book shall not be opened again this twelvemonth.—Huzza!—

CHAP. XLII.

— F IVE years with a bib under his chin;
Four years in travelling from Christ-cross-row to *Malachi*;[1]
A year and a half in learning to write his own name;
Seven long years and more **τυπ͞ω**-ing it, at Greek and Latin;[2]
Four years at his *probations* and his *negations*—the fine statue still lying in the middle of the marble block,[3]—and nothing done, but his tools sharpened to hew it out!—'Tis a piteous delay!—Was not the great *Julius Scaliger* within an ace of never getting his tools sharpened at all?——— Forty-four years old was he before he could manage his Greek;—and *Peter Damianus*, lord bishop of *Ostia*, as all the world knows, could not so much as read, when he was of man's estate.—And *Baldus*[4] himself, as

eminent as he turned out after, entered upon the law so late in life, that every body imagined he intended to be an advocate in the other world: no wonder, when *Eudamidas*, the son of *Archidamas*, heard *Xenocrates* at seventy-five disputing about *wisdom*, that he asked gravely,—*If the old man be yet disputing and enquiring concerning wisdom,—what time will he have to make use of it?*[5]

Yorick listened to my father with great attention; there was a seasoning of wisdom unaccountably mixed up with his strangest whims, and he had sometimes such illuminations in the darkest of his eclipses, as almost attoned for them:—be wary, Sir, when you imitate him.

I am convinced, *Yorick*, continued my father, half reading and half discoursing, that there is a North west passage[6] to the intellectual world; and that the soul of man has shorter ways of going to work, in furnishing itself with knowledge and instruction, than we generally take with it.—— But alack! all fields have not a river or a spring running besides them;— every child, *Yorick!* has not a parent to point it out.

——The whole entirely depends, added my father, in a low voice, upon the *auxiliary verbs*,[7] Mr. *Yorick*.

Had *Yorick* trod upon *Virgil*'s snake,[8] he could not have looked more surprised.—I am surprised too, cried my father, observing it,—and I reckon it as one of the greatest calamities which ever befell the republick of letters, That those who have been entrusted with the education of our children, and whose business it was to open their minds, and stock them early with ideas, in order to set the imagination loose upon them, have made so little use of the auxiliary verbs in doing it, as they have done ——So that, except *Raymond Lullius*, and the elder *Pelegrini*,[9] the last of which arrived to such perfection in the use of 'em, with his topics, that in a few lessons, he could teach a young gentleman to discourse with plausibility upon any subject, *pro* and *con*, and to say and write all that could be spoken or written concerning it, without blotting a word, to the admiration of all who beheld him—I should be glad, said *Yorick*, interrupting my father, to be made to comprehend this matter. You shall, said my father.

The highest stretch of improvement a single word is capable of, is a high metaphor,——for which, in my opinion, the idea is generally the worse, and not the better;——but be that as it may,—when the mind has done that with it—there is an end,—the mind and the idea are at rest,— until a second idea enters;——and so on.

Now the use of the *Auxiliaries* is, at once to set the soul a going by herself upon the materials as they are brought her; and by the versability[10] of this great engine, round which they are twisted, to open new tracks of enquiry, and make every idea engender millions.

You excite my curiosity greatly, said *Yorick*.

For my own part, quoth my uncle *Toby*, I have given it up.——The *Danes*, an' please your honour, quoth the corporal, who were on the left at the siege of *Limerick*, were all auxiliaries.——And very good ones, said my uncle *Toby*.—And your honour roul'd with them, captains with captains.—Very well, said the corporal.[11]—But the auxiliaries, my brother is talking about, answered my uncle *Toby*,—I conceive to be different things.——

——You do? said my father, rising up.

CHAP. XLIII.

M Y father took a single turn across the room, then sat down and finished the chapter.

The verbs auxiliary we are concerned in here, continued my father, are, *am*; *was*; *have*; *had*; *do*; *did*; *make*; *made*; *suffer*; *shall*; *should*; *will*; *would*; *can*; *could*; *owe*; *ought*; *used*; or *is wont*.—And these varied with tenses, *present*, *past*, *future*, and conjugated with the verb *see*,—or with these questions added to them;—*Is it? Was it? Will it be? Would it be? May it be? Might it be?* And these again put negatively, *Is it not? Was it not? Ought it not?*—Or affirmatively,—*It is*; *It was*; *It ought to be.* Or chronologically,—*Has it been always? Lately? How long ago?*—Or hypothetically,—*If it was*; *If it was not?* What would follow?——If the *French* should beat the *English?* If the *Sun* go out of the *Zodiac?*

Now, by the right use and application of these, continued my father, in which a child's memory should be exercised, there is no one idea can enter his brain how barren soever, but a magazine of conceptions and conclusions may be drawn forth from it.——Did'st thou ever see a white bear? cried my father, turning his head round to *Trim*, who stood at the back of his chair:—No, an' please your honour, replied the corporal.——But thou could'st discourse about one, *Trim*, said my father, in case of need?——

How is it possible, brother, quoth my uncle *Toby*, if the corporal never saw one?———'Tis the fact I want; replied my father,—and the possibility of it, is as follows.

A WHITE BEAR! Very well. Have I ever seen one? Might I ever have seen one? Am I ever to see one? Ought I ever to have seen one? Or can I ever see one?

Would I had seen a white bear? (for how can I imagine it?)

If I should see a white bear, what should I say? If I should never see a white bear, what then?

If I never have, can, must or shall see a white bear alive; have I ever seen the skin of one? Did I ever see one painted?—described? Have I never dreamed of one?

Did my father, mother, uncle, aunt, brothers or sisters, ever see a white bear? What would they give? How would they behave? How would the white bear have behaved? Is he wild? Tame? Terrible? Rough? Smooth?

—Is the white bear worth seeing?—

—Is there no sin in it?—

Is it better than a BLACK ONE?

END of the FIFTH VOLUME.

THE
L I F E
AND
O P I N I O N S
OF
TRISTRAM SHANDY,
GENTLEMAN.

Dixero si quid fortè jocosius, hoc mihi juris
Cum venia dabis.   HOR.

----- *Si quis calumnietur levius esse quam decet*
theologum, aut mordacius quam deceat Chris-
tianum----non Ego, sed Democritus dixit.-----
                 ERASMUS.

V O L. VI.

L O N D O N:

Printed for T. BECKET and P. A. DEHONDT,
in the Strand. MDCCLXII.

(Height of original type-page 123.5 mm.)

THE
LIFE and OPINIONS
OF
TRISTRAM SHANDY, Gent.

CHAP. I.

——WE'LL not stop two moments, my dear Sir,—only, as we have got thro' these five volumes, (do, Sir, sit down upon a set ——they are better than nothing) let us just look back upon the country we have pass'd through.———

——What a wilderness has it been! and what a mercy that we have not both of us been lost, or devoured by wild beasts in it.

Did you think the world itself, Sir, had contained such a number of Jack Asses?[1]——How they view'd and review'd us as we passed over the rivulet at the bottom of that little valley!——and when we climbed over that hill, and were just getting out of sight—good God! what a braying did they all set up together!

——Prithee, shepherd! who keeps all those Jack Asses? * * *

——Heaven be their comforter——What! are they never curried?—— Are they never taken in in winter?——Bray bray—bray. Bray on,— the world is deeply your debtor;——louder still—that's nothing;—in good sooth, you are ill-used:——Was I a Jack Asse, I solemnly declare, I would bray in G-sol-re-ut[2] from morning, even unto night.

CHAP. II.

WHEN my father had danced his white bear backwards and forwards through half a dozen pages, he closed the book for good an' all,—and in a kind of triumph redelivered it into *Trim*'s hand, with a nod to lay it upon the 'scrutoire where he found it.——*Tristram*, said he, shall be made to conjugate every word in the dictionary, backwards and forwards the same way;——every word, *Yorick*, by this means, you see, is converted into a thesis or an hypothesis;—every thesis and hypothesis have an offspring of propositions;—and each proposition has its own consequences and conclusions; every one of which leads the mind on again, into fresh tracks of enquiries and doubtings.——The force of this engine, added my father, is incredible, in opening a child's head.——'Tis enough, brother *Shandy*, cried my uncle *Toby*, to burst it into a thousand splinters.——

I presume, said *Yorick*, smiling,—it must be owing to this,——(for let logicians say what they will, it is not to be accounted for sufficiently from the bare use of the ten predicaments)[1]——That the famous *Vincent Quirino*, amongst the many other astonishing feats of his childhood, of which the Cardinal *Bembo* has given the world so exact a story,—should be able to paste up in the publick schools at *Rome*, so early as in the eighth year of his age, no less than four thousand, five hundred, and sixty different theses, upon the most abstruse points of the most abstruse theology;—and to defend and maintain them in such sort, as to cramp and dumbfound his opponents.——What is that, cried my father, to what is told us of *Alphonsus Tostatus*,[2] who, almost in his nurse's arms, learned all the sciences and liberal arts without being taught any one of them?——What shall we say of the great *Piereskius*?[3]—That's the very man, cried my uncle *Toby*, I once told you of, brother *Shandy*, who walked a matter of five hundred miles, reckoning from *Paris* to *Schevling*, and from *Schevling* back again, merely to see *Stevinus*'s flying chariot.——He was a very great man! added my uncle *Toby*; (meaning *Stevinus*) —He was so; brother *Toby*, said my father, (meaning *Piereskius*) ——and had multiplied his ideas so fast, and increased his knowlege[4] to such a prodigious stock, that, if we may give credit to an anecdote concerning him, which we cannot with-hold here, without shaking the authority of all anecdotes whatever—at seven

years of age, his father committed entirely to his care the education of his
younger brother, a boy of five years old,—with the sole management of
all his concerns.—Was the father as wise as the son? quoth my uncle
Toby.—I should think not, said *Yorick:*—But what are these, continued
my father—(breaking out in a kind of enthusiasm)—what are these, to
those prodigies of childhood in *Grotius, Scioppius, Heinsius, Politian, Pascal,
Joseph Scaliger, Ferdinand de Cordouè,*[5] and others—some of which left off
their *substantial forms*[6] at nine years old, or sooner, and went on reasoning
without them;—others went through their classics at seven;—wrote tra-
gedies at eight;—*Ferdinand de Cordouè* was so wise at nine,—'twas thought
the Devil was in him;——and at *Venice* gave such proofs of his knowlege
and goodness, that the monks imagined he was *Antichrist*, or nothing.——
Others were masters of fourteen languages at ten,—finished the course
of their rhetoric, poetry, logic, and ethics at eleven,—put forth their
commentaries upon *Servius* and *Martianus Capella*[7] at twelve,—and at
thirteen received their degrees in philosophy, laws, and divinity:——But
you forget the great *Lipsius*,[8] quoth *Yorick*, who composed a work* the day
he was born;——They should have wiped it up, said my uncle *Toby*, and
said no more about it.

CHAP. III.

WHEN the cataplasm[1] was ready, a scruple of *decorum* had
unseasonably rose up in *Susannah*'s conscience, about holding the
candle, whilst *Slop* tied it on; *Slop* had not treated *Susannah*'s distemper
with anodines,—and so a quarrel had ensued betwixt them.

——Oh! oh!——said *Slop*, casting a glance of undue freedom in

---

*Nous aurions quelque interêt, says *Baillet*, de montrer qu'il n'a rien de ridicule s'il étoit
véritable, au moins dans le sens énigmatique que *Nicius Erythræus* a tâché de lui donner. Cet
auteur dit que pour comprendre comme *Lipse*, a pû composer un ouvrage le premier jour de
sa vie, il faut s'imaginer, que ce premier jour n'est pas celui de sa naissance charnelle, mais
celui au quel il a commencé d'user de la raison; il veut que ç'ait été a l'age de *neuf* ans; et il
nous veut persuader que ce fut en cet âge, que *Lipse* fit un poem.——Le tour est ingenieux,
&c. &c.

Susannah's face, as she declined the office;——then, I think I know you, madam——You know me, Sir! cried *Susannah* fastidiously, and with a toss of her head, levelled evidently, not at his profession, but at the doctor himself,——you know me! cried *Susannah* again.——Doctor *Slop* clapped his finger and his thumb instantly upon his nostrils;—— *Susannah*'s spleen was ready to burst at it;——'Tis false, said *Susannah*.—Come, come, Mrs. Modesty, said *Slop*, not a little elated with the success of his last thrust, ——if you won't hold the candle, and look—you may hold it and shut your eyes:— That's one of your popish shifts, cried *Susannah:*—'Tis better, said *Slop*, with a nod, than no shift at all, young woman;——I defy you, Sir, cried *Susannah*, pulling her shift sleeve below her elbow.

It was almost impossible for two persons to assist each other in a surgical case with a more splenetic cordiality.

Slop snatched up the cataplasm,—— *Susannah* snatched up the candle; ——A little this way, said *Slop*; *Susannah* looking one way, and rowing another, instantly set fire to *Slop*'s wig, which being somewhat bushy and unctuous withal, was burnt out before it was well kindled.——You impudent whore! cried *Slop*,—(for what is passion, but a wild beast)— you impudent whore, cried *Slop*, getting upright, with the cataplasm in his hand;——I never was the destruction of any body's nose,[2] said *Susannah*,— which is more than you can say:——Is it? cried *Slop*, throwing the cataplasm in her face;——Yes, it is, cried *Susannah*, returning the compliment with what was left in the pan.——

CHAP. IV.

DOCTOR *Slop* and *Susannah* filed cross-bills against each other in the parlour; which done, as the cataplasm had failed, they retired into the kitchen to prepare a fomentation for me;—and whilst that was doing, my father determined the point as you will read.

CHAP. V.

YOU see 'tis high time, said my father, addressing himself equally to my uncle *Toby* and *Yorick*, to take this young creature out of these women's hands, and put him into those of a private governor. *Marcus Antoninus* [1] provided fourteen governors all at once to superintend his son *Commodus*'s education,—and in six weeks he cashiered five of them;—I know very well, continued my father, that *Commodus*'s mother was in love with a gladiator at the time of her conception, which accounts for a great many of *Commodus*'s cruelties when he became emperor;—but still I am of opinion, that those five whom *Antoninus* dismissed, did *Commodus*'s temper in that short time, more hurt than the other nine were able to rectify all their lives long.

Now as I consider the person [2] who is to be about my son, as the mirror in which he is to view himself from morning to night, and by which he is to adjust his looks, his carriage, and perhaps the inmost sentiments of his heart;—I would have one, *Yorick*, if possible, polished at all points, fit for my child to look into.——This is very good sense, quoth my uncle *Toby* to himself.

——There is, continued my father, a certain mien and motion of the body and all its parts, both in acting and speaking, which argues a man *well within*; and I am not at all surprized that *Gregory* of *Nazianzum*, upon observing the hasty and untoward gestures of *Julian*, should foretel he would one day become an apostate;——or that St. *Ambrose* should turn his *Amanuensis* out of doors, because of an indecent motion of his head, which went backwards and forwards like a flail;——or that *Democritus* should conceive *Protagoras* to be a scholar, from seeing him bind up a faggot, and thrusting, as he did it, the small twigs inwards.——There are a thousand unnoticed openings, continued my father, which let a penetrating eye at once into a man's soul; and I maintain it, added he, that a man of sense does not lay down his hat in coming into a room,—or take it up in going out of it, but something escapes, which discovers him.

It is for these reasons, continued my father, that the governor I make choice of shall neither* lisp, or squint, or wink, or talk loud, or look fierce,

*Vid. *Pellegrina*.

or foolish;——or bite his lips, or grind his teeth, or speak through his nose, or pick it, or blow it with his fingers.——

He shall neither walk fast,—or slow, or fold his arms,—for that is laziness;—or hang them down,—for that is folly; or hide them in his pocket, for that is nonsense.——

He shall neither strike, or pinch, or tickle,—or bite, or cut his nails, or hawk, or spit, or snift, or drum with his feet or fingers in company;—— nor (according to *Erasmus*) [3] shall he speak to any one in making water,— nor shall he point to carrion or excrement.——Now this is all nonsense again, quoth my uncle *Toby* to himself.——

I will have him, continued my father, cheerful, faceté, jovial; at the same time, prudent, attentive to business, vigilant, acute, argute, inventive, quick in resolving doubts and speculative questions;——he shall be wise and judicious, and learned:——And why not humble, and moderate, and gentle tempered, and good? said *Yorick:*——And why not, cried my uncle *Toby*, free, and generous, and bountiful, and brave?——He shall, my dear *Toby*, replied my father, getting up and shaking him by his hand.—Then, brother *Shandy*, answered my uncle *Toby*, raising himself off the chair, and laying down his pipe to take hold of my father's other hand,—I humbly beg I may recommend poor *Le Fever*'s son to you;——a tear of joy of the first water sparkled in my uncle *Toby*'s eye,—and another, the fellow to it, in the corporal's, as the proposition was made;——you will see why when you read *Le Fever*'s story:——fool that I was! nor can I recollect, (nor perhaps you) without turning back to the place, what it was that hindered me from letting the corporal tell it in his own words;—but the occasion is lost,—I must tell it now in my own.

CHAP. VI.

The Story of LE FEVER.

IT was some time in the summer of that year in which *Dendermond* was taken [1] by the allies,—which was about seven years before my father came into the country,—and about as many, after the time, that my uncle *Toby* and *Trim* had privately decamped from my father's house in town,

in order to lay some of the finest sieges to some of the finest fortified cities
in *Europe*——when my uncle *Toby* was one evening getting his supper,
with *Trim* sitting behind him at a small sideboard,——I say, sitting——for in
consideration of the corporal's lame knee (which sometimes gave him
exquisite pain)——when my uncle *Toby* dined or supped alone, he would
never suffer the corporal to stand; and the poor fellow's veneration for his
master was such, that, with a proper artillery, my uncle *Toby* could have
taken *Dendermond* itself, with less trouble than he was able to gain this
point over him; for many a time when my uncle *Toby* supposed the
corporal's leg was at rest, he would look back, and detect him standing
behind him with the most dutiful respect: this bred more little squabbles
betwixt them, than all other causes for five and twenty years together
——But this is neither here nor there—why do I mention it?——Ask
my pen,—it governs me,—I govern not it.[2]

He was one evening sitting thus at his supper, when the landlord of a
little inn in the village came into the parlour with an empty phial in his
hand, to beg a glass or two of sack; 'Tis for a poor gentleman,—I think,
of the army, said the landlord, who has been taken ill at my house four
days ago, and has never held up his head since, or had a desire to taste
any thing, till just now, that he has a fancy for a glass of sack and a thin
toast,——*I think*, says he, taking his hand from his forehead, *it would comfort
me.*——

——If I could neither beg, borrow, or buy such a thing,—added the
landlord,—I would almost steal it for the poor gentleman, he is so ill.
——I hope in God he will still mend, continued he,—we are all of us
concerned for him.

Thou art a good natured soul, I will answer for thee, cried my uncle
Toby; and thou shalt drink the poor gentleman's health in a glass of sack
thyself,—and take a couple of bottles with my service, and tell him he is
heartily welcome to them, and to a dozen more if they will do him good.

Though I am persuaded, said my uncle *Toby*, as the landlord shut the
door, he is a very compassionate fellow—*Trim*,—yet I cannot help
entertaining a high opinion of his guest too; there must be something more
than common in him, that in so short a time should win so much upon
the affections of his host;——And of his whole family, added the corporal,
for they are all concerned for him.——Step after him, said my uncle
Toby,—do *Trim*,—and ask if he knows his name.

——I have quite forgot it, truly, said the landlord, coming back into the parlour with the corporal,—but I can ask his son again:——Has he a son with him then? said my uncle *Toby.*—A boy, replied the landlord, of about eleven or twelve years of age;—but the poor creature has tasted almost as little as his father; he does nothing but mourn and lament for him night and day:——He has not stirred from the bedside these two days.

My uncle *Toby* laid down his knife and fork, and thrust his plate from before him, as the landlord gave him the account; and *Trim,* without being ordered, took away without saying one word, and in a few minutes after brought him his pipe and tobacco.

——Stay in the room a little, said my uncle *Toby.*——

Trim!——said my uncle *Toby,* after he lighted his pipe, and smoak'd about a dozen whiffs.—— *Trim* came in front of his master and made his bow;—my uncle *Toby* smoak'd on, and said no more.——Corporal! said my uncle *Toby*——the corporal made his bow.——My uncle *Toby* proceeded no farther, but finished his pipe.

Trim! said my uncle *Toby,* I have a project in my head, as it is a bad night, of wrapping myself up warm in my roquelaure, and paying a visit to this poor gentleman.——Your honour's roquelaure, replied the corporal, has not once been had on, since the night before your honour received your wound, when we mounted guard in the trenches before the gate of St. *Nicholas;*—— and besides it is so cold and rainy a night, that what with the roquelaure, and what with the weather, 'twill be enough to give your honour your death,[3] and bring on your honour's torment in your groin. I fear so; replied my uncle *Toby,* but I am not at rest in my mind, *Trim,* since the account the landlord has given me.——I wish I had not known so much of this affair,—added my uncle *Toby,*—or that I had known more of it:——How shall we manage it? Leave it, an't please your honour, to me, quoth the corporal;——I'll take my hat and stick and go to the house and reconnoitre, and act accordingly; and I will bring your honour a full account in an hour.——Thou shalt go, *Trim,* said my uncle *Toby,* and here's a shilling for thee to drink with his servant.——I shall get it all out of him, said the corporal, shutting the door.

My uncle *Toby* filled his second pipe; and had it not been, that he now and then wandered from the point, with considering whether it was not full as well to have the curtain of the tennaile a straight line, as a crooked one,—he might be said to have thought of nothing else but poor *Le Fever* and his boy the whole time he smoaked it.

CHAP. VII.

The Story of LE FEVER *continued.*

IT was not till my uncle *Toby* had knocked the ashes out of his third pipe, that corporal *Trim* returned from the inn, and gave him the following account.

I despaired at first, said the corporal, of being able to bring back your honour any kind of intelligence concerning the poor sick lieutenant—Is he in the army then? said my uncle *Toby*——He is: said the corporal—— And in what regiment? said my uncle *Toby*——I'll tell your honour, replied the corporal, every thing straight forwards, as I learnt it.—Then, *Trim*, I'll fill another pipe, said my uncle *Toby*, and not interrupt thee till thou hast done; so sit down at thy ease, *Trim*, in the window seat, and begin thy story again. The corporal made his old bow, which generally spoke as plain as a bow could speak it— *Your honour is good:*——And having done that, he sat down, as he was ordered,—and begun the story to my uncle *Toby* over again in pretty near the same words.

I despaired at first, said the corporal, of being able to bring back any intelligence to your honour, about the lieutenant and his son; for when I asked where his servant was, from whom I made myself sure of knowing every thing which was proper to be asked,—That's a right distinction, *Trim*, said my uncle *Toby*—I was answered, an' please your honour, that he had no servant with him;——that he had come to the inn with hired horses, which, upon finding himself unable to proceed, (to join, I suppose, the regiment) he had dismissed the morning after he came.—If I get better, my dear, said he, as he gave his purse to his son to pay the man,— we can hire horses from hence.——But alas! the poor gentleman will never get from hence, said the landlady to me,—for I heard the death-watch[1] all night long;——and when he dies, the youth, his son, will certainly die with him; for he is broken-hearted already.

I was hearing this account, continued the corporal, when the youth came into the kitchen, to order the thin toast the landlord spoke of;—— but I will do it for my father myself, said the youth.——Pray let me save you the trouble, young gentleman, said I, taking up a fork for the purpose, and offering him my chair to sit down upon by the fire, whilst I did it.

——I believe, Sir, said he, very modestly, I can please him best myself.
——I am sure, said I, his honour will not like the toast the worse for being toasted by an old soldier.——The youth took hold of my hand, and instantly burst into tears.——Poor youth! said my uncle *Toby*,—he has been bred up from an infant in the army, and the name of a soldier, *Trim*, sounded in his ears like the name of a friend;—I wish I had him here.

——I never in the longest march, said the corporal, had so great a mind to my dinner, as I had to cry with him for company:—What could be the matter with me, an' please your honour? Nothing in the world, *Trim*, said my uncle *Toby*, blowing his nose,—but that thou art a good natured fellow.

When I gave him the toast, continued the corporal, I thought it was proper to tell him I was Captain *Shandy*'s servant, and that your honour (though a stranger) was extremely concerned for his father;—and that if there was any thing in your house or cellar——(And thou might'st have added my purse too, said my uncle *Toby*) ——he was heartily welcome to it:——He made a very low bow, (which was meant to your honour) but no answer,—for his heart was full—so he went up stairs with the toast;—I warrant you, my dear, said I, as I opened the kitchen door, your father will be well again.——Mr. *Yorick*'s curate was smoking a pipe by the kitchen fire,—but said not a word good or bad to comfort the youth.
——I thought it wrong; added the corporal——I think so too, said my uncle *Toby*.

When the lieutenant had taken his glass of sack and toast, he felt himself a little revived, and sent down into the kitchen, to let me know, that in about ten minutes he should be glad if I would step up stairs.——I believe, said the landlord, he is going to say his prayers,——for there was a book laid upon the chair by his bedside, and as I shut the door, I saw his son take up a cushion.——

I thought, said the curate, that you gentlemen of the army, Mr. *Trim*, never said your prayers at all.——I heard the poor gentleman say his prayers last night, said the landlady, very devoutly, and with my own ears, or I could not have believed it.——Are you sure of it? replied the curate.
——A soldier, an' please your reverence, said I, prays as often (of his own accord) as a parson;——and when he is fighting for his king, and for his own life, and for his honour too, he has the most reason to pray to God, of any one in the whole world——'Twas well said of thee, *Trim*, said my uncle *Toby*.——But when a soldier, said I, an' please your reverence, has

been standing for twelve hours together in the trenches, up to his knees in cold water,—or engaged, said I, for months together in long and dangerous marches;—harrassed, perhaps, in his rear to-day;—harrassing others to-morrow;—detached here;—countermanded there;—resting this night out upon his arms;—beat up in his shirt the next;—benumbed in his joints;—perhaps without straw in his tent to kneel on;—must say his prayers *how* and *when* he can.—I believe, said I,—for I was piqued, quoth the corporal, for the reputation of the army,—I believe, an' please your reverence, said I, that when a soldier gets time to pray,—he prays as heartily as a parson,—though not with all his fuss and hypocrisy.——Thou shouldst not have said that, *Trim*, said my uncle *Toby*,—for God only knows who is a hypocrite, and who is not:——At the great and general review of us all, corporal, at the day of judgment, (and not till then)—it will be seen who has done their duties in this world,—and who has not; and we shall be advanced, *Trim*, accordingly.——I hope we shall, said *Trim*.——It is in the Scripture, said my uncle *Toby*; and I will shew it thee to-morrow:—In the mean time we may depend upon it, *Trim*, for our comfort, said my uncle *Toby*, that God Almighty is so good and just a governor of the world, that if we have but done our duties in it,—it will never be enquired into, whether we have done them in a red coat or a black one:——I hope not; said the corporal——But go on, *Trim*, said my uncle *Toby*, with thy story.

When I went up, continued the corporal, into the lieutenant's room, which I did not do till the expiration of the ten minutes,—he was lying in his bed with his head raised upon his hand, with his elbow upon the pillow, and a clean white cambrick handkerchief beside it:——The youth was just stooping down to take up the cushion, upon which I supposed he had been kneeling,—the book was laid upon the bed,—and as he rose, in taking up the cushion with one hand, he reached out his other to take it away at the same time.——Let it remain there, my dear, said the lieutenant.

He did not offer to speak to me, till I had walked up close to his bed-side:—If you are Captain *Shandy*'s servant, said he, you must present my thanks to your master, with my little boy's thanks along with them, for his courtesy to me;—if he was of *Leven*'s—said the lieutenant.—I told him your honour was—Then, said he, I served three campaigns with him in *Flanders*, and remember him,—but 'tis most likely, as I had not the honour of any acquaintance with him, that he knows nothing of me.——

You will tell him, however, that the person his good nature has laid under obligations to him, is one *Le Fever*, a lieutenant in *Angus*'s² ——but he knows me not,—said he, a second time, musing;——possibly he may my story—added he—pray tell the captain, I was the ensign at *Breda*,³ whose wife was most unfortunately killed with a musket shot, as she lay in my arms in my tent.——I remember the story, an't please your honour, said I, very well.——Do you so? said he, wiping his eyes with his handkerchief,— then well may I.—In saying this, he drew a little ring out of his bosom, which seemed tied with a black ribband about his neck, and kiss'd it twice——Here, *Billy*, said he,——the boy flew across the room to the bed-side,—and falling down upon his knee, took the ring in his hand, and kissed it too,—then kissed his father, and sat down upon the bed and wept.

I wish, said my uncle *Toby*, with a deep sigh,—I wish, *Trim*, I was asleep.

Your honour, replied the corporal, is too much concerned;—shall I pour your honour out a glass of sack to your pipe?——Do, *Trim*, said my uncle *Toby*.

I remember, said my uncle *Toby*, sighing again, the story of the ensign and his wife, with a circumstance his modesty omitted;—and particularly well that he, as well as she, upon some account or other, (I forget what) was universally pitied by the whole regiment;—but finish the story thou art upon:—'Tis finished already, said the corporal,—for I could stay no longer,—so wished his honour a good night; young *Le Fever* rose from off the bed, and saw me to the bottom of the stairs; and as we went down together, told me, they had come from *Ireland*, and were on their route to join the regiment in *Flanders*.——But alas! said the corporal,—the lieutenant's last day's march is over.——Then what is to become of his poor boy? cried my uncle *Toby*.

CHAP. VIII.

The Story of LE FEVER *continued.*

IT was to my uncle *Toby*'s eternal honour,——though I tell it only for the sake of those, who, when coop'd in betwixt a natural and a positive law,[1] know not for their souls, which way in the world to turn themselves ——That notwithstanding my uncle *Toby* was warmly engaged at that time in carrying on the siege of *Dendermond*, parallel with the allies, who pressed theirs on so vigorously, that they scarce allowed him time to get his dinner——that nevertheless he gave up *Dendermond*, though he had already made a lodgment upon the counterscarp;—and bent his whole thoughts towards the private distresses at the inn; and, except that he ordered the garden gate to be bolted up, by which he might be said to have turned the siege of *Dendermond* into a blockade,[2]——he left *Dendermond* to itself,—to be relieved or not by the *French* king, as the *French* king thought good; and only considered how he himself should relieve the poor lieutenant and his son.

——That kind BEING, who is a friend to the friendless, shall recompence thee for this.

Thou hast left this matter short, said my uncle *Toby* to the corporal, as he was putting him to bed,——and I will tell thee in what, *Trim*.——In the first place, when thou madest an offer of my services to *Le Fever*,—as sickness and travelling are both expensive, and thou knowest he was but a poor lieutenant, with a son to subsist as well as himself, out of his pay,—that thou didst not make an offer to him of my purse; because, had he stood in need, thou knowest, *Trim*, he had been as welcome to it as myself. ——Your honour knows, said the corporal, I had no orders;——True, quoth my uncle *Toby*,—thou didst very right, *Trim*, as a soldier,—but certainly very wrong as a man.

In the second place, for which, indeed, thou hast the same excuse, continued my uncle *Toby*,——when thou offeredst him whatever was in my house,—thou shouldst have offered him my house too:——A sick brother officer should have the best quarters, *Trim*, and if we had him with us,—we could tend and look to him:——Thou art an excellent nurse thyself, *Trim*,—and what with thy care of him, and the old woman's, and his boy's, and mine together, we might recruit him again at once, and set him upon his legs.————

————In a fortnight or three weeks, added my uncle *Toby*, smiling,—he might march.————He will never march, an' please your honour, in this world, said the corporal:————He will march; said my uncle *Toby*, rising up from the side of the bed, with one shoe off:————An' please your honour, said the corporal, he will never march, but to his grave:————He shall march, cried my uncle *Toby*, marching the foot which had a shoe on, though without advancing an inch,—he shall march to his regiment.————He cannot stand it, said the corporal;————He shall be supported, said my uncle *Toby*;————He'll drop at last, said the corporal, and what will become of his boy?————He shall not drop, said my uncle *Toby*, firmly.————A-well-o'day,—do what we can for him, said *Trim*, maintaining his point,—the poor soul will die:————He shall not die, by G——, cried my uncle *Toby*.

—The ACCUSING SPIRIT which flew up to heaven's chancery with the oath, blush'd as he gave it in;—and the RECORDING ANGEL as he wrote it down, dropp'd a tear upon the word, and blotted it out for ever.[3]

CHAP. IX.

—M Y uncle *Toby* went to his bureau,—put his purse into his breeches pocket, and having ordered the corporal to go early in the morning for a physician,—he went to bed, and fell asleep.

CHAP. X.

The Story of LE FEVER *concluded.*

THE sun looked bright the morning after, to every eye in the village but *Le Fever*'s and his afflicted son's; the hand of death press'd heavy upon his eye-lids,——and hardly could the wheel at the cistern turn round its circle,[1]—when my uncle *Toby*, who had rose up an hour before his wonted time, entered the lieutenant's room, and without preface or apology, sat himself down upon the chair by the bed-side, and independantly of all modes and customs, opened the curtain in the manner an old friend and brother officer would have done it, and asked him how he did,—how he had rested in the night,—what was his complaint,—where was his pain,—and what he could do to help him:——and without giving him time to answer any one of the enquiries, went on and told him of the little plan which he had been concerting with the corporal the night before for him.——

——You shall go home directly, *Le Fever*, said my uncle *Toby*, to my house,—and we'll send for a doctor to see what's the matter,—and we'll have an apothecary,—and the corporal shall be your nurse;——and I'll be your servant, *Le Fever*.

There was a frankness in my uncle *Toby*,—not the *effect* of familiarity,—but the *cause* of it,—which let you at once into his soul, and shewed you the goodness of his nature; to this, there was something in his looks, and voice, and manner, superadded, which eternally beckoned to the unfortunate to come and take shelter under him; so that before my uncle *Toby* had half finished the kind offers he was making to the father, had the son insensibly pressed up close to his knees, and had taken hold of the breast of his coat, and was pulling it towards him.——The blood and spirits of *Le Fever*, which were waxing cold and slow within him, and were retreating to their last citadel, the heart,—rallied back,—the film forsook his eyes for a moment,—he looked up wistfully[2] in my uncle *Toby*'s face,—then cast a look upon his boy,——and that *ligament*, fine as it was,—was never broken.——

Nature instantly ebb'd again,——the film returned to its place,——the

pulse fluttered——stopp'd——went on——throb'd——stopp'd again
——moved——stopp'd——shall I go on?——No.

CHAP. XI.

I Am so impatient to return to my own story, that what remains of young
Le Fever's, that is, from this turn of his fortune, to the time my uncle
Toby recommended him for my preceptor, shall be told in a very few
words, in the next chapter.—All that is necessary to be added to this
chapter is as follows.—

That my uncle *Toby*, with young *Le Fever* in his hand, attended the poor
lieutenant, as chief mourners, to his grave.

That the governor of *Dendermond* paid his obsequies all military
honours,—and that *Yorick*, not to be behind hand—paid him all ecclesiastic—for he buried him in his chancel:—And it appears likewise, he
preached a funeral sermon over him——I say it *appears*,—for it was
Yorick's custom, which I suppose a general one with those of his profession,
on the first leaf of every sermon which he composed, to chronicle down
the time, the place, and the occasion of its being preached: to this, he was
ever wont to add some short comment or stricture upon the sermon itself,
seldom, indeed, much to its credit:—For instance, *This sermon upon the
jewish dispensation—I don't like it at all*;—*Though I own there is a world of*
WATER-LANDISH *knowlege*[1] *in it,*—*but 'tis all tritical,*[2] *and most tritically put
together.*——*This is but a flimsy kind of a composition; what was in my head
when I made it?*

——N.B. *The excellency of this text is, that it will suit any sermon,*—*and of
this sermon,*——*that it will suit any text.*——

——*For this sermon I shall be hanged,*—*for I have stolen the greatest part of
it. Doctor* Paidagunes *found me out.* ☞ *Set a thief to catch a thief.*[3] ——

On the back of half a dozen I find written, *So, so*, and no more——and
upon a couple *Moderato*; by which, as far as one may gather from *Altieri*'s
Italian dictionary,[4]—but mostly from the authority of a piece of green
whipcord, which seemed to have been the unravelling of *Yorick*'s whip-lash,
with which he has left us the two sermons marked *Moderato*, and the half

dozen of *So, so*, tied fast together in one bundle by themselves,—one may safely suppose he meant pretty near the same thing.

There is but one difficulty in the way of this conjecture, which is this, that the *moderato*'s are five times better than the *so, so*'s;—shew ten times more knowlege of the human heart;—have seventy times more wit and spirit in them;—(and, to rise properly in my climax)—discover a thousand times more genius;—and to crown all, are infinitely more entertaining than those tied up with them;—for which reason, whene'er *Yorick*'s *dramatic* sermons[5] are offered to the world, though I shall admit but one out of the whole number of the *so, so*'s, I shall, nevertheless, adventure to print the two *moderato*'s without any sort of scruple.

What *Yorick* could mean by the words *lentamente*,[6]—*tenutè*,—*grave*,—and sometimes *adagio*,—as applied to theological compositions, and with which he has characterized some of these sermons, I dare not venture to guess.——I am more puzzled still upon finding *a l'octava alta!* upon one;——*Con strepito* upon the back of another;——*Scicilliana* upon a third;——*Alla capella* upon a fourth;——*Con l'arco* upon this;——*Senza l'arco* upon that.——All I know is, that they are musical terms, and have a meaning;——and as he was a musical man, I will make no doubt, but that by some quaint application of such metaphors to the compositions in hand, they impressed very distinct ideas of their several characters upon his fancy,—whatever they may do upon that of others.

Amongst these, there is that particular sermon which has unaccountably led me into this digression——The funeral sermon upon poor *Le Fever*, wrote out very fairly, as if from a hasty copy.—I take notice of it the more, because it seems to have been his favourite composition——It is upon mortality; and is tied length-ways and cross-ways with a yarn thrum, and then rolled up and twisted round with a half sheet of dirty blue paper,[7] which seems to have been once the cast cover of a general review, which to this day smells horribly of horse-drugs.——Whether these marks of humiliation were designed,—I something doubt;——because at the end of the sermon, (and not at the beginning of it)—very different from his way of treating the rest, he had wrote——

Bravo!

——Though not very offensively,——for it is at two inches, at least, and a half's distance from, and below the concluding line of the sermon, at the very extremity of the page, and in that right hand corner of it, which, you know, is generally covered with your thumb; and, to do it justice, it is wrote besides with a crow's quill so faintly in a small *Italian* hand,[8] as scarce to sollicit the eye towards the place, whether your thumb is there or not,—so that from the *manner of it*, it stands half excused; and being wrote moreover with very pale ink, diluted almost to nothing,—'tis more like a *ritratto*[9] of the shadow of vanity, than of VANITY herself—of the two, resembling rather a faint thought of transient applause, secretly stirring up in the heart of the composer, than a gross mark of it, coarsely obtruded upon the world.

With all these extenuations, I am aware, that in publishing this, I do no service to *Yorick*'s character as a modest man;—but all men have their failings! and what lessens this still farther, and almost wipes it away, is this; that the word was struck through sometime afterwards (as appears from a different tint of the ink) with a line quite across it in this manner, ~~BRAVO~~——as if he had retracted, or was ashamed of the opinion he had once entertained of it.

These short characters of his sermons were always written, excepting in this one instance, upon the first leaf of his sermon, which served as a cover to it; and usually upon the inside of it, which was turned towards the text;—but at the end of his discourse, where, perhaps, he had five or six pages, and sometimes, perhaps, a whole score to turn himself in,—he took a larger circuit, and, indeed, a much more mettlesome one;—as if he had snatched the occasion of unlacing himself with a few more frolicksome strokes at vice, than the straitness of the pulpit allowed.—These, though hussar-like, they skirmish lightly and out of all order, are still auxiliaries on the side of virtue—; tell me then, Mynheer Vander Blonederdonder-gewdenstronke,[10] why they should not be printed together?

CHAP. XII.

WHEN my uncle *Toby* had turned every thing into money, and settled all accounts betwixt the agent of the regiment and *Le Fever*, and betwixt *Le Fever* and all mankind,——there remained nothing more in my uncle *Toby*'s hands, than an old regimental coat and a sword; so that my uncle *Toby* found little or no opposition from the world in taking administration. The coat my uncle *Toby* gave the corporal;——Wear it, *Trim*, said my uncle *Toby*, as long as it will hold together, for the sake of the poor lieutenant——And this,——said my uncle *Toby*, taking up the sword in his hand, and drawing it out of the scabbard as he spoke—— and this, *Le Fever*, I'll save for thee,—'tis all the fortune, continued my uncle *Toby*, hanging it up upon a crook, and pointing to it,—'tis all the fortune, my dear *Le Fever*, which God has left thee; but if he has given thee a heart to fight thy way with it in the world,—and thou doest it like a man of honour,—'tis enough for us.

As soon as my uncle *Toby* had laid a foundation, and taught him to inscribe a regular polygon in a circle, he sent him to a public school, where, excepting *Whitsontide* and *Christmas*, at which times the corporal was punctually dispatched for him,—he remained to the spring of the year, seventeen; when the stories of the emperor's sending his army into *Hungary* against the *Turks*,[1] kindling a spark of fire in his bosom, he left his *Greek* and *Latin* without leave, and throwing himself upon his knees before my uncle *Toby*, begged his father's sword, and my uncle *Toby*'s leave along with it, to go and try his fortune under *Eugene*.—Twice did my uncle *Toby* forget his wound, and cry out, *Le Fever!* I will go with thee, and thou shalt fight beside me——And twice he laid his hand upon his groin, and hung down his head in sorrow and disconsolation.——

My uncle *Toby* took down the sword from the crook, where it had hung untouched ever since the lieutenant's death, and delivered it to the corporal to brighten up;——and having detained *Le Fever* a single fortnight to equip him, and contract for his passage to *Leghorn*,—he put the sword into his hand,——If thou art brave, *Le Fever*, said my uncle *Toby*, this will not fail thee,——but Fortune, said he, (musing a little)——Fortune may ——And if she does,—added my uncle *Toby*, embracing him, come back again to me, *Le Fever*, and we will shape thee another course.

The greatest injury could not have oppressed the heart of *Le Fever* more than my uncle *Toby*'s paternal kindness;——he parted from my uncle *Toby*, as the best of sons from the best of fathers——both dropped tears ——and as my uncle *Toby* gave him his last kiss, he slipped sixty guineas, tied up in an old purse of his father's, in which was his mother's ring, into his hand,—and bid God bless him.

CHAP. XIII.

*L*E *Fever* got up to the Imperial army just time enough to try what metal his sword was made of, at the defeat of the *Turks* before *Belgrade*;[1] but a series of unmerited mischances had pursued him from that moment, and trod close upon his heels for four years together after: he had withstood these buffetings to the last, till sickness overtook him at *Marseilles*, from whence he wrote my uncle *Toby* word, he had lost his time, his services, his health, and, in short, every thing but his sword;——and was waiting for the first ship to return back to him.

As this letter came to hand about six weeks before *Susannah*'s accident, *Le Fever* was hourly expected; and was uppermost in my uncle *Toby*'s mind all the time my father was giving him and *Yorick* a description of what kind of a person he would chuse for a preceptor to me: but as my uncle *Toby* thought my father at first somewhat fanciful in the accomplishments he required, he forbore mentioning *Le Fever*'s name,——till the character, by *Yorick*'s interposition, ending unexpectedly, in one, who should be gentle tempered, and generous, and good, it impressed the image of *Le Fever*, and his interest upon my uncle *Toby* so forceably, he rose instantly off his chair; and laying down his pipe, in order to take hold of both my father's hands——I beg, brother *Shandy*, said my uncle *Toby*, I may recommend poor *Le Fever*'s son to you——I beseech you, do, added *Yorick*——He has a good heart, said my uncle *Toby*——And a brave one too, an' please your honour, said the corporal.

——The best hearts, *Trim*, are ever the bravest, replied my uncle *Toby*. ——And the greatest cowards, an' please your honour, in our regiment, were the greatest rascals in it.——There was serjeant *Kumbur*, and ensign——

——We'll talk of them, said my father, another time.

CHAP. XIV.

WHAT a jovial and a merry world would this be, may it please your worships, but for that inextricable labyrinth of debts, cares, woes, want, grief, discontent, melancholy, large jointures, impositions, and lies!

Doctor *Slop*, like a son of a w——, as my father called him for it,—to exalt himself,—debased me to death,—and made ten thousand times more of *Susannah*'s accident, than there was any grounds for; so that in a week's time, or less, it was in every body's mouth, *That poor Master Shandy*

*　　*　　*　　*　　*　　*　　*　　*　　*　　*　　*

*　　*　　*　　*　　*　　*　　*　　* entirely.

—And FAME, who loves to double every thing,—in three days more, had sworn positively she saw it,—and all the world, as usual, gave credit to her evidence——"That the nursery window had not only *　　*　　*　　*　　*　　*　　*　　*

*　　*　　*　　*　　*　　*　　*　　*　　*

*　　*　　* ;——but that *　　*　　*　　*　　*

*　　*　　*　　*　　*　　* *'s also."

Could the world have been sued like a BODY-CORPORATE,—my father had brought an action upon the case, and trounced it sufficiently; but to fall foul of individuals about it——as every soul who had mentioned the affair, did it with the greatest pity imaginable;——'twas like flying in the very face of his best friends:——And yet to acquiesce under the report, in silence—was to acknowledge it openly,—at least in the opinion of one half of the world; and to make a bustle again, in contradicting it,—was to confirm it as strongly in the opinion of the other half.———

——Was ever poor devil of a country gentleman so hampered? said my father.

I would shew him publickly, said my uncle *Toby*, at the market cross.

——'Twill have no effect, said my father.

CHAP. XV.

——I'll put him, however, into breeches said my father,——let the world say what it will.

CHAP. XVI.

THERE are a thousand resolutions, Sir, both in church and state, as well as in matters, Madam, of a more private concern;——which, though they have carried all the appearance in the world of being taken, and entered upon in a hasty, hare-brained, and unadvised manner, were, notwithstanding this, (and could you or I have got into the cabinet, or stood behind the curtain, we should have found it was so) weighed, poized, and perpended——argued upon——canvassed through—— entered into, and examined on all sides with so much coolness, that the GODDESS of COOLNESS herself (I do not take upon me to prove her existence) could neither have wished it, or done it better.

Of the number of these was my father's resolution of putting me into breeches; which, though determined at once,——in a kind of huff, and a defiance of all mankind, had, nevertheless, been *pro'd* and *conn'd*, and judicially talked over betwixt him and my mother about a month before, in two several *beds of justice*,[1] which my father had held for that purpose. I shall explain the nature of these beds of justice in my next chapter; and in the chapter following that, you shall step with me, Madam, behind the curtain, only to hear in what kind of manner my father and my mother debated between themselves, this affair of the breeches,——from which you may form an idea, how they debated all lesser matters.

CHAP. XVII.

THE ancient *Goths* of *Germany*, who (the learned *Cluverius* is positive) were first seated in the country between the *Vistula* and the *Oder*, and who afterwards incorporated the *Herculi*, the *Bugians*,[1] and some other *Vandallick* clans to 'em,—had all of them a wise custom of debating every thing of importance to their state, twice; that is,—once drunk, and once sober:——Drunk—that their counsels might not want vigour;——and sober—that they might not want discretion.

Now my father being entirely a water-drinker,—was a long time gravelled almost to death, in turning this as much to his advantage, as he did every other thing, which the ancients did or said; and it was not till the seventh year of his marriage, after a thousand fruit-less experiments and devices, that he hit upon an expedient which answered the purpose;——and that was when any difficult and momen-tous point was to be settled in the family, which required great sobriety, and great spirit too, in its determination,——he fixed and set apart the first *Sunday* night in the month, and the *Saturday* night which immediately preceded it, to argue it over, in bed with my mother: By which contrivance, if you consider, Sir, with yourself, *   *   *   *
*   *   *   *   *   *   *   *   *   *
*   *   *   *   *   *   *   *   *   *
*   *   *   *   *   *.

These my father, humourously enough, called his *beds of justice*;—— for from the two different counsels taken in these two different humours, a middle one was generally found out, which touched the point of wisdom as well, as if he had got drunk and sober a hundred times.

It must not be made a secret of to the world, that this answers full as well in literary discussions, as either in military or conjugal; but it is not every author that can try the experiment as the *Goths* and *Vandals* did it ——or if he can, may it be always for his body's health; and to do it, as my father did it,—am I sure it would be always for his soul's.——

My way is this:——

In all nice and ticklish discussions,—(of which, heaven knows, there are but too many in my book)—where I find I cannot take a step without the danger of having either their worships or their reverences upon my back——I write one half *full*,—and t'other *fasting*;[2]——or write it all full,—and correct it fasting;——or write it fasting,—and correct it full, for they all come to the same thing:——So that with a less variation from my father's plan, than my father's from the *Gothick*——I feel myself upon a par with him in his first bed of justice,——and no way inferior to him in his second.——These different and almost irreconcileable effects, flow uniformly from the wise and wonderful mechanism of nature,—of which,—be her's the honour.——All that we can do, is to turn and work the machine to the improvement and better manufactury of the arts and sciences.——

Now, when I write full,—I write as if I was never to write fasting again as long as I live;——that is, I write free from the cares, as well as the terrors of the world.——I count not the number of my scars,—nor does my fancy go forth into dark entries and bye corners to antedate my stabs. ——In a word, my pen takes its course; and I write on as much from the fullness of my heart, as my stomach.——

But when, an' please your honours, I indite fasting, 'tis a different history. ——I pay the world all possible attention and respect,—and have as great a share (whilst it lasts) of that understrapping[3] virtue of discretion, as the best of you.——So that betwixt both, I write a careless kind of a civil, nonsensical, good humoured *Shandean* book, which will do all your hearts good——

——And all your heads too,—provided you understand it.

CHAP. XVIII.

WE should begin, said my father, turning himself half round in bed, and shifting his pillow a little towards my mother's, as he opened the debate——We should begin to think, Mrs. *Shandy*, of putting this boy into breeches.——

We should so,—said my mother.——We defer it, my dear, quoth my father, shamefully.——

CHAPTER XVIII

I think we do, Mr. *Shandy*,—said my mother.

——Not but the child looks extremely well, said my father, in his vests and tunicks.——

——He does look very well in them,—replied my mother.——

——And for that reason it would be almost a sin, added my father, to take him out of 'em.——

——It would so,—said my mother:——But indeed he is growing a very tall lad,—rejoin'd my father.

——He is very tall for his age, indeed,—said my mother.——

——I can not (making two syllables of it) imagine, quoth my father, who the duce he takes after.——

I cannot conceive, for my life,—said my mother.——

Humph!——said my father.

(The dialogue ceased for a moment.)

——I am very short myself,—continued my father, gravely.

You are very short, Mr. *Shandy*,—said my mother.

Humph! quoth my father to himself, a second time: in muttering which, he plucked his pillow a little further from my mother's,—and turning about again, there was an end of the debate for three minutes and a half.

——When he gets these breeches made, cried my father in a higher tone, he'll look like a beast in 'em.

He will be very aukward in them at first, replied my mother.——

——And 'twill be lucky, if that's the worst on't, added my father.

It will be very lucky, answered my mother.

I suppose, replied my father,—making some pause first,—he'll be exactly like other people's children.——

Exactly, said my mother.——

——Though I should be sorry for that, added my father: and so the debate stopped again.

——They should be of leather, said my father, turning him about again.—

They will last him, said my mother, the longest.

But he can have no linings to 'em, replied my father.——

He cannot, said my mother.

'Twere better to have them of fustian, quoth my father.

Nothing can be better, quoth my mother.——

——Except dimity,—replied my father:——'Tis best of all,—replied my mother.

——One must not give him his death, however,—interrupted my father.

By no means, said my mother:——and so the dialogue stood still again.

I am resolved, however, quoth my father, breaking silence the fourth time, he shall have no pockets in them.——

——There is no occasion for any, said my mother.——

I mean in his coat and waistcoat,—cried my·father.

——I mean so too,—replied my mother.

——Though if he gets a gig or a top——Poor souls! it is a crown and a scepter to them,—they should have where to secure it.——

Order it as you please, Mr. *Shandy*, replied my mother.——

——But don't you think it right? added my father, pressing the point home to her.

Perfectly, said my mother, if it pleases you, Mr. *Shandy*.——

——There's for you! cried my father, losing temper——Pleases me! ——You never will distinguish, Mrs. *Shandy*, nor shall I ever teach you to do it, betwixt a point of pleasure and a point of convenience.——This was on the *Sunday* night;——and further this chapter sayeth not.

CHAP. XIX.[1]

AFTER my father had debated the affair of the breeches with my mother,—he consulted *Albertus Rubenius*[2] upon it; and *Albertus Rubenius* used my father ten times worse in the consultation (if possible) than even[3] my father had used my mother: For as *Rubenius* had wrote a quarto express, *De re Vestiaria Veterum*,—it was *Rubenius*'s business to have given my father some lights.—On the contrary, my father might as well have thought of extracting the seven cardinal virtues out of a long beard,—as of extracting a single word out of *Rubenius* upon the subject.

Upon every other article of ancient dress,[4] *Rubenius* was very communicative to my father;—gave him a full and satisfactory account of

The Toga, or loose gown.
The Chlamys.

The Ephod.

The Tunica, or Jacket.

The Synthesis.

The Pænula.

The Lacerna, with its Cucullus.

The Paludamentum.

The Prætexta.

The Sagum, or soldier's jerkin.

The Trabea: of which, according to *Suetonius*, there were three kinds.——

——But what are all these to the breeches? said my father.

Rubenius threw him down upon the counter all kinds of shoes which had been in fashion with the *Romans*.——

There was,

> The open shoe.
>
> The close shoe.
>
> The slip shoe.
>
> The wooden shoe.
>
> The soc.
>
> The buskin.

And The military shoe[5] with hobnails in it, which *Juvenal* takes notice of.

There were, The clogs.

> The patins.[6]
>
> The pantoufles.
>
> The brogues.
>
> The sandals, with latchets to them.

There was, The felt shoe.

> The linen shoe.
>
> The laced shoe.
>
> The braided shoe.
>
> The calceus incisus.

And The calceus rostratus.

Rubenius shewed my father how well they all fitted,——in what manner they laced on,——with what points, straps, thongs, latchets, ribands, jaggs, and ends.——

——But I want to be informed about the breeches, said my father.

Albertus Rubenius informed my father that the *Romans* manufactured stuffs of various fabricks,——some plain,—some striped,—others diapered throughout the whole contexture of the wool, with silk and gold—— That linen did not begin to be in common use, till towards the declension of the empire, when the *Egyptians* coming to settle amongst them, brought it into vogue.

——That persons of quality and fortune distinguished themselves by the fineness and whiteness of their cloaths; which colour (next to purple, which was appropriated to the great offices) they most affected and wore on their birth-days and public rejoicings.——That it appeared from the best historians of those times, that they frequently sent their cloaths to the fuller, to be cleaned and whitened;——but that the inferior people, to avoid that expence, generally wore brown cloaths, and of a something coarser texture,—till towards the beginning of *Augustus*'s reign, when the slave dressed like his master, and almost every distinction of habiliment was lost,[7] but the *Latus Clavus*.

And what was the *Latus Clavus?* said my father.

Rubenius told him, that the point was still litigating amongst the learned: ——That *Egnatius, Sigonius, Bossius Ticinensis, Bayfius, Budæus, Salmasius, Lipsius, Lazius, Isaac Causabon,* and *Joseph Scaliger,*[8] all differed from each other,—and he from them: That some took it to be the button,—some the coat itself,—others only the colour of it:—That the great *Bayfius,*[9] in his Wardrobe of the ancients, chap. 12.—honestly said, he knew not what it was,—whether a fibula,[10]—a stud,—a button,—a loop,—a buckle,— or clasps and keepers.——

——My father lost the horse, but not the saddle[11]——They are *hooks and eyes,* said my father——and with hooks and eyes he ordered my breeches to be made.

CHAP. XX.

WE are now going to enter upon a new scene of events.——
——Leave we then the breeches in the taylor's hands, with my father standing over him with his cane, reading him as he sat at work a

lecture upon the *latus clavus*, and pointing to the precise part of the waistband, where he was determined to have it sewed on.——

Leave we my mother—(truest of all the *Poco-curante*'s[1] of her sex!)—careless about it, as about every thing else in the world which concerned her;—that is,—indifferent whether it was done this way or that,—provided it was but done at all.——

Leave we *Slop* likewise to the full profits of all my dishonours.——

Leave we poor *Le Fever* to recover, and get home from *Marseilles* as he can.——And last of all,—because the hardest of all——

Let us leave, if possible, *myself*.——But 'tis impossible,—I must go along with you to the end of the work.

CHAP. XXI.

IF the reader has not a clear conception of the rood and the half of ground which lay at the bottom of my uncle *Toby*'s kitchen garden, and which was the scene of so many of his delicious hours,—the fault is not in me,—but in his imagination;—for I am sure I gave him so minute a description, I was almost ashamed of it.

When FATE was looking forwards one afternoon, into the great transactions of future times,—and recollected for what purposes, this little plot, by a decree fast bound down in iron, had been destined,—she gave a nod to NATURE—'twas enough—Nature threw half a spade full of her kindliest compost upon it, with just so *much* clay in it, as to retain the forms of angles and indentings,—and so *little* of it too, as not to cling to the spade, and render works of so much glory, nasty in foul weather.

My uncle *Toby* came down, as the reader has been informed, with plans along with him, of almost every fortified town in *Italy* and *Flanders*; so let the Duke of *Marlborough*,[1] or the allies, have set down before what town they pleased, my uncle *Toby* was prepared for them.

His way, which was the simplest one in the world, was this; as soon as ever a town was invested—(but sooner when the design was known) to take the plan of it, (let it be what town it would) and enlarge it upon a scale to the exact size of his bowling-green; upon the surface of which, by means of a large role of packthread, and a number of small piquets driven into the ground, at the several angles and redans, he transferred the lines from his paper; then taking the profile of the place, with its works, to determine the depths and slopes of the ditches,—the talus of the glacis, and the precise height of the several banquets, parapets, &c.—he set the corporal to work——and sweetly went it on:——The nature of the soil,—the nature of the work itself,—and above all, the good nature of my uncle *Toby* sitting by from morning to night, and chatting kindly with the corporal upon past-done deeds,—left LABOUR little else but the ceremony of the name.

When the place was finished in this manner, and put into a proper posture of defence,—it was invested,—and my uncle *Toby* and the corporal began to run their first parallel.——I beg I may not be interrupted in my story, by being told, *That the first parallel should be at least three hundred toises distant from the main body of the place*,[2]—*and that I have not left a single inch for it*;——for my uncle *Toby* took the liberty of incroaching upon his kitchen garden, for the sake of enlarging his works on the bowling green, and for that reason generally ran his first and second parallels betwixt two rows of his cabbages and his collyflowers; the conveniences and inconveniences of which will be considered at large in the history of my uncle *Toby*'s and the corporal's campaigns, of which, this I'm now writing is but a sketch, and will be finished, if I conjecture right, in three pages (but there is no guessing)——The campaigns themselves will take up as many books; and therefore I apprehend it would be hanging too great a weight of one kind of matter in so flimsy a performance as this, to rhapsodize them, as I once intended, into the body of the work——surely they had better be printed apart,——we'll consider the affair——so take the following sketch of them in the mean time.

CHAP. XXII.

WHEN the town, with its works, was finished, my uncle *Toby* and the corporal began to run their first parallel——not at random, or any how——but from the same points and distances the allies had begun to run theirs; and regulating their approaches and attacks, by the accounts my uncle *Toby* received from the daily papers,——they went on, during the whole siege, step by step with the allies.

When the duke of *Marlborough* made a lodgment,——my uncle *Toby* made a lodgment too.——And when the face of a bastion was battered down, or a defence ruined,—the corporal took his mattock and did as much,—and so on;——gaining ground, and making themselves masters of the works one after another, till the town fell into their hands.

To one who took pleasure in the happy state of others,—there could not have been a greater sight in the world, than, on a post-morning,[1] in which a practicable breach had been made by the duke of *Marlborough*, in the main body of the place,—to have stood behind the horn-beam hedge, and observed the spirit with which my uncle *Toby*, with *Trim* behind him, sallied forth;——the one with the *Gazette*[2] in his hand,—the other with a spade on his shoulder to execute the contents.——What an honest triumph in my uncle *Toby*'s looks as he marched up to the ramparts! What intense pleasure swimming in his eye as he stood over the corporal, reading the paragraph ten times over to him, as he was at work, lest, peradventure, he should make the breach an inch too wide,—or leave it an inch too narrow ——But when the *chamade*[3] was beat, and the corporal helped my uncle up it, and followed with the colours in his hand, to fix them upon the ramparts ——Heaven! Earth! Sea!——but what avails apostrophes?——with all your elements, wet or dry, ye never compounded so intoxicating a draught.

In this track of happiness for many years, without one interruption to it, except now and then when the wind continued to blow due west for a week or ten days together, which detained the *Flanders* mail, and kept them so long in torture,—but still 'twas the torture of the happy——In this track, I say, did my uncle *Toby* and *Trim* move for many years, every year of which, and sometimes every month, from the invention of either the one or the other of them, adding some new conceit or quirk of improvement to their operations, which always opened fresh springs of delight in carrying them on.

The first year's campaign was carried on from beginning to end, in the plain and simple method I've related.

In the second year, in which my uncle *Toby* took *Liege* and *Ruremond*,[4] he thought he might afford the expence of four handsome draw-bridges, of two of which I have given an exact description, in the former part of my work.

At the latter end of the same year he added a couple of gates with portcullises:——These last were converted afterwards into orgues, as the better thing;[5] and during the winter of the same year, my uncle *Toby*, instead of a new suit of cloaths, which he always had at *Christmas*, treated himself with a handsome sentry-box, to stand at the corner of the bowling-green, betwixt which point and the foot of the glacis, there was left a little kind of an esplanade for him and the corporal to confer and hold councils of war upon.

——The sentry-box was in case of rain.

All these were painted white three times over the ensuing spring, which enabled my uncle *Toby* to take the field with great splendour.

My father would often say to *Yorick*, that if any mortal in the whole universe had done such a thing, except his brother *Toby*, it would have been looked upon by the world as one of the most refined satyrs upon the parade and prancing manner, in which *Lewis* XIV. from the beginning of the war, but particularly that very year, had taken the field——But 'tis not my brother *Toby*'s nature, kind soul! my father would add, to insult any one.

——But let us go on.

CHAP. XXIII.

I Must observe, that although in the first year's campaign, the word *town* is often mentioned,—yet there was no town at that time within the polygon; that addition was not made till the summer following the spring in which the bridges and sentry-box were painted, which was the third year of my uncle *Toby*'s campaigns,—when upon his taking *Amberg, Bonn,* and *Rhinberg,* and *Huy* and *Limbourg,*[1] one after another, a thought came into the corporal's head, that to talk of taking so many towns, *without one* TOWN *to show for it,*—was a very nonsensical way of going to work, and so proposed to my uncle *Toby*, that they should have a little model of a town built for them,—to be run up together of slit deals, and then painted, and clapped within the interior polygon to serve for all.

My uncle *Toby* felt the good of the project instantly, and instantly agreed to it, but with the addition of two singular improvements, of which he was almost as proud, as if he had been the original inventor of the project itself.

The one was to have the town built exactly in the stile of those, of which it was most likely to be the representative:——with grated windows, and the gable ends of the houses, facing the streets, &c. &c.—as those in *Ghent* and *Bruges*, and the rest of the towns in *Brabant* and *Flanders*.[2]

The other was, not to have the houses run up together, as the corporal proposed, but to have every house independant, to hook on, or off, so as to form into the plan of whatever town they pleased. This was put directly into hand, and many and many a look of mutual congratulation was exchanged between my uncle *Toby* and the corporal, as the carpenter did the work.

——It answered prodigiously the next summer——the town was a perfect *Proteus*[3]——It was *Landen*, and *Trerebach*, and *Santvliet*, and *Drusen*, and *Hagenau*,—and then it was *Ostend* and *Menin*, and *Aeth* and *Dendermond*.[4]——

——Surely never did any TOWN act so many parts, since *Sodom* and *Gomorrah*, as my uncle *Toby*'s town did.

In the fourth year, my uncle *Toby* thinking a town looked foolishly without a church, added a very fine one with a steeple.—— *Trim* was for having bells in it;——my uncle *Toby* said, the mettle had better be cast into cannon.

This led the way the next campaign for half a dozen brass field pieces,—to be planted three and three on each side of my uncle *Toby*'s sentry-box; and in a short time, these led the way for a train of somewhat larger,—and so on—(as must always be the case in hobby-horsical affairs) from pieces of half an inch bore, till it came at last to my father's jack boots.

The next year,[5] which was that in which *Lisle* was besieged, and at the close of which both *Ghent* and *Bruges* fell into our hands,—my uncle *Toby* was sadly put to it for *proper* ammunition;——I say proper ammunition ——because his great artillery would not bear powder; and 'twas well for the *Shandy* family they would not——For so full were the papers, from the beginning to the end of the siege,[6] of the incessant firings kept up by the besiegers,——and so heated was my uncle *Toby*'s imagination with the accounts of them, that he had infallibly shot away all his estate.

SOMETHING therefore was wanting, as a *succedaneum*,[7] especially in one or two of the more violent paroxysms of the siege, to keep up something like a continual firing in the imagination,——and this *something*, the corporal, whose principal strength lay in invention, supplied by an entire new system of battering of his own,—without which, this had been objected to by military critics, to the end of the world, as one of the great *desiderata*[8] of my uncle *Toby*'s apparatus.

This will not be explained the worse, for setting off, as I generally do, at a little distance from the subject.

CHAP. XXIV.

WITH two or three other trinkets, small in themselves, but of great regard, which poor *Tom*, the corporal's unfortunate brother, had sent him over, with the account of his marriage with the *Jew*'s widow ——there was

A *Montero*-cap[1] and two *Turkish* tobacco pipes.

The *Montero*-cap I shall describe by and bye.——The *Turkish* tobacco pipes had nothing particular in them, they were fitted up and ornamented as usual, with flexible tubes of *Morocco* leather and gold wire, and mounted at their ends, the one of them with ivory,—the other with black ebony, tipp'd with silver.

My father, who saw all things in lights different from the rest of the world, would say to the corporal, that he ought to look upon these two presents more as tokens of his brother's nicety, than his affection.—— *Tom* did not care, *Trim*, he would say, to put on the cap, or to smoak in the tobacco-pipe of a *Jew*.——God bless your honour, the corporal would say, (giving a strong reason to the contrary)—how can that be.——

The Montero-cap was scarlet, of a superfine *Spanish* cloth, died in grain, and mounted all round with furr, except about four inches in the front, which was faced with a light blue, slightly embroidered,—and seemed to have been the property of a *Portuguese* quartermaster, not of foot, but of horse, as the word denotes.

The corporal was not a little proud of it, as well for its own sake, as the sake of the giver, so seldom or never put it on but upon GALA-days; and yet never was a Montero-cap put to so many uses; for in all controverted points, whether military or culinary, provided the corporal was sure he was in the right,—it was either his *oath*,—his *wager*,—or his *gift*.

——'Twas his gift in the present case.

I'll be bound, said the corporal, speaking to himself, to *give* away my Montero-cap to the first beggar who comes to the door, if I do not manage this matter to his honour's satisfaction.

The completion was no further off, than the very next morning; which was that of the storm of the counterscarp betwixt the *Lower Deule*, to the right, and the gate St. *Andrew*,—and on the left, between St. *Magdalen*'s and the river.

As this was the most memorable attack in the whole war,—the most gallant and obstinate on both sides,—and I must add the most bloody[2] too, for it cost the allies themselves that morning above eleven hundred men,—my uncle *Toby* prepared himself for it with a more than ordinary solemnity.

The eve which preceded, as my uncle *Toby* went to bed, he ordered his ramallie wig,[3] which had laid inside out for many years in the corner of an old campaigning trunk, which stood by his bedside, to be taken out and laid upon the lid of it, ready for the morning;—and the very first thing he did in his shirt, when he had stepped out of bed, my uncle *Toby*, after he had turned the rough side outwards,—put it on:——This done, he proceeded next to his breeches, and having buttoned the waistband, he forthwith buckled on his sword belt, and had got his sword half way in,—when he considered he should want shaving, and that it would be very inconvenient doing it with his sword on,—so took it off:——In assaying to put on his regimental coat and waistcoat, my uncle *Toby* found the same objection in his wig,—so that went off too:—So that what with one thing, and what with another, as always falls out when a man is in the most haste,—'twas ten o'clock, which was half an hour later than his usual time, before my uncle *Toby* sallied out.

CHAP. XXV.

MY uncle *Toby* had scarce turned the corner of his yew hedge, which separated his kitchen garden from his bowling green, when he perceived the corporal had began the attack without him.——

Let me stop and give you a picture of the corporal's apparatus; and of the corporal himself in the height of this attack just as it struck my uncle *Toby*, as he turned towards the sentry box, where the corporal was at work,——for in nature there is not such another,——nor can any combination of all that is grotesque and whimsical in her works produce its equal.

The corporal——

——Tread lightly on his ashes, ye men of genius,——for he was your kinsman:

Weed his grave clean, ye men of goodness,—for he was your brother.—Oh corporal! had I thee, but now,—now, that I am able to give thee a dinner and protection,—how would I cherish thee! thou should'st wear thy Montero-cap every hour of the day, and every day of the week,—and when it was worn out, I would purchase thee a couple like it:—— But alas! alas! alas! now that I can do this, in spight of their reverences— the occasion is lost—for thou art gone;—thy genius fled up to the stars from whence it came;—and that warm heart of thine, with all its generous and open vessels, compressed into a *clod of the valley!*[1]

——But what——what is this, to that future and dreaded page, where I look towards the velvet pall, decorated with the military ensigns of thy master—the first—the foremost of created beings;——where, I shall see thee, faithful servant! laying his sword and scabbard with a trembling hand across his coffin, and then returning pale as ashes to the door, to take his mourning horse by the bridle, to follow his hearse, as he directed thee; ——where—all my father's systems shall be baffled by his sorrows; and, in spight of his philosophy, I shall behold him, as he inspects the lackered plate, twice taking his spectacles from off his nose, to wipe away the dew which nature has shed upon them——When I see him cast in the rosemary[2] with an air of disconsolation, which cries through my ears,——O *Toby!* in what corner of the world shall I seek thy fellow?

——Gracious powers! which erst have opened the lips of the dumb in his distress, and made the tongue of the stammerer speak plain[3]——when I shall arrive at this dreaded page, deal not with me, then, with a stinted hand.

CHAP. XXVI.

THE corporal, who the night before had resolved in his mind, to supply the grand *desideratum*, of keeping up something like an incessant firing upon the enemy during the heat of the attack,—had no further idea in his fancy at that time, than a contrivance of smoaking tobacco against the town, out of one of my uncle *Toby*'s six field pieces, which were planted on each side of his sentry-box; the means of effecting which occurring to his fancy at the same time, though he had pledged his cap, he thought it in no danger from the miscarriage of his projects.

Upon turning it this way, and that, a little in his mind, he soon began to find out, that by means of his two *Turkish* tobacco-pipes, with the supplement of three smaller tubes of wash-leather at each of their lower ends, to be tagg'd by the same number of tin pipes fitted to the touch holes, and sealed with clay next the cannon, and then tied hermetically with waxed silk at their several insertions into the *Morocco* tube,[1]——he should be able to fire the six field pieces all together, and with the same ease as to fire one.——

——Let no man say from what taggs and jaggs hints may not be cut out for the advancement of human knowlege. Let no man who has read my father's first and second *beds of justice*, ever rise up and say again, from collision of what kinds of bodies, light may, or may not be struck out, to carry the arts and sciences up to perfection.——Heaven! thou knowest how I love them;——thou knowest the secrets of my heart, and that I would this moment give my shirt——Thou art a fool, *Shandy*, says *Eugenius*,—for thou hast but a dozen in the world,—and 'twill break thy set.——

No matter for that, *Eugenius*; I would give the shirt off my back to be burnt into tinder, were it only to satisfy one feverish enquirer, how many sparks at one good stroke, a good flint and steel could strike into the tail of it.——Think ye not that in striking these *in*,—he might, peradventure, strike something *out?* as sure as a gun.——

——But this project, by the bye.

The corporal sat up the best part of the night in bringing *his* to perfection; and having made a sufficient proof of his cannon, with charging them to the top with tobacco,—he went with contentment to bed.

CHAP. XXVII.

THE corporal had slipped out about ten minutes before my uncle *Toby*, in order to fix his apparatus, and just give the enemy a shot or two before my uncle *Toby* came.

He had drawn the six field-pieces for this end, all close up together in front of my uncle *Toby*'s sentry-box, leaving only an interval of about a yard and a half betwixt the three, on the right and left, for the convenience of charging, &c.—and the sake possibly of two batteries, which he might think double the honour of one.

In the rear, and facing this opening, with his back to the door of the sentry-box, for fear of being flanked, had the corporal wisely taken his post:——He held the ivory pipe, appertaining to the battery on the right, betwixt the finger and thumb of his right hand,—and the ebony pipe tipp'd with silver, which appertained to the battery on the left, betwixt the finger and thumb of the other——and with his right knee fixed firm upon the ground, as if in the front rank of his platoon, was the corporal, with his montero-cap upon his head, furiously playing off his two cross batteries at the same time against the counterguard, which faced the counterscarp, where the attack was to be made that morning. His first intention, as I said, was no more than giving the enemy a single puff or two;—but the pleasure of the *puffs*, as well as the *puffing*, had insensibly got hold of the corporal, and drawn him on from puff to puff, into the very height of the attack, by the time my uncle *Toby* joined him.

'Twas well for my father, that my uncle *Toby* had not his will to make that day.

CHAP. XXVIII.

MY uncle *Toby* took the ivory pipe out of the corporal's hand,— looked at it for half a minute, and returned it.

In less than two minutes my uncle *Toby* took the pipe from the corporal again, and raised it half way to his mouth——then hastily gave it back a second time.

The corporal redoubled the attack,——my uncle *Toby* smiled,—— then looked grave,——then smiled for a moment,——then looked serious for a long time;——Give me hold of the ivory pipe, *Trim*, said my uncle *Toby*——my uncle *Toby* put it to his lips,——drew it back directly,—— gave a peep over the horn-beam hedge;——never did my uncle *Toby*'s mouth water so much for a pipe in his life.——My uncle *Toby* retired into the sentry-box with the pipe in his hand.——

——Dear uncle *Toby!* don't go into the sentry-box with the pipe,— there's no trusting a man's self with such a thing in such a corner.

CHAP. XXIX.

I Beg the reader will assist me here, to wheel off my uncle *Toby*'s ordnance behind the scenes,——to remove his sentry-box, and clear the theatre, *if possible*, of horn-works and half moons, and get the rest of his military apparatus out of the way;——that done, my dear friend *Garrick*,[1] we'll snuff the candles bright,—sweep the stage with a new broom,—draw up the curtain, and exhibit my uncle *Toby* dressed in a new character, throughout which the world can have no idea how he will act: and yet, if pity be akin to love,—and bravery no alien to it, you have seen enough of my uncle *Toby* in these, to trace these family likenesses, betwixt the two passions (in case there is one) to your heart's content.

Vain science! thou assists us in no case of this kind——and thou puzzlest us in every one.

There was, Madam, in my uncle *Toby*,[2] a singleness of heart which misled him so far out of the little serpentine tracks in which things of this nature usually go on; you can—you can have no conception of it: with this, there was a plainness and simplicity of thinking, with such an unmistrusting ignorance of the plies and foldings of the heart of woman;——and so naked and defenceless did he stand before you, (when a siege was out of his head) that you might have stood behind any one of your serpentine walks, and shot my uncle *Toby* ten times in a day, through his liver,[3] if nine times in a day, Madam, had not served your purpose.

With all this, Madam,—and what confounded every thing as much on the other hand, my uncle *Toby* had that unparalleled modesty of nature I once told you of, and which, by the bye, stood eternal sentry upon his feelings, that you might as soon——But where am I going? these reflections croud in upon me ten pages at least too soon, and take up that time, which I ought to bestow upon facts.

CHAP. XXX.

OF the few legitimate sons of *Adam*, whose breasts never felt what the sting of love was,—(maintaining first, all mysogynists to be bastards)—the greatest heroes of ancient and modern story have carried off amongst them, nine parts in ten of the honour; and I wish for their sakes I had the key of my study out of my draw-well,[1] only for five minutes, to tell you their names—recollect them I cannot—so be content to accept of these, for the present, in their stead.——

There was the great king *Aldrovandus*, and *Bosphorus*, and *Capadocius*, and *Dardanus*, and *Pontus*, and *Asius*,——to say nothing of the iron-hearted *Charles* the XIIth, whom the Countess of K*****[2] herself could make nothing of.——There was *Babylonicus*, and *Mediterraneus*, and *Polixenes*,[3] and *Persicus*, and *Prusicus*, not one of whom (except *Capadocius* and *Pontus*, who were both a little suspected) ever once bowed down his breast to the goddess——The truth is, they had all of them something else to do—and so had my uncle *Toby*—till Fate—till Fate I say, envying his name the glory of being handed down to posterity with *Aldrovandus*'s and the rest,——she basely patched up the peace of *Utrecht*. [4]

——Believe me, Sirs, 'twas the worst deed she did that year.

CHAP. XXXI.

AMONGST the many ill consequences of the treaty of *Utrecht*, it was within a point of giving my uncle *Toby* a surfeit of sieges; and though he recovered his appetite afterwards, yet *Calais* itself left not a deeper scar in *Mary*'s heart,[1] than *Utrecht* upon my uncle *Toby*'s. To the end of his life he never could hear *Utrecht* mentioned upon any account whatever,— or so much as read an article of news extracted out of the *Utrecht Gazette*, without fetching a sigh, as if his heart would break in twain.

My father, who was a great MOTIVE-MONGER, and consequently a very dangerous person for a man to sit by, either laughing or crying,—for he generally knew your motive for doing both, much better than you knew it yourself—would always console my uncle *Toby* upon these occasions, in a way, which shewed plainly, he imagined my uncle *Toby* grieved for nothing in the whole affair, so much as the loss of his *hobby-horse*.—— Never mind, brother *Toby*, he would say,—by God's blessing we shall have another war break out again some of these days; and when it does,— the belligerent powers, if they would hang themselves, cannot keep us out of play.——I defy 'em, my dear *Toby*, he would add, to take countries without taking towns,——or towns without sieges.

My uncle *Toby* never took this back-stroke of my father's at his hobby horse kindly.——He thought the stroke ungenerous; and the more so, because in striking the horse, he hit the rider too, and in the most dishonourable part a blow could fall; so that upon these occasions, he always laid down his pipe upon the table with more fire to defend himself than common.

I told the reader, this time two years, that my uncle *Toby* was not eloquent; and in the very same page gave an instance to the contrary: ——I repeat the observation, and a fact which contradicts it again.—He was not eloquent,—it was not easy to my uncle *Toby* to make long harangues,—and he hated florid ones; but there were occasions where the stream overflowed the man, and ran so counter to its usual course, that in some parts my uncle *Toby*, for a time, was at least equal to *Tertullus*[2]——but in others, in my own opinion, infinitely above him.

My father was so highly pleased with one of these apological orations of my uncle *Toby*'s, which he had delivered one evening before him and *Yorick*, that he wrote it down before he went to bed.

I have had the good fortune to meet with it amongst my father's papers, with here and there an insertion of his own, betwixt two crooks, thus [   ], and is endorsed,

My brother TOBY'*s justification of his own principles*
and conduct in wishing to continue the war.

I may safely say, I have read over this apological oration of my uncle *Toby*'s a hundred times, and think it so fine a model of defence,—and shews so sweet a temperament of gallantry and good principles in him, that I give it the world, word for word, (interlineations and all) as I find it.

CHAP. XXXII.

My uncle TOBY'*s apological oration.*[1]

I Am not insensible, brother *Shandy*, that when a man, whose profession is arms, wishes, as I have done, for war,—it has an ill aspect to the world;——and that, how just and right soever his motives and intentions may be,—he stands in an uneasy posture in vindicating himself from private views in doing it.

For this cause, if a soldier is a prudent man, which he may be, without being a jot the less brave, he will be sure not to utter his wish in the hearing of an enemy; for say what he will, an enemy will not believe him.——He will be cautious of doing it even to a friend,—lest he may suffer in his esteem:——But if his heart is overcharged, and a secret sigh for arms must have its vent, he will reserve it for the ear of a brother, who knows his character to the bottom, and what his true notions, dispositions, and principles of honour are: What, I *hope*, I have been in all these, brother *Shandy*, would be unbecoming in me to say:——much worse, I know, have I been than I ought,—and something worse, perhaps, than I think: But such as I am, you, my dear brother *Shandy*, who have sucked the same breasts with me,—and with whom I have been brought up from my cradle,—and from whose knowlege, from the first hours of our boyish pastimes, down to this, I have concealed no one action of my life, and scarce a thought in it——Such as I am, brother, you must by this time know me, with all my vices, and with all my weaknesses too, whether of my age, my temper, my passions, or my understanding.

Tell me then, my dear brother *Shandy*, upon which of them it is, that when I condemned the peace of *Utrecht*, and grieved the war was not carried on with vigour a little longer, you should think your brother did it upon unworthy views; or that in wishing for war, he should be bad enough to wish more of his fellow creatures slain,—more slaves made, and more families driven from their peaceful habitations, merely for his own pleasure:——Tell me, brother *Shandy*, upon what one deed of mine do you ground it? [*The devil a deed do I know of, dear* Toby, *but one for a hundred pounds, which I lent thee to carry on these cursed sieges.*]

If, when I was a school-boy, I could not hear a drum beat, but my heart beat with it—was it my fault?——Did I plant the propensity there?—— did I sound the alarm within, or Nature?

When *Guy*, Earl of *Warwick*, and *Parismus* and *Parismenus*, and *Valentine* and *Orson*, and the *Seven Champions of England*[2] were handed around the school,—were they not all purchased with my own pocket money? Was that selfish, brother *Shandy*? When we read over the siege of *Troy*, which lasted ten years and eight months,——though with such a train of artillery as we had at *Namur*, the town might have been carried in a week—was I not as much concerned for the destruction of the *Greeks* and *Trojans* as any boy of the whole school? Had I not three strokes of a ferula given me, two on my right hand and one on my left, for calling *Helena* a bitch for it? Did any one of you shed more tears for *Hector*? And when king *Priam* came to the camp to beg his body, and returned weeping back to *Troy* without it,[3]—you know, brother, I could not eat my dinner.——

——Did that bespeak me cruel? Or because, brother *Shandy*, my blood flew out into the camp, and my heart panted for war,—was it a proof it could not ache for the distresses of war too?

O brother! 'tis one thing for a soldier to gather laurels,—and 'tis another to scatter cypress.———[*Who told thee, my dear* Toby, *that cypress was used by the ancients on mournful occasions?*]

———'Tis one thing, brother *Shandy*, for a soldier to hazard his own life—to leap first down into the trench, where he is sure to be cut in pieces:———'Tis one thing, from public spirit and a thirst of glory, to enter the breach the first man,—to stand in the foremost rank, and march bravely on with drums and trumpets, and colours flying about his ears:———'Tis one thing, I say, brother *Shandy*, to do this—and 'tis another thing to reflect on the miseries of war;—to view the desolations of whole countries, and consider the intolerable fatigues and hardships which the soldier himself, the instrument who works them, is forced (for six-pence a day, if he can get it) to undergo.

Need I be told, dear *Yorick*, as I was by you, in *Le Fever*'s funeral sermon, *That so soft and gentle a creature, born to love, to mercy, and kindness, as man is, was not shaped for this?*———But why did you not add, *Yorick*,—if not by NATURE—that he is so by NECESSITY?———For what is war? what is it, *Yorick*, when fought as ours has been, upon principles of *liberty*, and upon principles of *honour*———what is it, but the getting together of quiet and harmless people, with their swords in their hands, to keep the ambitious and the turbulent within bounds? And heaven is my witness, brother *Shandy*, that the pleasure I have taken in these things,—and that infinite delight, in particular, which has attended my sieges in my bowling green, has arose within me, and I hope in the corporal too, from the consciousness we both had, that in carrying them on, we were answering the great ends of our creation.

CHAP. XXXIII.

I Told the Christian reader——I say *Christian*——hoping he is one ——and if he is not, I am sorry for it——and only beg he will consider the matter with himself, and not lay the blame entirely upon this book,——

I told him, Sir——for in good truth, when a man is telling a story in the strange way I do mine, he is obliged continually to be going backwards and forwards to keep all tight together in the reader's fancy——which, for my own part, if I did not take heed to do more than at first, there is so much unfixed and equivocal matter starting up, with so many breaks and gaps in it,—and so little service do the stars afford, which, nevertheless, I hang up in some of the darkest passages, knowing that the world is apt to lose its way, with all the lights the sun itself at noon day can give it ——and now, you see, I am lost myself!——

——But 'tis my father's fault; and whenever my brains come to be dissected, you will perceive, without spectacles, that he has left a large uneven thread, as you sometimes see in an unsaleable piece of cambrick, running along the whole length of the web, and so untowardly, you cannot so much as cut out a **, (here I hang up a couple of lights again)——or a fillet,[1] or a thumb-stall, but it is seen or felt.——

Quanto id diligentius in liberis procreandis cavendum, sayeth *Cardan*.[2] All which being considered, and that you see 'tis morally impracticable for me to wind this round to where I set out——

I begin the chapter over again.

CHAP. XXXIV.

I Told the Christian reader in the beginning of the chapter which preceded my uncle *Toby*'s apologetical oration,—though in a different trope from what I shall make use of now, That the peace of *Utrecht* was within an ace of creating the same shyness betwixt my uncle *Toby* and his hobby-horse, as it did betwixt the queen and the rest of the confederating powers.

There is an indignant way in which a man sometimes dismounts his horse, which as good as says to him, "I'll go afoot, Sir, all the days of my life, before I would ride a single mile upon your back again." Now my uncle *Toby* could not be said to dismount his horse in this manner; for in strictness of language, he could not be said to dismount his horse at all ——his horse rather flung him——and somewhat *viciously*, which made my uncle *Toby* take it ten times more unkindly. Let this matter be settled by state jockies as they like.——It created, I say, a sort of shyness betwixt my uncle *Toby* and his hobby-horse.—— He had no occasion for him from the month of *March* to *November*,[1] which was the summer after the articles were signed, except it was now and then to take a short ride out, just to see that the fortifications and harbour of *Dunkirk* were demolished, according to stipulation.[2]

The *French* were so backwards all that summer in setting about that affair, and Monsieur *Tugghe*, the deputy from the magistrates of *Dunkirk*, presented so many affecting petitions to the queen,—beseeching her majesty to cause only her thunderbolts to fall upon the martial works, which might have incurred her displeasure,—but to spare— to spare the mole,[3] for the mole's sake; which, in its naked situation, could be no more than an object of pity——and the queen (who was but a woman) being of a pitiful disposition,—and her ministers also, they not wishing in their hearts to have the town dismantled, for these private reasons, * * * * * * * * * * *
* * * * * * * * * * * * * * * * * *
* * * * * *————

    * * * * * * * * * * * * * * * * *
* * * * * * * * * * * * * * * * * *
* * * * * * *   *; so that the whole went heavily on with my uncle *Toby*; insomuch, that it was not within three full months, after he and the corporal had constructed the town, and put it in a condition to be destroyed, that the several commandants, commissaries, deputies, negotiators, and intendants, would permit him to set about it.——Fatal interval of inactivity!

The corporal was for beginning the demolition, by making a breach in the ramparts, or main fortifications of the town——No,—that will never do, corporal, said my uncle *Toby*, for in going that way to work with the town, the *English* garrison will not be safe in it an hour; because if the *French* are treacherous——They are as treacherous as devils, an' please your honour, said the corporal——It gives me concern always when I hear it, *Trim*, said my uncle *Toby*,—for they don't want personal bravery; and if a breach is made in the ramparts, they may enter it, and make themselves masters of the place when they please:——Let them enter it, said the corporal, lifting up his pioneer's spade in both his hands, as if he was going to lay about him with it,—let them enter, an' please your honour, if they dare.——In cases like this, corporal, said my uncle *Toby*, slipping his right hand down to the middle of his cane, and holding it afterwards truncheon-wise, with his forefinger extended,——'tis no part of the consideration of a commandant, what the enemy dare,—or what they dare not do; he must act with prudence. We will begin with the outworks both towards the sea and the land, and particularly with fort *Louis*, the most distant of them all, and demolish it first,—and the rest, one by one, both on our right and left, as we retreat towards the town; ——then we'll demolish the mole,—next fill up the harbour,—then retire into the citadel, and blow it up into the air; and having done that, corporal, we'll embark for *England.*——We are there, quoth the corporal, recollecting himself——Very true, said my uncle *Toby*——looking at the church.

CHAP. XXXV.

A Delusive, delicious consultation or two of this kind, betwixt my uncle *Toby* and *Trim*, upon the demolition of *Dunkirk*,—for a moment rallied back the ideas of those pleasures, which were slipping from under him:——still—still all went on heavily——the magic left the mind the weaker—STILLNESS, with SILENCE at her back, entered the solitary parlour, and drew their gauzy mantle over my uncle *Toby*'s head;—— and LISTLESSNESS, with her lax fibre and undirected eye, sat quietly down beside him in his arm chair.——No longer *Amberg*, and *Rhinberg*, and

Limbourg, and *Huy,* and *Bonn,* in one year,—and the prospect of *Landen,* and *Trerebach,* and *Drusen,* and *Dendermond,* the next,—hurried on the blood:—No longer did saps, and mines, and blinds, and gabions, and palisadoes, keep out this fair enemy of man's repose:——No more could my uncle *Toby,* after passing the *French* lines, as he eat his egg at supper, from thence break into the heart of *France,*—cross over the *Oyes,* and with all *Picardie* open behind him, march up to the gates of *Paris,* and fall asleep with nothing but ideas of glory:——No more was he to dream, he had fixed the royal standard upon the tower of the *Bastile,* and awake with it streaming in his head.

——Softer visions,—gentler vibrations stole sweetly in upon his slumbers;—the trumpet of war fell out of his hands,—he took up the lute, sweet instrument! of all others the most delicate! the most difficult!—— how wilt thou touch it, my dear uncle *Toby?*

CHAP. XXXVI.

NOW, because I have once or twice said, in my inconsiderate way of talking, That I was confident the following memoirs of my uncle *Toby*'s courtship of widow *Wadman,* whenever I got time to write them, would turn out one of the most compleat systems, both of the elementary and practical part of love and love-making, that ever was addressed to the world——are you to imagine from thence, that I shall set out with a description of *what love is?*[1] whether part God and part Devil, as *Plotinus* will have it——

——Or by a more critical equation, and supposing the whole of love to be as ten——to determine, with *Ficinus,* "*How many parts of it—the one,—and how many the other*;"—or whether it is *all of it one great Devil,* from head to tail, as *Plato* has taken upon him to pronounce; concerning which conceit of his, I shall not offer my opinion:—but my opinion of *Plato* is this; that he appears, from this instance, to have been a man of much the same temper and way of reasoning with doctor *Baynyard,*[2] who being a great enemy to blisters, as imagining that half a dozen of 'em on at once, would draw a man as surely to his grave, as a herse and six—

rashly concluded, that the Devil himself was nothing in the world, but one great bouncing *Cantharidis.*————

I have nothing to say to people who allow themselves this monstrous liberty in arguing, but what *Nazianzen* cried out *(that is polemically)* to *Philagrius*————

"᾿ΕΥΓΕ!" *O rare! 'tis fine reasoning, Sir, indeed!*—"ὅτι φιλοσοφεῖς ἐν Πάθεσι" —*and most nobly do you aim at truth, when you philosophize about it in your moods and passions.*[3]

Nor is it to be imagined, for the same reason, I should stop to enquire, whether love is a disease,——or embroil myself with *Rhasis* and *Dioscorides,* whether the seat of it is in the brain or liver;—because this would lead me on, to an examination of the two very opposite manners, in which patients have been treated——the one, of *Aëtius,* who always begun with a cooling glyster of hempseed and bruised cucumbers;—and followed on with thin potations of water lillies and purslane—to which he added a pinch of snuff, of the herb *Hanea*;—and where *Aëtius* durst venture it,—his topaz-ring.

——The other, that of *Gordonius,* who (in his cap. *15. de Amore*) directs they should be thrashed, "*ad putorem usque,*"——till they stink again.[4]

These are disquisitions, which my father, who had laid in a great stock of knowledge of this kind, will be very busy with, in the progress of my uncle *Toby*'s affairs: I must anticipate thus much, That from his theories of love, (with which, by the way, he contrived to crucify my uncle *Toby*'s mind, almost as much as his amours themselves)—he took a single step into practice;—and by means of a camphorated cerecloth, which he found means to impose upon the taylor for buckram, whilst he was making my uncle *Toby* a new pair of breeches, he produced *Gordonius*'s effect upon my uncle *Toby* without the disgrace.

What changes this produced, will be read in its proper place: all that is needful to be added to the anecdote, is this,——That whatever effect it had upon my uncle *Toby,*——it had a vile effect upon the house;—— and if my uncle *Toby* had not smoaked it down as he did, it might have had a vile effect upon my father too.

CHAP. XXXVII.

_____'TWILL come out of itself by and bye.——All I contend for is, that I am not *obliged* to set out with a definition of what love is; and so long as I can go on with my story intelligibly, with the help of the word itself, without any other idea to it, than what I have in common with the rest of the world, why should I differ from it a moment before the time?——When I can get on no further,—and find myself entangled on all sides of this mystick labyrinth,—my Opinion will then come in, in course,—and lead me out.

At present, I hope I shall be sufficiently understood, in telling the reader, my uncle *Toby fell in love:*

—Not that the phrase is at all to my liking: for to say a man is *fallen* in love,—or that he is *deeply* in love,—or up to the ears in love,—and sometimes even *over head and ears in it*,—carries an idiomatical kind of implication, that love is a thing *below* a man:—this is recurring again to *Plato*'s opinion, which, with all his divinityship,—I hold to be damnable and heretical;—and so much for that.

Let love therefore be what it will,—my uncle *Toby* fell into it.

——And possibly, gentle reader, with such a temptation—so wouldst thou: For never did thy eyes behold, or thy concupiscence covet any thing in this world, more concupiscible than widow *Wadman.*

CHAP. XXXVIII.

TO conceive this right,—call for pen and ink—here's paper ready to your hand.——Sit down, Sir, paint her to your own mind——as like your mistress as you can——as unlike your wife as your conscience will let you—'tis all one to me——please but your own fancy in it.

————Was ever any thing in Nature so sweet!—so exquisite!

——Then, dear Sir, how could my uncle *Toby* resist it?

Thrice happy book! thou wilt have one page, at least, within thy covers, which MALICE will not blacken, and which IGNORANCE cannot misrepresent.

CHAP. XXXIX.

AS *Susannah* was informed by an express from Mrs. *Bridget*, of my uncle *Toby*'s falling in love with her mistress, fifteen days before it happened,—the contents of which express, *Susannah* communicated to my mother the next day,—it has just given me an opportunity of entering upon my uncle *Toby*'s amours a fortnight before their existence.

I have an article of news to tell you, Mr. *Shandy*, quoth my mother, which will surprise you greatly.————

Now my father was then holding one of his second beds of justice, and was musing within himself about the hardships of matrimony, as my mother broke silence.————

"——My brother *Toby*, quoth she, is going to be married to Mrs. *Wadman*."

——Then he will never, quoth my father, be able to lie *diagonally* in his bed again as long as he lives.

It was a consuming vexation to my father, that my mother never asked the meaning of a thing she did not understand.

——That she is not a woman of science, my father would say—is her misfortune—but she might ask a question.——

My mother never did.——In short, she went out of the world at last without knowing whether it turned *round*, or stood *still*.——My father had officiously told her above a thousand times which way it was,—but she always forgot.

For these reasons a discourse seldom went on much further betwixt them, than a proposition,—a reply, and a rejoinder; at the end of which, it generally took breath for a few minutes, (as in the affair of the breeches) and then went on again.

If he marries, 'twill be the worse for us,—quoth my mother.

Not a cherry-stone, said my father,—he may as well batter away his means upon that, as any thing else.

——To be sure, said my mother: so here ended the proposition,—the reply,—and the rejoinder, I told you of.

It will be some amusement to him, too,——said my father.

A very great one, answered my mother, if he should have children.——

——Lord have mercy upon me,—said my father to himself——

* * * * * * * * * * * * * * * * * * *

* * * * * * * * * * * * * * * * * * *

* * * * * * * * *

CHAP. XL.

I Am now beginning to get fairly into my work; and by the help of a vegitable diet, with a few of the cold seeds,[1] I make no doubt but I shall be able to go on with my uncle *Toby*'s story, and my own, in a tolerable straight line. Now,

Inv.T.S   *Scul.T.S*

These were the four lines I moved in through my first, second, third, and fourth volumes.[2]——In the fifth volume I have been very good,—— the precise line I have described in it being this:

By which it appears, that except at the curve, marked A. where I took a trip to *Navarre*,—and the indented curve B. which is the short airing when I was there with the Lady *Baussiere* and her page,—I have not taken the least frisk of a digression, till *John de la Casse*'s devils led me the round you see marked D.—for as for *c c c c c* they are nothing but parentheses, and the common *ins* and *outs* incident to the lives of the greatest ministers of state; and when compared with what men have done,—or with my own transgressions at the letters A B D—they vanish into nothing.

In this last volume I have done better still—for from the end of *Le Fever*'s episode, to the beginning of my uncle *Toby*'s campaigns,—I have scarce stepped a yard out of my way.

If I mend at this rate, it is not impossible——by the good leave of his grace of *Benevento*'s devils——but I may arrive hereafter at the excellency of going on even thus;

which is a line drawn as straight as I could draw it, by a writing-master's ruler, (borrowed for that purpose) turning neither to the right hand or to the left.

This *right line*,—the path-way for Christians to walk in! say divines——

——The emblem of moral rectitude! says *Cicero*[3]——

——The *best line*! say cabbage-planters[4]——is the shortest line,[5] says *Archimedes*, which can be drawn from one given point to another.——

I wish your ladyships would lay this matter to heart in your next birth-day suits![6]

——What a journey!

Pray can you tell me,—that is, without anger, before I write my chapter upon straight lines——by what mistake——who told them so——or how it has come to pass, that your men of wit and genius have all along confounded this line, with the line of GRAVITATION.

END of the SIXTH VOLUME.

THE
LIFE
AND
OPINIONS
OF
TRISTRAM SHANDY,
GENTLEMAN.

Non enim excursus hic ejus, sed opus ipsum est.
PLIN. Lib. quintus Epistola sexta.

VOL. VII.

LONDON:

Printed for T. BECKET and P. A. DEHONT,
in the Strand. MDCCLXV.

(Height of original type-page 109.5 mm.)

THE

LIFE and OPINIONS

OF

TRISTRAM SHANDY, Gent.

CHAP. I.

NO——I think, I said, I would write two volumes every year, provided the vile cough which then tormented me, and which to this hour I dread worse than the devil, would but give me leave——and in another place—(but where, I can't recollect now) speaking of my book as a *machine*, and laying my pen and ruler down cross-wise upon the table, in order to gain the greater credit to it—I swore it should be kept a going at that rate these forty years if it pleased but the fountain of life[1] to bless me so long with health and good spirits.

Now as for my spirits, little have I to lay to their charge—nay so very little (unless the mounting me upon a long stick,[2] and playing the fool with me nineteen hours out of the twenty-four, be accusations) that on the contrary, I have much—much to thank 'em for: cheerily have ye made me tread the path of life with all the burdens of it (except its cares) upon my back; in no one moment of my existence, that I remember, have ye once deserted me, or tinged the objects which came in my way, either with sable, or with a sickly green; in dangers ye gilded my horizon with hope, and when DEATH himself knocked at my door—ye bad him come again; and in so gay a tone of careless indifference, did ye do it, that he doubted of his commission——

"——There must certainly be some mistake in this matter," quoth he.

Now there is nothing in this world I abominate worse, than to be interrupted in a story——and I was that moment telling Eugenius a most tawdry one[3] in my way, of a nun who fancied herself a shell-fish, and of a monk damn'd for eating a muscle, and was shewing him the grounds and justice of the procedure——

"—Did ever so grave a personage get into so vile a scrape?" quoth Death. Thou hast had a narrow escape, Tristram, said Eugenius, taking hold of my hand as I finish'd my story——

But there is no *living*, Eugenius, replied I, at this rate; for as this *son of a whore* has found out my lodgings——

—You call him rightly, said Eugenius,—for by sin, we are told, he enter'd the world[4]——I care not which way he enter'd, quoth I, provided he be not in such a hurry to take me out with him—for I have forty volumes to write, and forty thousand things to say and do, which no body in the world will say and do for me, except thyself; and as thou seest he has got me by the throat[5] (for Eugenius could scarce hear me speak across the table) and that I am no match for him in the open field, had I not better, whilst these few scatter'd spirits remain, and these two spider legs of mine (holding one of them up to him) are able to support me—had I not better, Eugenius, fly for my life? 'tis my advice, my dear Tristram, said Eugenius——then by heaven! I will lead him a dance he little thinks of—for I will gallop, quoth I, without looking once behind me to the banks of the Garonne; and if I hear him clattering at my heels——I'll scamper away to mount Vesuvius——from thence to Joppa,[6] and from Joppa to the world's end, where, if he follows me, I pray God he may break his neck——

—He runs more risk *there*, said Eugenius, than thou.

Eugenius's wit and affection brought blood into the cheek from whence it had been some months banish'd—'twas a vile moment to bid adieu in; he led me to my chaise——*Allons!*[7] said I; the post boy gave a crack with his whip——off I went like a cannon, and in half a dozen bounds got into Dover.

CHAP. II.

NOW hang it! quoth I, as I look'd towards the French coast—a man should know something of his own country too, before he goes abroad——and I never gave a peep into Rochester church, or took notice of the dock of Chatham, or visited St. Thomas at Canterbury,[1] though they all three laid in my way——

——But mine, indeed, is a particular case——

So without arguing the matter further with Thomas o'Becket, or any one else—I skip'd into the boat, and in five minutes we got under sail and scudded away like the wind.

Pray captain, quoth I, as I was going down into the cabin, is a man never overtaken by *Death* in this passage?

Why, there is not time for a man to be sick in it, replied he——What a cursed lyar! for I am sick as a horse, quoth I, already——what a brain!——upside down!——hey dey! the cells are broke loose one into another, and the blood, and the lymph, and the nervous juices, with the fix'd and volatile salts,[2] are all jumbled into one mass——good g—! every thing turns round in it like a thousand whirlpools——I'd give a shilling to know if I shan't write the clearer for it——

Sick! sick! sick! sick!——

——When shall we get to land? captain—they have hearts like stones——O I am deadly sick!——reach me that thing, boy——'tis the most discomfiting sickness——I wish I was at the bottom—Madam! how is it with you? Undone! undone! un—— O! undone! sir—What the first time?——No, 'tis the second, third, sixth, tenth time, sir,—hey-day——what a trampling over head!—hollo! cabin boy! what's the matter—

The wind chopp'd about! s'Death!—then I shall meet him full in the face.

What luck!—'tis chopp'd about again, master——O the devil chop it——

Captain, quoth she, for heaven's sake, let us get ashore.

CHAP. III.

I T is a great inconvenience to a man in a haste, that there are three distinct roads between Calais and Paris, in behalf of which there is so much to be said by the several deputies from the towns which lie along them, that half a day is easily lost in settling which you'll take.

First, the road by Lisle and Arras, which is the most about——but most interesting, and instructing.

The second that by Amiens, which you may go, if you would see Chantilly——

And that by Beauvais, which you may go, if you will.

For this reason a great many chuse to go by Beauvais.

CHAP. IV.

" N OW before I quit Calais," a travel-writer would say, "it would not be amiss to give some account of it."—Now I think it very much amiss—that a man cannot go quietly through a town, and let it alone, when it does not meddle with him, but that he must be turning about and drawing his pen at every kennel he crosses over, merely o'my conscience, for the sake of drawing it; because, if we may judge from what has been wrote of these things, by all who have *wrote and gallop'd*—or who have *gallop'd and wrote*, which is a different way still; or who for more expedition than the rest, have *wrote-galloping*, which is the way I do at present——from the great Addison[1] who did it with his satchel of school-books hanging at his a— and galling his beast's crupper at every stroke—there is not a galloper of us all who might not have gone on ambling quietly in his own ground (in case he had any) and have wrote all he had to write, dry shod, as well as not.[2]

For my own part, as heaven is my judge, and to which I shall ever make my last appeal—I know no more of Calais, (except the little my barber told me of it, as he was whetting his razor) than I do this moment of *Grand Cairo*; for it was dusky in the evening when I landed, and dark as pitch in the morning when I set out, and yet by merely knowing what is what, and by drawing this from that in one part of the town, and by spelling and putting this and that together in another—I would lay any travelling odds, that I this moment write a chapter upon Calais as long as my arm; and with so distinct and satisfactory a detail of every item, which is worth a stranger's curiosity in the town—that you would take me for the town clerk of Calais itself—and where, sir, would be the wonder? was not Democritus, who laughed ten times more than I—town-clerk of *Abdera?* and was not (I forget his name) who had more discretion than us both, town-clerk of Ephesus?³——it should be penn'd moreover, Sir, with so much knowledge and good sense, and truth, and precision——

—Nay—if you don't believe me, you may read the chapter for your pains.

CHAP. V.

C ALAIS, *Calatium, Calusium, Calesium.*¹
This town, if we may trust it's archives, the authority of which I see no reason to call in question in this place—was *once* no more than a small village belonging to one of the first Counts de Guines; and as it boasts at present of no less than fourteen thousand inhabitants, exclusive of four hundred and twenty distinct families in the *basse ville,* or suburbs ——it must have grown up by little and little, I suppose, to it's present size.

Though there are four convents, there is but one parochial church in the whole town; I had not an opportunity of taking its exact dimensions, but it is pretty easy to make a tolerable conjecture of 'em—for as there are fourteen thousand inhabitants in the town, if the church holds them all, it must be considerably large—and if it will not—'tis a very great pity they have not another—it is built in form of a cross, and dedicated to the Virgin Mary; the steeple which has a spire to it, is placed in the middle of the church, and stands upon four pillars elegant and light enough, but sufficiently strong at the same time—it is decorated with eleven altars, most of which are rather fine than beautiful. The great altar is a master-piece in its kind; 'tis of white marble, and as I was told near sixty feet high—had it been much higher, it had been as high as mount Calvary itself—therefore, I suppose it must be high enough in all conscience.

There was nothing struck me more than the great *Square*; tho' I cannot say 'tis either well paved or well built; but 'tis in the heart of the town, and most of the streets, especially those in that quarter, all terminate in it; could there have been a fountain in all Calais, which it seems there cannot, as such an object would have been a great ornament, it is not to be doubted, but that the inhabitants would have had it in the very centre of this square,—not that it is properly a square,—because 'tis forty feet longer from east to west, than from north to south; so that the French in general have more reason on their side in calling them *Places* than *Squares*, which strictly speaking, to be sure they are not.

The town-house seems to be but a sorry building, and not to be kept in the best repair; otherwise it had been a second great ornament to this place; it answers however its destination, and serves very well for the reception of the magistrates, who assemble in it from time to time; so that 'tis presumable, justice is regularly distributed.

I had heard much of it, but there is nothing at all curious in the *Courgain*;[2] 'tis a distinct quarter of the town inhabited solely by sailors and fishermen; it consists of a number of small streets, neatly built and mostly of brick; 'tis extremely populous, but as that may be accounted for, from the principles of their diet,—there is nothing curious in that neither.——A traveller may see it to satisfy himself—he must not omit however taking notice of *La Tour de Guet*,[3] upon any account; 'tis so called from its particular destination, because in war it serves to discover and give notice of the enemies which approach the place, either by sea or land;——but 'tis monstrous high, and catches the eye so continually, you cannot avoid taking notice of it, if you would.

It was a singular disappointment to me, that I could not have permission to take an exact survey of the fortifications, which are the strongest in the world, and which, from first to last, that is, from the time they were set about by Philip of France[4] Count of Bologne, to the present war, wherein many reparations were made, have cost (as I learned afterwards from an engineer in Gascony)—above a hundred millions of livres. It is very remarkable that at the *Tête de Gravelenes*,[5] and where the town is naturally the weakest, they have expended the most money; so that the outworks stretch a great way into the campaign,[6] and consequently occupy a large tract of ground.—However, after all that is *said* and *done*, it must be acknowledged that Calais was never upon any account so considerable from itself, as from its situation, and that easy enterance which it gave our ancestors upon all occasions into France: it was not without its inconveniences also; being no less troublesome to the English in those times, than Dunkirk has been to us, in ours; so that it was deservedly looked upon as the key to both kingdoms, which no doubt is the reason that there have arisen so many contentions who should keep it: of these, the siege of Calais, or rather the blockade (for it was shut up both by land and sea) was the most memorable, as it withstood the efforts of Edward the third a whole year, and was not terminated at last but by famine and extream misery; the gallantry of *Eustace de St. Pierre*, who first offered himself a victim for his fellow citizens, has rank'd his name with heroes. As it will not take up above fifty pages, it would be injustice to the reader, not to give him a minute account of that romantic transaction, as well as of the siege itself, in Rapin's own words:[7]

CHAP. VI.

—**B**UT courage! gentle reader!——I scorn it——'tis enough to have thee in my power——but to make use of the advantage which the fortune of the pen has now gained over thee, would be too much——No——! by that all powerful fire which warms the visionary brain, and lights the spirits through unworldly tracts! ere I would force a helpless creature upon this hard service, and make thee pay, poor soul! for fifty pages which I have no right to sell thee,—naked as I am, I would browse upon the mountains, and smile that the north wind brought me neither my tent or my supper.

—So put on, my brave boy! and make the best of thy way to Boulogne.

CHAP. VII.

——Boulogne!——hah!——so we are all got together——debtors and sinners before heaven; a jolly set of us—but I can't stay and quaff it off with you—I'm pursued myself like a hundred devils, and shall be overtaken before I can well change horses:——for heaven's sake, make haste——'Tis for high treason, quoth a very little man, whispering as low as he could to a very tall man that stood next him——Or else for murder; quoth the tall man——Well thrown size-ace![1] quoth I. No; quoth a third, the gentleman has been committing—— ——.

Ah! ma chere fille![2] said I, as she tripp'd by, from her matins—you look as rosy as the morning (for the sun was rising, and it made the compliment the more gracious)——No; it can't be that, quoth a fourth——(she made a curt'sy to me—I kiss'd my hand) 'tis debt; continued he: 'Tis certainly for debt; quoth a fifth; I would not pay that gentleman's debts, quoth *Ace*, for a thousand pounds; Nor would I, quoth *Size*, for six times the sum— Well thrown, Size-Ace, again! quoth I;—but I have no debt but the debt of Nature,[3] and I want but patience of her, and I will pay her every farthing I owe her——How can you be so hard-hearted, Madam, to arrest a poor traveller going along without molestation to any one, upon his lawful occasions? do stop that death-looking, long-striding scoundrel of a scare-sinner, who is posting after me——he never would have followed me but for you——if it be but for a stage, or two, just to give me start of him, I beseech you, madam—— ——do, dear lady——.

——Now, in troth, 'tis a great pity, quoth mine Irish host, that all this good courtship should be lost; for the young gentlewoman has been after going out of hearing of it all along——.

——Simpleton! quoth I.

——So you have nothing *else* in Boulogne worth seeing?

—By Jasus! there is the finest Seminary for the Humanities——.

—There cannot be a finer; quoth I.

CHAP. VIII.

WHEN the precipitancy of a man's wishes hurries on his ideas ninety times faster than the vehicle he rides in — woe be to truth! and woe be to the vehicle and its tackling (let 'em be made of what stuff you will) upon which he breathes forth the disappointment of his soul!

As I never give general characters either of men or things in choler, "*the most haste, the worst speed*;" was all the reflection I made upon the affair, the first time it happen'd; — the second, third, fourth, and fifth time, I confined it respectively to those times, and accordingly blamed only the second, third, fourth, and fifth post-boy for it, without carrying my reflections further; but the event continuing to befall me from the fifth, to the sixth, seventh, eighth, ninth, and tenth time, and without one exception, I then could not avoid making a national reflection of it, which I do in these words;

That something is always wrong in a French post-chaise upon first setting out.

Or the proposition may stand thus.

A French postilion has always to alight before he has got three hundred yards out of town.

What's wrong now? —— Diable! —— a rope's broke! —— a knot has slipt! —— a staple's drawn! —— a bolt's to whittle! —— a tag, a rag, a jag, a strap, a buckle, or a buckle's tongue, want altering. ——

Now true as all this is, I never think myself impower'd to excommunicate thereupon either the post-chaise, or its driver —— nor do I take it into my head to swear by the living G—, I would rather go a foot ten thousand times —— or that I will be damn'd if ever I get into another —— but I take the matter coolly before me, and consider, that some tag, or rag, or jag, or bolt, or buckle, or buckle's tongue, will ever be a wanting, or want altering, travel where I will —— so I never chaff, but take the good and the bad as they fall in my road, and get on: —— Do so, my lad! said I; he had lost five minutes already, in alighting in order to get at a luncheon of black bread which he had cramm'd into the chaise-pocket, and was remounted and going leisurely on, to relish it the better —— Get on, my lad, said I, briskly — but in the most persuasive tone imaginable, for I jingled a four and twenty sous piece against the glass, taking care to hold the flat side towards him, as he look'd back: the dog grinn'd intelligence from his right ear to his left, and behind his sooty muzzle discover'd such a pearly row of teeth, that *Sovereignty* would have pawn'd her jewels for them.——

Just heaven! $\left\{\begin{array}{l}\text{What masticators!}\text{——}\\\text{What bread!}\text{——}\end{array}\right.$

and so, as he finish'd the last mouthful of it, we enter'd the town of Montreuil.

CHAP. IX.

THERE is not a town in all France, which in my opinion, looks better in the map, than MONTREUIL;——I own, it does not look so well in the book of post roads; but when you come to see it—to be sure it looks most pitifully.

There is one thing however in it at present very handsome; and that is the inn-keeper's daughter:[1] She has been eighteen months at Amiens, and six at Paris, in going through her classes; so knits, and sews, and dances, and does the little coquetries very well.——

—A slut![2] in running them over within these five minutes that I have stood looking at her, she has let fall at least a dozen loops in a white thread stocking——Yes, yes—I see, you cunning gipsy!—'tis long, and taper— you need not pin it to your knee—and that 'tis your own—and fits you exactly.——

——That Nature should have told this creature a word about a *statue*'s *thumb!*[3]——

—But as this sample is worth all their thumbs——besides I have her thumbs and fingers in at the bargain if they can be any guide to me,— and as *Janatone* withal (for that is her name) stands so well for a drawing ——may I never draw more, or rather may I draw like a draught-horse, by main strength all the days of my life,—if I do not draw her in all her proportions, and with as determin'd a pencil, as if I had her in the wettest drapery.[4]——

—But your worships chuse rather that I give you the length, breadth, and perpendicular height of the great parish church, or a drawing of the fascade of the abbey of Saint Austreberte which has been transported from Artois hither[5]—every thing is just I suppose as the masons and carpenters left them,—and if the belief in Christ continues so long, will be so these fifty years to come—so your worships and reverences, may all measure them at your leisures——but he who measures thee, Janatone, must do it now—thou carriest the principles of change within thy frame; and considering the chances of a transitory life, I would not answer for thee a moment; e'er twice twelve months are pass'd and gone, thou mayest grow out like a pumkin, and lose thy shapes——or, thou mayest go off like a flower, and lose thy beauty——nay, thou mayest go off like a hussy— and lose thyself.——I would not answer for my aunt Dinah, was she alive ——'faith, scarce for her picture——were it but painted by Reynolds—

—But if I go on with my drawing, after naming that son of Apollo, I'll be shot——

So you must e'en be content with the original; which if the evening is fine in passing thro' Montreuil, you will see at your chaise door, as you change horses: but unless you have as bad a reason for haste as I have— you had better stop:—She has a little of the *devote*:[6] but that, sir, is a terce to a nine in your favour——

—L— help me! I could not count a single point: so had been piqued, and repiqued, and capotted[7] to the devil.

CHAP. X.

ALL which being considered, and that Death moreover might be much nearer me than I imagined——I wish I was at Abbeville, quoth I, were it only to see how they card and spin[1]——so off we set.
de Montreuil a Nampont – poste et demi de Nampont a Bernay – – – poste
de Bernay a Nouvion – – – poste
de Nouvion a ABBEVILLE poste
——but the carders and spinners were all gone to bed.

*Vid. Book of French post-roads,[2] page 36. edition of 1762.

CHAP. XI.

WHAT a vast advantage is travelling! only it heats one; but there is a remedy for that, which you may pick out of the next chapter.

CHAP. XII.

WAS I in a condition to stipulate with death, as I am this moment with my apothecary, how and where I will take his glister——I should certainly declare against submitting to it before my friends; and therefore, I never seriously think upon the mode and manner of this great catastrophe, which generally takes up and torments my thoughts as much as the catastrophe itself, but I constantly draw the curtain across it with this wish, that the Disposer of all things may so order it, that it happen not to me in my own house——but rather in some decent inn——at home, I know it,——the concern of my friends, and the last services of wiping my brows and smoothing my pillow, which the quivering hand of pale affection shall pay me, will so crucify my soul, that I shall die of a distemper which my physician is not aware of: but in an inn, the few cold offices I wanted, would be purchased with a few guineas, and paid me with an undisturbed, but punctual attention——but mark. This inn, should not be the inn at Abbeville——if there was not another inn in the universe, I would strike that inn out of the capitulation: so

Let the horses be in the chaise exactly by four in the morning——Yes, by four, Sir,——or by Genevieve![1] I'll raise a clatter in the house, shall wake the dead.

CHAP. XIII.

"*MAKE them like unto a wheel*,"[1] is a bitter sarcasm, as all the learned know, against the *grand tour*, and that restless spirit for making it, which David prophetically foresaw would haunt the children of men in the latter days; and therefore, as thinketh the great bishop Hall, 'tis one of the severest imprecations which David ever utter'd against the enemies of the Lord—and, as if he had said, "I wish them no worse luck than always to be rolling about"—So much motion, continues he, (for he was very corpulent)—is so much unquietness; and so much of rest, by the same analogy, is so much of heaven.

Now, I (being very thin) think differently; and that so much of motion, is so much of life, and so much of joy——and that to stand still, or get on but slowly, is death and the devil——

Hollo! Ho!——the whole world's asleep!——bring out the horses—— grease the wheels——tie on the mail——and drive a nail into that moulding——I'll not lose a moment——

Now the wheel we are talking of, and *whereinto* (but not *whereonto*, for that would make an Ixion's wheel[2] of it) he curseth his enemies, according to the bishop's habit of body, should certainly be a post-chaise wheel, whether they were set up in Palestine at that time or not——and my wheel, for the contrary reasons, must as certainly be a cart-wheel groaning round its revolution once in an age; and of which sort, were I to turn commentator, I should make no scruple to affirm, they had great store in that hilly country.

I love the Pythagoreans (much more than ever I dare tell my dear Jenny) for their "χωρισμὸν ἀπὸ τȣ̃ Σώμαȷος, εις το Καλῶς Φιλοσοφεῖν"—— [their] *"getting out of the body, in order to think well."* No man thinks right whilst he is in it; blinded as he must be, with his congenial humours, and drawn differently aside, as the bishop and myself have been, with too lax or too tense a fibre——REASON, is half of it, SENSE; and the measure of heaven itself is but the measure of our present appetites and concoctions[3]——

——But which of the two, in the present case, do you think to be mostly in the wrong?

You, certainly: quoth she, to disturb a whole family so early.

407

CHAP. XIV.

——But she did not know I was under a vow not to shave my beard till I got to Paris;——yet I hate to make mysteries of nothing;——'tis the cold cautiousness of one of those little souls from which *Lessius (lib.* 13. *de moribus divinis, cap.* 24.) hath made his estimate, wherein he setteth forth, That one Dutch mile, cubically multiplied, will allow room enough, and to spare, for eight hundred thousand millions, which he supposes to be as great a number of souls (counting from the fall of Adam) as can possibly be damn'd to the end of the world.

From what he has made this second estimate——unless from the parental goodness of God—I don't know——I am much more at a loss what could be in Franciscus Ribbera's head, who pretends that no less a space than one of two hundred Italian miles multiplied into itself, will be sufficient to hold the like number——he certainly must have gone upon some of the old Roman souls, of which he had read, without reflecting how much, by a gradual and most tabid decline, in a course of eighteen hundred years, they must unavoidably have shrunk, so as to have come, when he wrote, almost to nothing.[1]

In Lessius's time, who seems the cooler man, they were as little as can be imagined——

——We find them less *now*——

And next winter we shall find them less again; so that if we go on from little to less, and from less to nothing, I hesitate not one moment to affirm, that in half a century, at this rate, we shall have no souls at all; which being the period beyond which I doubt likewise of the existence of the Christian faith, 'twill be one advantage that both of 'em will be exactly worn out together——

Blessed Jupiter! and blessed every other heathen god and goddess! for now ye will all come into play again, and with Priapus[2] at your tails—— what jovial times!——but where am I? and into what a delicious riot of things am I rushing?[3] I——I who must be cut short in the midst of my days,[4] and taste no more of 'em than what I borrow from my imagination ——peace to thee, generous fool! and let me go on.

CHAP. XV.

———— "So hating, I say, to make mysteries of *nothing* "———— I intrusted it with the post-boy, as soon as ever I got off the stones; he gave a crack with his whip to balance the compliment; and with the thill-horse[1] trotting, and a sort of an up and a down of the other, we danced it along to *Ailly au clochers*,[2] famed in days of yore for the finest chimes in the world; but we danced through it without music————the chimes being greatly out of order—(as in truth they were through all France).

And so making all possible speed, from
Ailly au clochers, I got to Hixcourt,[3]
from Hixcourt, I got to Pequignay, and
from Pequignay, I got to AMIENS,
concerning which town I have nothing to inform you, but what I have informed you once before————and that was————that Janatone went there to school.

CHAP. XVI.

IN the whole catalogue of those whiffling vexations which come puffing across a man's canvass, there is not one of a more teasing and tormenting nature, than this particular one which I am going to describe————and for which, (unless you travel with an avance-courier,[1] which numbers do in order to prevent it)————there is no help: and it is this.

That be you in never so kindly a propensity to sleep————tho' you are passing perhaps through the finest country—upon the best roads,—and in the easiest carriage for doing it in the world————nay was you sure you could sleep fifty miles straight forwards, without once opening your eyes ————nay what is more, was you as demonstratively satisfied as you can be of any truth in Euclid, that you should upon all accounts be full as well asleep as awake————nay perhaps better————Yet the incessant returns of paying for the horses at every stage,——with the necessity thereupon of putting your hand into your pocket, and counting out from thence, three livres fifteen sous (sous by sous) puts an end to so much of the project, that you cannot execute above six miles of it (or supposing it is a post and a half, that is but nine)——were it to save your soul from destruction.

——I'll be even with 'em, quoth I, for I'll put the precise sum into a piece of paper, and hold it ready in my hand all the way: "Now I shall have nothing to do" said I (composing myself to rest) "but to drop this gently into the post-boy's hat, and not say a word."——Then there wants two sous more to drink——or there is a twelve sous piece of Louis XIV. which will not pass—or a livre and some odd liards[2] to be brought over from the last stage, which Monsieur had forgot; which altercations (as a man cannot dispute very well asleep) rouse him: still is sweet sleep retrievable; and still might the flesh weigh down the spirit,[3] and recover itself of these blows—but then, by heaven! you have paid but for a single post—whereas 'tis a post and a half; and this obliges you to pull out your book of post-roads, the print of which is so very small, it forces you to open your eyes, whether you will or no: then Monsieur le Curè[4] offers you a pinch of snuff——or a poor soldier shews you his leg——or a shaveling[5] his box——or the priestesse of the cistern will water your wheels——they do not want it——but she swears by her *priesthood* (throwing it back) that they do:——then you have all these points to argue, or consider over in your mind; in doing of which, the rational powers get so thoroughly awakened——you may get 'em to sleep again as you can.

It was entirely owing to one of these misfortunes, or I had pass'd clean by the stables of Chantilly[6]——

——But the postillion first affirming, and then persisting in it to my face, that there was no mark upon the two sous piece, I open'd my eyes to be convinced—and seeing the mark upon it, as plain as my nose—I leap'd out of the chaise in a passion, and so saw every thing at Chantilly in spite.—I tried it but for three posts and a half, but believe 'tis the best principle in the world to travel speedily upon; for as few objects look very inviting in that mood—you have little or nothing to stop you; by which means it was that I pass'd through St. Dennis,[7] without turning my head so much as on side towards the Abby——

——Richness of their treasury! stuff and nonsense!—bating their jewels, which are all false, I would not give three sous for any one thing in it, but *Judas*'s *lantern*——nor for that either, only as it grows dark, it might be of use.

CHAP. XVII.

CRACK, crack——crack, crack——crack, crack——so this is Paris![1] quoth I (continuing in the same mood)——and this is Paris! ——humph!——Paris! cried I, repeating the name the third time——

The first, the finest, the most brilliant——

—The streets however are nasty;

But it looks, I suppose, better than it smells——crack, crack——crack, crack——What a fuss thou makest!—as if it concern'd the good people to be inform'd, That a man with pale face, and clad in black, had the honour to be driven into Paris at nine o'clock at night, by a postilion in a tawny yellow jerkin turned up with red calamanco[2]——crack, crack—— crack, crack——crack, crack——I wish thy whip——

——But 'tis the spirit of thy nation; so crack—crack on.

Ha!——and no one gives the wall![3]——but in the SCHOOL of URBANITY herself, if the walls are besh—t—how can you do otherwise?

And prithee when do they light the lamps? What?—never in the summer months!——Ho! 'tis the time of sallads.——O rare! sallad and soup— soup and sallad—sallad and soup, *encore*——

——'Tis *too much* for sinners.

Now I cannot bear the barbarity of it; how can that unconscionable coachman talk so much bawdy to that lean horse? don't you see, friend, the streets are so villainously narrow, that there is not room in all Paris to turn a wheel-barrow? In the grandest city of the whole world, it would not have been amiss, if they had been left a thought wider; nay were it only so much in every single street, as that a man might know (was it only for satisfaction) on which side of it he was walking.

One—two—three—four—five—six—seven—eight—nine—ten. —Ten cook's shops! and twice the number of barber's! and all within three minutes driving! one would think that all the cooks in the world on

some great merry-meeting with the barbers, by joint consent had said—
Come, let us all go live at Paris: the French love good eating——they
are all *gourmands*——we shall rank high; if their god is their belly [4]——
their cooks must be gentlemen: and forasmuch as *the periwig maketh the
man*,[5] and the periwig-maker maketh the periwig——ergo, would the
barbers say, we shall rank higher still—we shall be above you all—we
shall be * Capitouls at least—pardi![6] we shall all wear swords——

—And so, one would swear, (that is by candle-light,—but there is no
depending upon it) they continue to do, to this day.

CHAP. XVIII.

THE French are certainly misunderstood:——but whether the
fault is theirs, in not sufficiently explaining themselves; or speaking
with that exact limitation and precision which one would expect on a
point of such importance, and which moreover, is so likely to be contested
by us——or whether the fault may not be altogether on our side, in not
understanding their language always so critically as to know "what they
would be at"——I shall not decide; but 'tis evident to me, when they
affirm, "*That they who have seen Paris, have seen every thing*," they must mean
to speak of those who have seen it by day-light.

As for candle-light—I give it up——I have said before, there was no
depending upon it—and I repeat it again; but not because the lights and
shades are too sharp—or the tints confounded—or that there is neither
beauty or keeping, &c. . . . for that's not truth—but it is an uncertain light
in this respect, That in all the five hundred grand Hôtels,[1] which they
number up to you in Paris—and the five hundred good things, at a modest
computation (for 'tis only allowing one good thing to a Hôtel) which by
candle-light are best to be *seen, felt, heard and understood* (which, by the bye
is a quotation from Lilly)[2]——the devil a one of us out of fifty, can get
our heads fairly thrust in amongst them.

This is no part of the French computation: 'tis simply this.

* Chief Magistrate in Toulouse, &c. &c. &c.

That by the last survey[3] taken in the year one thousand seven hundred and sixteen, since which time there have been considerable augmentations, Paris doth contain nine hundred streets; (viz.)

In the quarter called the *City*—there are fifty three streets.

In St. *James* of the Shambles, fifty five streets.

In St. *Oportune*, thirty four streets.

In the quarter of the *Louvre*, twenty five streets.

In the *Palace Royal*, or St. *Honorius*, forty nine streets.

In *Mont. Martyr*, forty one streets.

In St. *Eustace*, twenty nine streets.

In the *Halles*, twenty seven streets.

In St. *Dennis*, fifty five streets.

In St. *Martin*, fifty four streets.

In St. *Paul*, or the *Mortellerie*, twenty seven streets.

The *Greve*, thirty eight streets.

In St. *Avoy*, or the *Verrerie*, nineteen streets.

In the *Marais*, or the *Temple*, fifty two streets.

In St. *Antony*'s, sixty eight streets.

In the *Place Maubert*, eighty one streets.

In St. *Bennet*, sixty streets.

In St. *Andrews de Arcs*, fifty one streets.

In the quarter of the *Luxembourg*, sixty two streets.

And in that of St. Germain, fifty five streets, into any of which you may walk; and that when you have seen them with all that belongs to them, fairly by day-light—their gates, their bridges, their squares, their statues – – – – and have crusaded it moreover through all their parish churches, by no means omitting St. *Roche* and *Sulplice*[4] – – – and to crown all, have taken a walk to the four palaces, which you may see either with or without the statues and pictures, just as you chuse—

——Then you will have seen——

——but, 'tis what no one needeth to tell you, for you will read it yourself upon the portico of the Louvre,[5] in these words,

> *EARTH NO SUCH FOLKS!—NO FOLKS E'ER SUCH A TOWN
> AS PARIS IS!—SING, DERRY, DERRY, DOWN.

---

*Non Orbis gentem, non urbem gens habet ullam
———————————ulla parem.

The French have a *gay* way of treating every thing that is Great; and that is all can be said upon it.

CHAP. XIX.

IN mentioning the word *gay* (as in the close of the last chapter) it puts one *(i.e.* an author) in mind of the word *spleen*——especially if he has any thing to say upon it: not that by any analysis—or that from any table of interest or genealogy, there appears much more ground of alliance betwixt them, than betwixt light and darkness, or any two of the most unfriendly opposites in nature——only 'tis an undercraft[1] of authors to keep up a good understanding amongst words, as politicians do amongst men—not knowing how near they may be under a necessity of placing them to each other—which point being now gain'd, and that I may place mine exactly to my mind, I write it down here—

SPLEEN.

This, upon leaving Chantilly, I declared to be the best principle in the world to travel speedily upon; but I gave it only as matter of opinion, I still continue in the same sentiments—only I had not then experience enough of its working to add this, that though you do get on at a tearing rate, yet you get on but uneasily to yourself at the same time; for which reason I here quit it entirely, and for ever, and 'tis heartily at one's service—it has spoiled me the digestion of a good supper, and brought on a bilious diarrhæa, which has brought me back again to my first principle on which I set out——and with which I shall now scamper it away to the banks of the Garonne—

——No;——I cannot stop a moment to give you the character of the people—their genius—their manners—their customs—their laws—their religion—their government—their manufactures—their commerce—their finances, with all the resources and hidden springs which sustain them: qualified as I may be, by spending three days and two nights amongst them, and during all that time, making these things the entire subject of my enquiries and reflections——

Still—still I must away——the roads are paved—the posts are short—the days are long—'tis no more than noon—I shall be at Fontainbleau before the king——

—Was he going there? not that I know——

CHAP. XX.

NOW I hate to hear a person, especially if he be a traveller, complain that we do not get on so fast in France as we do in England; whereas we get on much faster, *consideratis, considerandis*;[1] thereby always meaning, that if you weigh their vehicles with the mountains of baggage which you lay both before and behind upon them—and then consider their puny horses, with the very little they give them—'tis a wonder they get on at all: their suffering is most unchristian, and 'tis evident thereupon to me, that a French post-horse would not know what in the world to do, was it not for the two words ****** and ****** in which there is as much sustenance, as if you gave him a peck of corn: now as these words cost nothing, I long from my soul to tell the reader what they are; but here is the question—they must be told him plainly, and with the most distinct articulation, or it will answer no end—and yet to do it in that plain way—though their reverences may laugh at it in the bed-chamber—full well I wot, they will abuse it in the parlour:[2] for which cause, I have been volving[3] and revolving in my fancy some time, but to no purpose, by what clean device or facete contrivance I might so modulate them, that whilst I satisfy *that ear* which the reader chuses to *lend* me—I might not dissatisfy the other which he keeps to himself.

——My ink burns my finger to try——and when I have——'twill have a worse consequence——it will burn (I fear) my paper.

——No;——I dare not——

But if you wish to know how the *abbess* of Andoüillets,[4] and a novice of her convent got over the difficulty (only first wishing myself all imaginable success)—I'll tell you without the least scruple.

CHAP. XXI.

THE abbess of Andoüillets, which if you look into the large set of provincial maps now publishing at Paris, you will find situated amongst the hills which divide Burgundy from Savoy, being in danger of an *Anchylosis* or stiff joint (the *sinovia*[1] of her knee becoming hard by long matins) and having tried every remedy——first, prayers and thanksgiving; then invocations to all the saints in heaven promiscuously——then particularly to every saint who had ever had a stiff leg before her——then touching it with all the reliques of the convent, principally with the thigh-bone of the man of Lystra,[2] who had been impotent from his youth ——then wrapping it up in her veil when she went to bed——then cross-wise her rosary——then bringing in to her aid the secular arm, and anointing it with oils and hot fat of animals——then treating it with emollient and resolving fomentations——then with poultices of marsh-mallows, mallows, bonus Henricus, white lillies and fenugreek——then taking the woods, I mean the smoak of 'em, holding her scapulary across her lap[3]——then decoctions of wild chicory, water cresses, chervil, sweet cecily and cochlearia——and nothing all this while answering, was prevailed on at last to try the hot baths of Bourbon——so having first obtain'd leave of the visitor-general to take care of her existence—she ordered all to be got ready for her journey: a novice of the convent of about seventeen, who had been troubled with a whitloe[4] in her middle finger, by sticking it constantly into the abbess's cast poultices, *&c.*—had gained such an interest, that overlooking a sciatical old nun, who might have been set up for ever by the hot baths of Bourbon, Margarita, the little novice, was elected as the companion of the journey.

An old calesh,[5] belonging to the abbesse, lined with green frize,[6] was ordered to be drawn out into the sun—the gardener of the convent being chosen muleteer, led out the two old mules to clip the hair from the rump-ends of their tails, whilst a couple of lay-sisters were busied, the one in darning the lining, and the other in sewing on the shreds of yellow binding, which the teeth of time had unravelled——the under-gardener dress'd the muleteer's hat in hot-wine-lees[7]——and a taylor sat musically at it, in a shed overagainst the convent, in assorting four dozen of bells for the harness, whistling to each bell as he tied it on with a thong——

——The carpenter and the smith of Andoüillets held a council of wheels; and by seven, the morning after, all look'd spruce, and was ready at the gate of the convent for the hot-baths of Bourbon—two rows of the unfortunate stood ready there an hour before.

The abbess of Andoüillets, supported by Margarita the novice, advanced slowly to the calesh, both clad in white, with their black rosaries hanging at their breasts——

——There was a simple solemnity in the contrast: they entered the calesh; the nuns in the same uniform, sweet emblem of innocence, each occupied a window, and as the abbess and Margarita look'd up—each (the sciatical poor nun excepted)—each stream'd out the end of her veil in the air—then kiss'd the lilly hand which let it go: the good abbess and Margarita laid their hands saint-wise upon their breasts—look'd up to heaven—then to them—and look'd "God bless you, dear sisters."

I declare I am interested in this story, and wish I had been there.

The gardener, who I shall now call the muleteer, was a little, hearty, broad-set, good natured, chattering, toping kind of a fellow, who troubled his head very little with the *hows* and *whens* of life; so had mortgaged a month of his conventical wages in a borrachio, or leathern cask of wine, which he had disposed behind the calesh, with a large russet coloured riding coat over it, to guard it from the sun; and as the weather was hot, and he, not a niggard of his labours, walking ten times more than he rode—he found more occasions than those of nature, to fall back to the rear of his carriage; till by frequent coming and going, it had so happen'd, that all his wine had leak'd out at the *legal* vent of the borrachio, before one half of the journey was finish'd.

Man is a creature born to habitudes. The day had been sultry—the evening was delicious—the wine was generous—the Burgundian hill on which it grew was steep—a little tempting bush[8] over the door of a cool cottage at the foot of it, hung vibrating in full harmony with the passions—a gentle air rustled distinctly through the leaves—"Come—come, thirsty muleteer—come in."

——The muleteer was a son of Adam. I need not say one word more. He gave the mules, each of 'em, a sound lash, and looking in the abbess's and Margarita's faces (as he did it)—as much as to say, "here I am"—he gave a second good crack—as much as to say to his mules, "get on"——so slinking behind, he enter'd the little inn at the foot of the hill.

The muleteer, as I told you, was a little, joyous, chirping fellow, who thought not of to-morrow, nor of what had gone before, or what was to follow it, provided he got but his scantling of Burgundy, and a little chit-chat along with it; so entering into a long conversation, as how he was chief gardener to the convent of Andoüillets, *&c. &c.* and out of friendship for the abbess and Mademoiselle Margarita, who was only in her noviciate, he had come along with them from the confines of Savoy, *&c. – – &c. – –* and as how she had got a white swelling[9] by her devotions ——and what a nation of herbs he had procured to mollify her humours, *&c. &c.* and that if the waters of Bourbon did not mend that leg—she might as well be lame of both— *&c. &c. &c.*—He so contrived his story as absolutely to forget the heroine of it—and with her, the little novice, and what was a more ticklish point to be forgot than both—the two mules; who being creatures that take advantage of the world, inasmuch as their parents took it of them—and they not being in a condition to return the obligation *downwards* (as men and women and beasts are)—they do it side-ways, and long-ways, and back-ways—and up hill, and down hill, and which way they can.——Philosophers, with all their ethics, have never considered this rightly—how should the poor muleteer then, in his cups, consider it at all? he did not in the least—'tis time we do; let us leave him then in the vortex of his element, the happiest and most thoughtless of mortal men——and for a moment let us look after the mules, the abbess, and Margarita.

By virtue of the muleteer's two last strokes, the mules had gone quietly on, following their own consciences up the hill, till they had conquer'd about one half of it; when the elder of them, a shrewd crafty old devil, at the turn of an angle, giving a side glance, and no muleteer behind them——

By my fig![10] said she, swearing, I'll go no further——And if I do, replied the other—they shall make a drum of my hide.——

And so with one consent they stopp'd thus——

CHAP. XXII.

——Get on with you, said the abbess.

——Wh – – – – ysh——ysh——cried Margarita.

Sh – – – a——shu – u——shu – – u—sh – – aw——shaw'd the abbess.

——Whu—v—w——whew—w—w—whuv'd Margarita, pursing up her sweet lips betwixt a hoot and a whistle.

Thump—thump—thump—obstreperated[1] the abbess of Andoüillets with the end of her gold-headed cane against the bottom of the calesh——

——The old mule let a f—

CHAP. XXIII.

WE are ruin'd and undone, my child, said the abbess to Margarita ——we shall be here all night——we shall be plunder'd——we shall be ravish'd——

——We shall be ravish'd, said Margarita, as sure as a gun.

Sancta Maria! cried the abbess (forgetting the O!)—why was I govern'd by this wicked stiff joint? why did I leave the convent of Andoüillets? and why didst thou not suffer thy servant to go unpolluted to her tomb?

O my finger! my finger! cried the novice, catching fire at the word *servant*—why was I not content to put it here, or there, any where rather than be in this strait?

——Strait! said the abbess.

Strait——said the novice; for terrour had struck their understandings ——the one knew not what she said——the other what she answer'd.

O my virginity! virginity! cried the abbess.

——inity!——inity! said the novice, sobbing.

CHAP. XXIV.

M Y dear mother, quoth the novice, coming a little to herself,——
there are two certain words, which I have been told will force any
horse, or ass, or mule, to go up a hill whether he will or no; be he never
so obstinate or ill-will'd, the moment he hears them utter'd, he obeys.
They are words magic! cried the abbess, in the utmost horrour—No;
replied Margarita calmly—but they are words sinful—What are they?
quoth the abbess, interrupting her: They are sinful in the first degree,
answered Margarita,—they are mortal—and if we are ravish'd and die
unabsolved of them, we shall both——but you may pronounce them to
me, quoth the abbess of Andoüillets——They cannot, my dear mother,
said the novice, be pronounced at all; they will make all the blood in one's
body fly up into one's face——But you may whisper them in my ear,
quoth the abbess.

Heaven! hadst thou no guardian angel to delegate to the inn at the
bottom of the hill? was there no generous and friendly spirit unemploy'd
——no agent in nature, by some monitory shivering, creeping along the
artery which led to his heart, to rouze the muleteer from his banquet?
——no sweet minstrelsy to bring back the fair idea of the abbess and
Margarita, with their black rosaries!

Rouse! rouse!——but 'tis too late—the horrid words are pronounced
this moment——

——and how to tell them—Ye, who can speak of every thing existing,
with unpolluted lips——instruct me——guide me——

CHAP. XXV.

A LL sins whatever, quoth the abbess, turning casuist in the distress
they were under, are held by the confessor of our convent to be
either mortal or venial: there is no further division. Now a venial sin being

the slightest and least of all sins,—being halved—by taking, either only the half of it, and leaving the rest—or, by taking it all, and amicably halving it betwixt yourself and another person—in course becomes diluted into no sin at all.

Now I see no sin[1] in saying, *bou, bou, bou, bou, bou,* a hundred times together; nor is there any turpitude in pronouncing the syllable *ger, ger, ger, ger, ger,* were it from our matins to our vespers: Therefore, my dear daughter, continued the abbess of Andoüillets—I will say *bou,* and thou shalt say *ger*; and then alternately, as there is no more sin in *fou* than in *bou*—Thou shalt say *fou*—and I will come in (like fa, sol, la, re, mi, ut,[2] at our complines) with *ter.* And accordingly the abbess, giving the pitch note, set off thus:

Abbess, } Bou – – bou – – bou – –
Margarita, } —— ger, – – ger, – – ger

Margarita, } Fou – – fou – – fou – –
Abbess, } —— ter, – – ter, – – ter.

The two mules acknowledged the notes by a mutual lash of their tails; but it went no further.——'Twill answer by an' by, said the novice.

Abbess, } Bou- bou- bou- bou- bou- bou-
Margarita, } —ger, ger, ger, ger, ger, ger.

Quicker still, cried Margarita.

Fou, fou, fou, fou, fou, fou, fou, fou, fou.

Quicker still, cried Margarita.

Bou, bou, bou, bou, bou, bou, bou, bou, bou.

Quicker still—God preserve me! said the abbess—They do not understand us, cried Margarita—But the Devil does, said the abbess of Andoüillets.

CHAP. XXVI.

WHAT a tract of country have I run!—how many degrees nearer to the warm sun am I advanced, and how many fair and goodly cities have I seen, during the time you have been reading, and reflecting, Madam, upon this story! There's FONTAINBLEAU, and SENS, and JOIGNY, and AUXERRE, and DIJON the capital of Burgundy, and CHALLON, and Mâcon the capital of the Mâconese, and a score more upon the road to LYONS——and now I have run them over——I might as well talk to you of so many market-towns in the moon, as tell you one word about them: it will be this chapter at the least, if not both this and the next entirely lost, do what I will——

—Why, 'tis a strange story! Tristram.

————Alas! Madam, had it been upon some melancholy lecture of the cross—the peace of meekness, or the contentment of resignation——I had not been incommoded: or had I thought of writing it upon the purer abstractions of the soul, and that food of wisdom, and holiness, and contemplation, upon which the spirit of man (when separated from the body) is to subsist for ever——You would have come with a better appetite from it——

——I wish I never had wrote it: but as I never blot any thing out[1]—— let us use some honest means to get it out of our heads directly.

——Pray reach me my fool's cap——I fear you sit upon it, Madam ——'tis under the cushion——I'll put it on——

Bless me! you have had it upon your head this half hour.——There then let it stay, with a

> Fa-ra diddle di
> and a fa-ri diddle d
> and a high-dum—dye-dum
> fiddle – – – dumb – c.

And now, Madam, we may venture, I hope, a little to go on.

CHAP. XXVII.

——All you need say of *Fontainbleau*[1] (in case you are ask'd) is, that it stands about forty miles (south *something*) from Paris, in the middle of a large forest——That there is something great in it——That the king goes there once, every two or three years, with his whole court, for the pleasure of the chase—and that during that carnival of sporting, any English gentleman of fashion (you need not forget yourself) may be accommodated with a nag or two, to partake of the sport, taking care only not to out-gallop the king[2]——

Though there are two reasons why you need not talk loud of this to every one.

First, Because 'twill make the said nags the harder to be got; and

Secondly, 'Tis not a word of it true.——*Allons!*

As for SENS——you may dispatch it in a word———" *'Tis an archi-episcopal see.*"

——For JOIGNY—the less, I think, one says of it, the better.

But for AUXERRE—I could go on for ever: for in my *grand tour* through Europe, in which, after all, my father (not caring to trust me with any one) attended me himself, with my uncle Toby, and Trim, and Obadiah, and indeed most of the family, except my mother, who being taken up with a project of knitting my father a pair of large worsted breeches—(the thing is common sense)—and she not caring to be put out of her way, she staid at home at SHANDY HALL, to keep things right during the expedition; in which, I say, my father stopping us two days at Auxerre, and his researches being ever of such a nature, that they would have found fruit even in a desert——he has left me enough to say upon AUXERRE: in short, wherever my father went——but 'twas more remarkably so, in this journey through France and Italy, than in any other stages of his life——his road seemed to lie so much on one side of that, wherein all other travellers had gone before him—he saw kings and courts and silks[3] of all colours, in such strange lights——and his remarks and reasonings upon the characters, the manners and customs of the countries we pass'd over, were so opposite to those of all other mortal men, particularly those of my uncle Toby and Trim—(to say nothing of myself)—and to crown all—the occurrences and scrapes which we were perpetually meeting and getting into, in consequence of his systems and opiniatry—they were of so odd, so mixed and tragicomical a contexture—That the whole put together, it appears of so different a shade and tint from any tour of Europe, which was ever executed—That I will venture to pronounce—the fault must be mine and mine only—if it be not read by all travellers and travel-readers, till travelling is no more,—or which comes to the same point—till the world, finally, takes it into it's head to stand still.——

——But this rich bale is not to be open'd now; except a small thread or two of it, merely to unravel the mystery of my father's stay at AUXERRE.

——As I have mentioned it—'tis too slight to be kept suspended; and when 'tis wove in, there's an end of it.

We'll go, brother Toby, said my father, whilst dinner is coddling—to the abby of Saint Germain, if it be only to see these bodies, of which monsieur Sequier has given such a recommendation.——I'll go see any body; quoth my uncle Toby; for he was all compliance thro' every step of the journey——Defend me! said my father—they are all mummies ——Then one need not shave; quoth my uncle Toby——Shave! no—cried my father—'twill be more like relations to go with our beards on—So out we sallied, the corporal lending his master his arm, and bringing up the rear, to the abby of Saint Germain.

Every thing is very fine, and very rich, and very superb, and very magnificent, said my father, addressing himself to the sacristan, who was a young brother of the order of Benedictines—but our curiosity has led us to see the bodies, of which monsieur Sequier has given the world so exact a description.—The sacristan made a bow, and lighting a torch first, which he had always in the vestry ready for the purpose; he led us into the tomb of St. Heribald——This, said the sacristan, laying his hand upon the tomb, was a renowned prince of the house of Bavaria, who under the successive reigns of Charlemagne, Louis le Debonair, and Charles the Bald, bore a great sway in the government, and had a principal hand in bringing every thing into order and discipline[4]——

Then he has been as great, said my uncle, in the field, as in the cabinet ——I dare say he has been a gallant soldier——He was a monk—said the sacristan.

My uncle Toby and Trim sought comfort in each others faces—but found it not: my father clapp'd both his hands upon his cod-piece, which was a way he had when any thing hugely tickled him; for though he hated

a monk and the very smell of a monk worse than all the devils in hell
——Yet the shot hitting my uncle Toby and Trim so much harder than
him, 'twas a relative triumph; and put him into the gayest humour in the
world.

——And pray what do you call this gentleman? quoth my father, rather
sportingly: This tomb, said the young Benedictine, looking downwards,
contains the bones of Saint MAXIMA,[5] who came from Ravenna on purpose
to touch the body——

——Of Saint MAXIMUS, said my father, popping in with his saint
before him—they were two of the greatest saints in the whole martyrology,
added my father——Excuse me, said the sacristan——'twas to touch the
bones of Saint Germain[6] the builder of the abby——And what did she
get by it? said my uncle Toby——What does any woman get by it? said
my father——MARTYRDOME; replied the young Benedictine, making a
bow down to the ground, and uttering the word with so humble, but
decisive a cadence, it disarmed my father for a moment. 'Tis supposed,
continued the Benedictine, that St. Maxima has lain in this tomb four
hundred years, and two hundred before her canonization——'Tis but a
slow rise, brother Toby, quoth my father, in this self same army of martyrs.
——A desperate slow one, an' please your honour, said Trim, unless
one could purchase——I should rather sell out entirely, quoth my uncle
Toby——I am pretty much of your opinion, brother Toby, said my
father.

——Poor St. Maxima! said my uncle Toby low to himself, as we turn'd
from her tomb: She was one of the fairest and most beautiful ladies either
of Italy or France, continued the sacristan——But who the duce has got
lain down here, besides her, quoth my father, pointing with his cane to a
large tomb as we walked on——It is Saint *Optat*,[7] Sir, answered the
sacristan——And properly is Saint Optat plac'd! said my father: And what
is Saint Optat's story? continued he. Saint *Optat*, replied the sacristan, was
a bishop——

——I thought so, by heaven! cried my father, interrupting him——
Saint Optat!——how should Saint *Optat* fail? so snatching out his pocket-
book, and the young Benedictine holding him the torch as he wrote, he
set it down as a new prop to his system of christian names, and I will be
bold to say, so disinterested was he in the search of truth, that had he
found a treasure in St. Optat's tomb, it would not have made him half so
rich: 'Twas as successful a short visit as ever was paid to the dead; and so

highly was his fancy pleas'd with all that had passed in it,—that he determined at once to stay another day in Auxerre.

—I'll see the rest of these good gentry to-morrow, said my father, as we cross'd over the square—And while you are paying that visit, brother Shandy, quoth my uncle Toby—the corporal and I will mount the ramparts.

CHAP. XXVIII.

—NOW this is the most puzzled skein of all[1]——for in this last chapter, as far at least as it has help'd me through *Auxerre*, I have been getting forwards in two different journies together, and with the same dash of the pen—for I have got entirely out of Auxerre in this journey which I am writing now, and I am got half way out of Auxerre in that which I shall write hereafter——There is but a certain degree of perfection in every thing; and by pushing at something beyond that, I have brought myself into such a situation, as no traveller ever stood before me; for I am this moment walking across the market-place of Auxerre with my father and my uncle Toby, in our way back to dinner——and I am this moment also entering Lyons with my post-chaise broke into a thousand pieces—and I am moreover this moment in a handsome pavillion built by Pringello*,[2] upon the banks of the Garonne, which Mons. Sligniac has lent me, and where I now sit rhapsodizing all these affairs.

——Let me collect myself, and pursue my journey.

---

*The same Don Pringello, the celebrated Spanish architect, of whom my cousin Antony has made such honourable mention in a scholium to the Tale inscribed to his name.

Vid. p. 129, small edit.

CHAP. XXIX.

I Am glad of it, said I, settling the account with myself as I walk'd into Lyons——my chaise being all laid higgledy-piggledy with my baggage in a cart, which was moving slowly before me——I am heartily glad, said I, that 'tis all broke to pieces; for now I can go directly by water to Avignon,[1] which will carry me on a hundred and twenty miles of my journey, and not cost me seven livres——and from thence, continued I, bringing forwards the account, I can hire a couple of mules—or asses, if I like, (for no body knows me) and cross the plains of Languedoc, for almost nothing ——I shall gain four hundred livres by the misfortune clear into my purse; and pleasure! worth—worth double the money by it. With what velocity, continued I, clapping my two hands together, shall I fly down the rapid Rhone, with the VIVARES on my right-hand, and DAUPHINY on my left, scarce seeing the ancient cities of VIENNE, *Valence*, and Vivieres. What a flame will it rekindle in the lamp, to snatch a blushing grape from the Hermitage and Cotê roti, as I shoot by the foot of them! and what a fresh spring in the blood! to behold upon the banks advancing and retiring, the castles of romance, whence courteous knights have whilome rescued the distress'd——and see vertiginous, the rocks, the mountains, the cataracts, and all the hurry which Nature is in with all her great works about her——

As I went on thus, methought my chaise, the wreck of which look'd stately enough at the first, insensibly grew less and less in its size; the freshness of the painting was no more—the gilding lost its lustre—and the whole affair appeared so poor in my eyes—so sorry!—so contemptible! and, in a word, so much worse than the abbess of Andoüillet's itself—that I was just opening my mouth to give it to the devil—when a pert vamping chaise-undertaker,[2] stepping nimbly across the street, demanded if Monsieur would have his chaise refitted——No, no, said I, shaking my head sideways—Would Monsieur chuse to sell it? rejoin'd the under-taker—With all my soul, said I—the iron work is worth forty livres— and the glasses worth forty more—and the leather you may take to live on.

——What a mine of wealth, quoth I, as he counted me the money, has this post chaise brought me in? And this is my usual method of book-keeping, at least with the disasters of life——making a penny of every one of 'em as they happen to me——

——Do, my dear Jenny, tell the world for me, how I behaved under one, the most oppressive of its kind which could befall me as a man, proud, as he ought to be, of his manhood——

'Tis enough, said'st thou, coming close up to me, as I stood with my garters in my hand, reflecting upon what had *not* pass'd——'Tis enough, Tristram, and I am satisfied, said'st thou, whispering these words[3] in my ear, **** ** **** *** ******;—**** ** ****——any other man would have sunk down to the center——

——Every thing is good for something, quoth I.

——I'll go into Wales for six weeks, and drink goat's-whey [4]——and I'll gain seven years longer life for the accident. For which reason I think myself inexcusable, for blaming Fortune so often as I have done, for pelting me all my life long, like an ungracious dutchess, as I call'd her, with so many small evils: surely if I have any cause to be angry with her, 'tis that she has not sent me great ones——a score of good cursed, bouncing losses, would have been as good as a pension to me.

——One of a hundred a year, or so, is all I wish——I would not be at the plague of paying land tax for a larger.

CHAP. XXX.

TO those who call vexations, VEXATIONS, as knowing what they are, there could not be a greater, than to be the best part of a day in Lyons,[1] the most opulent and flourishing city in France, enriched with the most fragments of antiquity——and not be able to see it. To be withheld upon *any* account, must be a vexation; but to be withheld *by* a vexation ——must certainly be, what philosophy justly calls

VEXATION
upon
VEXATION.

I had got my two dishes of milk coffee [2] (which by the bye is excellently good for a consumption, but you must boil the milk and coffee together—otherwise 'tis only coffee and milk)—and as it was no more than eight in the morning, and the boat did not go off till noon, I had time to see enough of Lyons to tire the patience of all the friends I had in the world with it. I will take a walk to the cathedral, said I, looking at my list, and see the wonderful mechanism of this great clock of Lippius of Basil, in the first place——

Now, of all things in the world, I understand the least of mechanism ——I have neither genius, or taste, or fancy—and have a brain so entirely unapt for every thing of that kind, that I solemnly declare I was never yet able to comprehend the principles of motion of a squirrel cage, or a common knife-grinder's wheel—tho' I have many an hour of my life look'd up with great devotion at the one—and stood by with as much patience as any christian ever could do, at the other——

I'll go see the surprising movements of this great clock, said I, the very first thing I do: and then I will pay a visit to the great library of the Jesuits, and procure, if possible, a sight of the thirty volumes of the general history of China, wrote (not in the Tartarian but) in the Chinese language, and in the Chinese character too.

Now I almost know as little of the Chinese language, as I do of the mechanism of Lippius's clock-work; so, why these should have jostled themselves into the two first articles of my list——I leave to the curious as a problem of Nature. I own it looks like one of her ladyship's obliquities; and they who court her, are interested in finding out her humour as much as I.

When these curiosities are seen, quoth I, half addressing myself to my *valet de place*,[3] who stood behind me——'twill be no hurt if WE go to the church of St. Ireneus, and see the pillar to which Christ was tied——and after that, the house where Pontius Pilate lived[4]——'Twas at the next town, said the *valet de place*—at Vienne; I am glad of it, said I, rising briskly from my chair, and walking across the room with strides twice as long as my usual pace——"for so much the sooner shall I be at the *Tomb of the two lovers*."[5]

What was the cause of this movement, and why I took such long strides in uttering this——I might leave to the curious too; but as no principle of clock-work is concern'd in it——'twill be as well for the reader if I explain it myself.

CHAP. XXXI.

O! There is a sweet æra in the life of man, when, (the brain being tender and fibrillous,[1] and more like pap than any thing else)——a story read of two fond lovers, separated from each other by cruel parents, and by still more cruel destiny——

> Amandus——He
> Amanda[2]——She——

each ignorant of the other's course,

> He——east
> She——west

Amandus taken captive by the Turks, and carried to the emperor of Morocco's court, where the princess of Morocco falling in love with him, keeps him twenty years in prison, for the love of his Amanda——

She—(Amanda) all the time wandering barefoot, and with dishevell'd hair, o'er rocks and mountains enquiring for Amandus——Amandus! Amandus!—making every hill and vally to echo back his name——

> Amandus! Amandus!

at every town and city sitting down forlorn at the gate——Has Amandus!—has my Amandus enter'd?——till,——going round, and round, and round the world——chance unexpected bringing them at the same moment of the night, though by different ways, to the gate of Lyons their native city, and each in well known accents calling out aloud,

> Is Amandus $\Big\}$ still alive?
> Is my Amanda

they fly into each others arms, and both drop down dead for joy.

There is a soft æra in every gentle mortal's life, where such a story affords more *pabulum*[3] to the brain, than all the *Frusts*, and *Crusts*, and *Rusts* of antiquity,[4] which travellers can cook up for it.

——'Twas all that stuck on the right side of the cullender in my own, of what Spon and others, in their accounts of Lyons, had *strained* into it; and finding, moreover, in some Itinerary, but in what God knows—— That sacred to the fidelity of Amandus and Amanda, a tomb was built without the gates, where to this hour, lovers call'd upon them to attest their truths,——I never could get into a scrape of that kind in my life, but this *tomb of the lovers*, would some how or other, come in at the close ——nay such a kind of empire had it establish'd over me, that I could seldom think or speak of Lyons—and sometimes not so much as see even a *Lyons-waistcoat*, but this remnant of antiquity would present itself to my fancy; and I have often said in my wild way of running on——tho' I fear with some irreverence——"I thought this shrine (neglected as it was) as valuable as that of Mecca,[5] and so little short, except in wealth, of the Santa Casa[6] itself, that some time or other, I would go a pilgrimage (though I had no other business at Lyons) on purpose to pay it a visit."

In my list, therefore, of *Videnda*[7] at Lyons, this, tho' *last*—was not, you see, *least*; so taking a dozen or two of longer strides than usual across my room, just whilst it passed my brain, I walked down calmly into the *Basse Cour*,[8] in order to sally forth; and having called for my bill—as it was uncertain whether I should return to my inn, I had paid it——had moreover given the maid ten sous, and was just receiving the dernier[9] compliments of Monsieur Le Blanc,[10] for a pleasant voyage down the Rhône——when I was stopped at the gate——

CHAP. XXXII.

——'TWAS by a poor ass who had just turned in with a couple of large panniers upon his back, to collect eleemosunary turnip tops and cabbage leaves; and stood dubious, with his two forefeet on the inside of the threshold, and with his two hinder feet towards the street, as not knowing very well whether he was to go in, or no.

Now, 'tis an animal (be in what hurry I may) I cannot bear to strike

——there is a patient endurance of sufferings, wrote so unaffectedly in his looks and carriage, which pleads so mightily for him, that it always disarms me; and to that degree, that I do not like to speak unkindly to him: on the contrary, meet him where I will—whether in town or country—in cart or under panniers—whether in liberty or bondage——I have ever something civil to say to him on my part; and as one word begets another (if he has as little to do as I)——I generally fall into conversation with him; and surely never is my imagination so busy as in framing his responses from the etchings of his countenance—and where those carry me not deep enough——in flying from my own heart into his, and seeing what is natural for an ass to think—as well as a man, upon the occasion. In truth, it is the only creature of all the classes of beings below me, with whom I can do this: for parrots, jackdaws, &c.——I never exchange a word with them——nor with the apes, &c. for pretty near the same reason; they act by rote, as the others speak by it, and equally make me silent: nay my dog and my cat, though I value them both——(and for my dog he would speak if he could)—yet some how or other, they neither of them possess the talents for conversation——I can make nothing of a discourse with them, beyond the *proposition*, the *reply*, and *rejoinder*, which terminated my father's and my mother's conversations, in his beds of justice——and those utter'd—there's an end of the dialogue——

—But with an ass, I can commune for ever.[1]

Come Honesty! said I,—seeing it was impracticable to pass betwixt him and the gate——art thou for coming in, or going out?

The ass twisted his head round to look up the street——

Well—replied I—we'll wait a minute for thy driver:

——He turned his head thoughtful about, and looked wistfully the opposite way——

I understand thee perfectly; answered I——if thou takest a wrong step in this affair, he will cudgel thee to death——Well! a minute is but a minute, and if it saves a fellow creature a drubbing, it shall not be set down as ill-spent.

He was eating the stem of an artichoke as this discourse went on, and in the little peevish contentions of nature betwixt hunger and unsavouriness, had dropt it out of his mouth half a dozen times, and pick'd it up again——God help thee, Jack! said I, thou hast a bitter breakfast on't—and many a bitter day's labour—and many a bitter blow, I fear, for its wages——'tis all—all bitterness to thee, whatever life is to others.——

And now thy mouth, if one knew the truth of it, is as bitter, I dare say, as soot—(for he had cast aside the stem) and thou hast not a friend perhaps in all this world, that will give thee a macaroon.——In saying this, I pull'd out a paper of 'em, which I had just purchased, and gave him one—and at this moment that I am telling it, my heart smites me, that there was more of pleasantry in the conceit, of seeing *how* an ass would eat a macaroon ——than of benevolence in giving him one, which presided in the act.

When the ass had eaten his macaroon, I press'd him to come in—— the poor beast was heavy loaded——his legs seem'd to tremble under him——he hung rather backwards, and as I pull'd at his halter, it broke short in my hand——he look'd up pensive in my face—"Don't thrash me with it—but if you will, you may"——If I do, said I, I'll be d——d.

The word was but one half of it pronounced, like the abbess of Andoüil-let's—(so there was no sin in it)—when a person coming in, let fall a thundering bastinado upon the poor devil's crupper, which put an end to the ceremony.

Out upon it!

cried I——but the interjection was equivocal——and, I think, wrong placed too—for the end of an osier which had started out from the contexture of the ass's pannier, had caught hold of my breeches pocket as he rush'd by me, and rent it in the most disasterous direction you can imagine——so that the

Out upon it! in my opinion, should have come in here——but this I leave to be settled by

The
REVIEWERS
of
MY BREECHES.

which I have brought over along with me for that purpose.

CHAP. XXXIII.

WHEN all was set to rights, I came down stairs again into the *basse cour* with my valet de place, in order to sally out towards the tomb of the two lovers, &c.—and was a second time stopp'd at the gate——not by the ass—but by the person who struck him; and who, by that time, had taken possession (as is not uncommon after a defeat) of the very spot of ground where the ass stood.

It was a commissary sent to me from the post-office, with a rescript in his hand for the payment of some six livres odd sous.

Upon what account? said I.——'Tis upon the part of the king, replied the commissary, heaving up both his shoulders——

——My good friend, quoth I——as sure as I am I—and you are you——

——And who are you? said he.——Don't puzzle me; said I.[1]

CHAP. XXXIV.[1]

——But it is an indubitable verity, continued I, addressing myself to the commissary, changing only the form of my asseveration——that I owe the king of France nothing but my good-will; for he is a very honest man, and I wish him all health and pastime in the world——

Pardonnez moi[2]—replied the commissary, you are indebted to him six livres four sous, for the next post from hence to St. Fons, in your rout to Avignion—which being a post royal,[3] you pay double for the horses and postillion——otherwise 'twould have amounted to no more than three livres, two sous——

——But I don't go by land; said I.

——You may if you please; replied the commissary——

Your most obedient servant——said I, making him a low bow——

The commissary, with all the sincerity of grave good breeding—made

434

me one, as low again.——I never was more disconcerted with a bow in my life.

——The devil take the serious character of these people! quoth I——(aside) they understand no more of IRONY than this——

The comparison was standing close by with his panniers——but something seal'd up my lips——I could not pronounce the name——

Sir, said I, collecting myself——it is not my intention to take post——

——But you may——said he, persisting in his first reply——you may take post if you chuse——

——And I may take salt to my pickled herring, said I, if I chuse——

——But I do not chuse——

——But you must pay for it, whether you do or no——

Aye! for the salt;[4] said I (I know)——

——And for the post too; added he. Defend me; cried I——

I travel by water——I am going down the Rhône this very afternoon——my baggage is in the boat——and I have actually paid nine livres for my passage——

C'est tout egal—'tis all one; said he.

Bon Dieu! what, pay for the way I go! and for the way I do *not* go!

——*C'est tout egal*; replied the commissary——

——The devil it is! said I——but I will go to ten thousand Bastiles first——

O England! England! thou land of liberty, and climate of good sense, thou tenderest of mothers——and gentlest of nurses, cried I, kneeling upon one knee, as I was beginning my apostrophè——

When the director of Madam Le Blanc's conscience coming in at that instant, and seeing a person in black, with a face as pale as ashes, at his devotions——looking still paler by the contrast and distress of his drapery——ask'd, if I stood in want of the aids of the church——

I go by WATER——said I——and here's another will be for making me pay for going by OYL.[5]

CHAP. XXXV.

AS I perceived the commissary of the post-office would have his six livres four sous, I had nothing else for it, but to say some smart thing upon the occasion, worth the money:

And so I set off thus——

——And pray Mr. commissary, by what law of courtesy is a defenceless stranger to be used just the reverse from what you use a Frenchman in this matter?

By no means; said he.

Excuse me; said I—for you have begun, sir, with first tearing off my breeches—and now you want my pocket——

Whereas—had you first taken my pocket, as you do with your own people—and then left me bare a—'d after—I had been a beast to have complain'd——

As it is——

——'Tis contrary to the *law of nature*.

——'Tis contrary to *reason*.

——'Tis contrary to the GOSPEL.

But not to this——said he—putting a printed paper into my hand.

PAR LE ROY.[1]

—— ——'Tis a pithy prolegomenon, quoth I—and so read on

— — — — — — — — — —
— — — — — — — — — —
— — — — — — — — — —
— — — — — — — — — —
— — — — — — — — — —

——By all which it appears, quoth I, having read it over, a little too rapidly, that if a man sets out in a post-chaise from Paris—he must go on travelling in one, all the days of his life—or pay for it.——Excuse me, said the commissary, the spirit of the ordinance is this—That if you set out with an intention of running post from Paris to Avignion, *&c.* you shall not change that intention or mode of travelling, without first satisfying the fermiers² for two posts further than the place you repent at—and 'tis founded, continued he, upon this, that the REVENUES are not to fall short through your *fickleness*——

——O by heavens! cried I—if fickleness is taxable in France—we have nothing to do but to make the best peace with you we can——

AND SO THE PEACE WAS MADE;³

——And if it is a bad one—as Tristram Shandy laid the corner stone of it—nobody but Tristram Shandy ought to be hanged.

CHAP. XXXVI.

THOUGH I was sensible I had said as many clever things to the commissary as came to six livres four sous, yet I was determined to note down the imposition amongst my remarks before I retir'd from the place; so putting my hand into my coat pocket for my remarks—(which by the bye, may be a caution to travellers to take a little more care of *their* remarks for the future) "my remarks were *stolen*"——Never did sorry traveller make such a pother and racket about his remarks as I did about mine, upon the occasion.

Heaven! earth! sea! fire! cried I, calling in every thing to my aid but what I should——My remarks are stolen!—what shall I do?—Mr. commissary! pray did I drop any remarks as I stood besides you?——

You dropp'd a good many very singular ones; replied he——Pugh! said I, those were but a few, not worth above six livres two sous—but these are a large parcel——He shook his head——Monsieur Le Blanc! Madam Le Blanc! did you see any papers of mine?—you maid of the house! run up stairs—François! run up after her——

——I must have my remarks——they were the best remarks, cried I, that ever were made—the wisest—the wittiest——What shall I do?— which way shall I turn myself?

Sancho Pança, when he lost his ass's FURNITURE, did not exclaim more bitterly.¹

CHAP. XXXVII.

WHEN the first transport was over, and the registers of the brain were beginning to get a little out of the confusion into which this jumble of cross accidents had cast them—it then presently occurr'd to me, that I had left my remarks in the pocket of the chaise—and that in selling my chaise, I had sold my remarks along with it, to the chaise-vamper.[1]

   I leave this void space that the reader may swear into it, any oath that he is most accustomed to——For my own part, if ever I swore a *whole* oath into a vacancy in my life, I think it was into that ——*** **** **, said I—and so my remarks through France, which were as full of wit, as an egg is full of meat, and as well worth four hundred guineas, as the said egg is worth a penny—Have I been selling here to a chaise-vamper—for four Louis d'Ors[2]—and giving him a post-chaise (by heaven) worth six into the bargain; had it been to Dodsley, or Becket,[3] or any creditable bookseller, who was either leaving off business, and wanted a post-chaise—or who was beginning it—and wanted my remarks, and two or three guineas along with them—I could have borne it——but to a chaise-vamper!—shew me to him this moment François—said I—the valet de place put on his hat, and led the way—and I pull'd off mine, as I pass'd the commissary, and followed him.

CHAP. XXXVIII.

WHEN we arrived at the chaise-vamper's house, both the house and the shop were shut up; it was the eighth of September, the nativity of the blessed Virgin Mary, mother of God—
——Tantarra – ra – tan – tivi——the whole world was going out a May-poling—frisking here—capering there—no body cared a button for me or my remarks; so I sat me down upon a bench by the door, philosophating upon my condition: by a better fate than usually attends

me, I had not waited half an hour, when the mistress came in, to take the papilliotes[1] from off her hair, before she went to the May-poles——

The French women, by the bye, love May-poles, *a la folie*[2]—that is, as much as their matins——give 'em but a May-pole, whether in May, June, July, or September—they never count the times——down it goes—— 'tis meat, drink, washing, and lodging to 'em——and had we but the policy, an' please your worships (as wood is a little scarce in France) to send them but plenty of May-poles——

The women would set them up; and when they had done, they would dance round them (and the men for company) till they were all blind.

The wife of the chaise-vamper step'd in, I told you, to take the papilliotes from off her hair——the toilet stands still for no man——so she jerk'd off her cap, to begin with them as she open'd the door, in doing which, one of them fell upon the ground——I instantly saw it was my own writing——

—O Seigneur! cried I—you have got all my remarks upon your head, Madam!——*J'en suis bien mortifiée*,[3] said she——'tis well, thinks I, they have stuck there—for could they have gone deeper, they would have made such confusion in a French woman's noddle—She had better have gone with it unfrizled, to the day of eternity.

Tenez[4]—said she—so without any idea of the nature of my suffering, she took them from her curls, and put them gravely one by one into my hat——one was twisted this way——another twisted that——ay! by my faith; and when they are published, quoth I,——

They will be worse twisted still.

CHAP. XXXIX.

AND now for Lippius's clock! said I, with the air of a man, who had got thro' all his difficulties——nothing can prevent us seeing that, and the Chinese history, *&c.* except the time, said François——for 'tis almost eleven—then we must speed the faster, said I, striding it away to the cathedral.

I cannot say, in my heart, that it gave me any concern in being told by one of the minor canons, as I was entering the west door,—That Lippius's great clock was all out of joints, and had not gone for some years——It will give me the more time, thought I, to peruse the Chinese history; and besides I shall be able to give the world a better account of the clock in it's decay, than I could have done in its flourishing condition——

——And so away I posted to the college of the Jesuits.

Now it is with the project of getting a peep at the history of China in Chinese characters—as with many others I could mention, which strike the fancy only at a distance; for as I came nearer and nearer to the point— my blood cool'd—the freak gradually went off, till, at length I would not have given a cherry-stone to have it gratified——The truth was, my time was short, and my heart was at the Tomb of the Lovers——I wish to God, said I, as I got the rapper in my hand, that the key of the library may be but lost; it fell out as well——

For all the JESUITS *had got the cholic*[1]—and to that degree, as never was known in the memory of the oldest practitioner.

CHAP. XL.

AS I knew the geography of the Tomb of the Lovers, as well as if I had lived twenty years in Lyons, namely, that it was upon the turning of my right hand, just without the gate, leading to the Fauxbourg de Vaise ——I dispatch'd François to the boat, that I might pay the homage I so long ow'd it, without a witness of my weakness.—I walk'd with all imaginable joy towards the place——when I saw the gate which intercepted the tomb, my heart glowed within me——

—Tender and faithful spirits! cried I, addressing myself to Amandus and Amanda—long—long have I tarried to drop this tear upon your tomb———I come———I come———

When I came—there was no tomb to drop it upon.

What would I have given for my uncle Toby to have whistled, Lillo bullero!

CHAP. XLI.

NO matter how, or in what mood—but I flew from the tomb of the lovers—or rather I did not fly *from* it—(for there was no such thing existing) and just got time enough to the boat to save my passage;—and e'er I had sailed a hundred yards, the Rhône and the Saôn met together, and carried me down merrily betwixt them.

But I have described this voyage down the Rhône, before I made it——

——So now I am at Avignion—and as there is nothing to see[1] but the old house, in which the duke of Ormond[2] resided, and nothing to stop me but a short remark upon the place, in three minutes you will see me crossing the bridge upon a mule, with François upon a horse with my portmanteau behind him, and the owner of both, striding the way before us with a long gun upon his shoulder, and a sword under his arm, least peradventure we should run away with his cattle. Had you seen my breeches in entering Avignon,——Though you'd have seen them better, I think, as I mounted—you would not have thought the precaution amiss, or found in your heart to have taken it, in dudgeon: for my own part, I took it most kindly; and determined to make him a present of them, when we got to the end of our journey, for the trouble they had put him to, of arming himself at all points against them.

Before I go further, let me get rid of my remark upon Avignon, which is this; That I think it wrong, merely because a man's hat has been blown off his head by chance the first night he comes to Avignon,——that he should therefore say, "Avignion is more subject to high winds than any town in all France:" for which reason I laid no stress upon the accident till I had inquired of the master of the inn about it, who telling me seriously it was so——and hearing moreover, the windyness of Avignion[3] spoke of in the country about as a proverb—I set it down, merely to ask the learned what can be the cause——the consequence I saw—for they are all Dukes, Marquisses, and Counts, there——the duce a Baron, in all Avignion——so that there is scarce any talking to them, on a windy day.

Prithee friend, said I, take hold of my mule for a moment——for I wanted to pull off one of my jack-boots, which hurt my heel—the man was standing quite idle at the door of the inn, and as I had taken it into my head, he was someway concerned about the house or stable, I put the bridle into his hand—so begun with my boot:—when I had finished the affair, I turned about to take the mule from the man, and thank him——

—— *But Monsieur le Marquis* had walked in——

CHAP. XLII.

I Had now the whole south of France, from the banks of the Rhône to those of the Garonne to traverse upon my mule at my own leisure— *at my own leisure*—— for I had left Death, the lord knows—— and He only—how far behind me—— "I have followed many a man thro' France, quoth he—but never at this mettlesome rate"—— Still he followed,—— and still I fled him——but I fled him chearfully——still he pursued— but like one who pursued his prey without hope—— as he lag'd, every step he lost, softened his looks—— why should I fly him at this rate?

So notwithstanding all the commissary of the post-office had said, I changed the *mode* of my travelling once more; and after so precipitate and rattling a course as I had run, I flattered my fancy with thinking of my mule, and that I should traverse the rich plains of Languedoc upon his back, as slowly as foot could fall.

There is nothing more pleasing to a traveller——or more terrible to travel-writers, than a large rich plain; especially if it is without great rivers or bridges; and presents nothing to the eye, but one unvaried picture of plenty: for after they have once told you that 'tis delicious! or delightful! (as the case happens)—that the soil was grateful, and that nature pours out all her abundance, *&c.* ... they have then a large plain upon their hands, which they know not what to do with—and which is of little or no use to them but to carry them to some town; and that town, perhaps, of little more, but a new place to start from to the next plain——and so on.

—This is most terrible work; judge if I don't manage my plains better.

CHAP. XLIII.

I Had not gone above two leagues and a half, before the man with his gun, began to look at his priming.

I had three several times loiter'd *terribly* behind; half a mile at least every time: once, in deep conference with a drum-maker, who was making drums for the fairs of *Baucaira* and *Tarascone*[1]—I did not understand the principles——

The second time, I cannot so properly say, I stopp'd——for meeting a couple of Franciscans straiten'd more for time than myself, and not being able to get to the bottom of what I was about——I had turn'd back with them——

The third, was an affair of trade with a gossip, for a hand basket of Provence figs for four sous; this would have been transacted at once; but for a case of conscience at the close of it; for when the figs were paid for, it turn'd out, that there were two dozen of eggs cover'd over with vine-leaves at the bottom of the basket—as I had no intention of buying eggs—I made no sort of claim of them—as for the space they had occupied—what signified it? I had figs enow for my money——

—But it was my intention to have the basket—it was the gossip's intention to keep it, without which, she could do nothing with her eggs ——and unless I had the basket, I could do as little with my figs, which were too ripe already, and most of 'em burst at the side: this brought on a short contention, which terminated in sundry proposals, what we should both do——

—How we disposed of our eggs and figs, I defy you, or the Devil himself, had he not been there (which I am persuaded he was) to form the least probable conjecture: You will read the whole of it——not this year, for I am hastening to the story of my uncle Toby's amours—but you will read it in the collection of those which have arose out of the journey across this plain——and which, therefore, I call my

Plain Stories.

How far my pen has been fatigued like those of other travellers, in this journey of it, over so barren a track—the world must judge—but the traces of it, which are now all set o'vibrating together this moment, tell me 'tis the most fruitful and busy period of my life; for as I had made no convention with my man with the gun as to time—by stopping and talking to every soul I met who was not in a full trot—joining all parties before me—waiting for every soul behind—hailing all those who were coming through cross roads—arresting all kinds of beggars, pilgrims, fiddlers, fryars—not passing by a woman in a mulberry-tree without commending her legs, and tempting her into conversation with a pinch of snuff——In short, by seizing every handle, of what size or shape soever, which chance held out to me in this journey—I turned my *plain* into a *city*[2]—I was always in company, and with great variety too; and as my mule loved society as much as myself, and had some proposals always on his part to offer to every beast he met—I am confident we could have passed through Pall-Mall or St. James's-Street for a month together, with fewer adventures—and seen less of human nature.

O! there is that sprightly frankness which at once unpins every plait of a Languedocian's dress—that whatever is beneath it, it looks so like the simplicity which poets sing of in better days—I will delude my fancy, and believe it is so.

'Twas in the road betwixt Nismes and Lunel, where there is the best Muscatto[3] wine in all France, and which by the bye belongs to the honest canons of Montpellier—and foul befall the man who has drank it at their table, who grudges them a drop of it.

——The sun was set—they had done their work; the nymphs had tied up their hair afresh—and the swains were preparing for a carousal[4]—— My mule made a dead point——'Tis the fife and tabourin, said I—— I'm frighten'd to death, quoth he——They are running at the ring of pleasure,[5] said I, giving him a prick——By saint Boogar,[6] and all the saints at the backside of the door of purgatory, said he—(making the same resolution with the abbesse of Andoüillets) I'll not go a step further—— 'Tis very well, sir, said I—I never will argue a point with one of your family, as long as I live; so leaping off his back, and kicking off one boot into this ditch, and t'other into that—I'll take a dance, said I——so stay you here.

A sun-burnt daughter of Labour rose up from the groupe to meet me as I advanced towards them; her hair, which was a dark chesnut, approaching rather to a black, was tied up in a knot, all but a single tress.

We want a cavalier, said she, holding out both her hands, as if to offer them——And a cavalier ye shall have; said I, taking hold of both of them.

Hadst thou, Nannette, been array'd like a dutchesse!

——But that cursed slit in thy petticoat!

Nannette cared not for it.

We could not have done without you, said she, letting go one hand, with self-taught politeness, leading me up with the other.

A lame youth, whom Apollo had recompenced with a pipe, and to which he had added a tabourin of his own accord, ran sweetly over the prelude, as he sat upon the bank——Tie me up this tress instantly, said Nannette, putting a piece of string into my hand——It taught me to forget I was a stranger——The whole knot fell down——We had been seven years acquainted.

The youth struck the note upon the tabourin—his pipe followed, and off we bounded——"the duce take that slit!"

The sister of the youth who had stolen her voice from heaven, sung alternately with her brother——'twas a Gascoigne roundelay.[7]

Viva la joia!
Fidon la tristessa!

The nymphs join'd in unison, and their swains an octave below them——

I would have given a crown to have it sew'd up—Nannette would not have given a sous—*Viva la joia!* was in her lips—*Viva la joia!* was in her eyes. A transient spark of amity shot across the space betwixt us——She look'd amiable!——Why could I not live and end my days thus? Just disposer of our joys and sorrows,[8] cried I, why could not a man sit down in the lap of content[9] here—and dance, and sing, and say his prayers, and go to heaven with this nut brown maid?[10] capriciously did she bend her head on one side, and dance up insiduous[11]——Then 'tis time to dance off, quoth I; so changing only partners and tunes, I danced it away from Lunel to Montpellier——from thence to Pesçnas, Beziers——I danced it along through Narbonne, Carcasson, and Castle Naudairy, till at last I danced myself into Perdrillo's pavillion,[12] where pulling a paper of black lines, that I might go on straight forwards, without digression or parenthesis, in my uncle Toby's amours——

I begun thus——

END of the SEVENTH VOLUME.

THE
LIFE
AND
OPINIONS
OF
TRISTRAM SHANDY,
GENTLEMAN.

Non enim excursus hic ejus, sed opus ipsum est.
PLIN. Lib. quintus Epistola sexta.

VOL. VIII.

LONDON:
Printed for T. BECKET and P. A. DEHONT,
in the Strand. M DCC LXV.

(Height of original type-page 108 mm.)

LIFE and OPINIONS

TRISTRAM SHANDY, Gent.

CHAP. I.

—— **B**UT softly—— for in these sportive plains, and under this genial sun, where at this instant all flesh is running out piping, fiddling, and dancing to the vintage, and every step that's taken, the judgment is surprised by the imagination, I defy, notwithstanding all that has been said upon *straight lines** in sundry pages of my book—I defy the best cabbage planter[1] that ever existed, whether he plants backwards or forwards, it makes little difference in the account (except that he will have more to answer for in the one case than in the other)—I defy him to go on cooly, critically, and canonically, planting his cabbages one by one, in straight lines, and stoical distances, especially if slits in petticoats are unsew'd up—without ever and anon straddling out, or sidling into some bastardly digression—— In *Freeze-land, Fog-land*[2] and some other lands I wot of—it may be done——

But in this clear climate of fantasy and perspiration, where every idea, sensible and insensible, gets vent—in this land, my dear Eugenius—in this fertile land of chivalry and romance, where I now sit, unskrewing my ink-horn to write my uncle Toby's amours, and with all the meanders of JULIA's track in quest of her DIEGO, in full view of my study window—if thou comest not and takest me by the hand——

What a work is it likely to turn out!

Let us begin it.

*Vid. Vol. VI. p. 152. (Page 391 in present edition.)

CHAP. II.

I T is with LOVE as with CUCKOLDOM——
——But now I am talking of beginning a book, and have long had a thing upon my mind to be imparted to the reader, which if not imparted now, can never be imparted to him as long as I live (whereas the COMPARISON may be imparted to him any hour in the day)——I'll just mention it, and begin in good earnest.

The thing is this.

That of all the several ways of beginning a book which are now in practice throughout the known world, I am confident my own way of doing it is the best——I'm sure it is the most religious——for I begin with writing the first sentence——and trusting to Almighty God for the second.

'Twould cure an author for ever of the fuss and folly of opening his street-door, and calling in his neighbours and friends, and kinsfolk, with the devil and all his imps,[1] with their hammers and engines, &c. only to observe how one sentence of mine follows another, and how the plan follows the whole.

I wish you saw me half starting out of my chair, with what confidence, as I grasp the elbow of it, I look up——catching the idea, even sometimes before it half way reaches me——

I believe in my conscience I intercept many a thought which heaven intended for another man.

Pope and his Portrait[*2] are fools to me——no martyr is ever so full of faith or fire——I wish I could say of good works too——but I have no

Zeal or Anger——or

Anger or Zeal——

And till gods and men agree together to call it by the same name——the errantest TARTUFFE,[3] in science—in politics—or in religion, shall never kindle a spark within me, or have a worse word, or a more unkind greeting, than what he will read in the next chapter.

[*] Vid. Pope's Portrait.

CHAP. III.

——Bon jour!——good-morrow!——so you have got your cloak on betimes!——but 'tis a cold morning, and you judge the matter rightly ——'tis better to be well mounted, than go o'foot——and obstructions in the glands are dangerous——And how goes it with thy concubine— thy wife—and thy little ones o'both sides? and when did you hear from the old gentleman and lady—your sister, aunt, uncle and cousins——I hope they have got better of their colds, coughs, claps, tooth-aches, fevers, stranguries, sciaticas, swellings, and sore-eyes.——What a devil of an apothecary! to take so much blood—give such a vile purge—puke— poultice—plaister—night-draught—glister—blister?——And why so many grains of calomel? santa Maria! and such a dose of opium! periclitat-ing,[1] pardi! the whole family of ye, from head to tail——By my great aunt Dinah's old black velvet mask![2] I think there was no occasion for it.

Now this being a little bald about the chin, by frequently putting off and on, *before* she was got with child by the coachman—not one of our family would wear it after. To cover the MASK afresh, was more than the mask was worth——and to wear a mask which was bald, or which could be half seen through, was as bad as having no mask at all——

This is the reason, may it please your reverences, that in all our numerous family, for these four generations, we count no more than one archbishop,[3] a Welch judge, some three or four aldermen, and a single mounte-bank——

In the sixteenth century, we boast of no less than a dozen alchymists.

CHAP. IV.

"IT is with Love as with Cuckoldom"[1]——the suffering party is at least the *third*, but generally the last in the house who knows any thing about the matter: this comes, as all the world knows, from having half a dozen words for one thing; and so long, as what in this vessel of the human frame, is *Love*——may be *Hatred*, in that—— *Sentiment* half a yard higher—— and *Nonsense*————no Madam,—not there——I mean at the part I am now pointing to with my forefinger——how can we help ourselves?

Of all mortal, and immortal men too, if you please, who ever soliloquized upon this mystic subject, my uncle Toby was the worst fitted, to have push'd his researches, thro' such a contention of feelings; and he had infallibly let them all run on, as we do worse matters, to see what they would turn out——had not Bridget's pre-notification of them to Susannah, and Susannah's repeated manifesto's thereupon to all the world, made it necessary for my uncle Toby to look into the affair.

CHAP. V.

WHY weavers, gardeners, and gladiators—or a man with a pined leg (proceeding from some ailment in the *foot)*—should ever have had some tender nymph breaking her heart in secret for them,[1] are points well and duely settled and accounted for, by ancient and modern physiologists.

A water-drinker, provided he is a profess'd one, and does it without fraud or covin, is precisely in the same predicament: not that, at first sight, there is any consequence, or shew of logic in it, "That a rill of cold water dribbling through my inward parts, should light up a torch in my Jenny's—"

——The proposition does not strike one; on the contrary it seems to run opposite to the natural workings of causes and effects——

But it shews the weakness and imbecility of human reason.

——"And in perfect good health with it?"

—The most perfect—Madam, that friendship herself could wish me——

——"And drink nothing!—nothing but water?"

—Impetuous fluid! the moment thou presses against the flood-gates of the brain——see how they give way!——

In swims CURIOSITY, beckoning to her damsels to follow—they dive into the centre of the current——

FANCY sits musing upon the bank, and with her eyes following the stream, turns straws and bulrushes into masts and bowsprits——And DESIRE, with vest held up to the knee in one hand, snatches at them, as they swim by her, with the other——

O ye water-drinkers! is it then by this delusive fountain, that ye have so often governed and turn'd this world about like a mill-wheel—grinding the faces[2] of the impotent—be-powdering their ribs—be-peppering their noses, and changing sometimes even the very frame and face of nature——

——If I was you, quoth Yorick, I would drink more water, Eugenius.—— And, if I was you, Yorick, replied Eugenius, so would I.

Which shews they had both read Longinus[3]——

For my own part, I am resolved never to read any book but my own, as long as I live.

CHAP. VI.

I Wish my uncle Toby had been a water-drinker; for then the thing had been accounted for, That the first moment Widow Wadman saw him, she felt something stirring within her in his favour—Something!— something.

——Something perhaps more than friendship—less than love—some-thing—no matter what—no matter where—I would not give a single hair off my mule's tail, and be obliged to pluck it off myself (indeed the villain has not many to spare, and is not a little vicious into the bargain) to be let by your worships into the secret——

But the truth is, my uncle Toby was not a water-drinker; he drank it neither pure nor mix'd, or any how, or any where, except fortuitously upon some advanced posts, where better liquor was not to be had——or during the time he was under cure; when the surgeon telling him it would extend the fibres, and bring them sooner into contact——my uncle Toby drank it for quietness sake.

Now as all the world knows, that no effect in nature can be produced without a cause and as it is as well known, that my uncle Toby, was neither a weaver—a gardener, or a gladiator——unless as a captain, you will needs have him one—but then he was only a captain of foot—and besides the whole is an equivocation——There is nothing left for us to suppose, but that my uncle Toby's leg——but that will avail us little in the present hypothesis, unless it had proceeded from some ailment *in the foot*—whereas his leg was not emaciated from any disorder in his foot—for my uncle Toby's leg was not emaciated at all. It was a little stiff and awkward, from a total disuse of it, for the three years he lay confined at my father's house in town; but it was plump and muscular, and in all other respects as good and promising a leg as the other.

I declare, I do not recollect any one opinion or passage of my life, where my understanding was more at a loss to make ends meet, and torture the chapter I had been writing, to the service of the chapter following it, than in the present case: one would think I took a pleasure in runing into difficulties of this kind, merely to make fresh experiments of getting out of 'em——Inconsiderate soul that thou art! What! are not the unavoidable distresses with which, as an author and a man, thou art hemm'd in on every side of thee——are they, Tristram, not sufficient, but thou must entangle thyself still more?

Is it not enough that thou art in debt, and that thou hast ten cart-loads of thy fifth and sixth volumes still—still unsold, and art almost at thy wit's ends, how to get them off thy hands.[1]

To this hour art thou not tormented with the vile asthma thou gattest in skating against the wind in Flanders? and is it but two months ago, that in a fit of laughter, on seeing a cardinal make water like a quirister [2] (with both hands) thou brakest a vessel in thy lungs, whereby, in two hours, thou lost as many quarts of blood; and hadst thou lost as much more, did not the faculty tell thee——it would have amounted to a gallon?——

CHAP. VII.

——But for heaven's sake, let us not talk of quarts or gallons——let us take the story straight before us; it is so nice and intricate a one, it will scarce bear the transposition of a single tittle; and some how or other, you have got me thrust almost into the middle of it——

——I beg we may take more care.

CHAP. VIII.

MY uncle Toby and the corporal had posted down with so much heat and precipitation, to take possession of the spot of ground we have so often spoke of, in order to open their campaign as early as the rest of the allies; that they had forgot one of the most necessary articles of the whole affair; it was neither a pioneer's spade, a pick-ax, or a shovel—

——It was a bed to lie on: so that as Shandy Hall was at that time unfurnished; and the little inn where poor Le Fever died, not yet built; my uncle Toby was constrained to accept of a bed at Mrs. Wadman's, for a night or two, till corporal Trim (who to the character of an excellent valet, groom, cook, sempster, surgeon and engineer, superadded that of an excellent upholsterer too) with the help of a carpenter and a couple of taylors, constructed one in my uncle Toby's house.

A daughter of Eve, for such was widow Wadman, and 'tis all the character I intend to give of her—

——"*That she was a perfect woman;*"
had better be fifty leagues off—or in her warm bed—or playing with a case-knife[1]—or any thing you please—than make a man the object of her attention, when the house and all the furniture is her own.

There is nothing in it out of doors and in broad day-light, where a woman has a power, physically speaking, of viewing a man in more lights than one—but here, for her soul, she can see him in no light without

mixing something of her own goods and chattels along with him——
till by reiterated acts of such combinations, he gets foisted into her
inventory——

——And then good night.

But this is not matter of SYSTEM; for I have delivered that above——
nor is it matter of BREVIARY——for I make no man's creed but my own
——nor matter of FACT——at least that I know of; but 'tis matter
copulative and introductory to what follows.

CHAP. IX.

I Do not speak it with regard to the coarseness or cleanness of them—
or the strength of their gussets——but pray do not night-shifts differ
from day-shifts[1] as much in this particular, as in any thing else in the
world; That they so far exceed the others in length, that when you are
laid down in them, they fall almost as much below the feet, as the day-shifts
fall short of them?

Widow Wadman's night-shifts (as was the mode I suppose in King
William's and Queen Anne's reigns) were cut however after this fashion;
and if the fashion is changed, (for in Italy they are come to nothing)——
so much the worse for the public; they were two Flemish ells[2] and a half
in length; so that allowing a moderate woman two ells, she had half an ell
to spare, to do what she would with.

Now from one little indulgence gain'd after another, in the many bleak
and decemberly nights of a seven years widowhood, things had insensibly
come to this pass, and for the two last years had got establish'd into one
of the ordinances of the bed-chamber—That as soon as Mrs. Wadman
was put to bed, and had got her legs stretched down to the bottom of it, of
which she always gave Bridget notice—Bridget with all suitable decorum,
having first open'd the bed-cloaths at the feet, took hold of the half ell of
cloath we are speaking of, and having gently, and with both her hands,
drawn it downwards to its furthest extension, and then contracted it again
side long by four or five even plaits, she took a large corking pin out of
her sleeve, and with the point directed towards her, pin'd the plaits all

fast together a little above the hem; which done she tuck'd all in tight at the feet, and wish'd her mistress a good night.

This was constant, and without any other variation than this; that on shivering and tempestuous nights, when Bridget untuck'd the feet of the bed, &c. to do this——she consulted no thermometer but that of her own passions; and so performed it standing—kneeling—or squatting, according to the different degrees of faith, hope, and charity, she was in, and bore towards her mistress that night. In every other respect the *etiquette* was sacred, and might have vied with the most mechanical one of the most inflexible bed-chamber in Christendom.

The first night, as soon as the corporal had conducted my uncle Toby up stairs, which was about ten——Mrs. Wadman threw herself into her arm chair, and crossing her left knee with her right, which formed a resting-place for her elbow, she reclin'd her cheek upon the palm of her hand, and leaning forwards, ruminated till midnight upon both sides of the question.

The second night she went to her bureau, and having ordered Bridget to bring her up a couple of fresh candles and leave them upon the table, she took out her marriage-settlement, and read it over with great devotion: and the third night (which was the last of my uncle Toby's stay) when Bridget had pull'd down the night-shift, and was assaying to stick in the corking pin——

——With a kick of both heels at once, but at the same time the most natural kick that could be kick'd in her situation——for supposing ****** *** to be the sun in its meridian, it was a north-east kick——she kick'd the pin out of her fingers——the *etiquette* which hung upon it, down——down it fell to the ground, and was shivered into a thousand atoms.

From all which it was plain that widow Wadman was in love with my uncle Toby.

CHAP. X.

MY uncle Toby's head at that time was full of other matters, so that it was not till the demolition of Dunkirk, when all the other civilities of Europe were settled, that he found leisure to return this.

This made an armistice (that is speaking with regard to my uncle Toby—but with respect to Mrs. Wadman, a vacancy)—of almost eleven years. But in all cases of this nature, as it is the second blow, happen at what distance of time it will, which makes the fray——I chuse for that reason to call these the amours of my uncle Toby with Mrs. Wadman, rather than the amours of Mrs. Wadman with my uncle Toby.

This is not a distinction without a difference.

It is not like the affair of *an old hat cock'd*[1] —— and *a cock'd old hat*, about which your reverences have so often been at odds with one another—— but there is a difference here in the nature of things——

And let me tell you, gentry, a wide one too.

CHAP. XI.

NOW as widow Wadman did love my uncle Toby——and my uncle Toby did not love widow Wadman, there was nothing for widow Wadman to do, but to go on and love my uncle Toby——or let it alone.

Widow Wadman would do neither the one or the other——

——Gracious heaven!——but I forget I am a little of her temper myself; for whenever it so falls out, which it sometimes does about the equinoxes, that an earthly goddess is so much this, and that, and t'other, that I cannot eat my breakfast for her——and that she careth not three halfpence whether I eat my breakfast or no——

——Curse on her! and so I send her to Tartary, and from Tartary to *Terra del Fuogo*,[1] and so on to the devil: in short there is not an infernal nitch where I do not take her divinityship and stick it.

But as the heart is tender, and the passions in these tides ebb and flow ten times in a minute, I instantly bring her back again; and as I do all things in extremes, I place her in the very centre of the milky-way——

Brightest of stars! thou wilt shed thy influence upon some one——

——The duce take her and her influence too——for at that word I lose all patience——much good may it do him!——By all that is hirsute and gashly![2] I cry, taking off my furr'd cap,[3] and twisting it round my finger——I would not give sixpence for a dozen such!

——But 'tis an excellent cap too (putting it upon my head, and pressing it close to my ears)—and warm—and soft; especially if you stroke it the right way—but alas! that will never be my luck——(so here my philosophy is shipwreck'd again)

——No; I shall never have a finger in the pye[4] (so here I break my metaphor)——

Crust and crumb

Inside and out

Top and bottom——I detest it, I hate it, I repudiate it——I'm sick at the sight of it——

'Tis all pepper,

garlick,

staragen,[5]

salt, and

devil's dung[6]——by the great arch cook of cooks, who does nothing, I think, from morning to night, but sit down by the fire-side and invent inflammatory dishes for us, I would not touch it for the world——

——O Tristram! Tristram! cried Jenny.

O Jenny! Jenny! replied I, and so went on with the twelfth chapter.

CHAP. XII.

——"Not touch it for the world" did I say——
Lord, how I have heated my imagination with this metaphor!

CHAP. XIII.

WHICH shews, let your reverences and worships say what you will of it (for as for *thinking*——all who *do* think—think pretty much alike, both upon it and other matters)——LOVE is certainly, at least alphabetically speaking,[1] one of the most

A gitating
B ewitching
C onfounded
D evilish affairs of life——the most
E xtravagant
F utilitous
G alligaskinish
H andy-dandyish
I racundulous (there is no K to it) and
L yrical of all human passions: at the same time, the most
M isgiving
N innyhammering
O bstipating[2]
P ragmatical
S tridulous
R idiculous—though by the bye the R should have gone first—
But in short 'tis of such a nature, as my father once told my uncle Toby upon the close of a long dissertation upon the subject——"You can

scarce," said he, "combine two ideas together upon it, brother Toby, without an hypallage"——What's that? cried my uncle Toby.

The cart before the horse, replied my father——

——And what has he to do there? cried my uncle Toby——

Nothing, quoth my father, but to get in——or let it alone.

Now widow Wadman, as I told you before, would do neither the one or the other.

She stood however ready harnessed and caparisoned at all points to watch accidents.

CHAP. XIV.

THE Fates, who certainly all foreknew of these amours of widow Wadman and my uncle Toby, had, from the first creation of matter and motion (and with more courtesy than they usually do things of this kind) established such a chain of causes and effects hanging so fast to one another, that it was scarce possible for my uncle Toby to have dwelt in any other house in the world, or to have occupied any other garden in Christendom, but the very house and garden which join'd and laid parallel to Mrs. Wadman's; this, with the advantage of a thickset arbour in Mrs. Wadman's garden, but planted in the hedge-row of my uncle Toby's, put all the occasions into her hands which Love-militancy wanted; she could observe my uncle Toby's motions, and was mistress likewise of his councils of war; and as his unsuspecting heart had given leave to the corporal, through the mediation of Bridget, to make her a wicker gate[1] of communication to enlarge her walks, it enabled her to carry on her approaches to the very door of the sentry-box; and sometimes out of gratitude, to make the attack, and endeavour to blow my uncle Toby up in the very sentry-box itself.

CHAP. XV.

IT is a great pity——but 'tis certain from every day's observation of man, that he may be set on fire like a candle, at either end[1]——provided there is a sufficient wick standing out; if there is not——there's an end of the affair; and if there is——by lighting it at the bottom, as the flame in that case has the misfortune generally to put out itself——there's an end of the affair again.

For my part, could I always have the ordering of it which way I would be burnt myself——for I cannot bear the thoughts of being burnt like a beast——I would oblige a housewife constantly to light me at the top; for then I should burn down decently to the socket; that is, from my head to my heart, from my heart to my liver, from my liver to my bowels, and so on by the meseraick veins and arteries, through all the turns and lateral insertions of the intestines and their tunicles, to the blind gut——

——I beseech you, doctor Slop, quoth my uncle Toby, interrupting him as he mentioned the *blind gut*,[2] in a discourse with my father the night my mother was brought to bed of me——I beseech you, quoth my uncle Toby, to tell me which is the blind gut; for, old as I am, I vow I do not know to this day where it lies.

The *blind gut*, answered doctor Slop, lies betwixt the *Illion*[3] and *Colon*——

——In a man? said my father.

——'Tis precisely the same, cried doctor Slop, in a woman——

That's more than I know; quoth my father.

CHAP. XVI.

——And so to make sure of both systems, Mrs. Wadman predetermined to light my uncle Toby neither at this end or that; but like a prodigal's candle, to light him, if possible, at both ends at once.

Now, through all the lumber rooms of military furniture, including both of horse and foot, from the great arsenal of Venice to the Tower of London (exclusive) if Mrs. Wadman had been rummaging for seven years together, and with Bridget to help her, she could not have found any one *blind* or *mantelet* so fit for her purpose, as that which the expediency of my uncle Toby's affairs had fix'd up ready to her hands.

I believe I have not told you——but I don't know——possibly I have ——be it as it will, 'tis one of the number of those many things, which a man had better do over again, than dispute about it—That whatever town or fortress the corporal was at work upon, during the course of their campaign, my uncle Toby always took care on the inside of his sentry-box, which was towards his left hand, to have a plan of the place, fasten'd up with two or three pins at the top, but loose at the bottom, for the conveniency of holding it up to the eye, &c. . . . as occasions required; so that when an attack was resolved upon, Mrs. Wadman had nothing more to do, when she had got advanced to the door of the sentry-box, but to extend her right hand; and edging in her left foot at the same movement,[1] to take hold of the map or plan, or upright, or whatever it was, and with outstretched neck meeting it half way,—to advance it towards her; on which my uncle Toby's passions were sure to catch fire——for he would instantly take hold of the other corner of the map in his left hand, and with the end of his pipe, in the other, begin an explanation.

When the attack was advanced to this point;——the world will naturally enter into the reasons of Mrs. Wadman's next stroke of generalship—— which was, to take my uncle Toby's tobacco-pipe out of his hand as soon as she possibly could; which, under one pretence or other, but generally that of pointing more distinctly at some redoubt or breast-work in the map, she would effect before my uncle Toby (poor soul!) had well march'd above half a dozen toises with it.

—It obliged my uncle Toby to make use of his forefinger.

The difference it made in the attack was this; That in going upon it, as in the first case, with the end of her forefinger against the end of my uncle Toby's tobacco-pipe, she might have travelled with it, along the lines, from Dan to Beersheba,[2] had my uncle Toby's lines reach'd so far, without any effect: For as there was no arterial or vital heat in the end of the tobacco-pipe, it could excite no sentiment——it could neither give fire by pulsation——or receive it by sympathy——'twas nothing but smoak.

Whereas, in following my uncle Toby's forefinger with hers, close thro' all the little turns and indentings of his works——pressing sometimes against the side of it——then treading upon it's nail——then tripping it up——then touching it here——then there, and so on——it set something at least in motion.

This, tho' slight skirmishing, and at a distance from the main body, yet drew on the rest; for here, the map usually falling with the back of it, close to the side of the sentry-box, my uncle Toby, in the simplicity of his soul, would lay his hand flat upon it, in order to go on with his explanation; and Mrs. Wadman, by a manœuvre as quick as thought, would as certainly place her's close besides it; this at once opened a communication, large enough for any sentiment to pass or repass, which a person skill'd in the elementary and practical part of love-making, has occasion for——

By bringing up her forefinger parallel (as before) to my uncle Toby's ——it unavoidably brought the thumb into action——and the forefinger and thumb being once engaged, as naturally brought in the whole hand. Thine, dear uncle Toby! was never now in it's right place——Mrs. Wadman had it ever to take up, or, with the gentlest pushings, protrusions, and equivocal compressions, that a hand to be removed is capable of receiving——to get it press'd a hair breadth of one side out of her way.

Whilst this was doing, how could she forget to make him sensible, that it was her leg (and no one's else) at the bottom of the sentry-box, which slightly press'd against the calf of his——So that my uncle Toby being thus attacked and sore push'd on both his wings——was it a wonder, if now and then, it put his centre into disorder?——

——The duce take it! said my uncle Toby.

CHAP. XVII.

THESE attacks of Mrs. Wadman, you will readily conceive to be of different kinds; varying from each other, like the attacks which history is full of, and from the same reasons. A general looker on, would scarce allow them to be attacks at all——or if he did, would confound them all together——but I write not to them: it will be time enough to be a little more exact in my descriptions of them, as I come up to them, which will not be for some chapters; having nothing more to add in this, but that in a bundle of original papers and drawings which my father took care to roll up by themselves, there is a plan of Bouchain[1] in perfect preservation (and shall be kept so, whilst I have power to preserve any thing) upon the lower corner of which, on the right hand side, there is still remaining the marks of a snuffy[2] finger and thumb, which there is all the reason in the world to imagine, were Mrs. Wadman's; for the opposite side of the margin, which I suppose to have been my uncle Toby's, is absolutely clean: This seems an authenticated record of one of these attacks; for there are vestigia of the two punctures partly grown up, but still visible on the opposite corner of the map, which are unquestionably the very holes, through which it has been pricked up in the sentry-box——

By all that is priestly! I value this precious relick, with it's *stigmata* and *pricks*, more than all the relicks of the Romish church—— always excepting, when I am writing upon these matters, the pricks which enter'd the flesh of St. *Radagunda* in the desert, which in your road from FESSE to CLUNY, the nuns of that name will shew you for love.[3]

CHAP. XVIII.

I Think, an' please your honour, quoth Trim, the fortifications are quite destroyed——and the bason is upon a level with the mole——I think so too; replied my uncle Toby with a sigh half suppress'd——but step into the parlour, Trim, for the stipulation——it lies upon the table.

It has lain there these six weeks, replied the corporal, till this very morning that the old woman kindled the fire with it—

——Then, said my uncle Toby, there is no further occasion for our services. The more, an' please your honour, the pity, said the corporal; in uttering which he cast his spade into the wheel-barrow, which was beside him, with an air the most expressive of disconsolation that can be imagined, and was heavily turning about to look for his pick-ax, his pioneer's shovel, his picquets and other little military stores, in order to carry them off the field——when a heigh ho! from the sentry-box, which, being made of

thin slit deal, reverberated the sound more sorrowfully to his ear, forbad
him.

————No; said the corporal to himself, I'll do it before his honour rises
to-morrow morning; so taking his spade out of the wheel-barrow again,
with a little earth in it, as if to level something at the foot of the glacis
————but with a real intent to approach nearer to his master, in order to
divert him————he loosen'd a sod or two————pared their edges with his
spade, and having given them a gentle blow or two with the back of it, he
sat himself down close by my uncle Toby's feet, and began as follows.

CHAP. XIX.

IT was a thousand pities————though I believe, an' please your honour,
I am going to say but a foolish kind of a thing for a soldier————

A soldier, cried my uncle Toby, interrupting the corporal, is no more
exempt from saying a foolish thing, Trim, than a man of letters————But
not so often; and please your honour, replied the corporal————My uncle
Toby gave a nod.

It was a thousand pities then, said the corporal, casting his eye upon
Dunkirk, and the mole, as *Servius Sulpicius*,[1] in returning out of Asia (when
he sailed from Ægina towards Megara) did upon Corinth and Pyreus————

—"It was a thousand pities, an' please your honour, to destroy these
works————and a thousand pities to have let them stood."————

————Thou art right, Trim, in both cases: said my uncle Toby————
This, continued the corporal, is the reason, that from the beginning of
their demolition to the end————I have never once whistled, or sung, or
laugh'd, or cry'd, or talk'd of pass'd done deeds, or told your honour one
story good or bad————

————Thou hast many excellencies, Trim, said my uncle Toby, and I
hold it not the least of them, as thou happenest to be a story-teller, that
of the number thou hast told me, either to amuse me in my painful hours,
or divert me in my grave ones—thou hast seldom told me a bad one————

————Because, an' please your honour, except one of a *King of Bohemia
and his seven castles*,—they are all true; for they are about myself————

I do not like the subject the worse, Trim, said my uncle Toby, on that score: But prithee what is this story? thou hast excited my curiosity.

I'll tell it your honour, quoth the corporal, directly—Provided, said my uncle Toby, looking earnestly towards Dunkirk and the mole again——provided it is not a merry one; to such, Trim, a man should ever bring one half of the entertainment[2] along with him; and the disposition I am in at present would wrong both thee, Trim, and thy story——It is not a merry one by any means, replied the corporal—Nor would I have it altogether a grave one, added my uncle Toby——It is neither the one nor the other, replied the corporal, but will suit your honour exactly—— Then I'll thank thee for it with all my heart, cried my uncle Toby, so prithee begin it, Trim.

The corporal made his reverence; and though it is not so easy a matter as the world imagines, to pull off a lank montero cap with grace——or a whit less difficult, in my conceptions, when a man is sitting squat upon the ground, to make a bow so teeming with respect as the corporal was wont, yet by suffering the palm of his right hand, which was towards his master, to slip backward upon the grass, a little beyond his body, in order to allow it the greater sweep——and by an unforced compression, at the same time, of his cap with the thumb and the two forefingers of his left, by which the diameter of the cap became reduced, so that it might be said, rather to be insensibly squeez'd—than pull'd off with a flatus——the corporal acquitted himself of both, in a better manner than the posture of his affairs promised; and having hemmed twice, to find in what key his story would best go, and best suit his master's humour—he exchanged a single look of kindness with him, and set off thus.

The Story of the king of Bohemia
and his seven castles.

THERE was a certain king of Bo – – he————
As the corporal was entering the confines of Bohemia, my uncle Toby obliged him to halt for a single moment; he had set out bare-headed, having since he pull'd off his Montero-cap in the latter end of the last chapter, left it lying beside him on the ground.

——The eye of Goodness espieth all things——so that before the corporal had well got through the first five words of his story, had my uncle Toby twice touch'd his Montero-cap with the end of his cane, interrogatively——as much as to say, Why don't you put it on, Trim? Trim took it up with the most respectful slowness, and casting a glance of humiliation as he did it, upon the embroidery of the fore-part, which being dismally tarnish'd and fray'd moreover in some of the principal leaves and boldest parts of the pattern, he lay'd it down again betwixt his two feet, in order to moralize upon the subject.

——'Tis every word of it but too true, cried my uncle Toby, that thou art about to observe——

"*Nothing in this world, Trim, is made to last for ever.*"

——But when tokens, dear Tom, of thy love and remembrance wear out, said Trim, what shall we say?

There is no occasion, Trim, quoth my uncle Toby, to say any thing else; and was a man to puzzle his brains till Doom's day, I believe, Trim, it would be impossible.

The corporal perceiving my uncle Toby was in the right, and that it would be in vain for the wit of man to think of extracting a purer moral from his cap, without further attempting it, he put it on; and passing his hand across his forehead to rub out a pensive wrinkle, which the text and the doctrine between them had engender'd, he return'd, with the same look and tone of voice, to his story of the king of Bohemia and his seven castles.

The story of the king of Bohemia and
his seven castles, continued.

THERE was a certain king of Bohemia, but in whose reign, except his own, I am not able to inform your honour——

I do not desire it of thee, Trim, by any means, cried my uncle Toby.

——It was a little before the time, an' please your honour, when giants were beginning to leave off breeding;—but in what year of our Lord that was——

——I would not give a half-penny to know, said my uncle Toby.

——Only, an' please your honour, it makes a story look the better in the face——

——'Tis thy own, Trim, so ornament it after thy own fashion; and take any date, continued my uncle Toby, looking pleasantly upon him—take any date in the whole world thou choosest, and put it to—thou art heartily welcome——

The corporal bowed; for of every century, and of every year[3] of that century, from the first creation of the world down to Noah's flood; and from Noah's flood to the birth of Abraham; through all the pilgrimages of the patriarchs, to the departure of the Israelites out of Egypt——and throughout all the Dynasties, Olympiads, Urbecondita's, and other memorable epochas of the different nations of the world, down to the coming of Christ, and from thence to the very moment in which the corporal was telling his story——had my uncle Toby subjected this vast empire of time and all its abysses at his feet; but as MODESTY scarce touches with a finger what LIBERALITY offers her with both hands open[4]——the corporal contented himself with the very *worst year* of the whole bunch; which, to prevent your honours of the Majority and Minority from tearing the very flesh off your bones in contestation, 'Whether that year is not always the last cast-year[5] of the last cast-almanack'——I tell you plainly it was; but from a different reason than you wot of——

——It was the year next him——which being the year of our Lord seventeen hundred and twelve,[6] when the duke of Ormond was playing the devil in Flanders——the corporal took it, and set out with it afresh on his expedition to Bohemia.

The story of the king of Bohemia and
his seven castles, continued.

IN the year of our Lord one thousand seven hundred and twelve, there was, an' please your honour——

——To tell thee truly, Trim, quoth my uncle Toby, any other date would have pleased me much better, not only on account of the sad stain upon our history that year, in marching off our troops, and refusing to cover the siege of Quesnoi, though Fagel was carrying on the works with such incredible vigour—but likewise on the score, Trim, of thy own story; because if there are—and which, from what thou hast dropt, I partly suspect to be the fact—if there are giants in it——

There is but one, an' please your honour——

——'Tis as bad as twenty, replied my uncle Toby——thou should'st have carried him back some seven or eight hundred years out of harm's way, both of criticks and other people; and therefore I would advise thee, if ever thou tellest it again——

——If I live, an' please your honour, but once to get through it, I will never tell it again, quoth Trim, either to man, woman, or child——Poo—poo! said my uncle Toby—but with accents of such sweet encouragement did he utter it, that the corporal went on with his story with more alacrity than ever.

The story of the king of Bohemia and his seven castles, continued.

THERE was, an' please your honour, said the corporal, raising his voice and rubbing the palms of his two hands cheerily together as he begun, a certain king of Bohemia——

——Leave out the date entirely, Trim, quoth my uncle Toby, leaning forwards, and laying his hand gently upon the corporal's shoulder to temper the interruption—leave it out entirely, Trim; a story passes very well without these niceties, unless one is pretty sure of 'em——Sure of 'em! said the corporal, shaking his head——

Right; answered my uncle Toby, it is not easy, Trim, for one, bred up as thou and I have been to arms, who seldom looks further forward than to the end of his musket, or backwards beyond his knapsack, to know much about this matter——God bless your honour! said the corporal, won by the *manner* of my uncle Toby's reasoning, as much as by the reasoning itself, he has something else to do; if not on action, or a march, or upon duty in his garrison—he has his firelock, an' please your honour, to furbish—his accoutrements to take care of—his regimentals to mend—himself to shave and keep clean, so as to appear always like what he is upon the parade; what business, added the corporal triumphantly, has a soldier, an' please your honour, to know any thing at all of *geography?*

——Thou would'st have said *chronology*, Trim, said my uncle Toby; for as for geography, 'tis of absolute use to him; he must be acquainted intimately with every country and its boundaries where his profession carries him; he should know every town and city, and village and hamlet, with the canals, the roads, and hollow ways which lead up to them; there is not a river or a rivulet he passes, Trim, but he should be able at first sight to tell thee what is its name—in what mountains it takes its rise—what is its course—how far it is navigable—where fordable—where not; he should know the fertility of every valley, as well as the hind who ploughs it; and be able to describe, or, if it is required, to give thee an exact map of all the plains and defiles, the forts, the acclivities, the woods

and morasses, thro' and by which his army is to march; he should know
their produce, their plants, their minerals, their waters, their animals, their
seasons, their climates, their heats and cold, their inhabitants, their customs,
their language, their policy, and even their religion.

Is it else to be conceived, corporal, continued my uncle Toby, rising
up in his sentry-box, as he began to warm in this part of his discourse—
how Marlborough could have marched[7] his army from the banks of the
Maes to Belburg; from Belburg to Kerpenord—(here the corporal could
sit no longer) from Kerpenord, Trim, to Kalsaken; from Kalsaken to
Newdorf; from Newdorf to Landenbourg; from Landenbourg to Mildenheim; from Mildenheim to Elchingen; from Elchingen to Gingen; from
Gingen to Balmerchoffen; from Balmerchoffen to Skellenburg, where he
broke in upon the enemy's works; forced his passage over the *Danube*;
cross'd the *Lech*—pushed on his troops into the heart of the empire,
marching at the head of them through Friburg, Hokenwert, and Schonevelt,
to the plains of Blenheim and Hochstet?——Great as he was, corporal,
he could not have advanced a step, or made one single day's march without
the aids of *Geography*——As for *Chronology*, I own, Trim, continued my
uncle Toby, sitting down again coolly in his sentry-box, that of all others,
it seems a science which the soldier might best spare, was it not for the
lights which that science must one day give him, in determining the
invention of powder;[8] the furious execution of which, renversing every
thing like thunder before it, has become a new æra to us of military
improvements, changing so totally the nature of attacks and defences both
by sea and land, and awakening so much art and skill in doing it, that the
world cannot be too exact in ascertaining the precise time of its discovery,
or too inquisitive in knowing what great man was the discoverer, and what
occasions gave birth to it.

I am far from controverting, continued my uncle Toby, what historians
agree in, that in the year of our Lord 1380, under the reign of Wencelaus,
son of Charles the fourth——a certain priest, whose name was Schwartz,
shew'd the use of powder to the Venetians, in their wars against the
Genoese; but 'tis certain he was not the first; because if we are to believe
Don Pedro the bishop of Leon—How came priests and bishops, an' please
your honour, to trouble their heads so much about gun-powder? God
knows, said my uncle Toby——his providence brings good out of every
thing—and he avers, in his chronicle of King Alphonsus, who reduced
Toledo, That in the year 1343, which was full thirty seven years before

that time, the secret of powder was well known, and employed with success, both by Moors and Christians, not only in their sea-combats, at that period, but in many of their most memorable sieges in Spain and Barbary—And all the world knows, that Friar Bacon had wrote expressly about it, and had generously given the world a receipt to make it by, above a hundred and fifty years before even[9] Schwartz was born—And that the Chinese,[10] added my uncle Toby, embarass us, and all accounts of it still more, by boasting of the invention some hundreds of years even before him——

——They are a pack of liars, I believe, cried Trim——

——They are some how or other deceived, said my uncle Toby, in this matter, as is plain to me from the present miserable state of military architecture amongst them; which consists of nothing more than a fossè with a brick wall without flanks—and for what they give us as a bastion at each angle of it, 'tis so barbarously constructed, that it looks for all the world————Like one of my seven castles, an' please your honour, quoth Trim.

My uncle Toby, tho' in the utmost distress for a comparison, most courteously refused Trim's offer—till Trim telling him, he had half a dozen more in Bohemia, which he knew not how to get off his hands—— my uncle Toby was so touch'd with the pleasantry of heart of the corporal ——that he discontinued his dissertation upon gunpowder——and begged the corporal forthwith to go on with his story of the King of Bohemia and his seven castles.

The story of the King of Bohemia and
his seven castles, continued.

THIS *unfortunate* King of Bohemia, said Trim——Was he unfortunate then? cried my uncle Toby, for he had been so wrapt up in his dissertation upon gun-powder and other military affairs, that tho' he had desired the corporal to go on, yet the many interruptions he had given, dwelt not so strong upon his fancy, as to account for the epithet——Was he *unfortunate* then, Trim? said my uncle Toby, pathetically——The corporal, wishing first the *word* and all its synonimas at the devil, forthwith began to run back in his mind, the principal events in the King of Bohemia's story; from every one of which, it appearing that he was the most fortunate man that ever existed in the world——it put the corporal to a stand: for not caring to retract his epithet——and less, to explain it——and least of all, to twist his tale (like men of lore) to serve a system——he looked up in my uncle Toby's face for assistance——but seeing it was the very thing, my uncle Toby sat in expectation of himself——after a hum and a haw, he went on——

The King of Bohemia, an' please your honour, replied the corporal, was *unfortunate*, as thus——That taking great pleasure and delight in navigation and all sort of sea-affairs——and there *happening* throughout the whole kingdom of Bohemia, to be no sea-port town whatever[11]——

How the duce should there—Trim? cried my uncle Toby; for Bohemia being totally inland, it could have happen'd no otherwise——It might; said Trim, if it had pleased God——

My uncle Toby never spoke of the being and natural attributes of God, but with diffidence and hesitation——

——I believe not, replied my uncle Toby, after some pause—— for being inland, as I said, and having Silesia and Moravia to the east; Lusatia and Upper Saxony to the north; Franconia to the west; and Bavaria to the south: Bohemia could not have been propell'd to the sea, without ceasing to be Bohemia——nor could the sea, on the other hand, have come up to Bohemia, without overflowing a great part of Germany, and destroying millions of unfortunate inhabitants who could make no defence against it——Scandalous! cried Trim—Which would bespeak, added my uncle Toby, mildly, such a want of compassion in him who is the father of it——that, I think, Trim——the thing could have happen'd no way.

The corporal made the bow of unfeigned conviction; and went on.

Now the King of Bohemia with his queen and courtiers *happening* one fine summer's evening to walk out——Aye! there the word *happening* is right, Trim, cried my uncle Toby; for the King of Bohemia and his queen might have walk'd out, or let it alone;——'twas a matter of contingency, which might happen, or not, just as chance ordered it.

King William was of an opinion, an' please your honour, quoth Trim, that every thing was predestined for us in this world; insomuch, that he would often say to his soldiers, that "every ball had it's billet." He was a great man, said my uncle Toby——And I believe, continued Trim, to this day, that the shot which disabled me at the battle of Landen, was pointed at my knee for no other purpose, but to take me out of his service, and place me in your honour's, where I should be taken so much better care of in my old age——It shall never, Trim, be construed otherwise, said my uncle Toby.

The heart, both of the master and the man, were alike subject to sudden overflowings;——a short silence ensued.

Besides, said the corporal, resuming the discourse—but in a gayer accent——if it had not been for that single shot, I had never, an' please your honour, been in love——

So, thou wast once in love, Trim! said my uncle Toby, smiling——

Souse! replied the corporal—over head and ears! an' please your honour. Prithee when? where?—and how came it to pass?——I never heard one word of it before; quoth my uncle Toby:——I dare say, answered Trim, that every drummer and serjeant's son in the regiment knew of it——Its high time I should——said my uncle Toby.

Your honour remembers with concern, said the corporal, the total rout and confusion of our camp and army at the affair of Landen;[12] every one was left to shift for himself; and if it had not been for the regiments of Wyndham, Lumley, and Galway, which covered the retreat over the bridge of Neerspeeken, the king himself could scarce have gain'd it—— he was press'd hard, as your honour knows, on every side of him——

Gallant mortal! cried my uncle Toby, caught up with enthusiasm— this moment, now that all is lost, I see him galloping across me, corporal, to the left, to bring up the remains of the English horse along with him to support the right, and tear the laurel from Luxembourg's brows, if yet 'tis possible——I see him with the knot of his scarfe just shot off, infusing fresh spirits into poor Galway's regiment—riding along the line—then wheeling about, and charging Conti at the head of it——Brave! brave by heaven! cried my uncle Toby—he deserves a crown——As richly, as a thief a halter;[13] shouted Trim.

My uncle Toby knew the corporal's loyalty;—otherwise the comparison was not at all to his mind——it did not altogether strike the corporal's fancy when he had made it——but it could not be recall'd——so he had nothing to do, but proceed.

As the number of wounded was prodigious, and no one had time to think of any thing, but his own safety—Though Talmash, said my uncle Toby, brought off the foot with great prudence——But I was left upon the field, said the corporal. Thou wast so; poor fellow! replied my uncle Toby——So that it was noon the next day, continued the corporal, before

I was exchanged, and put into a cart with thirteen or fourteen more, in order to be convey'd to our hospital.

There is no part of the body, an' please your honour, where a wound occasions more intolerable anguish than upon the knee——

Except the groin; said my uncle Toby. An' please your honour, replied the corporal, the knee, in my opinion, must certainly be the most acute, there being so many tendons and what-d'ye-call-'ems all about it.

It is for that reason, quoth my uncle Toby, that the groin is infinitely more sensible——there being not only as many tendons and what-d'ye-call-'ems (for I know their names as little as thou do'st)——about it—— but moreover * * *——

Mrs. Wadman, who had been all the time in her arbour—instantly stopp'd her breath—unpinn'd her mob[14] at the chin, and stood up upon one leg——

The dispute was maintained with amicable and equal force betwixt my uncle Toby and Trim for some time; till Trim at length recollecting that he had often cried at his master's sufferings, but never shed a tear at his own—was for giving up the point, which my uncle Toby would not allow ——'Tis a proof of nothing, Trim, said he, but the generosity of thy temper——

So that whether the pain of a wound in the groin (cæteris paribus)[15] is greater than the pain of a wound in the knee——or

Whether the pain of a wound in the knee is not greater than the pain of a wound in the groin——are points which to this day remain unsettled.

CHAP. XX.

THE anguish of my knee, continued the corporal, was excessive in itself; and the uneasiness of the cart, with the roughness of the roads which were terribly cut up—making bad still worse—every step was death to me: so that with the loss of blood, and the want of care-taking of me, and a fever I felt coming on besides——(Poor soul! said my uncle Toby) all together, an' please your honour, was more than I could sustain.

I was telling my sufferings to a young woman at a peasant's house, where our cart, which was the last of the line, had halted; they had help'd me in, and the young woman had taken a cordial out of her pocket and dropp'd it upon some sugar, and seeing it had cheer'd me, she had given it me a second and a third time——So I was telling her, an' please your honour, the anguish I was in, and was saying it was so intolerable to me, that I had much rather lie down upon the bed, turning my face towards one which was in the corner of the room—and die, than go on——when, upon her attempting to lead me to it, I fainted away in her arms. She was a good soul! as your honour, said the corporal, wiping his eyes, will hear.

I thought *love* had been a joyous thing, quoth my uncle Toby.

'Tis the most serious thing, an' please your honour (sometimes) that is in the world.

By the persuasion of the young woman, continued the corporal, the cart with the wounded men set off without me: she had assured them I should expire immediately if I was put into the cart. So when I came to myself ——I found myself in a still quiet cottage, with no one but the young woman, and the peasant and his wife. I was laid across the bed in the corner of the room, with my wounded leg upon a chair, and the young woman beside me, holding the corner of her handkerchief dipp'd in vinegar to my nose with one hand, and rubbing my temples with the other.

I took her at first for the daughter of the peasant (for it was no inn)— so had offer'd her a little purse with eighteen florins, which my poor brother Tom (here Trim wip'd his eyes) had sent me as a token, by a recruit, just before he set out for Lisbon——

——I never told your honour that piteous story yet——here Trim wiped his eyes a third time.

The young woman call'd the old man and his wife into the room, to shew them the money, in order to gain me credit for a bed and what little necessaries I should want, till I should be in a condition to be got to the hospital——Come then! said she, tying up the little purse—I'll be your banker—but as that office alone will not keep me employ'd, I'll be your nurse too.

I thought by her manner of speaking this, as well as by her dress, which I then began to consider more attentively—that the young woman could not be the daughter of the peasant.

She was in black down to her toes, with her hair conceal'd under a cambrick border, laid close to her forehead: she was one of those kind of nuns, an' please your honour, of which, your honour knows, there are a good many in Flanders which they let go loose——By thy description, Trim, said my uncle Toby, I dare say she was a young Beguine,[1] of which there are none to be found any where but in the Spanish Netherlands—except at Amsterdam——they differ from nuns in this, that they can quit their cloister if they choose to marry; they visit and take care of the sick by profession——I had rather, for my own part, they did it out of good-nature. ——She often told me, quoth Trim, she did it for the love of Christ—I did not like it.——I believe, Trim, we are both wrong, said my uncle Toby—we'll ask Mr. Yorick about it to-night at my brother Shandy's——so put me in mind; added my uncle Toby.

The young Beguine, continued the corporal, had scarce given herself time to tell me "she would be my nurse," when she hastily turned about to begin the office of one, and prepare something for me——and in a short time—though I thought it a long one—she came back with flannels, &c. &c. and having fomented my knee soundly for a couple of hours, &c. and made me a thin basin of gruel for my supper—she wish'd me rest, and promised to be with me early in the morning.——She wish'd me, an' please your honour, what was not to be had. My fever ran very high that night [2]—her figure made sad disturbance within me—I was every moment cutting the world in two—to give her half of it—and every moment was I crying, That I had nothing but a knapsack and eighteen florins to share with her——The whole night long was the fair Beguine, like an angel, close by my bedside, holding back my curtain and offering me cordials—and I was only awakened from my dream by her coming there at the hour promised, and giving them in reality. In truth, she was scarce ever from me, and so accustomed was I to receive life from her hands, that my heart sickened, and I lost colour when she left the room: and yet, continued the corporal, (making one of the strangest reflections upon it in the world)——

——"*It was not love*"——for during the three weeks she was almost constantly with me, fomenting my knee with her hand, night and day—I can honestly say, an' please your honour—that * * * * * * * * * * * * * once.

That was very odd, Trim, quoth my uncle Toby——

I think so too—said Mrs. Wadman.

It never did, said the corporal.

CHAP. XXI.

——But 'tis no marvel, continued the corporal—seeing my uncle Toby musing upon it—for Love, an' please your honour, is exactly like war, in this; that a soldier, though he has escaped three weeks compleat o'Saturday-night,—may nevertheless be shot through his heart on Sunday morning—— *It happened so here*, an' please your honour, with this difference only—that it was on Sunday in the afternoon, when I fell in love all at once with a sisserara[1]——it burst upon me, an' please your honour, like a bomb——scarce giving me time to say, "God bless me."

I thought, Trim, said my uncle Toby, a man never fell in love so very suddenly.

Yes, an' please your honour, if he is in the way of it——replied Trim.

I prithee, quoth my uncle Toby, inform me how this matter happened.

——With all pleasure, said the corporal, making a bow.

CHAP. XXII.

I Had escaped, continued the corporal, all that time from falling in love, and had gone on to the end of the chapter, had it not been predestined otherwise——there is no resisting our fate.

It was on a Sunday, in the afternoon, as I told your honour——

The old man and his wife had walked out——

Every thing was still and hush as midnight about the house——

There was not so much as a duck or a duckling about the yard——

——When the fair Beguine came in to see me.

My wound was then in a fair way of doing well——the inflammation had been gone off for some time, but it was succeeded with an itching both above and below my knee, so insufferable, that I had not shut my eyes the whole night for it.

Let me see it, said she, kneeling down upon the ground parallel to my knee, and laying her hand upon the part below it——It only wants rubbing a little, said the Beguine; so covering it with the bed cloaths, she began with the forefinger of her right-hand to rub under my knee, guiding her fore-finger backwards and forwards by the edge of the flannel which kept on the dressing.

In five or six minutes I felt slightly the end of her second finger—— and presently it was laid flat with the other, and she continued rubbing in that way round and round for a good while; it then came into my head, that I should fall in love—I blush'd when I saw how white a hand she had—I shall never, an' please your honour, behold another hand so white whilst I live——

——Not in that place: said my uncle Toby——

Though it was the most serious despair[1] in nature to the corporal—he could not forbear smiling.

The young Beguine, continued the corporal, perceiving it was of great service to me—from rubbing, for some time, with two fingers—proceeded to rub at length, with three—till by little and little she brought down the fourth, and then rubb'd with her whole hand: I will never say another word, an' please your honour, upon hands again——but it was softer than satin——

——Prithee, Trim, commend it as much as thou wilt, said my uncle Toby; I shall hear thy story with the more delight——The corporal thank'd his master most unfeignedly; but having nothing to say upon the Beguine's hand, but the same over again——he proceeded to the effects of it.

The fair Beguine, said the corporal, continued rubbing with her whole hand under my knee—till I fear'd her zeal would weary her——"I would do a thousand times more," said she, "for the love of Christ"——In saying which she pass'd her hand across the flannel, to the part above my knee, which I had equally complained of, and rubb'd it also.

I perceived, then, I was beginning to be in love——

As she continued rub-rub-rubbing—I felt it spread from under her hand, an' please your honour, to every part of my frame——

The more she rubb'd, and the longer strokes she took——the more the fire kindled in my veins——till at length, by two or three strokes longer than the rest——my passion rose to the highest pitch——I seiz'd her hand——

——And then, thou clapped'st it to thy lips, Trim, said my uncle Toby——and madest a speech.

Whether the corporal's amour terminated precisely in the way my uncle Toby described it, is not material; it is enough that it contain'd in it the essence of all the love-romances which ever have been wrote since the beginning of the world.

CHAP. XXIII.

A S soon as the corporal had finished the story of his amour—or rather my uncle Toby for him—Mrs. Wadman silently sallied forth from her arbour, replaced the pin in her mob, pass'd the wicker gate, and advanced slowly towards my uncle Toby's sentry-box: the disposition which Trim had made in my uncle Toby's mind, was too favourable a crisis to be let slipp'd——

——The attack was determin'd upon: it was facilitated still more by my uncle Toby's having ordered the corporal to wheel off the pioneer's shovel, the spade, the pick-axe, the picquets, and other military stores which lay scatter'd upon the ground where Dunkirk stood—The corporal had march'd—the field was clear.

Now consider, sir, what nonsense it is, either in fighting, or writing, or any thing else (whether in rhyme to it, or not) which a man has occasion to do—to act by plan: for if ever Plan, independent of all circumstances, deserved registering in letters of gold (I mean in the archives of Gotham)[1]—it was certainly the PLAN of Mrs. Wadman's attack of my uncle Toby in his sentry-box, BY PLAN——Now the Plan hanging up in it at this juncture, being the Plan of Dunkirk—and the tale of Dunkirk a tale of relaxation, it opposed every impression she could make: and besides, could she have gone upon it—the manœuvre of fingers and hands in the attack of the sentry-box, was so outdone by that of the fair Beguine's, in Trim's story—that just then, that particular attack, however successful before—became the most heartless attack that could be made——

O! let woman alone for this. Mrs. Wadman had scarce open'd the wicker-gate, when her genius sported with the change of circumstances.

——She formed a new attack in a moment.

CHAP. XXIV.

——I am half distracted, captain Shandy, said Mrs. Wadman, holding up her cambrick handkerchief to her left eye, as she approach'd the door of my uncle Toby's sentry-box——a mote——or sand——or something ——I know not what, has got into this eye of mine——do look into it— it is not in the white—

In saying which, Mrs. Wadman edged herself close in beside my uncle Toby, and squeezing herself down upon the corner of his bench, she gave him an opportunity of doing it without rising up———Do look into it— said she.

Honest soul! thou didst look into it with as much innocency of heart, as ever child look'd into a raree-shew-box;[1] and 'twere as much a sin to have hurt thee.

——If a man will be peeping of his own accord into things of that nature——I've nothing to say to it——

My uncle Toby never did: and I will answer for him, that he would have sat quietly upon a sopha from June to January, (which, you know, takes in both the hot and cold months) with an eye as fine as the Thracian[*] Rodope's[2] besides him, without being able to tell, whether it was a black or a blue one.

The difficulty was to get my uncle Toby, to look at one, at all.

'Tis surmounted. And

I see him yonder with his pipe pendulous in his hand, and the ashes falling out of it—looking—and looking—then rubbing his eyes——and looking again, with twice the good nature that ever Gallileo look'd for a spot in the sun.[3]

——In vain! for by all the powers which animate the organ——Widow Wadman's left eye shines this moment as lucid as her right——there is neither mote, or sand, or dust, or chaff, or speck, or particle of opake matter floating in it——there is nothing, my dear paternal uncle! but one lambent delicious fire, furtively shooting out from every part of it, in all directions, into thine——

[*] Rodope Thracia tam inevitabili fascino instructa, tam exacte oculis intuens attraxit, ut si in illam quis incidisset, fieri non posset, quin caperetur.——I know not who.

———If thou lookest, uncle Toby, in search of this mote one moment longer——thou art undone.

CHAP. XXV.

A N eye is for all the world exactly like a cannon, in this respect; That it is not so much the eye or the cannon, in themselves, as it is the carriage of the eye——and the carriage of the cannon, by which both the one and the other are enabled to do so much execution. I don't think the comparison a bad one: However, as 'tis made and placed at the head of the chapter, as much for use as ornament, all I desire in return, is, that whenever I speak of Mrs. Wadman's eyes (except once in the next period) that you keep it in your fancy.

I protest, Madam, said my uncle Toby, I can see nothing whatever in your eye.

It is not in the white; said Mrs. Wadman: my uncle Toby look'd with might and main into the pupil——

Now of all the eyes,[1] which ever were created——from your own, Madam, up to those of Venus herself, which certainly were as venereal a pair of eyes as ever stood in a head——there never was an eye of them all, so fitted to rob my uncle Toby of his repose, as the very eye, at which he was looking——it was not, Madam, a rolling eye——a romping or a wanton one—nor was it an eye sparkling—petulant or imperious—of high claims and terrifying exactions, which would have curdled at once that milk of human nature, of which my uncle Toby was made up—— but 'twas an eye full of gentle salutations——and soft responses—— speaking——not like the trumpet stop of some ill-made organ, in which many an eye I talk to, holds coarse converse——but whispering soft—— like the last low accents of an expiring saint——"How can you live comfortless, captain Shandy, and alone, without a bosom to lean your head on——or trust your cares to?"

It was an eye——

But I shall be in love with it myself, if I say another word about it.

——It did my uncle Toby's business.

CHAP. XXVI.

THERE is nothing shews the characters of my father and my uncle Toby, in a more entertaining light, than their different manner of deportment, under the same accident——for I call not love a misfortune, from a persuasion, that a man's heart is ever the better for it[1]——Great God! what must my uncle Toby's have been, when 'twas all benignity without it.

My father, as appears from many of his papers, was very subject to this passion, before he married——but from a little subacid kind of drollish impatience in his nature, whenever it befell him, he would never submit to it like a christian; but would pish, and huff, and bounce, and kick, and play the Devil, and write the bitterest Philippicks against the eye that ever man wrote——there is one in verse upon some body's eye or other, that for two or three nights together, had put him by his rest; which in his first transport of resentment against it, he begins thus:

> "A Devil 'tis——and mischief such doth work
> As never yet did Pagan, Jew, or Turk."[*2]

In short during the whole paroxism, my father was all abuse and foul language, approaching rather towards malediction——only he did not do it with as much method as Ernulphus——he was too impetuous; nor with Ernulphus's policy——for tho' my father, with the most intolerant spirit, would curse both this and that, and every thing under heaven, which was either aiding or abetting to his love——yet never concluded his chapter of curses upon it, without cursing himself in at the bargain, as one of the most egregious fools and coxcombs, he would say, that ever was let loose in the world.

My uncle Toby, on the contrary, took it like a lamb——sat still and let the poison work in his veins without resistance——in the sharpest exacerbations of his wound (like that on his groin) he never dropt one fretful or discontented word——he blamed neither heaven nor earth ——or thought or spoke an injurious thing of any body, or any part of it;

---

[*]This will be printed with my father's life of Socrates, &c. &c.[3]

he sat solitary and pensive with his pipe——looking at his lame leg——
then whiffing out a sentimental heigh ho! which mixing with the smoak,
incommoded no one mortal.

He took it like a lamb——I say.

In truth he had mistook it at first; for having taken a ride with my father,
that very morning, to save if possible a beautiful wood, which the dean
and chapter were hewing down to give to the poor*;[4] which said wood
being in full view of my uncle Toby's house, and of singular service to
him in his description of the battle of Wynnendale[5]——by trotting on too
hastily to save it——upon an uneasy saddle——worse horse, &c. &c. . .
it had so happened, that the serous part of the blood had got betwixt the
two skins, in the nethermost part of my uncle Toby——the first shootings
of which (as my uncle Toby had no experience of love) he had taken for
a part of the passion—till the blister breaking in the one case—and the
other remaining——my uncle Toby was presently convinced, that his
wound was not a skin-deep-wound——but that it had gone to his heart.

CHAP. XXVII.

THE world is ashamed of being virtuous——My uncle Toby knew
little of the world; and therefore when he felt he was in love with
widow Wadman, he had no conception that the thing was any more to be
made a mystery of, than if Mrs. Wadman, had given him a cut with a gap'd
knife[1] across his finger: Had it been otherwise——yet as he ever look'd
upon Trim as a humble friend; and saw fresh reasons every day of his life,
to treat him as such——it would have made no variation in the manner
in which he informed him of the affair.

"I am in love, corporal!" quoth my uncle Toby.

---

* Mr. Shandy must mean the poor *in spirit*;[6] inasmuch as they divided the money amongst
themselves.

CHAP. XXVIII.

IN love!——said the corporal—your honour was very well the day before yesterday, when I was telling your honour the story of the King of Bohemia—Bohemia! said my uncle Toby ————musing a long time ——— What became of that story, Trim?

—We lost it, an' please your honour, somehow betwixt us—but your honour was as free from love then, as I am——'twas, just whilst thou went'st off with the wheel-barrow—with Mrs. Wadman, quoth my uncle Toby——She has left a ball here—added my uncle Toby—pointing to his breast——

——She can no more, an' please your honour, stand a siege, than she can fly—cried the corporal——

——But as we are neighbours, Trim,—the best way I think is to let her know it civilly first—quoth my uncle Toby.

Now if I might presume, said the corporal, to differ from your honour——

—Why else, do I talk to thee Trim: said my uncle Toby, mildly——

—Then I would begin, an' please your honour, with making a good thundering attack upon her, in return—and telling her civilly afterwards—for if she knows any thing of your honour's being in love, before hand——L—d help her!—she knows no more at present of it, Trim, said my uncle Toby—than the child unborn——

Precious souls!——

Mrs. Wadman had told it with all its circumstances, to Mrs. Bridget twenty-four hours before; and was at that very moment sitting in council with her, touching some slight misgivings with regard to the issue of the affair, which the Devil, who never lies dead in a ditch, had put into her head—before he would allow half time, to get quietly through her *te Deum*[1]——

I am terribly afraid, said widow Wadman, in case I should marry him, Bridget—that the poor captain will not enjoy his health, with the monstrous wound upon his groin——

It may not, Madam, be so very large, replied Bridget, as you think—— and I believe besides, added she—that 'tis dried up——

———I could like to know—merely for his sake, said Mrs. Wadman———

—We'll know the long and the broad of it, in ten days—answered Mrs. Bridget, for whilst the captain is paying his addresses to you—I'm confident Mr. Trim will be for making love to me—and I'll let him as much as he will—added Bridget—to get it all out of him———

The measures were taken at once———and my uncle Toby and the corporal went on with theirs.

Now, quoth the corporal, setting his left hand a kimbo, and giving such a flourish with his right, as just promised success—and no more———if your honour will give me leave to lay down the plan of this attack———

———Thou wilt please me by it, Trim, said my uncle Toby, exceedingly—and as I foresee thou must act in it as my *aid de camp*, here's a crown, corporal, to begin with, to steep [2] thy commission.

Then, an' please your honour, said the corporal (making a bow first for his commission)—we will begin with getting your honour's laced cloaths out of the great campaign-trunk, to be well-air'd, and have the blue and gold taken up at the sleeves—and I'll put your white ramallie-wig fresh into pipes [3]—and send for a taylor, to have your honour's thin scarlet breeches turn'd———

—I had better take the red plush ones, quoth my uncle Toby———They will be too clumsy—said the corporal.

CHAP. XXIX.

———Thou wilt get a brush and a little chalk to my sword———'Twill be only in your honour's way, replied Trim.

CHAP. XXX.

——But your honour's two razors shall be new set—and I will get my Montero cap furbish'd up, and put on poor lieutenant Le Fever's regimental coat, which your honour gave me to wear for his sake—and as soon as your honour is clean shaved—and has got your clean shirt on, with your blue and gold, or your fine scarlet——sometimes one and sometimes t'other—and every thing is ready for the attack—we'll march up boldly, as if 'twas to the face of a bastion; and whilst your honour engages Mrs. Wadman in the parlour, to the right——I'll attack Mrs. Bridget in the kitchen, to the left; and having seiz'd that pass, I'll answer for it, said the corporal, snapping his fingers over his head—that the day is our own.

I wish I may but manage it right; said my uncle Toby—but I declare, corporal I had rather march up to the very edge of a trench——

—A woman is quite a different thing—said the corporal.

—I suppose so, quoth my uncle Toby.

CHAP. XXXI.

I F any thing in this world, which my father said, could have provoked my uncle Toby, during the time he was in love, it was the perverse use my father was always making of an expression of Hilarion the hermit;[1] who, in speaking of his abstinence, his watchings, flagellations, and other instrumental parts of his religion—would say—tho' with more face-tiousness than became an hermit—"That they were the means he used, to make his *ass* (meaning his body) leave off kicking."

It pleased my father well; it was not only a laconick way of expressing ——but of libelling, at the same time, the desires and appetites of the lower part of us; so that for many years of my father's life, 'twas his constant mode of expression—he never used the word *passions* once—but *ass* always instead of them——So that he might be said truly, to have been upon the bones, or the back of his own ass, or else of some other man's, during all that time.

I must here observe to you, the difference betwixt

My father's ass

and my hobby-horse—in order to keep characters as separate as may be, in our fancies as we go along.

For my hobby-horse, if you recollect a little, is no way a vicious beast; he has scarce one hair or lineament of the ass about him——'Tis the sporting little filly-folly which carries you out for the present hour—a maggot, a butterfly, a picture, a fiddle-stick—an uncle Toby's siege—or an *any thing*, which a man makes a shift to get a stride on, to canter it away from the cares and solicites of life—'Tis as useful a beast as is in the whole creation—nor do I really see how the world could do without it——

——But for my father's ass——oh! mount him—mount him—mount him—(that's three times, is it not?)—mount him not:—'tis a beast concupiscent—and foul befall the man, who does not hinder him from kicking.

CHAP. XXXII.

WELL! dear brother Toby, said my father, upon his first seeing him after he fell in love—and how goes it with your ASSE?

Now my uncle Toby thinking more of the *part* where he had had the blister, than of Hilarion's metaphor—and our preconceptions having (you know) as great a power over the sounds of words as the shapes of things, he had imagined, that my father, who was not very ceremonious in his choice of words, had enquired after the part by its proper name; so notwithstanding my mother, doctor Slop, and Mr. Yorick, were sitting in the parlour, he thought it rather civil to conform to the term my father had made use of than not. When a man is hemm'd in by two indecorums, and must commit one of 'em—I always observe—let him choose which he will, the world will blame him—so I should not be astonished if it blames my uncle Toby.

My A—e, quoth my uncle Toby, is much better—brother Shandy ——My father had formed great expectations from his Asse in this onset; and would have brought him on again; but doctor Slop setting up an intemperate laugh—and my mother crying out L— bless us!—it drove my father's Asse off the field—and the laugh then becoming general— there was no bringing him back to the charge, for some time——

And so the discourse went on without him.

Every body, said my mother, says you are in love, brother Toby—and we hope it is true.

I am as much in love, sister, I believe, replied my uncle Toby, as any man usually is——Humph! said my father——and when did you know it? quoth my mother——

——When the blister broke; replied my uncle Toby.

My uncle Toby's reply put my father into good temper—so he charged o'foot.

CHAP. XXXIII.

As the antients agree, brother Toby, said my father, that there are two different and distinct kinds of *love*, according to the different parts which are affected by it—the Brain or Liver——I think when a man is in love, it behoves him a little to consider which of the two he is fallen into.

What signifies it, brother Shandy, replied my uncle Toby, which of the two it is, provided it will but make a man marry, and love his wife, and get a few children.

——A few children! cried my father, rising out of his chair, and looking full in my mother's face, as he forced his way betwixt her's and doctor Slop's—a few children! cried my father, repeating my uncle Toby's words as he walk'd to and fro'——

——Not, my dear brother Toby, cried my father, recovering himself all at once, and coming close up to the back of my uncle Toby's chair— not that I should be sorry had'st thou a score—on the contrary I should rejoice—and be as kind, Toby, to every one of them as a father—

My uncle Toby stole his hand unperceived behind his chair, to give my father's a squeeze——

——Nay, moreover, continued he, keeping hold of my uncle Toby's hand—so much do'st thou possess, my dear Toby, of the milk of human nature, and so little of its asperities—'tis piteous the world is not peopled by creatures which resemble thee; and was I an Asiatick monarch, added my father, heating himself with his new project—I would oblige thee, provided it would not impair thy strength—or dry up thy radical moisture too fast—or weaken thy memory or fancy, brother Toby, which these gymnicks[1] inordinately taken, are apt to do—else, dear Toby, I would procure thee the most beautiful women in my empire, and I would oblige thee, *nolens, volens,*[2] to beget for me one subject every *month*——

As my father pronounced the last word of the sentence—my mother took a pinch of snuff.

Now I would not, quoth my uncle Toby, get a child, *nolens, volens,* that is, whether I would or no, to please the greatest prince upon earth——

——And 'twould be cruel in me, brother Toby, to compell thee; said my father—but 'tis a case put to shew thee, that it is not thy begetting a child—in case thou should'st be able—but the system of Love and marriage thou goest upon, which I would set thee right in——

There is at least, said Yorick, a great deal of reason and plain sense in captain Shandy's opinion of love; and 'tis amongst the ill spent hours of my life which I have to answer for, that I have read so many flourishing poets and rhetoricians in my time, from whom I never could extract so much——

I wish, Yorick, said my father, you had read Plato;[3] for there you would have learnt that there are two LOVES—I know there were two RELIGIONS, replied Yorick, amongst the ancients——one—for the vulgar, and another for the learned; but I think ONE LOVE might have served both of them very well—

It could not; replied my father—and for the same reasons: for of these Loves, according to Ficinus's comment upon Velasius, the one is *rational*——

——the other is *natural*——

the first ancient——without mother——where Venus had nothing to do: the second, begotten of Jupiter and Dione—

——Pray brother, quoth my uncle Toby, what has a man who believes in God to do with this? My father could not stop to answer, for fear of breaking the thread of his discourse——

This latter, continued he, partakes wholly of the nature of Venus.

The first, which is the golden chain[4] let down from heaven, excites to love heroic, which comprehends in it, and excites to the desire of philosophy and truth——the second, excites to *desire*, simply——

——I think the procreation of children as beneficial to the world, said Yorick, as the finding out the longitude——

——To be sure, said my mother, *love* keeps peace in the world——

——In the *house*—my dear, I own——It replenishes the earth; said my mother——

But it keeps heaven empty—my dear; replied my father.

——'Tis Virginity, cried Slop, triumphantly, which fills paradise.[5]

Well push'd nun! quoth my father.

CHAP. XXXIV.

MY father had such a skirmishing, cutting kind of a slashing way with him in his disputations, thrusting and ripping, and giving every one a stroke to remember him by in his turn—that if there were twenty people in company—in less than half an hour he was sure to have every one of 'em against him.

What did not a little contribute to leave him thus without an ally, was, that if there was any one post more untenable than the rest, he would be sure to throw himself into it; and to do him justice, when he was once there, he would defend it so gallantly, that 'twould have been a concern, either to a brave man, or a good-natured one, to have seen him driven out.

Yorick, for this reason, though he would often attack him—yet could never bear to do it with all his force.

Doctor Slop's VIRGINITY, in the close of the last chapter, had got him for once on the right side of the rampart; and he was beginning to blow up all the convents in Christendom about Slop's ears, when corporal Trim came into the parlour to inform my uncle Toby, that his thin scarlet breeches, in which the attack was to be made upon Mrs. Wadman, would not do; for, that the taylor, in ripping them up, in order to turn them, had found they had been turn'd before——Then turn them again, brother, said my father rapidly, for there will be many a turning of 'em yet before all's done in the affair——They are as rotten as dirt, said the corporal ——Then by all means, said my father, bespeak a new pair, brother—— for though I know, continued my father, turning himself to the company, that widow Wadman has been deeply in love with my brother Toby for many years, and has used every art and circumvention of woman to outwit him into the same passion, yet now that she has caught him——her fever will be pass'd it's height——

——She has gain'd her point.

In this case, continued my father, which Plato, I am persuaded, never thought of——Love, you see, is not so much a SENTIMENT as a SITU-ATION, into which a man enters, as my brother Toby would do, into a *corps*——no matter whether he loves the service or no——being once in it—he acts as if he did; and takes every step to shew himself a man of prowesse.

The hypothesis, like the rest of my father's, was plausible enough, and my uncle Toby had but a single word to object to it—in which Trim stood ready to second him——but my father had not drawn his conclusion——

For this reason, continued my father (stating the case over again) notwithstanding all the world knows, that Mrs. Wadman *affects*[1] my brother Toby—and my brother Toby contrariwise *affects* Mrs. Wadman, and no obstacle in nature to forbid the music striking up this very night, yet will I answer for it, that this self-same tune will not be play'd this twelvemonth.

We have taken our measures badly, quoth my uncle Toby, looking up interrogatively in Trim's face.

I would lay my Montero cap, said Trim——Now Trim's Montero-cap, as I once told you, was his constant wager; and having furbish'd it up that very night, in order to go upon the attack—it made the odds look more considerable——I would lay, an' please your honour, my Montero-cap to a shilling—was it proper, continued Trim (making a bow) to offer a wager before your honours——

——There is nothing improper in it, said my father—'tis a mode of expression; for in saying thou would'st lay thy Montero-cap to a shilling— all thou meanest is this—that thou believest——

CHAPTER XXXIV

———Now, What do'st thou believe?

That Widow Wadman, an' please your worship, cannot hold it out ten days———

And whence, cried Slop, jeeringly, hast thou all this knowledge of woman, friend?

By falling in love with a popish clergy-woman; said Trim.

'Twas a Beguine, said my uncle Toby.

Doctor Slop was too much in wrath to listen to the distinction; and my father taking that very crisis to fall in helter-skelter upon the whole order of Nuns and Beguines, a set of silly, fusty baggages———Slop could not stand it———and my uncle Toby having some measures to take about his breeches—and Yorick about his fourth general division[2]—in order for their several attacks next day—the company broke up: and my father being left alone, and having half an hour upon his hands betwixt that and bed-time; he called for pen, ink, and paper, and wrote my uncle Toby the following letter of instructions.

My dear brother Toby,

WHAT I am going to say to thee, is upon the nature of women, and of love-making to them; and perhaps it is as well for thee—tho' not so well for me—that thou hast occasion for a letter of instructions upon that head, and that I am able to write it to thee.

Had it been the good pleasure of him who disposes of our lots—and thou no sufferer by the knowledge, I had been well content that thou should'st have dipp'd the pen this moment into the ink, instead of myself; but that not being the case————Mrs. Shandy being now close besides me, preparing for bed——I have thrown together without order, and just as they have come into my mind, such hints and documents as I deem may be of use to thee; intending, in this, to give thee a token of my love; not doubting, my dear Toby, of the manner in which it will be accepted.

In the first place, with regard to all which concerns religion in the affair ——though I perceive from a glow in my cheek, that I blush as I begin to speak to thee upon the subject, as well knowing, notwithstanding thy unaffected secrecy, how few of its offices thou neglectest—yet I would remind thee of one (during the continuance of thy courtship) in a particular manner, which I would not have omitted; and that is, never to go forth upon the enterprize, whether it be in the morning or the afternoon, without first recommending thyself to the protection of Almighty God, that he may defend thee from the evil one.

Shave the whole top of thy crown clean, once at least every four or five days, but oftner if convenient; lest in taking off thy wig before her, thro' absence of mind, she should be able to discover how much has been cut away by Time——how much by Trim.

——'Twere better to keep ideas of baldness[3] out of her fancy.

Always carry it in thy mind, and act upon it, as a sure maxim, Toby——

"*That women are timid:*" And 'tis well they are——else there would be no dealing with them.

Let not thy breeches be too tight, or hang too loose about thy thighs, like the trunk-hose of our ancestors.

——A just medium prevents all conclusions.

Whatever thou hast to say, be it more or less, forget not to utter it in a low soft tone of voice. Silence, and whatever approaches it, weaves dreams of midnight secrecy into the brain: For this cause, if thou canst help it, never throw down the tongs and poker.[4]

Avoid all kinds of pleasantry and facetiousness in thy discourse with her, and do whatever lies in thy power at the same time, to keep from her all books and writings which tend thereto: there are some devotional tracts, which if thou canst entice her to read over—it will be well: but suffer her not to look into Rabelais, or Scarron,[5] or Don Quixote——

——They are all books which excite laughter; and thou knowest, dear Toby, that there is no passion so serious, as lust.

Stick a pin in the bosom of thy shirt, before thou enterest her parlour.

And if thou art permitted to sit upon the same sopha with her, and she gives thee occasion to lay thy hand upon hers—beware of taking it—— thou can'st not lay thy hand on hers, but she will feel the temper of thine. Leave that and as many other things as thou canst, quite undetermined; by so doing, thou will have her curiosity on thy side; and if she is not conquer'd by that, and thy ASSE continues still kicking, which there is great reason to suppose——Thou must begin, with first losing a few ounces of blood below the ears, according to the practice of the ancient Scythians, who cured the most intemperate fits of the appetite by that means.

Avicenna, after this, is for having the part anointed with the syrrup of hellebore, using proper evacuations and purges——and I believe rightly. But thou must eat little or no goat's flesh, nor red deer——nor even foal's flesh by any means; and carefully abstain——that is, as much as thou canst, from peacocks, cranes, coots, didappers, and water-hens——

As for thy drink—I need not tell thee, it must be the infusion of VERVAIN, and the herb HANEA, of which Ælian relates such effects—but if thy stomach palls with it—discontinue it from time to time, taking cucumbers, melons, purslane, water-lillies, woodbine, and lettice, in the stead of them.[6]

There is nothing further for thee, which occurs to me at present——

—Unless the breaking out of a fresh war——So wishing every thing, dear Toby, for the best,

> I rest thy affectionate brother,
> WALTER SHANDY.

CHAP. XXXV.

WHILST my father was writing his letter of instructions, my uncle Toby and the corporal were busy in preparing every thing for the attack. As the turning of the thin scarlet breeches was laid aside (at least for the present) there was nothing which should put it off beyond the next morning; so accordingly it was resolv'd upon, for eleven o'clock.

Come, my dear, said my father to my mother—'twill be but like a brother and sister, if you and I take a walk down to my brother Toby's ——to countenance him in this attack of his.

My uncle Toby and the corporal had been accoutred both some time, when my father and mother enter'd, and the clock striking eleven, were that moment in motion to sally forth—but the account of this is worth more, than to be wove into the fag end of the eighth volume of such a work as this.——My father had no time but to put the letter of instructions into my uncle Toby's coat-pocket——and join with my mother in wishing his attack prosperous.

I could like, said my mother, to look through the key-hole out of *curiosity*
——Call it by it's right name, my dear, quoth my father——
And look through the key-hole as long as you will.

End of the Eighth Volume.

THE
LIFE
AND
OPINIONS
OF
TRISTRAM SHANDY,
GENTLEMAN.

Si quid urbaniuscule lusum a nobis, per Musas et Cha-
ritas et omnium poetarum Numina, Oro te, ne me
male copias.

VOL. IX.

LONDON:
Printed for T. BECKET and P. A. DEHONDT,
in the Strand. MDCCLXVII.

(Height of original type-page 103 mm.)

A
DEDICATION
TO A
GREAT MAN. [1]

HAVING, *a priori*, intended to dedicate *The Amours of my uncle Toby* to Mr. *** —— I see more reasons, *a posteriori*,[2] for doing it to Lord *******.

I should lament from my soul, if this exposed me to the jealousy of their Reverences; because, *a posteriori*, in Court-latin, signifies, the kissing hands for preferment—or any thing else—in order to get it.

My opinion of Lord ******* is neither better nor worse, than it was of Mr. ***. Honours, like impressions upon coin, may give an ideal and local value to a bit of base metal; but Gold and Silver will pass all the world over without any other recommendation than their own weight.

The same good will that made me think of offering up half an hour's amusement to Mr. *** when out of place—operates more forcibly at present, as half an hour's amusement will be more serviceable and refreshing after labour and sorrow, than after a philosophical repast.

Nothing is so perfectly *Amusement* as a total change of ideas; no ideas are so totally different as those of Ministers, and innocent Lovers: for which reason, when I come to talk of Statesmen and Patriots, and set such marks upon them as will prevent confusion and mistakes concerning them for the future—I propose to dedicate that Volume to some gentle Shepherd,[3]

> Whose Thoughts proud Science never taught to stray,
> Far as the Statesman's walk or Patriot-way;
> Yet *simple Nature* to his hopes had given
> Out of a cloud-capp'd head a humbler heaven;
> Some *untam'd* World in depth of woods embraced—
> Some happier Island in the watry-waste—
> And where admitted to that equal sky,
> His *faithful Dogs* should bear him company.[4]

In a word, by thus introducing an entire new set of objects to his Imagination, I shall unavoidably give a *Diversion* to his passionate and love-sick Contemplations. In the mean time,

I am

The AUTHOR.

LIFE and OPINIONS

TRISTRAM SHANDY, Gent.

CHAP. I.

I CALL all the powers of time and chance,[1] which severally check us in our careers in this world, to bear me witness, that I could never yet get fairly to my uncle Toby's amours, till this very moment, that my mother's *curiosity*, as she stated the affair,——or a different impulse in her, as my father would have it——wished her to take a peep at them through the key-hole.

"Call it, my dear, by its right name, quoth my father, and look through the key-hole as long as you will."

Nothing but the fermentation of that little subacid humour, which I have often spoken of, in my father's habit, could have vented such an insinuation——he was however frank and generous in his nature, and at all times open to conviction; so that he had scarce got to the last word of this ungracious retort, when his conscience smote him.

My mother was then conjugally swinging with her left arm twisted under his right, in such wise, that the inside of her hand rested upon the back of his—she raised her fingers, and let them fall—it could scarce be call'd a tap; or if it was a tap——'twould have puzzled a casuist to say, whether 'twas a tap of remonstrance, or a tap of confession: my father, who was all sensibilities from head to foot, class'd it right—Conscience redoubled her blow—he turn'd his face suddenly the other way, and my mother supposing his body was about to turn with it in order to move homewards, by a cross movement of her right leg, keeping her left as its centre, brought herself so far in front, that as he turned his head, he met her eye——Confusion again! he saw a thousand reasons to wipe out the reproach, and as many to reproach himself——a thin, blue, chill, pellucid chrystal with all its humours so at rest, the least mote [2] or speck of desire might have been seen at the bottom of it, had it existed——it did not——and how I happen to be so lewd myself, particularly a little before the vernal and autumnal equinoxes——Heaven above knows—— My mother——madam——was so at no time, either by nature, by institution, or example.

A temperate current of blood ran orderly through her veins in all months of the year, and in all critical moments both of the day and night alike; nor did she superinduce the least heat into her humours from the manual effervescencies of devotional tracts, which having little or no meaning in them, nature is oft times obliged to find one——And as for my father's example! 'twas so far from being either aiding or abetting thereunto, that 'twas the whole business of his life to keep all fancies of that kind out of her head——Nature had done her part, to have spared him this trouble; and what was not a little inconsistent, my father knew it——And here am I sitting, this 12th day of August, 1766,[3] in a purple jerkin and yellow pair of slippers, without either wig or cap on, a most tragicomical completion of his prediction, "That I should neither think, nor act like any other man's child, upon that very account."

The mistake of my father, was in attacking my mother's motive, instead of the act itself: for certainly key-holes were made for other purposes; and considering the act, as an act which interfered with a true proposition, and denied a key-hole to be what it was———it became a violation of nature; and was so far, you see, criminal.[4]

It is for this reason, an' please your Reverences, That key-holes are the occasions of more sin and wickedness, than all other holes in this world put together.

——which leads me to my uncle Toby's amours.

CHAP. II.[1]

THOUGH the Corporal had been as good as his word in putting my uncle Toby's great ramallie-wig into pipes, yet the time was too short to produce any great effects from it: it had lain many years squeezed up in the corner of his old campaign trunk; and as bad forms are not so easy to be got the better of, and the use of candle-ends not so well understood, it was not so pliable a business as one would have wished. The Corporal with cheary eye and both arms extended, had fallen back perpendicular from it a score times, to inspire it, if possible, with a better air——had SPLEEN given a look at it, 'twould have cost her ladyship a smile——it curl'd every where but where the Corporal would have it; and where a buckle[2] or two, in his opinion, would have done it honour, he could as soon have raised the dead.

Such it was——or rather such would it have seem'd upon any other brow; but the sweet look of goodness which sat upon my uncle Toby's, assimulated every thing around it so sovereignly to itself, and Nature had moreover wrote GENTLEMAN with so fair a hand in every line of his countenance, that even his tarnish'd gold-laced hat and huge cockade of flimsy taffeta became him; and though not worth a button in themselves, yet the moment my uncle Toby put them on, they became serious objects, and altogether seem'd to have been picked up by the hand of Science to set him off to advantage.

Nothing in this world could have co-operated more powerfully towards this, than my uncle Toby's blue and gold——*had not Quantity in some measure been necessary to Grace:*[3] in a period of fifteen or sixteen years since they had been made, by a total inactivity in my uncle Toby's life, for he seldom went further than the bowling-green—his blue and gold had become so miserably too strait for him, that it was with the utmost difficulty the Corporal was able to get him into them: the taking them up at the sleeves, was of no advantage.——They were laced however down the back, and at the seams of the sides, &c. in the mode of King William's reign; and to shorten all description, they shone so bright against the sun that morning, and had so metallick, and doughty an air with them, that had my uncle Toby thought of attacking in armour,[4] nothing could have so well imposed upon his imagination.

As for the thin scarlet breeches, they had been unripp'd by the taylor between the legs, and left at *sixes and sevens*——

——Yes, Madam,——but let us govern our fancies. It is enough they were held impracticable the night before, and as there was no alternative in my uncle Toby's wardrobe, he sallied forth in the red plush.[5]

The Corporal had array'd himself in poor Le Fevre's[6] regimental coat; and with his hair tuck'd up under his Montero cap, which he had furbish'd up for the occasion, march'd three paces distant from his master: a whiff of military pride had puff'd out his shirt at the wrist; and upon that in a black leather thong clipp'd into a tassel beyond the knot, hung the Corporal's stick ——My uncle Toby carried his cane like a pike.

——It looks well at least; quoth my father to himself.

CHAP. III.

MY uncle Toby turn'd his head more than once behind him, to see how he was supported by the Corporal; and the Corporal as oft as he did it, gave a slight flourish with his stick—but not vapouringly; and with the sweetest accent of most respectful encouragement, bid his honour "never fear."

Now my uncle Toby did fear; and grievously too: he knew not (as my father had reproach'd him) so much as the right end of a Woman from the wrong, and therefore was never altogether at his ease near any one of them——unless in sorrow or distress; then infinite was his pity; nor would the most courteous knight of romance have gone further, at least upon one leg, to have wiped away a tear from a woman's eye; and yet excepting once that he was beguiled into it by Mrs. Wadman, he had never looked stedfastly into one; and would often tell my father in the simplicity of his heart, that it was almost (if not alout)[1] as bad as talking bawdy.——

——And suppose it is? my father would say.

CHAP. IV.

SHE cannot, quoth my uncle Toby, halting, when they had march'd up to within twenty paces of Mrs. Wadman's door—she cannot, Corporal, take it amiss.——

——She will take it, an' please your honour, said the Corporal, just as the Jew's widow at Lisbon took it of my brother Tom.——

——And how was that? quoth my uncle Toby, facing quite about to the Corporal.

Your honour, replied the Corporal, knows of Tom's misfortunes; but this affair has nothing to do with them any further than this, That if Tom had not married the widow——or had it pleased God after their marriage, that they had but put pork into their sausages, the honest soul had never been taken out of his warm bed, and dragg'd to the inquisition——'Tis a cursed place—added the Corporal, shaking his head,—when once a poor creature is in, he is in, an' please your honour, for ever.

'Tis very true; said my uncle Toby looking gravely at Mrs. Wadman's house, as he spoke.

Nothing, continued the Corporal, can be so sad as confinement for life—or so sweet, an' please your honour, as liberty.

Nothing, Trim——said my uncle Toby, musing——

Whilst a man is free—cried the Corporal, giving a flourish with his stick[1] thus——

A thousand of my father's most subtle syllogisms could not have said more for celibacy.

My uncle Toby look'd earnestly towards his cottage and his bowling green.

The Corporal had unwarily conjured up the Spirit of calculation with his wand; and he had nothing to do, but to conjure him down again with his story, and in this form of Exorcism, most un-ecclesiastically did the Corporal do it.

CHAP. V.

A S Tom's place, an' please your honour, was easy—and the weather warm—it put him upon thinking seriously of settling himself in the world; and as it fell out about that time, that a Jew who kept a sausage shop in the same street, had the ill luck to die of a strangury, and leave his widow in possession of a rousing trade——Tom thought (as every body in Lisbon was doing the best he could devise for himself) there could be no harm in offering her his service to carry it on: so without any introduction to the widow, except that of buying a pound of sausages at her shop—Tom set out—counting the matter thus within himself, as he walk'd along; that let the worst come of it that could, he should at least get a pound of sausages for their worth—but, if things went well, he should be set up; inasmuch as he should get not only a pound of sausages— but a wife—and a sausage-shop, an' please your honour, into the bargain.

Every servant in the family, from high to low, wish'd Tom success; and I can fancy, an' please your honour, I see him this moment with his white dimity waistcoat and breeches, and hat a little o'one side, passing jollily along the street, swinging his stick, with a smile and a chearful word for every body he met:——But alas! Tom! thou smilest no more, cried the Corporal, looking on one side of him upon the ground, as if he apostrophized him in his dungeon.

Poor fellow! said my uncle Toby, feelingly.

He was an honest, light-hearted lad, an' please your honour, as ever blood warm'd——

——Then he resembled thee, Trim, said my uncle Toby, rapidly.

The Corporal blush'd down to his fingers ends—a tear of sentimental bashfulness—another of gratitude to my uncle Toby—and a tear of sorrow for his brother's misfortunes, started into his eye and ran sweetly down his cheek together; my uncle Toby's kindled as one lamp does at another; and taking hold of the breast of Trim's coat (which had been that of Le Fevre's) as if to ease his lame leg, but in reality to gratify a finer feeling——he stood silent for a minute and a half; at the end of which he took his hand away, and the Corporal making a bow, went on with his story of his brother and the Jew's widow.

CHAP. VI.

WHEN Tom, an' please your honour, got to the shop, there was nobody in it, but a poor negro girl,[1] with a bunch of white feathers slightly tied to the end of a long cane, flapping away flies—not killing them.——'Tis a pretty picture! said my uncle Toby—she had suffered persecution, Trim, and had learnt mercy——

——She was good, an' please your honour, from nature as well as from hardships; and there are circumstances in the story of that poor friendless slut that would melt a heart of stone, said Trim; and some dismal winter's evening, when your honour is in the humour, they shall be told you with the rest of Tom's story, for it makes a part of it——

Then do not forget, Trim, said my uncle Toby.

A Negro has a soul? an' please your honour, said the Corporal (doubtingly).

I am not much versed, Corporal, quoth my uncle Toby, in things of that kind; but I suppose, God would not leave him without one, any more than thee or me——

——It would be putting one sadly over the head of another, quoth the Corporal.

It would so; said my uncle Toby. Why then, an' please your honour, is a black wench to be used worse than a white one?

I can give no reason, said my uncle Toby——

——Only, cried the Corporal, shaking his head, because she has no one to stand up for her——

——'Tis that very thing, Trim, quoth my uncle Toby,——which recommends her to protection——and her brethren with her; 'tis the fortune of war which has put the whip into our hands *now*——where it may be hereafter, heaven knows!——but be it where it will, the brave, Trim! will not use it unkindly.

——God forbid, said the Corporal.

Amen, responded my uncle Toby, laying his hand upon his heart.

The Corporal returned to his story, and went on———but with an embarrassment in doing it, which here and there a reader in this world will not be able to comprehend; for by the many sudden transitions all along, from one kind and cordial passion to another, in getting thus far on his way, he had lost the sportable[2] key of his voice which gave sense and spirit to his tale: he attempted twice to resume it, but could not please himself; so giving a stout hem! to rally back the retreating spirits, and aiding Nature at the same time with his left arm a-kimbo on one side, and with his right a little extended, supporting her on the other—the Corporal got as near the note as he could; and in that attitude, continued his story.

CHAP. VII.

AS Tom, an' please your honour, had no business at that time with the Moorish girl, he passed on into the room beyond to talk to the Jew's widow about love——and his pound of sausages; and being, as I have told your honour, an open, cheary hearted lad, with his character wrote in his looks and carriage, he took a chair, and without much apology, but with great civility at the same time, placed it close to her at the table, and sat down.

There is nothing so awkward, as courting a woman, an' please your honour, whilst she is making sausages——So Tom began a discourse upon them; first gravely,——"as how they were made——with what meats, herbs and spices"—Then a little gayly—as, "With what skins ——and if they never burst——Whether the largest were not the best" ——and so on—taking care only as he went along, to season what he had to say upon sausages, rather under, than over;——that he might have room to act in——

It was owing to the neglect of that very precaution, said my uncle Toby, laying his hand upon Trim's shoulder, That Count de la Motte lost the battle of Wynendale:[1] he pressed too speedily into the wood; which if he had not done, Lisle had not fallen into our hands, nor Ghent and Bruges, which both followed her example; it was so late in the year, continued my uncle Toby, and so terrible a season came on, that if things had not fallen out as they did, our troops must have perished in the open field.——

——Why therefore, may not battles, an' please your honour, as well as marriages, be made in heaven?[2]—My uncle Toby mused.——

Religion inclined him to say one thing, and his high idea of military skill tempted him to say another; so not being able to frame a reply exactly to his mind——my uncle Toby said nothing at all; and the Corporal finished his story.

As Tom perceived, an' please your honour, that he gained ground, and that all he had said upon the subject of sausages was kindly taken, he went on to help her a little in making them.——First, by taking hold of the ring of the sausage whilst she stroked the forced meat down with her hand ——then by cutting the strings into proper lengths, and holding them in his hand, whilst she took them out one by one——then, by putting them across her mouth, that she might take them out as she wanted them—— and so on from little to more, till at last he adventured to tie the sausage himself, whilst she held the snout.——

——Now a widow, an' please your honour, always chuses a second husband as unlike the first as she can: so the affair was more than half settled in her mind before Tom mentioned it.

She made a feint however of defending herself, by snatching up a sausage:——Tom instantly laid hold of another——

But seeing Tom's had more gristle in it——

She signed the capitulation——and Tom sealed it; and there was an end of the matter.

CHAP. VIII.

ALL womankind, continued Trim, (commenting upon his story) from the highest to the lowest, an' please your honour, love jokes; the difficulty is to know how they chuse to have them cut; and there is no knowing that, but by trying as we do with our artillery in the field, by raising or letting down their breeches, till we hit the mark.[1]——

——I like the comparison, said my uncle Toby, better than the thing itself——

——Because your honour, quoth the Corporal, loves glory, more than pleasure.

I hope, Trim, answered my uncle Toby, I love mankind more than either; and as the knowledge of arms tends so apparently to the good and quiet of the world——and particularly that branch of it which we have practised together in our bowling-green, has no object but to shorten the strides of AMBITION,[2] and intrench the lives and fortunes of the *few*, from the plunderings of the *many*——whenever that drum beats in our ears, I trust, Corporal, we shall neither of us want so much humanity and fellow-feeling as to face about and march.

In pronouncing this, my uncle Toby faced about, and march'd firmly as at the head of his company——and the faithful Corporal, shouldering his stick, and striking his hand upon his coat-skirt as he took his first step ——march'd close behind him down the avenue.

——Now what can their two noddles be about? cried my father to my mother——by all that's strange, they are besieging Mrs. Wadman in form, and are marching round her house to mark out the lines of circumvallation.

I dare say, quoth my mother——But stop, dear Sir——for what my mother dared to say upon the occasion——and what my father did say upon it——with her replies and his rejoinders, shall be read, perused, paraphrased, commented and discanted upon——or to say it all in a word, shall be thumb'd over by Posterity in a chapter apart——I say, by Posterity—and care not, if I repeat the word again—for what has this book done more than the Legation of Moses, or the Tale of a Tub,[3] that it may not swim down the gutter of Time along with them?

I will not argue the matter: Time wastes too fast: every letter I trace tells me with what rapidity Life follows my pen; the days and hours of it, more precious, my dear Jenny! than the rubies about thy neck, are flying over our heads like light clouds of a windy day, never to return more ——every thing presses on——whilst thou art twisting that lock,—— see! it grows grey; and every time I kiss thy hand to bid adieu, and every absence which follows it, are preludes to that eternal separation which we are shortly to make.[4]——

——Heaven have mercy upon us both!

CHAP. IX.

NOW, for what the world thinks of that ejaculation[1]——I would not give a groat.

CHAP. X.

MY mother had gone with her left arm twisted in my father's right, till they had got to the fatal angle of the old garden wall, where Doctor Slop was overthrown by Obadiah on the coach-horse: as this was directly opposite to the front of Mrs. Wadman's house, when my father came to it, he gave a look across; and seeing my uncle Toby and the Corporal within ten paces of the door, he turn'd about——"Let us just stop a moment, quoth my father, and see with what ceremonies my brother Toby and his man Trim make their first entry——it will not detain us, added my father, a single minute:"——No matter, if it be ten minutes, quoth my mother.

——It will not detain us half a one; said my father.

The Corporal was just then setting in with the story of his brother Tom and the Jew's widow: the story went on—and on——it had episodes in it——it came back, and went on——and on again; there was no end of it——the reader found it very long——

——G— help my father! he pish'd fifty times at every new attitude, and gave the corporal's stick, with all its flourishings and danglings, to as many devils as chose to accept of them.

When issues of events like these my father is waiting for, are hanging in the scales of fate, the mind has the advantage of changing the principle of expectation three times, without which it would not have power to see it out.

Curiosity governs the *first moment*; and the second moment is all œconomy to justify the expence of the first——and for the third, fourth, fifth, and sixth moments, and so on to the day of judgment—'tis a point of Honour.

I need not be told, that the ethic writers have assigned this all to Patience; but that Virtue methinks, has extent of dominion sufficient of her own, and enough to do in it, without invading the few dismantled castles which Honour has left him upon the earth.

My father stood it out as well as he could with these three auxiliaries to the end of Trim's story; and from thence to the end of my uncle Toby's panegyrick upon arms, in the chapter following it; when seeing, that instead of marching up to Mrs. Wadman's door, they both faced about and march'd down the avenue diametrically opposite to his expectation—he broke out at once with that little subacid soreness of humour which, in certain situations, distinguished his character from that of all other men.

CHAP. XI.

——"NOW what can their two noddles be about?" cried my father ‒ ‒ &c. ‒ ‒ ‒ ‒

I dare say, said my mother, they are making fortifications——

——Not on Mrs. Wadman's premises! cried my father, stepping back——

I suppose not: quoth my mother.

I wish, said my father, raising his voice, the whole science of fortification at the devil, with all its trumpery of saps, mines, blinds, gabions, fausse-brays and cuvetts——

——They are foolish things——said my mother.

Now she had a way, which by the bye, I would this moment give away my purple jerkin, and my yellow slippers into the bargain, if some of your reverences would imitate—and that was never to refuse her assent and consent to any proposition my father laid before her, merely because she did not understand it, or had no ideas to the principal word[1] or term of art, upon which the tenet or proposition rolled. She contented herself with doing all that her godfathers and godmothers promised for her[2]—but no more; and so would go on using a hard word twenty years together—and replying to it too, if it was a verb, in all its moods and tenses, without giving herself any trouble to enquire about it.

This was an eternal source of misery to my father, and broke the neck, at the first setting out, of more good dialogues between them, than could have done the most petulant contradiction——the few which survived were the better for the *cuvetts*——

—"They are foolish things;" said my mother.

——Particularly the *cuvetts*;[3] replied my father.

'Twas enough—he tasted the sweet of triumph—and went on.

—Not that they are, properly speaking, Mrs. Wadman's premises, said my father, partly correcting himself—because she is but tenant for life——

——That makes a great difference—said my mother——

—In a fool's head, replied my father——

Unless she should happen to have a child—said my mother——

——But she must persuade my brother Toby first to get her one—

——To be sure, Mr. Shandy, quoth my mother.

——Though if it comes to persuasion——said my father—Lord have mercy upon them.

Amen: said my mother, *piano*.

Amen: cried my father, *fortissimè*.

Amen: said my mother again——but with such a sighing cadence of personal pity at the end of it, as discomfited every fibre about my father— he instantly took out his almanack; but before he could untie it, Yorick's congregation coming out of church, became a full answer to one half of his business with it—and my mother telling him it was a sacrament day [4]—left him as little in doubt, as to the other part—He put his almanack into his pocket.

The first Lord of the Treasury thinking of *ways and means*, could not have returned home, with a more embarrassed look.

CHAP. XII.

UPON looking back from the end of the last chapter and surveying the texture of what has been wrote, it is necessary, that upon this page and the five following, a good quantity of heterogeneous matter be inserted, to keep up that just balance betwixt wisdom and folly, without which a book would not hold together a single year: nor is it a poor creeping digression (which but for the name of, a man might continue as well going on in the king's highway) which will do the business——no; if it is to be a digression, it must be a good frisky one, and upon a frisky subject too, where neither the horse or his rider are to be caught, but by rebound.

The only difficulty, is raising powers suitable to the nature of the service: FANCY is capricious—WIT must not be searched for—and PLEASANTRY (good-natured slut as she is) will not come in at a call, was an empire to be laid at her feet.

——The best way for a man, is to say his prayers——

Only if it puts him in mind of his infirmities and defects as well ghostly as bodily—for that purpose, he will find himself rather worse after he has said them than before—for other purposes, better.

For my own part there is not a way either moral or mechanical under heaven that I could think of, which I have not taken with myself in this case: sometimes by addressing myself directly to the soul herself, and arguing the point over and over again with her upon the extent of her own faculties——

——I never could make them an inch the wider——

Then by changing my system, and trying what could be made of it upon the body, by temperance, soberness and chastity:[1] These are good, quoth I, in themselves—they are good, absolutely;—they are good, relatively;—they are good for health—they are good for happiness in this world—they are good for happiness in the next——

In short, they were good for every thing but the thing wanted; and there they were good for nothing, but to leave the soul just as heaven made it: as for the theological virtues of faith and hope, they give it courage; but then that sniveling virtue of Meekness[2] (as my father would always call it) takes it quite away again, so you are exactly where you started.

Now in all common and ordinary cases, there is nothing which I have found to answer so well as this——

——Certainly, if there is any dependence upon Logic, and that I am not blinded by self-love, there must be something of true genius about me, merely upon this symptom of it, that I do not know what envy is: for never do I hit upon any invention or device which tendeth to the further-ance of good writing, but I instantly make it public; willing that all mankind should write as well as myself.

——Which they certainly will, when they think as little.

CHAP. XIII.

NOW in ordinary cases, that is, when I am only stupid, and the thoughts rise heavily and pass gummous[1] through my pen——

Or that I am got, I know not how, into a cold unmetaphorical vein of infamous writing, and cannot take a plumb-lift[2] out of it *for my soul*; so must be obliged to go on writing like a Dutch commentator[3] to the end of the chapter, unless something be done——

——I never stand confering with pen and ink one moment; for if a pinch of snuff or a stride or two across the room will not do the business for me—I take a razor at once; and having tried the edge of it upon the palm of my hand, without further ceremony, except that of first lathering my beard, I shave it off; taking care only if I do leave a hair, that it be not a grey one: this done, I change my shirt—put on a better coat—send for my last wig—put my topaz ring[4] upon my finger; and in a word, dress myself from one end to the other of me, after my best fashion.

Now the devil in hell must be in it, if this does not do: for consider, Sir, as every man chuses to be present at the shaving of his own beard (though there is no rule without an exception) and unavoidably sits overagainst himself the whole time it is doing, in case he has a hand in it—the Situation, like all others, has notions of her own to put into the brain.——

——I maintain it, the conceits of a rough-bearded man, are seven years more terse and juvenile for one single operation; and if they did not run a risk of being quite shaved away, might be carried up by continual shavings, to the highest pitch of sublimity—How Homer could write with so long a beard, I don't know——and as it makes against my hypothesis, I as little care——But let us return to the Toilet.

Ludovicus Sorbonensis[5] makes this entirely an affair of the body (εξωλερικη πραξις) as he calls it——but he is deceived: the soul and body are joint-sharers in every thing they get: A man cannot dress, but his ideas get cloath'd at the same time; and if he dresses like a gentleman, every one of them stands presented to his imagination, genteelized along with him—so that he has nothing to do, but take his pen, and write like himself.

For this cause, when your honours and reverences would know whether I writ clean and fit to be read, you will be able to judge full as well by looking into my Laundress's bill, as my book: there was one single month in which I can make it appear, that I dirtied one and thirty shirts with clean writing; and after all, was more abus'd, curs'd, criticis'd and confounded, and had more mystic heads shaken at me, for what I had wrote in that one month, than in all the other months of that year put together.

——But their honours and reverences had not seen my *bills*.

CHAP. XIV.

AS I never had any intention of beginning the Digression, I am making all this preparation for, till I come to the 15th chapter——I have this chapter to put to whatever use I think proper——I have twenty this moment ready for it——I could write my chapter of Button-holes[1] in it——

Or my chapter of *Pishes*, which should follow them——

Or my chapter of *Knots*, in case their reverences have done with them ——they might lead me into mischief: the safest way is to follow the tract of the learned, and raise objections against what I have been writing, tho' I declare before-hand, I know no more than my heels how to answer them.

And first, it may be said, there is a pelting kind of *thersitical* satire,[2] as black as the very ink 'tis wrote with——(and by the bye, whoever says so, is indebted to the muster-master general of the Grecian army, for suffering the name of so ugly and foul-mouth'd a man as *Thersites* to continue upon his roll——for it has furnished him with an epithet)—— in these productions he will urge, all the personal washings and scrubbings upon earth do a sinking genius no sort of good——but just the contrary, inasmuch as the dirtier the fellow is, the better generally he succeeds in it.

To this, I have no other answer——at least ready——but that the Archbishop of Benevento wrote his *nasty* Romance of the Galatea,[3] as all the world knows, in a purple coat, waistcoat, and purple pair of breeches; and that the penance set him of writing a commentary upon the book of the Revelations, as severe as it was look'd upon by one part of the world, was far from being deem'd so, by the other, upon the single account of that *Investment.*

Another objection, to all this remedy, is its want of universality; forasmuch as the shaving part of it, upon which so much stress is laid, by an unalterable law of nature excludes one half of the species entirely from its use: all I can say is, that female writers, whether of England, or of France, must e'en go without it——

As for the Spanish ladies——I am in no sort of distress——

CHAP. XV.

THE fifteenth chapter is come at last; and brings nothing with it but a sad signature of "How our pleasures slip from under us in this world;"[1]

For in talking of my digression——I declare before heaven I have made it! What a strange creature is mortal man! said she.

'Tis very true, said I——but 'twere better to get all these things out of our heads, and return to my uncle Toby.

CHAP. XVI.

WHEN my uncle Toby and the Corporal had marched down to the bottom of the avenue, they recollected their business lay the other way; so they faced about and marched up streight to Mrs. Wadman's door.

I warrant your honour; said the Corporal, touching his Montero-cap with his hand, as he passed him in order to give a knock at the door—— My uncle Toby, contrary to his invariable way of treating his faithful servant, said nothing good or bad: the truth was, he had not altogether marshal'd his ideas; he wish'd for another conference, and as the Corporal was mounting up the three steps before the door—he hem'd twice—a portion of my uncle Toby's most modest spirits fled, at each expulsion, towards the Corporal; he stood with the rapper of the door suspended for a full minute in his hand, he scarce knew why. Bridget stood perdue within, with her finger and her thumb upon the latch, benumb'd with expectation; and Mrs. Wadman, with an eye ready to be deflowered again, sat breathless behind the window-curtain of her bed-chamber, watching their approach.

Trim! said my uncle Toby——but as he articulated the word, the minute expired, and Trim let fall the rapper.

My uncle Toby perceiving that all hopes of a conference were knock'd on the head by it———whistled Lillabullero.

CHAP. XVII.

AS Mrs. Bridget's finger and thumb were upon the latch, the Corporal did not knock as oft as perchance your honour's taylor——I might have taken my example something nearer home; for I owe mine, some five and twenty pounds at least, and wonder at the man's patience——

——But this is nothing at all to the world: only 'tis a cursed thing to be in debt; and there seems to be a fatality in the exchequers of some poor princes, particularly those of our house, which no Economy can bind down in irons: for my own part, I'm persuaded there is not any one prince, prelate, pope, or potentate, great or small upon earth, more desirous in his heart of keeping streight with the world than I am——or who takes more likely means for it. I never give above half a guinea——or walk with boots——or cheapen tooth-picks——or lay out a shilling upon a band-box the year round; and for the six months I'm in the country, I'm upon so small a scale, that with all the good temper in the world, I out-do Rousseau,[1] a bar length[2]———for I keep neither man or boy, or horse, or cow, or dog, or cat, or any thing that can eat or drink, except a thin poor piece of a Vestal (to keep my fire in)[3] and who has generally as bad an appetite as myself——but if you think this makes a philosopher of me ——I would not, my good people! give a rush for your judgments.

True philosophy———but there is no treating the subject whilst my uncle is whistling Lillabullero.

——Let us go into the house.

CHAP. XVIII.

CHAP. XIX.

CHAP. XX.

———   *   *   *   *   *   *   *   *

*   *   *   *   *   *   *   *   *   *   *

*   *   *   *   *   *   *

*   *   *   *   *   *   *   *   *   *

*   *   *   *   *   *   *   *   *   *

*   *   *   *   *   *   *   *   *   *

*   *   *   *   *———

——You shall see the very place, Madam; said my uncle Toby.

Mrs. Wadman blush'd——look'd towards the door——turn'd pale ——blush'd slightly again——recovered her natural colour——blush'd worse than ever; which for the sake of the unlearned reader, I translate thus——

> "L—d! I cannot look at it——
> What would the world say if I look'd at it?
> I should drop down, if I look'd at it—
> I wish I could look at it——
> There can be no sin in looking at it.
> ——I will look at it."

Whilst all this was running through Mrs. Wadman's imagination, my uncle Toby had risen from the sopha, and got to the other side of the parlour-door, to give Trim an order about it in the passage——

*   *   *   *   *   *   *   *   *   *   *   *

*   *   *   *   *   *   ——I believe it is in the garret, said my uncle Toby——I saw it there, an' please your honour, this morning, answered Trim——Then prithee, step directly for it, Trim, said my uncle Toby, and bring it into the parlour.

The Corporal did not approve of the orders, but most chearfully obey'd them. The first was not an act of his will—the second was; so he put on his Montero cap, and went as fast as his lame knee would let him. My uncle Toby returned into the parlour, and sat himself down again upon the sopha.

——You shall lay your finger upon the place—said my uncle

Toby.——I will not touch it, however, quoth Mrs. Wadman to herself.

This requires a second translation:[1]—it shews what little knowledge is got by mere words—we must go up to the first springs.

Now in order to clear up the mist which hangs upon these three pages, I must endeavour to be as clear as possible myself.

Rub your hands thrice across your foreheads—blow your noses—cleanse your emunctories—sneeze, my good people!——God bless you——

Now give me all the help you can.

CHAP. XXI.

AS there are fifty different ends (counting all ends in——as well civil as religious) for which a woman takes a husband, she first sets about and carefully weighs, then separates and distinguishes in her mind, which of all that number of ends, is hers: then by discourse, enquiry, argumentation and inference, she investigates and finds out whether she has got hold of the right one——and if she has——then, by pulling it gently this way and that way, she further forms a judgment, whether it will not break in the drawing.

The imagery under which *Slawkenbergius* impresses this upon his reader's fancy, in the beginning of his third Decad, is so ludicrous, that the honour I bear the sex, will not suffer me to quote it——otherwise 'tis not destitute of humour.

"She first, saith Slawkenbergius, stops the asse, and holding his halter in her left hand (lest he should get away) she thrusts her right hand into the very bottom of his pannier to search for it—For what?—you'll not know the sooner, quoth Slawkenbergius, for interrupting me"——

"I have nothing, good Lady, but empty bottles;" says the asse.

"I'm loaded with tripes;" says the second.

——And thou art little better, quoth she to the third; for nothing is there in thy panniers but trunk-hose and pantofles—and so to the fourth and fifth, going on one by one through the whole string, till coming to the asse which carries it, she turns the pannier upside down, looks at it—

considers it—samples it—measures it—stretches it—wets it—dries it—then takes her teeth both to the warp and weft of it——

——Of what? for the love of Christ!

I am determined, answered *Slawkenbergius*, that all the powers upon earth shall never wring that secret from my breast.

CHAP. XXII.

WE live in a world beset on all sides with mysteries and riddles[1]— and so 'tis no matter——else it seems strange, that Nature, who makes every thing so well to answer its destination, and seldom or never errs, unless for pastime, in giving such forms and aptitudes to whatever passes through her hands, that whether she designs for the plough, the caravan, the cart—or whatever other creature she models, be it but an asse's foal, you are sure to have the thing you wanted; and yet at the same time should so eternally bungle it as she does, in making so simple a thing as a married man.

Whether it is in the choice of the clay——or that it is frequently spoiled in the baking; by an excess of which a husband may turn out too crusty (you know) on one hand——or not enough so, through defect of heat, on the other——or whether this great Artificer is not so attentive to the little Platonic exigences[2] *of that part* of the species, for whose use she is fabricating *this*——or that her Ladyship sometimes scarce knows what sort of a husband will do——I know not: we will discourse about it after supper.

It is enough, that neither the observation itself, or the reasoning upon it, are at all to the purpose——but rather against it; since with regard to my uncle Toby's fitness for the marriage state, nothing was ever better: she had formed him of the best and kindliest clay——had temper'd it with her own milk, and breathed into it the sweetest spirit——she had made him all gentle, generous and humane——she had fill'd his heart with trust and confidence, and disposed every passage which led to it, for the communication of the tenderest offices——she had moreover considered the other causes for which matrimony was ordained——

And accordingly   *   *   *   *   *   *
*   *   *   *   *   *   *   *   *   *
*   *   *   *   *   *   *   *   *   *
*   *   *   *   *   *   *.

The DONATION was not defeated[3] by my uncle Toby's wound.

Now this last article was somewhat apocryphal; and the Devil, who is the great disturber of our faiths in this world, had raised scruples in Mrs. Wadman's brain about it; and like a true devil as he was, had done his own work at the same time, by turning my uncle Toby's Virtue thereupon into nothing but *empty bottles, tripes, trunk-hose,* and *pantofles.*

CHAP. XXIII.

MRS. Bridget had pawn'd all the little stock of honour a poor chambermaid was worth in the world, that she would get to the bottom of the affair in ten days; and it was built upon one of the most concessible *postulatums* in nature: namely, that whilst my uncle Toby was making love to her mistress, the Corporal could find nothing better to do, than make love to her——"*And I'll let him as much as he will,*" said Bridget, "*to get it out of him.*"

Friendship has two garments; an outer, and an under one. Bridget was serving her mistress's interests in the one—and doing the thing which most pleased herself in the other; so had as many stakes depending upon my uncle Toby's wound, as the Devil himself——Mrs. Wadman had but one—and as it possibly might be her last (without discouraging Mrs. Bridget, or discrediting her talents) was determined to play her cards herself.[1]

She wanted not encouragement: a child might have look'd into his hand ——there was such a plainness and simplicity in his playing out what trumps he had——with such an unmistrusting ignorance of the *ten-ace*[2] ——and so naked and defenceless did he sit upon the same sopha with widow Wadman, that a generous heart would have wept to have won the game of him.

Let us drop the metaphor.

CHAP. XXIV.

————A ND the story too—if you please: for though I have all along
been hastening towards this part of it, with so much earnest
desire, as well knowing it to be the choicest morsel of what I had to offer
to the world, yet now that I am got to it, any one is welcome to take my
pen, and go on with the story for me that will—I see the difficulties of
the descriptions I'm going to give—and feel my want of powers.

It is one comfort at least to me, that I lost some fourscore ounces of
blood[1] this week in a most uncritical[2] fever which attacked me at the
beginning of this chapter; so that I have still some hopes remaining, it may
be more in the serous or globular[3] parts of the blood, than in the subtile
aura of the brain——be it which it will—an Invocation can do no hurt
——and I leave the affair entirely to the *invoked*, to inspire or to inject
me according as he sees good.

THE INVOCATION.

G ENTLE Spirit of sweetest humour, who erst didst sit upon the
easy pen of my beloved CERVANTES; Thou who glided'st daily
through his lattice, and turned'st the twilight of his prison into noon-day
brightness by thy presence——tinged'st his little urn of water with heaven-
sent Nectar, and all the time he wrote of Sancho and his master, didst cast
thy mystic mantle o'er his wither'd* stump, and wide extended it to all
the evils of his life[4]——

——Turn in hither, I beseech thee!——behold these breeches!——
they are all I have in the world——that piteous rent was given them at
Lyons——

* He lost his hand at the battle of Lepanto.

527

My shirts! see what a deadly schism has happen'd amongst 'em—for the laps are in Lombardy, and the rest of 'em here—I never had but six, and a cunning gypsey of a laundress at Milan cut me off the *fore*-laps of five—To do her justice, she did it with some consideration—for I was returning *out* of Italy.[5]

And yet, notwithstanding all this, and a pistol tinder-box which was moreover filch'd from me at Sienna, and twice that I pay'd five Pauls for two hard eggs, once at Raddicoffini, and a second time at Capua[6]—I do not think a journey through France and Italy, provided a man keeps his temper[7] all the way, so bad a thing as some people would make you believe: there must be *ups* and *downs*, or how the duce should we get into vallies where Nature spreads so many tables of entertainment.—'Tis nonsense to imagine they will lend you their voitures[8] to be shaken to pieces for nothing; and unless you pay twelve sous for greasing your wheels, how should the poor peasant get butter to his bread?—We really expect too much—and for the livre or two above par for your suppers and bed—at the most they are but one shilling and ninepence halfpenny——who would embroil their philosophy for it? for heaven's and for your own sake, pay it——pay it with both hands open, rather than leave *Disappointment* sitting drooping upon the eye of your fair Hostess and her Damsels in the gate-way, at your departure——and besides, my dear Sir, you get a sisterly kiss of each of 'em worth a pound——at least I did——

——For my uncle Toby's amours running all the way in my head, they had the same effect upon me as if they had been my own——I was in the most perfect state of bounty and good will; and felt the kindliest harmony vibrating within me, with every oscillation of the chaise alike; so that whether the roads were rough or smooth, it made no difference; every thing I saw, or had to do with, touch'd upon some secret spring either of sentiment or rapture.

——They were the sweetest notes I ever heard; and I instantly let down the fore-glass to hear them more distinctly——'Tis Maria;[9] said the postilion, observing I was listening———Poor Maria, continued he, (leaning his body on one side to let me see her, for he was in a line betwixt us) is sitting upon a bank playing her vespers upon her pipe, with her little goat beside her.

The young fellow utter'd this with an accent and a look so perfectly in tune to a feeling heart, that I instantly made a vow, I would give him a four and twenty sous piece, when I got to *Moulins*——

CHAPTER XXIV

————And who is *poor Maria?* said I.

The love and pity of all the villages around us; said the postillion——
it is but three years ago, that the sun did not shine upon so fair, so
quick-witted and amiable a maid; and better fate did *Maria* deserve, than
to have her Banns forbid, by the intrigues of the curate of the parish who
published them——

He was going on, when Maria, who had made a short pause, put the
pipe to her mouth and began the air again——they were the same notes;
——yet were ten times sweeter: It is the evening service to the Virgin,
said the young man——but who has taught her to play it—or how she
came by her pipe, no one knows; we think that Heaven has assisted her
in both; for ever since she has been unsettled in her mind, it seems her
only consolation——she has never once had the pipe out of her hand,
but plays that *service* upon it almost night and day.

The postillion delivered this with so much discretion and natural
eloquence, that I could not help decyphering something in his face above
his condition, and should have sifted out his history, had not poor Maria's
taken such full possession of me.

We had got up by this time almost to the bank where Maria was sitting:
she was in a thin white jacket with her hair, all but two tresses, drawn up
into a silk net, with a few olive-leaves twisted a little fantastically on one
side——she was beautiful; and if ever I felt the full force of an honest
heart-ache, it was the moment I saw her——

——God help her! poor damsel! above a hundred masses, said the
postillion, have been said in the several parish churches and convents
around, for her,——but without effect; we have still hopes, as she is
sensible for short intervals, that the Virgin at last will restore her to herself;
but her parents, who know her best, are hopeless upon that score, and
think her senses are lost for ever.

As the postillion spoke this, MARIA made a cadence so melancholy, so
tender and querulous, that I sprung out of the chaise to help her, and
found myself sitting betwixt her and her goat before I relapsed from my
enthusiasm.

MARIA look'd wistfully for some time at me, and then at her goat
——and then at me——and then at her goat again, and so on, alternately——

——Well, Maria, said I softly——What resemblance do you find?

I do intreat the candid reader to believe me, that it was from the humblest conviction of what a *Beast* man is,——that I ask'd the question; and that I would not have let fallen an unseasonable pleasantry in the venerable presence of Misery, to be entitled to all the wit that ever Rabelais scatter'd——and yet I own my heart smote me, and that I so smarted at the very idea of it, that I swore I would set up for Wisdom and utter grave sentences the rest of my days——and never——never attempt again to commit mirth with man, woman, or child, the longest day I had to live.[10]

As for writing nonsense to them——I believe, there was a reserve—but that I leave to the world.

Adieu, Maria!—adieu, poor hapless damsel!——some time, but not *now*, I may hear thy sorrows from thy own lips——but I was deceived; for that moment she took her pipe and told me such a tale of woe with it, that I rose up, and with broken and irregular steps walk'd softly to my chaise.

——What an excellent inn at Moulins!

CHAP. XXV.

WHEN we have got to the end of this chapter (but not before) we must all turn back to the two blank chapters, on the account of which my honour has lain bleeding this half hour——I stop it, by pulling off one of my yellow slippers and throwing it with all my violence to the opposite side of my room, with a declaration at the heel of it——

——That whatever resemblance it may bear to half the chapters which are written in the world, or, for aught I know, may be now writing in it—that it was as casual as the foam of Zeuxis his horse:[1] besides, I look upon a chapter which has, *only nothing in it*, with respect; and considering what worse things there are in the world——That it is no way a proper subject for satire——

——Why then was it left so? And here, without staying for my reply, shall I be call'd as many blockheads, numsculs, doddypoles, dunderheads, ninnyhammers, goosecaps, joltheads, nicompoops, and sh--t-a-beds——

and other unsavory appellations, as ever the cake-bakers of Lernè, cast in the teeth of King Gargantua's shepherds [2]——And I'll let them do it, as Bridget said, as much as they please; for how was it possible they should foresee the necessity I was under of writing the 25th chapter of my book, before the 18th, &c.

——So I don't take it amiss——All I wish is, that it may be a lesson to the world, *"to let people tell their stories their own way."*

The Eighteenth Chapter.

AS Mrs. Bridget open'd the door before the Corporal had well given the rap, the interval betwixt that and my uncle Toby's introduction into the parlour, was so short, that Mrs. Wadman had but just time to get from behind the curtain——lay a Bible upon the table, and advance a step or two towards the door to receive him.

My uncle Toby saluted Mrs. Wadman, after the manner in which women were saluted by men in the year of our Lord God one thousand seven hundred and thirteen——then facing about, he march'd up abreast with her to the sopha, and in three plain words——though not before he was sat down——nor after he was sat down——but as he was sitting down, told her, *"he was in love"*——so that my uncle Toby strained himself more in the declaration than he needed.

Mrs. Wadman naturally looked down, upon a slit she had been darning up in her apron, in expectation every moment, that my uncle Toby would go on; but having no talents for amplification, and LOVE moreover of all others being a subject of which he was the least a master——When he had told Mrs. Wadman once that he loved her, he let it alone, and left the matter to work after its own way.

My father was always in raptures with this system of my uncle Toby's, as he falsely called it, and would often say, that could his brother Toby to his processe have added but a pipe of tobacco——he had wherewithal to have found his way, if there was faith in a Spanish proverb,[3] towards the hearts of half the women upon the globe.

My uncle Toby never understood what my father meant; nor will I presume to extract more from it, than a condemnation of an error which the bulk of the world lie under——but the French, every one of 'em to a man, who believe in it, almost as much as the REAL PRESENCE, "*That talking of love, is making it.*"[4]

——I would as soon set about making a black-pudding[5] by the same receipt.

Let us go on: Mrs. Wadman sat in expectation my uncle Toby would do so, to almost the first pulsation of that minute, wherein silence on one side or the other, generally becomes indecent: so edging herself a little more towards him, and raising up her eyes, sub-blushing, as she did it ——she took up the gauntlet——or the discourse (if you like it better) and communed with my uncle Toby, thus.

The cares and disquietudes of the marriage state, quoth Mrs. Wadman, are very great. I suppose so—said my uncle Toby: and therefore when a person, continued Mrs. Wadman, is so much at his ease as you are—so happy, captain Shandy, in yourself, your friends and your amusements— I wonder, what reasons can incline you to the state——

——They are written, quoth my uncle Toby, in the Common-Prayer Book.[6]

Thus far my uncle Toby went on warily, and kept within his depth, leaving Mrs. Wadman to sail upon the gulph as she pleased.

——As for children—said Mrs. Wadman—though a principal end perhaps of the institution, and the natural wish, I suppose, of every parent—yet do not we all find, they are certain sorrows, and very uncertain comforts?[7] and what is there, dear sir, to pay one for the heart-aches— what compensation for the many tender and disquieting apprehensions of a suffering and defenceless mother who brings them into life? I declare, said my uncle Toby, smit with pity, I know of none; unless it be the pleasure which it has pleased God——

——A fiddlestick! quoth she.

𝕮𝖍𝖆𝖕𝖙𝖊𝖗 𝖙𝖍𝖊 𝕹𝖎𝖓𝖊𝖙𝖊𝖊𝖓𝖙𝖍.

NOW there are such an infinitude of notes, tunes, cants, chants, airs, looks, and accents with which the word *fiddlestick* may be pronounced in all such causes as this, every one of 'em impressing a sense and meaning as different from the other, as *dirt* from *cleanliness*—That Casuists (for it is an affair of conscience on that score) reckon up no less than fourteen thousand in which you may do either right or wrong.

Mrs. Wadman hit upon the *fiddlestick*, which summoned up all my uncle Toby's modest blood into his cheeks—so feeling within himself that he had somehow or other got beyond his depth, he stopt short; and without entering further either into the pains or pleasures of matrimony, he laid his hand upon his heart, and made an offer to take them as they were, and share them along with her.

When my uncle Toby had said this, he did not care to say it again; so casting his eye upon the Bible which Mrs. Wadman had laid upon the table, he took it up; and popping, dear soul! upon a passage in it, of all others the most interesting to him—which was the siege of Jericho—he set himself to read it over—leaving his proposal of marriage, as he had done his declaration of love, to work with her after its own way. Now it wrought neither as an astringent or a loosener; nor like opium, or bark, or mercury, or buckthorn, or any one drug which nature had bestowed upon the world—in short, it work'd not at all in her; and the cause of that was, that there was something working there before——Babbler that I am! I have anticipated what it was a dozen times; but there is fire still in the subject——allons.[8]

CHAP. XXVI.

IT is natural for a perfect stranger who is going from London to Edinburgh, to enquire before he sets out, how many miles to York; which is about the half way——nor does any body wonder, if he goes on and asks about the Corporation,[1] &c. ——

It was just as natural for Mrs. Wadman, whose first husband was all his time afflicted with a Sciatica, to wish to know how far from the hip to the groin; and how far she was likely to suffer more or less in her feelings, in the one case than in the other.

She had accordingly read *Drake*'s anatomy from one end to the other. She had peeped into *Wharton* upon the brain, and borrowed * Graaf upon the bones and muscles;[2] but could make nothing of it.

She had reason'd likewise from her own powers——laid down theorems ——drawn consequences, and come to no conclusion.

To clear up all, she had twice asked Doctor Slop, "if poor captain Shandy was ever likely to recover of his wound——?"

——He is recovered, Doctor Slop would say——

What! quite?

——Quite: madam——

But what do you mean by a recovery? Mrs. Wadman would say.

Doctor Slop was the worst man alive at definitions; and so Mrs. Wadman could get no knowledge: in short, there was no way to extract it, but from my uncle Toby himself.

There is an accent of humanity in an enquiry of this kind which lulls SUSPICION to rest——and I am half persuaded the serpent got pretty near it, in his discourse with Eve; for the propensity in the sex to be deceived could not be so great, that she should have boldness to hold chat with the devil, without it——But there is an accent of humanity—— how shall I describe it?—'tis an accent which covers the part with a garment, and gives the enquirer a right to be as particular with it, as your body-surgeon.

---

* This must be a mistake in Mr. Shandy; for Graaf wrote upon the pancreatick juice, and the parts of generation.

CHAPTER XXVI

"——Was it without remission?—

——Was it more tolerable in bed?

——Could he lie on both sides alike with it?

—Was he able to mount a horse?

—Was motion bad for it?" et cætera, were so tenderly spoke to, and so directed towards my uncle Toby's heart, that every item of them sunk ten times deeper into it than the evils themselves——but when Mrs. Wadman went round about by Namur to get at my uncle Toby's groin; and engaged him to attack the point of the advanced counterscarp, and *pêle mêle* with the Dutch to take the counterguard of St. Roch sword in hand—and then with tender notes playing upon his ear, led him all bleeding by the hand out of the trench, wiping her eye, as he was carried to his tent——Heaven! Earth! Sea!—all was lifted up—the springs of nature rose above their levels—an angel of mercy sat besides him on the sopha—his heart glow'd with fire—and had he been worth a thousand, he had lost every heart of them to Mrs. Wadman.

—And whereabouts, dear Sir, quoth Mrs. Wadman, a little categorically, did you receive this sad blow?——In asking this question, Mrs. Wadman gave a slight glance towards the waistband of my uncle Toby's red plush breeches, expecting naturally, as the shortest reply to it, that my uncle Toby would lay his fore-finger upon the place——It fell out otherwise ——for my uncle Toby having got his wound before the gate of St. Nicolas, in one of the traverses of the trench, opposite to the salient angle of the demi-bastion of St. Roch; he could at any time stick a pin upon the identical spot of ground where he was standing when the stone struck him: this struck instantly upon my uncle Toby's sensorium——and with it, struck his large map of the town and citadel of Namur and its environs, which he had purchased and pasted down upon a board by the Corporal's aid, during his long illness——it had lain with other military lumber in the garret ever since, and accordingly the Corporal was detached into the garret to fetch it.

My uncle Toby measured off thirty toises, with Mrs. Wadman's scissars, from the returning angle before the gate of St. Nicolas; and with such a virgin modesty laid her finger upon the place, that the goddess of Decency, if then in being—if not, 'twas her shade—shook her head, and with a finger wavering across her eyes—forbid her to explain the mistake.

Unhappy Mrs. Wadman!——

——For nothing can make this chapter go off with spirit but

an apostrophe to thee——but my heart tells me, that in such a crisis an apostrophe is but an insult in disguise, and ere I would offer one to a woman in distress—let the chapter go to the devil; provided any damn'd critick *in keeping*[3] will be but at the trouble to take it with him.

CHAP. XXVII.

MY uncle Toby's Map is carried down into the kitchen.

CHAP. XXVIII.

——AND here is the *Maes*—and this is the *Sambre*;[1] said the Corporal, pointing with his right hand extended a little towards the map, and his left upon Mrs. Bridget's shoulder—but not the shoulder next him—and this, said he, is the town of Namur——and this the citadel—and there lay the French—and here lay his honour and myself——and in this cursed trench, Mrs. Bridget, quoth the Corporal, taking her by the hand, did he receive the wound which crush'd him so miserably *here*——In pronouncing which he slightly press'd the back of her hand towards the part he felt for——and let it fall.

We thought, Mr. Trim, it had been more in the middle——said Mrs. Bridget——

That would have undone us for ever—said the Corporal.

——And left my poor mistress undone too—said Bridget.

The Corporal made no reply to the repartee, but by giving Mrs. Bridget a kiss.

Come—come—said Bridget—holding the palm of her left-hand parallel to the plane of the horizon, and sliding the fingers of the other over it, in a way which could not have been done, had there been the least wart or protuberance——'Tis every syllable of it false, cried the Corporal, before she had half finished the sentence——

——I know it to be fact, said Bridget, from credible witnesses.

————Upon my honour, said the Corporal, laying his hand upon his heart, and blushing as he spoke with honest resentment—'tis a story, Mrs. Bridget, as false as hell——Not, said Bridget, interrupting him, that either I or my mistress care a halfpenny about it, whether 'tis so or no———— only that when one is married, one would chuse to have such a thing by one at least——

It was somewhat unfortunate for Mrs. Bridget, that she had begun the attack with her manual exercise; for the Corporal instantly *   *
*   *   *   *   *   *   *   *   *   *   *
*   *   *   *   *   *   *   *   *   *   *
*   *   *   *   *.

CHAP. XXIX.

I T was like the momentary contest in the moist eye-lids of an April morning,[1] "Whether Bridget should laugh or cry."

She snatch'd up a rolling-pin——'twas ten to one, she had laugh'd——

She laid it down——she cried; and had one single tear of 'em but tasted of bitterness, full sorrowful would the Corporal's heart have been that he had used the argument; but the Corporal understood the sex, a *quart major to a terce*[2] at least, better than my uncle Toby, and accordingly he assailed Mrs. Bridget after this manner.

I know, Mrs. Bridget, said the Corporal, giving her a most respectful kiss, that thou art good and modest by nature, and art withal so generous a girl in thyself, that if I know thee rightly, thou wouldst not wound an insect, much less the honour of so gallant and worthy a soul as my master, wast thou sure to be made a countess of——but thou hast been set on, and deluded, dear Bridget, as is often a woman's case, "to please others more than themselves——"

Bridget's eyes poured down at the sensations the Corporal excited.

———— Tell me———— tell me then, my dear Bridget, continued the Corporal, taking hold of her hand, which hung down dead by her side,————
and giving a second kiss———— whose suspicion has misled thee?

Bridget sobb'd a sob or two———— then open'd her eyes———— the Corporal wiped 'em with the bottom of her apron———— she then open'd her heart and told him all.

CHAP. XXX.

MY uncle Toby and the Corporal had gone on separately with their operations the greatest part of the campaign, and as effectually cut off from all communication of what either the one or the other had been doing, as if they had been separated from each other by the *Maes* or the *Sambre*.

My uncle Toby, on his side, had presented himself every afternoon in his red and silver, and blue and gold alternately, and sustained an infinity of attacks in them, without knowing them to be attacks—and so had nothing to communicate————

The Corporal, on his side, in taking Bridget, by it had gain'd considerable advantages————and consequently had much to communicate————but what were the advantages————as well, as what was the manner by which he had seiz'd them, required so nice an historian that the Corporal durst not venture upon it; and as sensible as he was of glory, would rather have been contented to have gone barehead and without laurels for ever, than torture his master's modesty for a single moment————

————Best of honest and gallant servants!————But I have apostrophiz'd thee, Trim! once before————and could I apotheosize thee also (that is to say) with good company————I would do it *without ceremony* in the very next page.

CHAP. XXXI.

NOW my uncle Toby had one evening laid down his pipe upon the table, and was counting over to himself upon his finger ends, (beginning at his thumb) all Mrs. Wadman's perfections one by one; and happening two or three times together, either by omitting some, or counting others twice over, to puzzle himself sadly before he could get beyond his middle finger——Prithee, Trim! said he, taking up his pipe again,—— bring me a pen and ink: Trim brought paper also.

Take a full sheet[1]——Trim! said my uncle Toby, making a sign with his pipe at the same time to take a chair and sit down close by him at the table. The Corporal obeyed——placed the paper directly before him ——took a pen and dip'd it in the ink.

—She has a thousand virtues, Trim! said my uncle Toby——

Am I to set them down, an' please your honour? quoth the Corporal.

——But they must be taken in their ranks, replied my uncle Toby; for of them all, Trim, that which wins me most, and which is a security for all the rest, is the compassionate turn and singular humanity of her character—I protest, added my uncle Toby, looking up, as he protested it, towards the top of the ceiling——That was I her brother, Trim, a thousand fold, she could not make more constant or more tender enquiries after my sufferings——though now no more.

The Corporal made no reply to my uncle Toby's protestation, but by a short cough—he dip'd the pen a second time into the inkhorn; and my uncle Toby, pointing with the end of his pipe as close to the top of the sheet at the left hand corner of it, as he could get it——the Corporal wrote down the word

HUMANITY – – – – thus.

Prithee, Corporal, said my uncle Toby, as soon as Trim had done it ————how often does Mrs. Bridget enquire after the wound on the cap of thy knee, which thou received'st at the battle of Landen?

She never, an' please your honour, enquires after it at all.

That, Corporal, said my uncle Toby, with all the triumph the goodness of his nature would permit——That shews the difference in the character of the mistress and maid——had the fortune of war allotted the same

mischance to me, Mrs. Wadman would have enquired into every circumstance relating to it a hundred times——She would have enquired, an'
please your honour, ten times as often about your honour's groin——
The pain, Trim, is equally excruciating,——and Compassion has as much
to do with the one as the other——

——God bless your honour! cried the Corporal——what has a
woman's compassion to do with a wound upon the cap of a man's knee?
had your honour's been shot into ten thousand splinters at the affair of
Landen, Mrs. Wadman would have troubled her head as little about it as
Bridget; because, added the Corporal, lowering his voice and speaking
very distinctly, as he assigned his reason——

"The knee is such a distance from the main body—whereas the groin,
your honour knows, is upon the very *curtin* of the *place*."

My uncle Toby gave a long whistle——but in a note which could
scarce be heard across the table.

The Corporal had advanced too far to retire——in three words he
told the rest——

My uncle Toby laid down his pipe as gently upon the fender, as if it
had been spun from the unravellings of a spider's web——

——Let us go to my brother Shandy's, said he.

CHAP. XXXII.

THERE will be just time, whilst my uncle Toby and Trim are walking to my father's, to inform you, that Mrs. Wadman had, some
moons before this, made a confident of my mother; and that Mrs. Bridget,
who had the burden of her own, as well as her mistress's secret to carry,
had got happily delivered of both to Susannah behind the garden-
wall.

As for my mother, she saw nothing at all in it, to make the least bustle
about——but Susannah was sufficient by herself for all the ends and
purposes you could possibly have, in exporting a family secret; for she
instantly imparted it by signs to Jonathan——and Jonathan by tokens to
the cook, as she was basting a loin of mutton; the cook sold it with some

kitchen-fat to the postillion for a groat, who truck'd it with the dairy-maid for something of about the same value——and though whisper'd in the hay-loft, FAME caught the notes with her brazen trumpet and sounded them upon the house-top—In a word, not an old woman in the village or five miles round, who did not understand the difficulties of my uncle Toby's siege, and what were the secret articles which had delay'd the surrender.——

My father, whose way was to force every event in nature into an hypothesis, by which means never man crucified TRUTH at the rate he did——had but just heard of the report as my uncle Toby set out; and catching fire suddenly at the trespass done his brother by it, was demonstrating to Yorick, notwithstanding my mother was sitting by——not only, "That the devil was in women, and that the whole of the affair was lust;" but that every evil and disorder in the world of what kind or nature soever, from the first fall of Adam, down to my uncle Toby's (inclusive) was owing one way or other to the same unruly appetite.

Yorick was just bringing my father's hypothesis to some temper, when my uncle Toby entering the room with marks of infinite benevolence and forgiveness in his looks, my father's eloquence rekindled against the passion ——and as he was not very nice in the choice of his words when he was wroth——as soon as my uncle Toby was seated by the fire, and had filled his pipe, my father broke out in this manner.

CHAP. XXXIII.[1]

—— T HAT provision should be made for continuing the race of so great, so exalted and godlike a Being as man—I am far from denying—but philosophy speaks freely of every thing; and therefore I still think and do maintain it to be a pity, that it should be done by means of a passion which bends down the faculties, and turns all the wisdom, contemplations, and operations of the soul backwards——a passion, my dear, continued my father, addressing himself to my mother, which couples and equals wise men with fools, and makes us come out of our caverns and hiding-places more like satyrs and four-footed beasts than men.

I know it will be said, continued my father (availing himself of the *Prolepsis*) [2] that in itself, and simply taken——like hunger, or thirst, or sleep——'tis an affair neither good or bad—or shameful or otherwise. ——Why then did the delicacy of *Diogenes* and *Plato* [3] so recalcitrate [4] against it? and wherefore, when we go about to make and plant a man, do we put out the candle? and for what reason is it, that all the parts thereof— the congredients [5]—the preparations—the instruments, and whatever serves thereto, are so held as to be conveyed to a cleanly mind by no language, translation, or periphrasis whatever?

——The act of killing and destroying a man, continued my father raising his voice—and turning to my uncle Toby—you see, is glorious— and the weapons by which we do it are honourable——We march with them upon our shoulders——We strut with them by our sides——We gild them——We carve them——We in-lay them——We enrich them ——Nay, if it be but a *scoundril* cannon, we cast an ornament upon the breech of it.—

——My uncle Toby laid down his pipe to intercede for a better epithet ——and Yorick was rising up to batter the whole hypothesis to pieces——

——When Obadiah broke into the middle of the room with a complaint, which cried out for an immediate hearing.

The case was this:

My father, whether by ancient custom of the manor, or as improprietor of the great tythes, [6] was obliged to keep a Bull for the service of the Parish, and Obadiah had led his cow upon a *pop-visit* to him one day or other the preceeding summer——I say, one day or other—because as chance would have it, it was the day on which he was married to my father's house-maid——so one was a reckoning to the other. Therefore when Obadiah's wife was brought to bed—Obadiah thanked God——

——Now, said Obadiah, I shall have a calf: so Obadiah went daily to visit his cow.

She'll calve on Monday—on Tuesday—or Wednesday at the far-thest——

The cow did not calve——no—she'll not calve till next week—— the cow put it off terribly——till at the end of the sixth week Obadiah's suspicions (like a good man's) fell upon the Bull.

Now the parish being very large, my father's Bull, to speak the truth of him, was no way equal to the department; he had, however, got himself, somehow or other, thrust into employment—and as he went through the business with a grave face, my father had a high opinion of him.

——Most of the townsmen, an' please your worship, quoth Obadiah, believe that 'tis all the Bull's fault——

——But may not a cow be barren? replied my father, turning to Doctor Slop.

It never happens: said Dr. Slop, but the man's wife may have come before her time naturally enough——Prithee has the child hair upon his head?—added Dr. Slop——

——It is as hairy as I am;[7] said Obadiah.——Obadiah had not been shaved for three weeks——Wheu – – u – – – – u – – – – – – – – – cried my father; beginning the sentence with an exclamatory whistle——and so, brother Toby, this poor Bull of mine, who is as good a Bull as ever p—ss'd, and might have done for Europa herself in purer times——had he but two legs less, might have been driven into Doctors Commons [8] and lost his character——which to a Town Bull, brother Toby, is the very same thing as his life——

L – – d! said my mother, what is all this story about?——

A COCK and a BULL,[9] said Yorick——And one of the best of its kind, I ever heard.

The END of the NINTH VOLUME.

Notes

These annotations are based on Volume 3 of the Florida Edition of *The Works of Laurence Sterne: Tristram Shandy: The Notes*, ed. Melvyn New, with Richard A. Davies and W. G. Day (University Press of Florida, 1984); I gratefully acknowledge their kind permission to use materials in that volume. Readers interested in further pursuing information in the notes below are advised to consult the Florida *Notes*, since many details therein have necessarily been omitted here.

All annotators of *Tristram Shandy* must also pay homage to Sterne's first textbook annotator, James A. Work (Odyssey, 1940). Many of Work's identifications of historical persons are repeated verbatim in these notes, as they were in the Florida *Notes*.

All journals are abbreviated as in the *PMLA* Bibliography. Classical quotations and translations are taken from the Loeb Classical Library (Harvard University Press), unless otherwise indicated. Shakespeare is quoted from *The Riverside Shakespeare*, ed. G. Blakemore Evans, *et al.* (Houghton Mifflin, 1974). Scripture is quoted from the King James Version. In quoting Rabelais, Montaigne, Cervantes, Burton, Chambers, and other sources, I have used the translation or edition cited in the Florida *Notes*, but have not provided the detailed page references available in that volume.

Sterne's letters are quoted from the valuable edition of Lewis Perry Curtis (Clarendon Press, 1935). His forty-five sermons are cited by their sequential number in the seven volumes published between 1760 and 1769; the scholarly edition of the *Sermons* is the Florida Edition of *The Works of Laurence Sterne*, Volumes 4 and 5 (1996).

Assertion that a phrase is 'proverbial' is based on its appearance in *The Oxford Dictionary of English Proverbs*, 3rd ed., rev. F. P. Wilson (Clarendon Press, 1970) or Morris Palmer Tilley, *A Dictionary of the Proverbs in England in the Sixteenth and Seventeenth Centuries* (University of Michigan Press, 1950).

Conjectural alternative readings are indicated by an italicized question mark. Terms of fortification are defined at the end of this volume in a Glossary of Terms of Fortification.

Titles often referred to have been given short titles as follows:

ASJ   [Sterne], *A Sentimental Journey through France and Italy by Mr. Yorick*, ed. Gardner D. Stout, Jr. (University of California Press, 1967).

Burton   Robert Burton, *The Anatomy of Melancholy*, 5th ed. (Oxford, 1638).

Cash, *EMY*   Arthur H. Cash, *Laurence Sterne: The Early and Middle Years* (Methuen, 1975).

Cash, *LY*   Arthur H. Cash, *Laurence Sterne: The Later Years* (Methuen, 1986).

Chambers   Ephraim Chambers, *Cyclopædia: or, an Universal Dictionary of Arts and Sciences*, 5th ed., 2 vols. (1741, 1743).

Don Quixote Miguel de Cervantes, *Don Quixote*, trans. Peter Motteux, rev. John Ozell, 7th ed., 4 vols. (1743).

Montaigne   Michel de Montaigne, *Essays*, trans. Charles Cotton, 5th ed., 3 vols. (1738).

OED   *Oxford English Dictionary*.

Pope   John Butt, general ed., *The Twickenham Edition of the Poems of Alexander Pope* (Methuen, 1939–69).

Rabelais   *The Works of Francis Rabelais, M.D.*, trans. Thomas Urquhart and Peter Motteux, with notes by John Ozell, 5 vols. (1750).

Spectator   *The Spectator*, ed. Donald F. Bond (Clarendon Press, 1965).

Tindal   Paul Rapin de Thoyras, *The History of England*, trans. and continued by N. Tindal, 3rd ed., 4 vols. in 5 (1743–7).

Watt   [Sterne], *Tristram Shandy*, ed. Ian Watt (Riverside Editions, 1965).

Work   [Sterne], *Tristram Shandy*, ed. James A. Work (Odyssey, 1940).

Volume I

Frontispiece: First published in the second edition, engraved by Simon François Ravenet (*c.* 1706–74) after a drawing by William Hogarth (1697–1764). Almost immediately upon his arrival in London in the spring of 1760, Sterne wrote to an acquaintance asking him to solicit Hogarth for an illustration to 'clap at the Front of my next Edition . . .' A second state of the engraving, to which a grandfather's clock and a three-cornered hat have been added, is on p. 107, facing the passage it illustrates.

Motto: From the *Enchiridion* of the Stoic philosopher Epictetus (*c.* 55–*c.* 135): 'Men are tormented with the opinions they have of things, and not by the things themselves.' Donald Greene offers an alternative translation important for understanding *TS*: 'Not practicalities trouble human beings, but dogmas concerning them' ('Pragmatism versus Dogmatism: The Ideology of *Tristram Shandy*', in *Approaches to Teaching 'Tristram Shandy'* (Modern Language Association, 1989)).

DEDICATION

1. Mr. PITT: Dedication added to the second edition, published on 2 April 1760. William Pitt (1708–78) was enjoying particular popularity at this time for his political leadership during the Seven Years War.

2. bye corner: I.e., the village of Sutton-on-the-Forest, eight miles north of York, where Sterne lived from 1738 until 1760, when he was awarded the living of Coxwold (thirteen miles north of York); his home in Coxwold, which he called Shandy Hall, has been restored and is open to visitors.

3. ill health: Sterne was consumptive and troubled by ill-health during much of the writing of *TS*.

CHAPTER I

1. I Wish . . . me: That the conditions of conception determined the future of the child was a commonplace idea.

2. temperature: I.e., temperament; the two words were interchangeable throughout the eighteenth century.

3. humours: Sterne alludes to the medieval notion that character was determined by the balance of the four elements (earth, air, water, and fire) in the body; imbalance created four character types: sanguine, phlegmatic, choleric, or melancholic.

4. animal spirits: According to Chambers, Sterne's favourite source for arcane learning, the animal spirits were conceived as a 'fine subtile juice, or humour' intended to account for the interaction of mind and body; in the eighteenth century, the concept was under considerable sceptical scrutiny.

CHAPTER II

1. scattered . . . reception: Cf. Rabelais, III.31. Sterne was familiar with Rabelais (*c.* 1494–*c.* 1553) in the free-wheeling translation by Thomas Urquhart and Peter Motteux, with notes by John Ozell. The word 'Homunculus' ('little man') and the subsequent discussion reflect an ongoing eighteenth-century debate concerning procreation. The 'animalculists' believed male sperm contained the complete human being in miniature, the female egg merely providing nutriment for nine months; the 'ovulists' suspected the woman's egg had a more central role in procreation.

2. minutest philosophers: The phrase harks back to Cicero and connotes 'petty', rather than 'careful' or 'precise'.

3. skin . . . articulations: Sterne's list is borrowed from Rabelais, V.9.

4. Lord Chancellor: Chief administrator of justice in England.

5. *Tully, Puffendorff*: Marcus Tullius Cicero (106–43 B.C.), Roman orator and statesman; Samuel Pufendorf (1632–94), German jurist and philosopher. It is doubtful that Sterne had specific passages in mind; the names are invoked as typical legal authorities.

CHAPTER IV

1. *Pilgrim's Progress*: First published in 1678, John Bunyan's *Pilgrim's Progress* was the most popular Protestant work of piety throughout the eighteenth century.

2. *Montaigne*: Sterne alludes to 'Upon Some Verses of Virgil' in the *Essays* of Michel de Montaigne (1533–92). Like Rabelais and Cervantes, Montaigne (in Charles Cotton's translation) was a favourite author of Sterne.

3. as *Horace* says, *ab Ovo*: As Sterne – and all educated readers – well knew, Horace praises Homer for *not* beginning *ab ovo* (from the egg), but rather *in medias res* (in the middle of things); see *Ars Poetica*, lines 146ff. Cf. Tristram's comment: 'write as I will, and rush as I may into the middle of things, as *Horace* advises . . .' (p. 235). Horace (65–8 B.C.), masterly Roman odist and satirist, taught Sterne much about writing satire that stings rather than bites.

4. now made public: Stock bookseller's phrase.

5. *Turky* merchant: Member of the Turkey or Levant Company, trading in that area of the world.

6. *Locke*: Sterne alludes to John Locke's *Essay Concerning Human Understanding* (1690), in which Locke glances at the association of unconnected ideas in a negative light; see, e.g., II.33.5 and II.33.9. Locke (1632–1704), the great English empiricist, had an influence on *TS*, but its extent and nature have been much debated, ranging from those who believe *TS* is structured on Lockean principles to those who believe it is written *contra* Locke. To begin to explore this question, see W. G. Day, '*Tristram Shandy*: Locke May Not Be the Key', in *'Tristram Shandy': Riddles and Mysteries*, ed. V. G. Myer (Vision, 1984).

7. *Lady-Day*: Popular name for the Feast of the Annunciation, 25 March.

8. *Westminster* school: Favourite place for educating the sons of the aristocracy during the eighteenth century.

9. Sciatica: Pain in the lower back, buttocks, hips, etc.

CHAPTER V

1. ON the fifth . . . expected: The first of several playful, and probably meaningless, hints in *TS* that Walter may not be Tristram's father, since the gestation period is eight rather than nine months, assuming this version of the conception is accurate. November 5th was Sterne's deliberate choice: it is Guy Fawkes Day, officially celebrated in England until 1859 with bonfires and processions commemorating the discovery of the so-called gunpowder treason (1605), a Roman Catholic plot to blow up Parliament, and the inauguration of the Glorious Revolution of 1688 with the landing of William III in Torbay.

2. disasterous: As Watt (7, n. 1) notes, Sterne's misspelling of 'disastrous' reminds us that the word means 'ill-starred' from an astrological viewpoint; the analogy continues to the end of the chapter.

3. misadventures and cross accidents: A favourite and important expression of Sterne.

CHAPTER VI

1. *O diem præclarum*: 'O glorious day', a Latin commonplace.

CHAPTER VII

1. midwife: Sterne enters the ongoing debate in his age regarding midwives and male doctors, clearly on the side of the former. See Jean Donnison, *Midwives and Medical Men* (Schocken, 1977), and Donna Landry and Gerald MacLean, 'Of Forceps, Patents, and Paternity: *Tristram Shandy* ', *ECS* 23 (1990).

2. *rights ... whatsoever*: A legitimate legal phrase.

3. *Didius*: Traditionally associated with Dr Francis Topham (1713–70), a leading York lawyer who plays a central role as the villain (named Trim) in Sterne's pamphlet satire on the local ecclesiastical establishment, *A Political Romance*, written and suppressed at the end of 1758. The work triggered Sterne's creative juices, the first two volumes of *TS* appearing one year later. When *Didius* reappears in Volumes III and IV, he has lost all local representation and is a generalized representative of the legal profession. The name may refer to Julianus Didius, who, in 193, purchased the Roman Empire from the praetorian guards.

4. whim-wham: While the word may denote 'fantastic notion, odd fancy' (*OED*), Sterne found his purport in Ozell's note to Rabelais, IV.32: 'whim-whams, men's pissing tools'.

5. Dr. *Kunastrokius*: Sterne alludes to Richard Mead (1673–1754), an eminent London physician whose private sexual conduct became the subject of public comment. Sensitive to possible criticism for his recognizable satiric targets, Sterne prepared a defence in a letter to an unknown correspondent in late January 1760: 'If Kunastrokius after all is too sacred a character to be even smiled at ... he has had better luck than his betters:— In the same page ... I have said as much of a man of twice his wisdom—and that is Solomon, of whom I have made the same remark "That they were both great men—and like all mortal men had each their ruling passion." '

The name *Kunastrokius* bears comparison to Voltaire's *Cunegund*; Sterne invokes Voltaire in the next chapter.

6. HOBBY-HORSES: Among the meanings that come into play in Sterne's usage throughout *TS* are hobby, foible, pastime, amusement, obsession, ruling passion, child's toy (a stick with a horse's head attached, also used in country dances), and, as used in the seventeenth century, a wanton or prostitute. See David Oakleaf, 'Long Sticks, Morris Dancers, and Gentlemen: Associations of the Hobby-horse in *Tristram Shandy* ', *ECLife* 11 (1987).

7. running horses: Possibly bawdy, since the term was used in the eighteenth century for a venereal affliction.

8. pallets: Palettes.

9. maggots: Whimsical fancies, but also, possibly, an allusion to the growing scientific interest in insects and microscopic organisms, which may have appeared to Sterne – as to Pope and Swift – hobby-horsical.

CHAPTER VIII

1. *De gustibus non est disputandum*: There is no disputing about tastes.

2. fiddler and painter: Sterne was both; he wrote in his 'Memoirs' for his daughter, Lydia, that 'Books, painting, fiddling, and shooting' were his amusements (*Sterne's Memoirs*, ed. Kenneth Monkman (The Laurence Sterne Trust, 1985)). See Cash, *EMY*, 208–14.

3. pads: Horses.

CHAPTER IX

1. daubing: Perhaps a pun on a secondary meaning of daubing: 'The putting a false show on anything (*obs.*); hypocritical flattery' (*OED*). The primary meaning is bad painting.

2. painter's scale: Sterne's use in this paragraph of the 'painter's scale', the invention of Roger de Piles, a seventeenth-century authority on painting, has been usefully discussed in R. F. Brissenden, 'Sterne and Painting', in *Of Books and Humankind*, ed. John Butt (Routledge & Kegan Paul, 1964). De Piles awards grades (1–20) in several categories to fifty painters, including an 18 to Raphael for design; Tristram awards himself a 19, although the pun on *design* should be noted. An English translation, *The Principles of Painting*, appeared in 1743.

3. *tout ensemble*: In a painting, the 'harmony which results from the distribution of the several objects or figures, whereof it is composed' (Chambers).

4. Mr. *Dodsley*: Since Robert Dodsley (1703–64) retired from their thriving publishing firm in March 1759, his brother James (1724–97) is most likely referred to here. Robert had turned down Sterne's manuscript in the spring of 1759, but after Sterne published the first two volumes in York at his own expense, James bought the copyright for a second edition, as well as for Volumes III and IV, and two volumes of sermons.

5. CANDID and Miss CUNEGUND's affairs: The hero and heroine of Voltaire's *Candide*, published in January 1759 and translated into English soon thereafter.

CHAPTER X

1. *Rosinante*: Don Quixote's horse, described in I.I.1, I.III.1, etc., always unflatteringly as a 'jade' of a broken-down horse.

2. chaste deportment: *Don Quixote*, I.III.1; when the Yanguesian carriers bring some mares into his vicinity, Rozinante proves to be less chaste than was previously thought. Sterne used Peter Motteux's translation, revised by John Ozell.

3. demi-peak'd: 'Peak of about half the height of that of the older war-saddle' (*OED*).

4. *poudrè d'or*: Powdered with gold.

5. chuck-farthing and shuffle-cap: Games in which money is tossed into a hole or shaken in a hat.

6. true point of ridicule: Cf. Sterne's letter of 23 May 1759, describing to Dodsley the design of *TS*: 'The Plan . . . is a most extensive one,—taking in, not only, the Weak part of the Sciences, in wch the true point of Ridicule lies—but every Thing else, which I find Laugh-at-able in my way—.'

7. *de vanitate mundi et fugâ sæculi*: On the vanity of the world and the swift [frightful] passing of time. A commonplace; cf. Rabelais, I.42, where Friar John speaks of delivering a 'fine long sermon, de contemptu mundi, & fuga seculi' to drowning men.

8. death's head: A skull, a *memento mori*, the most famous of which is Yorick's, recovered by the gravedigger in *Hamlet*, V.i.

9. like wit and judgment: Cf. Tristram's 'Author's Preface' in III.xx: 'for that wit and judgment in this world never go together; inasmuch as they are two operations differing from each other as wide as east is from west.—So, says *Locke*,—so are farting and hickuping, say I.'

10. compose his cough: Tristram and Yorick share with Sterne the common characteristic of a pulmonary ailment.

11. broken-winded: Sterne lists several diseases of horses, common knowledge in an age when horses were the primary means of transportation.

12. *communibus annis*: In average or ordinary years.

13. knight of *La Mancha*: I.e., Don Quixote. The identification of Yorick with Cervantes's hero, which begins with the comparison of his horse to Rozinante, ends with the '*cervantick* tone' of his last words.

14. a fatality . . . men: Sterne perhaps recalls *Hamlet*, V.ii.10–11: 'There's a divinity that shapes our ends, / Rough-hew them how we will . . .'

CHAPTER XI

1. YORICK: Sterne brilliantly exploits the complexities of Shakespeare's jester—*memento mori* as a voice for his own work. Kenneth Monkman ('Sterne, Hamlet, and Yorick', in *The Winged Skull: Papers from the Laurence Sterne Bicentenary Conference*, ed. Arthur Cash and John M. Stedmond (Kent State University Press, 1971)) notes

Sterne's early fascination with *Hamlet* and also that the older pronunciation of *York* was *Yorick*. In the 'Rabelaisian Fragment', written just prior to *TS*, Sterne laments for his clerical protagonist, 'Alass poor *Homenas!*'; the sentence may have steered him to Yorick as his *alter ego*. He published sermons in 1760 and 1766 under the name Mr Yorick and used the name for his protagonist in *ASJ*.

2. reign of *Horwendillus*: Allusion to Shakespeare's source for the Hamlet story in the *Gesta Danorum* of Saxo Grammaticus (*c.* 1200), published in 1514; Horwendillus was Hamlet's (Amleth's) father. Yorick is never mentioned in the account.

3. *Noddy*'s: Generic name for a fool.

4. delectable narrative: Sterne never provides this, although he seems to have had some version of a continental tour in mind when he began *TS*, perhaps involving the Bishop of Gloucester, William Warburton, as Tristram's tutor. Warburton (1698–1779), author of the monumental *Divine Legation of Moses* (1738–41), editor of Pope, and a leading literary figure in the middle of the century, plays an important if covert role in *TS*, a repository of Sterne's hostility toward censorship and prudery.

5. goods and chattels: Common legal phrase.

6. crasis: Cf. Johnson, *Dictionary* (1755): 'Temperature; constitution arising from the various properties of humours.'

7. heteroclite . . . declensions: Warburton was perhaps the first to apply this metaphor of grammatical irregularity to Sterne himself, writing to Garrick in June 1760, 'I must not forget to thank you for the hints I received from you . . . concerning our heteroclite Parson.'

8. *gaité de cœur*: Gaiety of heart, mirthfulness.

9. bubbled: A popular term in the eighteenth century for being deceived or tricked by a deception or fraudulent scheme (a 'bubble' being both the scheme and the victim); Sterne uses it again at pp. 105, 164, 165.

10. a *French* wit: Sterne has in mind a maxim of François de la Rochefoucauld (1613–80), the cynical French wit; he borrowed his translation from the anonymous *Moral Maxims: by the Duke de la Roche Foucault* (1749), maxim 205.

11. But, in plain truth: The character of a truth-teller persecuted by enmity and gossip is one that Sterne returns to several times in his sermons, especially 17, 'Hezekiah and the messengers', and 31, 'St. Peter's character'; one suspects he identified himself with persecuted 'plain-dealers'.

12. unhackneyed: Inexperienced.

13. *bon mot*: Clever remark.

14. his gibes and his jests: Cf. *Hamlet*, V.i.189: 'Where be your gibes now . . . ?' asks Hamlet of Yorick's skull.

CHAPTER XII

1. upon all-four: Proverbial, although the usual import is that no simile or metaphor can 'run on all four (wheels)', i.e., can correspond.

2. book-debts: 'Amount debited to a person's account in a ledger' (*OED*); cf. p. 299 where Sterne, characteristically, literalizes the expression.

3. *Eugenius* 's: Name traditionally applied as a compliment in the eighteenth century, connoting good nature, good counsel, and good health. It is usually assumed that Sterne honoured his Cambridge and Yorkshire friend John Hall-Stevenson (1718–85) in the name, although doing so had an element of wit attached, since Hall-Stevenson was a hypochondriac and neither prudent nor sensible. Indeed, he made use of Sterne's success to publish some bawdy and unskilful scribblings that probably embarrassed Sterne. One might also consider Eugenius at this point as the *adversarius* in traditional verse satire (e.g., Horace's *Satire* II.i, Pope's *Epistle to Arbuthnot*), who tries (ironically) to discourage the poet's satiric instincts as impediments to success.

4. *When to . . . with*: Sterne's probable source is Thomas Tenison, 'Discourse by Way of Introduction', in *Baconiana, or Certain Genuine Remains of Sir Francis Bacon* (1679). Sterne's *'enew'* is Yorkshire dialect for 'enow', as is 'anew' at p. 230. Tenison has 'enough'.

5. tit: Small horse.

6. that when . . . him: Cf. *Henry VIII*, III.ii.355–8: 'The third day comes a frost, a killing frost, / And when he thinks, good easy man, full surely / His greatness is a-ripening, nips his root, / And then he falls as I do.' That the words are spoken by Cardinal Wolsey, an emblem of clerical vicissitudes at the highest level, provides Sterne with a rich irony in applying them to a country parson's disappointments; first noted by Watt (23, n. 5).

Sterne's narrative of Yorick's career has usually been considered an idealized autobiographical account, especially of his poor relationship with his uncle, Jaques Sterne (1695/6–1759), and his failure to advance in the church. The story of the relationship is told in Cash, *EMY*, 232–40 and *passim*.

7. *Sancho Pança*: Sterne alludes to Sancho Pança's reply to the idea of his wife's becoming a Queen in *Don Quixote*, I.I.7. Sterne often referred to his frustrated ambitions in the church with variants of this passage.

8. *cervantick* tone: One clue to Sterne's meaning is provided by his phrase '*Cervantick* gravity' to describe Walter's attitude when he traps Dr Slop into reading 'Ernulphus's Curse' in III.x; and another, by his reference to the amours of Toby as having a 'Cervantick' cast in IV.xxxii. In a letter written in the summer of 1759, he defines 'Cervantic humour' as 'describing silly and trifling Events, with the Circumstantial Pomp of great Ones'. Clearly, burlesque and irony (mock gravity) are a large part of Sterne's definition of '*cervantick* tone'.

9. faint picture . . . roar: Cf. *Hamlet*, V.i.189–91: 'Where be your gibes now, your

gambols, your songs, your flashes of merriment, that were wont to set the table on a roar?'

10. Alas, poor Y O R I C K : *Hamlet*, V.i.184. Sterne's black page may reflect an earlier elegiac tradition in which words were printed with white letters on black paper; Florida *Notes* gives details of several examples.

CHAPTER XIII

1. rhapsodical work: *OED* cites this passage as its last example: 'Of a literary work: Consisting of a medley of narratives, etc.; fragmentary or disconnected in style.' Cf. Montaigne, 'The Ceremony of the Interview of Princes', which opens: 'There is no Subject so frivolous, that does not merit a Place in this Rhapsody.'

2. out-edge: *OED* records two examples, this passage and one from *ASJ*.

3. compound-ratio: Sterne seems to mean 'inverse ratio'.

4. by way of commentary: One persistent characteristic of the putative author of Jonathan Swift's *A Tale of a Tub* is his (commercial) interest in the size of his volume and in the learned commentators who will be appointed to illuminate 'dark points'. Sterne learned much about the narrative voice of Tristram from his close reading of the *Tale*, a significant model for *TS*.

CHAPTER XIV

1. *Jack Hickathrift* or *Tom Thumb*: Chapbook stories of folk-tale figures. The Grub-street author of *A Tale of a Tub* had written a learned dissertation on *Tom Thumb*.

2. from *Rome . . . Loretto*: Santa Casa, or the Holy House of Loreto, one of the most famous shrines of Italy since the fifteenth century, is on the Adriatic Sea, about 125 miles north-east of Rome.

3. journey's end: Sterne returns to this idea in VII.xlii – xliii, when Tristram crosses the plains of Languedoc in search of 'adventures' and 'human nature'; and again in *ASJ*.

4. views and prospects: The idea recurs in several sermons, most particularly in 2, 'The house of feasting and the house of mourning': 'like travellers, though upon business of the last and nearest concern to us, [we] may surely be allowed to amuse ourselves with the . . . beauties of the country we are passing through'.

CHAPTER XV

1. ingress . . . regress: Legal formula; Sterne uses it again in IV.xxxi – with bawdy intent, as did many in his age.

2. *femme sole*: Single woman.

3. *toties quoties*: Repeatedly; as often as occasion requires. Sterne's legal language is an excellent parody, perhaps copied from an actual document.

4. swell of imagination: C. H. G. Macafee, 'The Obstetrical Aspects of *Tristram Shandy*', *Ulster Medical Journal* 19 (1950), calls this passage an accurate description of pseudocyesis, a condition in which the patient falsely believes herself to be pregnant and produces the objective signs by abdominal swelling.

CHAPTER XVI

1. wall-fruit: Fruit trees, especially those bearing soft fruit, benefit in England from being grown espaliered against a protective wall – hence 'wall-fruit'.

2. From *Stilton . . . Grantham*: Two post stages on the road from London to Edinburgh; Stilton is fifty-nine miles north of London, and Grantham twenty-eight miles farther north. The Trent crossed the post road at Newark-on-Trent, ten miles north of Grantham. York is approximately 200 miles north of London, midway to Edinburgh.

3. running divisions: The image is a musical one; *OED*, s.v. *Division*: 'The execution of a rapid melodic passage, originally conceived as the dividing of each of a succession of long notes into several short ones . . . *esp.* as a variation on, or accompaniment to, a theme or "plain song".' See a similar usage in III.xi.

4. stage: The distance between changes of horse during a journey.

CHAPTER XVII

1. thirteen months after: John A. Hay, 'Rhetoric and Historiography: Tristram Shandy's First Nine Kalendar Months', in *Studies in the Eighteenth Century II* (University of Toronto Press, 1973), points out the computational error in this sentence; it is only a little more than five months later that Tristram is conceived (the first Sunday in March 1718) and thirteen months later that he is born.

2. 'Tis known . . . one: Cf. Sir Thomas Browne, *Religio Medici* (1642): 'for obstinacy in a bad cause, is but constancy in a good'. The sentence has a proverbial aura, perhaps stretching as far back as Tacitus, *Germania*.

CHAPTER XVIII

1. Dr. *Maningham*: Sir Richard Manningham, M.D. (1690–1759), the leading English man-midwife of Sterne's day; since Sterne is discussing events in 1718, however, the allusion is anachronistic.

2. scientifick operator: Sterne's first overt allusion to John Burton, M.D. (1710–71), antiquary and physician of York, author of the *Essay towards a Complete New System of Midwifry* (1751). While Sterne certainly uses the opportunity to pillory an old adversary (see Cash, *EMY*, 159–78 and *passim*), he is also alluding, as noted

above, to the eighteenth-century debate regarding male and female midwives and to a second debate concerning the use of instruments for delivery. Male midwives were usually called only in difficult cases, meaning the need to extract a dead foetus or kill a live one that was endangering the mother's life. Cash, 'Birth' (see Further Reading), provides an excellent background for Sterne's portrait of Slop.

3. *March* 9, 1759: The first of four specific dates that Tristram provides for the writing of *TS*, coinciding with Sterne's own time of writing; the other dates are 26 March 1759 (I.xxi); 10 August 1761 (V.xvii); and 12 August 1766 (IX.i).

4. dear *Jenny*: Cash, *EMY*, 292, points out that the identification of Jenny with Catherine Fourmantel, the professional singer with whom Sterne was having a liaison during the autumn and winter of 1759–60, and who carried the York edition of Volumes I and II of *TS* to David Garrick in London, is unlikely to have been the mistress Sterne writes about in the spring of 1759, unless she was in York for the 1758–9 season as well – for which only supposition exists. More likely, he argues, Jenny is 'not Catherine . . . but a vague general figure of the confidante and mistress'. Yorick's statement in *ASJ* perhaps best solves the problem: '[I have] been in love with one princess or another almost all my life, and I hope I shall go on so, till I die, being firmly persuaded, that if ever I do a mean action, it must be in some interval betwixt one passion and another . . .'

5. heroine it: Recorded by *OED* as a nonce word.

6. He was . . . cases: Cf. Pope, 'Thoughts on Various Subjects' (LXXXIII): 'The people all running to the Capital city, is like a confluence of all the animal spirits to the heart; a symptom that the constitution is in danger.' The idea was a political commonplace by the middle of the century.

7. Squirality: The landed class, usually termed Squirearchy.

8. country-interest: Unrecorded in *OED*. This is the party that opposed Robert Walpole (1676–1745) and later Henry Pelham (1696–1754), and hence was linked with the Tory label. During Sterne's politically active period in the 1740s, he identified with the Whigs opposed to the country-interest. Possibly, however, Sterne simply means a general 'interest in the country's welfare' as distinct from these political divisions.

9. Grand Monarch: Louis XIV, the 'Sun-King'; Sterne's charge of a direct relation between the monarch's absolute power and France's poverty was often made by English observers during the century, from *Spectator* 180 to Edward Gibbon in *Memoirs*.

10. weaker vessels: See 1 Peter 3:7: 'giving honour unto the wife, as unto the weaker vessel'.

11. Sir *Robert Filmer*'s opinion: Although Walter's remarks are in accord with the ideas of the English conservative political writer Robert Filmer (d. 1653), as found in *Patriarcha*, there are no direct borrowings. Wilfred Watson, 'The Fifth Commandment: Some Allusions to Sir Robert Filmer's Writings in *Tristram Shandy*', *MLN*

62 (1947), makes the point that Sterne could have known Filmer's ideas primarily through Locke's *Two Treatises of Government*, or simply because Filmer's name continued well into the eighteenth century as representative of 'antiquated and hobby-horsical political thinking' about the divine rights of kings. See V.xxxi–xxxii for another allusion to Filmer.

12. *Te Deum*: *Te deum laudamus* (We praise thee, O God), the title and first words of a hymn attributed to St Ambrose and sung following a victory; and also in the Anglican morning service.

13. Surely, Madam . . . sex: Cf. Jean de la Bruyère, *The Characters, or the Manners of the Age* (1699): 'There may be a Friendship between persons of different Sexes, which may subsist without Enjoyment; yet a Woman will always look upon a Man as a Man, and so will a Man still look upon a Woman as a Woman.'

14. sentimental: More than any other author of the eighteenth century, Sterne has been credited with the introduction of the word *sentimental* to English literary consciousness; see Mullan in Further Reading. While Sterne's usage varies, the gist of this passage is captured in a letter he wrote from France in 1765: 'I carry on my affairs quite in the French way, sentimentally—"*l'amour*" (say they) "*n'est rien sans sentiment*"—Now notwithstanding they make such a pother about the *word*, they have no precise idea annex'd to it . . .' In *ASJ*, Sterne offers a neat turn on his French motto: '*Et le sentiment est encore moins sans amour*' (Love is nothing without sentiment. And sentiment is even less without love).

CHAPTER XIX

1. Christian names: Walter's theory provides occasion to suggest associations evoked by the names of the Shandy household.

'Shandy' in Yorkshire dialect lies somewhere between 'boisterous' and 'crack-brained'. 'Tristram' recalls the hero of Arthurian legend, whose difficult birth kills his mother, Elizabeth; before dying, she names him 'Tristram', meaning a 'sorrowful birth'. Sterne may also have had in mind a Renaissance tradition in which the name identified a libertine.

In French, the equivalent of 'Merry Andrew' (i.e., a clown) is 'Merry Walter'. 'Toby' was used during the eighteenth century for the posteriors, the buttocks; cf. *Tickletoby*, which Sterne borrows from Rabelais in III.xxxvi. 'Elizabeth' was not only the name of the Arthurian Tristram's mother, but also of Sterne's wife. Finally, 'Trim', in addition to being the villain's name in *A Political Romance* (playing on sycophant, i.e., a *trimmer*), also had connotations more in keeping with the Corporal, particularly being fit, competent, neat, in good order – a good name for a soldier or a servant; see also the suggestion by Ian Campbell Ross and Noha Saad Nassar that the name alludes to a bit of doggerel: 'Trim tram, / Like master, like man' (*N&Q* 36 (1989)).

2. DULCINEA's: Dulcinea del Toboso is the imaginary mistress of Don Quixote; he

dedicates his rare successes to her, and his many misconceptions to necromancers or magicians, who can make an army appear like a flock of sheep.

3. TRISMEGISTUS: Hermes Trismegistus, the name given to the Egyptian god Thoth, reputed author of the *Hermetica*, a compilation of mystical and alchemical writings from the first to the third centuries. For Sterne, hermetic lore probably connotes esoteric and useless knowledge.

4. ARCHIMEDES: Greek mathematician (*c.* 287–212 B.C.).

5. NYKY and SIMKIN: Nicknames for Nicholas and Simon or Simeon.

6. NICODEMUS'D: Sterne may have been looking at a note to a passage in Rabelais's 'Author's Prologue' (Volume I) while writing this section: 'Certain proper names have particular ideas affix'd to them for ridiculous reasons. For instance ... Nicodemus is a foolish fellow or ninny-hammer, from Nigaut and Nice ...' Sterne might also be referring to the Pharisee Nicodemus, whose actions in John 3:1–13 and 7:45–53 led to connotations of faintheartedness and weakness.

7. prejudices of education: A term used during the period by free-thinkers in their attacks on established religion.

8. *piano*: Softness.

9. *argumentum ad hominem*: Argument addressed to the man, i.e., to the character of one's opponent, rather than the issues.

10. Θεοδίδαχ7ος: Theodídaktos: Taught of God; see 1 Thessalonians 4:9.

11. that NATURE ... eloquent: Cf. Antony's 'This was the noblest Roman of them all' speech, *Julius Caesar*, V.v.73–5: 'His life was gentle, and the elements / So mix'd in him that Nature might stand up / And say to all the world, "This was a man!"'

12. *Cicero* ... commentator: Sterne's list includes some standard reading in rhetoricall studies, beginning with the great Roman orators, Cicero (see n. 5 to I.ii) and Marcus Fabius Quintilianus (*c.* 35–*c.* 95), author of the *Institutio Oratoria*. He then lists some earlier Greek authors, Isocrates (436–338 B.C.) and Aristotle (384–322 B.C.), whose *Rhetoric* was still standard fare in the eighteenth century. Longinus is the name Sterne's age gave to the author of *On the Sublime* (first century), a work Sterne returns to several times in *TS*. In his 'Rabelaisian Fragment', the central character is named Longinus Rabelaicus – the would-be author of a parodic treatise on writing sermons.

Gerhard Johann Voss (1577–1649), Francis Burgersdyk (1590–1635), Caspar Schoppe (1576–1649), and Petrus Ramus (1515–72) were continental rhetoricians (the first two were Dutch), while Thomas Farnaby (*c.* 1575–1647) and Richard Crakanthorpe (1567–1624) were English. Although such lists usually import dead learning, these authors were still read in the universities. *Dutch commentator*, commonplace for a verbose and weighty scholar.

13. argument *ad ignorantiam*: Argument that relies on the ignorance of one's opponents or their inability to offer a good counterargument.

14. *Jesus College*: Sterne took his B.A. degree from Jesus College, Cambridge, where he was in residence from 1733 to 1737; his M.A. degree was awarded in 1740. Sterne's

great-grandfather, Archbishop Richard Sterne, had been Master of the college during the Civil War. See Cash, *EMY*, 41–62.

15. *vive la Bagatelle*: Long live trifles (foolery). The phrase was closely associated with Swift, as in Pope's *Imitations of Horace*, Ep. I.vi: 'And Swift cry wisely, "Vive la Bagatelle!" / The Man that loves and laughs, must sure do well.'

16. *Epsom*: Presumably visited for the medicinal waters.

17. *Numps . . . Nick*: *OED* defines *Numps* as a 'silly or stupid person'. The Devil was referred to as *Nick* or *Old Nick*.

18. in *rerum naturâ*: In the nature or order of things.

19. EPIPHONEMA ... EROTESIS: Classical rhetorical terms, the first meaning a striking concluding statement, and the second, a rhetorical question.

CHAPTER XX

1. *Pliny*: Pliny the Younger (*c.* 61–*c.* 112) did say this in his *Epistolae*, but he was talking about his uncle, Pliny the Elder (23/24–79), the Roman naturalist.

2. *Parismus* and *Parismenus*: Popular figures of chivalric romance.

3. Seven Champions of *England*: Probably a slip for *The Seven Champions of Christendom*, tales of the national saints of England, France, Spain, Italy, Scotland, Ireland, and Wales, recounted in countless oral and written versions.

4. *The *Romish* Rituals*: Sterne found the 'Memoire' in Heinrich van Deventer's *Observations Importantes sur le Manuel des Accouchemens* (1734) and provided a footnote citation in the second edition. He found there as well the information offered in this footnote, Aquinas's verdict that 'A child still in the womb can in no way be baptized.' The question asked of the Sorbonne doctors was whether a child in the womb, where no bodily part was visible and the mother unable to deliver, could be baptized by means of a 'little injection-pipe' that would not harm the mother ('*par le moyen d'une* petite canulle . . . sans faire aucun tort à la mere'). In the 'Reply', the doctors note Aquinas's belief that the thing is impossible, since the *second* birth by baptism in Christ presupposes a *first* birth, but go on to suggest that the issue be reopened, by appeal to the Bishop and the Pope, since means now exist to conduct the baptism (*sous condition*: conditionally) without harm to the mother. Watt (47, n. 4), noting that 'conditional baptism' was the official term for baptizing an infant under unusual circumstances (e.g., when the 'conformation is so monstrous' as to cast doubt on its being human), suggests that to say someone was 'baptized conditionally' was a 'jocular reference' to extreme ugliness or stupidity.

For a discussion of Sterne's source for the 'Memoire', see Appendix 6 in the Florida *Text*; for a translation, see the Florida *Notes*.

5. *sans faire aucun tort a le pere*: Sterne's elaborate joke culminates in a sentence artfully, if ungrammatically, parallel to the key phrase of the 'Memoire': *sans faire aucun tort à la mere*. His proposal: baptize the homunculi while they are still in the male, by means of 'a little injection-pipe', *if it can be done without harm to the father!*

CHAPTER XXI

1. I think ... sentence: Tristram recalls his uncle later in this chapter, but does not allow him to finish his sentence until II.vi. The Russian formalist critic Viktor Shklovsky calls attention to this and similar interruptions in his famous essay 'A Parodying Novel: Sterne's *Tristram Shandy*' (1929) reprinted in *Laurence Sterne*, ed. John Traugott (Prentice-Hall, 1968).

2. *Dryden*: The 'long preface' is probably John Dryden's *Essay of Dramatick Poesie* (1668), in which he celebrates the triumph of English over French comedy, though not in climatic terms; nothing in Dryden comes closer, but note that the date of composition was twenty years *before* William's reign (1688–1702) began.

3. *Addison*: Joseph Addison (1672–1719), along with Richard Steele, published the *Spectator* from 1711 to 1714. Sterne may have in mind numbers 179 or 371, or both. That the British climate created the exceptional eccentricity of British character was a commonplace throughout the century.

4. Αχμὴ: Akmè: Acme, pinnacle. Sterne's endorsement of the progress of the 'moderns' is almost certainly ironic, in the manner of Swift in *A Tale of a Tub* and *The Battle of the Books*.

5. *As war ... peace*: A song or catch traced as far back as the sixth century. The full verse has a bearing on *TS*: 'War begets Poverty, / Poverty Peace: / Peace maketh Riches flow, / (Fate ne'er doth cease:) / Riches produceth Pride, / Pride is War's ground, / War begets Poverty, &c. / The World goes round.'

6. the females ... all: Cf. Pope, 'Epistle to a Lady', lines 1–2: 'NOTHING so true as what you once let fall, / "Most Women have no Characters at all." '

7. DINAH: Walter's comment on her name suggests the biblical story of Dinah's rape in Genesis 34:1–31.

8. *Fescue*: Teacher's pointer.

9. *Tacitus*: The Roman historian Tacitus (*c. 55–c.* 117) had a reputation throughout the eighteenth century for excessive subtlety.

10. modesty of nature: Don Quixote was also distinguished by his extreme modesty (II.III.44). Wayne Booth ('Did Sterne Complete *Tristram Shandy*?', *MP* 48 (1951)) points to this and similar passages in the first four volumes to argue that Sterne knew the end of his story would come – whatever else intervened – with the telling of Toby's amours.

11. siege of *Namur*: See II.i.

12. retrogradation of the planets: Apparent backward or westward movement of a planet in the zodiac; Sterne shows some comprehension of astronomical theory in that Copernicus's argument for a heliocentric universe was indeed 'fortified' by the observation of retrogradation.

13. *Amicus Plato ... sister*: Plato is my friend, but truth is a greater friend. The saying may be traced to Plato's *Phaedo* or Aristotle's *Nicomachean Ethics*.

14. in *Foro Scientiæ*: In the forum of science (or knowledge); Sterne's coinage, by

analogy with *in Foro Legis* (the outer forum, i.e., in the eyes of the law) and *in Foro Conscientiæ* (the inner forum, i.e., in the eyes of God, the conscience).

15. 'tis only DEATH: The anti-militaristic idea that 'he who kills one man is a murderer, while he who kills a thousand is a hero' seems to have been a commonplace; the distinction between 'killing' and 'murder' on the basis of malice is a legal principle.

16. *Lillabullero*: Immensely popular song originating in Ireland in 1687 or 1688 as an anti-papist ballad, supposedly written by Thomas Wharton; according to Anthony Collins (*A Discourse Concerning Ridicule and Irony in Writing* (1729)): 'King *James* II and *Popery* were *laugh'd* or *Lilli-bullero'd*' rather than argued out of Ireland. The music and lyrics are reproduced in the Florida *Notes*.

17. *Argumentum ad Verecundiam*: Argument addressed to one's modesty or reverence for authority.

18. *ex Absurdo*: Argument which dismisses a proposition by demonstrating the absurdity of its consequences.

19. *ex Fortiori*: Argument which offers a more conclusive proof than hitherto had been offered.

20. *Ars Logica*: Art of logic.

21. end of disputation: Sterne's attitude toward formal argumentation is paralleled by Locke's in his *Essay Concerning Human Understanding*, IV.17, where he reflects on modes of argumentation that 'Men in their Reasonings with others do ordinarily make use of, to prevail on their Assent; or at least so to awe them, as to silence their Opposition' (ed. Peter H. Nidditch (Clarendon Press, 1975)).

22. *Argumentum Fistulatorium*: Argument of one who plays upon a pipe, i.e., in the present instance, one who whistles. This and the remainder of the terms are not traditional.

23. *Argumentum Baculinum*: Argument of the stick, i.e., violence. Sterne may have borrowed it from *Spectator* 239.

24. *Argumentum ad Crumenam*: Argument directed to the purse (avarice or need) of one's opponent.

25. *Argumentum Tripodium*: Argument addressed to the third leg. Taken with *Argumentum ad Rem*, an argument addressed to 'the *thing*', we are clearly in the realm of Shandean bawdy.

CHAPTER XXII

1. Bishop *Hall*: The work so carefully cited has never been located, although John Beale did publish some works by Joseph Hall (1574–1656), Bishop, successively, of Exeter and Norwich. Hall was a prolific author and one of Sterne's primary sources when composing his sermons. Kenneth Monkman supplied Florida *Notes* with the sentence Sterne possibly had in mind, from Hall's *Meditations and Vowes* (1624): 'It is a vaine-glorious flatterie for a man to praise himselfe.'

2. digressive skill: Many eighteenth-century authors praised digression in a similar

manner, including Swift in 'A Digression in Praise of Digressions' (*A Tale of a Tub*, sect. VII) and Fielding in *Tom Jones*, I.2.

3. like a bridegroom: See Psalm 19:5 and Joel 2:16.

4. brings in variety ... fail: Perhaps recalling Shakespeare's famous description of Cleopatra's 'infinite variety'; *Antony and Cleopatra*, II.ii.234−7.

CHAPTER XXIII

1. *Momus*'s glass: Momus is the Greek personification of mockery and fault-finding. Sterne alludes to the story told by Lucian in *Hermotimus or Concerning the Sects*, although his direct source may have been Robert Burton, *Anatomy of Melancholy*, 'Democritus Junior to the Reader': 'How would *Democritus* have been moved, had he seene the secrets of their hearts? If every man had a window in his breast, which *Momus* would have had in *Vulcans* man ...' According to Lucian, Momus found fault with Hephaestus (Vulcan) for creating man without such a window. Burton (1577−1640) is another author of whom Sterne was particularly fond, but unlike his open acknowledgements of Rabelais, Montaigne, and Cervantes, he never mentions him (although the second motto to Volume V, acknowledging Democritus, is a hint to the learned); while *Anatomy* (1621) is considered a classic today, in Sterne's day it was deemed esoteric.

2. window-money: Tax on house windows, in effect in England from 1696 until the middle of the nineteenth century.

3. dioptrical: Capable of being seen through, and usually, as here, connected to see-through windows on beehives.

4. the planet *Mercury*: Had Sterne consulted Chambers, he would have learned that by Newton's computations the heat on Mercury was seven times greater than on Earth.

5. efficient cause ... final cause: Terms from Aristotelian logic, used here with typical Sternean facetiousness. The 'efficient cause' is that which produces an effect, and the 'final cause', the end for which any act is taken; both terms were subject to endless debate over definition and significance.

6. more: mere?

7. play the fool ... house: Cf. *Hamlet*, III.i.131−2: 'Let the doors be shut upon him, that he may play the fool no where but in 's own house.'

8. *Virgil ... Æneas*: In *Aeneid*, IV, Virgil describes the many tongues of Fame (Rumour) as she spreads the report of Dido and Aeneas. The illustration of the passage in Dryden's translation (1697) shows Fame in her traditional posture of blowing one trumpet while holding another. Samuel Butler, in *Hudibras*, II.i.69−74, describes Fame's instruments with the same bawdy implications as Sterne: 'Two Trumpets she does sound at once, / But both of clean contrary tones. / But whether both with the same wind, / Or one before, and one behind, / We know not; onely this can tell, / The one sounds vilely, th'other well.'

9. the *Italians*: Allusion to the Italian *castrati*, whose appearance on the English opera stage at this time was causing considerable stir; see, e.g., Charles Churchill, *The Rosciad* (1761), lines 721–2: 'But never shall a TRULY BRITISH Age / Bear a vile race of EUNUCHS on the stage.'

10. *forte* or *piano*: Loud (strong) or soft (low).

11. *ad populum*: To the people.

12. *Non-Naturals*: Work's definition (76, n. 8) is good: 'A term formerly used by physicians to indicate the six things which because they do not enter into the composition of the body are not "natural" yet which are essential to animal life and health and which by accident or abuse often cause disease: air, meat and drink, excretion and retention, sleep and waking, motion and rest, and the affections of the mind.' The examination of waste matter, a part of diagnostic medicine from ancient times, was always vulnerable to satire, as in Swift's *Gulliver's Travels*, Book III.

13. Pentagraphic: Sterne's definition may have come from Chambers.

14. in the *Camera*: Sterne plays on *in camera*, 'in a private room or chamber' (a legal term, in contrast to 'in open court'), and *camera obscura*, defined in Chambers as 'a machine, or apparatus representing an artificial eye; whereon the images of external objects received through a double convex glass, are exhibited distinctly . . .' As did the pentagraph, it allowed people without artistic talent to reproduce objects accurately.

15. pencil: I.e., paintbrush in eighteenth-century usage.

16. HOBBY-HORSE: Cf. Sterne's letter of January 1760, defending *TS*: 'The ruleing passion *et les egarements du cœur* [and the wanderings of the heart], are the very things which mark, and distinguish a man's character;—in which I would as soon leave out a man's head as his hobby-horse.' Cf. his comments in sermon 9, on Herod, concerning the way to understand character: 'distinguish . . . the principal and ruling passion which leads the character—and separate that, from the other parts of it. . . . [W]e often think ourselves inconsistent creatures, when we are the furthest from it, and all the variety of shapes and contradictory appearances we put on, are in truth but so many different attempts to gratify the same governing appetite.'

The classic eighteenth-century statement on the ruling passion is Pope's in his *Essay on Man*, II. Whether Sterne's hobby-horse and Pope's ruling passion are the same remains, however, an open question.

CHAPTER XXIV

1. reality of motion: Thomas Stanley, *The History of Philosophy*, 4th ed. (1743), offers a version of this well-known rebuttal in his chapter on scepticism: 'one of the Cynicks, an Argument being propounded to him to take away Motion, made no Answer, but rose up and walk'd, shewing by Action and Evidence, that there is

Motion'. The argument originated with Zeno of Elea (*c.* 490–*c.* 430 B.C.), and the rebuttal is usually assigned to Diogenes of Sinope (*c.* 400–*c.* 325 B.C.); Sterne's suggestion that they are both in the same room is poetic licence.

CHAPTER XXV

1. *oss pubis . . . oss illeum*: Cf. Chambers, s.v. *Coxæ, coxendicis*: 'In infants, each of these [hipbones] consists of three distinct bones, separated by cartilages; which, in adults, grow up, and constitute one firm, solid bone; whose parts, however, retain three distinct names . . . *viz.* the *os ilium*, . . . [the] *os coxendicis*, and the *os pubis.*' Chambers's anatomical chart makes clear that the wound site is as close as possible to the groin without a direct hit.

2. The history . . . wound: *Spectator* 105 describes a military pedant who always talks about 'storming Towns, making Lodgments, and fighting Battels', and 371 alludes to one of those 'dull Generation of Story-tellers' who spends an entire day discussing the siege of Namur. This comic aspect of uncle Toby would seem to have been familiar ground to an eighteenth-century audience.

Volume II

CHAPTER I

1. siege of *Namur*: The siege of Namur is described at length in Sterne's probable source for much of his historical information, Paul Rapin de Thoyras, *The History of England*, trans. and continued by N. Tindal; Sterne's extensive use of this work was first noted by Theodore Baird, 'The Time-Scheme of *Tristram Shandy* and a Source', *PMLA* 51 (1936).

A sample of Tindal's account will demonstrate Sterne's use of his source:

The *English* and *Scots* commanded by Major-general *Ramsey* and Brigadier *Hamilton* came out of the trenches to the right, and attacked the point of the foremost counterscarp, which inclosed the sluice or water-stop. The enemy received them with a furious discharge, which however did not hinder them from going on briskly. . . . [T]he *English* [were] exposed to the shot of the counter-guard and demi-bastion of St. *Roche*, which they sustained and answered with incredible resolution. . . . The *Dutch* lodged themselves upon the counter-guard; and thus both they and the *English* preserved the foremost covered-way before *St. Nicholas* 's gate from the *Maese* to the water-stop. . . . [T]he *French* officers behaved themselves like men of true courage, exposing themselves on the glacis of the counterscarp . . . with their swords in their hands . . .

Tindal includes a map of Namur, as does the Florida *Notes*. Although detailed newspaper reports of the battles of the Seven Years War (1757–63) provided Sterne with a contemporary audience more familiar with this jargon than modern readers, we still must suspect he was more interested in baffling and bemusing readers than allowing Toby's delineations to enlighten them.

King William's wars began with his accession in November 1688 and ended with the Peace of Ryswick in 1697. Between 1689 and 1691 the arena was primarily Ireland, where William successfully defeated the Jacobite threat; the decisive Battle of the Boyne in July 1690 prepared the way for the fall of Limerick in 1691, a campaign in which Toby and Trim participated. William then turned to the continent, where France had taken the offensive in Flanders and captured Namur in 1692. William's recapture of the citadel in 1695 was England's major success in the war and also its turning-point.

2. *Hippocrates*: Hippocrates (469–399 B.C.), the most famous of Greek physicians.

3. Dr. *James Mackenzie*: James Mackenzie (*c*. 1680–1761), Scottish physician and author of *History of Health, and the Art of Preserving It* (1758), is quoted extensively by Sterne in V.xxxiv. Sterne may have had in mind Mackenzie's advice that whoever wants good health 'must previously learn to conquer his passions', because 'unhappy passions, if indulged to excess, will prevail over all his regularity, and prevent the good effects of his temperance ...'

4. digestion: Sterne puns on digestion's now obsolete meaning, 'the process of maturing an ulcer or wound'.

CHAPTER II

1. *Locke*'s Essay ... Understanding: In the ensuing discussion, Sterne paraphrases the *Essay*, II.29.3:

The *cause of Obscurity* in simple *Ideas*, seems to be either dull Organs; or very slight and transient Impressions made by the Objects; or else a weakness in the Memory, not able to retain them as received. ... If the Organs, or Faculties of Perception, like Wax over-hardned with Cold, will not receive the Impression of the Seal, from the usual impulse wont to imprint it; or, like Wax of a temper too soft, will not hold it well, when well imprinted; or else supposing the Wax of a temper fit, but the Seal not applied with a sufficient force, to make a clear Impression: In any of these cases, the print left by the Seal, will be *obscure*.

2. *Malbranch*: Sterne's invocation of Nicolas Malebranche (1638–1715) perhaps alludes to his *De la recherche de la vérité* (1674–5), translated by T. Taylor in 1694 as *Father Malebranche's treatise concerning the search after truth*.

3. brass-jack: Not recorded in *OED*, but probably a reference to a counterfeit coin.

4. *Arthur*'s: Well-known London club.

5. 'yclept: I.e., called, named; Sterne's use of archaisms (see above, 'eke [i.e., also] the thimble') is worth noting.

6. Gentle critick ... space: Sterne continues to borrow from Locke's *Essay*: 'When it is considered, what a pudder is made about *Essences*, and how much all sorts of

Knowledge, Discourse, and Conversation, are pester'd and disorder'd by the careless, and confused Use and Application of Words, it will, perhaps, be thought worth while th[o]roughly to lay [the subject] open' (III.5.16; see also III.3.9 and III.10.2). Sterne's Greek may be translated interchangeably as 'essence' or 'substance', a distinction much debated among scholastic metaphysicians.

CHAPTER III

1. feet of the elephant: W. E. Buckley, *N&Q* 6th ser. 5 (1882), suggests that the title of Toby's map was adorned with a cartouche, 'among the ornaments of which an elephant was introduced', a common decoration in the eighteenth century.

2. *Gobesius* 's: Perhaps, as suggested by C. Deedes, *N&Q* 10th ser. 5 (1906), an allusion to Leonhard Gorecius (*fl. c.* 1577), author of *Descriptio Belli Ivoniæ* (*Account of the War in Spain*); or Sterne may have invented the name, since the other 'experts' mentioned are found in Chambers. *Pyroballogy* is the 'study of the art of casting fire', i.e., of artillery.

3. *Maes . . . Salsines*: Cf. Tindal: 'the Elector of *Bavaria* . . . passed [the *Sambre*] amidst the enemy's continual fire, and possessed himself of the abbey of *Salsines*, a post of great importance, and which favoured the attack of *Vauban* 's line . . .' For Vauban, see n. 6 to this chapter.

4. assimulation: Cf. pp. 122 and 503 for similar misspelling; Sterne may have found the error useful, embodying 'assimilation' and 'stimulation' in one word.

5. incumbition: *OED* cites this passage as its sole illustration of figurative use: 'the action of lying or pressing upon'.

6. *Ramelli . . . Blondel*: Toby's list of military authorities is culled from Chambers, s.v. *Fortification*, as first noted by Sir Edward Bensly, 'A Debt of Sterne's', *TLS* (1 November 1928). Sterne's entire knowledge of fortification could have come from Chambers, Tindal, and the daily gazettes; there is no reason to believe, based on the discussions in *TS*, that he read the experts he mentions – which is, of course, his joke.

Baron Menno van Coehoorn (1641–1704), Dutch engineer, and Sébastien le Prestre de Vauban (1633–1707), Marshal of France and the most celebrated of military engineers, were the designers of the fortifications of Namur.

7. invaded his library: See *Don Quixote*, I.I.6: 'There they found above a hundred large Volumes neatly bound, and a good Number of small ones . . .'

8. the third year: Sterne's chronology is confused. Since Toby was wounded in late July 1695, August 1699 would be the beginning of the fifth year, unless it took Toby two years to reach London from Namur.

9. *N. Tartaglia*: Again a borrowing from Chambers, this time from entries under *Projectile* and *Gunnery*: e.g., 'N. Tartaglia was the first who perceived the mistake, and maintained the path of the bullet to be a crooked line . . .'; and again, 'there

are certain rules, founded on geometry, for all these things: most of which we owe to Gallileo ... and his disciple Torricellius'.

10. *latus rectum*: Straight line; Sterne found the term in Chambers.

11. mases: I.e., mazes. For an excellent study of mazes and labyrinths in *TS*, see Soud in Further Reading.

12. fly ... serpent: Ecclesiasticus 21:2: 'Flee from sin as from the face of a serpent ...'

13. Is it fit ... age: Sterne borrows this passage from his 'Rabelaisian Fragment', two chapters of an abortive effort to write a parodic 'Art of Sermon-writing' similar to Pope's *Peri Bathous*; see New, 'Sterne's Rabelaisian Fragment: A Text from the Holograph Manuscript', *PMLA* 87 (1972). Radical moisture is a medieval medical term for that which nourishes and preserves the vital flame of life.

CHAPTER IV

1. I Would ... groat: Proverbial; the groat was not coined after 1662, but remained a term for a very small sum.

2. *cum grano salis*: With a grain of salt.

3. clean shirt: A daily clean shirt was the century's sign of respectability.

4. Monsieur *Ronjat*: Étienne Ronjat, first surgeon to William III.

CHAPTER V

1. WHEN a man ... discretion: Cf. Swift, *A Tale of a Tub*, sect. IX: 'But when a Man's Fancy gets *astride* on his Reason, when Imagination is at Cuffs with the Senses, and common Understanding, as well as common Sense, is Kickt out of Doors; the first Proselyte he makes, is Himself ...' (ed. A. C. Guthkelch and D. Nichol Smith, 2nd ed. (Clarendon Press, 1958)).

2. incarnate: To cause flesh to grow on or in (a wound or sore); to heal over.

3. The sound ... mind: Sterne touches on Lockean concepts of duration and the succession of ideas, discussed more fully in III.xviii.

4. 'Change: The Royal Exchange, London's trading centre, built in 1669.

5. demigration: Migration.

6. *James Butler*: Second Duke of Ormonde (1665–1745). He replaced Marlborough as General of the Army in 1712 and pursued the orders of Anne and Bolingbroke in implementing the Treaty of Utrecht, for which he was impeached when the Whigs returned to power in 1715. Like Trim, he was wounded at Landen in 1693 and took part in the battle of Namur.

7. broke no squares: Proverbial for 'made no difference'; its origin is military, i.e., breaking ranks.

8. ichnography: In Sterne's *Political Romance* one character offers a solution to the 'allegory' based on the 'Ichnography and Plan' of Gibraltar, but another character

protests that he does not understand the word; it evidently struck Sterne as a difficult – or humorous – word.

9. sit down before: Trim puns on the military usage of *sit*, meaning 'to encamp *before* a town, etc., in order to besiege it; to begin *to* a siege' (*OED*).

10. mark me the polygon: John Muller, *A Treatise . . . of Fortification* (1746), makes the point that the first step in planning a fortification is to 'inscribe in a circle a polygon of as many sides as the fortification is designed to have fronts'.

11. campaign: Tract of open country, a plain.

12. something like a tansy: *OED* cites this passage as its last illustration of the phrase: 'properly, fittingly, perfectly'. *Tansy* is the name of a plant and, by extension, of a pudding or omelette flavoured with its juice.

13. red as scarlet: This comparison occurs in the Commination service in the *Book of Common Prayer*: 'For tho' our sins be as red as scarlet, they shall be made white as snow.'

14. bowling-green: In a possible precursor to *TS*, the anonymous *Life and Memoirs of Mr. Ephraim Tristram Bates* (1756), the hero practises the use of his firelock on a 'Bowling-green . . . so surrounded with a Hedge-row that no one suspected any People there at that Time'. When he dies, people pass his grave and cry 'Alas! poor Bates'. The argument of an influence is made by Helen Sard Hughes in *JEGP* 17 (1918).

15. retina: *OED* cites this passage as its first illustration of figurative usage.

16. epitasis: Traditional second part of a drama in which the plot or action is complicated.

CHAPTER VI

1. *Susannah . . . ravish her*: Probably an allusion to the apocryphal story of Susanna, who bathes in her garden while two elders spy on her and later attempt her virtue.

2. pudding's end: Sterne has something more bawdy in mind than the knotted end of a sausage, i.e., a trifle; the trumpeter's wife in 'Slawkenbergius's Tale' calls Diego's nose a 'pudding's end'.

3. My sister . . . her ****: A very real problem for man-midwives, as suggested by the contemporary pamphlet *Man-Midwifery Analysed* (1764): 'I desire every woman . . . to consider whether she be strictly entitled to the appellation of . . . a modest woman, after she has admitted a male operator thus to insult her person.'

4. *Aposiopesis*: The sudden breaking-off in mid-course. Sterne was especially interested in this rhetorical figure and concludes *ASJ* with one of the most famous examples in literature:

So that when I stretch'd out my hand, I caught hold of the Fille de Chambre's

END OF VOL. II.

5. *Poco piu . . . Poco meno*: The little more and the little less. Brissenden, 'Sterne and Painting', traces Sterne's discussion to Hogarth's *The Analysis of Beauty* (1753), where Hogarth alludes to 'what the Italians call, Il poco piu (*the little more* that is expected from the hand of a master)'. 'The precise line of beauty' also alludes to Hogarth, his argument that all beauty can be associated with the sinuous curvatures (the serpentine line) represented by a wire twisted round a cone.

Sterne's inclusion of *poco meno*, a term not used in art criticism, indicates familiarity with the origin of both terms in musical notation.

6. *et cætera*: Here as elsewhere, an allusion to sexual parts, usually female.

CHAPTER VII

1. natural philosopher: A term denotatively equivalent to *scientist* or *physicist* today, but its connotation, in unsympathetic hands, might have suggested a dabbler or amateur.

2. demolition of *Dunkirk*: In 1713. It is described at length in VI.xxxiv; the shock Toby receives is described in IX.xxxi.

3. *Aristotle's Master-Piece*: Not in *Aristotle's Master-Piece*, but in another pseudo-Aristotle, often bound with it, *Aristotle's Book of Problems*. These popular works served the eighteenth century as sex manual, midwife's guide, book of remedies, and compendium of folk-science, and were reprinted well into the nineteenth century.

4. ANALOGY: Cf. Chambers: 'a certain relation, proportion, or agreement, which several things, in other respects different, bear to each other'.

CHAPTER VIII

1. IT is . . . bell: Only Chapters vi and vii have occurred since the ringing of the bell. Toby was interrupted mid-sentence in I.xxi, and is allowed to conclude his thought with the suggestion to ring the bell only at the beginning of II.vi; this is the 'hour and a half' of reading to which Sterne alludes.

2. unity . . . of time: Watt's note (79, n. 1) is useful: 'One of the three neo-classical dramatic unities, the unity of time required that the events in a play take no longer than they would in real life. Aristotle, in the *Poetics*, stated that the events in a plot should be *probable*; this may account for Sterne's reference to probability.'

3. duration . . . ideas: Sterne again anticipates his discussion of duration in III.xviii. The issue is treated in Locke's *Essay* in a chapter entitled 'Of Duration, and its simple Modes' (II.14).

4. between the acts: By 1720 the practice of a full evening of entertainment, with entr'acte performances, was well established on the London stage.

CHAPTER IX

1. IMagine . . . height: See n. 2 to I.xviii. As Cash notes, the real John Burton appears to have been 'a tall Well sett' person, and not a Roman Catholic (*EMY*, 180); Sterne's portrait is imaginary in its most salient details. Cf. the opening paragraph of *The Adventures of Gil Blas*, trans. Tobias Smollett: 'Figure to yourself a little fellow, three feet and a half high, as fat as you can conceive, with a head sunk deep between his shoulders, and you have my uncle to the life.'

2. sesquipedality: Literally, foot-and-a-half long, usually applied to long words, here, obviously, to Slop's equal girth and height.

3. three strokes: Cf. Hogarth, *Analysis of Beauty*: 'The general idea of an action, as well as of an attitude, may be given with a pencil in very few lines. . . . [T]wo or three lines at first are sufficient to shew the intention of an attitude . . .' Work (104, n. 3) finds this passage a 'graceful compliment' to Hogarth, but William V. Holtz, *Image and Immortality* (Brown University Press, 1970), sees Sterne primarily critical of *Analysis*.

4. fardel: Cf. *Hamlet*, III.i.75–6: 'who would fardels bear, / To grunt and sweat under a weary life . . .' *Hamlet* is clearly on Sterne's mind in the next chapter.

5. this description: Writing to a friend who had suggested he retrench his wit, Sterne singles out this description: 'I will reconsider Slops fall & my too Minute Account of it—but in general I am perswaded that the happiness of the Cervantic humour arises from this very thing—of describing silly and trifling Events, with the Circumstantial Pomp of great Ones . . .'

6. *Whiston*'s comets: In *New Theory of the Earth* (1696), William Whiston (1667–1752) argued that the biblical flood was caused by the near approach of a comet to the earth; the fear that other comets might destroy the earth (and the reappearance of Halley's comet in early 1759 makes the discussion timely) became associated with Whiston, often disparagingly.

7. hydrophobia: *OED* cites this passage as the first illustration of usage in the etymological sense, i.e., dread of water, as opposed to the disease associated with rabies.

8. imprompt: *OED* cites this passage as its sole illustration: 'Not ready or prepared; unready.'

9. beluted: Covered with mud (lute) or dirt. Sterne's slighting reference to the Roman Catholic doctrine of transubstantiation should be noted.

CHAPTER X

1. *unwiped* . . . him: Cf. *Hamlet*, I.v.74–9: '*Ghost*. Thus was I . . . / Cut off even in the blossoms of my sin, / Unhous'led, disappointed, unanel'd, / No reck'ning made, but sent to my account / With all my imperfections on my head.' The ghost stands 'motionless and speechless' in I.i.41–9 and I.iv.38–57. The clever alteration of

'disappointed' to 'unappointed' takes into account that the midwife, not Dr Slop, has the position of trust with regard to the delivery. *Unanealed*, i.e., not having received extreme unction.

2. majesty of mud: Sterne recalls the mud-diving contest in the *Dunciad* (A), II.302: 'Lo Smedley rose, in majesty of mud!' First noted by Gwin J. Kolb, *N & Q* 196 (1951).

3. mental reservation: Roman Catholic doctrine that under certain circumstances equivocations with 'mental reservations' may be made use of; from the eighteenth-century Protestant viewpoint the doctrine was 'the great refuge of religious hypocrites; who use them to accommodate their consciences with their interests' (Chambers).

4. *Argumentum ad hominem*: See n. 9 to I.xix.

5. sensorium: *OED* cites this passage as its first example of playful usage: 'in non-technical writing (sometimes for "brain" or "mind")'. It is a favourite word with Sterne; see pp. 120, 122, 188, 535; and the famous passage in *ASJ*, where God is addressed as the 'great SENSORIUM of the world'.

6. *Stevinus*: Simon Stevinus (1548–1620), Dutch mathematician, one of the military engineers Sterne lists out of Chambers in II.iii.

CHAPTER XI

1. pumps: Soft shoes worn by acrobats and running footmen.

2. stay thy obstetrick hand: Another allusion to Pope's *Dunciad* (B), IV.393–4: 'There all the Learn'd shall at the labour stand, / And Douglas lend his soft, obstetric hand'; noted by Brady (see Further Reading).

3. *Lucina*: Facet of the goddess Juno, that which makes the child see the light of day; and also, possibly, an allusion to Lucina's relationship with Hecate as the author of nightmares (see Schulze in Further Reading).

4. *Pilumnus*: One of three deities who protected a woman in labour from the god of uncultivated land, Silvanus.

5. thy *tire-tête* ... thee: Sterne's 'salvation and deliverance' are ironic, since the primary function of the *tire-tête* (head-puller) and the *crotchet* (little hook) was to extract a foetus by crushing or attaching its skull. Burton was very proud of his newly-invented forceps, but others deemed it unworkable and dangerous. See Cash, 'Birth', in Further Reading. The '*squirt*' is not a real instrument, but alludes to the '*petite canulle*' of the Sorbonne doctors, and hence is a means of 'salvation' only from the Roman Catholic viewpoint.

6. bays: Baize.

CHAPTER XII

1. argument *Ad Crumenam*: See n. 24 to I.xxi.

2. *Dennis*: John Dennis (1657–1734) reveals his antipathy towards punning in, among other writings, his *Remarks on Rape of the Lock* (1728); his attitude was proverbial throughout the century. Slop's pun is on the 'horns' figuratively adorning the head of a faithless wife's spouse (i.e., the cuckold).

3. the curtins: Toby's discussion of curtins is lifted from Chambers, s.v. *Curtin*, along with the allusion to Charles du Fresne du Cange (1610–88), French philologist and historian. Sterne then turned to entries under *Ravelin* and *Half-Moon* to confuse the issue thoroughly: '*Half moons* are sometimes raised before the curtin ... in which case it is much the same with a ravelin; only that the gorge of an *half-moon* is ... chiefly used to cover the point of the bastion; whereas ravelins are always placed before the curtin.—But they are both defective, as being ill flanked.' The distinction confused many commentators.

4. *Accoucheur*: French for man-midwife; Burton frequently uses the word in his *Letter to William Smellie, M.D.* (1753), a work Sterne parodies later in this volume (Ch. xix).

5. fifth chapter: Actually in the second chapter; 'fifth' may be a vestige of chapters deleted when Sterne, on the advice of friends and, perhaps, Dodsley, 'Burn'd More wit' than he published.

6. *Literæ humaniores*: The humanities.

7. one half of my philanthropy: Cf. Sterne's preface to Volumes I and II of *Sermons* (1760): 'the sermons turn chiefly upon philanthropy, and those kindred virtues to it, upon which hang all the law and the prophets ...'

8. rash humour ... me: Cf. *Julius Caesar*, IV.iii.119–21: '*Cassius*. [to Brutus] Have not you love enough to bear with me, / When that rash humour which my mother gave me / Makes me forgetful?' Cf. II.xiv.

CHAPTER XIII

1. family-way: *OED* defines *in a family-way* as 'with the freedom of members of the same family; without ceremony'. Closely related is *in the family-way*: 'pregnant'. Slop may have both meanings in mind.

CHAPTER XIV

1. sailing chariot: Sterne borrows his discussion of the sailing chariot (a wheeled carriage with sails constructed by Simon Stevinus (see n. 6 to II.x)) from John Wilkins, *Mathematical Magick* (1680): 'I have often wondred, why none of our Gentry who live near great Plains, and smooth Champions, have attempted any thing to this purpose. The experiments of this kind being very pleasant, and not costly:

what could be more delightful or better husbandry, than to make use of the *wind* (which costs nothing, and eats nothing) instead of *horses?'* (first noted by Kolb). Wilkins fails to mention that Stevinus was engineer to Prince Maurice of Orange, a fact Sterne perhaps found in Chambers. Peireskius, cited by Wilkins, is Fabrici de Peiresc (1580–1637), collector and antiquarian; his name became a byword for such activities well into the eighteenth century.

CHAPTER XV

1. the next Halberd: Reading and writing were required for advancement in the military, in this instance, promotion to sergeant, denoted by the 'Halberd'.

CHAPTER XVII

1. his attitude: See Brissenden, 'Sterne and Painting', for a discussion of Sterne's use in his description of Trim's stance of Hogarth's *Analysis* and Leonardo da Vinci's *Treatise of Painting* (English edition, 1721). Leonardo predicts that unless the figure is drawn in accordance with the laws of gravity, it 'of necessity must tumble to the Ground'.

2. cyclopædia ... sciences: Tristram's several hints that he is writing a book of universal knowledge seem to point to Swift, especially *A Tale of a Tub*, sect. I: 'I have been prevailed on ... to travel in a compleat and laborious Dissertation upon the prime Productions of our Society, which ... have darkly and deeply couched under them, the most finished and refined Systems of all Sciences and Arts.' The attack on system-making is central to Scriblerian satire – and to Sterne's.

3. line of beauty: See n. 5 to II.vi; Hogarth defines this central concept of *Analysis* in ch. 7.

4. The SERMON: 'Abuses of conscience' was first preached in York Minster on 29 July 1750, at the close of the summer assizes (court sessions) in York. It appeared as a sixpenny pamphlet less than two weeks later, printed in York; the version in *TS* is an almost verbatim reproduction of that earlier publication. The sermon appeared again as the final sermon in Volume IV of the *Sermons of Mr. Yorick* (1766). See the Florida *Text*, Appendix 7, for an account of the three versions.

5. old house over his head: Proverbial for getting into trouble.

6. architecture: Sly allusion, perhaps, to Burton's recent publication of *Monasticon Eboracense*, an account of the architecture of churches and abbeys in the York area.

7. I never ... before: Sterne makes a rare slip here, since Trim tells Toby the entire story in 1713 (IX.iv–vii), five years before this scene.

8. *hardly ... before us*: Wisdom 9:16.

9. plann'd: placed?

10. Now ... good also: This paragraph owes much – as does the entire sermon –

to Swift's sermon on the same subject; see *Prose Works* (Blackwell, 1939–68), Vol. 9; both authors echo 1 John 3:20–22.

11. scripture assures it may: Proverbs 28:14, Hebrews 3:13.

12. or was ... darkness: Sterne borrows from 'Difficulty of knowing one's self', attributed to Swift in the eighteenth century, but considered of unknown authorship today; behind the image is the biblical commonplace 'clouds and thick darkness' (e.g., Deuteronomy 4:11, Psalm 97:2). And cf. *A Tale of a Tub*, sect. IX, the discussion about vapours and the brain. Sterne's combining of scripture and scepticism reveals his profound debt to a tradition splendidly outlined by Wehrs and Parnell (see Further Reading).

13. *Elijah ... awoke*: 1 Kings 18:27.

14. Seven: Anglicanism recognizes two sacraments, Baptism and Communion. To these, Roman Catholicism adds Confirmation, Penance, Orders, Matrimony, and Extreme Unction.

15. Seven golden ... planets: Seven golden candlesticks are mentioned in Revelation 1:12, 20, and 2:1. In the Ptolemaic system, seven planets were identified (Moon, Mercury, Venus, Sun, Mars, Jupiter, and Saturn), each with its own heaven, hence seven heavens. For the seven plagues, see Revelation 15–16.

16. Shall not ... *before me*: Sterne alludes to the parable of the Pharisee and the publican, Luke 18:10–12.

17. Letter of the Law: Romans 7:6, 2 Corinthians 3:6.

18. mental reservation: See n. 3 to II.x.

19. the wound digests there: See n. 4 to II.i.

20. the heart ... things: Jeremiah 17:9; Sterne alludes to this text in several sermons, including 4, 'Self knowledge', an early version of 'Abuses of conscience'.

21. speak ... no peace: Scriptural formula; e.g., Jeremiah 6:14, Ezekiel 13:10, etc.

22. I must ... dishonour: Again, Sterne borrows from Swift's 'Difficulty of knowing one's self'.

23. When *David* ... done: See 1 Samuel 24:4–5, 2 Samuel 11:2–12:14. David ordered that Uriah, the husband of Bathsheba, be slain so that he could marry her.

24. So that ... they: See Swift, 'Testimony of conscience'; the paragraph embodies an essential component of Anglican thinking in its balancing of 'reason' and 'religion' (revelation). The question 'What is written in the law of God' is from Luke 10:26.

25. if thy heart ... *God*: 1 John 3:21.

26. *Blessed is ... high*: Sterne conflates and paraphrases Ecclesiasticus 14:1–2, 13:24–26, 37:14.

27. Temple: Temple Church, located in the section of London associated with the legal profession.

28. *Corps de Garde*: Sentry duty and those who comprise the detail, usually under a corporal's command.

29. *Coup de main*: Sudden, resolute assault.

30. two *tables*: The stone tablets on which the Ten Commandments were inscribed;

the two tables refer to the division of the decalogue into religious and moral duties. See Exodus 32:15ff.

31. I said ... life: Cf. Swift, 'On the testimony of conscience' for the substance of this entire discussion; however, where Swift uses a tradesman and lawyer for his examples, Sterne, considering his audience, substitutes a banker and a physician.

32. instrumental parts of religion: Commonplace Anglican term (also, 'instrumental duties') for the rituals or outer forms of religious practice, often with negative associations to Pharisees and Roman Catholics.

33. *This likewise ... sun*: Ecclesiastes 5:13.

34. history of the *Romish* Church: Sterne's Inquisition scene is patched together from a sermon by Richard Bentley (1715) and *The Religion of Nature Delineated* (1722) by William Wollaston. As with Trim's reading, Bentley's sermon was delivered on 5 November, Guy Fawkes Day, when anti-Roman Catholic oratory was part of the observance. Sterne's anti-Catholicism would have been shared by most – if not all – Anglican clergymen of his day, especially after the Jacobite uprising in 1745.

Trim's reaction should be considered alongside Adam Smith's *Theory of Moral Sentiments* (1759); see also Kenneth MacLean, 'Imagination and Sympathy: Sterne and Adam Smith', *JHI* 10 (1949).

35. saint-errant: Cf. knight-errant; Sterne uses this compound, connoting misguided religious zeal, in several sermons.

36. tricker: Trigger.

37. something more contempt: something more of contempt?

38. *Portugal*: Portugal had a particularly bad reputation for inquisitorial cruelty.

39. *By their ... them*: Matthew 7:20.

40. *Asiatick* Cadi: Turkish counterpart to a Justice of the Peace.

41. eloquence of our pulpits: Cf. Sterne's discussion of proper sermonizing in 'Rabelaisian Fragment' and again in IV.xxvi. His interest in simplicity, directness, and affectiveness is echoed by Anglican preachers throughout the century.

42. *a priori*: Argument from cause to effect (deductive reasoning), as opposed to *a posteriori*, argument from effect to cause (inductive).

43. Ill-fated ... story: The account is intended, perhaps, to recall the Apostles' Creed, a central part of the Anglican morning and evening service: 'Christ ... was crucified, dead, and buried: He descended into Hell; The third day he rose again from the dead ...'; see Sharon Damoff, *Scriblerian* 25.1 (1992).

44. *Yorick*'s ghost ... *walks*: Cf. *Hamlet*, I.v.9–10: '*Ghost.* I am thy father's spirit, / Doom'd for a certain term to walk the night.'

45. sample of his sermons: In May 1760, Sterne published two volumes of previously written sermons with the title *Sermons of Mr. Yorick*. In the preface he wrote: 'THE sermon which gave rise to the publication of these, having been offer'd to the world as a sermon of *Yorick*'s, I hope the most serious reader will find nothing to offend him, in my continuing these two volumes under the same title: lest it should be otherwise, I have added a second title page with the real name of the author ...'

Despite the ploy of two title-pages, some were appalled, including the *Monthly Review* 22 (May 1760): 'we consider [this] the greatest outrage against Sense and Decency, that has been offered since the first establishment of Christianity ...' In general, however, the reception was favourable, and the two volumes were reprinted seven times before Sterne's death in 1768.

CHAPTER XVIII

1. *en Soveraines*: As sovereigns.

CHAPTER XIX

1. What I ... elsewhere: Sterne reflects a similar moment in *A Tale of a Tub*, sect. VI: 'I ought in Method, to have informed the Reader about fifty Pages ago, of a Fancy *Lord Peter* took. ... Now, this material Circumstance, having been forgot in due Place; as good Fortune hath ordered, comes in very properly here ...'

2. stage ... childishness: Sterne is thinking of Jaques's ages-of-man speech in *As You Like It*, II.vii.139ff.

3. steel-yard: Because of the concluding remark, Chambers is worth quoting: 'in mechanics, a kind of balance ... by means whereof, the gravity of different bodies are found by the use of one single weight. ... But the instrument being very liable to deceit, is [not] ... countenanced in commerce.'

4. *in infinitum*: To infinity.

5. truth ... her well: Proverbial expression, traced to Democritus.

6. out of joint: Proverbial. Cf. *Hamlet*, I.v.188.

7. sorites: Cf. Chambers: 'a kind of argument, wherein a number of propositions are gradually, and minutely laid together; and something inferred from the whole. ... This method of disputing prevailed much among the stoicks; especially with Zeno, and Chrysippus. But it is very captious, and sophistical.' The *sorites* consists of a chain of argument whereby the predicate of the first link becomes the subject of the next. Zeno of Citium (335–263 B.C.) founded the Stoic school; Chrysippus (*c.* 280–207 B.C.) was a later leader.

8. Why ... corrupted: Walter echoes Bishop George Berkeley, 'Essay Towards Preventing the Ruin of Great Britain' (1721), who concludes, 'Neither the plain reason of the thing, nor the experience of past ages, nor the examples we have before our eyes, can restrain us from imitating, not to say surpassing, the most corrupt and ruined people, in those very points of luxury that ruined them.'

9. our poverty ... consent: Cf. *Romeo and Juliet*, V.i.75: 'My poverty, but not my will, consents.'

10. an ounce ... people's: Sterne plays on the proverbial expression: 'an ounce of wit is worth a pound of learning.'

11. Now, as ... place: Walter rushes in where Locke, refusing to explore the why

of uneven capacities, feared to tread (*Essay*, IV.20.5). René Descartes (1596–1650) was bolder, although Sterne's learning here is derived from Chambers, not Descartes; see B. L. Greenberg, 'Laurence Sterne and Chambers' *Cyclopædia*', *MLN* 69 (1954). Under *Soul*, Sterne discovered Descartes and the pineal gland; under *Pineal gland*, he was led to *Conarium*, and the definition 'a small gland, about the bigness of a pea'; thence to *Brain*, where experiments are recounted of pigeons and dogs surviving after the cerebellum was removed. Returning to *Soul*, he read about 'Borri, a milanese physician, in a letter to Bartholine, [who] asserts, that in the brain is found a certain, very subtile, fragrant juice, which is the principal seat or residence of the reasonable *soul* . . .' The tradition in which this discourse of mock learning thrives (see the important essay by Jefferson in Further Reading) is made clear when one notes that Martinus Scriblerus (*Memoirs*, ch. 12) makes a similar attempt to locate the soul – and also reaches Descartes's conclusion.

12. battle of *Landen*: 29 July 1693; Trim receives his wound during the retreat (VIII.xix).

13. If death . . . Q. E. D.: Chambers, s.v. *Death*, has a similar definition. Q.E.D.: *Quod erat demonstrandum* (which was to be proved), usually reserved for mathematical theorems.

14. *Borri . . . Bartholine*: Sterne found Joseph Francis Borri (1627–95), Italian physician, and Thomas Bartholine (1616–80), Danish physician, in Chambers. *Coglionissimo* is Sterne's play on *coglione* = testicle.

15. *Metheglingius*: Type of mead, made by fermenting honey and water; hence, perhaps, Sterne's coinage for a besotted philosopher.

16. *Animus . . . Anima*: Philosophy and theology had long considered the possibility of two souls, in order to explain the difference between 'life' or 'soul' (*anima*) and 'mind' or 'spirit' (*animus*).

17. *Dutch* anatomists: Sterne may be offering a compliment to the Dutch medical establishment of the first half of the eighteenth century when Hermann Boerhaave (1668–1738) turned Leyden into the medical centre of Europe. But there is also the connotation of 'Dutch logician or commentator' (see n. 12 to I.xix).

18. seven senses: 'Speech' and 'understanding' are most often listed (cf. Ecclesiasticus 17:5) as the additional 'senses'.

19. *Causa sine quâ non*: Indispensable cause or condition, a cause without which a certain effect is impossible.

20. *Lithopædus . . . difficili*: In 1751, John Burton published his *Essay towards a Complete New System of Midwifry*, only to be upstaged by William Smellie's far better received *Treatise on the Theory and Practice of Midwifery* (1752). Burton struck back in a 250-page *Letter to William Smellie, M.D.* (1753), in which he minutely criticizes the *Treatise* for such errors as Smellie's slip of mistaking the title of an illustration (of a petrified child, i.e., *Lithopædion*) for the name of an author (*Lithopædus*); the details of Sterne's footnote are from Burton's *Letter*, which carps on the error throughout the work as indicative of Smellie's untrustworthiness. Cordaeus and Albosius were sixteenth-

century French physicians, and Trincavellius an Italian physician of the same period, all mentioned by Burton. *Smelvogt* is probably Sterne's play or slip on another name from Burton, Johann Adrian Slevogt (1653–1726), professor of anatomy at Jena.

21. 470 pounds: Sterne's figure is a gross exaggeration, the force being between 32 and 50 pounds.

22. piece of dough: The metaphor is perhaps derived from Burton, *Letter*, who writes of the head's assuming the shape of a 'Sugar Loaf, nine and forty Times in fifty'; it may, however, be a commonplace.

23. mothery: Full of sediment.

24. Angels . . . us: Cf. *Hamlet*, I.iv.39.

25. extracted by the feet: Sterne parodies Burton's discussion of difficult births, although, to be fair, Burton advocated the podalic version (feet-first delivery) only in extreme cases. On the other hand, Burton does criticize Smellie for waiting too long for nature to take its course.

26. *Cæsarian* section: Sterne returns to Chambers for the substance of his discussion, including the anatomical terms *epigastrium* (the part of the abdomen lying over the stomach) and *matrix* (uterus or womb), and the allusions to Julius Cæsar, Scipio Africanus, Manlius, and Edward VI. '*Manlius Torquatus*' (consul in the third century B.C.) is Sterne's 'learned' error, caused by Chambers's misspelling; the proper citation would have been to *Manilius* Manius, who invaded Carthage in 149 B.C., as noted by Work (152, n. 10). Mrs Shandy has every right to pale at Walter's suggestion: the first recorded successful caesarean operation in England (i.e., the mother surviving) occurred in 1793. Before then it was associated with Roman Catholicism's interest in saving the unbaptized child rather than the already baptized mother.

Sterne's addition of Hermes Trismegistus to Chambers's list seems unjustified, except for foreshadowing the christening scene (IV.xiv).

27. *oss coxcygis*: Sterne's unorthodox spelling for *coccygis*, the four bones at the end of the spinal column. Note that Volume I ends with an attempt to locate Toby's wound between the *os pubis* and the *coxendix*, and Volume II with a similar anatomical survey of the female, the pudendum being between the *os pubis* in front and the *os coccygis* behind.

28. sage *Alquife* . . . truth: Sterne borrows from a footnote to *Don Quixote*, I.I.5; *Don Belianis of Greece*, sixteenth-century Spanish romance, still popular in Sterne's day.

Volume III

Frontispiece: Two engraved versions of this Hogarth illustration exist, the first by Ravenet (reproduced here), the second by J. Ryland (see below, p. 237).

Motto: Sterne borrowed his motto, in all probability, from Motteux's preface to Rabelais, I. John of Salisbury (*c.* 1115–80), Bishop of Chartres (not Lyons, as '*Lugdun*' suggests), wrote the sentence, here slightly altered, in his *Policraticus*, Book 8, ch. 25. Sterne's version may be translated: 'I do not fear the opinions of the ignorant crowd; nevertheless, I ask they spare my little work, in which it has always been my purpose to pass from humour to seriousness and from seriousness back to humour.' The original does not contain the final clause.

CHAPTER I

1. chapter of wishes: Never written; the opening chapters of Volumes I and III begin with the same words: 'I wish . . .'

CHAPTER II

1. *India* handkerchief: From cloth made in India.
2. *Reynolds*: Sterne sat for Sir Joshua Reynolds (1723–92) in March and April 1760, one sign of his celebrity status following the publication of Volumes I and II of *TS* (for details of his London stay, see Cash, *LY*, ch. 1). The result is one of Reynolds's best portraits. Sterne's compliment to him is implied by 'great and gracefully', since these qualities were thought to be rarely combined modes of excellence.

CHAPTER III

1. zig-zaggery: *Zigzag* is an approach towards a besieged place in short turns or 'zigzags', so as not to be enfiladed by the defenders.

CHAPTER IV

1. gum-taffeta: Taffeta stiffened with gum was known quickly to wear out; hence the expression 'to fret like gum-taffeta' became proverbial.
2. *Zeno . . . Montaigne*: Sterne's list is lifted from Chambers, s.v. *Stoicks*. Sterne adds two names, 'Dyonisius Heracleotes' and Montaigne; the first may be a joke, since Dionysius (*c.* 328–248 B.C.) is best known for abandoning Stoicism because of a painful ailment. The inclusion of Montaigne is problematic, but perhaps Sterne recalled 'Of Experience', where Montaigne insists that his bouts with kidney stones affected his body, but never his soul.
3. nine months together: I.e., since the publication of Volumes I and II; Sterne may be referring to reviewers (see next note) or bothersome imitators, of which there were many.
4. monthly Reviewers: The *Monthly Review* and the *Critical Review* were favourably inclined towards the first volumes of *TS*, but when Sterne published his sermons under the name Mr. Yorick (in May 1760), some reconsideration occurred (see n. 45

to II.xvii). Alan B. Howes, *Sterne: The Critical Heritage* (Routledge & Kegan Paul, 1974), is an excellent sourcebook for early responses to *TS*.

CHAPTER V

1. redden'd ... colour: In ch. 14 of *Analysis of Beauty*, Hogarth sets forth a system of colouring on a scale of 1 to 7; if Sterne is alluding to this, he is describing a red face indeed, one half tint from the darkest possible red. *OED* cites this passage as its sole illustration of a burlesque nonce word formed by blending *scientifically* and *tint*.

2. Avison's Scarlatti: Twelve concertos by the Italian composer Domenico Scarlatti (1685–1757), published in 1744 by Charles Avison (1709–70), English composer and author of *An Essay on Musical Expression*. The second movement of the sixth concerto is indeed to be played *con furia*, i.e., with fury. *Con strepito*, i.e., noisily.

CHAPTER VI

1. cornish: I.e., cornice.

2. buccinatory: The *buccinator* is the 'chief muscle employed in the act of blowing' (*OED*).

CHAPTER VII

1. *Hymen*: Mythological god of marriage and virginity; in that he is connected with the 'marriage song', he may be frightened away by Obadiah's 'music'; of course, the jangling instruments of birthing are themselves an argument against marriage.

2. patriots: The word had negative connotations from the mid-1740s, as noted in Johnson's *Dictionary*: 'a factious disturber of the government'. Cf. V.ii, where Walter instructs Obadiah to saddle 'PATRIOT', and is informed that 'PATRIOT is sold.'

CHAPTER VIII

1. obstretical: The misspelling is retained since Sterne's intention may be the 'tical' endings; cf. I.xxi, where a similar list is offered.

2. caball-istical: Play on *cabalistic* and *caballus* (Latin for pack-horse, nag).

CHAPTER IX

1. GREAT wits jump: I.e., great minds agree or coincide.

2. the thought ... side: Common image, receiving an elegant statement in Pope's *Essay on Man*, II.105–8: 'The rising tempest puts in act the soul, / Parts it may

ravage, but preserves the whole. / On life's vast ocean diversely we sail, / Reason the card, but Passion is the gale ...'

CHAPTER X

1. Mr. *Hammond Shandy*: Perhaps an allusion to the hanging of Haman ('hanged as high as Haman' being proverbial) in the Book of Esther 7:9–10.

2. duke of *Monmouth*'s affair: James Scott, Duke of Monmouth (1649–85), bastard son of Charles II, returned from exile in the late spring of 1685 to claim the throne from James II. The attempt ended in disaster and he was executed.

3. *implication*: Sterne puns on the Latin *implico*: 'to enfold, embrace, join', with the idea of intimacy.

4. *knots*: Sterne's elaborate emphasis on knots and knives alludes to several folk ideas, including the marriage (love)-knot and the avoidance of knives which could cut it; and the untying of knots in a house where childbirth was occurring in order to 'ensure' an easy birth. See Ehlers in Further Reading. 'To knot' is also a euphemism for copulation, and 'knife' yet another phallus-shaped object.

5. the nails ... close: To avoid injury to the mother during delivery.

6. cut my thumb: Cf. Swift, *Polite Conversation*, ed. Eric Partridge (Oxford University Press, 1963): '*Col.* Ods so, I have cut my Thumb with this cursed Knife. *Lady Answ.* Ay, that was your Mother's Fault; because she only warned you not to cut your Fingers. *Lady Sm.* No, no; 'tis only Fools cut their Fingers, but Wise Folks cut their Thumbs.' Partridge comments on the proverbial thrust of this: 'the follies of the wise are prodigious'. John Burton's forceps required expert use of the thumb to keep the blades properly separated.

7. *Injuries ... heart*: Sterne's italics and quotation marks indicate a borrowing, but the closest Florida *Notes* was able to come is *Henry V*, IV.viii.46: 'All offences, my lord, come from the heart.' Cf. Ecclesiasticus 19:16: 'There is one that slippeth in his speech, but not from his heart ...'

8. *Cervantick* gravity: Cf. n. 8 to I.xii ('*cervantick* tone'). Pope, *Dunciad* (A), I.19–20, captures the age's perception of the pose of Cervantes, attributing it to Swift: 'Whether thou chuse Cervantes' serious air, / Or laugh and shake in Rab'lais' easy Chair.' Swift reflects on his own method in 'Verses on the Death of Dr. Swift' (lines 315–16): 'His Vein, ironically grave, / Expos'd the Fool, and lash'd the Knave.'

9. form of excommunication: Thomas Hearne's edition of the *Textus Roffensis* (1720) was Sterne's likely source for the Latin version of the Bishop of Rochester's twelfth-century 'Excommunication'. The English version was probably taken from the *Gentleman's Magazine* (September 1745); see William A. Jackson, 'The Curse of Ernulphus', *Harvard Library Bulletin* 14 (1960) and Appendix 8 in the Florida *Text*. Its reappearance in 1745 is linked to anti-Roman Catholic sentiment resulting from the Jacobite uprising.

CHAPTER XI

1. *vel* os: Standard rubric allowing the Bishop to adapt the curse to the singular or (*vel*) plural. 'N.N.' abbreviates *Nomen, Nomina* (i.e., name, names); Slop supplies Obadiah's name.

2. *Dathan* and *Abiram*: See Numbers 16:1–35 and Psalm 106:17.

3. heavenly armies: Sterne changes the source's 'heavenly host' in order to mount Toby on his hobby-horse. Similarly, he alters 'top of the head' to 'vertex' and 'interior parts' to 'purtenance', words with Shandean overtones.

4. John the Baptist: As the Latin indicates, the two St Johns are the same person; Sterne may be laughing at the multiplicity of saints in Roman Catholicism – or simply have made an error.

5. *minim*: Half-note; along with 'division' and 'running bass' it constructs a musical metaphor.

6. By the . . . establishment: Cf. Burton, 3.4.1.3:

The *Romans* borrowed from all, besides their own gods, which were *majorum* and *minorum gentium*, as *Varro* holds, certaine and uncertaine; some cœlestial select and great ones . . . : gods of all sorts, for all functions; some for the Land, some for Sea; some for Heaven, some for Hel; some for passions, diseases, some for birth. . . . And not good men only do they thus adore, but tyrants, monsters, divels, . . . beastly women, and arrant whores amongst the rest. . . . [M]ale and female gods, of all ages, sexes, and dimensions, with beards, without beards. . . . *Hesiodus* reckons up at least 30000 gods, *Varro* 300 *Jupiters*.

Marcus Terentius Varro (116–27 B.C.), Roman scholar; Sterne cites him (III.iv) in his list of Stoics borrowed from Chambers.

7. *Cid Hamet*: Cid Hamet Benengeli, the reputed chronicler of many of Don Quixote's adventures, swears that 'by *Mahomet*, he would have given the best Coat of two that he had . . .' (II.III.48). Sterne forgets that Tristram is not a parson.

8. to all eternity: Revelation 20:10.

CHAPTER XII

1. *befetish'd*: *OED* records this passage as its sole example.

2. *Garrick*: David Garrick (1717–79), the greatest actor of the century, with whom Sterne struck up an immediate acquaintance when he came to London in the winter of 1760, having previously sent copies of *TS* to him by means of Catherine Fourmantel (see n. 4 to I.xviii); see Cash, *EMY*, 294–6 and *LY*, 47–52. Sterne refers to Garrick again in *TS* (pp. 169, 228–9, 377), always with a compliment. Here he parodies contemporary criticisms of Garrick, e.g., Thomas Fitzpatrick's in *An Enquiry into the Real Merit of a Certain Popular Performer* (1760): 'it was agreed that we should go to . . . Hamlet this evening, and each man, furnished with a printed play

and a pencil, mark such improprieties, in respect of speaking, as Mr. G------ might possibly fall into'; twenty faults are then listed.

3. new book: I.e., *TS*, though the most famous such statement would be made by Samuel Johnson fifteen years later: 'Nothing odd will do long. "Tristram Shandy" did not last.'

4. *Bossu's*: René Le Bossu's *Traité du poëme épique* (1675) was translated into English as *Treatise of the Epick Poem* in 1695, and long proved influential. Like Sterne, Pope attacked Le Bossu's rigidities, both in the prefatory matter to the *Dunciad* and in ch. 15 of *Peri Bathous*.

5. daub: 'A coarsely executed, inartistic painting' (*OED*).

6. *pyramid* ... group: Sterne's connoisseur is indebted to Reynolds, *Idler* 76 (29 September 1759): ' "Here," says he, "are twelve upright figures; what a pity it is that Raffaelle was not acquainted with the pyramidal principle ..." ' (ed. W. J. Bate, *et al.* (Yale University Press, 1963)).

7. colouring ... of *Angelo*: Sterne again borrows from *Idler* 76: '[the connoisseur's] mouth [was] full of nothing but the grace of Raffaelle, the purity of Domenichino, the learning of Poussin, the air of Guido, the greatness of taste of the Characbes, and the sublimity and grand contorno of Michael Angelo.' Sterne adds Titian, Rubens, and Correggio to the list, three painters often grouped in eighteenth-century art criticism; he may have looked, e.g., into Daniel Webb, *An Inquiry into the Beauties of Painting*, 2nd ed. (1761), where Titian is considered the 'greatest master' of colouring, or into de Piles, *The Principles of Painting* (see n. 2 to I.ix), where Titian is given 18 out of 20 points for colouring and Rubens 17 for 'expression'. Webb also comments that 'among us any action that is singularly graceful, is termed Correggiesque'. Both Reynolds and Sterne are satirizing the reduction of these great Renaissance artists to trite and hackneyed labels.

8. I would ... wherefore: Cf. *Idler* 76: 'for these rules being always uppermost ... instead of giving up the reins of their imagination into their author's hands, their frigid minds are employed in examining whether the performance be according to the rules of art'.

9. Great *Apollo*: In his role as the god of learning, poetry, and music, as opposed to Mercury, the god of science and commerce. Sterne later calls Reynolds 'that son of *Apollo* ' (VII.ix).

10. St. *Paul*'s ... *fish*: As is evident in Shakespeare's *Richard III*, Richard's habit of swearing by St Paul was common knowledge. Work (182, n. 4) notes that Charles II swore by ' 'Od's fish' (i.e., a corruption of 'God's fish', itself a corruption of 'God's flesh').

11. orientality: 'Eastern style or character' (*OED*).

12. *Justinian* ... digest: Sterne's learning is from Chambers, s.v. *Civil Law*: 'Lastly, Justinian [*c.* 482–565], finding the authority of the Roman law almost abolished in the west, by the declension of the empire; resolved to make a general collection, of the whole Roman jurisprudence; and committed the care thereof to his chancellor

Tribonianus [d. *c.* 542]. . . . See DIGEST, and CODE. . . . The same year he published an abridgment thereof . . . under the title of *institutes.* See INSTITUTES.' The resultant *Corpus Juris Civilis* is the basis of western jurisprudence. Digests and institutes of *all* knowledge were a favourite target for the Scriblerians.

13. *By the splendour of God*: Cf. Tindal: '[William] was so provoked . . . he swore by the *Splendor of God*, his usual Oath . . .'

CHAPTER XIII

1. julap: I.e., julep, a medicinal drink, usually the base for other medicines.

2. reduction . . . year Ten: Not in 1710, but in December 1708; Sterne dates it correctly in VI.xxiii. A mutiny over bread took place at Ghent in 1712.

CHAPTER XIV

1. *in petto*: In the breast; in secret.

2. *Tully*'s second *Philippick*: The longest of the fourteen diatribes Cicero delivered against Mark Antony. The most memorable use of the cloak, however, was Mark Antony's, when he produces Caesar's 'pink'd' mantle and will from under his (see *Julius Caesar*, III.ii.169ff.).

3. by head and shoulders: Proverbial; here and elsewhere, the humorous literalism of many of Sterne's proverbial expressions is noteworthy.

4. *trunk-hose*: Loose-fitting breeches of the previous century, sometimes stuffed with wool, as opposed to the tighter breeches of the eighteenth century, which could not be stuffed.

CHAPTER XVII

1. difficult to know: Cf. Burton, *Letter to Smellie*: 'how is it possible that you can tell the Head of the Child from its Breech or Knees. . . . It is an Observation of the best Operators, that . . . the Knees greatly resemble the Head, and are not easily distinguishable from it . . .'

CHAPTER XVIII

1. pantoufles: Slippers.

2. *duration and its simple modes*: Ch. 14 of Book II of *An Essay Concerning Human Understanding* is entitled 'Of Duration, and its simple Modes'. This passage is Sterne's most extensive borrowing from Locke.

3. rapid succession: Locke never quite ties the length of duration to the speed of the succession of ideas, but the notion had become a commonplace; see *Essay*, II.14.3−4.

4. the ideas . . . us: The ideas that do *not* concern Toby are precisely those of most interest to Locke.

5. INFINITY . . . NECESSITY: While all these topics are discussed by Locke, Chambers, s.v. *Prescience*, directs the reader to 'liberty' and 'necessity'. One must always suspect Sterne in instances of this kind.

6. To understand . . . *preconceived*: Cf. *Essay*, II.14.3, quoted almost verbatim. Sterne invents the phrase '*and so according to that preconceived*' to create a sense of interruption; he had actually completed Locke's passage with '*our thinking*'.

7. 'Tis owing . . . all: Cf. Locke, II.14.19. The parenthetical comment may glance at a phenomenon reported in *The Clockmakers Outcry*, one of many imitations of *TS* to appear in 1760, namely, that the inquiry 'Sir, will you have your clock wound-up?' had become popular among street-walkers; hence Walter's (or Sterne's) comment. Or perhaps Walter is simply lamenting the association established in I.i.

8. regular . . . candle: Cf. *Essay*, II.14.9: '[is it] not probable that our *Ideas* do, whilst we are awake, succeed one another in our Minds at certain distances, not much unlike the Images in the inside of a Lanthorn, turned round by the Heat of a Candle'.

9. smoak-jack: *OED* credits Sterne with a new, figurative meaning for this word, 'The head, as the seat of confused ideas.' The jack was used to turn a roasting-spit by means of the hot air rising from the fire.

CHAPTER XIX

1. *Lucian* . . . *Cervantes*: Cf. Fielding, *Tom Jones*, XIII.1: 'Come thou, that hast inspired thy *Aristophanes*, thy *Lucian*, thy *Cervantes*, thy *Rabelais* . . .' These are the writers one would traditionally summon as Muses for a work of comedy or satire. Lucian of Samosata (*c.* 120–after 180), the model for much subsequent prose satire, especially the dialogue and the fantastic voyage.

2. devoutly . . . for: Cf. *Hamlet*, III.i.62–3.

3. *Ontologic*: Ontology is the study of Being and abstractions.

CHAPTER XX

1. siege of *Messina*: Messina in Sicily, held by Spain, was besieged in July 1719 and taken in October. That Toby and Trim have this information eight months before it happens may be a simple error, a play with the malleability of time, or – as suggested in Ch. xxv – a bit of military acumen, although that discussion ends with Walter convincing Toby that the campaign would *not* be in Sicily.

2. *Agelastes*: One who never laughs; a name in Rabelais.

3. *Triptolemus*: Greek hero and demigod, taught the arts of agriculture by Ceres; Plato and Tully name him as a judge of the dead. Why Sterne includes him among these invented names is not known.

4. *Phutatorius*: Copulator; he will receive the hot chestnut in his lap at the Visitation dinner, IV.xxvii.

5. wit and judgment: Sterne's refusal to separate the two is reminiscent of Pope's similar refusal in his *Essay on Criticism*, lines 82–3: 'For *Wit* and *Judgment* often are at strife, / Tho' meant each other's Aid, like *Man* and *Wife*.' The opposite view was embraced by both Hobbes and Locke; see *Leviathan*, ch. 8, and *Essay*, II.11.2 and III.10.34. In so far as Sterne's critics were accusing him of having too much wit, too little judgement, the 'Author's Preface' is a retort to them, rather than a serious engagement with Locke.

6. *de fartandi ... fallaciis*: Literally, 'concerning the deceptions of farting and illustration'. Didius: see n. 3 to I.vii.

7. opacular: *OED* cites this passage as its sole illustration; Sterne seems to mean 'opaque'.

8. thrice able critics: Comic mode of address borrowed from Rabelais.

9. *Monopolos ... Somnolentius*: Sterne's inventions: a monopolist, lick-spittle (less politely, ass-kisser), big-belly, and sleeper. The last three reappear at the Visitation dinner.

10. several receptacles ... out: Cf. Rabelais, III.31: 'the more promptly, dexterously, and copiously to suppeditate, furnish, and supply him with store of spirits, sufficient to replenish, and fill up the ventricles, seats, tunnels, mansions, receptacles, and celluls of the common sense ...' Here, and in what follows, Sterne has in view Rabelais's description of the glorious world that will ensue when all men are lenders (see III.3–4).

11. satire and sarcasm: In sermon 18, 'The Levite and his concubine', Sterne offers some strictures on men of 'wit and parts' who make 'shrewd and sarcastick reflections upon whatever is done in the world.... [I]t has helped to give wit a bad name, as if the main essence of it was satire: certainly there is a difference between *Bitterness* and *Saltness*,—that is,——between the malignity and the festivity of wit,——the one is a mere quickness of apprehension, void of humanity,—and is a talent of the devil; the other comes down from the Father of Spirits, so pure and abstracted from persons, that willingly it hurts no man ...'

12. milk and honey: Scriptural commonplace.

13. compass of his cave: Thomas Salmon, *Modern History*, 3rd ed. (1744), points out that winters in the north are nine months long and that in Nova Zembla (Arctic islands off the coast of eastern Russia), the inhabitants must 'escape to some cave and shelter themselves' if they are to survive them.

14. where the spirits ... itself: Another glance at the theory that climate and national character are linked; see I.xxi.

15. Angels ... defend us: *Hamlet*, I.iv.39; '*plentiful a lack* of wit' is also from *Hamlet*, II.ii.199.

16. run a match: A horse-race.

17. *Norway ... Tartary*: Sterne almost certainly traced this voyage on a map. From

Russia's Novaya Zemlya islands (*Nova Zembla*), between the Kara and Barents Seas, he moves south-west across the northernmost regions of Scandinavia and Finland (*North Lapland*); reaching Norway, he turns nearly 180 degrees and moves east, crossing Sweden through the northern district of Angermania to the Gulf of Bothnia, between Sweden and Finland, and then enters Russia just north of the Gulf of Finland, at the easternmost point of which is St Petersburg. Carelia is the area north of St Petersburg, Ingria the area south. Sterne then continues eastward in Russia.

18. luxuriant island: An earlier statement of these commonplaces – that climate and national character are interrelated, and that England's changeable weather produces eccentric characters – is found in William Temple's essay 'Of Poetry', quoted at length in the Florida *Notes*.

19. *height . . . necessities*: Cf. Swift, *A Tale of a Tub*, sect. IX: 'For, what Man in the natural State, or Course of Thinking, did ever conceive it in his Power, to reduce the Notions of all Mankind, exactly to the same Length, and Breadth, and Height of his own?' The sufficiency of our faculties to our needs is discussed by Locke, *Essay*, II.23.12, a section Pope paraphrases in his *Essay on Man*, I.193–206. See also Locke, IV.14.2.

20. *dialectick induction*: Cf. Chambers, s.v. *Induction*: 'Suidas reckons three kinds of *induction*; that . . . which concludes or gathers some general proposition from an enumeration of all the particulars of a kind, he calls the *dialectic induction*.' We now know *Suidas* is the name of a Greek lexicon rather than its author.

21. reverences and worships: Sterne's common mode of address to embrace clergy and nobility.

22. *How d'ye*: Earlier in the century servants called on their master's or mistress's acquaintances to ask, with their compliments, 'How do ye?' – equivalent to leaving a card.

23. I tremble . . . kennels: Cf. Swift, *A Tale of a Tub*, sect. XI: 'HE would shut his Eyes as he walked along the Streets, and if he happened to bounce his Head against a Post, or fall into the Kennel (as he seldom missed either to do one or both) . . .' The serious side of both passages is suggested by scriptural echoes (Isaiah 59:9–10, Job 5:14, Luke 6:39, John 3:19–20) amidst the comedy. Stinks: sinks? Kennels = gutters.

24. full butt: Point-blank meeting, violent collision.

25. like hogs: Cf. Pope, *Dunciad* (B), IV.525: 'The vulgar herd turn off to roll with Hogs.'

26. In this . . . one: A typical witticism at the expense of doctors, found in Swift, Pope, and Fielding, but perhaps most succinctly in Sancho Pança's proverb, 'A Doctor gives his Advice by the Pulse of your Pocket.' Aesculapius was for both Greeks and Romans the god of medicine.

27. coalition of the gown: I.e., the legal profession; hence the 'spacious HALL' = Westminster Hall.

28. *John o'Nokes . . . Tom o'Stiles*: Fictitious names for parties in a legal action.

29. centumvirate: Body of one hundred men.

30. contrist: Make sad: Sterne may have found this rare word in Rabelais; cf. *Trist*ram.

31. for what . . . chair: Copied verbatim from Rabelais, III.16. Sterne adds the 'cane chair' from which he creates his argument; mittain = mitten.

32. *to answer one another*: As a principle in painting, 'embellishments' answering one another were less desirable among connoisseurs than variety. Cf. IV.xxxi, where the water-mill on one side of the river is to be 'answered' by a wind-mill on the other.

33. sow with one ear: Sterne conflates three proverbial expressions: 'You cannot make a silk purse out of a sow's ear'; 'To have the sow by the right [or wrong] ear'; and 'To take the right [or wrong] sow by the ear.'

34. good fame or feeding: In his January 1760 letter defending *TS*, Sterne argues that he 'wrote not [to] be *fed*, but to be *famous* ', inverting Colley Cibber's 'I wrote more to be Fed than be Famous' (*A Letter from Mr. Cibber to Mr. Pope* (1742)).

35. thousand vulgar errors: Thomas Browne, in his preface to the best known collection of vulgar (common) errors, *Pseudodoxia Epidemica* (1646), cites numerous forerunners in the tradition, but perhaps the most famous is Burton's *Anatomy*. Locke defines himself in his *Essay* as '*employed as an Under-Labourer in clearing Ground a little, and removing some of the Rubbish, that lies in the way to Knowledge . . .*'

CHAPTER XXI

1. handy-cuffs: Blows with the hands, i.e., fisticuffs.

2. Inconsistent . . . man is: Sterne borrows the observations of this paragraph from John Norris, *Practical Discourses upon Several Divine Subjects, Volume Three* (1693):

Do [men] not disquiet themselves about Phantastick and Imaginary Goods. . . . [T]here is no Man but who vainly disquiets *himself.*

Poor unhappy Creature that he should do so! Are there not necessary and unavoidable Causes of Trouble sufficient, but he must needs add Voluntary Afflictions to his heap of Misery, . . . disquiet himself, and that too in Vain, without Reason, and without Measure . . .

John Norris of Bemerton (1657–1711), philosopher, poet, and cleric, was an important source for Sterne's sermons; for example, the idea of this passage is repeated in sermon 22 ('History of Jacob'):

If there is an evil in this world, 'tis sorrow and heaviness of heart.——The loss of goods, ——of health,——of coronets and mitres, are only evil, as they occasion sorrow;—— take that out——the rest . . . dwelleth only in the head of man.

Poor unfortunate creature that he is! as if the causes of anguish in the heart were not enow——but he must fill up the measure, with those of caprice; and not only walk in a vain shadow,——but disquiet himself in vain too.

3. pouring in oyl: Cf. the parable of the good Samaritan (Luke 10:33–34).

CHAPTER XXII

1. our government . . . hinges: Almost certainly a reference to the sudden death of
George II on 25 October 1760.
2. jack-boots: Riding boots of the gentry and the military, and a likely allusion to
Lord Bute, who was already beginning his rapid rise to power as George III's most
trusted minister; John Bute was easily corrupted into Jack Boot, his iconographic
as well as cognomenal representation in political prints and pamphlets.
3. cut off the entail: Legal expression meaning to put an end to the limitation of an
inheritance to a particular line of heirs; one rightly suspects a bawdy play. A
perpetuity in law is considered odious because it prevents the circulation of property
and wealth; cf. Pope, *Imitations of Horace*, Ep. II.ii.246–7: 'The Laws of God, as well
as of the Land, / Abhor, a *Perpetuity* should stand.'
4. Sir *Roger . . . Marston-Moor*: Marston Moor, eight miles west of York, scene of
Cromwell's greatest victory of the Civil War (July 1644). Sterne's great-grandfather,
Dr Richard Sterne (1596–1683), later Archbishop of York, became famous during
the war for loyalist activities. Roger Sterne, Laurence's father, was a soldier.

CHAPTER XXIII

1. retrograde planet: Astrological term for a planet that moves (apparently) contrary
to the succession of signs and degrees, i.e., east to west; birth under such a planet
was deemed unlucky.

CHAPTER XXIV

1. *Bridget*: In addition to the play on *bridge*, Sterne may have in mind a connection
with St Brigid, patroness of Ireland, for whom Bridewell Hospital, the London
house of correction for wayward women, was named. 'Mrs' was used for both
married and unmarried women in the eighteenth century.
2. tagging of points: Fastening metal ends to laces; i.e., trivial tasks.
3. opificers: *OED*: 'One who makes or constructs a work'; this passage is its last
example of a word Johnson says is 'not received'.
4. *Aristotle . . . Ricaboni*: The question of single versus multiple plots was of great
importance to neoclassical critics, all of whom started with Aristotle's *Poetics*. Le
Bossu (see n. 4 to III.xii) has a chapter in his *Treatise* entitled '*Of the Vicious
Multiplication of* Fables'. Luigi Riccoboni (1676–1753), playwright and theatrical
historian, comments on the subject in his work. Why Sterne also cites the Roman
tragedian Marcus Pacuvius (220–*c.* 130 B.C.) is unclear.

5. *vis* a *vis*: Light carriage for two persons sitting face to face (correctly: *vis à vis*). Madame de Pompadour (1721–64), mistress of Louis XV.

6. trumpet of Fame: See n. 8 to I.xxiii.

7. soss: *OED* cites this passage as its sole illustration of usage as an adverb: 'with a heavy fall or dull thud'. Now considered dialect.

8. break his leg: Eric Partridge, *A Dictionary of Slang and Unconventional English*, 7th ed. (Macmillan, 1970), records the colloquial meaning, 'give birth to a bastard'.

9. BATTERING-RAMS: Most of this information is found in Chambers, but differences in wording suggest Sterne had another source. The *scorpion* was used to launch arrows, the *catapulta*, javelins, the *ballista*, stones, and the *pyraboli*, flaming arrows. *Battering rams* and the *terebra* were used to knock down walls; the *vinea* was a shelter protecting those approaching the wall. Chambers notes that Marcellinus (*c.* 330–*c.* 395), a Greek historian of Rome, described the *ballista* and also wrote that the *catapulta* was the invention of the Syrians. Tyre fell to Alexander the Great in 332 B.C.

10. sally port: Opening in a fortification allowing troops to conduct raiding parties (sallies); the term almost certainly had bawdy connotations.

CHAPTER XXV

1. cardinal *Alberoni*'s intrigues: In chronicling the events of 1718–19, culminating in the retaking of Messina (see n. 1 to III.xx), Tindal notes in his margin: '*Intrigues of* Spain', and below it: 'Alberoni*'s practices discovered in* France.' Giulio Alberoni (1664–1752), prime minister of Philip V of Spain, involved him in a disastrous war against England, France, Holland, and Austria (the Quadruple Alliance). The 'pre-engagements' refer to the Treaty of Utrecht's guarantee of the neutrality of Italy, violated by Spain.

2. For . . . itself: Almost all of Sterne's details in this paragraph are found in Chambers, s.v. *Bridge*, including references to the work of Jacques Bernouilli (1654–1705) and Guillaume-François Antoine de l'Hospital (1661–1704), both mathematicians; however, Chambers does not mention the bridges at Spires and Brisac (Breisach). For an insightful essay that ties Sterne's interests in cycloids and parabolas to his interest in 'bridging' gaps in communication, see Burckhardt in Further Reading.

    Act. Erud. Lips., i.e., *Acta Eruditorium, Leipzig*, a learned journal cited by Chambers.

CHAPTER XXVI

1. *Savoyard*'s box: Possibly a hurdy-gurdy, but more likely a 'raree-shew box' also associated with Savoyards (see n. 1 to VIII.xxiv).

CHAPTER XXIX

1. hit the longitude: Methods to determine longitude at sea occupied scientific minds throughout the century, culminating in success in Sterne's day.

CHAPTER XXXI

1. the word *Nose*: That 'nose' does not simply mean 'nose' is obvious, but in addition to its phallic implications, there is a classical tradition wherein the length of one's nose is equated to the extent of one's wit. Of his 'chapter of noses' Sterne wrote to a friend in late 1760: 'I am not much in pain upon what gives my kind friends ... so much on the chapter of *Noses*—because, as the principal satire throughout that part is levelled at those learned blockheads who, in all ages, have wasted their time and much learning upon points as foolish—it shifts off the idea of what you fear [excessive bawdiness?], to another point.'

CHAPTER XXXII

1. island of ENNASIN: In Rabelais, IV.9, Pantagruel and his company arrive at the island of Ennasin, where the 'men, women, and children, have their noses shap'd like an ace of clubs'. The word itself suggests 'noseless' or 'flat-nosed'.

CHAPTER XXXIII

1. saving the mark: Proverbial, from 'God save the mark'; used by way of apology when something obscene or horrible has been mentioned.
2. *Michaelmas* and *Lady day*: Michaelmas is celebrated on 29 September and Lady-day (Feast of the Annunciation) on 25 March; in England, they are two of the four quarter-days on which rents and various other fiscal responsibilities are discharged.
3. cawl: I.e., caul, the netted substructure of a wig.
4. lay down in their tents: Perhaps an echo of Numbers 16:26 or Psalm 84:10.
5. mother's milk: The idea is as old as Cicero's observation that we take in the errors and prejudices of our world at the breast (*Tusculan Disputations*).
6. turn'd up trumps: From whist, where the final card dealt is turned up to establish the trump suit. Clubs were considered unlucky.

CHAPTER XXXIV

1. *ex confesso*: Confessedly.
2. The apple ... could: Sterne closely borrows from Locke's chapter on property in *Of Civil Government*, 2.5.27–8.
3. *Tribonius*: See n. 12 to III.xii.

4. *Gregorius ... Des Eaux*: Cf. Chambers, s.v. *Code*:

In 506, Alaric, king of the Goths, made a new collection of the Roman laws, taken from the three former *Codes*, the *Gregorian*, *Hermogenian*, and *Theodosian*, which he likewise published under the title of the *Theodosian Code* ...

   There have been various other later *Codes*, particularly of the ancient Gothic, and since of the French kings; as the ... *Code* Louis ... *Code* des Eaux, *&c.*

See n. 12 to III.xii. Sterne misread 'des Eaux' as a person; it is a code governing rivers and forests, as noted by Work (222, n. 3).

5. exsudations: I.e., exudations, oozings.

6. wafted: The first edition's 'wasted' makes no sense in context and has been emended.

7. service: Work (224), following the 1780 edition, emends to 'sorrows', but 'service', the reading of the first edition, is abundantly meaningful.

CHAPTER XXXV

1. *Bruscambille*'s prologue: Sterne probably did not read Bruscambille (the theatrical name of le Sieur Deslauriers, comedian and author of *Prologues tant sérieux que facécieux* (1610)), but simply lifted the reference from Ozell's note to Rabelais, I.40: 'Bruscambille has repeated it in his prologue on large noses.' Two other 'authorities' cited by Walter are found in another of Ozell's footnotes to I.40:

Bouchet [Guillaume Bouchet (*c.* 1513–93), publisher of a collection of witty domestic conversations] in his 24th serée (which I take to mean his evenings conferences, for I never saw the book) says that friar John's answer is not altogether a joke; for that the famous surgeon, Ambrose Paræus [Ambrose Paré (1510–90), French surgeon, considered the 'father of modern surgery'], has maintain'd, that the hardness of a nurse's breast may make the child have a flat nose.

Sterne's 'Andrea' is either a slip for 'Ambrose' or belongs with Scroderus (cf. p. 190), but was poorly marked in the manuscript. *Prignitz* and *Scroderus* seem to be comic names, related to the authorities cited in a footnote to 'Slawkenbergius's Tale', i.e., 'J. Scrudr.', 'J. Tubal', and 'Von Jacobum Koinshoven'. *Hafen Slawkenbergius* is also invented, based on German words for chamber-pot and pile of offal (manure).

2. *Coleman*-street: In the heart of London's financial district in the mid-eighteenth century, and today (EC2).

3. he solaced ... mistress: Walter's enjoyment bears comparison to Toby's decampment for the bowling-green: 'Never did lover post down to a belov'd mistress, etc.' (II.v).

CHAPTER XXXVI

1. celebrated dialogue: 'De Captandis Sacerdotiis' ('Of Benefice-Hunters') from the *Colloquia Familiaria* of Desiderius Erasmus (1466–1536), author of *Praise of Folly* (1509), a work comparable to *TS* in significant ways.

2. *Tickletoby* 's mare: Rabelais tells the story of Francis Villon's vengeance on Friar Tickletoby in IV.13; Sterne shortens the passage, and avoids the outcome, where Tickletoby has his brains 'dash'd out'. *Tickletoby* is a cant term for 'penis' or 'a wanton', according to Partridge, *Dictionary*; cf. *Toby* = buttocks.

3. *ab urb. con.*: Events in Roman history were dated 'from the founding of the city' (*ab urbe condita*) of Rome in 753 B.C. The second Punic War began in 218 B.C., or 535 *ab urb. con.*

4. reader! read: Cf. p. 231, where we are told to read Longinus with similar insistence; the parallel is interesting in view of the main character, Longinus Rabelaicus, in Sterne's 'Rabelaisian Fragment'.

5. saint *Paraleipomenon*: See *OED*, s.v. *Paralipomena*: things omitted from the body of the work and appended in a supplement; Cervantes uses the singular (as does Sterne), in II.III.40, where '*Sir* Paralipomenon, *Knight of the three Stars* ' is mentioned.

6. penetrate the moral: Cf. *Political Romance*, where Sterne talks about the meanings found under the 'dark Veil of its Allegory, [as many] as ever were discovered in ... *Gargantua* and *Pantagruel* '. He is recalling Motteux's preface: 'THE ingenious of our age ... have been extreamly desirous of discovering the truths which are hid under the dark veil of allegories in that incomparable work.'

7. motly: The obvious meaning, 'variegated, parti-coloured', should not make us forget the word's association with the costumes of court jesters and clowns. On the preparation of the marbled leaf for the first edition, see W. G. Day, '*Tristram Shandy*: The Marbled Leaf', *Library* 27 (1972); and Diana Patterson, 'Tristram's Marblings and Marblers', *Shandean* 3 (1991); the most important point is that every marbled page is unique.

CHAPTER XXXVII

1. *NIHIL me* ... fail: Sterne quotes from Erasmus's dialogue between Pamphagus and Cocles and translates (loosely) as he goes. The line on which Walter sets to work is 'Conducet excitando foculo, si desuerit follis' (If you haven't a bellows, it [a nose] will serve to stir the fire). Work (229, n. 3) suggests that Walter's emendation of *focum* to either *ficum* (fig) or *locum* (place) would provide additional bawdiness, both words having sexual connotations.

2. ambidexterity: *OED* cites this passage as its first illustration of figurative use: 'superior dexterity or cleverness'.

3. nautical uses: Erasmus suggests use as a grappling-hook in a sea-fight and as an anchor.

CHAPTER XXXVIII

1. *Disgrázias*: Unpleasant accidents, misfortunes.

2. *Whitfield*'s disciples: George Whitefield (1714–70), along with John Wesley, a founder of Methodism and a fiery preacher. Sterne directs several sermons against excesses he perceived in the movement. See New, 'Swift and Sterne', in Further Reading.

3. to gird up myself: Scriptural; e.g., Job 38:3, Jeremiah 1:17.

4. dilucidating: I.e., elucidating.

5. charnel houses in *Silesia*: In so far as three-quarters of the population of Silesia (presently divided between Poland and the Czech Republic) was said to have been killed during the Thirty Years War, its charnel houses a century later might well be singled out.

6. *Crim Tartary*: Cf. Chambers, s.v. *Nose*: 'The Crim-Tartars break the *noses* of their children while young, as thinking it a great piece of folly to have their *noses* stand before their eyes.' This perhaps explains why the hero of 'Slawkenbergius's Tale' will return to '*Crim-Tartary*' (Crimea) after his journey to Frankfort.

7. bating . . . heaven: A commonplace observation of travellers to Turkey was the reverence given to fools and madmen as inspired by God.

8. *Ambrose Paræus*: Paré served several kings, but not Francis IX – who never existed. He attributed to Gaspare Tagliacozzi (1545–99) an operation for the restoration of the nose (its loss usually the effect of the mercury used to treat venereal disease) by grafting skin from the arm. Although Tagliacozzi responded on several occasions that the procedure was not his, the eighteenth century, on the basis of Paré's testimony, made Tagliacozzi a subject of ridicule, as in Butler's *Hudibras* and *Tatler* 260. That Sterne knew Paré was in error indicates he read more deeply on this issue than was his usual practice.

9. efficient cause: Sterne elaborates on Friar John's explanation for his long nose (Rabelais, I.40): 'according to the true monastical philosophy, it is because my nurse had soft teats, by virtue whereof, whilst she gave me suck, my nose did sink in, as in so much butter'. It is to this passage that Ozell adds the footnotes quoted above.

10. *puisne*: Puny (legalism for inferior).

11. *ad mensuram suam legitimam*: At its proper size.

12. refocillated: *OED* cites this passage as its last example: 'to revive, refresh, reanimate, comfort'.

13. ratios: Rations.

14. *crucifix'd*: *OED*'s last illustration is dated 1635; Sterne uses the far more common *crucified* in IX.xxxii.

15. *Ponocrates* and *Grangousier*: Ponocrates is Gargantua's tutor; Grangousier, his father. Along with Friar John, they attempt to answer Gargantua's question: 'What is the cause . . . that friar John hath such a goodly nose?' Friar John's answer is

quoted in n. 9 to this chapter; Grangousier's is given at p. *195*. Ponocrates's solution may have inspired 'Slawkenbergius's Tale': 'Because . . . he came with the first to the fair of noses, and therefore made choice of the fairest and the greatest.'

CHAPTER XL

1. syllogize by their noses: According to Montaigne ('Apology for Raimond de Sebonde'), a dog syllogizes by his nose in this manner: '*I have followed my Master by the Foot to this Place, he must of necessity be gone one of these three Ways, he is not gone this Way, nor that, he must then infallibly be gone this other.*'
2. *Locke . . . juxta-position*: Sterne paraphrases Locke, *Essay*, IV.17.18: 'the principal Act of Ratiocination is the finding the Agreement, or Disagreement of two *Ideas* one with another, by the intervention of a third. As a Man, by a Yard, finds two Houses to be of the same length, which could not be brought together to measure their Equality by *juxta*-position.' Sterne's alterations set up several bawdy possibilities. *Medius terminus*: term in a syllogism not appearing in the conclusion.

CHAPTER XLI

1. *quære*: Query; common Latinism.
2. *Grangousier*'s solution: Cf. Rabelais, I.40: 'What is the cause . . . that friar John hath such a goodly nose? Because, said Grangousier, that God would have it so . . .'

CHAPTER XLII

1. contrited and attrited: *OED* cites this passage as its last example of *contrited* (crushed, ground to pieces); and its first example of *attrited* (worn down by continued friction).

Volume IV

SLAWKENBERGIUS'S TALE

1. FABELLA: Sterne's Latin is quite accurate and almost certainly his translation of his own invented tale.
2. *Strasburg*: The setting of Strasbourg exploits its surprise capture by the French in 1681 and the fact that within its history are not only the varying fortunes of French and German (Austrian) masters, but of Lutheran and Catholic theologians as well, a perfect focus for the scholastic arguments Sterne ridicules.
3. scabbard: Sterne's humour is served by the Latin *vaginam*.
4. *Crepitare*: Sterne may have been aware of an additional meaning, 'to fart'.

5. *Rem penitus explorabo*: The bawdiness of 'I'll know the bottom of it' is abetted by the association of *penitus* (as an adverb) with *penis*, and the usual play on *rem*, i.e., *thing*.

6. *Benedicity*: Bless me!

7. saint *Nicolas*: Patron saint of Russia and of children, sailors, and, more generally, travellers.

8. Περιζομαῖὲ: perizomatè: Girdle worn round the loins as in Jeremiah 1:17; cod-piece, an ornamented flap for the crotch area of tight trousers, is not, as Sterne well knew, an equivalent.

9. *Minime tangetur*: 'It never shall be touched' is too strong; more accurately: 'It shall be touched as little as possible.'

10. saint *Radagunda*: St Radegund (*c.* 520–87), founder of the monastery of Our Lady of Poitiers in 552, known to Sterne in her role as patroness of his alma mater, Jesus Collège, Cambridge.

11. turpentine: Sterne was probably aware that the turpentine of Strasbourg was the most commonly used in England; and perhaps, also, that turpentine was used for clearing blocked urinary passages.

12. queen *Mab*: Usually considered an invention of Shakespeare; cf. *Romeo and Juliet*, I.iv.54, 70–71, where she is described as the 'fairies' midwife' who 'gallops night by night / Through lovers' brains, and then they dream of love . . .'

13. abbess of *Quedlingberg*: Sterne perhaps chooses Quedlingberg (in Saxony) because the women of the famous abbey located there were at one time governors of the city as well. Here, as elsewhere, inconsistencies in the spelling of names are preserved in the belief that Sterne was self-consciously nonchalant about spelling them 'correctly'; this decision does, at times, preserve compositors' errors, but the alternative, to normalize Sterne's erratic spellings, seems the greater violation of his text in most instances.

14. placket holes: Openings in the outer skirt, giving access to the pocket within; obscene connotations adhered to them from the beginning of the seventeenth century.

15. third . . . *Francis*: Lay order of men and women, the first and second orders being fully professed men and women. It was founded by St Francis in 1221.

16. nuns of mount *Calvary*: Benedictine order, founded in 1617 at Poitiers.

17. *Præmonstratenses*: Augustinian order founded in 1120.

18. *Clunienses*: Benedictine order founded in 890. St Odo (879–942) was the second Abbot of Cluny (927–42). A nunnery was not established by the order until 1056; where Sterne garnered his misinformation is not known.

19. *Carthusians*: Contemplative order founded at Chartreuse in 1084.

20. flead: Flayed.

21. saint *Antony* . . . fire: Erysipelas, marked by inflammation of the skin; also known as St Anthony's fire, from the belief that his intercession is efficacious.

22. nuns of saint *Ursula*: Either the Ursulines, founded at Brescia in 1535, or the

Society of the Sisters of St Ursula of the Blessed Virgin, founded in 1606. Ursula was accompanied in martyrdom by 11,000 other virgins.

23. capitulars: Members of an ecclesiastical chapter.

24. domiciliars: Canons of a minor order having no voice in a chapter.

25. butter'd buns: Cant expression for a woman who has intercourse with several men in quick succession, or, more simply, a whore.

26. *Chrysippus* and a *Crantor*: Chrysippus was second only to Zeno in establishing the Stoic philosophy; see n. 7 to II.xix and n. 2 to III.iv. The Stoics derived their name from the Greek word for *porch* or *portico*, the covered arcade in Athens where they gathered. Crantor (*c.* 335–*c.* 275 B.C.) was the first commentator on Plato.

27. bottom of the well: See n. 5 to II.xix.

28. faculty: I.e., medical doctors.

29. It was . . . time: Chambers notes that the foetus is first 'head upwards' but after eight months, as the head becomes heavier than the body, it 'tumbles in the liquor which contains it', and turns head downwards; Sterne's 'statical' seems a foreshortening of *hydrostatical*, alluding to the pressures of this 'liquor' or fluid.

30. stamina: Cf. Chambers: 'those simple, original parts, which existed first in the embryo, or even in the seed . . .' In the following discussion about *sanguification*, Sterne again seems to gather his 'learning' from Chambers.

31. *petitio principii*: Begging the question – a fallacy in logic consisting of arguing from a premise that depends on the conclusion it is used to prove.

32. Now death . . . blood: Cf. Chambers: 'generally considered as the separation of the soul from the body. . . . Physicians usually defined death by a total stoppage of the circulation of the blood . . .'

33. civilians: I.e., practitioners of civil law as opposed to commissaries, practitioners in the ecclesiastical courts. For Sterne's career as a commissary, see Cash, *EMY*, 243–61.

34. *ex mero motu*: Of his own accord.

35. two universities: Whether the University of Strasbourg was founded by Jacobus (1489–1553) or Johannes (1507–89) Sturmius was in doubt in Sterne's day, although the year, 1538, was agreed on. Sterne or his source guessed correctly: Jacobus, a leading figure in Strasbourg's senate, was the more instrumental. There was no 'Popish' university in Strasbourg until some twenty years after the French victory when the Catholic University at Molsheim was moved there by Louis XIV; Archduke Leopold (1586–1632), Bishop of Strasbourg and Passau, had been an early patron. Sterne's source is unknown.

36. *Martin Luther*'s damnation: Sterne found the entire debate, as well as a suggestion for connecting it to Strasbourg, in Pierre Bayle, *Dictionary*, 5 vols. (1734–8), s.v. *Luther* (first noted by Work, 261 n. •). Bayle annotates his sentence '[They] have even falsified the day of his birth, in order to frame a scheme of his nativity to his disadvantage' with his customary elaborateness:

Martin Luther was born the tenth of November, betwixt eleven and twelve of the clock at night, at Isleben [a note informs us that Isleben is in the county of Mansfeld].... [His mother] being examined ... concerning the year she was brought to bed ... answered ... she only knew the day and the hour. It is therefore out of pure malice, that Florimond de Remond places his birth on the twenty second of October. He thought thereby to confirm the astrological predictions of Junctinus.... This Astrologer was strongly confuted by a professor of Strasburg, who shewed, that, by the rules of Astrology, Luther was to be a great man.

Bayle traces the debate at length, and Sterne copies his discussion, including the Latin note and its wonderful error 'religiosissimus' for 'irreligiosissimus', the Catholic astrologer being said to have found Luther dying wholly *religious*, a slip Sterne may have wanted to retain, assuming he noticed it. Bayle translates himself: '*This is strange, indeed terrible, five planets being in conjunction in Scorpio, in the ninth house which the Arabians allotted to religion, made [Luther] a sacrilegious Heretic, a most bitter and most prophane enemy to the Christian faith. It appears from the horoscope directed to the conjunction of Mars, that he died without any sense of religion, his soul steeped in guilt sailed to hell, there to be lashed with the fiery whips of Alecto, Tisiphone, and Megera thro' endless ages.*' Lucas Gauricus (1476–1558), Bishop of Civitate and noted astrologer; Sterne's reference to his *Astrological Treatise on the Past Accidents of Many Men, by Means of an Examination of their Nativities* (1552) was taken from Bayle's margin. Alecto, Tisiphone, and Megæra, the Greek Erinyes (Roman Furies) responsible for avenging crimes, here and hereafter.

37. *Nonnulli ... Idea: Sterne's meaningless footnote imitates the nonsensical argumentation of Bridlegoose in Rabelais, III.39–42, though the actual legalisms may have been borrowed from Henry Swinburne's *A Briefe Treatise of Testaments and Last Willes* (1590), cited in IV.xxix.

38. *Alexandrian* library: Most important library in antiquity, supposedly burned by Julius Caesar in 47 B.C., but not fully destroyed until 640.

39. doubled the cape: Partridge, *Dictionary*, s.v. *Double Cape Horn*: 'To be made a cuckold.'

40. distribute their types: Technical printing term: 'To remove (type that has been "composed" or set up) from the forme, and return each letter into its proper box or compartment in the case' (*OED*).

41. square cap: The present-day academic mortarboard regularly worn by church-men and members of universities.

42. implies contradictions: Cf. Chambers, s.v. *Imply a contradiction*: 'a phrase used among philosophers, in speaking of the object of divine omnipotence'. The problem was a central one in scholastic logic, the intersection of God's omnipotence with his created world and its laws of operation.

43. He can make two and two five: The first and second editions read 'cannot', but it seems evident that the 'Popish' position is the 'Nosarian' position ('God's power

is infinite') as opposed to the 'Lutheran' or 'Antinosarian' position ('It extends only to all possible things'). Descartes is commonly associated with the specific assertion that God can make two and two five.

44. he can ... *Strasburg*: Rabelais similarly defends the birth of Gargantua from the left ear of Gargamelle: 'if it had been the will of God, would you say that he could not do it? ... I tell you, nothing is impossible with God; and, if he pleased, all women henceforth should bring forth their children at the ear' (I.6). All contemporary accounts of Strasbourg mention its famous steeple.

45. the *Parchmentarians*: Chambers, s.v. *Lutheranism*, lists some of the 'thirty nine different sects, which at different times have sprung up among the Lutherans', including the Antinomians, Antidiaphorists, Antiswenkfeldians, and Antiosiandrians.

46. like *Pantagruel* ... sight: In the 'Explanatory Remarks' to Rabelais, IV.1, we are told that Pantagruel and his attendants 'embarked for the oracle of the holy bottle'.

47. beguines: Sisterhood founded in the twelfth century. The members were free to quit the cloister and to marry. They flourished in much of western Europe, so there is little validity to Toby's claim (VIII.xx) that they were found only in the Spanish Netherlands and Amsterdam. Trim falls in love with a beguine, VIII.xx–xxii.

48. Haste ... them: Sterne's divisions are traditional, though post-Aristotelian. Chambers's definitions are useful: *Protasis*: 'the first part ... wherein the several persons of the play are shewn, their characters and manners intimated, and the action ... entered upon'; *Epitasis*: 'the second part ... wherein the plot, or action ... was carried on, heightened ... till it arrived at its state, or height'; *Catastasis*: 'wherein the intrigue, or action set on foot in the epitasis, is supported ... till it be ripe for the unravelling'; and *Catastrophe*: 'the fourth, and last part ... immediately succeeding the catastasis'. Chambers discusses peripeteia (reversal of fortune) as part of the catastrophe.

49. rest and quietness: Not in Aristotle's *Poetics* but part of the received commentary.

50. *Valadolid*: Cf. Cervantes, I.IV.2: 'for I have known several Men in my Time go by the Names of the Places where they were born, as [e.g.,] ... *Diego de Valladolid*'.

51. dying *un*——: Florida *Notes* suggests 'undone' (see IX.xxviii) rather than '*unconvinced*', but New, 'Swift and Sterne' (see Further Reading), argues the relevance of 'conviction' to the 'Tale'.

52. eased his mind: Partridge, *Dictionary*, suggests *easing oneself* was used euphemistically for *ejaculation*; the more usual suggestion of *defecation* (*urination*) might also be in play.

53. As this ... tale: Sterne is accurate in saying the fall of Strasbourg was often spoken of – always with awe over Louis XIV's treachery and scorn for Strasbourg's pride and unpreparedness; see, e.g., Gilbert Burnet, *Some Letters Containing an Account of ... Travelling through Switzerland, Italy, Some Parts of Germany*, 2nd ed. (Rotterdam, 1687):

One seeth, in the ruin of this *City*, what a mischievous thing the popular pride of a *free City* is: they fancied they were able to defend themselves, and so they refused to let an *Imperial Garrison* come within their *Town.* . . . [T]he *Town* thought this was a Diminution of their Freedom, and so chose rather to pay a *Garrison* of three thousand *Souldiers*, which . . . ex[h]austed their *Revenue*, and brought them under great *Taxes.* . . . The *Town* begins to sink in its *Trade*, notwithstanding the great circulation of *Money* . . . for it is impossible for a *Place of Trade*, that is to have alwayes eight or ten thousand *Souldiers* in it, to continue long in a Flourishing State.

54. Universal Monarchy: The term was often used in relation to Louis XIV, but not 'every body' attributed the scheme to Jean-Baptiste Colbert (1619–83), his finance minister.

CHAPTER I

1. pupilability: *OED* cites this passage as its sole example and notes the pun on the pupils of the eyes.
2. not worth stooping for: Cf. *Twelfth Night*, II.ii.14–15, where Malvolio tosses Olivia's ring at Viola's feet: 'If it be worth stooping for, there it lies . . .'

CHAPTER III

1. *Makay*'s regiment: Hugh Mackay (*c.* 1640–92), general in the army of William III, killed at the head of his regiment at Steinkirk, a battle recounted in V.xxi.

CHAPTER IV

1. I can have . . . world: Sterne glances at several proverbial expressions, epitomized in Bacon's famous opening sentence to 'Of Marriage and Single Life': 'He that hath wife and children hath given hostages to fortune.'

CHAPTER VI

1. Attitudes . . . all: Sterne perhaps borrows his idea from Charles Avison, *An Essay on Musical Expression*, 2nd ed. (1753): 'As the proper Mixture of Light and Shade . . . is, indeed, essential to the Composition of a good Picture; so the judicious Mixture of Concords and Discords is equally essential to a musical Composition. . . . [T]he *Preparations* and *Resolutions* of Discords, resemble the soft Gradations from Light to Shade, or from Shade to Light in Painting.'

CHAPTER VII

1. WHEN . . . inheritance: Sterne borrows from the opening of sermon 34, 'Trust in God':

WHOEVER seriously reflects upon the state and condition of man, and looks upon that dark side of it, which represents his life as open to so many causes of trouble;—when he sees, how often he eats the bread of affliction, and that he is born to it as naturally as the sparks fly upwards;—that no rank or degrees of men are exempted from this law of our beings . . . when one sits down and looks upon this gloomy side of things, with all the sorrowful changes and chances which surround us,—at first sight,—would not one wonder,—how the spirit of a man could bear the infirmities of his nature, and what it is that supports him, as it does, under the many evil accidents which he meets with in his passage through the valley of tears?

Sterne borrowed these sentences from an obscure cleric, Walter Leightonhouse. Scriptural echoes in them include: 'bread of affliction' (Deuteronomy 16:3, 1 Kings 22:27); 'Yet man is born unto trouble, as the sparks fly upward' (Job 5:7); and 'Is there yet any portion or inheritance for us in our father's house?' (Genesis 31:14; see also Joshua 17:14, Psalm 16:5).

2. Zooks: Gadzooks, a corruption of 'God's hooks', the nails of the crucifixion.

3. 'Tis . . . Almighty God: Toby maintains 'Grangousier's solution'; see n. 2 to III.xli.

4. cutting the knot: Behind Sterne's metaphor is the proverbial cutting of the Gordian knot. In sermon 45, 'The ingratitude of Israel', Sterne condemns those who believe it 'idle to bring in the Deity to untie the knot, when [the causes of earthquakes] can be resolved easily into natural causes': 'Vain unthinking mortals!— As if natural causes were any thing else in the hands of God,—but instruments which he can turn to work the purposes of his will . . .' Sterne's glances at his sermons in these chapters are noteworthy.

5. school of *Athens*: Cf. Jonathan Richardson the younger, *An Account of Some of the Statues, . . . and Pictures in Italy* (1722): 'Even the Manner of the Reasoning of *Socrates* is Express'd; he holds the Fore-finger of his Left-hand between that, and the Thumb of his Right, and seems as if he was saying, You grant me This, and This . . .'; noted by Brissenden, 'Sterne and Painting'. The painting, housed in the Vatican, was often alluded to in the eighteenth century.

6. *Garrick*: Cf. Sterne's letter to Garrick, 27 January 1760: 'I sometimes think of a Cervantic Comedy upon these & the Materials of ye 3^d & 4th Vol^s which will be still more dramatick . . .'

CHAPTER VIII

1. THOUGH ... within us: Sterne continues to borrow from 'Trust in God': 'This expectation [that we 'shall ... live to see better days'] ... imposes upon the sense ... and like a secret spring in a well-contrived machine, though it cannot prevent, at least it counterbalances the pressure,—and so bears up this tottering, tender frame under many a violent shock and hard justling, which otherwise would unavoidably overwhelm it.' Sterne's point in the sermon is that 'self-love', the usual counterbalance to the world's evils, is always insufficient; the only *true* counterbalance is 'trust in God'.

2. GEORGE or EDWARD: Sterne alludes, by way of compliment, to George III and his brother Edward, Duke of York; he had been in the Duke's company during his spring 1760 visit to London.

3. *Trismegistus*: See n. 3 to I.xix.

CHAPTER X

1. story of a roasted horse: Proverbial expression for nonsense stories or histories, tales of a tub, cock and bull stories; perhaps derived from 'amounting to no more than the tail of a roasted horse'.

2. fifty other cold conceits: Cf. IX.xiii, where Tristram writes of 'a cold unmetaphorical vein of infamous writing'; and *ASJ*: 'I confess I do hate all cold conceptions, as I do the puny ideas which engender them ...'

3. you must read *Longinus*: Sterne alludes to the discussion of bombast and puerilities in sect. III of *On the Sublime*, and specifically to a note in the English translation by William Smith (1739) to Longinus's mention of a writer of 'empty simple Froth'. To exemplify this 'frigid' writing, the note offers his explanation of why Diana's temple at Ephesus burned to ashes the night Alexander the Great was born: the goddess, he wrote, was too busy assisting the midwife and 'had no leisure to extinguish the Flames'. The sentence became a commonplace in discussions of bad writing. In sermon 42, 'Search the Scriptures', Sterne calls Longinus 'the best critic the eastern world ever produced'. See Lamb, *Sterne's Fiction*, in Further Reading.

4. *Avicenna* and *Licetus*: As indicated in his footnote, Sterne borrows his learning from Adrien Baillet's *Des enfans célèbres*, published as Volume VI of *Jugemens des Savans sur les Principaux Ouvrages des Auteurs* (1722). Avicenna (980–1037), Arabian physician and philosopher, was said by Baillet to have read Aristotle's *Metaphysics* forty times without understanding it. No evidence exists that Licetus (1577–1657) had similar difficulty. He did, however, have a premature birth and, according to Baillet, was nineteen years old when he composed a treatise on the origin of the soul, entitled *Gonopsychanthropologia*. Sterne's footnote is copied verbatim from Baillet and tells of a foetus no larger than the palm of the hand, the father's consultation with the learned, and his placing the child in an oven (the method of

hatching chickens in Egypt) with the temperature regulated. The success of this effort was attested to by the fact that Licetus lived eighty years and composed eighty works; hence, concludes Baillet, one must grant that incredible things are not necessarily untrue, and that *appearance is not always on the side of truth*, a phrase Sterne uses to conclude his joke in Ch. xv. Sterne borrows from Baillet again in VI.i.

5. *de omni scribili*: Concerning all kinds of writing or scribbling (*scribili* is a nonce word); Sterne plays on the Latin commonplace *de omni scibili*, concerning all knowable things.

6. picking straws: Proverbial for pointless activity.

CHAPTER XII

1. *Job*'s stock of asses: Job begins with 500 she asses, doubled to 1,000 at the end of his sufferings.

CHAPTER XIII

1. chairman: One of two men carrying a sedan chair, a common mode of city transport in the century.

2. *day-tall*: I.e., *day-taler*, 'a worker engaged and paid by the day' (*OED*).

3. biographical writer: Montaigne makes a similar observation, in his essay 'Of Vanity': 'Who does not see that I have taken a Road, in which, incessantly and without labour I shall proceed, so long as there shall be Ink and Paper in the World?'

4. as *Horace* advises: See n. 3 to I.iv.

5. this propitious reign: See n. 1 to III.xxii.

CHAPTER XV

1. But for sleep: This discourse on sleep suggests Sterne kept a commonplace book; the sentiments of the first paragraph are so typical that identifying particular sources is unlikely.

2. set . . . bad matter: Sterne plays with the proverbial 'setting a good face on a bad matter'.

3. God's blessing . . . cloak: Cf. *Don Quixote*, II.III.68: 'Now Blessings light on him that first invented this same Sleep: It covers a Man all over, Thoughts and all, like a Cloak . . .'

4. what *Montaigne* advances: Sterne combines two distant passages from Montaigne's 'Of Experience': 'They enjoy the other Pleasures as they do that of Sleep, without knowing it; to the End, that even Sleep itself should not so stupidly escape from me, I have formerly caus'd my self to be disturb'd in my Sleep, that I might the

better and more sensibly relish and taste it.' The second passage occurs twenty pages earlier: 'I love to lie hard, and alone, even without my Wife, as Kings and Princes do, but well cover'd with Cloaths.... My Body is capable of a firm, but not of a violent or sudden Agitation. I evade of late all violent Exercises.... I can stand a whole Day together, and am never weary of walking: but from my Youth, I never loved to ride upon Pavements.' Sterne's ironic re-ordering juxtaposes Baillet's sentence (see n. 4 to IV.x) with 'even without my Wife'.

CHAPTER XVII

1. riddles and mysteries: Cf. p. 525: 'WE live in a world beset on all sides with mysteries and riddles ...' Sterne's wording for this passage has roots in two sermons, 44, 'The ways of Providence justified to man': 'Nay, have not the most obvious things that come in our way dark sides, which the quickest sight cannot penetrate into; and do not the clearest and most exalted understandings find themselves puzzled, and at a loss, in every particle of matter?'; and 19, 'Felix's behaviour towards Paul': 'That in many dark and abstracted questions of mere speculation, we should err——is not strange: we live amongst mysteries and riddles, and almost every thing which comes in our way, in one light or other, may be said to baffle our understandings.'

The source for both passages is Norris, *Practical Discourses ... Volume Two* (1691): 'We live among Mysteries and Riddles, and there is not one thing that comes in at our Senses, but what baffles our Understandings; but though (as the Wise Man [Wisdom 9:16] complains,) *hardly do we guess aright at the things that are upon Earth, and with labour do we find the things that are before us ...*' Behind Norris and Sterne is Locke, *Essay*, IV.3.22: 'He that knows anything, knows this in the first place, that he need not seek long for Instances of his Ignorance. The meanest, and most obvious Things that come in our way, have dark sides, that the quickest Sight cannot penetrate into. The clearest, and most enlarged Understandings of thinking Men find themselves puzzled, and at a loss, in every Particle of Matter.'

2. *Pythagoras ... Mahomet*: The names, excepting Mahomet, would occur to any eighteenth-century writer preparing a list of legal authorities.

CHAPTER XVIII

1. *James Butler*: See n. 6 to II.v.

CHAPTER XIX

1. my own ... *Shandy*-family: Walter echoes Exodus 20:5: 'for I the LORD thy God am a jealous God, visiting the iniquity of the fathers upon the children'.
2. child of wrath: Scriptural phrase; see Ephesians 2:3.

3. book of embryotic evils: *OED* cites this passage for its first recorded usage and refers to *embryonic*, 2 *fig.*: 'Immature, undeveloped.' The context, however, points to *embryonic*, 1: 'Pertaining to ... an embryo.'

4. radical heat: Chambers, s.v. *Flame* (*vital*), defines 'radical heat' as the 'fine, warm, ignious substance, supposed ... to reside in the hearts of animals, as necessary to life, or rather, as that which constitutes life itself'. For 'radical moisture' see n. 13 to II.iii.

5. stamina: See n. 30 to IV.S.T.

6. non-naturals: See n. 12 to I.xxiii.

7. There she gave vent: Sterne perhaps plays on *vent*; cf. p. 270, where the mother is referred to in legal parlance as the *venter*.

CHAPTER XX

1. undertaking criticks: Work's note (298, n. 1), with an eye on Swift, is useful: 'Enterprising; used here in the derogatory sense of officious, over-reaching.' Cf. p. 293.

2. splash'd a bishop: Almost certainly an allusion to Warburton (see n. 4 to I.xi), who liked the first instalment of the work so well he gave Sterne a purse, along with advice to tone down his bawdiness. As each instalment proved equally bawdy, the Bishop lost patience with the 'heteroclite parson', soon referring to him as an 'irrecoverable scoundrel'. Sterne evokes Warburton directly only once in *TS* (IX.viii), where the *Divine Legation* and *A Tale of a Tub* are linked with *TS*, but there are numerous covert allusions; see New, 'Sterne, Warburton', in Further Reading.

3. doctors of the Sorbonne: The doctors responsible for the 'Memoire' on intrauterine baptism, I.xx.

CHAPTER XXI

1. state*: Sterne cites the *Menagiana* (1693), a collection of gossip and *bons mots*, by Gilles Ménage (1613–92), and elaborates greatly on the one sentence that tells this story. Francis I (1494–1547) ruled France from 1515 until his death.

2. *Shadrach*, *Mesech*, and *Abed-nego*: The three friends of Daniel delivered from the fiery furnace; see Daniel 1:7, 3:1–30.

3. By saint *Peter*'s girdle: Nonce oath, such as Rabelais created: e.g., by St Winifrid's placket, by St Anthony's hog, etc.

4. pulling up his breeches: Louis XIV was infamous for conducting state business while sitting at stool.

CHAPTER XXII

1. *disport*: *OED* cites this passage as its sole illustration: 'bearing, carriage, deportment'.

2. *Francis* the Ninth: See n. 8 to III.xxxviii.

3. the duke of *Ormond*: See n. 6 to II.v.

4. If 'tis ... duodenums: This assertion of purpose, to make us laugh, has often been considered Sterne's own view of his work. In diction, he parodies the mechanistic bent of his age's medical science: e.g., 'from the above-mention'd *Communication between the Plexus Nervosus peculiar to Man, and the Nervus Diaphragmaticus*, the true Cause appears, why *Risibility* is *a Property of human* Nature; which is, because the Diaphragm, as well as the Heart ... is drawn upward by the Intercourse of the Nerves ... and the Lungs are likewise mov'd; then, because the same Intercostal nerve is continued upward, etc.' (from Thomas Willis, *Anatomy of the Brain*). That laughter was effective against the spleen was a truism; cf. Swift's labelling *A Tale of a Tub* 'A dangerous treatise writ against the spleen' ('The Author upon Himself '). *OED* cites this passage as its last illustration of 'inimicitious': 'unfriendly, hostile'.

CHAPTER XXIII

1. these great dinners: On the institution of the visitation dinner, see Cash, *EM Y*, 128–32. Goldsmith, *Citizen of the World*, letter 58, describes it thus: 'it was formerly the custom here for the ... [bishops] to go about the country once a year, and examine upon the spot whether those of subordinate orders did their duty ...' He describes the dinners as orgies of feasting. Sterne's **** in Ch. xxv represents York.

CHAPTER XXV

1. chasm of ten pages: The first edition skips nine pages (147–55), resulting in even-numbered right-hand pages for the remainder of Volume IV; to avoid this anomaly, which would have to continue to the end of modern one-volume editions, ten pages are usually skipped, as in this edition.

2. *Turpilius ... Basil*: Turpilius (first century) and Hans Holbein (1497–1543), left-handed painters, often linked for that reason alone.

3. *bend dexter*: In heraldry, the bend dexter is the diagonal band drawn across the shield from the top left (looking at the shield), or dexter chief, to the lower right (sinister base); when the band is drawn in the opposite direction, it is called the bend sinister and indicates bastardy.

4. blot in my escutcheon: Play on the literal and figurative meanings of the phrase, i.e., stain on a person's reputation.

5. by siege: Sterne plays with the bawdy usage of the word for the anus.

6. *Homenas*: Name of a clergyman in the 'Rabelaisian Fragment'. Sterne borrowed

it from Rabelais's Bishop of Papimany, annotated (IV.48) thus: 'They use it in Languedoc, when they would say, a great loggerheaded booby, that has neither wit nor breeding.' It may, however, be a simple play on 'homilist'.

7. as *Montaigne* complained: In 'Of the Education of Children', Montaigne complains that introducing a passage from an ancient author highlighted the insipidity of the book he was reading.

CHAPTER XXVI

1. SEE . . . pipes: In *Spectator* 46, Addison describes how the Spectator misplaces his notes in Lloyd's Coffee-house (cf. VII.xxxvi), and how, regaining possession, he 'twisted [the paper] into a kind of Match, and litt [his] Pipe with it'.

2. *Kysarcius*: See n. 9 to III.xx; the mock geographical reference underscores the obscenity.

3. head instead of my heart: Sterne often uses this formula, as in his preface to Volumes I and II of *Sermons*: 'I trust [these sermons] will be no less felt, or worse received, for the evidence they bear, of proceeding more from the heart than the head.' The preference was stated almost universally in the eighteenth-century Anglican pulpit in reaction to the polemical and divisive theologizing of the previous century.

4. To preach . . . heart: Cf. Sterne's sermon 42, 'Search the Scripture', in which he compares the eloquence of Scripture with false rhetoric consisting of 'an over-curious and artificial arrangement of figures, tinsel'd over with a gaudy embellishment of words, which glitter, but convey little or no light to the understanding'. The language is borrowed from Anthony Blackwall, *The Sacred Classics Defended and Illustrated* (1725).

CHAPTER XXVII

1. ZOUNDS: God's wounds, i.e., Christ's wounds on the cross.

2. *Phutatorius*: See n. 4 to III.xx.

3. twelve-penny oath: According to the Profane Oaths Act of 1746, the penalties for swearing were determined by the class of speaker rather than the oath uttered. Twelve pence was the fine for the lower orders; gentlemen paid more. Sterne would have been familiar with the act, since it was required to be read in church on four Sundays each year.

4. a yard below: Sterne puns on yard = penis.

5. *Gastripheres*: See n. 9 to III.xx, for this and other names at the visitation dinner.

6. *Johnson*'s dictionary: The 'chaste' words in the eighteenth century were *flap* or *fall*, but Johnson's *Dictionary* does indeed fail us.

7. temple of *Janus*: Janus, Roman god of doors and beginnings; closing the temple doors signified peace, opening them, war.

8. *Acrites* or *Mythogeras*: Respectively, 'confused, undiscriminating' and 'tale-bearer'.
9. *de Concubinis retinendis*: *On Keeping Concubines.*
10. compursions: *OED* cites this passage as its sole example: humorously, 'A pursing together.'
11. *Asker*: Common name, in West Midlands and Yorkshire dialect, for a newt.
12. aposiopestick-break: See n. 4 to II.vi.
13. trifles light as air: Cf. Iago's comment on leaving Desdemona's handkerchief in Cassio's lodging: 'Trifles light as air / Are to the jealous confirmations strong / As proofs of holy writ . . .' (*Othello*, III.iii.322–4).
14. *Euclid*'s demonstrations: See n. 1 to V.xxx.
15. worth stooping for: See n. 2 to IV.i.
16. as *Shakespear . . . jest*: *Hamlet*, V.i.184–5: 'Alas, poor Yorick! I knew him, Horatio, a fellow of infinite jest, of most excellent fancy.' The echoing of *Hamlet* here suggests that 'dreams of philosophy' is also a recall (I.v.166–7): 'There are more things in heaven and earth, Horatio, / Than are dreamt of in your philosophy.'

CHAPTER XXVIII

1. take out the fire: Sterne plays on the 'heat' of venereal infection; cf. the eighteenth-century term *fire-ship* for a prostitute.
2. make a very devil: Pun on 'printer's devil', the errand-boy in a printing shop.
3. *de re concubinariâ*: 'On the thing of a concubine'; cf. *Argumentum ad Rem*, p. 57.

CHAPTER XXIX

1. Had a priest . . . last: Sterne borrows his discussion from Ozell's note to Rabelais, I.19. Had he pursued Ozell's citation he would have discovered, as Work notes (327, n. 2), that Pope Zachary (741–52), not Pope Leo III (795–816), issued the decree; in all likelihood, Sterne cited his authority at random. At stake is whether or not grammatical errors (here, wrong declensional endings) invalidate a baptism. The correct Latin is *in nomine patris et filii et spiritus sancti* (in the name of the Father and of the Son and of the Holy Ghost).
2. *John Stradling*'s: Like Tom-o'Stiles above, Stradling was a conventional fictitious name for a party in a lawsuit.
3. best lawyers: As Sterne's first note indicates, he copies this dispute from Henry Swinburne's *Briefe Treatise*, the work used to create his nonsense footnote in 'Slawkenbergius's Tale' (see n. 37 to IV.S.T.). The notes here are culled from Swinburne's margins; although Kysarcius asserts that 'reason' is strongly on the side of the determination, Swinburne believed the opposite.
4. civilians: Civil lawyers.
5. jactitation: *OED* cites this passage as its sole illustration of an obsolete usage: 'discussion; bandying to and fro'.

6. *Triptolemus*: See n. 3 to III.xx.

7. Lord *Coke*: Sir Edward Coke (1552–1634), English jurist. *Brook* refers to Sir Robert Broke (d. 1558), another jurist cited by Swinburne.

8. juris-consulti: Legal counsellors.

9. juris-prudentes: Persons learned in the law.

10. consistory and prerogative courts: The function of these ecclesiastical courts is discussed by Cash, *EMY*, ch. 12.

11. *Liberi . . . liberorum*: Sterne translates this immediately above: 'that the child may be of the blood . . . etc.', except that, following Swinburne's translation rather than the Latin, he twice adds 'seed' to 'blood'.

12. *Mater non . . . signific*: The mother is not numbered among the blood relations. The sentence is from Swinburne, as is the reference to Pietro Baldi de Ubaldis (*c.* 1327–1400), Italian jurist.

13. levitical law: Although Leviticus 18:6ff. prohibits numerous cohabitations, it does not specify grandparents. The Book of Common Prayer, however, ends with a table of prohibited marriages, headed by grandmother and grandfather.

14. *Selden*: See *Table Talk of John Selden* (1689), ed. Sir Frederick Pollock (Quaritch, 1927): 'The King . . . [charged them with treason because they] charged my Lord of Canterbury & S^r. George Ratcliffe . . . with as much Logick as the boy that would have layen with his Grandmother said to his father, You lay with my Mother & why should I not lye with yo^{rs}.' Selden (1584–1654), English jurist and orientalist.

15. *Argumentum commune*: Cicero discusses the *exordium commune*, an exordium 'equally applicable to both sides of the case', and perhaps Sterne had this in mind; *argumentum commune* appears to be an invented term.

CHAPTER XXX

1. said: sad?

CHAPTER XXXI

1. loop of his hat: Since the cocked hats in fashion during the century were made by turning up (i.e., 'cocking') the brim on three sides and securing it with buttons and loops, to 'let down one loop' suggests dishevelment, perhaps mourning.

2. *Hippocrates*: As previously (p. 68), Sterne has his Hippocrates via Mackenzie's *History of Health*: 'MODERATE joy and anger, on the other hand, and those passions and affections of the mind which partake of their nature . . . invigorate the nerves, accelerate the circulating fluids, promote perspiration, and assist digestion.'

3. build a wind-mill: Gene Washington, *Scriblerian* 25 (1992), suggests a proverbial allusion – 'he has windmills in the head' – derived from *Don Quixote*, and meaning 'full of projects or plans'.

4. the *Missisippi*-scheme: The Mississippi Company reached its peak in the winter

of 1719–20 and collapsed in the spring, one of several trading-company schemes in the first decades of the century that turned sour, with great loss to speculators.

5. whinny: Covered or abounding with whins or furze-bushes.

6. ingress ... regress: Legal term, with bawdy connotations long before Sterne's usage.

7. feather ... cap: Proverbial; the earlier meaning of 'honour without profit' is closer to Sterne's intention than the more favourable connotations of present usage.

8. *tantum valet ... sonat*: It's worth as much as it sounds.

CHAPTER XXXII

1. choicest morsel: Cf. p. 527, where Tristram again refers to Toby's amours with these words.

2. akes dismally: Rabelais makes a similar complaint in concluding Book II: 'My head aches a little, and I perceive that the registers of my brain are somewhat jumbled and disordered with the septembral juice.'

3. True *Shandeism*: Cf. Sterne's letter to Hall-Stevenson in June 1761: 'I have not managed my miseries like a wise man—and if God, for my consolation under them, had not poured forth the spirit of Shandeism into me, which will not suffer me to think two moments upon any grave subject, I would else, just now lay down and die—die——and yet, in half an hour's time, I'll lay a guinea, I shall be as merry as a monkey—and as mischievous too ...' Shandeism bears comparison with Rabelais's 'Pantagruelism', as, e.g., Rabelais's concluding words to Book II: 'And if you desire to be good Pantagruelists, that is to say, to live in peace, joy, health, making yourselves always merry, never trust those men that always peep out at one hole' (II.34), i.e., narrow-minded persons.

4. like *Sancho Pança*: Cf. *Don Quixote*, I.IV.2, where Sancho, considering the fact that 'the People, over whom he was to be Governor, were all to be black', decides that the only remedy is 'loading a Ship with 'em, and having 'em into *Spain* ', where he would be able to sell them.

5. vile cough: Sterne had opened *TS* with an allusion to his ill-health, but he recovered somewhat during 1760, when writing Volumes III and IV. Within the next year, however, his health failed to the point of sending him, in January 1762, to the south of France in pursuit of a more congenial climate. See Cash, *LY*, 104–5.

6. pluck at your beards: In the Renaissance a gesture of contempt, but Sterne's usage is softer.

Volume V

Mottoes: The two mottoes of the first edition are borrowed from Burton's *Anatomy* and alert readers to the frequent presence of Burton in Volumes V and VI. Burton's introductory 'Democritus Junior to the Reader' explores, among other subjects, the use of a satiric voice or ironic persona and the freedom it affords; Sterne found his mottoes in one paragraph of this discussion: 'If I have overshot my selfe in this which hath beene hitherto said, or that it is, which I am sure some will object, too phantasticall, *too light and comicall for a Divine, too satyricall for one of my profession*, I will presume to answer with *Erasmus*, in like case, 'Tis not I, but *Democritus, Democritus dixit* [Burton's marginal note here reads: '*Mor. Encom. si quis calumnietur levius esse quam decet Theologum, aut mordacius quam deceat Christianum*']: you must consider what it is to speake in ones owne or anothers person ... and what liberty those old Satyrists have had, it is a *Cento* collected from others, not I, but they that say it. *Dixero si quid fortè jocosius, hoc mihi juris / Cum veniâ dabis.*' The concluding verses are from Horace, *Satires*, I.iv.104–5: 'if in my words I am too free, perchance too light, this bit of liberty you will indulgently grant me'. The passage from Erasmus's *Praise of Folly* is from the introductory letter to Sir Thomas More, translated by W. Kennett (4th ed., 1724): '*And it is a Chance if there be wanting some Quarrelsome Persons that will shew their Teeth, and pretend these Fooleries are either too Buffoon-like for a grave* Divine, *or too Satyrical for a Meek* Christian.*'

Sterne added a third motto to the second edition (1767), borrowed from the Second Council of Carthage (or an intermediate source not yet discovered): 'Si quis clericus aut monachus verba scurrilia jocolatoria, risumque moventia loquitur, acerrime corripiatur' (If any priest or monk speak words which are scurrilous, jesting, and exciting to laughter, let him be very sharply rebuked). Sterne alters this somewhat to 'If any priest or monk uses jesting words, exciting laughter, let him be denounced.' On the actual title-page, '*visum*' is a misprint for '*risum*'.

Dedication: Sterne's friendship with John Spencer (1734–83) began in 1761 and continued until Sterne's death. The great-grandson of the Duke of Marlborough, Spencer was created Baron of Althorp in 1761. The fair copy of Le Fever's story that Sterne sent to Lady Spencer, misplaced at the British Library for a century, has resurfaced; see New, 'A Manuscript of the Le Fever Episode in *Tristram Shandy*', *Scriblerian* 23 (1991).

CHAPTER I

1. Stilton to Stamford: Two towns, separated by twelve miles, on the post road from London to York and Edinburgh.

2. Shall we ... pace: As Work (342, n. 1) notes, following John Ferriar, the first diligent searcher into Sterne's sources (*Illustrations of Sterne* (1798)), this is a 'character-

istic example of Sterne's roguishness', since his attack on plagiarists is *plagiarized* from Burton's introduction: 'As Apothecaries we make new mixtures everie day, poure out of one vessell into another' and 'but we weave the same web still, twist the same rope again and again'. Gene Washington (*Scriblerian* 23 (1991)) points to the myth of Ocnus behind the second image: Ocnus's wife spends all he earns, so that in hell he endlessly plaits a rope which a she-ass continually eats; a myth of useless work.

3. Who made ... Aristotle: Sterne continues his game with Burton by echoing the opening paragraph of *Anatomy*. The phrase Sterne attributes to Aristotle, Burton attributes to Plato. Zoroaster is the name given to several cloudy figures of the pre-Hellenistic period; one book (Sterne provides the title in Greek) ascribed to the name was *On Nature*. St John Chrysostom (*c.* 354–407), important figure in the Greek Orthodox Church, used the concept of the *Shekinah* (Hebrew for the dwelling-place of God), but not the word. How Sterne came to know this is unknown; it is not in Burton. For Moses, see Genesis 1:26–27.

4. Horace ... occasion: In *Epistles*, I.xix.19–20: 'O you mimics, you slavish herd! How often your pother has stirred my spleen, how often my mirth!'

5. farcy: *OED* cites this passage as its first example of this disease of animals, especially horses, being applied to men – the 'catachresis', or misuse, that Tristram alludes to; a pun can be assumed in view of 'farcical' in the next phrase.

6. *shag-rag and bob-tail*: Contemptuous term for a number of persons of various sorts and conditions, perhaps borrowed from Rabelais.

7. in *mort main*: Under posthumous control; perpetual possession.

8. Tartufs: Tartuffe, the sanctimonious hypocrite in Molière's comedy of that name (1664).

9. queen of *Navarre*: Margaret of Valois (1552–1615), first wife of Henry IV, King of France and Navarre; first noted by William Jackson, *The Four Ages* (1798), who found Rebours and La Fosseuse named as members of her court in Bayle's *Dictionary*. Bayle characterizes Margaret as 'a princess of infinitely more wit and beauty than virtue', and Sterne may have had access to one or more of the scandalous accounts published about her. The identification of this queen with Margaret of Angoulême, author of the *Heptameron*, is incorrect.

10. St. *Antony* ... *Bridget*: For St Antony and St Ursula, see nn. 21, 22 to IV.S.T. St Francis (1181–1226), St Dominick (1170–1221), and St Bennet, i.e., Benedict (*c.* 480–*c.* 550) founded the three monastical orders that bear their names. St Basil (*c.* 330–79) established the rules by which monasteries of the Eastern Orthodox Church were run. For St Bridget, see n. 1 to III.xxiv.

11. lady *Baussiere* rode on: Sterne parodies an episode in Burton, 3.1.3.3, in which a person rides on impervious to cries for charity, and even ignores the 'Host' (communion bread).

12. order of mercy: Order of Our Lady of Mercy, founded in Spain in 1218 to solicit funds for ransoming Christians during the Crusades.

13. The best . . . combinations: Cf. *A Tale of a Tub*, sect. VII, where Swift comments on 'that highly celebrated Talent among the *Modern* Wits, of deducing Similitudes, Allusions, and Applications, very Surprizing, Agreeable, and Apposite, from the *Pudenda* of either Sex, together with *their proper Uses* '.

14. curate of *d'Estella*: Diego d'Estella (*c.* 1524–78), Franciscan from Navarre and author of *Contempt of the World and the Vanities Thereof*, which went through numerous English editions during the seventeenth century. Near its conclusion is a chapter entitled '*Against idle wordes* ', parts of which, attacking 'ribauld speeches', may be apropos. Just as likely, however, Sterne may be using the name as a pseudonym for himself, based on an etymology he offers, in part, in *ASJ*: Sterne = starn (starling) = star = stella; he may have used the name as early as 1739–40, during his courtship of Elizabeth, although the letter cited in evidence has a disputed date; see Cash, *EMY*, 81, n. 3.

15. trouse: Work (348, n. 7) suggests 'close-fitting, short breeches', but Sterne may have intended the long trousers worn by soldiers and artisans in lieu of the more common knee breeches.

CHAPTER II

1. PATRIOT: Possibly a political allusion, with the 'Scotch horse' representing Lord Bute and the Patriot as Pitt, who had lost office as part of the political changes surrounding the death of George II in 1760.

2. *Sanson* 's: Nicolas Sanson (1600–1667), cartographer to Louis XIV.

3. *Nevers*: The pun is perhaps too obvious.

4. When *Agrippina* . . . work: Cf. Burton, 2.3.5: 'as *Tacitus* [reported] of *Agrippina*, not able to moderate her passions. So when she heard her sonne was slaine, she abruptly broke off her work, changed countenance and colour, tore her haire, and fell a roaring down right . . .' This borrowing from Burton's chapter, '*Against sorrow for death of friends* . . . *&c.* ', begins the sustained collection of borrowed sentiments from which Walter creates his oration; Burton is the dominant source, but Bacon, Joseph Hall, and Montaigne are also pilfered. Ferriar was the first to note many of these debts.

CHAPTER III

1. 'Tis . . . *Barnard*: Sterne borrows from Burton, 2.3.1.1, who stops 'to collect and gleane a few remedies, and comfortable speeches out of our best Orators, Philosophers, Divines, and fathers of the Church . . .' In sermon 15, 'Job's expostulation with his wife', Sterne strongly endorses the notion that Christian consolations for death far surpass those of the ancients, the primary 'moral' of this chapter as well.

Sterne picked names selectively from Burton's much longer list: Jerome Cardan (1501–76), Italian physician, the most famous of his era; Budæus, i.e., Guillaume

Budé (1468–1540), highly regarded French classicist; and Petrarch (1304–74), the most important Italian poet after Dante, singled out for his sonnets on the death of Laura or his posthumous *De Contemptu Mundi*. For Stella, i.e., Diego d'Estella, see n. 14 to V.i. St Austin, i.e., Augustine (354–430); St Cyprian (d. 258), Bishop of Carthage; and St Barnard, i.e., Bernard (1091–1153), are major ecclesiastics.

2. who affirms ... children: Burton, 2.3.5, quoting Plutarch.

3. *Seneca* ... channel: Sterne is *positive* about the attribution to Seneca (the Elder) on Burton's authority.

4. *David* ... death: Cf. Burton, 1.2.4.7 and 2.3.5. The mingling of classical figures (Antinous, favourite of the emperor Hadrian) with biblical (David and Absalom; see 2 Samuel 18:33–19:4) and mythological (Niobe weeps for her children even after being turned to stone) is Burton's doing, but Sterne turns to another section for the death of Socrates to complete the hodgepodge.

5. neither wept ... *Germans*: Cf. Burton, 2.3.5: 'The *Italians* most part sleep away care and grief ...; *Danes, Dutchmen, Polanders* and *Bohemians* drink it down ...'

6. When *Tully* ... me: Sterne again combines two separate parts of *Anatomy* to produce his paragraph, 1.2.4.7 and 2.3.5. The reference to Pliny is to *Letters*; to Cicero, either *Tusculan Disputations* or *Letters to Atticus*.

7. A blessing ... him: Tristram's calculus owes much to William Wollaston, *The Religion of Nature Delineated* (1722): '*When pleasures and pains are equal, they mutually destroy each other: when the one exceeds, the excess gives the true quantity of pleasure or pain.* For nine degrees of pleasure, less by nine degrees of pain, are equal to nothing: but nine degrees of one, less by three degrees of the other, give six of the former *net* and *true*.' The last phrase, 'as it never ...', may be helped by emending to 'as if it never ...'

8. *Attic* salt: 'Refined, delicate, poignant wit' (*OED*, citing this passage). Cf. Sterne's distinction between the 'bitterness' and 'saltness' of wit in sermon 18, quoted in n. 11 to III.xx.

9. 'Tis an ... die: Verbatim borrowing from Burton, 2.3.5.

10. If my son ... with us: Cf. Joseph Hall, *Epistles* (1624): 'If they could not have dyed, it had been worthy of wonder; not at all, that they are dead. ... Lo, all Princes and Monarchs daunce with us in the same ring.'

11. tombs ... horizon: Sterne begins an extensive borrowing from Burton, 2.3.5; the original letter was from the Roman statesman Servius Sulpicius Rufus (d. 43 B.C.) to Cicero on the death of his daughter. Sterne almost certainly knew that Scarron's parody of Sulpicius had been singled out by Warburton in his 'Dedication to Free Thinkers' (*Divine Legation of Moses*) to reinforce his argument against Shaftesbury's theory of 'ridicule as the test of truth'. The most 'natural and humane Reflexion' could be turned to ridicule, Warburton noted, disapprovingly. Swift, too, wrote a parody of Sulpicius's letter, his short poem 'Shall I repine'.

12. *evolutions*: Cf. Chambers: 'in the art of war ... a term applied to the diverse figures, turns, and motions, made by a body of soldiers'.

13. *Mitylenæ*: Typical of his practice as a borrower, Sterne adds one city to Sulpicius's roll-call: Mytilene, chief city of Lesbos, home of Sappho.

14. *Zant*: Island in the Ionian Sea off the coast of Greece; in Walter's day it was owned by Venice and served for trade with Turkey and the East. 'Archipelago' had specific reference in the century to the Aegean Sea.

15. wandering *Jew*: The Jew who, according to legend, taunted Christ on his way to Calvary and was condemned to wander the earth until Judgment Day.

16. Labour ... life: Cf. Burton, 2.3.2: 'And therefore with good discretion, *Iovianus Pontanus* caused this short sentence to be engraven on his tombe in *Naples*: *Labour, sorrow, grief, sickness, want and woe, to serve proud masters, bear that superstitious yoke, and bury your dearest friends, &c. are the sawces of our life.*'

17. My son is dead: Throughout Walter's oration, Sterne may have had in mind Gargantua's lament over his wife's death (II.3): 'My wife is dead, well, by G—— ... I shall not raise her again by my crying: she is well; she is in paradise at least. ... What tho' she be dead, must not we also die? The same debt ... hangs over our heads; nature will require it of us, and we must all of us, some day, taste of the same sauce.'

18. 'tis a shame ... anchor: Burton, 2.3.5, attributes the sentence to Seneca.

19. He is got ... world: Cf. Burton, 2.3.5: '*he had risen*, saith *Plutarch, from the midst of a feast*, before he was drunk. ... *Why dost thou lament my death* ...? *what misfortune is befalne me? Is it because I am not bald* ...? The *Thracians* wept still when a child was born, feasted and made mirth when any man was buried ...' Plutarch is quoted from *Moralia*; the second sentence is from Lucian, 'On Funerals'; the third, from Herodotus, *Persian Wars*.

20. Death opens ... after it: From Bacon's 'Of Death'.

21. Shew me ... liberty: Cf. Hall, *Epistles*: 'Shew mee ever any man that knew what life was, and was loth to leave it. I will shew you a prisoner that would dwell in his Goale [*sic*], a slave that likes to be chained to his Galley.'

22. Is it not ... life: Cf. Burton, 2.3.5: '*Is it not much better not to hunger at all then to eat: not to thirst then to drink to satisfie thirst: not to be cold then to put on clothes to drive away cold? You had more neede rejoyce that I am freed from diseases, agues, cares, ... love ...* ' The sentiment is from Lucian, 'On Funerals'.

23. a galled ... afresh: Cf. Burton, 2.3.5: 'thou dost him great injury to desire his longer life. *Wilt thou have him crased & sickly still*, like a tired traveller that comes wearie to his Inne, beginne his journey afresh ...'

24. There is ... bed: Sterne combines Bacon, 'Of Death': 'Groanes and Convulsions, and a discoloured Face, and Friends weeping, and Blackes, and Obsequies, and the like, shew *Death* Terrible' with Montaigne, 'Of Experience': 'Death is more abject, more languishing and painful in *Bed* than in Battle'; cf. the index heading for this passage: '*Death is more glorious in a Battle than in a Bed* '. Cf. Trim's similar sentiment, p. 301.

25. mutes: Professional attendants at a funeral; hired mourners. Walter's list is

traditional; cf. John Gay, *Trivia*, III.231–2: 'Why is the Herse with 'Scutcheons blazon'd round, / And with the nodding Plume of Ostrich crown'd?'

26. when we *are . . . not*: Cf. Burton, 2.3.5: '*When we are, death is not, but when death is, then we are not . . .*' Burton cites Seneca; the more likely source is Epicurus or Cicero.

27. For this . . . wife: Sterne takes his examples from Bacon's 'Of Death'; all five figures were Roman emperors. The jest of Vespasianus (9–79) was 'I think I'm becoming a god.' Galba (*c.* 3 B.C.–69) told his assassins: 'Strike, if it be for the good of the Roman people.' Septimius Severus (146–211) died while asking his attendants to make haste if anything was left for him to do; Sterne miscopied or plays with Bacon's 'in dispatch'. Tiberius (42 B.C.–37) pretended continued strength and health while dying. And Augustus Caesar (63 B.C.–14) died asking his wife, Livia, not to forget the days of their marriage.

In a letter a few weeks before his death, Sterne wrote: 'But I brave evils.—et quand Je serai mort, on mettra mon nom dans le liste de ces Heros, qui sont Morts en plaisantant [and when I shall have died, my name will be placed in the list of those heroes who have died in jest].'

CHAPTER IV

1. *Cornelius Gallus*: Sterne borrows the anecdote from Montaigne, 'That to study philosophy, is to learn to die': 'And betwixt the very Thighs of Women, *Cornelius Gallus*, the *Prætor . . .*' is Montaigne's terse description of the untimely incident, chronicled by Pliny. Cf. p. 350, where Le Fever tells of his wife's death in his arms and Toby remembers a 'circumstance his modesty omitted'.

CHAPTER V

1. listening slave: The well-known classical statue *Arrotino* ('Whetter') in the Uffizi Gallery in Florence.

2. as *Rapin . . .* church: This is one of two overt allusions in *TS* to Paul Rapin de Thoyras's *L'Histoire d'Angleterre* (see n. 1 to II.i). Rapin de Thoyras (1661–1725) has a separate entry on church history at the end of many sections.

CHAPTER VI

1. upon the tapis: An absorption of the French idiom *sur le tapis* ('on the table[cloth]'), i.e., under discussion.

CHAPTER VII

1. Well might *Locke* ... words: As indeed Locke did, *Essay*, III.9.

2. Now as ... eloquence: Possibly an allusion to Thomas Sheridan (1719–88), who wrote and lectured extensively on oratory during the 1750s and 1760s, and made similarly grandiose claims.

3. I said ... confess: An important idea in Sterne; his language here is echoed in sermon 43 ['Efficacy of prayer']:

> in the present state we are in, we find such a strong sympathy and union between our souls and bodies, that the one cannot be touched or sensibly affected, without producing some corresponding emotion in the other.—Nature has assigned a different look, tone of voice, and gesture, peculiar to every passion and affection we are subject to; and, therefore, to argue against this strict correspondence which is held between our souls and bodies,—is disputing against the frame and mechanism of human nature.—We are not angels, but men cloathed with bodies, and, in some measure, governed by our imaginations, that we have need of all these external helps which nature has made the interpreters of our thoughts.

For 'seven senses', see n. 18 to II.xix.

4. the eye: In philosophy's various orderings of the senses, primacy has almost always been awarded to either sight or touch. *Barbati*, i.e., bearded ones, philosophers or goats; a classicism.

CHAPTER VIII

1. *green-gowns, and old hats*: 'To give a green-gown' is to 'tumble a woman on the grass' (Partridge, *Dictionary*), as in Robert Herrick's '*Corrina*'s going a Maying': 'Many a green-gown has been given; / Many a kisse, both odde and even.' Partridge also has an entry for *old hat*: 'The female pudend ... Because frequently felt.' Cf. VIII.x: 'the affair of *an old hat cock'd—and a cock'd old hat*'.

CHAPTER IX

1. Are we ... corruption: Sterne has Trim echo the Order for the Burial of the Dead from the *Book of Common Prayer*, made up of several scriptural passages – e.g., Psalm 90:5–6, Job 14:1–2, Isaiah 40:6–8 (Peter 1:24), and 1 Corinthians 15, especially 15:42. 'So also is the resurrection of the dead. It is sown in corruption; it is raised in incorruption.'

2. pumkin for his head: The man impervious to love, according to Burton, 3.2.1.2, 'is not a man but a block, a very stone ... he hath a gourd for his head, a pepon for his heart ...' The entire paragraph contains an idea central to Sterne's thought: 'there is nothing unmixt in this world' (*ASJ*).

CHAPTER X

1. In battle ... this: Cf. Montaigne, 'That to study philosophy, is to learn to die': 'I
have often consider'd with myself whence it should proceed, that in War, the Image
of Death ... appear[s] less dreadful than at Home ...'
2. in hot ... felt: Cf. Bacon, 'On Death': 'He that dies in an earnest Pursuit, is like
one that is wounded in hot Bloud; who, for the time, scarce feeles the Hurt ...'
3. And could ... nature: Sterne returns to Montaigne: 'if a Man could by any Means
avoid it, tho' by creeping under a Calf's Skin, I am one that should not be ashamed
of the Shift ...'

CHAPTER XI

1. I Am ... Nile: Sterne taps into a hoary tradition that Nile mud spontaneously
generates life forms; see, e.g., Dryden, All for Love, V.i.153–6.

CHAPTER XII

1. her curiosity: Cf. VIII.xxxv.
2. oration of Socrates: Sterne did not go to Plato's Apology for his account, but to
Montaigne's version in 'Of Physiognomy', interweaving it with the famous
soliloquy in Hamlet, III.i.55ff.
3. Life of Socrates: John Gilbert Cooper's scholarly Life of Socrates (1749) was written
primarily to prove that Socrates believed in the immortality of the soul, confuting
a major contention in Warburton's Divine Legation. Cooper also attacked Warburton's
comments on Scarron's parody of Sulpicius (see n. 11 to V.iii), criticizing the Bishop's
failure to distinguish between true ridicule and its abuse. A typical Warburtonian
paper-war ensued; Sterne's allusion here, and in VIII.xxvi, may have this quarrel
in mind.
4. That we ... of India: Typically enough, Sterne's citation of Flavius Josephus
(37–c. 95), author of The Jewish Wars, is misleading, since his source was almost
certainly John Donne's Biathanatos. Sterne misread Donne's reference to the Indian
philosophers, attributing to them a sentiment not found in Josephus. See W. G.
Day, N&Q 215 (1970).
5. died at Babylon: Alexander's death in 323 B.C. is recorded by Plutarch; Alexander
returned to Babylon despite omens presaging his death.
6. from Greece ... round: Sterne mocks the growing mythology of the 'progress' of
western civilization from the Middle East to Greece and westward.
7. By water ... Coptos: The journey begins where the Ganges empties into the Bay
of Bengal, proceeds south around the tip of India, and then north-west into the
Red Sea and the Gulf of Suez at its northern end. Tor is at the southern end of
the Gulf, Suez at the northern. Joddah (Jidda) is the port city of Mecca, on the

eastern shore of the Red Sea; Coptos was a trade centre south of Tor. Sterne's geography is not absolutely clear. For the Alexandrian library, see n. 38 to IV.S.T.
Karrawans: i.e., caravans.

CHAPTER XIII

1. in case . . . man: Sterne again baits Warburton, since a primary argument of the *Divine Legation* is that the Book of Job was written after the patriarchs (by Ezra), and was an *allegory* of the Captivity, an argument countered by Bishop Robert Lowth and others who believed Job to be historical rather than allegorical. For Sterne's original plan to 'run up' an allegory on the 'Writers on the Book of Job', and its implications for *TS*, see Zimmerman in Further Reading; see also Jonathan Lamb, 'The Job Controversy, Sterne, and the Question of Allegory', *ECS* 24 (1990).

CHAPTER XV

1. a farce: In the 'Life of Rabelais' prefixed to Ozell's edition, Rabelais's last words are reported: 'Let down the curtain, the farce is done.' The sentiment has been attributed to others as well.
2. *Calliope*: Muse of epic poetry; in creating his oppositions, Sterne contrasts the lightest and freest of musical forms with the most dignified of the muses, similar to the contrast between a Cremona (for a town in Lombardy where Amati and Stradivari violins were made) and a Jew's trump (or Jew's harp, played with the mouth and one finger).

CHAPTER XVI

1. *Xenophon*: Xenophon (*c.* 428–*c.* 354 B.C.), Greek philosopher and historian, set out his ideas on education primarily in *Cyropaedia*. Cornelius Scriblerus, before the birth of his son, 'composed two Treatises of Education' (*Memoirs of Martinus Scriblerus*).
2. collecting . . . adolescence: See n. 12 to III.xii. Sterne begins his parody of Obadiah Walker's *Of Education* (1673) with a glance at Walker's prefatory comment: 'I have therefore rather chused to gather up disorderly, and bind together, such scattered Counsels and Notions, as have occurred either in Observation, or in some *Italian Writers*, not ordinary amongst us.' See John M. Turnbull, 'The Prototype of Walter Shandy's *Tristrapaedia*', *RES* 2 (1926).
3. *Tartaglia*: See n. 9 to II.iii.
4. hussive: I.e., housewife: pocket-case for needles, pins, thread.
5. *John de la Casse*: From a few facts – Giovanni della Casa (1503–56) was the Archbishop of Benevento and did write a famous Renaissance conduct book called the *Galateo* (1558) – Sterne spins an elaborate fictional web. In all likelihood, he

never read the *Galateo*, but rather found references to della Casa in Burton, Bayle, and Rabelais, all of whom mention his youthful celebration of sodomy. Sterne seems to have confused this with the *Galateo*, which, in IX.xiv, he calls della Casa's '*nasty* Romance'. No evidence exists that della Casa held the theory of composition attributed to him.

6. *Rider*'s Almanack: Usually no more than twenty small pages, while the *Galateo* is perhaps four or five times that size.

7. fed ... famous: Cf. p. 164 and n. 34 to III.xx.

8. Term-time: When the law courts are in session.

9. life of a writer: Sterne may again be parodying Warburton, *Remarks on Several Occasional Reflections* (1744): 'The state of Authorship, whatever that of Nature be, is certainly a state of war: in which, especially if it be an *holy war*, every man's hand is set, not against his enemy, but his *brother*.' Pope had called the life of a wit a 'warfare upon earth' (preface to *Works*, 1717).

10. retrograde: Backward, slow.

11. Prejudice ... milk: Cf. n. 7 to I.xix and n. 5 to III.xxxiii. And see Montaigne's 'Of Custom' for a similar account, including the observation that 'by Reason that we suck it in with our Milk, and that the Face of the World presents itself in this Posture to our first Sight, it seems as if we were born upon Condition to pursue this Practice ...'

12. drawing a sun-dial: Proverbial for useless activity.

CHAPTER XVII

1. some men ... wires: Proverbial, importing the making of mountains from molehills.

2. *August* the 10th, 1761: In June, Sterne wrote to Hall-Stevenson that he was beginning Volume V and on 21 September, to another acquaintance, that he was 'scribbling away' at the work.

CHAPTER XVIII

1. all ... principals: True of high treason, but not of murder in English law.

CHAPTER XIX

1. prevented: Forestalled, anticipated.

2. like *Lewis* ... &c.: The armies of the day considered church-bells as war-booty because the metal was valuable for recasting into ordnance.

3. the lead ... too: Proverbial; to be cut into pieces like meat for the pot; to be ruined or destroyed.

CHAPTER XX

1. *Steenkirk*: Sterne's account of the allied defeat at Steinkirk (24 July 1692) is taken, often verbatim, from Tindal.

2. count *Solmes*: Heinrich Maastricht, Count Solms (1636–93), commanded the main body of allied troops in the battle; according to Tindal, he held back his troops because he was jealous that the Prince of Wirtemberg had command of the entire attack; his failure to engage caused the allied defeat.

3. made . . . to it: Michael O. Houlahan, *N&Q* 217 (1972), notes that Sterne parodies the advice Warburton gave him in June 1760: 'You say you will continue to laugh aloud. In good time. But one . . . would wish to laugh in good company, where priests and virgins may be present . . .' His giving this advice seems to have been public knowledge.

CHAPTER XXI

1. picquetted: A military punishment, one hand being tied as high as possible, while the victim stands with the opposite toe on a pointed stake.

2. *Cutts*'s . . . *Leven*'s: All listed in Tindal. In Le Fever's story (VI.vii), we are told that Toby and Trim served in Leven's regiment (David Melville, third Earl of Leven (1660–1728)), while Le Fever was a lieutenant under Angus (James Hamilton, Earl of Angus, killed at Steinkirk). In all, the Allies suffered 2,000 men killed and 3,000 wounded or taken prisoner. For useful accounts of eighteenth-century warfare, see David Chandler, *The Art of Warfare in the Age of Marlborough* (Hippocrene, 1976), and David McNeil, *The Grotesque Depiction of War and the Military in Eighteenth-Century English Fiction* (University of Delaware Press, 1990).

3. *Landen*: For a description of this battle (July 1693), in which Trim received his wound, see n. 12 to VIII.xix. Solms's injury was fatal, a fact Trim omits.

CHAPTER XXV

1. *Confucius*: Florida *Notes* suggests a trap for allusion-hunting by annotators, and then offers a possible allusion to Oliver Goldsmith's 'Chinese philosopher', Lien Chi Altangi, who had attacked *TS* in numbers 51 and 53 of *Citizen of the World* (1760).

CHAPTER XXVI

1. FIFTY . . . devils: Cf. Rabelais, 'Author's Prologue' to Vol. II: 'even as I give myself fairly to an hundred thousand panniers full of devils'; and again, III.22: 'his soul goeth infallibly to thirty thousand panniers full of devils'.

2. bitter *Philippick*: Cf. n. 2 to III.xiv.

CHAPTER XXVII

1. lint and basilicon: For excellent readings of Mrs Shandy's role in *TS*, see Ehlers, Loscocco, and Ostovich in Further Reading. Basilicon: an ointment.

2. *Spencer*: Sterne's source is John Spencer's *De Legibus Hebræorum Ritualibus* (*On the Ritual Laws of the Hebrews*) (1685). One section (I.iv.3), entitled '*De sede vel subjecto Circumcisionis*' ('*On the foundation or subject of circumcision*'), provides the first two Greek footnotes; the next section, the list of practising nations and the last two footnotes. Spencer provides Latin translations for his Greek.

3. *Maimonides*: Moses ben Maimon (1135–1204), the greatest Jewish scholar of the Middle Ages; cited by Spencer.

4. as follows: Sterne uses the device of the lacuna again, pp. 323, 359, 361, 384, 391, 436, 523, 526, 537. Swift employs it frequently in *A Tale of a Tub*.

5. CAPADOCIANS: As is his practice, Sterne adds an additional name to Spencer's list; perhaps these remote societies reminded him of the biblical list in Acts 2:9 (see n. 1 to VI.xxx). Cappadocia and Colchis were territories in Asia Minor. Troglodytes is a name applied to various ancient tribes.

6. SOLON and PYTHAGORAS: Sterne read about Pythagoras (*c.* 582–*c.* 500 B.C.) in Spencer, but his reason for including Solon (*c.* 638–*c.* 559 B.C.) among the circumcised is unknown; Sterne had listed both together as 'lawgivers' in IV.xvii.

CHAPTER XXVIII

1. the trine . . . genitures: Sterne parodies legitimate catch-phrases from the vocabulary of astrology.

2. *apothecaries . . . washer-women: Each Greek footnote calls forth one of Yorick's associations; hence, the first refers to 'a terrible disease, hard to cure, called anthrax', and Yorick thinks of 'apothecaries'; the second remarks that circumcised nations are the 'most prolific and populous', hence 'statesmen'; and the third is simply the phrase 'for the sake of cleanliness', calling forth Yorick's 'washer-women'. Sterne miscites the source of this third note, reading the wrong marginal citation; it is from Herodotus, historian of the Persian Wars. The first two are from Philo Judaeus (*c.* 20 B.C.–*c.* 40), the Jewish philosopher.

3. ILUS: Again Sterne borrows from Spencer, including this note, which Spencer translates into Latin, and Sterne paraphrases in this sentence. Sanchuniathon is an ancient Phoenician authority. The history of Pharaoh-neco (reigned 610–594 B.C.) is told in 2 Kings 23:29, 24:1–7, etc.; he was defeated by Nebuchadnezzar, King of Babylon, in 604, and retired into Egypt for the rest of his reign. If Ilus lived at all, he did so in the fourteenth or thirteenth century B.C. and hence could not have served in Neco's army.

4. polemic divines: One year after the publication of Volumes V and VI, Warburton delivered a strong defence of polemical divinity in the closing pages of *Doctrine of*

Grace (1763), lamenting, in particular, 'any well-meaning Clergyman of affected taste and real ignorance' who ridicules polemic divines just to be in fashion when, in reality, the term simply means those who study the doctrines of their faith.

5. practical divinity: Sterne's division between polemic and practical divinity appears throughout his sermons; despite Warburton, it marks no abatement of religious commitment, but rather is the legacy of seventeenth-century latitudinarians, who argued that, because polemical divinity had underwritten a century of religious warfare in England, it was time to eschew doctrinal disputes. This was the position of mainstream Anglicanism throughout the eighteenth century.

6. *Gymnast* and captain *Tripet*: Sterne borrows the passage, describing Gymnast's antics to convince the opposing army that he is insane, from Rabelais (I.35); in Sterne's hands, it is potent ridicule of religious polemicists.

CHAPTER XXIX

1. *en croup*: On the crupper or rear of a horse, behind the saddle.

2. demi-pommadas: The *pomada* is a vault on or over a horse by placing one hand on the pommel of the saddle; a *demi-pomada* is a half-vault. Sterne takes the term from Rabelais.

CHAPTER XXX

1. clear ... *Euclid*: Probably a commonplace; see p. 266. Euclid (*fl. c.* 300 B.C.), Greek mathematician; his *Elements* contains the fundamentals of all geometrical demonstration.

2. scrutoir: Escritoire, desk.

3. snuff'd the candle: Trim is not putting out the candle, the meaning of *snuff* most familiar to modern readers, but brightening its flame by freeing the candle from its excess wick, either by pinching or cutting off its *snuff* (the part of the wick partially consumed in burning).

CHAPTER XXXI

1. CHAP. XXXI: Watson (see n. 11 to I.xviii) argues the presence of Filmerian thought in this chapter and the next, both in the discussion of the origins of government and in the arguments concerning the 'natural relation between a father and his child' and the meaning of the fifth commandment. Specifically, Locke had undercut Filmer's interpretation of the fifth commandment as endorsing absolute patriarchal authority by reminding him that the commandment says 'honour thy father *and* thy mother'.

2. *Politian*: Angelo Poliziano (1454–94), noted Italian scholar and poet, tutor in the

household of Lorenzo de Medici. Although it is probable he somewhere expresses this often-repeated idea of society's conjugal origins, Sterne's most likely source is the opening section of Aristotle's *Politics*, which includes the quotation from Hesiod's *Works and Days* (*c.* 700 B.C.). Yorick's translation is correct: 'First and foremost a house and a wife and an ox for the ploughing.'

3. origin of fortification: Toby's argument is traditional, a staple of contemporary works on fortification.

4. argutely: Sharply, shrewdly.

5. *not the principal agent*: Filmer's opinion.

6. Institutes of *Justinian*: As Work notes (392, n. 5), *The Institutes*, I.xi.10, supports only Walter's first statement, that the mother has no power; for Justinian, see n. 12 to III.xii.

CHAPTER XXXII

1. Every thing ... out: Cf. George Herbert, 'The Church-porch,' lines 239–40: 'All things are bigge with jest: nothing that's plain, / But may be wittie, if thou hast the vein'; noted by Herbert Rauter (*Anglia* 80 (1962)).

2. bear-leaders: Tutors for young men on tour.

3. SCIENCES MAY ... NOT: Cf. Walker, *Of Education*: 'to *be learned* is *not to be wise....* Besides, Sciences are easily learned, being taught by rote and course; but *Wisdom* requires greater *Advertency*...'

4. determinate idea annexed: Locke defines 'determinate idea', a central concern in *Essay*, in his prefatory 'Epistle to the Reader'. Basically, he means words definitively attached to single and consistent ('clear or distinct') objects or ideas.

5. *Talmud*: Collection of post-biblical writings based on academic discussions of Jewish law by scholars and jurists over several centuries and in several countries. *Decalogue*: Ten Commandments.

CHAPTER XXXIII

1. O Blessed ... treasure: Cf. Burton, 1.2.4.7: 'O blessed health! *thou art above all gold and treasure*'; cf. Ecclesiasticus 30:15.

2. radical moisture: See n. 13 to II.iii and n. 4 to IV.xix.

CHAPTER XXXIV

1. CHAP. XXXIV: In this chapter and the next, Sterne again borrows from Mackenzie, *The History of Health*, including the allusions to Francis Bacon (Lord Verulam), the epithet 'nostrum-mongers', the famous first aphorism of Hippocrates ('art is long, and life is short'), and the entire discussion of the causes of a shortened life. He did not need to consult Bacon's *Historia Vitæ et Mortis* (1623) at this point.

2. stage-loads: Unrecorded in *OED*; Sterne alludes to the stage on which medical quacks and mountebanks exhibited themselves and their medicines.

3. glisters: Enemas. Succedaneums: inferior substitutes, but often misused, as here, to mean remedies.

CHAPTER XXXV

1. spicula: Small splinter-like bodies.

CHAPTER XXXVI

1. *Van Helmont*: Sterne seems to have borrowed his entire discussion from the Duchess of Newcastle's *Life of William Cavendish* (1667), as noted by Wilfred Watson, 'Sterne's Satire on Mechanism: A Study of *Tristram Shandy*' (Ph.D. dissertation, University of Toronto, 1951). Jean-Baptiste van Helmont (1577–1644), Flemish physician and chemist, quoted extensively by the Duchess.

2. *Quod omne* ... triste: After coition, every creature is dejected. The maxim, commonly attributed to Aristotle, is usually followed by bawdy exceptions, e.g., 'except women', or 'except priests'.

CHAPTER XXXVII

1. siege of *Limerick*: In August 1690; an account, including the flooded trenches, is given by Tindal.

CHAPTER XXXIX

1. *phimosis*: Contraction of the foreskin so that it cannot be retracted.

CHAPTER XL

1. I infer ... death: John Pringle, *Observations on the Diseases of the Army* (1752), devotes many pages to dampness and dysentery (flux), frequent concomitants of siege warfare. He supports both the drinking and burning (vaporizing) of spirits (gin) to take off dampness and as a general indulgence because of the hardships of soldiers. 'Vapours' may mean both moisture in the air and low spirits.

2. *Slop* had not forgot: An allusion to Trim's remark, *five* years earlier, that the 'Abuses of conscience' was 'wrote upon neither side ... for 'tis only upon *Conscience*' (II.xvii), a tribute to Slop's memory or a slight slip on Sterne's part.

3. *occludents*: Chambers, s.v. *Life*, summarizes Bacon's opinions and concludes: 'this mollifying of the parts without, is to be performed by consubstantials [similar substances], impriments [piercing substances], and occludents [closing substances].

See LONGÆVITY.' The phrase appears in Bacon's *Historia Vitæ et Mortis*, canon 26; for Bacon, whatever hardens the body moves towards death; whatever softens (mollifies) it, lengthens life.

4. *emperic discourse*: Based on experience and practice, rather than learning and doctrine. According to Chambers, 'empiric' was equivalent to '*charletan*, or *quack* '.

CHAPTER XLI

1. *Come . . . land*: A sentence attributed to Diogenes, as in *Spectator* 582: 'I have often admired a humorous Saying of *Diogenes*, who reading a dull Author to several of his Friends, . . . finding he was almost come to . . . the end of it, cried, *Courage, Lads, I see Land*.'

CHAPTER XLII

1. *Christ-cross-row to Malachi*: I.e., from learning the alphabet, always preceded in horn-books by a cross, to reading the last book of the Old Testament.

2. *Seven . . . Latin*: The Greek, **τυπʾlω**, tupto: pounding, slogging away (and perhaps a bilingual pun: tiptoe-ing), was used as a paradigm of the Greek verb. *Probations* and *negations* are terms in logic.

3. *the fine . . . block*: Commonplace, sometimes traced to Aristotle, but more likely Michelangelo's notion of the statue that the sculptor discovers within the marble block.

4. *Scaliger . . . Baldus*: Cf. Walker: '*Jul. Scagiler* [*sic*] began not to learn *Greek* till 40 years old, and then mastered it in a very few months. . . . *Pet. Damianus* learned not to read till Mans Estate. . . . *Baldus* entred so late upon the Law, that they told him he intended to be an Advocate in the other World.' Baillet provides very similar information in a section on 'contrary examples' to his discussion of prodigies. Julius Caesar Scaliger (1484–1558), Italian author and philosopher; St Pietro Damiani (*c.* 1007–72), Benedictine monk; Baldus (see n. 12 to IV.xxix). Walker does not indicate that Damianus was Bishop of Ostia; the name was probably unfamiliar to Sterne, and required some 'index-learning', perhaps from Bayle.

5. *when Eudamidas . . . of it*: Plutarch tells the story in his *Moralia* ('Sayings of Spartans'). Eudamidas (King of Sparta, *fl. c.* 330 B.C.), son of Archidamas (King of Sparta, *c.* 361–338 B.C.). Xenocrates (396–314 B.C.) headed the Platonic Academy at Athens.

6. *North west passage*: 'A passage for vessels along the north coast of America, formerly thought of as a possible channel for navigation between the Atlantic and the Pacific' (*OED*, which records figurative usage from 1670).

7. *auxiliary verbs*: The theory of auxiliary verbs parodies Walker's reliance on them as a pedagogic instrument, the use of which he explains at interminable length in *Of Education*, ch. II. The full extent of Sterne's borrowing is recorded in the Florida

Notes. Sterne's citations of '*Lullius*' (Raymond Lull, *c.* 1232–1315, Spanish theologian and author of a mechanical learning aid similar to Pellegrini's) and '*Pelegrini*' (Matteo Pellegrini, 1595–1652, Italian humanist, whose system of predication forms the basis of Walker's chapter) are almost surely derived from Walker, rather than from a direct reading of either.

Walker illustrates his method with a 'Battel', which Sterne alters because the subject must be 'barren' for Trim. What 'white bear' signifies is undecided; one possibility is an allusion to Pope's *Imitations of Horace*, Ep. II.i.320–23, where Pope complains of the corruption of the stage by spectacle: 'With laughter sure Democritus had dy'd, / Had he beheld an Audience gape so wide. / Let Bear or Elephant be e'er so white, / The people, sure, the people are the sight!' Democritus and the white elephant are Horace's, but the white bear is Pope's invention.

8. *Virgil*'s snake: Cf. *Aeneid*, Book II, where Virgil describes the reaction of the Greek warrior Androgeos when he discovers himself amidst the enemy.

9. elder *Pelegrini*: Walker makes no mention of there being an 'elder' or 'younger' Pellegrini; one always suspects parodic invention when Sterne's 'learning' goes beyond his source.

10. versability: *OED* cites this passage as its last example: 'aptness or readiness to be changed or turned (round)'. The word occurs in Walker, but differently defined: the speedy comparison of all circumstances as a function of wit.

11. And your honour ... corporal: The second edition of Volume V adds these two sentences to the discussion of the Danish auxiliaries, the *only* major substantive variation from the first edition of *TS* in subsequent lifetime editions. Its significance is not known, but since the addition entailed rewriting the next sentence as well, it was not simply omitted by the compositor's oversight. According to *OED*, s.v. *roll*, citing a military dictionary, 'to roul' was used for officers of equal quality, engaged in similar duties; one would not '[en]roul' with inferior officers. Hence, Sterne compliments the Danes, whose auxiliaries did play a gallant part at Limerick, according to Tindal.

Volume VI

CHAPTER I

1. Jack Asses: The representation of hostile critics as asses has a noble lineage; e.g., see *Don Quixote*, II.III.25 (the aldermen's braying contest); Swift, *A Tale of a Tub*, 'A Digression Concerning Criticks'; and Pope, *Dunciad* (B), II.247ff.

2. G-sol-re-ut: Designates the fifth note of the diatonic scale of C major in the hexachord system of notation invented by the eleventh-century monk Guido of Arezzo; it came to signify a particularly shrill sound, as in Rabelais, e.g., II.31, IV.19.

CHAPTER II

1. ten predicaments: Aristotle's ten predicaments represented the categories of all knowledge: substance, quantity, quality, relation, action, passion, time, place, situation, and habit (the nine 'accidents' of 'substance'). According to Chambers, s.v. *Category*, they are 'now almost out of doors; and, in effect, are of little use'. Walker's system is based on them.

2. *Quirino... Tostatus*: Sterne's survey of prodigies interweaves details from Walker's *Of Education* and Adrien Baillet's *Des enfans célèbres*; see the full extent of these borrowings in Florida *Notes*. Vincenzo Quirino, Cardinal Pietro Bembo, and Alfonso Tostado were learned figures of the fifteenth- and early sixteenth-century European Renaissance; who they were was of little concern to Sterne, however, since he was copying illustrative examples more or less randomly.

3. *Piereskius*: See n. 1 to II.xiv. The story of Peireskius's becoming a tutor for his younger brother is told by Baillet.

4. knowlege: A consistent misspelling in the first edition of Volume VI and thus retained.

5. *Grotius... Cordouè*: Baillet has entries on each of these learned figures, including the report that Ferdinand de Cordouè (1422–*c*. 1480), Spanish theologian and physician, must 'necessarily have been *the Antichrist and that he had been born of no other father than the Devil* ', so wise was he at an early age.

6. *substantial forms*: Like the ten predicaments, this was another exploded Aristotelian attempt to classify knowledge that came under severe attack throughout the seventeenth century, culminating in Locke's *Essay*, III.6.10: 'Those therefore who have been taught, that the several *Species* of Substances had their distinct internal *substantial Forms*... were led yet farther out of the way, by having their Minds set upon fruitless Enquiries after *substantial Forms*, wholly unintelligible ...'

7. *Servius ... Capella*: Sterne is looking in Walker and Baillet; the famous Dutch jurist Grotius (1583–1645) wrote on Martianus Capella, a fifth-century author; the Italian classicist Philippe Beroaldi (1453–1505) on Marius Servius Honoratus (*fl.* 400), himself a commentator on Virgil.

8. *Lipsius*: Sterne's footnote quotes part of Baillet's entry on Justus Lipsius (1547–1606), Flemish philologist and critic; Baillet suggests that in order to understand what is meant by Lipsius's having composed a work 'the first day of his life' we must understand the phrase (as Nicius Erythræus did) as figurative, the first day in which he used his reason, suggested to be when he wrote a poem at the age of nine.

CHAPTER III

1. cataplasm: Application of a warming medicinal compress to the injured part, as is 'a fomentation'.

2. destruction . . . nose: Allusion to the damage inflicted on the mucous membranes of the nose and mouth by the use of mercury in the treatment of venereal disease.

CHAPTER V

1. *Marcus Antoninus*: Sterne borrows the anecdote from Walker. Commodus (161–92) was a vicious emperor despite the efforts of his father, Marcus Aurelius Antoninus (121–80), whose Stoicism guided his own reign.

2. the person: Sterne borrows his discussion of a proper tutor from Walker; Florida *Notes* quotes the relevant passages. Sterne's note, 'Vid. *Pellegrina*', is a deliberate misdirection, since the Italian humanist (see n. 7 to V.xlii) has nothing to do with the list.

3. according to *Erasmus*: In the first of his *Familiar Colloquies*.

CHAPTER VI

1. *Dendermond* was taken: By Marlborough, in September 1706.

2. Ask my . . . not it: Cf. Sterne's letter written in 1767 to a friend: 'Now, I take heav'n to witness, after all this *badinage* my heart is innocent—and the sporting of my pen is equal, just equal, to what I did in my boyish days, when I got astride of a stick, and gallop'd away—The truth is this—that my pen governs me—not me my pen.'

3. your death: I.e., 'your death of cold', equivalent to the colloquial 'catch one's death (of cold)'.

CHAPTER VII

1. death-watch: Any of the wood-boring beetles, the clicking sound of which, particularly audible in the silence of a sickroom, was thought to presage death.

2. *Leven*'s . . . *Angus*'s: Both regiments served at Steinkirk; see V.xxi.

3. *Breda*: Town in the Netherlands where prisoners were held, probably also used for winter quarters by the allies.

CHAPTER VIII

1. a natural . . . law: Natural law is derived by the use of human reason; positive law is revealed by divinity.

2. siege . . . blockade: Tindal notes that Marlborough turned the blockade of Dendermond into a siege; Toby here reverses the action. In a blockade, one does

not construct trenches or carry on an attack. Marlborough's retaking of Dendermond (Louis XIV captured it in 1701) was a minor skirmish; Ramillies was the campaign's decisive victory in 1706.

3. The ACCUSING ... ever: The idea of a book of deeds probably derives for Sterne from Revelation 20:12, although it is also in the Jewish tradition (e.g., the 'book of remembrance' in Malachi 3:16). The passage won immediate acclaim from those who admired Sterne's sentimental vein; see, e.g., his letter to an admirer in early 1762: 'the thought of the accusing spirit flying up [to] heaven's chancery with the oath, you are kind enough to say is sublime—my friend, Mr. Garrick, thinks so too ...'

CHAPTER X

1. the wheel ... circle: Cf. Ecclesiastes 12:6: 'the wheel broken at the cistern'; the entire twelfth chapter is about death. Sterne seems to have borrowed important elements of Le Fever's death scene from John Norris, *Practical Discourses ... Volume Two* (1691), as noted by J. T. Parnell, privately to the editor.

2. wistfully: The first edition's 'wishfully' is emended, based on the manuscript Sterne presented to Lady Spencer (see A Note on the Text).

CHAPTER XI

1. WATER-LANDISH *knowlege*: Sterne's coinage, based on Daniel Waterland (1683–1740), prolific Anglican polemicist and chancellor of York Cathedral in the period immediately before Sterne's arrival in the area.

2. *tritical*: Cf. Swift's 'A Tritical Essay upon the Faculties of the Mind', which makes clear *OED*'s definition 'of a trite or commonplace character; *trite*, with play on *critical*'.

3. *For this ... thief*: Cf. Sterne's 'Rabelaisian Fragment', where the preacher Homenas is caught in the act of plagiarizing. Sterne's own sermons frequently contain passages from the works of Tillotson, Hall, Norris, and others. Eighteenth-century preachers, however, were encouraged to borrow from more successful sermon-writers rather than risk leading their congregations into error – or sleep. The Florida *Sermons* offers considerable evidence of this aspect of Sterne's sermon-writing. Paidagunes, i.e., a pedagogue; more correctly, Paedagunes.

4. *Altieri*'s *Italian* dictionary: Ferdinando Altieri's English–Italian dictionary (1726) was the standard until Baretti published his in 1760. Sterne's Italian, however, seems derived from his knowledge of music, not a dictionary.

5. *Yorick*'s *dramatic* sermons: In the first advertisement for Volumes I and II of the *Sermons* (*York Courant*, 4 March 1760), Sterne entitled them *The Dramatick Sermons of Mr. Yorick*; '*Dramatick*' was dropped from the London notices.

6. *lentamente*: Slowly; *tenutè*: sustained; *grave*: slow, solemn; *adagio*: gracefully; *a*

l'octava alta: in the high octave; *Con strepito*: boisterously; *Scicilliana*: slow (as for a Sicilian dance; Sterne means 'Siciliana', but his spelling is consistent with his practice – i.e., 'Scicily' (p. 172)); *Alla capella*: without instrumental accompaniment; *Con l'arco*: with the bow; *Senza l'arco*: without the bow (also *pizzicato*).

7. dirty blue paper: Work (429, n. 4) suggests a 'sly jab at the blue-covered *Critical Review*, which had given Sterne unfavorable reviews, and at its contentious editor, Tobias Smollett', who was trained as a doctor. Actually, *CR* was more favourable to Sterne than the *Monthly Review*; Florida *Notes* suggests the swipe is Sterne's response to *CR* 's attacks not on himself, but on Hall-Stevenson's writing and anti-Bute politics.

8. small *Italian* hand: I.e., the handwriting used in Europe and America today, as opposed to Gothic.

9. *ritratto*: Picture, portrait.

10. Blonederdondergewdenstronke: A parody, obviously, of a 'Dutch commentator' (see n. 12 to I.xix).

CHAPTER XII

1. the emperor's ... *Turks*: Sterne chose a perfect campaign for Le Fever's son; Prince François Eugène of Savoy's campaign against the Turks in the Balkans (1716–18) was seen as a modern crusade, and attracted volunteers from all over Europe. Prince Eugène (1663–1736) was Marlborough's ally in the War of the Spanish Succession; they shared honours as the age's greatest generals.

CHAPTER XIII

1. defeat ... *Belgrade*: August 1717.

CHAPTER XVI

1. *beds of justice*: Based on the *lit de justice*, the throne on which the King of France sat when attending some sessions of parliament.

CHAPTER XVII

1. THE ancient ... *Bugians*: Sterne cites Philip Cluwer (i.e., '*Cluverius* ') (1580–1623), German geographer and historian, but he probably had an English source not yet identified – perhaps, at least for some portion, William Temple, *Observations upon the United Provinces of the Netherlands* (1663), as Work (434, n. 1) suggests. Sterne's '*Herculi* ' and '*Bugians* ' are errors; the correct tribal names are *Heruli* and *Rugians*. One might suspect parodic intent, however, and the Florida *Text* retains the spellings of the first edition.

2. half *full . . . fasting*: Cf. Rabelais, Prologue to Volume III: 'Ennius drinking wrote, and writing drank. . . . Homer never wrote fasting, and Cato never wrote till after he had drank.'

3. understrapping: Of a subordinate or inferior character.

CHAPTER XIX

1. CHAP. XIX: This chapter owes something in spirit to ch. 5 of *Memoirs of Martinus Scriblerus*, in which Martin's father establishes the classical antecedents of his playthings. It is worth recalling that throughout the century boys and girls wore dresses until the age of four or five.

2. *Albertus Rubenius*: Sterne's citation of Rubenius (Albert Rubens (1614–57), son of the great painter and author of *De Re Vestiaria Veterum, Præcipue de Lato Clavo* [*Of the Clothing of the Ancients, Particularly of the Latus Clavus*]) is deceptive. Although he may have glanced at its table of contents and first chapter, he also had an English source, possibly Lefèvre de Morsan's *The Manners and Customs of the Romans. Translated from the French* (1740). It, and similar works, served as school textbooks throughout the century, so that terms esoteric to us were common schoolboy fare; e.g., the debate over the *Latus Clavus* is mentioned by Lefèvre: 'The Senators had under [the Prætexta] a tunic ample enough, called *Latus-clavus*, which was long taken literally for an habit adorned with large studs of purple like nail-heads, but has since been discovered to signify only a stuff with large stripes of purple.'

3. even: ever?

4. ancient dress: Lefèvre points out that the toga was to be properly tied, since a 'loose gown' was a 'mark of dissolute manners'. *Chlamys*: like the *Paludamentum*, a military robe worn over other clothes. *Ephod*: probably Sterne's joke, since it is the robe worn by Jewish priests, not discussed in works on Roman costume. *Tunica*: sleeveless, knee-length vest worn under the toga. *Synthesis*: large robe or cloak, for festivals and banquets. The *Pænula*: short, thick woollen or leather coat, worn in cold or rainy weather and for travelling. *Lacerna*, with its *Cucullus*: cloak for bad weather, with its hood. The first edition has 'Lacema', but that seems to be a compositor's error; the Florida *Text* repeats the error, which is here corrected. *Prætexta*: robe trimmed with purple, worn by magistrates. *Sagum*: vest worn by soldiers. *Trabea*: a little shorter than the toga and striped with purple and white. The reference to Suetonius (second-century Roman biographer, historian, and author of *De Genere Vestium*) may have been taken from Rubens, but it also appeared in textbooks.

5. military shoe: The reference is to Juvenal, *Satires*, 16, lines 23–5: 'you must have a mulish brain . . . to provoke so many jack-boots, and all those thousands of hobnails'.

6. patins: Wooden shoes (pattens); *pantoufles*: slippers (pantofles); *calceus incisus*: cutwork shoe; *calceus rostratus*: shoe with a point turned upward or backward. Lefèvre discusses most of the shoes on the list.

7. That persons ... lost: Lefèvre's discussion is very similar:

The most general colour of the Roman habits was white, which, except purple peculiar to the great offices, was deemed the most honourable. The citizens in public rejoicings generally appeared in white robes, to denote their joy.... Persons of quality were distinguished ... by the fineness, neatness, and whiteness of their habits: and we find in authors of those times, that they often sent their robes to the fuller to be cleaned and whitened. The inferior people, to avoid that expence, generally wore brown cloths. Appian informs us, that from Julius Cæsar's time, distinction of habit was no longer observed at Rome; ... that the slave was drest like his master ...

Lefèvre had already observed the introduction of linen by the Egyptians, and he goes on to discuss the Latus-clavus, but Sterne has a few additional observations not in Lefèvre; one assumes he had a second source or a work in the family of textbooks to which Lefèvre belongs.

8. *Egnatius ... Scaliger*: Fifteenth- and sixteenth-century Renaissance scholars, garnered from Rubens or a similar source.

9. *Bayfius*: Sterne perhaps found this reference in Rubens's first chapter: 'Some understand the clavi to be clasps, either gold balls or purple ones, which were either sewn on the breast of the tunic or on the edges. Bayfius [Lazare de Baïf (*c.* 1496–1547), French scholar], in ch. 7 of his work *On Clothing*, seems to agree with these writers, though in ch. 12 he frankly confesses himself to have some doubts' (translated by the editor).

10. *fibula*: Clasp, buckle, brooch.

11. lost the ... saddle: Play on the proverbial expression 'to win the horse or lose the saddle'.

CHAPTER XX

1. *Poco-curante*'s: *OED* cites this passage as its first example: 'careless or indifferent person; one who shows little interest'; from Voltaire's Lord Pococurante in ch. 25 of *Candide*.

CHAPTER XXI

1. Duke of *Marlborough*: John Churchill (1650–1722), first Duke of Marlborough, Commander-in-Chief of the British army under William III and Anne.

2. *the first ... place*: Sterne's italics indicate a quotation; cf. John Muller, *A Treatise ... of Fortification* (1746), where it is observed of parallels that 'there are generally three in an attack; the first is about 300 toises from the covert-way ...'

CHAPTER XXII

1. post-morning: *OED* cites this passage as its sole example: 'indicating the time at which the mail leaves or arrives'.

2. the *Gazette*: The *London Gazette*, official government newspaper, published thrice weekly beginning in 1666.

3. *chamade*: Signal, by drum or trumpet, for retreat or parley.

4. *Liege* and *Ruremond*: Towns captured by Marlborough in October 1702.

5. portcullises ... thing: See Glossary; according to Chambers, s.v. *Portcullice*, 'now-a-days, the orgues are more generally used, as being found to answer the purpose better'.

CHAPTER XXIII

1. *Amberg ... Limbourg*: All taken in 1703. The first three are in Germany; Huy and Limburg are in the Netherlands.

2. *Ghent ... Flanders*: Ghent and Bruges, captured by the Allies in 1708, are in Flanders; Brabant, an area of the Netherlands west and north of Flanders, containing both Brussels and Antwerp.

3. *Proteus*: Minor sea-god with power to assume different shapes.

4. *Landen ... Dendermond*: Sterne may have intended Landen, where Trim was wounded in 1693, but probably he (or the compositor) misread Landau, a town in Germany taken by Marlborough in 1704. Sterne gathered his towns from the margins of Tindal; e.g., '*Drusen*' occurs because he failed to notice the name 'Drusenheim' was hyphenated in the narrow margin. These campaigns took place in 1704–6.

5. The next year: I.e., 1708.

6. end of the siege: Sterne again plays on the early usage of 'siege' for 'anus' (*OED*); he has just mentioned Sodom and Gomorrah (the wicked cities of Genesis 19) and the many 'parts' they acted.

7. *succedaneum*: Substitute.

8. *desiderata*: Things desired.

CHAPTER XXIV

1. *Montero*-cap: Spanish cap worn by hunters; Sterne confused '*montero*' (Spanish for hunter or *mount*aineer) with the notion of a 'mounted' (i.e., on horseback) soldier. Gala days = holidays.

2. most bloody: Winston Churchill called the siege of Lille 'the greatest siege ... since the invention of gunpowder'. There were 23,000 dead and wounded among the 110,000 participants.

3. ramallie wig: Named in commemoration of Marlborough's victory at Ramillies

in 1706, it had a long plait of hair behind, tied with one or two black ribbon bows.

CHAPTER XXV

1. *clod of the valley*: Job 21:33.
2. cast in the rosemary: Cf. *Hamlet*, IV.v.175: 'There's rosemary, that's for remembrance.'
3. lips . . . plain: See Isaiah 32:4 and 35:6.

CHAPTER XXVI

1. *Morocco* tube: I.e., of Moroccan leather (see p. 372); Trim rigs his two water pipes (hookahs) so that when he inhales, smoke is sent from each pipe's main tube through three small wash-leather tubes, each attached to a cannon.

CHAPTER XXIX

1. *Garrick*: See n. 2 to III.xii.
2. my uncle *Toby*: In the memoir of his family Sterne wrote for his daughter in 1758, there is a sketch of his father in similar language: 'he was . . . of a kindly, sweet disposition, void of all design; and so innocent in his own intentions, that he suspected no one; so that you might have cheated him ten times in a day, if nine had not been sufficient for your purpose'.
3. through his liver: According to tradition the liver is the seat of the passions, especially of love.

CHAPTER XXX

1. the key . . . draw-well: See the opening paragraph of Volume V: Tristram's vow to lock his study door and throw the key into the draw-well. Without access to his library, his list of misogynists is a comic mix of real and fictitious (mostly geographical) names, including a play on 'Cappadocia, in Pontus, and Asia' of Acts 2:9. The King of Sweden, Charles XII (1682–1718), was noted for his misogyny, but the other possibly 'real' person, Ulisse Aldrovandi (1522–1605), an Italian naturalist (but not a king), was not. Charles became a symbol of vain military ambition, as in Johnson's famous couplet in *Vanity of Human Wishes*: 'He left the Name, at which the World grew pale, / To point a Moral, or adorn a Tale.'
2. Countess of K*****: The Countess of Königsmark, renowned for wit and beauty, was sent to Charles to negotiate a peace, but he refused a meeting; the story is told by Voltaire and others. Sterne was probably unaware that the Countess was a governor of the Abbey of Quedlingberg, as noted by Fritz W. Schulze (see Further Reading).

3. *Polixenes*: Possibly Sterne confused Shakespeare's Polixenes with his fellow king, Leontes, whose misogyny precipitates the action of *The Winter's Tale*.

4. peace of *Utrecht*: The end of the War of the Spanish Succession was proclaimed on 4 May 1713.

CHAPTER XXXI

1. *Mary* 's heart: Mary, Queen of England (1553–8), was widely reported to have said that the loss of Calais (1558), England's last possession in France, was etched in her heart, as would be discovered after her death.

2. *Tertullus*: Orator in Acts 24:1–8, who speaks against Paul and is answered by him; cf. sermon 19, 'Felix's behaviour towards Paul': 'Spare thy eloquence, Tertullus!'

CHAPTER XXXII

1. TOBY'*s apologetical oration*: Sterne combines elements of Don Quixote's elevation of knight-errantry over the profession of scholar (I.IV.10–11) with Burton's diatribe against war in the opening pages of *Anatomy*, sources that might influence our understanding of Toby's self-justification.

2. *Guy . . . England*: Chapbook and ballad heroes, based on romance literature.

3. *Helena . . .* without it: Helen, whose abduction precipitated the Trojan War; Hector, the Trojan hero. In Homer's account (*Iliad*, 24), Priam, Hector's father, is successful in recovering his body.

CHAPTER XXXIII

1. fillet: Headband or ribbon. Thumb-stall: pad to protect the thumb.

2. *Quanto id . . . Cardan*: Sterne borrows from Burton, 1.2.1.6, but misreads the attribution, which is not to Cardan (see n. 1 to V.iii), but to Jean Fernel (1497–1558), French physician and author of *Universa medicina* (1554); the sentence may be translated: 'How much more careful then should we be in begetting our children.'

CHAPTER XXXIV

1. *March* to *November*: Troops were kept inactive in winter.

2. according to stipulation: Sterne copies his account of the slow dismantling of Dunkirk from Tindal. *Tugghe* is identified therein as a 'Deputy from the Magistrates of *Dunkirk*'. The full account is provided in the Florida *Notes*.

3. spare the mole: It is possible to quarrel with the Florida *Notes*' annotation of 'mole' as slang for 'penis' (Partridge, *Dictionary*), if Partridge's 'mole' refers only to the animal and not possibly to a large pier or breakwater, the meaning of 'mole' here. Annotating Sterne's bawdy is difficult, but when one reads that the queen

was beseeched to 'spare the mole, for the mole's sake; which, in its naked situation, etc.', one may be forgiven for believing that a mole is not always a mole in *TS*, as a nose is not always a nose.

CHAPTER XXXVI

1. *what love is*: Chapter xxxvi is heavily dependent on Burton's discussion of 'Love Melancholy' in the third partition of *Anatomy*. Plotinus (205–69/70) and Marsilio Ficino (1433–99) are important commentators on Plato and major neoplatonic philosophers in their own right. Watt (354, nn. 1, 3) suggests Sterne is in error in using 'devil' where platonists use 'daimon', a spirit between the divine and the human. The error, however, is Burton's.

2. doctor *Baynyard*: Sterne borrows from Sir John Floyer and Edward Baynard, *The History of Cold-Bathing* (1702), who lament the over-use of 'cantharides' (a blistering agent) by calling it 'the Devil himself'. In Sterne's day, and long before, cantharides, a preparation of Spanish flies, was also known – as it is today – as an aphrodisiac.

3. I have ... *passions*: Work (467, n. 5) identifies this as a comment by St Gregory Nazianzen (329–89), a father of the Eastern Church, to his friend and correspondent Philagrius: 'Bravo! that you philosophize in your sufferings'; one suspects Sterne had an intermediate source.

4. Nor is ... again: Sterne continues to borrow from Burton and at least one other source, perhaps Jacques Ferrand, *Erotomania* (1640). The opinion of Gordonius (Bernard de Gordon, French physician (*fl. c.* 1283–*c.* 1308)) is clearly from the latter. Rhasis (*fl.* 925), Arabian physician; Dioscorides (*fl.* 75) and Aëtius (*fl.* 540), Greek physicians, are often mentioned by both, as are refrigerants (cooling substances), although 'hanea' is mentioned only by Burton, his probable error for another herb. Camphor and topaz were thought to calm the passions; Tristram puts on a topaz ring in IX.xiii.

CHAPTER XL

1. cold seeds: Seeds of the cucumber, gourd, pumpkin, etc.; George Cheyne, *The English Malady* (1733), makes it clear that a diet of them was a remedy of last resort for extreme disorders of mind or body.

2. These ... fourth volumes: The abbreviations 'Inv.' and 'Scul.' appear below most engravings; here they mean the illustration was 'invented' (*invenit*) and 'engraved' (*sculpsit*) by Tristram Shandy ('T. S').

3. says *Cicero*: Cicero often invokes the *'Recta via'* or 'the right path' in his moral writings.

4. cabbage-planters: Sterne almost certainly alludes to the sexual usage of both *planting* (intercourse) and *cabbage* (the female pudendum) in his day. Cf. VIII.i.

5. the shortest line: Famous first assumption of Archimedes in *On the Sphere and Cylinder*.

6. birth-day suits: Attire worn on the king's birthday, but possibly – as in modern usage – nakedness.

Volume VII

Motto: From the *Epistles* of Pliny the Younger, who defends a digression of his own by arguing that although a writer's first duty is to stick to his theme, a digression such as Homer's description of the arms of Achilles is acceptable because it is 'his main subject [the work itself] and not a digression' ('Non enim excursus hic eius, sed opus ipsum est').

CHAPTER I

1. fountain of life: Cf. Proverbs 13:14: 'The law of the wise is a fountain of life, to depart from the snares of death.' Cf. Proverbs 14:27 and Psalm 36:9.

2. mounting . . . stick: Image of the hobby-horse, probably as old as Horace (*Satires*, II.iii).

3. most tawdry one: Work (480, n. 2) suggests a passage in Burton (1.1.3.2): 'as of him that thought himselfe a shell-fish; of a Nunne, and of a desperate Monk, that would not be perswaded but that he was damned'. A passage in Hall-Stevenson's *Makarony Fables* (1768) may offer a clue to the bawdy joke now lost to us: 'Lobsters ought not to think like oysters; / They were not made to be confin'd, / And spend their days like them in cloysters; / To stand when they should stir and bustle, / Gaping and studying like a muscle.' Muscle = mussel.

4. by sin . . . world: Romans 5:12.

5. by the throat: Cash convincingly argues that Sterne lost his voice in the spring of 1762 and never recovered its full use; see *LY*, 148–50.

6. Joppa: Port city of ancient Israel (modern Jaffa) from which Jonah went to sea to escape God's mission (Jonah 1:3); and where Peter received the vision that allowed him to continue preaching to the Gentiles (Acts 11:5–17).

7. *Allons*: Let's go!

CHAPTER II

1. Rochester . . . Canterbury: Three towns on the road between London and Dover. Thomas à Becket (*c*. 1118–70) was murdered and enshrined in Canterbury Cathedral.

2. nervous juices . . . salts: Chambers, s.v. *Nervous Spirit or Juice*: 'a pure, subtile, volatile humour, better known by the name of *animal spirits* . . .' They were thought to convey sensation and motion through the body, but Chambers is dubious about

their existence. Salts, meaning any solid, soluble, non-inflammable substance, one of the five constituent elements of all bodies, were divided as *fixed* and *volatile*, the latter being those that rise when distilled.

CHAPTER IV

1. Addison: See Addison's introductory comments in *Remarks on Several Parts of Italy* (1705); he writes of comparing scenes of his travels with classical accounts read beforehand.

2. dry shod ... not: Cf. *ASJ*: 'much grief of heart has it oft and many a time cost me, when I have observed how many a foul step the inquisitive Traveller has measured to see sights and look into discoveries; all which, as Sancho Pança said to Don Quixote, they might have seen dry-shod at home'. The allusion is to *Don Quixote*, II.III.5, but the ultimate source is Joseph Hall's *Quo Vadis?* (1617).

3. Democritus ... Ephesus: Democritus (*c.* 460–*c.* 357 B.C.), Greek physical philosopher, native of Abdera in Thrace, called the laughing philosopher, in contrast to Heraclitus (i.e., the 'town clerk of Ephesus' (*c.* 540–*c.* 480 B.C.)), the weeping philosopher. That Burton uses the pseudonym 'Democritus Junior' plays a significant part in Sterne's invocation.

CHAPTER V

1. CALAIS ... *Calesium*: See Van R. Baker, 'Sterne and Piganiol de la Force: The Making of Volume VII of *Tristram Shandy*', *CLS* 13 (1976), for a full account of Sterne's extensive use of Jean Aimar Piganiol's *Nouveau Voyage de France* (1724) for details of his journey, beginning with this description of Calais; Florida *Notes* provides the relevant parallel passages. Sterne opens his parodic use of Piganiol by repeating his pedantic list of former Latin spellings of the town.

2. the *Courgain*: Literally, 'small gain', a name Piganiol attributes to the poverty of its inhabitants, poor fishermen. Sterne adds to Piganiol's account the longstanding belief in the power of seafood to increase sexual potency.

3. *La Tour de Guet*: Watchtower.

4. Philip of France: Philippe VI (1293–1350).

5. *Tête de Gravelenes*: The fortifications facing the lower town of Gravelines.

6. campaign: Tract of open country; a plain.

7. Rapin's own words: I.e., Sterne's primary historical source, Paul Rapin de Thoyras's *L'Histoire d'Angleterre* (see n. 1 to II.i). His account of the siege of Calais (1347–8) is actually less than a page, but Sterne is reading Piganiol's account of the valour of '*Eustache de saint Pierre*, the most eminent person in the town', who volunteered with five others to offer themselves to King Edward III with nooses around their necks in order to save the town.

CHAPTER VII

1. size-ace: Six and one on dice. For an entertaining note on the number seven in this seventh chapter of the seventh volume, see Harold Love, *N&Q* 216 (1971).
2. ma chere fille: My dear girl!
3. debt of NATURE: I.e., death.

CHAPTER IX

1. inn-keeper's daughter: Sterne mentions her again in *ASJ*, leading some to argue that he had a particular young woman in mind.
2. slut: In Sterne's day, an affectionate word.
3. *statue*'s *thumb*: Perhaps an allusion to the classical notion of the 'model statue', the *Doryphorus* (*Boy Carrying a Spear*) of Polyclitus, which supposedly established ideal measures for the human body, including the rule that the thumb and nose (!) should be equal.
4. wettest drapery: Sterne probably knew that wet drapery, used by ancient sculptors, was deemed inappropriate for painters.
5. the abbey ... hither: Sterne's detail of the abbey's transposition comes from Piganiol.
6. *devote*: In *ASJ*, Yorick defines three stages in the life of a French woman, viz., coquette, deist, and *devoté*, the last being when she turns herself over to religion.
7. terce ... capotted: Terms from the game of piquet; 'terce to a nine', the lowest three cards of a suit, i.e., seven, eight, and nine; to hold them can be a very minor advantage. To be 'piqued' is to have one's opponent win on cards and play before you begin to score; to be 'repiqued' is to have the opponent win on cards alone (hence, one cannot be piqued and repiqued in the same game). To be 'capotted' is to have one's opponent win everything.

CHAPTER X

1. card and spin: Abbeville was famous for its weaving; Sterne's conclusion perhaps glances at the motto on the royal arms of France: '*Lilia non laborant neque nent*' (They toil not, neither do they spin).
2. Book of French post-roads: *Liste générale des postes de France*, official guide to the post-roads of France, published annually from 1708 to 1779. A *poste et demi* is a 'post and a half', approximately nine miles.

CHAPTER XII

1. Genevieve: St Genevieve (*c.* 422–*c.* 500), patron saint of Paris.

CHAPTER XIII

1. *MAKE them ... wheel*: See Joseph Hall, *Quo Vadis?*: 'None of the least imprecations, which *David*, makes against Gods enemies, is, *Make them like unto a wheele, o Lord* [Psalm 83:13]: Motion is ever accompanied with unquietnesse; and both argues, and causes imperfection, whereas the happy estate of heaven is described by rest.' Sterne plays on his own thinness, a body ravaged by tubercular disease; whether Bishop Hall (see n. 1 to I.xxii) was more corpulent than a bishop should be is unknown.

2. Ixion's wheel: In Greek mythology, Ixion was tied to an ever-revolving wheel as a punishment for insulting Jupiter and Juno.

3. I love ... concoctions: Sterne found his sentence not in the Pythagoreans, but in John Norris (see n. 2 to III.xxi), *Practical Discourses ... Volume Two* (1691). The italicized words translate the Greek; Norris has a somewhat different version: 'that they must separate and unwind themselves even from their very Bodies, if they would be good Philosophers'. Norris attributes the sentence to the Pythagoreans, but gives no details. Sterne's 'too lax or too tense a fibre' offers a standard medical truism of the period: good health depends on a balance in which the nerves of the body are neither too tight nor too loose. 'Congenial humours' means something like 'our inclinations or dispositions'; as in sermon 28, 'Our conversation in heaven', Sterne follows Norris's argument that we prepare ourselves for the pleasures of heaven, *pace* the Pythagoreans, by a *proper* enjoyment of this life; that 'REASON, is half of it, SENSE' is not an invitation to hedonism but a recognition of the intimate relationship between body and soul in the postlapsarian human being, who nevertheless seeks 'heaven'.

CHAPTER XIV

1. But she ... nothing: Sterne borrows these two paragraphs from Burton, 2.2.3; they originated in John Wilkins, *The Discovery of a World in the Moon* (1638), whence Burton appropriated them for the fifth edition of *Anatomy*. Leonardus Lessius (1554–1623) and Francisco Ribera (1537–91) were Jesuit theologians. Dutch mile = about 4.4 English miles; Italian mile = not quite an English mile. Tabid: wasting, decaying.

2. Priapus: Greek god of male potency, usually represented with an enormous phallus.

3. where am ... rushing: Cf. Burton, 1.3.2.4: 'But where am I? Into what subject have I rushed? What have I to do with Nunnes, Maids, Virgins, Widows? I am a Batcheler my self, and lead a Monastick life in a Colledge ...' On Sterne's bachelor (if not monastic) life during this period, see Cash, *L Y*, ch. 5.

4. midst of my days: Scriptural phrase; see Psalm 102:24, Jeremiah 17:11.

CHAPTER XV

1. thill-horse: Last horse in a carriage shaft.
2. *Ailly au clochers*: Piganiol mentions Ailli aux Clochers, but says nothing about the chimes; Sterne may simply be playing on *cloche*: 'bell'; *clocher*: 'steeple, belfry'.
3. Hixcourt: Error for Flixcourt.

CHAPTER XVI

1. avance-courier: Sterne's error for an *avant-courier*: one who rides before; a herald.
2. liards: Smallest French coin, worth about half a farthing; the *livre* contained twenty sous, about ten pence. Tristram's difficulties are compounded by a general recoinage in 1738, hence the Louis XIV twelve-sous piece that 'will not pass'.
3. flesh . . . spirit: Galatians 5:17.
4. Monsieur le Curè: Parish priest.
5. shaveling: Contemptuous term for a tonsured friar; the box is for gathering alms.
6. stables of Chantilly: Built by the Duke of Bourbon, they contained stalls for 1,000 horses, and were considered a benchmark of French extravagance.
7. St. Dennis: The Benedictine Abbey of St Denis held many treasures, including the cup and lantern used by Judas on the night of Jesus's betrayal (see John 18:3); as a Protestant, Sterne deems such 'relics' ridiculous.

CHAPTER XVII

1. so this is Paris: Tristram's attitude towards Paris and Parisians is replete with traditional English prejudices regarding the dirtiness, narrowness, and darkness of its streets; the ill-treatment of its horses, never very strong anyway (compared with English horses); and the meticulous attention to food that was nevertheless considered inferior to English fare.
2. calamanco: Glossy Flemish woollen cloth.
3. gives the wall: Allusion to the long tradition whereby courtesy was shown by allowing another pedestrian the side farthest from the gutter, and superiority by claiming that side for oneself.
4. their god is their belly: Philippians 3:18–19.
5. *the periwig maketh the man*: Sterne wrote to an acquaintance in 1765: 'It is a terrible thing to be in Paris without a perriwig to a man's head!'
6. pardi: I.e., *pardieu*: by God!, Heavens!

CHAPTER XVIII

1. grand Hôtels: Palaces of the nobility.

2. quotation from Lilly: Sterne quotes the definition of *noun* from *A Short Introduction of Grammar* by William Lily and John Colet, first published in 1549 and still in use in the eighteenth century as *Lily's Grammar*.

3. the last survey: Extracted verbatim from Germain Brice's *Description de la Ville de Paris* (1752). Sterne's date, 1716, comes from misapplying a sentence therein concerning the increase in Paris hôtels since 1716.

4. St. *Roche* and *Sulplice*: Outstanding examples of the French classical style, completed in the middle of the eighteenth century. *Sulplice* should be *Sulpice* (from Sulpice II, Bishop of Bourges (d. 647)), but the error is retained as a likely confusion with 'surplice', the clerical garment.

5. portico of the Louvre: The complete sentence reads: '*Non orbis gentem, non urbem gens habet ullam, / Urbsve Domum, Dominum nec Domus ulla parem*' (The world holds no race, no race a city, or any city a house, or any house a master equal [to these]).

CHAPTER XIX

1. undercraft: *OED* cites this passage as its last example: 'a sly, underhand trick'.

CHAPTER XX

1. *consideratis, considerandis*: All things considered.

2. though … parlour: About *ASJ*, Sterne wrote to an acquaintance: 'the women will read this book in the parlour, and Tristram in the bed-chamber'.

3. volving: *OED* cites this passage as its last example: 'to turn over in the mind; to consider'.

4. Andoüillets: 'Little sausages'; both Rabelais and Sterne play on the bawdy possibilities of sausages as phallic objects (see IX.v–vii).

CHAPTER XXI

1. *sinovia*: Lubricating fluid secreted in the joints.

2. man of Lystra: Acts 14:8: 'And there sat a certain man at Lystra, impotent in his feet, being a cripple from his mother's womb, who never had walked.'

3. scapulary across her lap: Sterne is perhaps consulting a *Pharmacopoeia* or medical handbook for his collection of herbal remedies. One assumes the prioress holds her scapulary across her lap to prevent the smoke from reaching her nostrils.

4. whitloe: Inflammation or swelling; cf. 'white swelling' (p. 418 and n. 9 to this chapter). The difficulties of reading (and annotating) a teasing passage such as this in a work intent on showing that nothing human can be immunized from sexual

play are discussed by New, ' "At the backside of the door of purgatory": A Note on Annotating *Tristram Shandy* ', in *'Tristram Shandy': Riddles and Mysteries*.

5. calesh: I.e., calash, small covered carriage.

6. frize: I.e., frieze, coarse woollen cloth.

7. hot-wine-lees: Sediment from wine, used to scour material such as felt.

8. tempting bush: Sign of an inn.

9. white swelling: Swelling without redness, but also a colloquial term for pregnancy.

10. By my fig: By this point in the nuns' story, 'fig' as a bawdy allusion to a woman's pudendum almost certainly comes into play – perhaps a bilingual pun as well, i.e., *pudendum muliebre*.

CHAPTER XXII

1. obstreperated: *OED* cites this passage as its sole illustration: 'to make a noise or clamour'.

CHAPTER XXV

1. I see no sin: Sterne's joke is based on the indecency of *foutre* (to fuck) and the ambiguity of *bouger* (to stir, budge, move), with a probable allusion to *bougre* (bugger). Sterne labelled France 'foutre-land' in a letter to Hall-Stevenson.

2. fa ... mi, ut: The names given by Guido of Arezzo to the six notes of the hexachord system; see n. 2 to VI.i. Complines: the last of the seven daily canonical services.

CHAPTER XXVI

1. I never ... out: Cf. Ben Jonson's famous comment in *Timber* (1641): '*I remember, the Players have often mentioned it as an honour to Shakespeare, that ... hee never blotted out a line. My answer hath beene, would he had blotted a thousand.*'

CHAPTER XXVII

1. *Fontainbleau*: Sterne's joke juxtaposes the excessive magnificence of this royal palace with Tristram's lack of comment.

2. out-gallop the king: This was, in fact, the rule.

3. silks: The counsels of the various kings and courts, *silks* being used allusively in recognition of their silk gowns.

4. We'll go ... discipline: Sterne returns to Piganiol for these two paragraphs on the Abbey of St Germain and its tombs. 'Sequier' is his consistent misspelling for Dominique Séguier, Bishop of Auxerre (1593–1659). St Héribalde, abbot of the monastery of St Germain and eventually Bishop of Auxerre (d. *c.* 857). Charlemagne

ruled France from 768 to 814, succeeded by his son, Louis the Debonair, in turn succeeded by his son, Charles the Bald, who ruled from 840 until his death in 877.

5. Saint MAXIMA: Piganiol does refer to a St Maxima buried in the Abbey, but the name was held by numerous saints, as was Maximus, about whom Piganiol says nothing; Sterne introduces him in order to play on the masculine and feminine forms and Walter's bilingual pun, 'the greatest saints'.

6. Saint Germain: Bishop of Auxerre (*c.* 380–448), died at Ravenna, which accounts for the origin of St Maxima's pilgrimage.

7. Saint *Optat*: Bishop of Auxerre (d. *c.* 530). Latin *optatus*: longed for, desired, welcomed.

CHAPTER XXVIII

1. most puzzled skein of all: Tristram's multiple journeys through Auxerre comprise perhaps the single most discussed passage in *TS* among mid-twentieth-century critics. For example, in *The Winged Skull: Papers from the Sterne Bicentenary Conference*, ed. Cash and Stedmond, three of the first four essays discuss it.

2. pavillion built by Pringello: Hall-Stevenson (see n. 3 to I.xii), called Antony within his circle (in ironic contrast to St Antony, the founder of Christian asceticism), tried to profit from Sterne's success with a collection of very silly (and bawdy) stories in verse, *Crazy Tales* (1762). Each is narrated by a member of the so-called Demoniacs, Sterne's circle of north Yorkshire friends; the tale by Don Pringello, 'The Fellowship of the Holy Nuns; or the Monk's Wise Judgment', is a particularly tasteless tale, followed by a 'scholium' praising 'Pringello' as the architect (now thought to be Sir William Chambers (1726–96)) who helped renovate Hall-Stevenson's 'Crazy Castle'.

Since Sterne's actual journey ended in Toulouse, it has been assumed that 'Mons. Sligniac' might be the landlord mentioned in a letter written in August 1762, and that the pavilion is part of the country house Sterne describes as 'an excellent house well furnish'd, and elegant'; see Cash, *L Y*, 152–6.

CHAPTER XXIX

1. by water to Avignon: Tristram's journey down the Rhône passes the area to the west known as Vivarais and the area to the east, Dauphiné, as well as the three cities mentioned. The Hermitage and Côte Rôtie were the most famous vineyards of the Rhône valley.

2. chaise-undertaker: *OED* cites this passage as its only recorded example: 'One who undertakes to renovate chaises, a dealer in second-hand chaises.'

3. whispering these words: It is unlikely that Sterne has definite words in mind, despite the division of the asterisks; in contrast, note the ease with which one fills in the words in V.xvii.

4. goat's-whey: Prescribed in the eighteenth century for good health generally, and to aid in potency most particularly, as in the *Memoirs of Martinus Scriblerus*.

CHAPTER XXX

1. Lyons: Tristram's excessive praise for the *second* city of France is at Paris's expense. Lippius's clock (and its inoperative condition), the library with the general history of China, and the pillar in the Church of St Ireneus were all gleaned from Piganiol.
2. milk coffee: Coffee was considered medicinal in the eighteenth century, but it was probably the milk (or cream) that Sterne had with it that eased his pulmonary illness.
3. *valet de place*: A guide to strangers or tourists.
4. Pilate lived: Sterne's account does not come from Piganiol, but other travel writers mention the house, said to have belonged to Pontius Pilate in exile, a confusion over a local resident named Pilati and the town's desire for a 'relic'. This is the explanation given by the famous antiquarian Jacob Spon (1647–85), cited by Sterne in the next chapter; Sterne probably never consulted him.
5. *Tomb of the two lovers*: Although Sterne credits Spon, he is translating Piganiol's account (which cites Spon), a typical Sternean gesture. Piganiol notes that the tomb was demolished in 1707; exactly why it was erected remains a question, but travel writers did refer to it, often as the 'tomb of the lovers'.

CHAPTER XXXI

1. fibrillous: This occurrence is the last cited by *OED*; a fibril is a small fibre.
2. Amandus ... Amanda: Masculine and feminine forms in Latin for 'one who must be loved'.
3. *pabulum*: *OED* cites this passage as its first example of figurative usage: 'that which nourishes and sustains the mind or soul; food for thought'. Sterne's meaning is perhaps closer to *pap*, i.e., nonsense.
4. *Frusts ... antiquity*: *OED* cites this passage for the first occurrence of *Frust*: 'a fragment'. '*Rusts*' alludes to the value supposedly placed by antiquarians on layers of encrusted oxidation.
5. Mecca: Holiest city of Islam, birthplace of Mohammed and the destination of pilgrimages.
6. Santa Casa: In Loreto, Italy, said to have been the home of the Virgin Mary in Nazareth, miraculously relocated by angels; it remains a popular objective of Roman Catholic pilgrimages.
7. *Videnda*: *OED* cites this passage as its first illustration: 'things worth seeing or which ought to be seen'.
8. *Basse Cour*: Lower court, stable-yard.

9. dernier: Last.

10. Monsieur Le Blanc: Boswell (*On the Grand Tour*, 2 January 1766) mentions the house of Le Blanc in Lyons, a place he takes for three livres a day because 'the best places were taken'. If the two Le Blancs are the same person, it suggests that Sterne did not stay in the 'best places' during his travels.

CHAPTER XXXII

1. But with ... for ever: Sancho Pança wishes for an ass with which he might 'commune' (I.III.11).

CHAPTER XXXIII

1. Don't puzzle me; said I: Cf. *ASJ*: 'THERE is not a more perplexing affair in life to me, than to set about telling any one who I am ...'

CHAPTER XXXIV

1. CHAP. XXXIV: Behind this chapter is a joke told by Ozell in a note to Rabelais, II.7, about a curate who is told he must pay the tax for keeping a woman (the so-called custom of 'couillage'), whether he has a mistress or not.

2. *Pardonnez moi*: Pardon me.

3. post royal: Any post from Paris or Lyons or from any place where the king actually resided, the fee for which was double.

4. for the salt: The *gabelle*, tax on salt, one of four primary taxes in eighteenth-century France.

5. WATER ... OYL: Sterne plays on the Roman Catholic practice of anointing with oil in the Sacrament of Unction of the Sick, often called Extreme Unction because it became associated with last rites; the Anglican church abandoned the custom in 1552.

CHAPTER XXXV

1. PAR LE ROY: By [order of] the king.

2. fermiers: Tax collectors, i.e., farmers of taxes, notorious in pre-Revolutionary France.

3. THE PEACE WAS MADE: The Peace of Paris in 1763 that ended the Seven Years War.

CHAPTER XXXVI

1. Sancho Pança . . . bitterly: See *Don Quixote*, I.III.9, a passage Sterne refers to again in *ASJ*. Sancho loses the ass along with everything else.

CHAPTER XXXVII

1. chaise-vamper: I.e., chaise-undertaker (see n. 2 to VII.xxix).
2. Louis d'Ors: Gold pieces worth about a guinea.
3. Dodsley, or Becket: Sterne turned from Dodsley to Thomas Becket and P. A. Dehondt in December 1761, and they remained his publishers to the end of his life – publishing Volumes V–IX of *TS*, Volumes III–IV of the *Sermons* (1766), and *ASJ* (1768).

CHAPTER XXXVIII

1. papilliotes: Curl-papers.
2. *a la folie*: Madly; to excess.
3. *J'en suis bien mortifiée*: I am simply mortified.
4. *Tenez*: Here, take them!

CHAPTER XXXIX

1. JESUITS . . . *cholic*: I.e., the suppression of the Jesuit order in France, beginning in early 1762.

CHAPTER XLI

1. nothing to see: Sterne ignores, by design, the famous papal residence at Avignon.
2. duke of Ormond: He spent thirty years in exile in Avignon. While other travel writers ignored this landmark, Sterne's interest in the Treaty of Utrecht, the cause of Ormond's exile (see n. 6 to II.v and n. 6 to VIII.xix), explains his mention of it.
3. windyness of Avignion: I.e., the mistral, the north-west wind that sweeps down the Rhône valley and is especially felt by the towns at the southern end, Avignon and Orange. Only one proverb was found concerning this: 'Avignon venteuse, sans vent contagieuse' (Avignon is windy, but when not windy, contagious).

CHAPTER XLIII

1. *Baucaira* and *Tarascone*: Towns on the Rhône, just south of Avignon. Sterne mentions the famous fair at Beaucaire in a letter from Toulouse, 14 August 1762.
2. *plain* into a *city*: One of Sterne's most persistent ideas, receiving a fine restatement

in *ASJ*: '—What a large volume of adventures may be grasped within this little span of life by him who interests his heart in every thing, and who, having eyes to see, what time and chance are perpetually holding out to him as he journeyeth on his way, misses nothing he can *fairly* lay his hands on.'

3. the best Muscatto: I.e., muscatel.

4. carousal: Fit of carousing. The word was often confused with *carousel*, a 'tournament in which knights, divided into companies . . . engaged in various plays and exercises'. Sterne may combine both meanings.

5. running . . . pleasure: Chivalric exercise in which a rider attempts to pass his lance through a suspended ring, but here, as in Rabelais, also a sexual image; Sterne uses it again in *ASJ*.

6. saint Boogar: Play on 'bugger' (cf. *bouger* in VII.xxv), elaborated by 'pricks', 'ring of pleasure', and 'backside of the door of purgatory'; typical of *TS*, this outrageous bawdiness and Nannette's cursed slit in her petticoat (a term either borrowed from Samuel Butler, *The Genuine Remains* (1759), or available to both Butler and Sterne as a phrase of recognizably bawdy intent) are intertwined with one of the most pastoral and innocent scenes in all of Sterne.

7. Gascoigne roundelay: The *rondel* is a song in alternate parts, as Sterne indicates, designed to accompany a dance in the round (*ronde* or *rondel*). 'Long live joy! Fie on sadness'; *fidon* = *fi-donc*, which, Work conjectures (538, n. 3), was the Provençal accent as Sterne heard it.

8. Just disposer . . . sorrows: Cf. 'The Grace' in *ASJ*, where Yorick sees '*Religion* mixing in the dance' of a peasant family; and sermon 20, 'The prodigal son', where Sterne writes: 'When the affections so kindly break loose, Joy, is another name for Religion. . . . Was it not for this that GOD gave man musick to strike upon the kindly passions; that nature taught the feet to dance to its movements . . .'

9. lap of content: Cf. Sterne's letter dated 16 November 1764: 'I shall spend every winter of my life, in the same lap of contentment, where I enjoy myself now—and wherever I go—we must bring three parts in four of the treat along with us—In short we must be happy within—and then few things without us make much difference—This is my Shandean philosophy.—You will read a comic account of my journey from Calais thro' Paris to the Garonne, in these volumes . . .'

10. nut brown maid: Phrase previously made commonplace by the popular old ballad, 'The Nut-Brown Maid'.

11. insiduous: *OED* considers this an erroneous spelling of *insidious*; it occurs in one of Sterne's earliest letters as well, where 'insidious' is clearly the meaning.

12. Perdrillo's pavillion: Almost certainly Sterne's erroneous recall of 'Pringello', the name assigned to Hall-Stevenson's architect; see n. 2 to VII.xxviii. The place-names trace a 200-mile journey from Nîmes to Toulouse, similar to one Sterne and his family took in July 1762; they settled in Toulouse for a year (see Cash, *L Y*, ch. 4).

Volume VIII

CHAPTER I

1. cabbage planter: See n. 4 to VI.xl.
2. *Freeze-land, Fog-land*: Nonce words.

CHAPTER II

1. the devil ... imps: Proverbial: 'No marvel it is if the imps follow when the devil goes before.'
2. Pope and his Portrait*: An allusion, perhaps, to one of the several allegorical engravings of Alexander Pope (1688–1744), receiving inspiration from the muses, that appeared in the collected works edited by Warburton; or to a passage in Julien Offray de La Mettrie's *L'homme machine* (1747), translated as *Man a Machine*: 'Let us view the picture of the famous Mr. Pope.... The efforts and nerves of his genius are strongly represented in his physiognomy; it seems to be all in a sort of convulsion ... because the source of the nerves is ... in labour, and the whole body ... feels the pangs of a painful delivery.'
3. TARTUFFE: See n. 8 to V.i. Sterne includes several catch-words of religious controversy, including 'faith or fire', 'good works', and 'Zeal'; cf. a letter he wrote in 1767: 'This nasty gout! ... I wish it was the portion of splenetic philosophers, and Tartuffe's of all denominations.'

CHAPTER III

1. periclitating: *OED* cites this passage as its last example of usage as a transitive verb: 'endangering'. Sterne may have found the word in Rabelais. For 'pardi', see n. 6 to VII.xvii.
2. black velvet mask: Since wearing masks in public was a mark of disrepute, great-aunt Dinah's slip (I.xxi) is being recalled.
3. one archbishop: Sterne's great-grandfather, Dr Richard Sterne (*c.* 1596–1683), was Archbishop of York from 1664 until his death. The meaning of 'Welch judge' has eluded annotation.

CHAPTER IV

1. IT is ... Cuckoldom: Play on the proverbial wisdom that a cuckold (i.e., the husband of an adulterous wife) is the last person to learn of it.

CHAPTER V

1. WHY weavers ... them: Cf. Montaigne, 'Of Cripples', wherein he contemplates the longstanding notion that, as the marginal note puts it, '*Lame People best at the Sport of* Venus.' Pined, i.e., wasted.

2. grinding the faces: Cf. Isaiah 3:15: 'What mean ye that ye ... grind the faces of the poor?'

3. Longinus: In *On the Sublime*, Longinus asserts that 'the greatest Thoughts are always uttered by the greatest Souls' and illustrates his point thus: 'When *Parmenio* cried, "I would accept these Proposals if I was *Alexander*," *Alexander* made this noble Reply, "And so would I, if I was *Parmenio*." ' For Sterne's interest in Longinus, see n. 3 to IV.x.

CHAPTER VI

1. ten cart-loads ... hands: Of the 4,000 copies printed of Volumes V and VI, some 1,000 remained unsold fifteen months after publication – much to Sterne's chagrin; see Cash, *LY*, 149–50.

2. quirister: Chorister, choirboy.

CHAPTER VIII

1. case-knife: Knife with a sheath, a rather obvious sexual analogy.

CHAPTER IX

1. day-shifts: Nonce word, contrasting 'night-shifts', i.e., night-shirts.

2. Flemish ells: Variable measure, about 27 inches. A corking pin is a pin of the largest size.

CHAPTER X

1. *old hat cock'd*: See n. 1 to V.viii.

CHAPTER XI

1. *Terra del Fuogo*: Tierra del Fuego, the archipelago off the southern tip of South America; literally, land of fire. In light of the remainder of the sentence, Sterne's bawdiness here may also include a play on 'fugo', an eighteenth-century colloquialism for the anus.

2. gashly: *OED* cites this passage to illustrate an obsolete form meaning 'ghastly, horrid'. More likely, Sterne had in mind an adjectival form of *gash*.

3. furr'd cap: In a letter to a friend, Sterne joked: 'When you have got to your fireside ... and are so much a sovereign as to sit in your furr'd cap (if you like it, tho' I should not, for a man's ideas are at least the cleaner for being dress'd decently) ...'

4. finger in the pye: Proverbial, although perhaps not in Sterne's bawdy usage here. Despite many contemporary attacks on Sterne for his bawdiness, this chapter is blatantly licentious – a signal that he would defy tartuffery to the end.

5. staragen: Tarragon, a seasoning.

6. devil's dung: Asafoetida, a particularly foul-smelling drug, but also used in cooking.

CHAPTER XIII

1. alphabetically speaking: Cervantes, I.IV.7, has an alphabetical list of the require-ments of a good lover that may have inspired Sterne's. Some of Sterne's entries are nonce words: 'Futilitous', rooted in 'futile'; 'Galligaskinish', derived from 'galli-gaskins', ludicrous term for loose breeches; 'Handy-dandyish', probably an allusion to the child's game in which one guesses the hand that holds an object; and 'Iracundulous', meaning 'inclined to anger; irascible'.

2. Obstipating: Constipating.

CHAPTER XIV

1. wicker gate: Probably a solecism for *wicket gate*, a small gate opening on to a field or enclosed space for those on foot.

CHAPTER XV

1. set on fire ... end: Sterne brings new life to a proverbial expression, 'to burn or light a candle at both ends', signifying prodigality or sociability.

2. *blind gut*: The discussion here bears comparison to those in I.xxv, on the location of Toby's wound, II.xix, on the advantages of the '*Cæsarian* section', and, of course, II.vi, on Toby's ignorance concerning the right and wrong end of a woman. The play is on 'blind gut' as a term for the *cæcum* (the beginning of the large intestine), and, generally, for any tubular passage with one end closed.

3. *Illion*: Ileum, the lowest part of the small intestine.

CHAPTER XVI

1. movement: moment?

2. from Dan to Beersheba: Scriptural formula (Judges 20:1, 2 Samuel 24:2), marking the boundaries of Canaan, north and south.

CHAPTER XVII

1. Bouchain: The siege of Bouchain (August 1711) was one of Marlborough's great triumphs, the well-fortified town surrendering in just twenty days. A foldout map is provided in Tindal.

2. snuffy: Soiled with snuff.

3. the pricks ... love: For St Radegund, see n. 10 to IV.S.T.; she was particularly known for her self-inflicted physical punishments. Eric Rothstein (*Systems of Order and Inquiry in Later Eighteenth-Century Fiction* (University of California Press, 1975)) calls attention to the bilingual puns ('Fesse' and 'clunis', French and Latin, respectively, for 'buttock') and the implication that 'this spiritual voyage becomes a shifting of hams with "pricks" *in media re* '.

CHAPTER XIX

1. *Servius Sulpicius*: See V.iii and nn.

2. half of the entertainment: Sterne recalled this passage in response to a complimentary letter he received a month before his death: 'a true feeler,' he wrote, 'always brings half the entertainment along with him. His own ideas are only call'd forth by what he reads, and the vibrations within, so entirely correspond with those excited, 'tis like reading *himself* and not the *book*.'

3. every year: The 'science' of chronology, still taken very seriously in Sterne's day, built complex chronological tables for biblical and parallel events in the ancient world; hence creation took place on 23 October 4004 B.C., the flood began on 7 December 2349, Abraham was born in 1996, and the Israelites departed Egypt on 5 May 1491. Parallel dates were derived by several methods, including Greek Olympiads, the 'years of Nabonnassar' (the first King of Babylonia, perhaps alluded to in Sterne's 'Dynasties'), and the founding of Rome (*ab urbe condita*).

4. MODESTY ... open: As noted by W. G. Day ('A Novel Compliment', *BSECS Newsletter* 5 (1974)), Sterne alludes to Guido Reni's painting, variously called 'Liberality and Modesty' or 'Generosity and Modesty', perhaps as a compliment to John Spencer (see n. to Vol. V, dedication), who owned a studio version.

5. cast-year: Constructed (as is 'cast-almanack') by analogy perhaps to cast-clothes, i.e., something discarded.

6. seventeen hundred and twelve: Sterne borrows from Tindal the events of the closing campaign of the War of the Spanish Succession, marked by the Duke of Ormond's refusal to support Prince Eugène and the Dutch General François Nicolas Fagel (1655–1718) at their siege of Quesnoy because of 'orders' from Queen Anne or Marlborough. The precise nature of those 'orders' was the subject of Ormond's later impeachment trial. Contemporary accounts suggest that the army shared Toby's anger at what was considered a gross dereliction of duty; Roger Sterne, Laurence's father, was among the troops disbanded by the cessation of hostilities.

7. how Marlborough ... marched: Sterne condenses four double-column folio pages from Tindal describing Marlborough's march into Germany; Sterne (or his compositor) altered the spelling of many of the place-names, but the entire list appears in one form or another in Tindal.

8. invention of powder: Sterne takes his discussion primarily from Chambers, s.v. *Gunpowder*. Wenceslaus (1361–1419) became Holy Roman Emperor in 1378; the account of Berthold Schwartz, a German monk, is taken verbatim from Chambers. Don Pedro, Bishop of Leon, died in 1112; Sterne misread Chambers, and gives us the account of another authority on the events of 1343. 'Friar Bacon' is Roger Bacon (*c.* 1214–*c.* 1294), father of English philosophy.

9. even: ever?

10. the Chinese: Many of the military treatises Toby studied gave attention to the invention of gunpowder, repeating the information in Chambers, and adding the Chinese claim as well. In view of Trim's question, 'How came priests and bishops ... to trouble their heads so much about gun-powder?', one notes that Bishop Warburton discusses the history of gunpowder in *Julian, or A Discourse Concerning the Earthquake* (1750); Sterne may again be tweaking Warburton's nose.

11. kingdom of Bohemia ... whatever: Familiar trope for a never-never-land setting, as in *The Winter's Tale*; the coastline of a landlocked Bohemia was a common joke.

12. affair of Landen: Sterne's account of the Battle of Landen (29 July 1693) is taken from Tindal. It was a costly battle, with some 20,000 casualties. The three regimental generals, Hugh Wyndham (d. 1708); Henry Lumley (1660–1722); and the Earl of Galway (1648–1720), are all mentioned by Tindal, as are the Prince de Conti (1664–1709), who led the French cavalry, and François-Henri de Montmorency, duc de Luxembourg (1628–95), the Marshal of France and head of its army at Landen. Thomas Talmash, or Tollemache (*c.* 1651–94), was a lieutenant-general who fought at Limerick and Steinkirk.

13. he deserves ... halter: Possibly proverbial: 'As well worth it as a thief is worth a rope.'

14. mob: Informal head-covering, with a puffed crown and side pieces that could be tied under the chin or left dangling.

15. cæteris paribus: Other things being equal.

CHAPTER XX

1. Beguine: See n. 47 to IV.S.T.

2. My fever ... night: In his 'Journal to Eliza' Sterne comments on the 'truth' of this description: 'Twas a prophetic Spirit, wch dictated the Acc^t of Corp^l Trim's uneasy night when the fair Beguin ran in his head,—for every night & almost every Slumber of mine, since the day We parted, is a repe[ti]tion of the same description ...'

CHAPTER XXI

1. sisserara: I.e., siserary: with a vengeance, suddenly.

CHAPTER XXII

1. despair: Some modern editors emend to 'affair', perhaps a better reading.

CHAPTER XXIII

1. archives of Gotham: 'As wise as a man of Gotham' was proverbial, usually meaning a mask of folly to disguise real wisdom.

CHAPTER XXIV

1. raree-shew-box: Often called a Savoyard's box (see n. 1 to III.xxvi); a scenic representation (often of battles) with moving figures. 'Raree'. is supposedly a Savoyard's attempt at *rare*, indicating connection with the wandering inhabitants of Savoy.

2. Thracian * Rodope's: Sterne borrows his footnote from a marginal note in Burton, 3.2.2.3, itself lifted from Heliodorus's *An Æthiopian History*; Thomas Underdowne's popular Renaissance translation may also have caught Sterne's attention: 'Rhodopis . . . [was] perfectly instructed in all Venerious entisements [cf. the widow's 'venereal' eyes], and wanton behaviour, so that it was possible for none that looked on her, not to be intangled with her love, of such an unavoidable force, was the whorish allurement that proceeded from her eyes.' Rhodopis of Thrace, Greek courtesan of the sixth century B.C.

3. Gallileo . . . sun: Sterne's century credited Galileo (1564–1642) with the discovery of sunspots.

CHAPTER XXV

1. the eyes: Sterne covers much-travelled ground in his praise of eyes as the seat of love, but Burton's discussion in 3.2.2.2–3 is still on his mind; e.g., 'it is not the eye of it selfe that entiseth to lust, but an *adulterous eye*, as *Peter* termes it [2 Peter 2:14], a wanton, a rolling, lascivious eye'.

CHAPTER XXVI

1. for I call . . . for it: Cf. *ASJ*: '[I have] been in love with one princess or another almost all my life, and I hope I shall go on so, till I die, being firmly persuaded, that if ever I do a mean action, it must be in some interval betwixt one passion and another . . .'

2. A Devil ... Turk: Borrowed from Burton, 3.2.4, who quotes from Robert Tofte's (d. 1620) translation of Benedetto Varchi's *Blazon of Jealousie* (1615).

3. life of Socrates, *&c. &c.*: See n. 3 to V.xii.

4. to save ... poor: Sterne wrote to Hall-Stevenson in November 1764: ' 'Tis a church militant week with me, full of marches, and countermarches—and treaties about Stillington common, which we are going to inclose ...' Whether Sterne is alluding to this or some other particular action by the dean and chapter of York is unknown.

5. battle of Wynnendale: End of September 1708; the wooded surroundings are made clear in Tindal, both in his description and map.

6. the poor *in spirit*: Matthew 5:3.

CHAPTER XXVII

1. gap'd knife: *OED* cites this passage to illustrate *Gapped*: 'Having the edge notched or serrated.' Possibly Sterne meant *gaped*, i.e., 'opened'.

CHAPTER XXVIII

1. *te Deum*: See n. 12 to I.xviii.

2. steep: *OED*: 'To ... initiate or celebrate by a drink' (jocular).

3. pipes: Small tubes made of pipe-clay used to keep curls in periwigs. Chalk was used to polish metal.

CHAPTER XXXI

1. expression ... hermit: Cf. Burton, 3.2.5.1, where St Jerome's account of St Hilarion (291–371) is quoted: 'by this meanes [deprivation] *Hillarion made his Asse, as he called his own body, leave kicking ...*'

CHAPTER XXXIII

1. gymnicks: I.e., gymnastics, but Sterne borrows the word from Burton, 2.2.2, where the meaning seems delimited to sexual acrobatics.

2. *nolens, volens*: Unwilling or willing; willing or not.

3. read Plato: Sterne is reading Burton, 3.1.1.2, not Plato or his commentators, Valesius (Francisco de Vallés (1524–92), Spanish physician) and Ficino (see n. 1 to VI.xxxvi; having lived a century before de Vallés, Ficino could not have commented on him). *Symposium* is the work being cited. The concept of 'two religions', the so-called 'double doctrine', played an important part in Warburton's writings, among others; it held that Greek philosophers had one religion for themselves, another for the masses.

4. golden chain: From Homer to Milton, an image of love, concord, harmony, extending from heaven to earth.

5. procreation ... paradise: A good example of Sterne's turning borrowed material to new purposes. He combines two passages in Burton, separated by 150 pages, for his joke; the first is a sentence of Ficino: '*procreation of children is as necessary as that finding out of truth*' (3.1.1.2); for Slop's response, he borrows from an unrelated discussion in 3.2.5.3: 'Consider the excellency of Virgins ... marriage replenisheth the earth, but virginity Paradise ...'

CHAPTER XXXIV

1. *affects*: *OED* cites this passage as its last example of an obsolete usage: 'To be drawn to, have affection or liking for.'

2. fourth general division: Allusion to one of several methods (most recommending *three* divisions) by which sermons were to be organized.

3. ideas of baldness: Plentiful hair suggested sexual energy; baldness, the opposite.

4. tongs and poker: Cf. III.xx, where Trim bores 'touch holes with the point of a hot poker'. The aural pun of 'poker' is obvious; an additional play on 'tong[ue]' is probable.

5. Scarron: Paul Scarron (1610–60), author of *Le Roman comique* (trans. by Tom Brown as *The Comical Romance* (1700)), a work that bears comparison with *TS*.

6. Thou must ... them: Another borrowing from Burton, 3.2.5.1 and 1.2.2.1; similar prescriptions for controlling sexual appetite are given by the physician Rondibilis to Panurge in Rabelais, III.31. Claudius Ælianus (*fl. c.* 200), Roman author. Sterne takes his reference to *De Natura Animalium* – where it is reported that Athenian women put 'hanea' in their beds to relieve the pains of sexual abstinence – from Burton.

Volume IX

Motto: Sterne combines two sentences from Burton's preface to his discussion of 'love-melancholy' (3.1.1.1), the section from which he derived much of the conclusion of Volume VIII: 'Though you might prefer a somewhat more polite amusement, by the Muses and Charities and the grace of all poets, do not think badly of me.'

DEDICATION

1. GREAT MAN: Sterne again addresses William Pitt, to whom he had dedicated the second edition of Volumes I and II in 1760. He alludes to his having become in 1766 Viscount Pitt and Earl of Chatham; Pitt had been 'out of place [i.e., office]' between 1761 and 1766.

2. *a posteriori*: Sterne plays on the terms of logic, here meaning, more or less, 'before and after the fact', but also, in conjunction with 'exposed' and 'kissing . . . any thing else', a play on 'posterior' as well.

3. gentle Shepherd: As pointed out by Morris Golden ('Periodical Context in the Imagined World of *Tristram Shandy*', *Age of Johnson* 1 (1987)), Sterne alludes to a nickname for George Grenville (first Lord of the Treasury, 1763–5), originated by Pitt in 1763. Grenville made a speech asking where he was to find tax revenues, 'tell me where, tell me where', and Pitt responded with the words of a popular song, 'Gentle Shepherd, Tell Me Where'. Sterne exploits the humour of a well-known episode centred on the words 'tell me where' to preface a volume in which 'where?' is the most pressing question.

4. Whose . . . him company: Sterne appropriates Pope's description of the 'poor Indian' in *An Essay on Man*, I.99–112.

CHAPTER I

1. time and chance: Ecclesiastes 9:11: 'time and chance happeneth to them all', Sterne's text for sermon 8, 'Time and Chance'.

2. least mote: Matthew 7:3: 'And why beholdest thou the mote that is in thy brother's eye, but considerest not the beam that is in thine own eye?'

3. And here . . . 1766: Cf. Sterne's letter of 23 July 1766: 'at present I am in my peaceful retreat, writing the ninth volume of Tristram—I shall publish but one this year, and the next I shall begin a new work of four volumes [i.e., *ASJ*, only two volumes of which were written], which when finish'd, I shall continue Tristram with fresh spirit'.

4. The mistake . . . criminal: In his notes to the earlier Penguin edition of *TS* (1967), Graham Petrie credits J. C. Maxwell with suggesting that this passage is a 'ludicrous but perfectly fair application of the moral theory' of Wollaston, *The Religion of Nature Delineated*: 'Therefore nothing can interfere with any proposition that is true, but it must likewise interfere with nature . . . and consequently be *unnatural*, or *wrong in nature*.' Sterne quotes from Wollaston's work many times in his sermons, always with approbation.

CHAPTER II

1. CHAP. II: The format of Volume IX is unique in that each chapter begins on a new page rather than a few spaces below the preceding chapter, a format duplicated in the Florida *Text* but not here. This created a good deal of white space in the original and served to emphasize its slightness and, possibly, the weariness of its author.

2. buckle: Side curls of a wig, from the French 'boucle'.

3. *had not . . . Grace*: Cf. Hogarth, *Analysis of Beauty*: 'The grandeur of the Eastern

dress, which so far surpasses the European, depends as much on quantity as on costliness. In a word, it is quantity which adds greatness to grace.'

4. attacking in armour: Eighteenth-century term for using a condom.

5. red plush: Florida *Notes* cites examples from *Spectator* 129 and William Wycherley's *The Plain Dealer*, II.i, which indicate Toby was not alone in thinking 'red plush' the proper outfit for courtship.

6. Le Fevre's: Only in this volume does Sterne spell Le Fever thus; it became, however, the preferred spelling in the nineteenth century.

CHAPTER III

1. alout: Usually *allout* (i.e., all out, completely), probably obsolete by Sterne's day.

CHAPTER IV

1. flourish with his stick: Trim's flourish seems to resemble eighteenth-century illustrations of the motions of a spermatozoon.

CHAPTER VI

1. poor negro girl: On 21 July 1766, a former slave, Ignatius Sancho, wrote to Sterne in praise of his writings and in particular a passage in sermon 10 lamenting slavery. Sancho asks him to 'give half an hours attention to slavery' in his next work. Sterne immediately responded that the letter had arrived just as he was writing 'a tender tale of the sorrows of a friendless poor negro-girl', and that he would try to 'weave' it into the work he was writing. We may have here part or all of that 'tender tale'.

2. sportable: *OED* cites this passage as its sole illustration: 'capable of being sportive'. Cf. *ASJ*: 'I have something within me which cannot bear the shock of the least indecent insinuation: in the sportability of chit-chat I have often endeavoured to conquer it . . .'

CHAPTER VII

1. battle of Wynendale: See n. 5 to VIII.xxvi. The French lost between 6,000 and 7,000 men in the two-hour battle, the Allies 912, according to Tindal.

2. Why therefore . . . heaven: Trim plays on the proverb that marriages are made in heaven.

CHAPTER VIII

1. ALL womankind ... mark: Somewhere behind Trim's humour lurks a couplet recorded by John Ray, *A Collection of English Proverbs* (1678): 'He that woes a maid must fain, lie and flatter: / But he that woes a widow, must down with his breeches and at her.'

2. strides of AMBITION: Cf. Sterne's sermon 9, on the character of Herod: 'Consider what havock ambition has made ... where not only the innocence of childhood ——or the grey hairs of the aged, have found no protection——but whole countries without distinction have been put to the sword ...' And again, sermon 10: 'Consider the dreadful succession of wars in one part or other of the earth, perpetuated from one century to another with so little intermission, that mankind have scarce had time to breathe from them, since ambition first came into the world ...' Sterne's italicized '*few*' and '*many*' may well indicate an ironic tone.

3. Legation ... Tub: The sly linking of Warburton's monumental work with Swift's magnificent satire (dedicated to Prince Posterity) is discussed by New, 'Sterne, Warburton' (see Further Reading).

4. I will not ... make: Scriptural echoes give this paragraph an intensity that sets it apart from the humour surrounding it. See, e.g., Psalm 78:39: 'For he remembered that they were but flesh; a wind that passeth away, and cometh not again'; Job 7:9: 'As the cloud is consumed and vanisheth away: so he that goeth down to the grave shall come up no more'; and Proverbs 31:10: 'Who can find a virtuous woman? for her price is far above rubies.'

CHAPTER IX

1. ejaculation: Cf. *ASJ*, where Yorick breaks his oath of silence in the 'Case of Delicacy' and then declares his 'O my God!' was merely 'an ejaculation' (*OED*: 'a short prayer ... in an emergency').

CHAPTER XI

1. had no ... word: Emendation might seem called for, but in all likelihood Sterne is using, as Work notes (613, n. 2), a Lockean idiom meaning 'no ideas associated with or annexed to the word'.

2. her godfathers ... her: On behalf of a child in the Anglican baptismal ritual, the godfathers and godmothers promise to renounce the devil and all his works, and to have the child taught all 'things which a Christian ought to know and believe to his soul's health'.

3. the *cuvetts*: In so far as *cuvettes* are trenches, Walter is repeating the joke in VIII.xxx; *cuvette* also means 'bedpan'.

4. sacrament day: Sterne alludes to the ideal practice of administering Communion

on the first Sunday of each month (the same day Walter is expected to deal with other 'family concernments'). In reality, Communion was usually administered less frequently.

CHAPTER XII

1. temperance . . . chastity: Sterne echoes a portion of the response in the Anglican catechism to the question, 'What is thy duty towards thy neighbour?': 'To keep my body in temperance, soberness, and chastity.'

2. sniveling virtue of Meekness: Any Christian text would offer a contrary view of meekness, as in sermon 25, 'On humility', a fit commentary on Walter's character: 'Christianity, when rightly explained and practised, is all meekness and candour, and love and courtesy . . .'

CHAPTER XIII

1. gummous: *OED* cites this passage as its only recorded example of figurative usage: 'gum-like'.

2. plumb-lift: Not recorded in *OED*; Sterne seems to mean a perpendicular motion, straight up or straight down.

3. Dutch commentator: See n. 12 to I.xix.

4. topaz ring: See n. 4 to VI.xxxvi.

5. Ludovicus Sorbonensis: Sterne's invention, with a glance at the Sorbonne. The Greek means 'an external matter'.

CHAPTER XIV

1. chapter of Button-holes: In IV.xiv, Tristram promises to write chapters on chamber-maids, pishes, and button-holes. In V.viii he asks for credit for the first and last, based on V.vii, a chapter, he says, 'of *chamber-maids, green-gowns, and old hats* '. In IV.ix, he mentions a chapter of knots; here as elsewhere, 'knots' have sexual connotations.

2. *thersitical* satire: Sterne alludes to the Homeric character Thersites, described in Chapman's *Iliad*, II, as the 'filthiest fellow' of all, 'squint-eyd' and 'crooke-backt'. His speeches are characterized by vicious and abusive language, thus, the archetypal railer.

3. *nasty* . . . Galatea: See n. 5 to V.xvi. That Sterne had not read the *Galateo* is clear from his epithet 'nasty', but less clear is the source of his information about della Casa's penance; Walker, *Of Education*, has a brief account of his falling into disfavour because of his licentious verses, but another person is said to have 'paraphras'd the Gospel of S. *John* ' (not Revelation) in penance for his writings. *Investment* is a play on della Casa's being a bishop, as are the allusions to 'purple'.

CHAPTER XV

1. How our . . . world: Commonplace, but perhaps Sterne was looking at Volume I of *Sermons* while writing this part of *TS*. In sermon 1, 'Inquiry after happiness', he writes: 'our pleasures and enjoyments slip from under us in every stage of our life'; and in sermon 2, he exclaims: 'So strange and unaccountable a creature is man! he is so framed, that he cannot but pursue happiness—and yet unless he is made sometimes miserable, how apt is he to mistake the way . . .'

CHAPTER XVII

1. Rousseau: Although Sterne never met the French philosopher Jean-Jacques Rousseau (1712–78), they had mutual acquaintances, including Diderot and David Hume. Praise for a natural and simple life is so quintessentially Rousseau it is impossible to identify a particular source.
2. bar length: *OED* notes the competitive tossing of a thick rod of iron or wood, the contest being measured in lengths of the bar.
3. Vestal (to keep my fire in): Sterne plays on the perpetual fire burning in Roman temples in honour of Vesta and the virgins assigned to keep that fire burning.

CHAPTER XX

1. second translation: In the chapter 'The Translation. Paris' in *ASJ*, Sterne explores more fully the 'secret so aiding to the progress of sociality'—that of mastering 'this *short hand*, and . . . rendering the several turns of looks and limbs, with all their inflections and delineations, into plain words'.

CHAPTER XXII

1. WE live . . . riddles: See n. 1 to IV.xvii.
2. Platonic exigences: Cf. Chambers, s.v. *Platonic love*: 'denotes a pure, spiritual affection, subsisting between the different sexes, abstracted from all carnal appetites. . . . The world has a long time laugh'd at Plato's notions. . . . In effect, they appear arrant chimera's, contrary to the intentions of nature . . .'
3. defeated: Work has 'defended' (626), which cannot be justified and is probably a simple – though misleading – error.

CHAPTER XXIII

1. play her cards herself: Proverbial for making good use of one's resources or opportunities.

2. *ten-ace*: In whist, to have the ten-ace is to possess the first and third best cards while being the last player, a decided advantage.

CHAPTER XXIV

1. fourscore ounces of blood: Cf. Sterne's letter dated ?7–9 January 1767: 'I miscarried of my tenth Volume by the violence of a fever, I have just got thro'—I have however gone on to my reckoning with the ninth, of wch I am all this week in Labour pains . . .' Sterne often links images of giving birth with publication.

2. uncritical: *OED* defines this usage of 'uncritical' as 'not critical; lacking in judgment'; more likely, the word here refers to the crisis or turning-point of a disease, although the passage's precise meaning remains obscure.

3. serous or globular: Blood was considered separable into two parts, the more glutinous and solid, called the 'globular', and the more thin and fluid, called the 'serous'.

4. GENTLE . . . life: In his preface, Cervantes calls his work '*the Child of Disturbance, engendered in some dismal Prison, where Wretchedness keeps its Residence, and every dismal Sound its Habitation*'. In the account of Cervantes prefixed to the Motteux-Ozell translation, Sterne could discover that he lost his hand at the battle of Lepanto. Near the end of *Don Quixote* (II.III.45) Cervantes invokes the Sun, 'by whose assistance Man begets Man, on thee I call for help! Inspire me, I beseech thee, warm and illumine my gloomy Imagination, that my Narration may keep pace with the Great *Sancho Pança*'s Actions . . .'

5. cunning . . . Italy: Sterne was in Italy from November 1765 to May 1766; see Cash, *LY*, ch. 6. The anecdote told here was reported in the *St. James Chronicle* (14–17 June 1766) as having actually happened to Sterne, the perpetrator being a pregnant laundress who thought the laps would make comfortable 'head cloathes' for her baby, and perhaps inspire it with 'Wit and Humour'. One suspects, however, a more bawdy meaning in Sterne's rendition, given the italicized *fore* and *out*, a meaning clarified in this bit of eighteenth-century verse: 'For now tormented sore with scalding Heat / Of Urine, dread fore-runner of a Clap! / With Eye repentant, he surveys his Shirt / Diversify'd with Spots of yellow Hue, / Sad Symptom of ten Thousand Woes to come!'

6. Sienna . . . Capua: Capua, just north of Naples, on the road to Rome; Raddicoffini (Radicofani), site of a famous castle seventy miles north of Rome; Sienna, forty miles farther north, on the road to Florence. Pauls: *paolo*, obsolete Italian coin.

7. keeps his temper: Sterne's comments here are directed at Smollett, whose account of his own European tour, *Travels through France and Italy* (1766), is a target in *ASJ* as

well, where he is characterized as Smelfungus: 'he set out with the spleen and jaundice, and every object he pass'd by was discoloured or distorted—He wrote an account of them, but 'twas nothing but the account of his miserable feelings.' Typically, Smollett said of Sienna that they were lodged in a 'house that stunk like a privy'.

8. voitures: Carriages.

9. 'Tis Maria: In *ASJ*, Yorick feels compelled to visit the poor Maria, whom 'my friend, Mr. Shandy, met with near Moulines'. It is possible that Sterne used the scene to 'advertise' *ASJ*, certainly in his thoughts during the composition of Volume IX. Maria, by herself, or with Yorick (Tristram), was the single subject of Sterne's fiction most often illustrated by artists in the next century.

10. I would . . . live: Cf. Sterne's letter to Elizabeth Montagu in 1764: 'Would Apollo . . . had planted me within a League of Mrs Mountague this Summer, I could have taken my horse & gone & fetch'd Wit & Wisdome as I wanted them—as for nonsense—I am pretty well provided myself both by nature & Travel.'

CHAPTER XXV

1. foam . . . his horse: Pliny (*Natural History*) tells of the painter Protogenes (fourth century B.C.), who created foam on a dog's mouth by throwing his sponge, and then adds that Nealces (*fl.* 245 B.C.), another Greek painter, did the same to represent a horse's foam. The story appears often in literature as an illustration of chance, but why Sterne assigns it to Zeuxis, another celebrated fourth-century Greek painter, is unknown.

2. Gargantua's shepherds: In Rabelais, I.25, we are offered some forty such 'unsavory appellations', from which Sterne selects his small handful.

3. Spanish proverb: Several proverbs can be suggested, none definitively. Sancho Pança offers 'a buen entendedor, pocas palabras' (II.III.37), which may be idiomatically translated as the proverbial 'A word to the wise is enough.' Another proverb, 'A shut mouth catches no flies', was known in England as a 'Spanish proverb'. Work (633, n. 1) offers Lope de Vega's 'Brief words are a sign of love'; and Ian Campbell Ross, in his annotation for the Oxford edition of *Tristram Shandy* (1983), offers yet another suggestion, from Calderón: 'En las venturas de amor / dice más el que más calla' (In affairs of love, the less said the better).

4. condemnation . . . *making it*: Cf. *ASJ*, where Yorick condemns the French practice of 'making love by *sentiments*' and comments: 'I should as soon think of making a genteel suit of cloaths out of remnants . . .' 'Real presence' here refers to the Roman Catholic doctrine that the body and blood, soul and divinity, of Christ are really and substantially present in the Eucharist, a doctrine held to be 'repugnant to the plain words of Scripture' in article 28 of the Thirty-Nine Articles.

5. black-pudding: A sausage made of blood and suet, and sometimes meat.

6. They are written . . . Book: The Solemnization of Matrimony in the Book of Common Prayer lists three reasons: 'First, it was ordained for the procreation of

children. . . . Secondly, it was ordained for a remedy against sin, and to avoid fornication, that such persons as have not the gift of continency, might marry. . . . Thirdly, it was ordained for the mutual society, help, and comfort, that the one ought to have of the other . . .'

7. they are . . . comforts: Proverbial.

8. allons: Let's go!

CHAPTER XXVI

1. the Corporation: Self-governing body of York, which received ratification in 1212.

2. She had . . . muscles: Tristram borrows most of his authorities from Chambers; the footnote, typically enough, parodies the appearance of learning in the text. James Drake (1667–1707) wrote *Anthropologia Nova, or a New System of Anatomy*, Thomas Wharton (1614–73) discussed the nature of the brain in his *Adenographia*, and Regnier de Graaf (1641–73), Dutch physician, wrote, according to Chambers, on 'the pancreatic juice, and the parts of generation', precisely as the *editor's* 'correction' of 'Mr. Shandy' indicates.

3. critick *in keeping*: Cf. Pope's comment, in a letter of 1704 to Wycherley, that 'no Beggar is so poor but he can keep a Cur, and no Author is so beggarly but he can keep a Critic'. Sterne may also be thinking of 'critics' (i.e., the stable of hacks) kept by publishing houses; cf. 'keeping a mistress'.

CHAPTER XXVIII

1. *Maes . . . Sambre*: Cf. n. 1 to II.i.

CHAPTER XXIX

1. IT was . . . morning: Cf. *Two Gentlemen of Verona*, I.iii.84–7: 'O, how this spring of love resembleth / The uncertain glory of an April day, / Which now shows all the beauty of the sun, / And by and by a cloud takes all away.'

2. *quart major to a terce*: In piquet, a quart-major is the sequence of ace, king, queen, and knave, while a terce is simply any three successive cards in one suit. The phrase implies considerable superiority.

CHAPTER XXXI

1. Take a full sheet: Cf. Sterne's sermon 5, a charity sermon: 'let any number of us here imagine ourselves at this instant engaged in drawing the most perfect and amiable character. . . . I appeal to your own thoughts, whether the first idea which offered itself to most of our imaginations, would not be that of a compassionate benefactor . . .' And cf. sermon 3 ('Philanthropy recommended'): 'I think there needs no stronger argument to prove how universally and deeply the seeds of ... compassion are planted in the heart of man, than ... that from the general propensity to pity the unfortunate, we express that sensation by the word *humanity*, as if it was inseparable from our nature. That it is not *inseparable*, I have allowed in the former part of this discourse ...' The source of the second passage is Sterne's favourite sermon-writer, John Tillotson.

CHAPTER XXXIII

1. CHAP. XXXIII: Sterne borrows his discussion of human sexuality from Pierre Charron's *Of Wisdome*, trans. Samson Lennard (1612), first noted by Françoise Pellan, 'Laurence Sterne's Indebtedness to Charron', *MLR* 67 (1972). Charron attempts to systematize the writings of his master, Montaigne, but Sterne is clearly reading *Of Wisdome* and not Montaigne at this point; the passage is so central to the meaning of *TS* that it must be recorded at length:

Carnell Love is a fever and furious passion, and very dangerous unto him that suffereth himselfe to be carried by it. ... As it is naturall, so is it violent and common to all, and therefore in the action thereof it equalleth and coupleth fooles and wise men, men and beasts together. It maketh all the wisdome, resolution, contemplation & operation of the soule beastly and brutish ...

Philosophie speaketh freely of all things. ... [A]ll the motion of the world resolveth and yeeldeth to this copulation of the male and female: on the other side it causeth us to accuse, to hide our selves, to blush for shame, as if it were a thing ignominious and dishonest. We call it a shamefull act, and the parts that serve thereunto our shamefull parts. But why shamefull, since naturall ...

This action then in itselfe, and simply taken, is neither shamefull nor vitious, since it is naturall and corporall ...: yea, if it be well ordered, it is just, profitable, necessarie, at the least, as it is to eat and drinke.

The first point and proofe of the miserie of man is his birth; his entrance into the world is shamefull, vile, base, contemptible; his departure, his death, ruine, glorious and honorable: whereby it seemeth that he is a monster and against nature, since there is shame in making him, honor in destroying him. ... The action of planting and making man is shamefull, and all the parts thereof, the congredients, the preparations, the instruments, and whatsoever serves thereunto is called and accounted shamefull, and there is nothing more uncleane in the whole nature of man. The action of destroying and killing him honourable, and that which serves thereunto glorious: we gild it, we inrich it, we adorne our selves with it, we carrie it by our sides, in our hands, upon our shoulders. ... When we goe about to make a man, we hide our selves, we put out the candle, we do it by stealth. It is a glorie and a pompe to unmake a man, to kill him ...

Perhaps no other borrowing by Sterne in *TS* encompasses more of the meaning of his work than this.

2. *Prolepsis*: Figure in rhetoric by which one anticipates or prevents objections.

3. *Diogenes* and *Plato*: Such sentiments abound in Plato's writings, but why Sterne chose Diogenes (see n. 1 to I.xxiv) is unclear; perhaps his answer to the question of when to marry stuck in his mind: 'For a young man not yet: for an old man never at all.'

4. recalcitrate: *OED* cites this passage as its first illustration: 'to show strong objection or repugnance'.

5. congredients: Component parts, ingredients.

6. great tythes: Church revenues derived from major produce of the soil – corn, hay, wood, and fruit. An 'impropriator' was a layman in possession of those revenues; Sterne implies that possession entailed obligations, such as keeping the town bull.

7. as hairy as I am: Charles Parish, 'The Shandy Bull Vindicated', *MLQ* 31 (1970), argues that this sentence convinces Walter that Obadiah's child was sired by the bull and hence that the bull can be cleared of the charge of impotence. The implication of bestiality is tied to a similar suggestion in V.iii, where Obadiah is accused of siring a mule; it is reinforced by the allusion to Europa, who was carried away by Zeus after he had taken the form of a bull.

The argument is based, however, on the assumption that hairiness is a sign of full-term birth, when in fact it is more often associated with pre-term birth – i.e., the lanugo covering which comes in the fifth month and disappears before the ninth. Walter's response, then, may indicate relief that Obadiah's wife has 'come before her time' and that the bull may yet prove potent.

8. Doctors Commons: Area near St Paul's where ecclesiastical courts heard various civil cases, including divorces.

9. A COCK and a BULL: Story without direction, rambling, idle, often incredible; the term was associated with both prose and verse satire, and with tales of a tub or a roasted horse (and the French *coq-à-l'âne*); see Wayne C. Booth, 'Did Sterne Complete *Tristram Shandy*?', *MP* 48 (1951). That Sterne ends *TS* with a bawdy revivification of a proverbial expression is particularly characteristic.

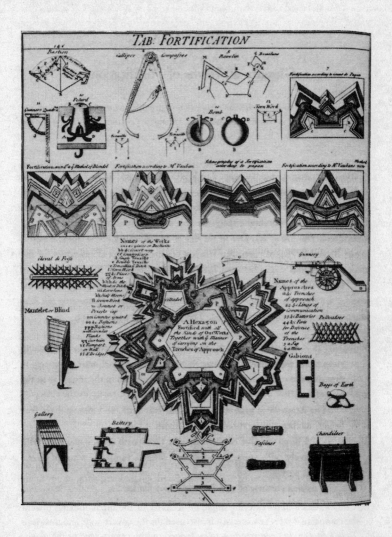

TAB: FORTIFICATION

Appendix

GLOSSARY OF TERMS OF FORTIFICATION

Generally the definitions herein are quoted directly from Chambers; in two instances, recourse is had to John Muller, *A Treatise Containing the Elementary Part of Fortification* (1746). The plate is from Chambers.

BANQUETTE 'A little foot-bank, or elevation of earth forming a path which runs along the inside of a parapet; by which the musqueteers get up, to discover the counterscarp, or to fire on the enemies in the moat, or in the covert-way. The *banquette* is generally a foot and a half high, and almost three foot broad; having two or three steps to mount it by.'

BASTION 'A huge massive of earth usually faced with sods, sometimes with brick, rarely with stone, standing out from a rampart, whereof it is a principal part. A *bastion* consists of two faces and two flanks. . . . The union of the two faces makes the outmost or saliant angle, called also the *angle of the bastion*.' See plate, figures o and p.

BLINDS 'Defences usually made of oziers, or branches interwoven and laid across, between two rows of stakes about the height of a man, and four or five foot apart; used particularly at the heads of trenches, when they are extended in front towards the glacis; serving to shelter the workmen, and prevent their being overlooked by the enemy.' See plate for illustration.

BREASTWORKS See PARAPET.

CIRCUMVALLATION 'A line or trench, with a parapet, thrown up by the besiegers, encompassing all their camp, to defend it against any army that may attempt to relieve the place. This line is to be cannon-shot distant from the place.'

COUNTERGUARD (s.v. *Envelope* in Chambers) 'A mount of earth, sometimes raised in the ditch of a place, and sometimes beyond it; being either in form of a simple parapet, or of a small rampart bordered with a parapet. These *envelopes* are made, where weak places are only to be covered with single lines; without advancing towards the field.'

COUNTERSCARP 'The exterior slope, or acclivity of the ditch, looking towards the campaign. COUNTER-SCARP is also used for the covert-way, and the glacis. *To be lodged on the counterscarp*, is to be lodged on the covert-way, or the glacis.'

COVERED WAY (s.v. *Covert Way* in Chambers) 'A space of ground level with the adjoining country, on the edge of the ditch, ranging quite round the half-moons, and other works without-side the ditch . . . One of the greatest difficulties in a siege, is to make a lodgment on the *covert way*; because, usually, the besieged pallisade it along the middle, and undermine it on all sides.' See plate, figure b.

CROSS BATTERIES (s.v. *Battery* in Chambers) 'Two batteries at a considerable distance from each other, which play a-thwart one another at the same time, and upon the same point, forming right angles.'

CURTIN 'That part of a wall, or rampart, which is between two bastions; or which joins the flanks thereof . . . The *curtin* is usually bordered with a parapet five foot high; behind which the soldiers stand to fire upon the covert way, and into the moat.' See plate, figure q. See also above, n. 3 to II.xii.

CUVETTE (s.v. *Cunette* in Chambers) 'A deep trench, about three or four fathom wide, sunk along the middle of a dry moat, to lade out the water; or to make the passage more difficult to the enemy.'

DEMI-BASTION 'A kind of fortification, that has only one face, and one flank.'

DEMI-CULVERIN 'A piece of ordnance commonly 4½ inches bore, 10 foot long, 2700 pound weight; its charge is 7 pound 4 ounces of powder; and it carries a shot of 10 pounds 11 ounces; and shoots point blank 175 paces.'

DITCH 'Called also *Foss*, and *Moat*, a trench dug round the rampart, or wall of a fortified place, between the scarp, and counterscarp. Some *Ditches* are dry; others full of water: each whereof have their advantages.' See plate, figure h.

DOUBLE TENAILLE See TENAILLE.

EPAULEMENT 'A side-work hastily thrown up, to cover the cannon, or the men. It is made either of earth thrown up, of bags filled with sand or earth, or of gabions, fascines, &c. with earth.

'EPAULEMENT, is also used for a demi-bastion . . . placed at the point of a horn or crown-work.'

ESPLANADE See GLACIS.

FACE 'FACES *of a bastion*, are the two foremost sides, reaching from the flanks to the point of the bastion, where they meet. . . . FACE *of a place*, denotes the interval between the points of two neighbouring bastions, containing the curtain, the two flanks, and the two *Faces* of the bastions that looked towards one another. This is otherwise called the *tenaille* of the place.'

FAUSSE-BRAYE 'An elevation of earth, two or three fathoms broad, round the foot of the rampart on the outside, defended by a parapet which parts it from the berme [i.e., the space between the ditch and the base of the parapet], and the edge of the ditch: its use is for the defence of the ditch. . . . It is of little use where ramparts are faced with wall, because of the rubbish which the cannon beats down into it. For this reason, engineers will have none before the faces of the bastions.'

FLANK 'A line, drawn from the extremity of the face, towards the inside of the work. . . . Or, *Flank* is that part of the bastion, which reaches from the curtin to the face, and defends the opposite face, the *Flank*, and the curtin.'

FOSS(E) 'A ditch, or moat.'

GABIONS 'Large baskets, made of osier twigs, woven of a cylindrical form, six foot high, and four wide; which being filled with earth, serve as a defence, or shelter from the enemy's fire.' See plate for illustration.

GAZONS 'Turfs, or pieces of fresh earth covered with grass, cut in form of a wedge, about a foot long, and half a foot thick: to line or face the outside of works made of earth, in order to keep up the same, and prevent their mouldering.'

GLACIS The slope or declivity of the counterscarp; 'being a sloping bank which reaches from the parapet of the counterscarp, or covert-way, to the level side of the field'. See plate, figure a. Also called ESPLANADE.

GORGE 'The entrance of a bastion; or of a ravelin, or other outwork.... The GORGE *of a bastion*, is what remains of the sides of the polygon of a place, after retrenching the curtins: in which case it makes an angle in the centre of the bastion.... GORGE *of a half moon*, or *ravelin*, is the space between the two ends of their faces next the place.'

HALF-MOON 'An outwork, consisting of two faces, forming together a saliant angle, whose gorge is turned like an *half moon*. ... *Half moons* are sometimes raised before the curtin, when the ditch is wider than it ought to be; in which case it is much the same with a ravelin; only that the gorge of an *half-moon* is made bending in like a bow, or crescent, and is chiefly used to cover the point of the bastion; whereas ravelins are always placed before the curtin.—But they are both defective, as being ill flanked.' See plate, figures 5 (top) and k. See also above, n. 3 to II.xii.

HORN-WORK 'A sort of out-work, advancing toward the field, to cover and defend a curtin, bastion, or other place suspected to be weaker than the rest.... It consists of two demi-bastions ... joined by a curtin.' See plate, figures 9 and f.

ICHNOGRAPHY 'The plan or representation of the length and breadth of a fortress, the distinct parts of which are marked out, either on the ground itself, or upon paper.'

INVESTING 'The opening a siege, and the incamping of an army round the place, to block up its avenues, and prevent all ingress and egress.... It is the cavalry that always begins to *invest* a place.'

LODGMENT 'A work cast up by the besiegers, during their approaches, in some dangerous post, which they have gained, and where it is absolutely necessary to secure themselves against the enemies fire; as in a covert-way; in a breach, the bottom of a moat, or any other part gained from the besieged. *Lodgments* are made by casting up earth, or by gabions, or palisades, ... mantelets, or any thing capable of covering soldiers in the place they have gained, and are determined to keep.'

MANTELET See BLINDS.

MINE 'A subterraneous canal, or passage dug under the wall, or rampart of a fortification, intended to be blown up by gun-powder.'

MOLE 'A massive work formed of large stones laid in the sea by means of coffer-dams, extended either in a right line or an arch of a circle, before a port; which it serves to close; to defend the vessels in it from the impetuosity of the waves, and prevent the passage of ships without leave.'

ORGUES 'Thick long pieces of wood pointed and shod with iron, and hung each by a separate rope over the gateway of a city, ready on any surprize or attempt of the enemy to be let down to stop up the gate.' See above, n. 5 to VI.xxii.

OUT-WORKS 'All those works made without side the ditch of a fortified place, to cover and defend it.... *Outworks*, called also *advanced* and *detached works*, are those which not only serve to cover the body of the place, but also to keep the enemy at a distance, and prevent his taking advantage of the cavities and elevations usually found in the places about the counterscarp.... Such are, ravelins, tenailles, hornworks.'

OUVRAGE DE CORNE See HORN-WORK.

PADERERO (s.v. *Pedrero* in Chambers) 'A small piece of ordnance, used on board ships for the discharging of nails, broken iron, or partridge shot on an enemy attempting to board.'

PALISADO (s.v. *Palisade* in Chambers) 'An inclosure of stakes, or piles driven into the ground, six or seven inches square, and eight foot long; three whereof are hid under ground.... *Palisades* are used to fortify the avenues of open forts, gorges, half-moons, the bottoms of ditches, the parapets of covert-ways; and in general all posts liable to surprize, and to which the access is easy.' See plate.

PARALLELS 'Deep trenches 15 or 18 feet wide, joining the several attacks together; they serve to place the guard of the trenches in, to be at hand to support the workmen when attacked. There are generally three in an attack; the first is about 300 toises from the covert-way, the second 160, and the third near or on the glacis' (Muller, 227–8).

PARAPET 'A defence or skreen, on the extreme of a rampart, or other work, serving to cover the soldiers, and the cannon from the enemy's fire.... *Parapets* are raised on all works, where it is necessary to cover the men from the enemy's fire; both within and without the place, and even the approaches.... The *Parapet* of the wall is sometimes of stone.—The *Parapet* of the trenches is either made of the earth dug up; or of gabions, fascines, barrels, sacks of earth, or the like.'

PETARD 'A brass pot fixed upon a strong square plank, which has an iron hook to fix it against a gate or palisades; this pot is filled with powder, which when fired, breaks every thing about it, and thereby makes an opening for an enemy to enter the place' (Muller, 228).

PLACE 'A general name for all kinds of fortresses, where a party may defend themselves.'

PORTCULLICE 'An assemblage of several great pieces of wood laid or joined across one another, like an harrow; and each pointed at the bottom with iron.... These formerly used to be hung over the gate-ways of fortified places, to be ready to let down in case of a surprize, when the enemy should come so quick, as not to allow time to shut the gates. But now-a-days, the orgues are more generally used, as being found to answer the purpose better.'

RAMPART 'A massy bank, or elevation of earth raised about the body of a place, to cover it from the great shot; and formed into bastions, curtins, &c.' See plate, figure r.

RAVELIN 'A detached work, composed only of two faces, which make a salient angle, without any flanks; and raised before the curtin on the counterscarp of the place.... It's use before a curtin, is to cover the opposite flanks of the two next bastions. It is used also to cover a bridge or a gate; and is always placed without the moat. What the engineers call a *ravelin*, the soldiers generally call a *demi-lune*, or half-moon.' See plate, figures 5 (top) and i.

REDANS (s.v. *Redens* in Chambers) 'A kind of work indented in form of the teeth of a saw, with saliant and re-entering angles; to the end that one part may flank or defend another.'

REDOUBT 'A small square fort, without any defence but in front; used in trenches, lines of circumvallation, contravallation, and approach; as also for the lodging of corps de garde, and to defend passages.' See plate, figure 4 (bottom).

RETURNING ANGLE (s.v. *Angle, Re-entering* in Chambers) 'That whose vertex is turned inwards, towards the place.'

SALIENT ANGLE (s.v. *Angle, Saillant* in Chambers) 'That which advances its point toward the field.'

SAP 'A work carried on under ground, to gain the descent of a ditch, counterscarp, or the like.' See plate, figure 5 (bottom).

SCARP 'The interior slope of the ditch of a place; that is, the slope of that side of a ditch which is next to the place, and faces the campaign.'

SODS See GAZONS.

TALUS 'The slope or diminution allowed to [a bastion or rampart]; whether it be of earth, or stone; the better to support its weight ... The *exterior Talus* of a work, is its slope on the side towards the country ... The *interior Talus* of a work, is its slope on the inside, towards the place.'

TENAILLE 'A kind of out-work, consisting of two parallel sides, with a front, wherein is a re-entering angle ... 'In strictness, that angle, and the faces which compose it, are the *tenaille* ...

  'Double, or flanked TENAILLE, is a large out-work consisting of two simple *tenailles*, or three salians, and two re-entering angles ...' See plate, figures 8, 9, e.

TERRACE (or Terras) 'An earth-work usually lined, and breasted with a strong wall, in compliance with the natural inequality of the ground.'

TOISE 'A French measure, containing six of their feet, or a fathom.'

TRAVERSE 'A trench with a little parapet, sometimes two, one on each side, to serve as a cover from the enemy that might come in flank.'

READ MORE IN PENGUIN

In every corner of the world, on every subject under the sun, Penguin represents quality and variety – the very best in publishing today.

For complete information about books available from Penguin – including Puffins, Penguin Classics and Arkana – and how to order them, write to us at the appropriate address below. Please note that for copyright reasons the selection of books varies from country to country.

In the United Kingdom: Please write to *Dept. EP, Penguin Books Ltd, Bath Road, Harmondsworth, West Drayton, Middlesex UB7 ODA*

In the United States: Please write to *Consumer Sales, Penguin Putnam Inc., P.O. Box 12289 Dept. B, Newark, New Jersey 07101-5289*. VISA and MasterCard holders call 1-800-788-6262 to order Penguin titles

In Canada: Please write to *Penguin Books Canada Ltd, 10 Alcorn Avenue, Suite 300, Toronto, Ontario M4V 3B2*

In Australia: Please write to *Penguin Books Australia Ltd, P.O. Box 257, Ringwood, Victoria 3134*

In New Zealand: Please write to *Penguin Books (NZ) Ltd, Private Bag 102902, North Shore Mail Centre, Auckland 10*

In India: Please write to *Penguin Books India Pvt Ltd, 11 Community Centre, Panchsheel Park, New Delhi 110017*

In the Netherlands: Please write to *Penguin Books Netherlands bv, Postbus 3507, NL-1001 AH Amsterdam*

In Germany: Please write to *Penguin Books Deutschland GmbH, Metzlerstrasse 26, 60594 Frankfurt am Main*

In Spain: Please write to *Penguin Books S. A., Bravo Murillo 19, 1° B, 28015 Madrid*

In Italy: Please write to *Penguin Italia s.r.l., Via Benedetto Croce 2, 20094 Corsico, Milano*

In France: Please write to *Penguin France, Le Carré Wilson, 62 rue Benjamin Baillaud, 31500 Toulouse*

In Japan: Please write to *Penguin Books Japan Ltd, Kaneko Building, 2-3-25 Koraku, Bunkyo-Ku, Tokyo 112*

In South Africa: Please write to *Penguin Books South Africa (Pty) Ltd, Private Bag X14, Parkview, 2122 Johannesburg*

PENGUIN AUDIOBOOKS

A Quality of Writing That Speaks for Itself

Penguin Books has always led the field in quality publishing. Now you can listen at leisure to your favourite books, read to you by familiar voices from radio, stage and screen. Penguin Audiobooks are produced to an excellent standard, and abridgements are always faithful to the original texts. From thrillers to classic literature, biography to humour, with a wealth of titles in between, Penguin Audiobooks offer you quality, entertainment and the chance to rediscover the pleasure of listening.

You can order Penguin Audiobooks through Penguin Direct by telephoning (0181) 899 4036. The lines are open 24 hours every day. Ask for Penguin Direct, quoting your credit card details.

PENGUIN AUDIOBOOKS

The Hound of the Baskervilles by Sir Arthur Conan Doyle, read by Freddie Jones

Middlemarch by George Eliot, read by Harriet Walter

Tom Jones by Henry Fielding, read by Robert Lindsay

The Great Gatsby by F. Scott Fitzgerald, read by Marcus D'Amico

Madame Bovary by Gustave Flaubert, read by Claire Bloom

Mary Barton by Elizabeth Gaskell, read by Clare Higgins

Jude the Obscure by Thomas Hardy, read by Samuel West

Far from the Madding Crowd by Thomas Hardy, read by Julie Christie

The Scarlet Letter by Nathaniel Hawthorne, read by Bob Sessions

Les Misérables by Victor Hugo, read by Nigel Anthony

A Passage to India by E. M. Forster, read by Tim Pigott-Smith

The Iliad by Homer, read by Derek Jacobi

The Dead and Other Stories by James Joyce, read by Gerard McSorley

On the Road by Jack Kerouac, read by David Carradine

Sons and Lovers by D. H. Lawrence, read by Paul Copley

The Prince by Niccolò Machiavelli, read by Fritz Weaver

Animal Farm by George Orwell, read by Timothy West

Rob Roy by Sir Walter Scott, read by Robbie Coltrane

Frankenstein by Mary Shelley, read by Richard Pasco

Of Mice and Men by John Steinbeck, read by Gary Sinise

Kidnapped by Robert Louis Stevenson, read by Robbie Coltrane

Dracula by Bram Stoker, read by Richard E. Grant

Gulliver's Travels by Jonathan Swift, read by Hugh Laurie

Vanity Fair by William Makepeace Thackeray, read by Robert Hardy

Lark Rise to Candleford by Flora Thompson, read by Judi Dench

The Invisible Man by H. G. Wells, read by Paul Shelley

Ethan Frome by Edith Wharton, read by Nathan Osgood

The Picture of Dorian Gray by Oscar Wilde, read by John Moffatt

Orlando by Virginia Woolf, read by Tilda Swinton

READ MORE IN PENGUIN

A CHOICE OF CLASSICS

Armadale   Wilkie Collins

Victorian critics were horrified by Lydia Gwilt, the bigamist, husband-poisoner and laudanum addict whose intrigues spur the plot of this most sensational of melodramas.

Aurora Leigh and Other Poems   Elizabeth Barrett Browning

Aurora Leigh (1856), Elizabeth Barrett Browning's epic novel in blank verse, tells the story of the making of a woman poet, exploring 'the woman question', art and its relation to politics and social oppression.

Personal Narrative of a Journey to the Equinoctial Regions of the New Continent   Alexander von Humboldt

Alexander von Humboldt became a wholly new kind of nineteenth-century hero – the scientist–explorer – and in *Personal Narrative* he invented a new literary genre: the travelogue.

The Pańćatantra   Visnu Sarma

The Pańćatantra is one of the earliest books of fables and its influence can be seen in the *Arabian Nights*, the *Decameron*, the *Canterbury Tales* and most notably in the *Fables* of La Fontaine.

A Laodicean   Thomas Hardy

The Laodicean of Hardy's title is Paula Power, a thoroughly modern young woman who, despite her wealth and independence, cannot make up her mind.

Brand   Henrik Ibsen

The unsparing vision of a priest driven by faith to risk and witness the deaths of his wife and child gives *Brand* its icy ferocity. It was Ibsen's first masterpiece, a poetic drama composed in 1865 and published to tremendous critical and popular acclaim.

READ MORE IN PENGUIN

A CHOICE OF CLASSICS

READ MORE IN PENGUIN

A CHOICE OF CLASSICS

William Hazlitt	**Selected Writings**
George Herbert	**The Complete English Poems**
Thomas Hobbes	**Leviathan**
Samuel Johnson/	
James Boswell	**A Journey to the Western Islands of Scotland** and **The Journal of a Tour of the Hebrides**
Charles Lamb	**Selected Prose**
George Meredith	**The Egoist**
Thomas Middleton	**Five Plays**
John Milton	**Paradise Lost**
Samuel Richardson	**Clarissa**
	Pamela
Earl of Rochester	**Complete Works**
Richard Brinsley	
Sheridan	**The School for Scandal and Other Plays**
Sir Philip Sidney	**Selected Poems**
Christopher Smart	**Selected Poems**
Adam Smith	**The Wealth of Nations** (Books I–III)
Tobias Smollett	**The Adventures of Ferdinand Count Fathom**
	Humphrey Clinker
	Roderick Random
Laurence Sterne	**The Life and Opinions of Tristram Shandy**
	A Sentimental Journey Through France and Italy
Jonathan Swift	**Gulliver's Travels**
	Selected Poems
Thomas Traherne	**Selected Poems and Prose**
Henry Vaughan	**Complete Poems**